The Path thro' the Woods

The Path thro' the Woods

Victoria Landers

The Path thro' the Woods
Victoria Landers

Design © 131 Design Ltd
www.131design.org
Text © Victoria Landers

ISBN 978-1-909660-55-7
ebook ISBN 978-1-909660-41-0

A CIP catalogue record for this book is
available from the British Library.

Published 2016 by Tricorn Books,
131 High Street, Old Portsmouth,
PO1 2HW

www.tricornbooks.co.uk

Printed & bound in UK

To J & D
With fondest love
And remembering Vicky
1942-2015

This downhill path is easy, but there's no turning back
Christina Rossetti, *Amor Mundi*

Victoria Landers has lived in East Devon most of her life. She worked for a Perfumery House, a merchant bank and nursed in a cottage hospital. She spent a year in the walled city of York and was enchanted by the surrounding countryside, historical buildings, abbeys, stately homes and the whole picturesque seaboard from Flamborough Head to Staithes. She now lives within sight of the sea but, at every opportunity will sneak across the Tamar to either surf the north coast of Cornwall, explore the secret hidden coves to the south or spend as long as possible on the Isles of Scilly – which she thinks is Britain's best kept secret.

Her first book, *Twenty Three Days* was published in 2013.

Contents

	Page
Prologue	11
Part I	17
Chapter 1	19
Chapter 2	42
Chapter 3	64
Chapter 4	76
Chapter 5	104
Chapter 6	121
Chapter 7	142
Chapter 8	158
Chapter 9	174
Chapter 10	188
Chapter 11	210
Chapter 12	229
Chapter 13	248
Chapter 14	270
Chapter 15	286
Chapter 16	307
Chapter 17	326
Chapter 18	351
Part II	369
Chapter 19	370
Chapter 20	387
Chapter 21	403
Chapter 22	423
Chapter 23	434
Chapter 24	449
Chapter 25	463

Chapter 26   481
Chapter 27   492
Chapter 28   512
Chapter 29   522
Chapter 30   539
Chapter 31   555
Chapter 32   569
Chapter 33   586

Journey's End   591

Prologue

If you look closely you might see a movement in the trees above the inlet known as Pont Pill, in Cornwall. A young girl climbs down towards the lazily surging tide. She checks her watch, then stops in some shade and sits, with her knees drawn up beneath her chin, staring intently across the water. In the distance, to her left, is the wide mouth of the river with its froth of choppy wavelets reflecting the deep blue of the overhead sky. It's a perfect day with the odd tuft of white cumulus cloud edging the periphery of the horizon and is undisturbed by the light breezes that are allowing the dozens of dinghies and stately yachts to criss-cross the river, sailing either towards the sea or enabling them to practise complicated manoeuvres in front of the prestigious Royal Fowey Yacht club.

The girl's gaze eventually fixes on a boat with a brown sail that is steadily beating its way up towards the cove where she sits. She hesitantly watches it coming ever nearer until it is close beneath her. She sees a young lad spring out and competently beach it. And only then does she stand and walk the few dozen yards to meet him. They meet; a relieved grin on his face and a wide, beaming smile on hers. Within seconds they climb aboard and the youngster takes the craft about and sails out of the creek and off down the river towards the sheltered village of Polruan that nestles beneath the trees, just around the bend.

As Jenny could explain, it all started in a relatively simple way. She arrived in the village of Polruan on a sunny, late June morning – not knowing exactly where she was. Her father drove them down, through the night, from Essex and, although quite honestly she didn't particularly want to accompany her parents on this holiday, she had reluctantly agreed. After getting deeply buried in a book through most of the environs of Middlesex and Surrey, she must have fallen asleep – either in Wiltshire or on the borders of Devon – because she has no recollection of the rest of the journey until she woke, bleary eyed, outside a small cottage clinging to a hillside and overlooking an expanse of water.

Her parents had taken a cottage by the River Fowey for a few weeks that summer and, after poring over a map in the library, she has the dreadful suspicion it will be as quiet here as it was at home – the only difference being that she has lots of friends back home, so there it wouldn't matter. For the past two days she has walked around the tiny village of Polruan; climbed its massively steep hill and wandered across the cliffs, before taking the ferry across the river to the sailing mecca that is Fowey, on the other side. That, at least, is more interesting, with its winding streets, thronged with holidaymakers, its varied shops and busy, upbeat attitude. It also has a decent beach, which will enable her to sunbathe – with a good book – and maybe even swim. So, after discovering a bookshop opposite the Tourist Information Centre, she decides to invest in a little Cornish culture by purchasing two second-hand paperbacks – a Daphne du Maurier novel and a light, local tale by Sir Arthur Quiller-Couch – that the shop assistant recommends. She then makes her way back on the bustling, fussy little ferry and arrives home just in time for lunch.

After eating, she joins her parents on the veranda overlooking the river, for their usual cup of coffee, then manages to escape and make her way towards the ruined, castle-like building she has noticed on the headland. She has no idea it is an ancient chain tower, constructed in 1380, to protect the two ports from attack by any Spanish, Dutch or French marauders who constantly roamed the high seas. At one time its heavy chain had stretched across the mouth of the river connecting it to the Fowey blockhouse on the far side, and could be raised and lowered at will. Jenny is frankly bored and it seems like an excellent idea to expend some energy, be off by herself and explore what appears to be a picturesque castle.

She strolls past other holiday cottages near a grey church, and then catches sight of the romantic ruin standing on a promontory, overlooking a deep blue sea. A rough path leads her towards what would have been the massive front door but is now only an empty opening. She ducks under it and finds wide, rectangular apertures, narrowing to slits, obviously gun ports. There is the beginning of a spiral staircase that would have given access to the first floor, long since disappeared, and she's surprised to find a large fireplace close to a mullioned window that faces upriver. On the far side of the sturdy building is another huge entry and she peers out to see an uneven path that leads steeply down to the rocks below. The whole place is warmly somnolent and, apart from the surge of the sea and the drone of a nearby bee, she is drowsily alone. She relaxes in the sunshine, drapes herself in the doorway and stares out across the river to Readymoney Cove and St Catherine's Point opposite. A small boat is making its way past her and she dreamily thinks of Tristan waiting for Iseult and smiles. The lad in the boat catches her smile and waves his hand in response. She has always been shy and she feels an idiot but, as the sea divides them, she dares to wave back.

That evening – as if on cue – he is waiting for her by the pontoon on the quay. She recognises his craft first, by its distinctive brown sail. He grins at her and leaves his friends to walk across the square to talk to her. They exchange names and she learns his is Andrew Lanyon and admits to hers being Jennifer Fairburn. They are too young to visit The Lugger Inn so they sit in a sheltered corner, in the evening sun, and talk as if their lives depended on it. They both know this has been a fortuitous accident and suddenly they are determined to spend as much time together as is humanly possible. Andrew introduces her to the love of his life – his beloved boat, *The Shy Curlew* – and she points out where she is staying. She is strangely wary of taking him back to meet her parents. She has never had a serious male friend before and she is conscious her parents may be subtly jealous and could try to sever this fragile relationship. So she meets him on the quay most mornings and he plans their days accordingly. It is always somewhere in *The Shy Curlew* and she revels in her improving crewing ability. He jubilantly takes her to his home – this is the highest accolade he can offer this girl. She is introduced to his boat-building family – his widowed father, his two older brothers and his adored sister-in-law, Deborah, who has looked after and loved him as if she were his mother. By then they are inseparable and both quietly dread this holiday ending. Neither talks about the limit on their time together as if, by ignoring it, their separation will not become a fact.

He shows her secret places that no other visitors will even suspect exist. They sail around the coast and he points out every rock and headland he has known since a boy. They land wherever it suits them and lounge indolently on pristine beaches, after swimming in the sea or digging around in rock pools. Occasionally they will explore busy harbour-side villages like Mevagissey, Polperro or Looe and wander round hand in hand.

He proudly takes her to visit the cliff-side garden at "The Headland" that is open every Thursday in the summer for charity. She takes her camera with her, as she does wherever they go, and records all the intimate sheltered corners where sub-tropical plants flourish and the seats are just perfect for intimate conversations. The owner encourages them both to go down to the tiny, sandy, bathing cove at the foot of the cliffs and they return, starving, to be welcomed by a delicious cream tea, which they devour with gusto.

During their solitary conversations they both share their hopes and aspirations for the future. Jenny has just left school and will be going on to college with her parents' blessing. Andrew, after being away from home for a few years, has chosen not to join the rest of his family in their boat building business; but has decided he wants to go to sea and has fixed his sights on studying to become a Radio Officer. He is hoping to join the Merchant Navy after he has passed exams in radio and radar. He will be going to Plymouth University but will return home at weekends. Jenny, who has no idea what career path she will finally decide on, is also going to study locally and, therefore, will still live at home. So their next few years are planned and catered for. She is fascinated by Andrew's dedication and certainty; she also resolves to aim for something equally important and rewarding.

She tells him two days before she is due to go that she is leaving. He says little and her hopes and confidence in sharing a future together dissipate as morning mist is devoured by sunshine. Her parents are upbeat to be leaving Cornwall as they have rarely seen their daughter and have been a little bored with each other's company. They consider she must be going through a strange, secretive and introverted stage in her life and hope, by returning home to her friends and family, she will become their cheerful, obedient child once more.

They leave late one Sunday afternoon, in unaccustomed rain, and Jenny, screwed up in the back of their comfortable car, deliberately keeps her eyes averted so she won't have to see all the achingly familiar haunts that she has been so happy to be part of for the past few weeks. The car arrives at the four-way turning by The Russell Inn: the driver hesitates before turning sharp right and accelerating up the long, steep hill. The girl refuses to look towards the quay and rigidly stares down at her well-washed jeans, so she misses the young lad striding down the hill. He casts a glance at the unknown, expensive car as it passes but fails to notice the dejected girl sitting hunched up behind her father. He is missing her presence already; but it is not in his nature to express these feelings to anyone.

Her mother speaks brightly and bracingly over her shoulder, including both daughter and husband in her idle chatter. It seems important to dispel the sullen atmosphere that she only vaguely detects, but is unable to comprehend, so she prattles thoughtlessly on. Her daughter feigns sleep until it becomes a reality – and their car speeds ever eastward towards another life, and their comfortable home.

Part I

Chapter 1

*

It all began on a cool but sunny Saturday afternoon near the end of September. Chris had been visiting for the weekend. Since his return to the UK, to oversee the small empire he was rapidly building, he had managed to inveigle himself slyly into our mundane lives for a couple of long weekends. We had all watched *Match of the Day* – sitting rather uncomfortably in front of the television, each with a huge plate of fish and chips balanced on a tray on our knees and washed down with copious cans of lager.

I had deliberately arranged this to remind him of times gone by when we had both done this most Saturday afternoons on a regular basis. I suppose it was to point out to him that there was more to life than increasing his substantial bank balance and influencing his well-heeled colleagues. It obviously had the desired effect because he laughingly reminisced about it and said he had never done it since he had left. I thought it would not hurt him to see how the other half lived – in Britain, anyway. For years now he had spent his life in other parts of the world, where it had not been the norm, and I wanted him to realise there could be more to life back in this country than high-powered conferences ending with a round of golf at the weekend or an invitation to a house party with some industrialist or politician.

I wanted him to be aware that, although Robin and I could cope with the lavish meals in sumptuous restaurants that he had introduced us to recently, we could also enjoy a cracking game of football to spice up a takeaway meal. We watched until the credits rolled and the music faded away, then the three of us retired to a sheltered corner in the garden with a pot of coffee. We sat back and rested and Chris and I returned to our conversation.

That was how it all started. I think by then Robin was half asleep. He'd had a really busy week with all sorts of irritating misdemeanours overshadowed by a particularly nasty double murder that had the police baffled, and it was taking all their already overstretched manpower with very little to show for it. Chris and I talked quietly and I became even more aware of how our paths had sharply diverged since he had left me all those years ago. Luckily I had managed to submerge myself in the nursing profession vowing I need never trust, or rely on, a man ever again.

My fervent vow had lasted all of three years, until Robin came along and quietly undermined all my jaundiced views. He was everything I did not need. Younger than me by an indecent number of years and holding down a stressful job that he was rarely able to discuss. We also had the added complication of both doing shift work, so often our only communication would be through scribbled notes plastered on the refrigerator door. Even after he moved in with me I was still mouthing that marriage was only for fools. That was until he finally convinced me that, maybe, this time it could possibly be different.

Chris, on the other hand, for all his inconsistency, had always kept in touch since his swift departure that Sunday so long ago. In the beginning he was probably only keeping an eye on me, by turning up at odd unexpected times to take me out for a meal or a show, until I finally had the courage to escape from the house we had so lovingly chosen together in Kent and purchased a purpose-built flat in town to show him I was quite capable of being on my own and, indeed, I even preferred it that way. Generous and lavish until the end, my ex-husband then insisted on having the apartment carpeted and, from then on, he only appeared when he had a new car or was seeking my approval about another mad scheme that would, hopefully, make his fortune.

When Robin appeared on the scene, Chris came and took a long cold look at him, listened to my usual formula that living together was one thing and marriage another, then swiftly went on his way. It was only then that he took off for pastures new with Hannelore, the woman he left me for. The fact that she looked so like me, and could have been my sister, always left me feeling slightly bemused.

She must have had something that I could never supply though because, through his monumental hard work, his business ventures suddenly became very successful.

They then moved out to a large house in one of the nicest parts of Surrey and it went very quiet. My parents in Devon would keep me up to date with the news as the pair frequently turned up at their modest bungalow every time Chris purchased a new and more expensive car and my father would regale us with the details. By the time the latest one was reported to be a Rolls Royce I wondered what Robin's reaction would be; but it never seemed to worry him one way or the other. I found it quietly amusing that Chris refused to marry the woman who had taken my place; but this was obviously his way of letting me know he was at last getting his heart's desire – success. I was genuinely pleased for him whilst being equally amazed that Robin and I were happily settling into a good life of our own. I would still wonder if it was doomed to end the way of my first partnership, but not as sharply as I had at the beginning.

Then something happened. I have no idea what. Chris maybe made some mistake, possibly stretched himself too far, cut a corner, twisted the law to suit himself: suddenly they were both gone like a puff of wind. They then made their home in Switzerland, which was where Hannelore hailed from, and Chris went off to try and make a second fortune anywhere in the world that offered lucrative employment. They decided to marry but this was probably to provide economic stability in a foreign country – his wife's country. Finally Robin and I also decided to move – to the West Country. My parents were becoming increasingly more vulnerable and frail and I felt I should be closer. Robin and I also elected to tie the knot and I started believing in us a little after all.

From then on, three or four times a year, Chris would call me from strange places all around the world. Some I had only heard of, others I would not be able to place my finger on accurately with an open atlas in front of me. I would blithely answer the telephone, rattling off our number expecting to hear Robin, a girlfriend or a message from the hospital, only to be greeted with Chris's light voice pitching down the line saying, 'Hi, it's me!'

It always gave me a warm frisson of pleasure to hear him. I suppose it was nice to know he still cared. Life was not all that exciting in our little country town and his news inevitably enlivened an uneventful day. Somehow, against all odds, we had remained good friends so my first thoughts were always how he was and *where* he was. He would then give me a résumé of his wanderings since he had last telephoned. Strange, exotic places that I had barely heard of – like Cambodia, Vietnam, the Philippines and even, once, Bolivia. Sometimes it was a more mundane location like Australia or South Africa, doing all sorts of jobs from sheep farming to gold mining. It all sounded improbable to me but then I knew that Chris would never bother to lie. Relationships with other women: yes, he had pulled the wool over my eyes whenever he thought it necessary - straight downright lies to get out of an awkward predicament maybe – but never just for the hell of it. Once, he was in some odd little backwater in China. In that instance he said how much he disliked the country – feeling lost and depressed in its vastness. But usually he recounted some amusing anecdotes about the strange places or customs he had encountered, or the tasks he had been tackling, and how he had dealt with them, against all odds, adequately and with competence.

I would listen and marvel silently – scribbling place names down so I would remember and could relay them to Robin later that evening. Strangely, Robin would be genuinely interested because, over the years, I had truly convinced him of my indifference as to what my former husband was doing. And the huge distance between us had somehow lent stability to my own strong and reliable relationship.

We would often discuss the odd occupations Chris was managing to carve out for himself. Jobs like oil exploration or gold mining seemed so exotic compared to *our* simple lives. How had he ever managed to convince a potential employer he was capable of such tasks, we asked ourselves? From my quiet niche in the West Country I marvelled at the bizarre locations that Chris would sound quite at home in. He would give graphic thumbnail descriptions of people and places, and I would be amazed at his adaptability. It seemed every time he rang the locations became even more far flung until, eventually, there seemed few places he had not visited or worked in.

Then one wintry morning I was having a lie-in after a rather frantic previous evening. We had been run ragged at the hospital with a very sick patient needing resuscitation, two more suffering second heart attacks and a visitor having a rather nasty accident on her way to the car park. So it was a good excuse to take my breakfast back to bed and settle down with a decent book. The telephone gave a loud jangle and, with a sigh, I padded out to the kitchen and picked it up on its third ring.

Chris's first words were, 'Guess where I am?'

I randomly suggested Israel or Australia off the top of my head. He laughed and told me he was in Henley-on-Thames, on his way to the office.

'What office?' I asked. This brought me up short. 'In the UK? Good heavens!'

He then moaned about the weather and the traffic. He was on his way to work, he told me, and was using one of the new mobile telephones while he sat in the usual traffic jam. In those days a telephone in a car was a luxurious asset and I was suitably impressed.

'What office?' I asked again, stupidly thinking I must have missed something. 'And what do you mean by the *usual* traffic jam?' What was he doing over here behaving like a middle-class citizen instead of a renegade pirate in a second-rate film?

He explained he had returned to Britain two weeks previously.

'Thought it was time I took a closer look at one of those factories I jointly own. See exactly how it all works. Think I am getting a little too old for all these outlandish places, foreign food and bad water,' he said, laughing. 'Still, I never reckoned or remembered quite how cold and damp it can be in England at this time of the year.'

'But how can you own a company over here when you are now a Swiss citizen?' I asked naively.

'Easily, my dear. I have always retained dual nationality. One never knows when a British passport might be a necessity in a sticky situation.'

I suddenly realised all these escapades, whilst amusing to us, may occasionally have had their serious side, too. I must have still sounded puzzled as to the reason why he was returning to the UK, for he then proceeded to list the other three companies he either owned or had an interest in. I took much of what he said with a pinch of salt – knowing his penchant for exaggeration of old; but, even so, it sounded impressive. I listened intently and wondered what Robin would make of it that evening.

I noticed, from that morning on, he would regularly contact me two or three times a week; usually when I would be on a late shift and had little to do at home. I had innocently explained my duties and I could well visualise him, bored, sitting in some traffic chaos, tapping his fingers on the steering wheel of his car. I was under no illusion that I was one of the few people he could use in this way as we chatted about inconsequential subjects while he subtlety educated me regarding the new person he had become. He would be delightfully amused at my unworldly questions. I am sure they gave his ego a great boost. It was obvious he had certainly taken to this new, urban way of life as a duck to water and I was amazed and flattered that, for now, he wanted to share it with me.

I asked about his wife and family. He appeared dismissive of their claims on him. The two girls had remained behind with their mother in Switzerland, he said, because he preferred the superior education he considered they would receive out there. Hannelore was always busy, so it suited him to take a flight shuttle to Geneva most Friday nights and return late on the Sunday. It sounded a very hectic and tiring life to me.

As the months went by Chris contacted me more and more. It appeared so casual, but I was never sure of his intentions. At one time he told me he would be coming to our part of the world for a conference. He and his chauffeur would be staying at one of the better hotels in Taunton and he smoothly asked if Robin and I would join him for a meal that first evening. Of course we went. Me, to see how much he had changed in the intervening years we had been apart and Robin simply out of interest. I had told my husband how, as a youngster, Chris had been one of the local lads, from one of the poorer areas of London, just fighting shy of getting into trouble with the law. This, to a quiet girl like me, had the effect of making him appear more exciting and glamorous to my untutored eyes.

He had been given a bad start in life. He was just five when he and his two sisters were taken into care. They had been living with their parents in a high-rise London flat; their mother had fallen ill and it had swiftly turned to pneumonia and, as the illness progressed, his father had disappeared. Neighbours had found the children in a cold room, crying. Their mother had been rushed away to the nearest district hospital and the three children had been sent to a London County Council children's home in one of the nicest parts of Essex. Chris's particular house-parents, Mr and Mrs Hughes, were an exceptional couple. They lived in an untidy, rambling old house in the extensive grounds of the Home along with their own three children and two other fostered young lads. He slotted into that life as if he belonged and they obviously enjoyed having him.

His two sisters were not quite so lucky, or as happy; but at least they had each other and the Home was run in an easy-going, pleasant way with reasonable schooling, and the children were always allowed to see each other as often as they liked. Chris soon grew to love and respect his carers who were middle-aged, fair and friendly and, for a while, he became the youngest member of their 'family'. Due to their care and attention he obtained a reasonable education but, even though they tried to persuade him against it, he elected to leave at sixteen. His two sisters had returned to the family home much earlier and it was some years before he rejoined them. I always had the sneaking suspicion that the job he obtained, with its basic salary, may have been part of the attraction in his returning to the family as far as his parents were concerned.

When we were first married Chris always insisted we attended the Home's annual garden party for all the old students and I was only too pleased to agree. The reunion gave the youngsters a chance to talk about their recent endeavours – to show off, or commiserate, or to simply gossip as one would do at any family gathering – and I soon noticed Chris was invariably in a happy frame of mind all the following week. We would drive into the car park shortly after lunch and there would be the diminutive Mr and Mrs Hughes – or Phyl and Jack as they always insisted we call them – waiting expectantly with bright, smiling faces. At over six feet, Chris would crush them with a hug and immediately proceed to tell them what he had been up to the previous twelve months. Eager listeners, they always brought out the best in him and suddenly he would sound like a well-adjusted member of society. A young man they could be proud of and accept as one of their own.

We would then stay for a couple of hours, walking around the displays proudly made by the current children and chatting with other ex-pupils and staff. The atmosphere was always congenial with afternoon tea on the vast lawns in the sunshine or in the cosy, slightly shabby, family room if it were overcast or wet. I would feel relaxed knowing Chris would be contented for the rest of the week. It was as if the seal of approval from his surrogate family made his entire world happier for a while.

Looking back, it was amazing that Chris and I ever met. We had been born miles apart and were from very different levels of society. He was the son of a nomadic family who rarely stayed long in their rented accommodation, moving around some of the most run-down parts of London. I, on the other hand, was a shy college student and the daughter of a staid, middle-aged couple from the leafy suburbs. My parents certainly were not rich but they had saved over the years and, by then, owned their comfortable, small three-bedroomed, semi-detached house, which must have seemed like riches to Chris and his family. Surrounded by gardens, with a garage and an old car, this must, I am sure, have been enough to raise us all in his estimation.

Blame my young cousin for twisting the probability of us ever meeting. Dee had always been quite different from the rest of us; she had scorned exams at school and only longed to begin work and 'live' – as she put it. For some obscure reason she had settled into a humdrum job for an engineering union in scruffy Kentish Town, which was miles away from where we lived. I think the work entailed little more than answering the telephone and typing up minutes for the delegates. She appeared to enjoy it though, especially as she had caught the eye of Bryn, a bright young fellow, who was always in and out of her office on some pretext.

They became besotted with one another to the extent that every evening he would catch the long-distance bus out to our quiet, pleasant neighbourhood. No one, and especially a young man, wants to travel miles alone every evening, so he would drag along his best friend Chris and expect Dee to provide suitable company to keep him amused. Despite their backgrounds, both lads were attractive and prepossessing. Now we would say they 'scrubbed up well'! They had the advantage of being tall and slim, they dressed in the latest fashions without going to extremes, and they had the quick repartee inherited from birth. Chris had dark, curly hair and Bryn was a very fiery redhead. Certainly neither would go unnoticed. Their slightly raffish air and devastating smiles, which they used knowingly, stood them in good stead in their own environment and, in our part of the world, they impressed Dee's friends by their very difference from the quieter lads we were used to.

Usually Dee had little difficulty in supplying Chris with a blind date most evenings. Weekends were sometimes more of a problem and occasionally, if all else failed, she would call on me – the quiet, older, studious cousin who lived next door – and badger me until I succumbed. My boyfriend was always many miles away so there were few reasonable excuses I could make. No one, apart from me, was even certain he was still in circulation. My natural shyness meant I never talked about our correspondence and scarcely even mentioned my visits to him. He rarely made appearances at our house, and then only fleetingly, so I was never allowed to use him as an excuse not to make up a foursome.

For what else had I to do, reasoned my cousin?

I had been lonely since childhood, mainly because I was so often ill and, while other children were forging friendships and having fun, I was languishing in bed. Because of this I had been a late developer during my latter years at school; luckily I was then able to become a solitary student at a nearby college. All my friends chose to leave school and seek their fortunes, with the fond hope they would soon secure the perfect marriage. It was every girl's dream in those days. Career women were the exception, and certainly did not come from our strata of society, where there were few professional parents who expected, or encouraged, their female offspring to carve out a niche in the business world. I knew of no female would-be solicitors, doctors or bank officials in my school, street or town. Females were there mostly to complement their male counterparts in a domestic setting and a partnership producing two or three children, within that marriage, was the goal of most girls.

My college was a completely alien environment and it was taking all my time just to stay abreast of the flow of information that was being thrust at us. Somehow I had to accept the brash mixture of studentalia that surrounded me in my new noisy life, keep my own counsel and remain steadfast. It was all so different from my quiet, solemn, straight-laced school where one was taught and not lectured to. It had been made clear on our first day that we were now considered adults; and whether we chose to learn or not was purely our own concern. No one would be chasing us, no one would care if we completed assignments or not and, if we fell by the wayside and left tomorrow, our places would be filled without a ripple affecting the educational pond.

None of this was helped by the fact that, just before I was accepted at college, I went on holiday and met a boy and, of course, fell madly in love with him. Andrew was intelligent, he was handsome but most important of all, he was nice. He came from a boat-building family who could trace their lineage back to the Fowey Gallants – swashbuckling privateers from the fourteenth century who could be relied upon to provide the Crown with a fleet of merchant ships to fight wars against a foreign enemy, transport soldiers to war, whether it be at home or abroad and carry sufficient victuals to feed them. Occasionally these merchant sailing ships would run foul of the King's temper when they, mistakenly, took the law into their own hands and attacked friendly foreign vessels. Immediately they then would be labelled pirates and punished accordingly. The rest of the time they peacefully traded staples of tin, cloth and wool with Normandy and Brittany, returning with salt, wine and iron. Another lucrative business for several of these vessels was to carry pilgrims to Spain. This became a popular pastime in the late fifteenth century when at least six Fowey ships sailed – and one included the local Vicar on its manifest!

Gradually as the years passed I learned snippets of Andrew's historical family background but, for the moment, all I recognised was they were a thoroughly down-to-earth, hard-working family who had the sea and boat building in their blood. His mother had died shortly after Andrew was born and, although his father was head of the family, he had long since retired and it was his two elder sons who actually ran the Polruan boatyard. Hugh was the designer of the small and large craft they built; but it was Mark who converted Hugh's ideas to reality. Andrew, as the youngest, was encouraged to join them but, like Ratty in *Wind in the Willows*, he preferred to sail and mess around in boats, so no one was surprised when he chose to interest himself in naval matters and took himself off to be educated.

What *did* surprise them, though, was the decision he made to take himself off to the other end of southern England. Browsing in a Fowey bookshop, he had found an article that told of an organisation known as the Shaftesbury Homes and, in particular, the four-masted training ship *Arethusa*, based on the River Medway in Upnor, Kent. The brainchild of the Earl of Shaftesbury, the Homes accepted boys from disadvantaged homes and trained them for posts in any of the Armed Services, but with a special emphasis on the Royal or Merchant Navy.

Lord Ashley, the 7th Earl of Shaftesbury, was born at the beginning of 1800 and educated at Harrow and Oxford. With that sort of aristocratic upbringing it was amazing he came into contact with the poor, and enabled him to notice the huge chasm that existed between their conditions and those of the people that surrounded *him*. As a young man of twenty-five he entered Parliament and immediately fought for factory reforms that included better conditions for its workers and a ten-hour day. He then turned his attention to the coal mines and fought to keep women, and children under 13, from being forced to do such terrible work. He supported Florence Nightingale in her new ideas to reform nursing and made sure the poor had affordable lodgings. Like so many kind-hearted men of his time he could see the great divide between rich and poor and was determined to close it.

One day his friend, a William Williams, was in Plymouth and spoke to some shackled lads on a train bound for deportation. He heard their awful stories about lack of work and famine that haunted most of them and their families. He and Lord Ashley decided they would provide education, food and homes for these boys, enabling them to go on and seek active employment. Thus the Shaftesbury centres came into being. They bought up decommissioned ships and moored them around the country where they considered was the most need. Each one was re-christened *Arethusa*. It was a hard life but it trained the lads to be self-reliant and to accept responsibility and, later, most of them would enjoy a decent career.

How Andrew persuaded his family to accept his plan and then to pull strings to enable him to apply we shall never know. Was he really disadvantaged or deprived? Hardly. At twelve years old he may not have had a mother; but his family provided him with a stable home life and, even though it may not have been particularly affluent, it was comfortable and he had lots of friends and pastimes.

Possibly it was his insatiable love of the sea that influenced the authorities, or his determination to join the navy, but something struck a chord in that crusty selection committee and a cool September day saw him alighting from the Cornwall-to-London train and catching the connection to Strood, in Kent. As he walked through the ticket barrier he heard another young lad ask the way to Lower Upnor and that was the beginning of a friendship with Rod that was to last until they both left the *TS Arethusa* at fifteen.

****

When I met Andrew he had been back in Cornwall a year and we were both on holiday from school. Two youngsters in one of the loveliest settings in England meant we were probably both ripe for a perfect friendship. My childhood suddenly dropped away from me. My hormones must have been flowing wildly because, what started as a light-hearted six-week interlude, became a deep-seated affair with both of us writing daily. Certainly, from my end, no one guessed how swiftly it would become serious. I was far too shy to boast about it to my parents or friends. Surprisingly, it lasted all of five years – during which time I left college and started my nursing career and Andrew left home for Plymouth polytechnic, then Southampton University; finally joining the Merchant Navy as a radio officer. I was delighted with his decision, as I knew he was happiest at sea. I was also well aware that my deep, unusual friendship with him meant most of my friends had drifted away towards their own concerns, while I would be subject to a very lonely period – until I was able to adjust.

Our writing continued – the only difference being that, now Andrew was away at sea, his letters did not now come regularly, but in large batches – posted as soon as he arrived at such destinations as Cape Town, Wellington or Buenos Aires. And I could imagine a similar pile of mine waiting for him, sent on by the line he worked for, once he arrived in port for any length of time.

This arrangement did not deter my cousin Dee from calling on my services when she was unable to find a girl to make up a regular foursome with Bryn, her new boyfriend, and Chris, his best mate. Maybe a couple of times a month, if I was at home, I would be expected to don my nicest clothes, put on some make-up accompanied by a decent perfume and enjoy myself. It was not hard and Dee rarely listened to any of my half-hearted excuses. And Chris was a nice enough lad who had certainly learned how to treat a girl with all the courtesy my parents could hope for. In contrast, the boys we usually associated with could have learned a lot from him and his friends. Somehow Chris never changed in that respect – as he matured he just became more practised and polished.

I was fast approaching my twenty-first birthday when it suddenly dawned on me that I was still that small-town girl, existing on the paltry sums hospitals doled out to their nurses and had the effrontery to call salaries. We were expected to be grateful that we had somewhere to live and were reasonably well fed. We certainly could afford no luxuries and, although we laughed, it was a struggle to make ends meet.

Andrew, on the other hand, had finished his training and was already reaping the benefits of all those years of study. He had a good job and was well paid for it. The work, he told me, was not arduous. Once he had learned his craft it was mostly routine. Even though his post was a solitary one he enjoyed the masculine company of his fellow officers and was settling into the long trips that go to make up a merchantman's life. In contrast, on entering port his ship would usually be given a rapturous welcome with various parties laid on by local dignitaries. It was an accepted fact that unmarried girls would be pressed into service, students and nurses to the fore, so, wearing his glamorous uniform, he would undoubtedly have an enjoyable time.

I began to see the writing on the wall. What incentive is there in writing to a girl on the other side of the world when one could speak to, and touch, a real live girl with no effort whatsoever? My friendship was now restricting him and I suddenly wondered if his bright letters were concealing thoughts of boredom. We had been such close friends for so long that I found it easy to imagine myself in his place. How would *I* react in a similar situation?

Possibly it was my fertile imagination but, once I had thought along these lines, I was unable to ignore my worries. I would soon become an encumbrance – like a clinging wife who needs constant reassurance. Was Andrew like an errant husband who removed his wedding band on leaving port and only replaced it on his finger the day he returned? Andrew had already described these seafaring colleagues who used their tours of duty as glorified holidays with no marital restrictions until they returned home to their humdrum lives.

I am ashamed to say Pride reared her ugly head and within a few days I had convinced myself. No sooner had I made up my mind than I wrote a brief note informing Andrew it was all over. I had to do it convincingly, and the only way, I decided, was to mention a new man in my life. I thought about some of the junior doctors but that would entail lots of embarrassing explanations. They would enjoy it, but I knew I wouldn't. Should I choose one I actually worked with or invent a fictitious character? I decided the simplest explanation would be an unknowing Chris. I had often talked about him to Andrew. I had never hidden from him that we occasionally went out together. I had said he was an ideal escort, so it all sounded reasonable and possible. The one thing I forgot to take into account was that Dee might relay all this to Chris as one huge joke.

In all honesty, Chris was not my type and never would be. We were as different as a rich gateau is to plain bread and butter. The quiet, studious nurse as opposed to the flamboyant, extrovert lad – what on earth had we in common? A night at the cinema was my idea of relaxation, while his was attending a dance hall, surrounded by a contingent of boisterous friends, chatting up and dancing with any girl who took his fancy. What had I done?

I now have no doubt that Chris was intrigued as to my motives and, from that moment, set out to woo me seriously. As far as he was concerned I had given him the go-ahead. Andrew had always been shy and reticent, the perfect gentleman, so I, having never been courted in such a determined way before, found it all strangely flattering.

Andrew returned at last from New Zealand and we arranged to meet for one last time. Chris obligingly decided he would take all three of us out for a meal. He borrowed his brother-in-law's old

Jaguar and did it in style. He acted the part perfectly, relaxed and calm, playing the role of 'mine host' to perfection as he escorted us to our local inn. We sat in a quiet, secluded alcove as he carefully arranged for Andrew and I to face one other while he sat comfortably beside me, his arm loosely across the back of my chair. Andrew and I barely picked at our food as, with a proprietary air, Chris took over proceedings. He smoothly ordered three courses with the appropriate wine to match. He never actually told Andrew that the two of us were an item but it was made abundantly clear that he considered we were. He kept the chat light and flowing while Drew and I barely spoke. Before we reached the cheese and biscuits stage, Andrew aligned his knife and fork neatly and stood up.

'I have to be off,' he said, barely glancing at his watch. 'Good luck, Jenny. I won't be getting in touch again.'

I was unable to raise my head. 'This is how Judas must have felt' fleetingly passed through my mind.

'No, please don't get up,' he said as Chris made to stand. 'I'll get a cab from here back to the Docks.' And then he quietly turned away and walked out of our lives.

I sat there with my head bent, breathing in the scent of a steak that I hadn't wanted and had been unable to eat. I knew it would be my least favourite dish for as long as I lived. Chris began on his crackers and cheese, but at least he had the good sense not to discuss the scene he had orchestrated and arranged to his own satisfaction. He took me home a short while afterwards and, apart from a swift kiss on the cheek, allowed me to walk indoors alone. I drearily climbed the stairs and sat on my bed completely drained of emotion.

Within days the massive gap that Andrew had always filled to overflowing left me dull-witted, wan and vulnerable. I missed the warm and chatty letters, his quirky view of this new world that he was seeing for the first time – and I felt lost when I had to disregard all the snippets of news I would normally have saved up and passed on to him. No more would I gleefully hoard up the smallest incidents to relate to him – silly things that only he would appreciate. Never again would I read his whimsical utterances, and either agree or argue violently with him. I never felt so lonely. I had become used to my cosy little rut and now I began to feel raw and lost. Before long, the reaction set in and I was naively thinking the gratitude and affection I felt for Chris must really be love.

We were engaged and married all within six months – much to my parents' dismay – and sadly, within the first week of marriage, I knew I had made a grave error. Nevertheless, I turned my back on common sense, deciding I would keep my side of the bargain without admitting to anyone my true feelings. I had made my bed and now I must lie on it. I certainly felt foolish but for some strange reason I decided that if I stuck rigidly to all the things a perfect housewife did, then I couldn't go far wrong. I was determined to love, honour and obey, as I had promised so glibly before my family and friends in our elegant parish church. I immediately knuckled down; I shopped for food, cleaned our flat to within an inch of its life, learned to cook passably well and even managed to put an iron around my husband's shirts – after asking for a crash-course on ironing from my mother-in-law.

By then I had completed my nursing training, while Chris had been trying out various jobs – from carpet fitting to ambulance driving. We managed to find a two-bedded flat in a run-down, seedy corner of London. Luckily, I had no time to take note of our surroundings as married life took up so much of my time and energy. At the hospital I might be dressing a nasty leg ulcer, as well as keeping an eye on a tricky blood transfusion, while cudgelling my brain as to what to rustle up for dinner later that evening. It was a delicate balance and one I was determined to get used to swiftly.

In the beginning we were so short of cash that we both had to supplement our earnings. When I was off duty I often baby-sat for a friend's small children – they were proper little scamps but I thoroughly enjoyed their company – and Chris found work in a West End theatre doing odd jobs. An aunt had suggested he apply, as she had lots of contacts in the theatrical world. We were relieved at even this small amount of extra money and, as neither job was onerous, we were grateful. Sometimes we returned home at the same time but often I would hand over Meryl's two sleeping angels as Chris might be sweeping a littered stage after a final curtain call. Occasionally we would meet on the number 12 bus home, both sinking into our seats and drifting into a tired reverie – but not for long. On arriving indoors I would have to swiftly conjure up a basic meal. The cheapest, and easiest, would be spam and mashed potatoes accompanied by a spoonful of frozen peas. Some nights, if I'd had a long and exhausting day, I was unable to face even boiling the potatoes and would proffer a few spam sandwiches, which we would wolf down with huge mugs of tea before falling thankfully into bed. Because Chris's money could not always be relied on, I would economise by buying *Lifebuoy* washing soap instead of the much more expensive toilet soap. I would hack each tablet into three and we would pretend we much preferred its smell and colour. I would haunt the shelves of our small supermarket and choose food that would soon be out of date. These small economies enabled us to pay the rent and keep our clapped-out Ford Prefect on the road.

The extra work took its toll and we were pushing ourselves to our limits. We were too proud to discuss it with my parents and, quite often, my mother would be sharp with me for looking tired and listless on the odd precious day we did get off. She did not know I'd get up at the crack of dawn to clean the flat, take our washing down to the launderette as soon as it opened and then snatch up some shopping from the corner shop before racing across London to join them for a leisurely meal. She invariably made a few pointed remarks about me looking bored, while all *I* longed to do was put my head down between the dishes and descend into blessed sleep!

Chris's parents had drifted off in their inimitable way. On the rare times we visited them his father had often downed too many pints at the local pub and would arrive home for Sunday lunch red-faced and maudlin. His mother would disregard the signals and brightly serve up a roast meal in the hope he would manage to eat some of it. The rest of the family ignored him. Chris and I were always starving, after waiting for him, and we would clear our plates long before the others in the hope there might be a substantial pudding to follow.

Most of my set sat, and passed, our exams. I commiserated with my friend, Cassie, who had to sit part of hers again due to her being off for two months with a nasty bout of glandular fever. Eventually I breathed a sigh of relief when I applied for, and was offered, the post of a junior staff nurse at a nearby hospital. Chris went on his meandering way, trying various jobs but settling to none. We rubbed along well enough. Once I earned a decent salary, I started to save for a house and had vague thoughts about raising a family in country surroundings. This decision had no firm basis in reality. What did I really know of the country? I had lived in a town all my life where the roads were mostly lined with trees but there was never a field, a hedge or a cow in sight.

My dream was shattered sooner than I expected. One evening we had friends round for a meal and I had been bragging how we would soon be on the lowest rung of the property ladder. I was still hazy about where this home would be. I leaned towards village greens and pleasant countryside, even though there was nothing remotely like that anywhere near the hospital that employed me. Chris never uttered a word.

Imagine my bewilderment when, the next night, he rushed home from work, bubbling over with excitement and insisted I accompany him to view a surprise. Downstairs, outside our shabby flat, there was a sparkling green and cream Hillman estate car. I stood there puzzled. He proudly admitted to having traded in the little second-hand car that we still owed money on, and announced we were the proud owners of this new vehicle that we could not afford to buy – let alone run.

'Oh yes we can,' he announced triumphantly. 'I spent our savings on it!'

He had spent the house money I had been so patiently putting aside for months and months. I stood, with the blustery wind and rain raking my face, speechless. Luckily the weather hid my bitter tears. It was then that I knew my fond dream had never been his. He had played lip service to my wants and needs, but my priorities were never his and maybe never would be. I slowly walked back up the stairs.

The second time around I made sure it was *my* savings and that they were well hidden along with the gas and electricity money. In fact, in the case of these utilities, I finally had pre-payment meters installed to prevent temptation. I had soon discovered Chris's weak points. It had been all too easy to go to a drawer and 'borrow' a few pounds with the intention of returning them later. Too often I would go to pay a bill and find the drawer's contents sadly depleted. From then on all our financial dealings became my concern and we were both a lot happier (or at least *I* was!).

By dint of saving every extra penny, I eventually raised the deposit once again and, with the help of the local council, who gave us a generous mortgage, we moved to a modern bungalow in the depths of Kent. Slowly, it became clear that neither of us could afford the daily journey to London. Our budget was already over-stretched. I settled down at a hospital in Chatham and Chris went on his merry way picking up work here and there as it suited him.

He had returned to driving an ambulance but missed the glamour and excitement of accident work in London. The incidents that had always seemed so stirring, when recounted by him or his colleagues at some of the London parties we attended, were absent. Now, in sleepy Kent, one gory road collision would be equalled by fifteen daily runs, taking old folk to the hospital or clinic, and it was only the odd stroke or heart attack victim he attended that would enliven his day.

As he so succinctly put it, 'Taking old dears along to have their toenails clipped is not my idea of an essential career!' So he became bored and, sadly, looked around to relieve his boredom. He found Rosamund who, by chance, was a workmate of mine. She was blonde and beautiful with an irresistible smile, and he was a pushover from the very start. And, worse, her trim figure was enhanced by our smart uniform. He was unable to help himself: and so began a tantalising liaison that only ground to a halt when she told him she was pregnant. Sadly, I was oblivious to this drama.

To me, he had made up some cock-and-bull story of having a mid-life crisis. If he could go away for a while he knew, as soon as he felt better, he would be able to return. I was harassed with work, running a home and wondering bitterly if I could keep everything together on my salary alone – so it never occurred to me to challenge these odd statements. I plodded on, refusing to tell my parents, who had escaped to Devon to enjoy a well-deserved retirement. I also wanted to give them no ammunition with which to taunt me.

I rang his parents and, like me, they accepted his abnormal behaviour. I *did* insist he gave me his new address, in case of emergency, and this he did reluctantly. I noticed it was only in the next town, so then I relaxed slightly.

From then on he would return home an average of once a week, in the evening, giving me a welcome lift back from the hospital. He would often stay and have the odd cup of coffee before rushing off. I would see his fellow ambulance drivers at the hospital but they rarely mentioned him, and, as I was so busy with my workload, plus keeping the bungalow in apple-pie order, I had little time to ponder on it. Now I know they were probably too embarrassed about the situation and, I'm sure, they didn't want to be involved, so found it easier to look the other way and ignore us both.

Chris told me he was staying with a fellow driver and his wife. The man was older, and I knew him vaguely, therefore I never queried his explanation. Naively, I hoped the wife would mother him but I also wondered if he was causing them too much disruption. Little did I realise the true state of affairs!

As the weeks went by, gradually his visits became more frequent. He would stay later – drinking coffee and munching a hastily made sandwich. He would often tell me how clean and neat the house looked. Why wouldn't it, I reflected, when I was rarely there to make it messy?

Then one evening, possibly finding me as obtuse as ever after all the hints he was dropping, he put his head in his hands and told me the truth. In the split second before he blurted it all out, I guessed exactly what he would say. I then saw Chris for what he was. A liar and a weak man, tall in stature, with good looks and a kindliness shining out of his face, easy-going to a fault and more easily led than leading. Always good company in a crowd; but he had never shown determination or commitment to me, his wife, ever. The lad I had married had never really grown up – he still wanted to be a Peter Pan and be well thought of by his peers – a good laugh and a good friend to everyone. None of this now measured up to my standards and I felt incredibly sad.

He begged me to take him back. When I had got over the shock and embarrassment that all this was happening at the place where I worked, and with a close colleague at that, it raised other questions in my head. Did all my fellow nurses know? He assured me not. We argued back and forth and I reminded him of the baby Rosamund would soon be having. Surely it would be better to start again and marry her – if only for the baby's sake? He explained it had all been a sorry mistake and it was really me he loved. Looking back, I realise how stupid I was to listen to his facile excuses. We sat in the kitchen and I argued, and he pleaded, through most of the night until finally, tired and worn out with reasoning, I agreed to try and make a go of our marriage once more. I could see Chris's relief as he made his way to his car for the return journey back to Rosamund, just as dawn was breaking. I knew he hoped that this would solve all his problems – but, for me, I guessed it would never be that simple.

I was on the late shift at the hospital the next day. I was extremely tired and in a state of bemusement and dread. But nothing seemed to have changed since the previous day and no one took any particular notice of me. I felt there was little reason to celebrate Chris's return. I was still uncertain as to how we were going to carry on and patch up our sad marriage. Chris, somehow, had got off very lightly; both Rosamund and I would be suffering from this terrible mess for as long as I could foresee. She more than me. For she would shortly have a new life to look after with no reliable future on which to base her and her baby's needs.

I told my closest friend, Jess, who had worked with me since I had arrived in Kent, and we both decided it was nobody else's business. Would I ever be able to trust Chris again, she asked? I had no idea. We pressed on with the afternoon clinic and I managed to smother my turbulent feelings by concentrating on a stream of very sick patients.

These feelings gradually changed into a cold rage as two weeks went by and I heard nothing from my errant husband. I refused to contact him and waited impatiently until one evening when my telephone rang. I reached for it, expecting it to be Chris, and discovered it was my cousin Dee, in floods of tears. I listened while she explained that Bryn, the boy she had been madly in love with, had left his job and gone off accompanied by two back- packing pals, to New Zealand.

'I'm sure they had been planning it for months,' she wailed. 'He must have because, along with his passport, he showed me a letter offering him employment that was dated weeks ago. And, to add insult to injury, he expected me to wish him well!'

I commiserated and refrained from telling her my news. There would be time for that when Chris and I had sorted out our differences – or not. But what struck me as most ironical was, if

Dee hadn't set off the chain of events by being irresistibly attracted to Bryn, the boy in her office, I would never have even *met* Chris, let alone *married* him. Chance happenings can cause momentous results, I suddenly discovered. It wouldn't have altered the fact that Andrew and I had drifted apart and I would almost certainly have finished my relationship with him; but I would now only be a lonely, single woman and not a married fool caught up in a web of deceit and unhappiness. I knew Paul, a lad Dee had known since they were both in primary school together, would always be on hand to pick up the pieces for her. Kind, faithful Paul could always be relied on to cushion her misery and bring her consolation.

On cue Chris came breezily back and expected us to resume our old life together, but by then I had hardened my heart against him. His tolerant, hard-working partner had changed and, sadly, she had become less naive and far more vigilant. So, two weeks later, when I came upon a racy letter crushed in his uniform pocket from the wife of the ambulance driver who had befriended him when he had left me, my suspicions were confirmed. She had attended an impromptu party at our house one night and, after her husband left to begin a late shift at the ambulance station, she had asked if she could stay over. The next morning I had left her sleeping and quietly gone off to work. From the crumpled letter I retrieved I learned their affair had begun almost as soon as Chris had been taken in by her and her husband and it had culminated in a very pleasant day, spent mostly in our bed, I deduced. So not only had my newly returned husband been unfaithful to me but to his new love, Rosamund, as well! I felt for his helpful colleague who had offered him shelter and had inherited immense troubles.

I went straight to a solicitor friend in the hope that our divorce would be swift and unhindered. This concluded one blustery day in October. I was ordered to attend The Royal Courts of Justice to go through the traumatic (as it was in those days) experience of divorce. Kindly to the end, Chris had insisted he took me in our car and, having no one else to turn to, I reluctantly agreed. Alone on the witness stand, I stood calmly and listened dispassionately as my barrister told how my husband had admitted adultery – not once but twice – and all within a short space of time. He disclosed how the first liaison had produced a child and the second culminated in a lady spending a night in my home on the flimsiest pretext. I reminded myself that having my secrets revealed in court was a small price to pay for freedom and, when I walked out of court with my solicitor, I felt truly liberated. Chris, civilised and thoughtful to the end, took me for a pleasant meal at the Swiss Centre and then put me on the last train from Waterloo to spend the weekend with my parents in Devon.

The relief was immeasurable. I pulled the tatters of my old life around me once more. My close friends began to telephone again and, suddenly, every free weekend was taken up with visits or company. Laughter, agreeable companions and good food made my world a better place. I held my head up and straightened my spine. Chris had decided to return to his carpet-planning ventures and Rosamund disappeared from both our lives. I had no idea what happened to his second paramour. She had been the last act in our ten-year play and I was satisfied, when the final curtain came down, that it was for good.

Once I began to visit Devon again, I refused to talk about past years and gently led my parents' conversations away from my old life with Chris as if it had been a bad dream. Gradually they came to accept the new me. I had become stronger, I was whole once more and slowly they recognised I was an individual with valid opinions of my own.

It took time but gradually I became an interesting woman once again. I had ideas and views that did not always coincide with those around me. I was not pedantic, but I was firm. I would never knowingly let anything spoil my life ever again. Little did I know that I would eventually meet a man called Robin and my whole jaundiced outlook on marriage and happiness would change under his friendly persuasion.

And little did I guess that my life would finally swing round in a full circle and surprise everyone – especially me!

Chapter 2

*

It had finally grown cold in the garden so the three of us returned to the sitting room to spread out on our rather shabby, comfortable furniture while Chris and I carried on discussing our past life together. Robin, probably bored, had wandered off to write up a long overdue report.

Looking back, I suppose my marriage to Chris was not half as bad as I felt it had been at the time. In the beginning there had been lots of good times. We had found a sturdy Victorian maisonette in London's Peckham with high ceilings and draughty windows. Our landlady was a gossip and jealous of our modest, but newer, furnishings; while her husband was kind and fair, actually reducing our rent by five shillings a week because he could obviously see the struggle we were having even to exist

I learned to cook simply by trial and error, and usually we were so hungry we would eat almost anything – cremated or half raw. Quite often I would arrive home tired and worn out from a long day on the wards only to discover I had forgotten the bread, or we had left the milk out on the table and it had become rancid in the sunshine, and all I could do was fume at my own stupidity. In those days there were few late-night corner shops or supermarkets open, as we know them, so we invariably went without the forgotten item and I would vow to do better the next time.

But, on the other side of the coin, I had lots of friends at the hospital and we would visit each other's homes with a bottle of cheap wine and a galaxy of jokes. Impromptu parties that had us all dancing to the latest discs were a feature of our lives and gave us a lot of pleasure. Any children would be put upstairs to sleep and we would take it in turns to creep up and make sure all was serene.

As my culinary skills improved we would host small dinner parties for our special friends. Often it would be simple sausage-and-mash eaten around our scarred kitchen table while we put the world to rights and told the Government what they should be doing. We could not afford to go to the local pub so we sat there and chattered into the small hours of the morning.

Sometimes there would be wild gatherings of Chris's ambulance friends, maybe for a birthday or a promotion, and we would dance the night away. We were young enough to be able to drape ourselves over whatever we found most comfortable at the end of the night and drop asleep. I remember one night finding a spot on a friend's stairs and stiffly waking the next morning with my head awkwardly cramped against my cousin's knees and my feet resting on a stranger's lap.

Somehow we always managed to pull ourselves together, stagger home in time for a swift bath, a cup of black coffee and race off and present ourselves at work. Now the thought of being so profligate with sleep sends shudders through me. I would be unable to keep up such a frenetic pace. Now I need a reasonable amount of rest, a comfortable bed plus a cup of tea before I can greet the coming day with anything like good grace. Blame that on the passing years as well as sensible living away from the bright lights of London.

'Do you remember the morning we all walked down to the Thames at about 5am after a wild ambulance "knees-up"?' asked Chris with a grin.

'No, but I remember doing a conga in the East End of London one New Year's Eve. It was coming up to midnight and we danced in and out of strangers' houses while all the boats on the Thames sounded off eerily in celebration. The cacophony of mournful hoots and klaxons from the Docks blended in with our shouts and singing as we stomped in through wide open front doors and out through the backs.'

'How about the night we went to our local cinema and a fight broke out down in the front stalls?' I reminded him.

'Yes, and you made me wade in and separate the two kids who were punching hell out of each other. At that time I was petrified that the rest of them would decide to turn on me just for the fun of it,' he said with a rueful grin. 'I may have been tall but I was never invincible and there were dozens of them.'

I had never guessed he felt like that. He had always seemed like an indestructible giant to me and it had never entered my head that he was no Sir Galahad wanting to put the world to rights.

'What about that lad on his bicycle who hurtled into our stationary Ford Prefect?' I asked.

'And after that awful bang we thought we had at least been hit by a lorry – until we saw the dent his head had made in the back of our tatty little car!' We laughed together at the memory.

By then we were in the kitchen and I was swiftly preparing our evening meal. The recollections were coming thick and fast as we delved back into our chequered 10-year history. I brought out a bottle of wine and we shared it as we chatted. We'd had very little money. At one time we had both done two jobs to supplement our incomes and to keep ourselves from literally going hungry. The car that had been damaged by the young cyclist had been clapped out when we bought it but we had both been determined to keep it on the road to give ourselves some independence.

So it was with great mellow benevolence we finished an excellent dinner accompanied by a selection of wines Chris had supplied. Finally I pushed everything in the dishwasher and brought in a tray of coffee as Robin placed a decent bottle of brandy near at hand and we relaxed. I curled up on the settee while the two men lay back on reclining chairs, when suddenly Chris asked that all-important question. The question that was to change the rest of my life!

Taking an appreciative sip of brandy he said, 'Is there anything you've ever regretted doing – or not doing – in your life, Jenny?'

For a second I could think of nothing. The ten years I had been with Chris had mostly been enjoyable as long as I discounted the short indiscretions he was prone to. In his eyes they were just light dalliances that had meant very little to him. Whether this applied to each person he had centred his attentions on may have been questionable. All I could remember was that none of these liaisons had lasted – until the very last two.

We'd often been poor and had to work extremely hard but we were both healthy and I am sure it had never hurt us. We had certainly learnt the value of money as well as always managing to extract fun with our young friends and neighbours who were as strapped for cash as we were. Life had had its ups and downs but had never been boring and both Chris and I had managed to part on cordial terms.

My father had told me to expect men to act like this and to get on with my marriage and forget his escalating infidelities. I said, 'Not my men!' and visited a solicitor. I was thankful we managed to keep bitterness out of our divorce and had parted as disinterested companions.

I mused carefully on Chris's words. Had I regretted anything over the years? Not really. All in all I'd had a pretty good life. Nursing is never an easy career but it is certainly never dull and I had made some steadfast chums over the years. I regretted that Robin and I had never started a family but I had always enjoyed our friends' offspring on holidays, or days out, so had seldom felt deprived. Robin and I enjoyed each other's company but we both had our own particular pastimes. We gave each other space.

Holidays were always looked forward to and we rarely re-visited old haunts, preferring to extend our horizons. We enjoyed being together yet we always made loose friendships on foreign holidays – occasionally staying in touch once we returned but often waving goodbye at the airport without a backward glance.

Maybe it was the seductive, velvety brandy that caused me to be so truthful. I had one regret that had haunted me all down the years. Andrew's face suddenly slipped into my mind and I was jolted into awareness. I remembered how shabbily I had treated him. The night I had told those awful lies with such calmness and watched him crumble. How his white face and staccato speech had bravely hidden his massive hurt. I remember watching his face and the tears that stung my throat.

Clearly I could remember him quietly wishing us goodnight and swiftly walking out of that pleasant restaurant all those years ago. Neither of us had enjoyed or finished our meal under Chris's benign gaze and, as Andrew walked away and I watched him disappear from my life, a sick, leaden weight settled on my stomach. I longed to race after him and tell him it was all a silly lie to prevent me losing face. How Chris and I were both lying. How I was unable to bear the thought of never seeing him again, never hearing his voice or reading his letters. But I let him go and had spent the rest of my life feeling vaguely ashamed at my cruelty.

I had never heard from Andrew again. As the months went by the emptiness I felt had increased. It was as if he had vanished off the face of the earth. So many times I would lift the office telephone, desperate to hear his warm Cornish accent, and would then force myself to replace the receiver before actually dialling his number which, I felt, was burnt in my brain. I had stopped myself from listening for the postman with our early morning mail. I knew he would not be writing.

So often I would see his profile as a head was turned in front of me on London Bridge, a face looking down at a morning newspaper would make me catch my breath in the Underground or I would watch a tall, slim blond lad pushing his way through the crowds in Regent Street. A man, in naval uniform, crossing at the changing lights in Oxford Circus would cause me to hurry forward – only to be disappointed. It was never Andrew.

Eventually the blind longing had lessened and finally died as I forced myself to forget this man who had once been the cornerstone of my life. It helped that I had managed to erase every trace of him at home. Photos and old letters had been easily dealt with; but other things, like the warm gloves he had given me, a special letter opener from Jamaica, tiny silver charms on my bracelet, a bookmark at the back of a drawer, a tiny silver locket, scribbled notes on a map, a programme from a show we had enjoyed together, even a Cornish bus ticket I found nestled in a favourite book, all appeared as time went by, one by one, to haunt me and I had had to remove them immediately to prevent myself from contacting him. After a couple of years I had convinced myself I had eradicated all trace of him. In the meantime I had gradually eased myself back into a life that had contained mostly Chris with his warmth and fun outlook on everything. He always managed to be around when I needed him and, quite often, when I didn't! Every day he would be in touch either by telephone or accompanying Bryn, Dee's erstwhile boyfriend, on his nightly visits next door until, eventually, my parents and I had come to accept him almost as a member of our family.

My mother would prepare extra food for evening meals and somehow, often at weekends, Chris was expected to join us for our

Sunday roast as well as the light supper we always had later on in the evening after my parents returned from church. He would help my father in the garden, wheeling barrow-loads of leaf mould to mulch around the roses, assisting him to build a dry-stone wall and he had even spent weeks painting a fence. He would chat with my grandmother and, one day, I had even caught him carrying shopping bags for my mother.

I am sure his aim had been to become indispensable, in one way or another, to all of us. He would escort me to the cinema as often as I was willing to go. We would take a bus and go for long romantic walks in the countryside that spring and later, if I had a summer weekend, we would take a huge picnic up to our local open-air swimming pool and stay all day. Dee, Bryn and other friends would join us and we would wander home in the dusk pleasantly tired and extremely happy. That had been my perfect courtship.

It had seemed only a short step from there to accepting that, at some time in the near future, we would be married. In fact I honestly do not remember Chris actually proposing. He had taken me out for a sumptuous meal one evening and on the table, along with an exquisite long-stemmed dark red rose, had been a small velvet box. I had opened it gingerly and discovered a Victorian antique ring. A garnet surrounded by seed pearls had been nestling inside. I had been entranced and if I had thought of Andrew at all, it would have been to marvel at how he had never spoken of our future together. Both of us had been far too shy to even discuss our hopes and aspirations. Chris, on the other hand, suffered none of these inhibitions and I had been charmed by his clear-sighted decisiveness.

We had been engaged for six months and married shortly after. I had wanted a simple wedding but Chris and my parents had persuaded me that an impressive ceremony in the local parish church, followed by a huge reception, was perfect for an only daughter. The wedding invitation list had become longer and longer. Chris's family had been sparse by comparison; but he had made up for it by inviting all his friends and work colleagues so that I had known that both sides of the church would be crowded with guests.

It had not pleased my mother when I had quietly gone out and chosen my own wedding dress. The first one I had tried on looked perfectly fine to me. The assistant had come back with a suitable veil and modest tiara and I had accepted them both immediately. I, who had always hated fuss, had been amazed when I had emerged from the fitting room to find a circle of ladies I had never seen before waiting to admire the bride, which had caused me to blush deeply. My three bridesmaids had not been difficult either. This time my mother had insisted on accompanying me. We had taken along Chris's young sister and found her a suitable, puff-sleeved little voile dress that hid her fragile figure and had delighted her into the bargain. Meryl, my best friend, and Dee, my cousin, were both my size so I had modelled two similar-coloured dresses and had chosen them swiftly on their behalf. I had then selected modest headdresses as I had decided that small white prayer books with simple fresh-flower bookmarks would be suitable for them to carry. I considered none of my attendants would want to clutch bunches of flowers.

I had decided on pale apricot as a suitable colour for their dresses. It would enhance all of them even though I had known for certain that the two elder girls would never want to wear theirs again once the ceremony was over. So often had I attended weddings where the bride looked absolutely stunning. Sadly, often the bridesmaids might looked washed out in their chosen finery, almost as if it had been selected deliberately, or the dresses would show up bulges or bumps better hidden, or maybe the colour clashed with one girl's hair. It then often crossed my mind, when standing watching, that the poor attendants may have wished they were somewhere else on that particular day! I had wanted no disgruntled sentiments like that on my special day so I had chosen pretty, elegant dresses they would all feel comfortable in.

The elder girls would all wear their own white, high-heeled summer sandals. Who cared if they were in slightly differing styles? I had bought a pretty pair of soft white pumps for Chris's small sister, Molly, with three pairs of white gloves and had decided that was my shopping finished for the day. My mother had appeared to be slightly hurt and puzzled at the speed I had located and decided on my purchases. There had been no wandering around great departmental stores and trying on every dress they had in the place – just for the fun of it. No dreaming of fairy-tale creations that would have cost more than our furniture. To me it had been a simple matter of logistics. My wedding was going to be the *beginning* of my married life - not a grand finale to wow a captured audience. Therefore, anything simple and becoming would have done, as I'd had no interest in studying bridal books or shopping around in boutiques for that exclusive, perfect, creation. No, dragging out the whole matter over several weeks had not been not my idea of fun. How some women could spend months and months, even years, to provide a spectacle equal to a Royal Wedding always amazed me. I had paid for everything and then gently led my mother just off Oxford Street to a nearby bistro to feed and water her. She had soon cheered up.

We hadn't chosen her outfit with quite the same speed; but I had made sure it was suitable and a reasonable price before I'd let her purchase it. I had known my father would not be impressed by her presenting him with a huge bill. *He* always looked debonair and immaculate but he never expected her to look anything but understated and presentable. He also would not have admired her in one of the huge millinery creations she espied when we walked to St Christopher's Place, and I had persuaded her to choose a simple hat which enhanced her face and blended in perfectly with the elegant lavender and white dress and jacket she had chosen.

* * * * * * *

Suddenly I returned from daydreaming to the present. Chris was still nursing his brandy and waiting for my reply to his casual question, 'Is there anything you have ever regretted doing – or not doing – in your life, Jenny?'

I hesitated, wondering if I should answer him truthfully or not. Why not? Chris was nothing to me now and all my adult life I had wrestled with the guilt that I had hurt a person who could have been my dearest friend forever. 'Yes, there is one thing that I have always regretted and that remorse has never left me.' I swallowed painfully. 'Lying so blatantly to Andrew that night in the restaurant will always remain with me. I have often thought maybe I should do my best to find him and tell him the truth. It would probably mean little to him now. I suspect he will have forgotten it totally, but it would certainly salve my conscience to put right the one mistake I have ever knowingly made in my life.'

I glanced across the room as I said it. Never have I seen a man move so swiftly. Suddenly he was towering above me, his face incandescent with rage. Robin and I watched in amazement as he leaned towards me and I flinched as I wondered if he would strike me. His face filled my startled vision and I cowered back in my chair, fearful.

He spoke quietly, which made his fury all the more menacing. 'Don't ever say that again. There is no way you will find him. No way you will contact him. Do you understand?' He was breathing heavily as if he had run up many flights of stairs.

I laughed shakily, 'Don't talk rubbish, Chris. This has nothing to do with you. If I decide I want to talk to him and explain, I will certainly do so,' I countered.

'I forbid you to speak to him. Do you hear me?' By now he was shouting with suppressed fury. Robin and I sat stunned at the outburst. What on earth had upset him so? Never had I seen him so disturbed. The easy-going young man who had always been quick to laugh and be loved had disappeared and in his place was this implacable despot whose words were low and threatening. A man used to getting his own way and never being thwarted. We glowered at each other. I was breathing rapidly now but neither of us backed down or apologised.

Robin broke the impasse by leaning forward and topping up our glasses with more brandy. Silently he handed me mine and I shakily downed a huge mouthful and immediately coughed. Nothing further was said but, in the tense silence, we were all uncomfortable and, after Robin looked obviously at his watch, we found ourselves bidding each other good night. It seemed the easiest way to put this stupid scene behind us and we all trailed along to our two separate rooms. I was relieved I had put Chris at the end of the corridor overlooking the garden. I felt shaken and unnerved. It had happened so suddenly and I hated the thought that I could still be affected by him after so long.

As Robin and I slid between the cool sheets we deliberately said nothing, knowing Chris was only a few doors away. The silence of the house settled around us. Robin dropped into a deep sleep almost immediately, but I stayed awake for quite some time mulling over the events of the evening.

The next morning I busied myself preparing a huge breakfast and nothing more was said amid the flurry of preparations for my ex-husband to leave. He was attending some important conference up in the Midlands and was anxious to be off. To be honest I was relieved. There would be no more embarrassing confrontations. I still had no idea what Robin thought of Chris's fit of temper and, as I had never discussed Andrew or any other previous boyfriend with him, he must have wondered why we had both become so upset about a virtual stranger. I began ramming dirty dishes into the dishwasher, only stopping to wave Chris's car off.

Autumn arrived accompanied by high winds and floods so that Chris's dire threats soon faded from my mind as I allowed hard work and pleasure to take over my life once more.

I had forgotten our discussion that fateful weekend until I finally decided to take early retirement many years later. We lived in a lovely part of Britain. So many people took holidays in our part of the country and yet, because we were both so busy, we hardly had time to enjoy and take advantage of beautiful rolling hills and secret sandy coves that were often only a short drive away. We decided money wasn't everything. We neither had any dependants so why did we need to both have a career and tie ourselves down for no reason?

Robin was still on shift work with the Police so we both decided, if I gave up my erratic hours, we could spend any spare time together and enjoy the pastimes, like bird-watching and swimming, that we had relinquished.

We had always enjoyed surfing and the closeness of North Devon and the well-known beaches in Cornwall meant we could take advantage whenever the sun was set fair. Also, for many years we had promised ourselves we would learn to sail. We had no grandiose ideas and a simple dinghy would probably satisfy our needs. Any time we could get away for a few days we felt sailing would be an ideal way of relaxing. In preparation we took a course with our local sailing club and asked an old hand to advise us as to a suitable boat – one our car would be able to tow. Now we were ready to enjoy life.

I decided I would slip away quietly from the NHS. Not for me the bustling hospital party with the press faithfully recording every anecdote, photos of bouquets and smutty asides from the doctors. I had noticed over the years how each Head of the Hospital felt incumbent to mouth a few platitudes as to how one would be missed while stealing glances at their watch knowing they would be late for a meeting. It was all rubbish. No one is indispensable and least of all nurses. I had told everyone I would be retiring quietly on my birthday and wanted no fuss or formal presentation. I would slip away quietly and no one would even notice my going. They were not happy but I insisted.

The girls on my ward arranged a party at a nearby pub and, alone, we managed to let our hair down and say our fond farewells. I was among friends who had worked with me for years. We were a small, closely knit group who relied on, and appreciated, each other's skills and expertise. These would be the workmates I would miss, not the hierarchy that wields a lot of power but does very little work to make a hospital run smoothly and successfully.

At first it felt as if I was on holiday and I would have an awful guilty feeling as I waved Robin off to work. Suddenly there were no deadlines to meet, no life-and-death decisions to be taken, no boring training to keep one abreast with the latest medical knowledge, and no getting up almost in the middle of the night to be at work at some ungodly hour. Soon it began to feel pretty good.

I quickly adjusted to a comfortable routine of meeting odd friends for coffee, walking our old dog, Crumble, giving the occasional dinner party or arranging some out-of-town shopping sprees. Even doing the ironing ceased to be a deadly chore. Where before it had stretched me to my physical limits after a busy day on the wards and, as Robin was always fond of quoting that 'I became like a bear with a sore head', suddenly I was able to gently press warm, fragrant cloth, smooth it with pleasure, and not feel hard done by.

One pleasant afternoon I was sitting, daydreaming, in the garden, listening to the drone of a questing bee and sipping a welcome cup of tea. The house was clean and tidy and I had no gardening chores to finish. Suddenly, unbidden, the words I had spoken so defiantly to Chris returned to haunt me. Why had I voiced my thoughts and why had I been so upset that evening, I wondered. How could something that had happened so long ago cause him to frantically react in such a way? He appeared to accept Robin and I as a couple, so why should the memory of a boy who I had first known in my teens, make him behave so strangely? I was puzzled as I mused over it in my head - I also hated to be told what I should or shouldn't do.

A gleam of warm sunshine speckled my arms under the gnarled apple tree as I began to sketch in my mind how I could set about contacting Andrew. Of course he could be anywhere in the world by now, I surmised. The last time I had heard from him was many years after we parted. He had written to my family home. My parents had been long gone by then and his letter had chased them to their new place of retirement. For some reason my mother had not mentioned it during one of our weekly telephone conversations and, strangely, my father had re-addressed the letter to the hospital where I worked, instead of sending it to Chris and I in our new marital home.

The packet contained half a dozen old black-and-white photographs of the two of us and was accompanied by a very short note. He had written to say he had been clearing out and I might like to keep the enclosed. He mentioned he now had two young children and that he was a schoolmaster in York. I had smiled as, in typical Andrew fashion, he had described himself as a schoolmaster and not a schoolteacher. In his mind there would be a subtle difference and he wanted me to appreciate it. Nothing was said about his decision to transfer from the Merchant Navy to the teaching profession and neither did he speak of his wife.

For some reason I decided not to mention it to Chris and I quietly shoved the letters and the photos out of sight, right at the bottom of my work box – the one place he would never have occasion to look. Even though I seldom opened the packet over the years, I knew it was there and derived a sort of comfort from my small act of hidden defiance.

I had never spoken of Andrew once since we had married. What was the point? But, as the years went by, I noticed Chris would behave tensely once we set out on our annual holiday to the West Country. Strangely, it had always been Chris who suggested a few days in Cornwall.

From the beginning it was almost as if he had decided to tease me. Or even taunt me. Maybe he wanted to force me to remember and speak of Andrew. He would drive me quite close to his village and then, often when we were within a quarter of a mile of it, he would pretend to change his mind and swing the car around and head in another direction. One day he had surprised me by actually driving down to the estuary and parking the car. We had alighted in the hot sunshine and, as if pulled by a magnet, I had walked eagerly towards the once familiar river with its gaggle of moored yachts and dinghies all jinking and bobbing on the incoming tide. I had felt him watching me and I'd immediately tried not to look around to prevent myself catching the eye of an unwary villager who might have recognised me and want to chat about days gone by. How embarrassed I would feel if I had to explain why I never visited the village any longer and had to suffer Chris's knowing, twisted smile boring into the back of my head. So that particular day it had been me who'd suggested we drive on to Mevagissey – thereby breaking the tension between us.

Suddenly I knew I *would* do exactly what Chris had forbidden. A devil egged me on. Chris had forfeited any influence over me many years before. Surely, even though Andrew had probably moved on, some of his extensive family must still live in Cornwall? I pondered the best way to get in touch. It didn't seem unreasonable to write to their local newspaper. In such a small community someone would surely know their whereabouts and I should soon trace them? I quickly checked my memory for the names of his brothers and sister-in-law and went into our cool study to draft a suitable enquiry. As I sat staring at the blank sheet of paper, wondering how to begin, I hesitated and picked up the telephone instead. Could he *still* be living in York, I mused? Highly unlikely, but it was worth a try, so I dialled directory enquiries.

I reeled off the only information I had gleaned all those years ago and, within seconds, I was given a number which I swiftly scribbled down. Before I could lose my nerve, I dialled it and was asked by a cool calm voice on an answering machine to leave my message and either Andrew or Fay would get back to me. I gave all the relevant details and then added, for good measure, that, if none of this made any sense to the Lanyon family, would they please disregard my garbled enquiry. Within half an hour I was speaking with Andrew!

He rang me straight back and rattled off my full name – Jennifer Dawn Fairburn – as if the previous years had never existed. He sounded breathless as if he had run upstairs; but I probably sounded equally as winded as we both took a deep breath and formally greeted each other. Then we both laughed and started speaking at the same time. Within seconds we were taking it in turns to list where we had been and to explain and channel our information about what we had been doing with our lives since that disastrous night when we had parted.

I had difficulty in keeping up with his words. I had grabbed a pencil and was frantically scribbling down places and occupations as he mentioned them, on the back of an old envelope. We laughed and tripped over our words in an effort to tell all and keep nothing back. Our enthusiasm then became infectious as we finally came around to times gone by and we kept triggering the other off on another round of memories and anecdotes. Anyone listening to us would have expected to see two teenagers chattering inconsequential nothings on the telephone – not two middle-aged people who should have known better. I kept offering to ring him back as I was conscious the call could be costing a small fortune and I was the one who had instigated it, but he impatiently brushed me off saying, 'Oh for goodness sake this is the most fun I've had in years.'

I was saddened that he had done so much with his life, visiting so many locations and changing the course of his career while I, by comparison, had done very little apart from training to be a nurse, marrying twice and finally moving to the West Country. My life appeared pale by contrast.

Andrew told me he had decided to leave the Navy shortly after our last fateful meeting. Up until then he had become settled and comfortable in his job – albeit it could be a lonely one at times. One is in a strange position aboard a merchant ship. Once they are fully trained, a Radio Officer will work alone and is only responsible to the Captain. The duties may not be onerous but they are always solitary. There is no one else trained to do the job so, if one is ill, it's a case of plodding on until one recovers. Andrew told me how, on his first single posting, he was violently seasick for days on end and he had to learn to cope with the wretched nausea along with the work.

He had never divulged these secrets all those years ago and I now realised how my enthusiasm had probably kept him silent. *His* misgivings had been swamped by my passion. My love of the sea and my intense desire to travel had clouded my judgement. As a child, I had listened avidly to my naval grandfather all those years ago until his dreams became mine. It was a career I would have chosen if I had been a lad; but maybe the reality would have brought me down to earth had I ever been given the opportunity. My imagination had not taken into account the everyday boredom that was inevitable from the sheer drudgery of a routine that seldom changed.

I had not thought of the small circle of personnel that one would be forced to live with – sometimes for months on end – on even the largest vessel. There is never a guarantee that every member of the ship's crew would be pleasant and stimulating. Indeed, it is highly unlikely. Imagine living in close proximity, day by day, with a fellow officer who was a bore, or a hectoring bully, both of which one would dislike intensely. Or a mess feud that emerges out of nowhere but can divide the men and cause an uncomfortable atmosphere from which there is no escape – apart from work or retiring to one's solitary cabin. None of this had ever occurred to me all those years ago.

I had only visited Andrew aboard ship once. From the dockside I had been awed by such a huge vessel but, on alighting from the gangplank where he stood to welcome me, I'd found an enclosed world of corridors, steep stairways leading to various decks and many doors – all closed. There had been a rarefied, claustrophobic atmosphere and, by the time I had walked down endless passages and finally stepped over the threshold into his cabin, all that had registered was how clean, neat and small it all was. A narrow bunk under a small bookshelf and a simple desk and chair had dominated the room. I remember, fleetingly, being shocked at seeing his small cache of paperback books residing on their pristine shelf. I had been able to saunter into any library and bring out a satisfying armful of books any time I'd wanted; but Andrew had been restricted to this tiny room with its own small library. My nautical rose-coloured spectacles had obviously been jolted into clarity that day!

Andrew went on to tell me that he had soon realised that only an exceptional partnership could weather being apart for long periods with only letters forming a bridge of communication.

'I thought maybe ours could,' he said. 'We had spent so many years communicating daily by letter, with the odd phone call being thrown in for good measure. And, if we met once or twice a year, we considered ourselves lucky. Of course, what I hadn't taken into consideration was that it wouldn't be a case of a letter-a-day arriving via our cheery postman, but silent gaps with no news at all and then a bundle of letters – sometimes weeks old – all languishing at our latest port of call and waiting to be picked up. It was either a feast or a famine and it always left me feeling dissatisfied and disgruntled.'

I knew that feeling well. I found it impossible to explain, that evening on the telephone, that I had always been prepared for being constantly separated but could not accept my growing conviction that he was leaving me rapidly behind, in more than distance, on his new adventurous journey. He had talked so casually about the Bahamas, North America, South Africa, New Zealand and Australia as if they were resorts on the south coast of England. But, sadly he had also spoken as casually about our relationship – and that had hurt me the most.

I explained *I* had no such exciting stories to tell him in return. I had had to cudgel my brains to dredge some happening at the hospital that sounded even remotely interesting in my letters. Who wants to hear about painful dressings, ward rounds and fussy Ward Sisters who find dust in the most inaccessible places?

I had soon learned that at every port they entered they had been entertained by the locals; stories of wild parties thrown in their honour may have been exaggerated but they had only served to make me even more despondent. I am sure his determination to sound happy had had the reverse effect on me and deepened my growing conviction he had been having fun and growing tired of our distant relationship.

While he was explaining it saddened me to think his great dream had turned to dust through a decision I had made, halfway across the world, and carried out with such forcefulness. It had never occurred to me my decision would be changing *his* life as well as my own. I had told him my thoughts when he was in New Zealand and he had accepted them instantly. He had offered no pleading or arguing. This very attitude had reinforced my certainty that we had been due to split up anyway and maybe he had been relieved that I had taken the initiative.

It comforted me to hear him say that at least his previous, rigorous naval training had stood him in good stead. His radio expertise and clean bill of health in background checks enabled him to join the Foreign Office and, after taking a course in Russian, and then Chinese, he had been posted to various capital cities around the world. After a lone, solitary existence on board a ship he had begun to enjoy a full and rewarding social life. Heady stuff for a young man who came from a small village in Cornwall, I surmised. He told me it had been a sensitive time when the threat of an atomic bomb exploding in our midst was a distinct possibility. Powerful nations had mistrusted each other and threatened annihilation at the touch of a button. Andrew's prime concern, at that time, had been with the aftermath of the Bay of Pigs confrontation in Cuba; but it was in Stockholm that he had met his future wife-to-be, Fay.

Her father was a foreign attaché. She had been an only child and her mother had always faithfully followed her husband around the world to where the vagaries of fortune had taken them, dragging Fay along in their wake. Andrew went on to explain that, where he had travelled the world by sea, Fay had seen and sampled it first hand, and in depth. Living sometimes in exotic, sometimes primitive, surroundings had made her either receptive or, occasionally, judgemental. Her parents had always found suitable schools or provided private tuition for their daughter.

'One thing she did find easy,' he said with a laugh, 'was that she could absorb foreign languages as effortlessly as other children enjoy listening to bedtime stories.'

'Was she spoilt and precocious?' I longed to ask but dared not. 'I guess you'd met your match?' I said instead.

Here was an attractive young girl who was as intelligent as him and equally as well travelled. There had seemed no reason not to marry immediately. Fay had kept herself busy using her language skills but neither she nor Andrew had been particularly happy in Sweden. Apart from her parents being close by there had seemed little to keep them there. Andrew's arduous hours had played havoc with their social life (which he said Fay had hated and had often led to many heated arguments) so, as his tour of duty neared its end, it had been decided that maybe a complete change of direction in their careers was in order. They had decided to return to England where Fay had acquired a position teaching at a prestigious language school and Andrew had finally decided to take the plunge and return to University to obtain a degree which would enable him to teach also.

They had chosen York for no better reason than it was a small, romantic, walled city where housing was inexpensive. They'd had two children in quick succession. Fay had given up her job and Andrew had supplemented his grant by working nights in a bakery and doing relief milking in his college holidays. He had been constantly tired but had enjoyed the challenge. It had been a busy but happy life.

I told him about my advanced hospital training and we smiled at how similar our chosen careers had been. Both studying hard, trying to be frugal within the limited budgets available to us, while we attained our goals.

He then went on to tell me how their funds had finally run out before he had obtained his degree. Fay had always been used to a comfortable lifestyle and she had finally rebelled when her eldest child and her husband both needed new shoes and couldn't afford them. It had been the final straw. In desperation she had taken her two young sons back to her parents' welcoming home. His in-laws had been enjoying a comfortable life in Washington DC at the time and were always asking their beloved daughter to join them. As it was only to be for a short time Andrew had encouraged Fay to go alone.

'I knew I could concentrate on my studies and they would be well looked after – spoiled even. Fay had cheered up immediately and it was a great relief and worry off my mind.'

He told me how he had accompanied them, plus a mountain of baggage, to Heathrow and waved them off. The two little boys, their arms clasping his neck and their childish voices ringing in his ears, had been as upset as he was. He had turned away immediately their mother walked them through the Departure Lounge.

Suddenly he hesitated and the line went quiet for a few seconds.

I broke in with, 'Yes, and then what happened? Did you get your degree but, more importantly, how did you manage without shoes?'

'Oh yes, I obtained a respectable degree', he said softly, 'and immediately started looking around for a lucrative job. Two small children, a wife and a mortgage saw to that. Fay had made some contacts in Washington and she encouraged me to join the Army.'

'The Army?' If he had become an MP or swam the Channel I could not have been more surprised. I was puzzled. He had always assured me the regimental structure of any of the Armed Forces had never interested him. He had chosen the Merchant Navy for that very reason and enjoyed the freedom it gave him. He would laugh when he told me how the sight of an entire crew lining the deck of a Royal Naval vessel as it left port had always amused him. His preference was for a few deckhands nonchalantly slipping the moorings of a huge tanker, with no ceremony whatsoever, as it slid out of a harbour on the tide. Quite often he would listen indulgently when I told him tales about my grandfather's experiences in the Royal Navy. *He* had begun his career as a humble able seaman, working his way up the naval ladder, only to be reduced to the ranks by some minor misdemeanour when he invariably broke one or other of the Royal Navy's sacred rules.

'Oh, never fear, I only joined the Army in a loose capacity. It was suggested I apply to teach in one of the military schools abroad. My background meant I would probably be accepted without too much red tape. We were offered various postings and Fay and I chose Hong Kong. A decent salary, a pleasant lifestyle and lots of household help; what more could anyone demand? Fay was delighted. Sun, sea and a good social life with help thrown in – who wouldn't be?'

Silently I agreed with him. It was a far cry from the long hours and backbreaking duties I'd endured in a bustling general hospital. In fact it sounded like one long holiday to me, but I'm sure it wasn't.

'Teaching became a pleasure. I applied for various posts – and was usually successful. After a few years I was given my own school and attained the honorary rank of Major.'

'And then what?' I asked eagerly. Once again the line went quiet and I wondered if we had been cut off.

'Nothing much,' he said eventually. 'I learned to sail competitively, the kids swam like fishes and it was a pretty good life.' There was a longer silence and I waited expectantly.

'We stayed there six years and then we moved to Germany,' he said abruptly.

'*Germany*? Surely that was a bit different?' A real cultural shock, I surmised.

'Well they taught me to ski and, being back in Europe, it allowed us to explore France and Spain, even down as far as Greece. We also spent some time in the north – in Holland and Norway for instance.'

I was extremely impressed. 'Were you still a headmaster?'

'Oh yes, I had definitely found my niche in life.'

I asked if he had missed the sun and the sea of Hong Kong as well as the lifestyle.

'No, I made some solid friendships in Germany.'

Somehow, I couldn't put my finger on it but there seemed much being left unsaid and I didn't know him well enough to ask searching questions. Suddenly the atmosphere had changed. I felt he had become withdrawn and I had no idea why. Shortly after, I tentatively said I had to go and he agreed instantly saying, 'Have you a computer? If so, I'll send a long e-mail and attach a few photos. Would you like that?'

As a matter of fact I had only just begun to use a second-hand computer. I had been railroaded into one by a journalist friend who had threatened to throw his old one onto the tip – knowing full well my frugal nature would never allow that. For the past couple of years I had raised excuse after excuse not to buy one. Life was a lot simpler without one, I would say firmly. Robin used one at work but we had never felt the need to own one personally. Now was my opportunity. I knew, as soon as Andrew wrote, I would answer. I just hoped I could make a reasonably good effort and not look like an ignorant amateur when I tried to reply to him.

So that's how it all began. What started as an innocuous enquiry soon became a raging forest fire that neither Andrew nor I wanted to extinguish. We should have remembered the first time around and how the instant attraction and rapport had taken hold of both of us.

It had never occurred to me that the quiet pace of my life could ever be altered. I was the middle-aged friend who ran errands for my neighbours, changed their light bulbs and unscrewed their jars. I'd fix dodgy radiators and could usually manage to sort out their TV channels. I looked after gardens when holidays loomed, lugging slopping buckets of water when there was a drought and dead-heading flowers when there wasn't. I would be roped in to meet a kiddie from school when mum was unavailable and I *always* ended up delivering Neighbourhood Watch leaflets.

I attended a library club once a month and firmly expressed my opinion on our current read; I would sit in at boring council meetings to bulk out the number of protesters and could always be relied on to help provide cakes for the stall at our annual Goosey Fayre. '*Ask Jenny*' seemed to be the watchword as I would invariably ransack our house and put out the obligatory bag of old clothes for a good cause. I normally opted out of playing darts at our local pub but, unless I could think of a good reason, I was expected to attend the scouts' hall whist drives and patiently explain what was trumps to all those who could never remember.

Ask anyone and they would have said I was just a reliable member of our village society who usually was willing to help when other people found excuses not to.

I was 'good old Jenny' who now enjoyed a pleasant life, had an easy-going husband and too much leisure. I was always sanguine and up for a laugh. In the end I was more than ready to slowly submerge myself into this deadening limbo and accept that I was past it, settle into a life of stagnation with a gradual closing of my mind to anything new – be it ideas or pastimes.

I don't know if Andrew's life had developed along similar lines but, if it had, we were both of us in for a great shock. I doubt if we realised at that point, but nothing was ever going to be quite the same for us ever again.

I went fizzing with excitement to report back to Robin and he listened patiently as I relayed all the news I had discovered about my oldest and dearest friend whom he had never met. Did he feel a frisson of doubt as I sparkled and chattered? I doubt it. It probably wouldn't have crossed his mind – I was always so transparently honest, never having reason not to be. Gradually this would all change; but that evening I am certain neither of us was aware what was about to happen.

Chapter 3

*

True to his word Andrew sent a full resumé of his life and times in Hong Kong and Germany in a lengthy e-mail and accompanied it with lots of interesting photographs. Studying them closely, I watched his children grow from blond, plump little cherubs to cheeky, lean scamps. They obviously spent most of their formative years with their father as there were lots of photos of him teaching them to swim like dolphins, as well as to sail and windsurf in a bright, sunny climate. In later pictures I noticed they were into skiing and rock climbing. It was clear that living abroad had given them many advantages over similar children in this country and I could see by their animated faces that they were children who enjoyed a full and active life.

There were other snaps; of his father, two brothers and Deborah – shielding her eyes from the sun. Most of them were taken around their harbour-side cottage and often included grandchildren. I examined them carefully and decided they all looked happy and content. There were a few of Andrew and Fay. Taken on more formal occasions and posed for official photographers by the look of it. As far as I could tell they were probably standing with her parents at two embassy functions; everyone looked extremely elegant in full evening dress and I envied them their poise and self-assurance. It was obviously a different life from the humdrum one Robin and I had led. I mused that Andrew had certainly come a long way from the lad who taught me how to handle a small dinghy off the coast of Fowey – bellowing at me to keep my head down as we tacked back and forth in a choppy sea

It had always surprised me, when we first met as teenagers, how Andrew's family had accepted me – a girl from 'up-country' who could have tempted their bright son with ideas about moving away and embarking on a more interesting and lucrative career, far in excess of anything available in the West Country at that time. But he had not needed any encouragement from me. He had decided, long before we met, that there was a bright future out there and all he had to do was grasp it. Strangely enough, I was the staid, shy one who would have accepted life as it came: he was the inquisitive explorer who would go on to make a stable and successful future for himself and his family.

I was extremely surprised when I found a few photographs that I recognised. Obviously he had been lying, all those years ago, when he assured me the photos he had returned from York were the remains of his entire collection. Here were half a dozen more that I had forgotten even existed. So even Andrew wasn't quite as honest as I had always believed; he *also* had his Achilles heel. One of the snaps had been taken by a friend while we had been sailing off St George's Island. Andrew was gazing down intently at me and I was looking away in embarrassment. That just about summed me up at seventeen!

Finally there were two others he had decided to include. A current one of him looking all of his 55 years – settled deeply in a comfortable armchair, obviously immersed in *The Times* crossword, and a second one captioned MY 50th BIRTHDAY. The second was a slightly younger Andrew, looking slim and handsome, surrounded by five adoring middle-aged women, as he beamed down on his birthday cake. Would I have recognised this man if I had passed him in a busy street? I'm not sure. Maybe not. I spent ages, scrolling back and forth, scrutinising all those photographs. It was only later, when I learned how to print them off, that I was able to study them closely. Suddenly it was late and time for me to prepare the evening meal. I chatted about my old Cornish friend all the way through our steak-and-kidney pudding followed by cheese and biscuits. Robin was obviously tired but he made suitable replies before he settled down in front of our faithful television for what was left of the evening. I cleared away, and it was only then that I was able to return to my slumbering computer to learn the rest of Andrew's story.

He appeared to skim over their later years in Germany, apart from telling me he and Fay had a villa built in a relatively quiet part of Spain. Fay's parents had retired by then and decided they would like to spend the rest of their life on the Mediterranean seaboard and Spain afforded a pleasant climate that would suit them all. They chose adjoining villas to enable her parents to keep a watchful eye on theirs when they returned home; and it also, he wrote dryly, had the added benefit that her parents could use it as an annexe when they invited their many friends to stay. They and the boys spent most of their holidays there – just messing around in boats. The boys were in their element and it was a relatively easy journey by car from Germany to southern Spain. I had the feeling it was easier to go along with Fay and her parents' plans than choose another option that might lead to opposition. It was only on her parents' deaths that they sold their holiday home but, by then, Andrew was back in a British school with a preference for holidays to different destinations. He said it seemed pointless using it once or twice a year, so they sold it and paid off their UK mortgage.

His account brought me up to date. He had taken early retirement and was leading a full life with more interests than he could comfortably fit in. He told me he played golf all year with a bunch of similarly aged cronies plus bridge in winter; this was also the time he could indulge in one of his greatest loves – amateur radio. It enabled him to use Morse code to speak with interesting people all over the world. He also liked to surf the Internet with his new state-of-the-art computer, take photos and sketch or paint whenever the weather was suitable. Recently he had been tracing his family history and had gone back to the seventeenth century. Added to that, he and Fay enjoyed as many holidays as they were able to cram in between visiting their children and grandchildren.

I gulped – by comparison I was doing virtually nothing. Two holidays a year, helping out at our local charity shop when they needed me, walking with our rambling club as long as the weather was suitable and the walk not too long, maybe sailing whenever Robin managed to snatch a couple of days off, and thinking vaguely about learning to dance now I had the time and energy. After working extremely hard in a busy hospital, as well as running my small house to the best of my ability, I now knew that the life I was leading was not exactly scintillating. I felt as if I had been winding down in preparation for my old age. I had accepted it as I had accepted all the other stages of my life; I had worked my way patiently through all of them – some happily and some uncomfortably – but always knowing I was heading for retirement and relaxation. It was a bit of a shock to realise it didn't have to be like that – if I so chose. Did I want to accept a comfortable lifestyle and virtual stagnation? I wasn't sure. I felt fired up enough to sit down and answer Andrew's e-mail immediately but, deciding I would look too eager, opted to wait until the following morning.

The next morning I made myself clear away the breakfast debris and fill the washing machine before I allowed myself to return to my computer and settle down once again. There were as many questions as answers bubbling irrepressibly through my mind and, although my fingers were slow and clumsy, I persevered. It was my first serious foray into the world of computing and I was so lost and ponderous. Trying to locate a letter took me ages and then placing actual sentences within a suitable format that looked presentable would have made any office worker laugh. How people made a living at this sort of thing I would never understand. I remembered *now* why I had taken up nursing and never trained for a clerical job – no patience with machinery and a strong dislike for a sedentary life, I guess.

I was also aware that, at the touch of a button, I could wipe my whole output off the screen and I would painstakingly have to start from scratch again. It made me super careful. It took me the whole of that first morning to get my reply looking like a proper letter. And, on reading it back, I realised it only amounted to a page and a half - a few meagre, stilted lines that said virtually nothing. Where had my usual happy, breezy style disappeared to? I normally had no trouble dashing off a decent letter. It was also ludicrous because, when I finally dared push the button to send it, I was not even certain that it had actually left my machine. Well, I concluded, it was the best I could do and Andrew would have to accept my inept effort or go scratch. Serve him right! Then I had a brilliant idea. I would cheat. In desperation I rustled up my usual writing pad and immediately scribbled off a warm and newsy letter to make up for the stiff and laboured one that would tell Andrew so very little.

One thing that *had* troubled me during our telephone conversation was when he informed me that my thoughtless action, all those years ago, had led to him leaving the Merchant Navy. He had reached his third tour of duty and had been away many months at a time for each. He had seen all those places I longed to visit – the USA, the West Indies, South Africa, Australia and New Zealand – and had appeared to be getting established and settled. Maybe I had meant more to him at that time than I had appreciated. He had seldom expressed this in his letters. Just the usual *I miss you no end, darling. Especially those daily letters you used to send without fail. These only come in occasional piles now and, however much I try to eke them out, they never last until we are once again in port to collect the next batch.* The main part of his letter would then normally contain a brief run-down of what had been happening on board, who was arguing with who, who was having difficulty with his love life, who had got away with murder but had managed to dodge the Captain's wrath, what books he had been reading and, finally, their next port of call, the address to write to and what would be happening on their arrival. As I say, it had all sounded a busy and exciting life to one who was studying hard, had very little money and was expected to appear bright and receptive every morning before tackling a very long day on the wards.

I had imagined he was drawing away from me as he had become immersed in his new and demanding career. He had told a story of being invited one evening to a mess dinner on board another ship that was berthed alongside theirs in Cape Town. I think it may have been a Swedish vessel because he had recounted how a couple of the officers were blonde, voluptuous ladies who had looked superb in their glamorous uniforms. After various courses, all the men had spaced themselves around the wardroom but Andrew, so he had told me, had tipped his cap over his eyes and rested in a comfortable armchair. Too much wine may have induced him to doze off.

Most of his fellow officers had been clustering around the two girls, vying for their attention. It obviously had gone against the grain, he'd surmised, that one of their colleagues could be disinterested after so long at sea and, from then on, the prettiest of the two had been all over him like a rash. He hadn't gone into details but I'd been easily able to fill in the picture for myself. A young, slim, good-looking officer feigning indifference would have been a great challenge to a beautiful woman and I am sure Andrew hadn't tried too hard to resist

I had then begun to imagine him climbing the social ladder that exists in the Navy as he settled into his chosen career. He had an ease and assurance that belied his modest upbringing and I had been certain he would soon find his place in that rarefied society with a suitable partner. From there it had not taken much working out to realise that partner would probably not be *me*. I later learned that he had done exactly as I'd expected, which proved my theory, but maybe not in quite the way I had originally envisaged. He had soon found Fay, a diplomat's daughter, so perhaps my reasoning had not been so far off the mark, after all!

Within two days of me sending off my stilted e-mail, and posting my accompanying letter, Andrew's reply dropped with a satisfying *thunk* on our doormat. He began by urging me to persevere with my new computer, pointing out they were the perfect medium for busy people. E-mails could be compiled at home and sent in seconds without resorting to pens and paper, rooting around for stamps or walking to find a post box – as we had always done all those years ago. In my heart I knew he was right so, as usual, I obeyed his wishes and, without fully noticing, our correspondence began in earnest and then grew in volume.

It was so easy to dash home with a neighbour's groceries, or cut short a shopping trip with a friend, snatch a quick cup of tea, and then sit down at the computer to check my mail and answer it before preparing the evening meal. If Robin noticed a change in my routine he didn't say anything and, on the evenings he was working late, or working all night, I would take my time and enjoy the freedom it gave me to type out great reams of memories, ask dozens of questions and tell Andrew my thoughts about anything and everything as it occurred to me. Gradually our correspondence became my prime reason for getting up in the morning and, knowing Andrew as I had, I suspected he was feeling the same way too.

Suddenly it was just like the old days; we must have both noticed it but we said nothing. What we had failed to take on board was that we were two staid, middle-aged people who both had responsibilities and family – not a pair of starry-eyed teenagers who were answerable to nobody and had no obligations whatsoever. We were living in a fragile dream world.

Not long after our correspondence began in earnest, Robin and I spent a well-deserved holiday on the idyllic island of Skiathos. We rented an old rambling apartment, covered in rampant greenery, on a quiet beach. It was the perfect place for a relaxing holiday and I fell in love with it. The solitude was a revelation after our bustling, small market town in Devon. The low rambling building had two terraces and this gave us the option of either sun or shade as we ate our breakfast, breathing in the sparkling warm air and gazing at the glinting dark blue ocean; or when we were sipping our cool wine in the still of a velvety dark evening. We would long for one or the other as we came home to shower, ravenously hungry, after lazing most of the day on a sandy crescent of beach or swimming in a pellucid Aegean sea. Occasionally, we would scramble up steep cliffs to visit a dusty monastery and even dustier monks. It was the perfect away-from-it-all holiday and Robin and I regained a timeless joy in each other's company. Our evening walks mainly consisted of watching endless sunsets and eating delicious, dawdling meals in remote tavernas. Hours later we would wander back home under the glow of a huge, orange moon, replete and contented.

We returned home rested and refreshed to find a scribbled postcard among the junk mail littering our doormat.

Monday 15th May

Hi! Was in Cornwall for my grammar school reunion on Sat. Spent Sun at home meeting family and friends and am now in Honiton High Street sampling a coffee and admiring where you live, Jenny. Tried phoning a few times but I guess you are on your hols. Now off to Gatwick to meet Fay. We fly out to San Diego, California for 5 weeks on Wed. Sorry to have missed you – but I tried!

Andrew.

Inevitably, we had both talked vaguely about meeting up. It was a tantalising thought and one we had often returned to in our e-mails. I was puzzled that he had not mentioned, in a previous communication, that he would be visiting the West Country shortly. Not that I would have contemplated changing our holiday dates; but it would have been sensible to let us know. Maybe he wanted to surprise me, but instead we had missed each other by just a few days. He had written in one of his earlier missives:

I do hope we meet one of these days. I don't I think it would harm anyone for us to chat over a glass of wine. But do be aware that, although it might sound like innocent fun to us, it will probably appear quite bizarre to everyone around us! You'll love retirement, Jenny – I do. There are no rules. It is a time to look back and, as in our case, mend fences. It is also a golden period, which we mustn't allow to erode away. I bought a beer mat in Exeter Cathedral last year. "ENJOY LIFE, THIS IS NOT A REHEARSAL." Trite, but it will do for me!

I listened carefully to Andrew's thoughts, so much so that I also reached out to enjoy my retirement. His words affected me deeply and I began to look on my life not as an end but as a beginning – a beginning with opportunities, and time to take advantage of these opportunities. First of all I decided to luxuriate in doing very little, only what suited me, as Andrew had advised. Maybe my new motto should be, I decided: *I can always put off until tomorrow what I should have done yesterday – or the day before*! It gave me a great feeling of liberation. When that strategy paled, I then planned my days to take advantage of the free time I had managed to carve out for myself. I was still always available when I was needed, but suddenly I structured my free time to do all the things I had constantly put off down the years. Personally I now felt rested and every morning I would wake eagerly to greet a new day. I went to the theatre in Exeter and Taunton. I made a point of going to art exhibitions in London and visited as many National Trust properties as I could cram in. Friends remarked I had an extra spring in my step and I always knew my smile was only a blink away.

That September Robin and I made our usual pilgrimage to Cornwall. We packed our surfboards and were lucky enough to enjoy two perfect weeks in Trebarwith Strand. The weather was kind, the surf good and the onshore breeze was warm and not sharply fierce – as it can so often be on the north Cornish coast. We frolicked in the white, tumbling waves like a pair of kids and arrived home at our small guesthouse every evening ravenous and spent.

We would take a quick shower and drag ourselves down to the local pub for a simple meal and a couple of halves of cider. We would then amble back to our beds in the soft twilight in order to rise bright and early to repeat it all again the next day.

I had told Andrew our destination and he told me he might be visiting friends at Dartmouth around the same time. I think we both knew the inevitable was about to happen. Although neither of us would admit it, we had been building up to this for some months. Robin had to return to work, of course, but there was no such restriction on my time. I had often stayed on for a few extra days when my hospital duties had allowed so, as usual, I was quite open with Robin and told him I might be seeing this old friend. I had casually mentioned the name Andrew for months and I don't think it crossed Robin's mind that there was anything suspect or sinister about this meeting.

Robin and I had lots of friends of both sexes from our previous jobs and also from our past lives. Neither of us were people who would form a friendship and then allow it to dissolve as we moved on. If we had enjoyed a friend's company we never forgot them. A deep and lasting friendship is hard to duplicate. I had stayed in contact with school and college chums, and also with two sets of neighbours of ours in Kent when I was married to Chris. Robin and I had carried on visiting them when we toured the Home Counties and, occasionally, if they came down to the West Country on holiday, they might come and see us, or even stay with us for a few days. It was a pleasure that we always encouraged. Robin had a particular friend from his school days, a probation officer, and we always made a point of seeing Derek and his wife when we were in London. He had also trained, or worked with, many policemen and women over the years so his circle of friends was also wide and varied. It was an informal arrangement but one that worked well.

Quite honestly, as the holiday in Trebarwith drew to a close, I was undecided if this meeting with Andrew was such a good idea. I was excited at the thought of a reunion but anxious as to the outcome. Say all our old rapport had disappeared? We might dislike each other on sight. He might think I was only a boring housewife and I might find him an insufferable snob. Who was to say? And after so many years apart it was inevitable that we should have both changed physically, as it was certain we had both changed intellectually. Say I didn't even recognise him when we met? Or worse still, that we just stared at each other and could find little to say. The awkwardness and embarrassment would be unbearable. All these possibilities spun through my mind until I felt hot and flustered just thinking about them. Were we both making a great mistake?

Slowly our leisurely vacation drew to a close. Robin would be returning to his busy police station and I could tell his mind was already sliding back to his colleagues and his work mode groove. I reminded him again, that last night, that I would be staying on for a few days and he made little comment, apart from saying if I rang him he would make arrangements to come down and pick me up.

Early next morning I tightly packed our largest suitcase while Robin secured our surfboards onto the roof rack of the car. I had kept back the smaller of the two suitcases as I explained that it would be easier for travelling if I could return with a minimum of luggage. I was hoping, if Andrew came at all, he would be willing to run me back home, but if not I was quite capable of getting to the nearest station and catching a train back. Robin reminded me again he would be quite willing to make another journey over the border from Devon to rescue me. He would be only too willing to do it and this I found a tempting thought.

Straight after breakfast Robin gave me a light kiss then, with a brisk wave of his hand, he drove swiftly away. I stood very still and, as I watched our car vanish into the distance. I slowly dialled Andrew on his mobile phone to check if he *would* be able to join me for a few days. I hesitated and then, on the spur of the moment, I changed my plans. Trebarwith Strand was a small village with only a beautiful beach, plus a romantic island standing out in the bay, to recommend it There was little to do and few places in which to dine. It was one thing to relax with one's husband in just such a place, but imagine trying to amuse a man who was used to travelling the world? What would he think of it? I cringed at the thought he might find it all very parochial and homespun. Bustling Newquay would be a better option, I decided. It was the end of the season so it would undoubtedly be quieter, the lager louts would all have departed, and the vast range of accommodation meant there would be a reasonable selection. Robin and I had been there so often over the years that I was sure I could secure a decent hotel with en-suite accommodation overlooking The Island and Andrew would easily find something similar around The Crescent, which bordered it.

I was very aware the situation was open to interpretation and I didn't want him to have the cynical thought that, at my age, I was blatantly asking him to spend an illicit few days with me. I quickly dialled his number before I could change my mind. As I had guessed, he agreed to get in the car and come immediately. I was certain he had been waiting for my call. What excuse he gave his friends I have no idea, but he must have spent some time pre-planning this jaunt because his determination reminded me of the old Andrew I had known all those years ago.

I caught the bus to Newquay and arrived there late morning on an unusually calm September day. Yes of *course* The Faulkner could accommodate me. They showed me to a spacious room overlooking the beach and I gazed out of the window to admire some surfers sitting on the swell and waiting for the perfect wave to work its magic and speed them ashore. I suspected this might be the hotel's honeymoon suite, as the four-poster bed was covered in crisp white lace and the whole elegant room had a luxurious feel to it.

I unpacked swiftly before strolling up Marcus Hill towards the parish church where I had arranged to meet Andrew. My mind was elated and resigned by turns. This would be our first opportunity to speak freely, face to face, and be absolutely honest with each other. I could at long last tell the unvarnished truth, which would be a great relief. On the other hand, this could be the worst decision either of us had ever made. Maybe Andrew had changed out of all recognition. He might have turned into a fussy old man, with no sense of humour and a tedious, boring view of life; or he might have thought I was there for only one reason and be too forward with his attentions. Maybe it was me who had changed over the years and he would be horrified when we met. It was in the lap of the gods, so

I forced myself to sit on the warm sunny church steps as I tried to concentrate on the paperback I had brought with me – but, instead, I watched the fringe of plump cumulus clouds that edged the deep blue of the horizon and simply daydreamed.

Chapter 4

*

Suddenly Andrew came bounding up the steps. I rose with uncertainty, not sure if he would expect us to shake hands formally or not, but he grabbed me firmly by the shoulders and kissed me warmly on the lips. I was taken aback; we hadn't seen each other for over thirty years and his deep kiss felt excessive. In fact he almost tumbled me backwards down those steps as his arms tightened around me. He had obviously forgotten my poor sense of balance. It was one of my greatest failings and one I had never been able to conquer. Shyly we both pulled back and looked at one another. Suddenly the old infectious grin lit up his face and, at last, I knew everything was going to be all right. Here was my one-time best friend, confidant and mentor and we were going to spend three fabulous days together. I returned his beaming smile. He stood on the church steps, shading his eyes, looking towards the tangled town spread beneath us and on towards the sparkling, distant sea. He stretched in the sunshine and, with a deep sigh, he turned slowly, threaded my arm through his and we strolled back the way he had come.

We decided to leave his bags in the parked car and I led him down towards The Crescent. I pointed out a small hotel I knew from past experience to be excellent. He turned and looked at me quizzically as I hastily explained I was booked into one close by. One could never pull the wool over Andrew's eyes; I knew he had guessed my thoughts and also my reticence to appear too eager for us to be together in the same hotel. I felt myself reddening. I realised that I had suddenly become embarrassed at my own forwardness. I hated to be judged presumptuous. It was not in my nature – I was normally reserved and shy and no way did I want Andrew to think I had changed, so as soon as he had registered, I suggested I wait downstairs in the hotel lounge with a coffee, while he returned for his car and settled in. In no time at all he was running lightly down the curving staircase, ready to go out in the bright sunshine to explore the beckoning panorama of cliffs and beach.

We left the hotel and strolled to the top of the steps that lead down to the smooth sand around The Island. I gazed across to the half-dozen beaches that stretched away north into the hazy distance. This was one of my favourite views in the whole of Newquay and always made me catch my breath – whether in the teeth of a ferocious gale, when ribbons of cloud streaked across the sky, leaving a white cauldron of surf seething at the base of the cliffs and around the jagged rocks, or even on a sullen grey day when the sea looked like swollen molten lead that neither advanced nor retreated. Occasionally, one encountered the odd deceptively calm day with a deep cobalt sky and a sea with only a fine lacy edging of crisp white that appeared to be teasing the miles of fine golden sand. No good for surfing, although it was then one could be forgiven for mistaking it for a glowing Mediterranean resort. But my favourite day has always had an onshore breeze briskly blowing, a hurtling, fizzing constant gust of wind, kicking up spume and spray that races across a dark azure sea and sets the spindrift smoking. Out in the bay there were always dozens of poised surfers, all waiting to catch that supreme crest of a wave that allowed them to skid and slide down translucent waterfalls at incredible speed. They ducked and dived, and we watchers caught our breath in the hope the display would go on forever. But it never did – for once they reached shallower water they would immediately turn tail and repeat the process all over again!

Closer to shore would be the inevitable body-boarders, their boards held high and their heads turned towards the toppling waves. If they were lucky they would catch the perfect surge which would grab them and bump them down two or three separate waves as they were caught up and forced to race ashore faster and faster. One would hear the whoops and screams as their excitement mounted. Once surfing fever is caught, I can assure you, the malady never diminishes as one is unable to forget the elation and thrill that is always hovering at the sight of a towering wave of water.

As we reached the top of the steps overlooking Great Western beach I noted the tide was out – on the horizon was a ribbon of blue, edged by a frothy white crescent of foam. Impulsively, I grabbed Andrew's hand and dragged him joyfully down those steps. Turning left I pulled him across the firm golden sands of busy Towan Beach; we stepped over a few slippery rock pools to make our way up the far steps that led to the harbour. Here the boats were angled deep in the rippled sand as they awaited the incoming tide. Like a pair of children we skipped over half-buried anchor ropes, and around kiddies with buckets and spades, as we made our way up the footpath that led to the Harbour Hotel perched on the granite rocks above us.

As always, the hotel provided us with a selection of satisfying snacks to quell our appetite. We gave our order and flopped down with contented sighs. Soon a plate of sandwiches and two huge steaming pasties magically appeared, accompanied by a bottle of chilled white wine, as we settled into the armchairs to enjoy the sparkling view, a late lunch and a long overdue conversation.

'Tell me everything,' I ordered, 'from the moment we parted until now.'

'That's a tall order,' he said, 'but I'll do the best I can.'

Andrew could always string together a good account and I settled down to be enthralled, my feet tucked under me; until, suddenly, we couldn't stop talking, and asking, and answering, and laughing. Words tumbled out as we remembered and interrupted one another. It was all heady stuff and we sat with our heads close together like two teenagers at their first meeting. Finally he turned to me, his eyes serious.

'You know Mark - my brother - died, Jenny?'

Of course I hadn't known. It seemed impossible that the mainstay of their family had gone. Mark, the eldest, who, along with Deborah his wife, had cared for them all. Even their elderly father had relied on him and, while he was at the helm, the business had been strong, successful and flourishing. As time passes I notice it is often difficult to imagine good friends getting older, ailing or even dying. In one's mind they remain the same forever until one learns the truth that, just as one's own life slips by and progresses or diminishes, nothing ever *does* remain just as it was. I looked at him in shock.

'He was only forty and died of a sudden, and unexpected, heart attack. We had no idea anything was ever wrong. He worked alongside the men in the Yard until the end and I never heard him complain of not feeling well in all his life. Dad gently lost his life to leukaemia shortly after. It all happened so quickly. I was in Hong Kong at the time and only got back in time for Mark's funeral. Hugh was doing the best he could to run the business as Deborah had her hands full with my father, who was swiftly losing his hold on life. It was the saddest homecoming ever. I asked for compassionate leave from the Army and Deborah and I nursed Dad until the end. I had left Fay and the two boys behind as I thought a sick, sorrowing house wasn't a suitable place to bring two boisterous scamps. It was all over very quickly and I returned to my post in Hong Kong within three weeks.'

'How could you bear it? You must have felt the comfortable, loving home you had left would be there forever? A lifestyle that no one expected would ever change.'

I recalled Andrew's house as I had first seen it. Three young men and an elderly father meant it had always appeared shabby and untidy. I had loved the easy-going atmosphere – so different from my home where everything ran on well-oiled wheels. Meals had been haphazard and hastily prepared by whoever was "on duty" that day. It had seemed to work very well, with only some amicable grumbling thrown in for good measure by the two younger boys. Shortly after I'd arrived on the scene, Mark had married his childhood sweetheart and immediately the whole family's style of living had changed. Deborah had quietly taken over the management and the casual, disorderly routine had become smoothly organised. The sprawling home had lost none of its charming warmth and happiness but, from then on, the boys had always looked well cared for, well fed and far more relaxed.

I remembered noisy Sunday teas with Mark and Hugh both bragging about their conquests, or adventures, of the night before. Their father would be shaking his head in horrified disbelief and try and remonstrate with them. Most times Andrew and I would sit like mice, close together, listening intently. It had been a different world for us. We had been only halfway to full adulthood and, to us, his brothers had seemed so worldly-wise and certain of themselves. Occasionally one of them would indulgently hand us some money to enjoy ourselves and we would race off to the local flea-pit of a cinema or spend it on a bus ride.

Sometimes we would sit out on the cliffs near Ready Money Cove and I would question Andrew about what *he* got up to when I was safely out of the way, back home. I had often seen glances of mild dislike directed towards me by local girls when I had been sitting in an animated group on the Quay with Andrew and some of his friends. We would all be chattering and laughing, pretending not to notice as a few of them would saunter by, arm in arm, casting sharply acid glances in my direction. It had all been so different from the town I'd lived in. This had been a small community where everyone was either related to their neighbours or knew their neighbour's business intimately. Nothing could remain hidden here for long.

Andrew had always insisted that he and Dan, his best friend, were quite capable of dealing with these girls, and I had always been naive enough to believe him! The fact that it would have been absolutely natural for two young lads, on the threshold of manhood, to surely enjoy these encounters – out of season when the village was quiet – had often entered my head; but there had been nothing I could do about it, from so many miles away, so I had always forced myself to resolutely put these corrosive thoughts from my mind and forget them.

* * * * * * *

Time fled by that afternoon as Andrew and I watched the incoming tide flood across Newquay harbour to set all the craft bobbing and rocking as we stared at the distant golden beaches with their suddenly gathering surf. We could see small figures sitting astride slim boards, all waiting the perfect moment to launch themselves and ride those newly curling waves. I could conjure up the excitement these surfers felt but I was unable to wish myself with them on that particular day. Andrew and I couldn't stop talking. It was as if we had uncorked a genie and were incapable of restraining it and returning it to its bottle. We both decided it would be easier to book a meal here at the Harbour Hotel for later and, instead of returning to our individual hotels to shower and dress, we would sit it out and watch the day end.

So we asked for another pot of tea and settled down to discuss Andrew's ever-diminishing family. I was intrigued as to what had happened to them. He explained that Deborah and Hugh had tried to keep the family business together.

'Hugh had so many ideas that he was eager to get off his drawing board, and get built and launched on our slipway. That is the way one keeps one's customers happy and returning for more. At that time we were the flavour of the month in so many magazines. Mark was turning Hugh's ideas into reality and it appeared they could do no wrong. The Boat Show in London would be the culmination of all their hard work every year, and it was always an exciting time for my family. Their order book would steadily fill with work for the next year to eighteen months. Nothing was too much trouble. They produced everything from tiny clinker-built dinghies, sturdy crabbers and simple family craft to Atlantic racing catamarans and classy elegant six-berth yachts. Both of my brothers were in their element and my Dad, until that last year, was so proud of their achievements.'

'What about Deborah? With Mark gone was she at a loose end or did she try and replace him at work?' I couldn't imagine Deborah without her quiet, steady husband. They had apparently been inseparable as children and, once married, Deborah had slotted into their busy lives as if she had been trained for it.

'Hugh did his best, but his forte was ideas and solutions – never the building side of the business,' said Andrew. 'They decided to employ a manager in the boatyard, but even that was never terribly successful. Mark had no successor already working for the company so they went outside for a candidate. Martin came from Millbrook and had served his apprenticeship at the Dockyard in Plymouth. He should have been perfect for the job. He was a nice enough lad, but often he and Hugh fell out over some design that he thought was too avant-garde for the yachting community stalwarts. He was probably right. Mark was always a calming influence on Hugh - he could talk him around - and together they would produce yet another success for a happy customer. Hugh had always listened to Mark, but Martin would grate on him like sandpaper with both of them refusing to back down. Deborah told me their spats were frequent and long lasting.'

'It came to a head when Hugh was poached by a prestigious boat-building company in Boston, Massachusetts. Deborah said he and Martin had been arguing for days over the set and rake of a spinnaker. Hugh came home and, over their evening meal, he tiredly told her he felt he was being stifled over unimportant details when all he longed to do was design the most perfect craft and have someone else work out the logistics and build it. Deborah took three days to mull it over before she told him to go ahead. They sold the yard as a going concern with the provision that the new owners keep on their workforce and, within nine months Hugh went to the States and Deborah accepted the post of matron at a public school in Wellington, Somerset. Later she returned to Cornwall – to a school in Mevagissey.'

'Do you see either of them often?' I enquired.

'Rarely,' said Andrew. 'Fay and I go to the States for a month most years. Hugh is terribly busy doing a job he adores and we always visit him for at least one week. He married a ditzy blonde with a happy disposition and they now have two little rascals that are the apple of their parents' eyes. Hugh is happy and says it's the best decision Deborah ever made for him.'

'And Deborah? Is *she* OK? Is she happy?'

He looked at me thoughtfully. 'I'm not sure. She appears to love her school kids and is so sad to see them leave her care at eighteen, or when their parents are posted to another part of the world but, as to happiness, who can say? I see a sadness always lurking in her eyes. Fay says I'm imagining it, that I'm a romantic idiot with a vivid imagination. But then Fay had always found it difficult to understand another person's feelings.' He looked across the harbour, shading his eyes, and I had the feeling he regretted admitting that. 'Oh, I know Deborah tried dating various eligible masters at both schools – but it was never successful, she said, and one date was always enough. She also became friendly with a chap a few years her junior but, when he decided to return to New Zealand, I notice she made no move to accompany him. She tells me little now, maybe thinking a happily married couple would not want to be dragged down by her sadness. Perhaps she tells Hugh her troubles. I have never asked him.'

'Do you see the rest of your relations back home?' I enquired. His huge interwoven family seemed to encompass most of the town's inhabitants. I had never learned all his tangled family history – try as I might. Everyone we met seemed to be related to him, in some way, and my head would spin with these complex ramifications.

'Rarely,' said Andrew. 'We don't have a lot in common now. Occasionally we will all meet up at a family wedding or funeral but, since Dad died, we mostly go our own separate ways. I keep in contact with a cousin who was also in the navy at roughly the same time and I hear from a couple of aunts who still live in the town, but Fay is not terrible interested so, unless I make a point of coming down, like now, I rarely see them from one year to the next.'

By carefully listening, and reading between the lines, I was beginning to understand that, by chance or design, his life had diverged sharply from the rest of his family's. Likewise, his friends had faded into the background – as so often happens when one moves on to a completely different way of life. I have often noticed that men are more prone to cease communication when distance intervenes. And it certainly had in Andrew's case. He had passed to go to the local grammar school on the hill at eleven but, shortly afterwards he had persuaded his family that he was desperate to pursue a career at sea. One brother designed boats, the other built them; but Andrew was convinced his destiny was to seek adventure across the oceans of the world.

Somehow he had heard of a training ship called the *Arethusa*. She was owned and run by The Shaftesbury Society which, in years gone by, had provided places for up to two hundred and forty poor-law boys to be trained for careers in the armed services. The lads served their apprenticeship on board one of their many ships moored around the coast of the British Isles and then most went on to serve in the Royal, or Merchant, navy. The *Arethusa* was a four-masted steel barque moored at Upnor, on the River Medway, in Kent. Originally named the SS *Peking*, she had carried out sterling work moving grain around Cape Horn until she had ended her life in the service of the Shaftesbury Homes. She was an ideal ship for the boys to train on.

Andrew had often told me about the five happy years he had spent on the *"Are"*. I had met him just before he had been due to go to Plymouth to train for the Merchant Navy proper. As our light-hearted holiday ended he had started a course at the Polytechnic in Plymouth, where he had trained to be a Radio Officer; he then had gone on to Southampton University, to pass a Radar course, before embarking on his first ship. It had been on his third tour of duty that I had told him my unwelcome news that our five-year romantic affair was at an end. I now wanted him to tell me more.

'Tell me about your two sons', I asked. 'Do they look like you and have they followed in your footsteps?'

'Yes, they were both accepted into universities. Peter spent three profitable years at St Andrew's and Mark followed me to York and is now teaching in Manchester. They are both happily settled with children of their own.'

I could see a satisfied glow around Andrew and I recognised it as one so many parents have when they describe their prowess in extending their families. Procreation "boasting" seems to bring out the worst in so many people. Do they not realise how hurtful this can so often be to childless couples who have tried to conceive children, but with no success? I am not talking about those people who brag they would rather die than propagate their species; or the ones that put themselves selfishly first in everything to the exclusion of allowing any other person to enter their tight little liaison with their partner. I am speaking of ordinary, sincere folk who look with longing at close-knit, happy families. When one thinks about it, there are no stiff exams that need to be passed, and no one has to fulfil any complicated criteria to obtain this reward or even do anything of great merit. No one needs to be clever – or fit – or even honest. So how does one person appease the gods and not another? Apparently anyone *can* produce a child if they are lucky – and sometimes if they are *unlucky* – but the bragging about their hordes of children, grandchildren and great grandchildren, by smug grandparents is, to me, a guaranteed red rag to a bull.

How often we have heard pontificating idiots mention they consider childless marriages are incomplete, almost as if they think people who are unable to produce offspring should not even consider this act of union. Is love not the perfect basis for marriage? Too often I have seen warring parents who are indifferent to the suffering of their children. I have dealt with mentally or physically abused children and, down at the other end of the scale, severely ignored children. They are all damaged children. Is this acceptable in a world where thoughtless, complacent bigots truly believe their cruel utterances?

I glanced at Andrew dreading to see these opinions, set in stone, in his mind also. I guessed our new-found friendship might easily founder at this very juncture, but all he did was describe his mixed bunch of kids, with fond love glowing in his eyes.

'I guess brats or angels, as the mood takes them, would probably sum them up.'

I grinned back and relaxed. He was still the same old Andrew. Much later, as we ate our Dover sole, I discovered we had both remembered to sort out, and bring, some snapshots that had recorded some of the intervening years we had spent apart. They were back at our hotels, so we agreed to fetch them with us, the next night, when we knew we would meet again for a slow, leisurely meal. With that settled, we walked out into the warm balmy night.

As we strolled across the cliffs, feeling as if we needed to duck under the low-hanging, swollen moon, I asked, 'What do you want to do tomorrow? We have all day but we mustn't waste it. It will all pass so very quickly.' I was conscious already how time was spilling, like a fast-flowing stream rushing towards a deep weir. The swiftness was frightening me.

'I would love to stay here and hire surfboards – but how about we go back to my old home and wander instead? I need to go to the museum and ask them some questions and, of course, have a darn good yarn with them all. Maybe, afterwards, we could go on to Lansallos and poke around the churchyard? I need to swot up on a bit more family history and it seems a shame to waste this opportunity. Have you anything you especially want to do, Jenny?'

Going back to Fowey raised warning bells in my mind, so I immediately voiced some objections. It was doubtful if anyone would recognise *me* after all the intervening years, I reckoned. I had changed and inevitably they would have done too – but I was certain that word would soon get out that cousin Andrew was back in town and that he was accompanied by some strange woman. And surely they would know that woman was not his wife, Fay?

'Quit worrying,' he said, as he lightly held my arm. 'Fay has not been down to Cornwall for years – no one will even notice.'

I privately knew they might *say* nothing but that there is *always* someone who notices. I decided, there and then, to keep a low profile. Luckily visitors throng the busy streets all through the year; so that would be my camouflage. I would act the passing acquaintance, or maybe a work colleague, and, if anyone became too nosy, I would swiftly ease away and find my way down to the river where there would be enough sailing craft to absorb my interest. That was the best plan I could come up with on the spur of the moment. I would have to play it by ear, but I was determined Andrew would have no awkward questions to answer on my behalf.

With that we kissed warmly, as only old friends can, and made our separate ways across the green to our respective hotels. A great jumble of reflections were rushing through my head as I eased my weary body into the crisp "honeymoon" bed and snuggled down with a sigh. I had imagined another sleep-disturbed night after discussing so many memories during the day, but I drifted off remembering another glorious day, years ago, on those sands when we had revelled in the sparkling waves together, on our beaten up old surfboards, until we had been so tired that all we had been able to do was stretch out and fade into sleep. It was only when I awoke to sunshine streaming through my window early the next morning that I realised I had slept deeply and dreamlessly.

I hastened through my satisfying breakfast and raced back upstairs to gather my things together for the day. Glancing idly through the window I saw Andrew lounging against the hotel wall and I guessed he was waiting impatiently for me. His car was already standing outside the front entrance to the hotel; I dived inside and we were able to make a quick getaway in the fresh morning air. As we drew away from the kerb I watched a tumbling, gauzy surf, framed in the car's rear mirror, and longed, fleetingly, to be part of it. I guessed Andrew would choose the tiny village of Polkerris, on the sheltered south coast, for our mid-morning coffee. I was amazed at how it had grown during the intervening years – from a small unknown hamlet, with one narrow, steep winding road, leading down to a simple grassy sward that overlooked a small modest harbour. Now it was a colourful, bijou holiday resort. The last time I had visited, with a crowd of friends, we had been on our way to a youth hostel in St Austell. Then Polkerris had boasted one typically dour granite inn, surrounded by a scattering of cottages, and very little else. Now it was bustling, with visitors crowding the beach and offshore dinghies racing around in the glittering choppy water as they tacked and dodged each other under a freshening breeze.

We queued for some delicious filtered coffee from a café doing a roaring trade, and took it with us to sit on the plain little harbour wall and admire the view. I wondered if Fowey would have changed to the same extent and if Polruan, across the river, with its narrow, steep and winding streets would still be as modest. Would I recognise these resorts or had they been spoilt by unlimited tourists and the necessity to house them? I passionately hoped not.

We left little Polkerris behind, made our way onto the main road and took the right-hand turning towards Fowey and Andrew's old home. I noticed Four Turnings was still the resting place for the seven-foot granite monolith that was once the gravestone of King Mark's nephew. Tristan's actual grave was reputedly nearer Castle Dore but, seeing the huge stone once again, it only served to remind me of him and the beautiful Iseult, or Isolde, falling in love and it all ending, like Shakespeare's Romeo and Juliet, in tragic death. We dropped down the road towards Fowey and I could see the river nestling down below us, with Pont Pill, the Hall Walk and Polruan making a pleasant backdrop across the water. Andrew decided we would leave the car at Readymoney Cove and walk back through the town. As we stepped out into the sunshine by St Catherine's Castle I glanced back towards Polridmouth Bay and The Grotto – above which, I knew, the one-time house of Daphne Du Maurier, *Menabilly,* lay hidden snugly in the woods. In those far off days "Priddy" had been our favourite walk and I would often think of Daphne brooding over her complex characters in *Rebecca* or *Frenchman's Creek* whenever we rambled there. We turned eastwards and took a leisurely stroll into town, the wooded seashore on our right and the uneven sprawl of Victorian villas and hotels climbing high across the land to our left.

Nothing seemed to have changed vastly. There were no new pubs or amusement arcades to offend us or spoil our walk, thank goodness. We made our way towards Place House, the home of the Treffry family, and the parish church of St Fimbarrus. In the busiest part of town we discovered a tiny bistro offering a vast selection of appealing meals. We made our way through the chattering families and were directed upstairs. We sat down gratefully, under a gaily striped umbrella, on a small, bleached wooden balcony, overlooking a sea of chimney pots that crowned the centre of Fowey. We each ordered a deliciously warm pasty and washed it down with a cool half pint of ale. It was such a pleasant day so we sat talking quietly, admiring the view, until it was time to go. We made our way round the corner, past The Ship Inn – once the home of the influential Rashleigh family – and crossed the square towards the small intimate museum that had once been the Town Hall.

I had almost decided to go against my instincts, and join Andrew on his fact-finding mission, when we suddenly heard a shout from across the street, outside the King of Prussia Inn. Within seconds, I was certain this would not be a good or suitable place for awkward introductions and it was high time for me to make my escape. I muttered, 'You don't need me to cramp your style, Drew. I'll take the next ferry to Polruan and get back to meet you at Readymoney Cove by three o'clock at the latest.' I then skipped between a cycle and an overladen car and was gone before Andrew could respond.

Andrew grinned in agreement while raising his hand to a grey-haired gentleman who was bustling importantly across the road. I smartly turned away, lost myself in the drifting melee of visitors, and was on the foot ferry that plies back and forth constantly between Fowey and Polruan, within minutes. I watched Place House and the crowded Town Quay drop astern, and in no time I was alighting at the Old Coal Wharf slip opposite the Lugger Inn. Immediately I was in another world – peaceful and hushed. There was no hammering or whining from the boatyard, for once, and only a few dinghies, with their sails unfurled, making their way swiftly towards the sea. The few passengers who had arrived with me had purposefully made their way up the steep hill towards their homes, or the bus that would take them on towards Polperro or Looe. I followed them, but then turned right past the Russell Inn and walked on until I could see over the rooftops of Polruan, towards Fowey and the wide estuary spread beneath. I studied the Hall Walk in the distance and could just make out the giant memorial hidden in the trees above Penleath Point. It had been raised to Sir Arthur Quiller-Couch and was set beneath the skyline. Later on I hoped Andrew would make a detour and take me to view it before we made our way, by car, yet further eastwards towards Lansallos and the churchyard he was hoping to explore.

I continued walking towards the headland and the fifteenth-century ruined castle we had always called The Blockhouse. It faced a twin stronghold across the estuary and, during the time of the Armada, a huge chain was slung between the two, hoping to protect the river entrance from marauding Spaniards. I stood inside the fortress and looked out of the deep embrasures at the swirling blue sea's restless pull against the rocks below. I studied the ruined staircase that led nowhere now, imagining I was a soldier guarding the people of Fowey and Polruan in time of war, and having to live in this primitive, draughty castle with few comforts and scant food. I walked back out into the sunshine and made my way along Battery Lane, towards St Saviour's Point where I knew there was a ruined chapel, built in the Middle Ages, and used ever since as a landmark by sailors returning to a safe harbour. The lovely landscaped garden that tumbled down the hillside at this point had always drawn Andrew and I like a magnet. We called it the *secret* garden all those years ago because it was so well hidden away. It had every sort of bench or seat imaginable, placed in snug warm corners, surrounded by unusual plants and protected from any winds. Many level grassy swards were all cunningly connected by paths and these would lead one through rocky archways and down more meandering steps until one arrived at a tiny, sandy cove that looked across to the larger, more well-known Readymoney Cove. I gazed across as a yacht glided gently by in the light breeze – and I was at peace.

I thought it must be time to make my way back towards the ferry, but on examining my watch I decided I still had time to take a look at the boatyard where a besotted Andrew had first introduced me to the love of his life – his dinghy. That year he and his elder brother had rescued it from a scrapyard and, after much pleading, he had been given it as a late Christmas present. He had then spent the rest of that year lovingly scraping, caulking and varnishing it. It was an International 14 and had been built by Fairey Marine just before the Second World War. The cottage my parents had rented was only a few hundred yards from where I was standing. I had formally met Andrew after watching him sailing at a distance, shortly after I arrived. Later, I had been sitting on a wall throwing stones at a worn stump of wood that may have once been part of a jetty. Andrew had squatted down near me and we'd begun talking. At least, *he* had asked the questions and I had answered them. I think that had been the standard procedure with the local lads. Find out who she was, where she came from and how long would she be staying! I must have volunteered all the right answers because, when he had offered to show me his boat and teach me how to sail, he had been extending one of the highest compliments he could have devised.

So it was from their family boatyard I had learned the rudiments of sailing: hauling the mainsail sheets, tacking, jibing and going about until it had all become second nature. We spent hours that holiday exploring the lovely Fowey River and all its tributaries. From Pont Pill we would make our way upriver towards Daphne du Maurier's old family home at Bodinnick, past Mixtow Pill and on to Penpoll Creek, then drift towards Golant and, if the tide was right, turn towards Lerryn. Occasionally, on a good day, we would take *The Shy Curlew* out to sea past Blackbottle Rock and anchor off Lantic Bay, or sail on past Pencarrow Head towards the fishing havens of Polperro or Looe. That had been really exciting. Sometimes, being lazy, we would just ferry ourselves across the river and tie up at the Quay, and then walk up through the town to Readymoney Cove and on to our quiet little "Priddy", deeply hidden away in the woods. It hadn't mattered what we did as long as we were together and, in my innocence, I had hoped this magnetic attraction would last forever.

I had no intention of not keeping my promise to Andrew, so I joined the sparse queue waiting for the Polruan ferry and was back outside the King of Prussia Inn in no time. It was still ten minutes to three o'clock as I smartly swung through the town, dodging all the sun-saturated holidaymakers, who so often meandered indecisively on holiday, and retracing our steps of that morning. Andrew was leaning against the car, soaking up the sunshine. He opened one eye.

'And about time, too,' he couldn't resist saying with a big cheeky grin.

I swiftly glanced down to check my watch, but of course I wasn't late. Within minutes we were sweeping once more across town and on our way to catch the Bodinnick ferry. As we queued behind three other cars, I asked if it would be possible to visit the memorial the good people of Fowey had raised to the memory of Sir Arthur Quiller-Couch? I knew it would not take us far out of our way and I longed to see it again. I love crossing the river at this point; it is as if I know a short cut to a secret part of Cornwall that few visitors find - it also gives me chance to study Daphne du Maurier's old family home, for the few minutes it takes to cross, and ponder over her childhood there. Which one would have been her bedroom? I wondered if she had attended the local school in the town, or had her parents employed a governess? I *do* know that she had expressed scathing remarks about those village children because she admitted, years later, to making up a cryptic language to exclude them from her and her siblings' games and fun. That always seemed rather cruel, to me.

We "curtsied" off the ferry and chugged into The Old Ferry Inn car park to ask permission from the landlord to leave our car while we took a swift foray into the nearby woods. He agreed with a smile, on the promise we would return for a well-earned pint later. We turned towards the indentation on the river that marked the beginning of Pont Pill. It was a tough climb up a really steep hill, until we turned right, passed through a gate and discovered the path of the National Trust Hall Walk – so beloved of ramblers. From here we could see the river spread deeply beneath us with the twin towns of Polruan and Fowey forming a backdrop in the hazy distance. Everything became very quiet, with only the occasional birdsong to break the silence. The first monument we came across was the rugged marker that commemorated the men and women from this corner of Cornwall who gave their lives in two world wars. It seemed a fitting tribute to have placed it in such a beautiful setting.

We walked deeper into the trees, still following the path, until, on our right, we came across a giant granite obelisk, surmounted by a huge Q, set on a steep hillside. It was at least eighteen feet high and towered over our heads. I walked around the front to read the plaque – most of which I had learned by heart. Sir Arthur Quiller-Couch had been a classical professor at Cambridge and had been famous for his critiques and anthologies. He had edited an Oxford Book of English Verse in the 1900s and had published many essays. In my ignorance I had never heard of him before I visited Cornwall that first time, but I *had* just met Andrew and when I began my two-year stint at college, I had stumbled by chance across his "Troy Town" stories. This was a distinctly different facet of Quiller-Couch's character; suddenly he was no longer the austere genius of literature as I was being taught. I had eagerly devoured thinly disguised tales about the town of Fowey that I'd rapidly recognised. They had been warm and intriguing, and I had immediately fallen under the spell of a far less scholarly and classical "Q". These had recounted tales about Cornish folk and their customs, in a magical land that *I* was beginning to love almost as much as he had. These books had opened up a whole new world for me.

The writing on the granite monolith was very simple. It stated that he had been born in Bodmin in 1863 and died in his beloved Fowey in 1944. Among the many and varied positions he had held was an honorary fellowship at Trinity College, Oxford and a similar one in Cambridge; as well as being Professor of English Literature at Cambridge, it went on to say, he brought honour to his county as well as education to Cornwall. He lived in Fowey for over fifty years. It concluded with these words: COURTEOUS IN MANNER, CHARITABLE IN JUDGEMENT AND CHIVALROUS IN ACTION. What better praise could anyone ever hope for?

It was time to go. We hurried back to The Ferry Boat Inn, to down our promised pints and resume the journey. As soon as we reached the top of the steep and winding hill, we turned back towards the coast and finally, in the distance, we could see the untouched golden shingle triangle of Lantic Bay. By common accord we parked the car and alighted to breathe in the clear air and admire the stunning view. Who, coming this way, wouldn't want to scramble down to such an enticing beach? I suspected it would often only be locals, as most visitors would probably want to get to their better-known destinations and wouldn't spare the time. Andrew and I had often sailed around the headland and picnicked on its shore. I remember, one spring day, coming with Andrew's two brothers, and a few close friends, on their motor cycles and having an impromptu barbecue on the beach. It had been such fun; especially as the two of us had been the youngest and had only been included as an afterthought.

But there was no time to waste if we were to visit the local church to enable Andrew to do some more research into his family history. We left Lantic Bay behind us and made our way to the village of Lansallos. Although it was so small and hidden away in a remote corner of Cornwall it had been chosen as the parish church, along with Talland Bay church to the far side of Polperro, to record births, marriages and deaths for the whole area. I wondered if, at one time, many more people had not lived and farmed around here. Most of Andrew's ancestors had originally come from the surrounding farms and had been baptised, married or buried here and, as soon as we walked through the churchyard, I decided to leave him to search for his forebears' memorials in peace while I entered the church. I learned it was named after Saint Ildierna and little is known of her apart from the fact that she was a virgin. I shivered; the interior was cold and bare and it looked as if it had suffered some recent fire damage. The roof timbers were blackened in places and I noticed new carving had replaced old. I wondered who would harm such an isolated building. Walking around I discovered little of interest, apart from an intriguing grey memorial stone attached to a wall. The lady depicted looked like a rather trim Queen Elizabeth I, with a neat stomacher, a high ruff, shoulder pads and an elegant headdress. Her hands were primly clasped and two neatly shod feet peeped out from beneath her sumptuous dress. She looked like a Royal Courtier and totally out of place in this simple church. I wondered who she was and if she was any relation to Andrew. So often we are told family fortunes can go from rags to riches in a few generations: and revert just as swiftly. I shivered and turned to go.

Andrew came strolling towards me as I emerged into the evening sunshine with a sheaf of notes clutched in his hand. 'Corn in Egypt,' he exclaimed. 'Quite a few of my lot seem to be buried here although it's sometimes difficult to decipher the words on the bases of some of the oldest graves, due to the tall grasses and lichen-covered stonework.'

The whole burial ground looked like a billowy sea of lush green grass crowned with white, wild garlic. There were crosses, leaning monuments and even one pretty granite lantern enveloped in this surging tide that threatened to engulf them. I could see his dilemma. One could either take a couple of days to quarter the whole churchyard methodically, to be absolutely certain no important epitaph or gravestone had been missed; or take a cursory look and hope most family members would have been buried in close proximity to each other, and therefore would be easy to spot. And, sadly, we did not have two or three days.

Andrew took my arm. 'Let's take a walk down to the beach, darling. This is all a bit serious and dull for you and I want you to see how my smuggling ancestors made their nefarious forays ashore to take brandy for the parson and baccy for the clerk.'

He opened the wrought iron gate that led from the churchyard and walked through what looked like the garden of a deserted manse. I hoped we were not trespassing and prepared myself for a wrathful vicar racing out to order us off his property. Nothing happened and all remained quiet and peaceful. It did not take much searching before we found the gently meandering National Trust footpath that dropped down through the lush woods and finally led one to the beach. We strolled beside a trickling stream until the path opened out and I could hear falling water. Andrew explained this was Reed Waterfall, but he had no idea why it was so named. We walked the last few yards between a deeply hollowed-out rock and I glimpsed the crashing torrent away to my right. It fell onto a beach that appeared grey and deserted. We wandered down and walked among the flat pebbles – some as big and round as dinner plates. Not a very welcoming place, I surmised. Andrew walked me towards the sea and then turned me around and pointed out why this particular spot had been chosen as a smugglers' haven.

'It is miles away from anywhere, even now. Remember the Revenue men were just ordinary chaps who had probably little seafaring experience, but had been employed by the authorities to stamp out smuggling. Most of them would be unlikely to know the area at all; they would likely be from "up country" and there would be no help from the local population. I expect they were longing to get back to their homes and families in places like Plymouth or Exeter. The smugglers, on the other hand, were well organised. They knew this coast and every route inland, from birth. There was a lot of money involved and a lot at stake, provided by people who were willing to equip them with swift boats and even protect them if an operation went wrong. In those days smuggling was considered fair game for everyone – from the Lords of the Manor, the clergy, schoolteachers, inn owners and clerics to the women who performed menial tasks like salting and pickling pilchards or working in the tin mines, as well as their husbands who worked the land or fished these waters. Many luxury items – like lace, brandy and tobacco – had always been imported from France for those who could afford them. Suddenly these same goods attracted a ridiculous excise duty – probably because the King at the time was anxious to pay for one of his numerous wars. The local fishermen were still employed to import these goods but suddenly the taxation was exorbitant and everyone considered it unreasonable and preposterous. That, my darling, was how smuggling was born.'

He then drew me towards the rear of the beach and pointed out where deep grooves had been worn into the rock through constant use. 'Imagine how many hundreds of trips would be needed regularly, on any dark night, to cause this. Goods worth thousands of pounds would be manhandled off this beach and put into dozens of carts, year after year, to be trundled up this narrow gully towards the fields above, where every able-bodied man available would be waiting to transport them inland as quickly and quietly as possible. Usually, before a Revenue Cutter could find its way into this cove, the whole operation would be completed and the contraband dispersed throughout the area, silently and competently. Every cottage and manor house would have its hidden room – built for just such a purpose – that could be used as required; caves had secret hide-outs, that might be right under a searcher's eyes, caches concealing dozens of barrels of spirits and no one, but *no one*, ever told. It was the Cornish version of *Omerta*. Us against them!'

'Didn't you and your Dad once find a secret room in *your* house by the river?' I innocently asked.

'Yes, we were painting the back cob wall when we both suddenly realised there was an odd space which we couldn't account for indoors. We found it in the end. It was between the smallest upstairs bedroom and the kitchen. We set to with a will and, after taking up the lino and the floorboards, we eventually uncovered a trap door. Deborah wasn't very pleased when she returned,' he said ruefully. 'She was furious at the mess we had made – and we certainly didn't find any brandy or tobacco stashed away!'

As we walked up the steep path, back towards the church and our car, Andrew swung my hand in his and chanted Rudyard Kipling's poem which talks of '*brandy for the parson and baccy for the clerk.*' He finished it with '*so Watch the wall, my darling, as the Gentlemen go by.*'

We had both been so absorbed in each other that neither of us had noticed the day softly waning. It would soon be dark and I was suddenly aware I was ravenous after such an early lunch so, instead of stopping on the way back, we both decided to return to our respective hotels, to shower and change and go straight out for an evening meal.

I found myself singing in the shower. As I looked in the mirror to comb my hair I noticed I was glowing with good health and happiness. I made a quick telephone call to reassure Robin and then I knew I was free to give the rest of the evening to a man who had once been my best friend, comforter and advisor.

Andrew and I were almost identical in age and yet it was he who had taught me how to make the transition between childhood and maturity with ease and delight. He had refused to allow me to be ashamed of my sexuality. I had learned from him it was entirely natural, and not something to hide and be embarrassed about. He had managed to undo all the silly, puritanical ideas my parents had installed in my head from an early age – that sex was dangerous and I should steer well clear of it. I now know the reason behind their homilies – their beloved daughter should be protected from any lad who, in their estimation, would be only too eager to sow his wild oats. Cutting off a young girl from normal interaction with suitable young men meant they would also be depriving her of a routine, essential growing-up process. How could one ever form a natural relationship with someone of the opposite sex if it was drummed into them that a man is only interested in one thing – namely to have his wicked way – and then expect that person to terminate the relationship at another's insistence? Looking back, I wondered how I was ever expected to know anyone - how could I judge anyone and how on earth was I expected to eventually fall in love and look forward to marriage and a family? If I had been a daughter of a high-caste Muslim family, Royalty or Spanish, and closely chaperoned, I could not have been subjected to more strict, albeit gentle, rules and regulations. And sadly, all this had been done by my parents with the best of intentions and a deep love for me.

Andrew had taught me that exuberance was natural and fun. I had been a teenager and should act like one. I'd had my whole life in front of me and it had been in my own hands as to what I was going to do with it. With his gentle tutoring I had grown up and yet regained my earlier, innocent view of life. I had responded to *his* ideas as I'd gradually learned to think for myself. This Cornish lad had been like a breath of fresh air all those years ago and I had forgotten how I had missed the honest sharing of our thoughts and hopes which had always been such an integral part of our correspondence over those years. I snatched up the packet of photographs I had remembered to pack in my suitcase and stuffed them in my handbag. I grabbed a light wrap and was ready. I glanced out of the window. I should have guessed – he was always there ahead of me when we made plans – and that evening was no different.

He had asked the helpful receptionist at his hotel to recommend a decent restaurant. It was within walking distance and enabled us to stroll across the cliffs enjoying the warm, velvety evening air. The breeze had dropped, as it can so often do at this time of an evening, and we could have been in Sorrento or Cannes under a roseate moon. Andrew gently took my hand and I smiled back at him with immense pleasure. His receptionist had chosen well. The dining area was upstairs in a large pleasant room overlooking the bay. Did the maître d' guess our longing for solitude, because he showed us to a secluded, yet cosy, alcove with a perfect view up the coast to Bedruthan Steps? Lights were strung like a glistening diamond necklace along the seashore as far as one could see, reflecting the white foamy incoming tide and creating a veritable fairyland. We both settled back with a comfortable sigh; suddenly there was no reason to hurry, the night stretched ahead of us and I knew we were both going to enjoy it.

Maybe we *did* drink too much red wine that evening but who cares? It served to relax and refresh us and we ended up chattering and laughing comfortably about anything and everything that took our fancy. Our three courses slowly melted before our eyes and, by the time we reached the cheese board, we had laughed and questioned each other until gradually all our inhibitions disappeared and we could have been twenty again and just Drew and Jenny, as it had always been.

By then we had become friendly with our attentive waiter and he suggested, when we asked for a pot of coffee, that it could be served in their comfortable lounge. We explained we hadn't met for years and we wanted to look at old photographs undisturbed and reminisce some more, so once again we were shown to a commodious corner with conker-brown, deep-seated leather armchairs and settled before a huge, low coffee table with a brandy each – courtesy of the management.

Andrew began by spreading dozens of well-worn pictures of his children, his grandchildren, his dog and, finally, a few of Fay his wife, across the table. I found it difficult to get them straight. As far as I could work out Rosy, Leigh and Perkin belonged to Peter, his eldest son; and Ben and Camilla were Mark's children. Their mothers' names and descriptions were a mystery too far for me and I mentally switched off as Andrew tried to explain the ramifications of his immediate family. I recognised his parents' photos and also his two brothers and one sister-in-law, all of whom I had known in Cornwall but, once again, I became a bit muddled regarding Hugh's wife, who he had married much later, and *their* two children. I also could barely place his best friend, Dan, who looked as if he had changed significantly. Blame the brandy!

When it was my turn it was far simpler. I had brought a couple of photos of my parents at my two weddings. In a group photo Andrew instantly recognised Dee, my cousin, and my good friend, Meryl, as bridesmaids at the first one. He remembered Chris my first husband, of course, from his ill-fated meeting in the pub that evening all those years ago. He idly asked if I had found him changed when he had returned to the UK and had stayed with us for those few weekends.

'Still tall – very assured – fatter – richer – and losing his hair,' I told him shortly.

From his slight smirk, I knew Andrew was amused. I then passed across two photographs I had remembered to bring of my second wedding. Robin is of average height and only tops me by half a dozen inches. This ceremony had been a lot more relaxed than my first attempt at getting married. No long trains, tiaras and trailing bouquets. No cute little flower girls, with bouncy curls, holding tightly to the hands of elegant bridesmaids. No best man shaking hands and no tier upon tier of two families all standing tall and proud in their wedding finery. No unbelievably huge hats and no grey morning suits.

No, this was obviously a low-key affair. Robin was wearing his best grey "interview" suit and I had chosen a long dress, one I had only worn once before at a dinner and dance at The Talk of the Town in London. Luckily the dress was demure, so absolutely ideal. Heavy white Nottingham lace over pale turquoise silk, the long, slim fitting A-line skirt was offset by short sleeves, cut high under the bust, and both were edged with crisp white appliquéd daisies. I had felt dainty and attractive – and it showed. All of us were relaxed and smiling at the cameraman. My first wedding had been to satisfy my parents and this time I had wanted it to be personal to both Robin and me. We had only invited fourteen of our family and friends to join us. Dee and Paul, her husband, were standing chatting to Meryl, Adam and their two children. My parents were looking reasonably happy, even if slightly bewildered, and Robin was solely represented by his sister, Alexis, and flanked by his two nephews, Owen and Cameron. We had asked my oldest hospital friend, Cassie, to join us and two of Robin's police colleagues. That was it.

The girls had chosen long, Laura Ashley type, sprigged muslin, pinafore dresses which were all the rage at that time. Alexis and Dee both wore circular straw Scarlett O'Hara hats and I had found a lacy white one that had been floating around our house since the previous summer. I had tarted it up with a pale turquoise chiffon scarf. In all, my wedding finery had cost me absolutely nothing and, in lots of ways that had summed up the whole day. We all looked comfortable and relaxed – even the children. The second photograph showed Robin cringing while Alexis held onto her brother with one hand as she stuffed confetti down his neck with the other. The rest of us were falling about laughing. As soon as the ceremony was over we had all set out in a convoy of assorted cars to where Robin had booked us into a simple restaurant for lunch. And there the jollity had continued until it was time for Robin and me to escape our guests' clutches by deliberately ignoring our car, which we were certain would have been sabotaged, and taking a taxi to catch the train to the Lake District for a few days.

I explained all this to Andrew as he examined all the pictures closely. We had almost talked ourselves to a standstill; but, before the evening was over, I was determined to find out about Andrew's wife, Fay. She was turning into something of an enigma. He had talked extensively, with glowing love, about his two sons and his grandchildren. He had told me about their funny ways and sayings; and he told me how he missed the kiddies, especially now both families had moved to the far side of the Pennines. I could see how proud he was of them all. He had also mentioned both sons' wives who he described as sensible as well as likeable; but he had said almost nothing about his wife. I stretched across and studied the photographs of her carefully. One showed a young and beautiful, windswept Fay who had been cheekily grinning up at the photographer. She appeared to be sitting outside an inn and downing half a pint of beer or cider. The second had been taken on their wedding day. They were standing and cutting a huge four-tiered cake with what looked like a ceremonial sword. Andrew, looking young and unsure, had his hand over hers and she was smiling up at him prettily. The final snap was obviously more recent. In it she was looking slightly matronly in a long, dark winter's coat with a large black velvet cocked hat set at a becoming angle. I noticed that her hair, over the years, had changed from a thick dark brown to an immaculate, stylish, coiffured blonde – courtesy of her hairdresser, I suspected.

I began to ask Andrew about her but he was either too tired, or just plain reticent, because he changed the subject and immediately suggested he settle the bill so we could leave. I was delighted, as we strolled outside, to find the evening air was still warm and somnolent but I also reflected that another precious day was almost over. I tried to push away the thought that soon we would be going our separate ways; and Andrew seemed to feel the same way, too, because he stopped, clasped my hands in his warm ones, and hugged me to him.

We stood close together, overlooking the harbour, and I found myself telling him how, all those years ago, I had come here with Chris for two weeks during the second year of our marriage. At our wedding we'd had very little money and, by necessity, had done without a proper honeymoon. The next year things had not been a lot better and we could only afford to holiday somewhere inexpensive. I described how the small Cornish guest house we had booked was full when we'd arrived and by chance we had been sent along to Mabel and Fred's cottage. By coincidence, it was a few minutes away from where we were standing. In fact, I said, I could even take him there.

It always surprises me that so often, in large busy towns, there may be secret, quiet little corners, possibly only a short way away from a busy thoroughfare, just waiting to be discovered by the adventurous. And so it was here; behind the town's main street, invariably thronged by noisy holidaymakers, one can find a small cul de sac that is Broad Street. I led Andrew to the far end to where the Tregennas had lived all their married life. Just a simple whitewashed cottage in a small unmade road. Very few people, I am sure, ever discovered this peaceful backwater and certainly very few ever stayed there. It looked unpretentious, but the love and warmth, dispensed along with the most delicious Cornish fare, had been a revelation to both Chris and myself.

I went on to tell Andrew how both Fred and Mabel had welcomed us to their home and treated us like one of their large family. I also explained how I had relied on the couple when, after ten years, my marriage had started to unravel. Mabel's simple philosophy had seen me through the bad times, as well as my shattering divorce, until, after years of holidaying alone, I had dared to bring Robin down to meet them. They had accepted him immediately and, from then on, insisted we spend our annual surfing holidays with them; and, finally, when I'd agreed to marry Robin, they had welcomed us once again. Neither Robin nor I had ever longed for expensive hotels with elegant service, so to spend two weeks every year with our friends had suited us both perfectly. Sadly, a few years ago Fred had died and Mabel, well into her nineties by then, had gone to live with her son. We were then forced to find other accommodation, but we always made a point of visiting the Tregenna family as soon as we crossed the border into Cornwall. It became our pleasurable ritual.

I hoped I hadn't bored Andrew with my rustic descriptions of the Life and Times of Jenny Fairburn. Compared with his worldly wanderings, my fifty years had been tame and insipid. Maybe I was only demonstrating how dull and provincial I had become. I roused myself from my musings and tugged at his hand.

'Come on, let's get back to civilisation. It must be really late and we are now down to our last day tomorrow. What do you want to do, Drew? Do you have anything planned?'

I dreaded him suggesting we should make an early start so we could both arrive home in good time. Maybe he had made plans to be with his friends. Arrangements that could neither be altered nor cancelled. Then I would know, without doubt, exactly how much I had bored him and how he was longing to get back to his own people – people he knew and liked. I waited, trying not to show him I cared, to hear his decision.

'Would you mind too much accompanying me to Truro?' he asked.

'No, of course not,' I said, my heart singing. 'But what are you planning to do in Truro?'

'It will be a perfect opportunity to visit the Cornwall Record Office. I have wanted to visit it for such a long time. I do loads of stuff, online, via my computer, of course. I also have a cousin who often supplies me with huge chunks of our family history but it would be stimulating to talk with real live, intelligent Cornishmen, maybe pick their brains, and actually find out just what info *is* on offer there. Would you be willing to help me, Jenny? I promise to have you back home by late afternoon – scout's honour.'

I hadn't realised I had been holding my breath. That sounded to me as the most wonderful idea. Maybe the holiday hadn't been as tedious for him as I had imagined. I would scribble reams for him if it meant we could be together for a little longer. We beamed at each other as I turned towards my hotel. The dark cliffs formed a perfect backdrop and, across the bay, a silver shaft of moonlight bit deep into a restless, inky sea. The Island stood four square, rooted deep in the surging waves, and, for a few seconds, looked like a miniature image of Camelot. It was a magical moment and I found it difficult to turn away casually and run up the hotel steps, waving a nonchalant goodbye. He blew me a kiss and turned to walk across the Green with a satisfied smile of contentment lighting his face. I went smiling and humming to my room, and flung myself on my "honeymoon" bed with gay abandon. I had been granted a reprieve: one more day to savour his company. I perceived then with a blinding clarity what I should have guessed that first afternoon when we had ended up comfortably chatting and laughing in the warm sunshine overlooking the busy harbour. There was some strange affinity, a bond that had always linked us together and, as far as I was concerned, it was as potent as it had always been. Almost forty years had not diminished it and, I would have to take care not to allow it to overwhelm me and tarnish my love and future with Robin.

It was a sobering thought and I wondered fleetingly whether Andrew felt the same tug of nostalgia and yearning as I did, for times past and opportunities missed. There was no way I would ever know and I would always be too proud to ever question him. I was not in the least bit sleepy but, if I was to be up bright and early for our foray into the world of ancestors, family trees and parish registers, I had best get to bed and stop dreaming about what might have been, all those years ago.

Chapter 5

*

I made sure my case was packed and waiting when Andrew came to pick me up that last morning. I was so determined not to waste a minute of our precious time together that I had come down for breakfast as soon as the dining room opened. I said my last goodbyes to the staff and lugged my case to the top of the outside steps. Andrew walked up and took it from me and heaved it into his car boot.

'What on earth's *in* this, Jenny?' he grunted. 'It feels like a ton of iron ore plus two pregnant elephants.'

'How did you guess?' I grinned happily, and swung my legs into the car. That was typical Andrew, forgetting I had been on holiday for almost three weeks and that he had only been down for a few days. But it was lovely to hear him teasing me – just like the old days.

We drove off with a flourish and I silently said my fond farewells to Newquay. We arrived in Truro, at the Cornish Record Office, within the hour. I love the approaches to this city; it appears modest and unpretentious until, suddenly, the pale grey twin towers of the west front of the cathedral rise dramatically above the houses and shops, and immediately Truro begins to work its magic on me.

Andrew found the record office with no trouble and produced his membership card. It probably made a change for the staff to see a fellow Cornishman and he was welcomed with a beaming smile. I am sure it is mostly relatives from other parts of the UK, or from across the seas, spending their precious holiday time trying to track down an ancestor or two. I would imagine most people, who pass through their doors, need only quick and concise information and spend little time chatting and relaxing with the workforce supplying the information. Andrew pulled me forward and introduced me to the man and woman behind the counter. They vetted me thoroughly and then signed me in for the day. All very painless, I decided. In the hushed atmosphere, that could have been a monastery, we were taken around their library, told about their extensive archives and finally shown how to operate the various machines. Andrew asked them for the records of births, marriages and deaths from 1800 until 1850 and settled me at a desk to record every Lanyon, Toms, Rashleigh, Kittow and Treffry that I could find. He supplied me with a sharpened pencil and a large wad of foolscap paper and I became immersed immediately in the assignment he had set me.

He then went off with one of the assistants and I could hear their muted murmur in another room until it went very quiet and silence reigned once more. I filled in line after line of information regarding his family until gradually I saw a certain pattern and sequence emerging. It was a fascinating task and I soon became absorbed in their occupations, where they had lived, their children and their complex intermarrying. I did not know it at the time, but Andrew was looking up the Lansallos Parish Records for the same period. His aim was to weave the two together and maybe obtain a more detailed account of the lives of his numerous ancestors during that time.

I was scribbling away contentedly when a light touch on my shoulder brought me back to the present. A plump, jolly little lady was standing smiling at me.

'How are you doing, my dear? Are you discovering what you want? I hope your hubby is doing as well,' she whispered, nodding towards where Andrew had disappeared.

'Oh, we aren't married,' I answered, embarrassed. 'He's just a good friend.'

She shrugged and walked away, saying as an afterthought, 'If you want a short break for a cup of coffee, my lover, just go off into the Staff Room and help yourself.'

I thanked her but decided it was more important to carry on. If I was lucky, maybe I could finish before Andrew wanted to leave. And then I could be satisfied with a job well done. I put my head down and continued. But, blow me down, within two minutes I was interrupted again. A balding, middle-aged man – probably the lady's husband – sidled up to me. I looked enquiringly at him.

'Your husband is having a right old time with those parish records. He's scribbling away as if the Devil himself is on his tail. He's racing through at a rate of knots - you'd think there was no tomorrow!'

'For us there isn't,' I instantly thought. Tomorrow we would both be back with our respective families and in another world. I tried once again to explain we were just good friends, but he only laughed indulgently as if he didn't believe me, raised his hands in the air and walked away.

'What is the matter with these people?' I wondered. Obviously we had given the wrong impression; but did it really matter? I decided it didn't, and lowered my head once more.

I had three more entries to record when Andrew arrived back to whisk me away for lunch. I hate to leave any task unfinished, so I insisted on completing my mission before raising my hands above my head and stretching my aching limbs that had remained cramped all morning. Andrew was scanning my output with interest.

'Is that it?' I asked.

'Yep! You have done a sterling job and I am really grateful, Jenny. Let's go and find you a decent meal. I'm starving and we definitely both deserve it.'

We collected our coats while thanking and waving farewell to our helpers. They watched us go after recommending The Globe as a decent place for lunch. It turned out to be a pleasant hostelry and the Record Office Staff were right – it produced an excellent meal. We had salmon en croute surrounded by half a dozen seasonal vegetables, followed by strawberries with mounds of clotted cream, all washed down with a glass of Riesling. While we were enjoying our coffee afterwards, we sat back and examined our morning's work. We had both produced dozens of pages of detailed material. I guessed this would keep Drew amused and busy for quite some time.

'What do you find so interesting about all this information?' I asked.

'Not the boring facts, that's for sure, but the odd little quirks that suddenly put the flesh on the bones. I noticed, as I was going through, that one of my ancestors had been drowned at sea, leaving a young wife and half a dozen children. Later, I might discover that, as well as earning his living as a fisherman, he might have been one of the many smugglers that worked around our coast. Most red-bloodied Cornishmen would supplement their earnings in this way, if the need arose, and just about everyone in the County would condone the trade that went on so blatantly. I have no idea, but maybe he needed extra money to keep his young family from starvation. He could have possibly come into conflict with the 'Excise Men', who were probably from 'up country', and would automatically be bitterly disliked by all the locals. Smugglers didn't always win these cat-and-mouse games they constantly played and he may have been shot and fallen overboard from his vessel, and drowned. You can bet it would have all been hushed up for the sake of his family. This might be borne out in the parish records where I *might* learn that his now destitute family had been forced to apply to the parish for help and it would, in all probability, immediately be given. See what I mean? This is all conjecture, Jenny, and nothing may ever have happened like this at all – but suddenly these dry and dusty ancestors become real people and not just a statistic in a dog-eared ledger.'

I nodded. I could see how this sort of interest could become addictive. It made me want to go home and start looking at my own family archives. See what family skeletons *I* could uncover.

'Well come on,' he said briskly. 'That's my sermon over for today. It's about time we were on our way.'

In the car we both fell silent. This was so unusual because, up until then, we had never stopped chattering and laughing. I think the silence made him feel uncomfortable, too, because he switched on some low 60s music. I curled up in my seat and pretended to doze.

We crossed the Cornish border on the far side of Launceston with neither of us saying a word. I stared unseeingly out at the scenery as I could feel us racing back towards separation and a nothingness that threatened to engulf me. I dreaded returning home. I felt sick at the thought. Why? I had a kindly and thoughtful husband who would be delighted to see me but all I could feel was a deep melancholy submerging all the happiness I had wrapped around myself for the past three days. I knew I was being ridiculous, as well as morbid, as I tried to remember the good life I would be returning to. There were my elderly neighbours who were always pleased to see me. Sometimes they traded on my good nature but, to balance that, I enjoyed listening to their fascinating memories while sharing a cup of tea or coffee with them. And there were my friends who I relied on heavily. There was my pleasant garden, all the pastimes I enjoyed, as well as my darling old faithful dog that I always missed immensely. What on earth was the matter with me?

We were almost on the outskirts of Exeter when Andrew snapped out of his reverie and quietly said, 'Look, let's not go home just yet. Where would you like to go? How about north Devon? I keep seeing signs to north Devon. Is it far?'

I shot up in my seat. 'Of *course* it is,' I answered. 'Don't be ridiculous. We can't possibly go there. It is nowhere near Honiton and definitely in the opposite direction to Dartmouth! And what about your friends, will they not expect you back soon?'

He turned and glanced at my indignation. We glared at each other for some seconds before he sharply spun the steering wheel and we turned off – not to the north, as I had expected – but south and what turned out to be an extremely long and winding road.

'Where on earth are you taking us?' I demanded. He shrugged.

I immediately lowered my feet to the floor and sat up straighter. I had absolutely no idea where we were heading. I was certain I had never travelled this road before, and there were no signposts to enable me to get my bearings. It felt as if we had arrived in the middle of nowhere, but I later learned we were travelling through the Teign Valley. Tall, dark trees lined either side of the deserted roadway and I wondered how many people actually ever came this way. Once again our closeness had disappeared. Andrew drove on in silence as I stared around me at the narrow, winding road and finally, after an extremely tight, sharp bend, we entered the small village of Drewsteignton. On my left I noticed a pleasant, flower-bedecked inn and wondered if we were coming here for tea. Obviously not. Andrew, glancing at a prominent signpost, accelerated once again. I clung on grimly. Finally it appeared his search was over. He turned sharply left and we swept up a wide drive and came to an abrupt halt outside a huge, grey granite castle. Like a sturdy casket placed on a ledge and overlooking a misty valley. It looked very theatrical and I wondered if it was as solid as it appeared. The car ticked into silence and I felt a calmness descend on me. The unrelieved greyness of the building was lightened by crenellated battlements and we both sat there absorbing the peace that surrounded us.

Andrew then explained it was supposedly the last castle to be constructed in the British Isles. He went on, 'This place was designed and built by Edwin Lutyens – the man who provided us with the Cenotaph in London and with some of the best architecturally designed governmental buildings in Delhi. He did England and the Raj proud. I have wanted to explore it for ages but, since wandering around stately homes has never been Fay's bag, she has always persuaded me to keep on driving and I have long been thwarted.'

I looked long and hard at this strange building set bleakly above the Teign Gorge. The very greyness made it look forbidding and, even though it looked across rolling moors, I wondered just what it would be like to be marooned here in the depths of winter with no other signs of human habitation. But, being me, I was willing to give it a try so I swung my legs out of the car and marched through the plain front door.

Andrew produced his National Trust card and, as mine was packed securely in my suitcase, paid for my entrance. Inside, we discovered a home – warm and cosy and strangely modern. Built early in the twentieth century by the foremost modern architect of the age; it had been commissioned by Julius Drewe, who had conceived his dream of a medieval, grand castle. His fortune had been made via the Home & Colonial stores that populated the British Isles at that time and perhaps he fancied himself as a Joseph Lipton of his day because, as Lipton raced huge prestigious yachts across oceans, maybe Julius Drewe wanted to make a more permanent mark with a bizarre fortress set deep in the moors of Devon.

Inside we found much modern luxury; but also huge rooms decorated with seventeenth-century tapestries. In the dining room one couldn't help being stunned by a monumental portrait of Julius dwarfing the dining table. He looked like Gilbert Harding to me and I had the distinct impression he was a man who knew his own mind, brooked no argument and whose will always prevailed. I noticed his wife's pleasant portrait had been done earlier, when they still lived on their Sussex estate. I wondered if she had hated the difference between leafy Sussex and this often bleak, wild place when, I suspect, he would often be away from home and attending to his vast food empire.

We learned, against good advice from his architect, that Julius Drewe had insisted on single walls with no damp proofing – as one would expect in a real medieval castle. I am sure he had ruefully regretted that insistence because, ever since, the family, and now the National Trust, had battled against rising damp and had never found a cure.

We had swiftly walked through the warm and pleasant house. Sadly, we had little time to spare so Andrew insisted we went to the new café in the Visitor Centre for one last cream tea. Neither of us was able to do it justice, but we did manage a cup of tea as we toyed with our golden scones. It seemed a fitting end to a long and busy day. I suggested gently that he settle the bill so we could leave. I took his hand as we walked out of the building. I understood his feelings. To me, it was as if our world was rushing towards us far too quickly. I knew my attitude was childish and I had done my utmost not to let him guess it. It had never occurred to me he might feel the same way, too. Back in the car I placed my hand on his knee, as a sort of comfort, and we travelled the rest of the way to Honiton, chatting easily.

I directed Andrew to my home. It was nothing spectacular – a solid, cheerful bungalow with no pretensions – just like Robin and me, I suppose one would say. As we turned into our close, a simple ten-house cul-de-sac, I could sense a tension building in Andrew. He pulled up sharply by the kerb when I indicated and, within seconds, was out of the car and heaving my red suitcase from the boot. He strode down the footpath and deposited it outside the white front door that always looked, at that time of the year, as if it were drowning in showers of tumbling yellow roses. I hurried after him. I was aiming to check if Robin was at home, so I could introduce them to each other. He strode back to the car in an instant. To keep him a few minutes longer, I offered to accompany him to the main road once more. I said it would enable me to direct him back towards Dartmouth. He appeared to calm down as we moved away from my house and, in the next road, I asked him to stop so we could say our goodbyes.

We chatted quietly for a few minutes. He promised to keep in touch after warning me that within a few days he would be going to stay overnight in London, with family, before flying off to California for five weeks. We kissed gently and he hugged me to him as if he was unable to let me go. I slowly slipped out of his arms and eased myself out of the car. He put it in gear and allowed it to drift steadily down the hill. The whole way down the road I could see his hand raised, almost in benediction, out of the window. I lifted mine in salute until he became a veritable dot in the distance and then, mercifully, he turned the corner and disappeared. Various emotions coursed through me – happiness that we had met once again, of course, sadness that he had left me so suddenly, warmth that maybe our friendship could continue and endure, desolation that I should feel so bereft after such a short time. I allowed myself a few tears as I walked back across the park towards my home.

My case was still standing forlornly outside the porch where Andrew had so abruptly placed it. I flung open the door and thrust it inside. I shouted for Robin but in my heart I had known all along the house was empty. It had that dead, warm, eerie silence that I particularly notice when returning home from every holiday. Even the carpet smelt, and felt different – unfamiliar – alien. I dumped my case in our bedroom and left it to be unpacked later. Right then I only needed a cheering cup of tea so I pulled myself together and went towards the kitchen to brew one.

I wondered if Robin was still at work. I decided to ring him on his mobile. He took ages to answer but, when he did, all I could hear was a lot of background noise and laughter. I discovered he was only a street away, at his best friend Kevin's house, and it sounded as if an impromptu party was in full swing. I asked what they were up to.

Robin bellowed, 'Come over and find out.'

I wondered how many beers they had consumed. I ditched my cup of tea and went straight round. The door was opened by Hazel, Kevin's wife, who looked at me with questioning eyes. She had always been inclined to be curious and was often slightly malicious.

'And where have you been to, young lady?' she asked.

I normally employ the maxim that attack always proves the best form of defence with this sort of person. I calmly followed her back into their sitting room where about six other friends were sitting or standing around clutching various glasses. I wondered what they were celebrating.

'I'll have you know I have been working my socks off most of today. I spent all morning in the Cornish Record Office in Truro copying down dozens of statistics that meant nothing to me whatsoever. I was then treated to a late lunch, which I badly needed. We spent most of this afternoon – in traffic – travelling back.' The last statement was a lie but it slipped out simply and easily.

I watched a glazed look of boredom slipping across their faces. I guessed there wouldn't be too many questions about what I had been up to during the past few days, and I breathed a sigh of relief. I asked for a gin and tonic and settled down next to Pete and Denise who only wanted to talk about a new caravan they had bought the previous weekend. I tried to make intelligent conversation but my heart wasn't in it. I could only think of a certain car winging its way towards Dartmouth. Was Andrew playing a favourite CD, or perhaps listening to a world affairs programme, or maybe even just staring moodily through the windscreen as he drove westward once again? Stupidly I hoped the latter. I wondered if he felt as dejected as I did. It was childish to feel like that after we had enjoyed such a wonderful few days together. Rather we should both be feeling elated and satisfied and, although I laughed and joked for the next two hours, inside I was at another place and reliving every second of our time together.

The next day I came down to earth with a bump. Robin went off to work at some unearthly hour, nursing a well-deserved hangover. I shoved a mountain of dirty laundry through the washing machine before going to check on my next-door neighbour. I had found her a suitable gift, as always, and regaled her with tales of our fantastic surfing holiday at Trebarwith. I ended by telling her about my busy interlude in Newquay. Rose had become almost a recluse since her husband had died and she always enjoyed hearing about our escapades. She was fascinated when I told her about Andrew and asked lots of searching questions – most of which I answered truthfully, but not in too much depth. I then took her shopping list, along with my own, and went off to Tesco's to shop for both of us.

I managed to cut the front lawn and trim the edges before Robin came home, tired out, from work. I was satisfied I had managed to fill in my day with lots of hard work and the fatigue, I felt, had helped to dull my thoughts of Andrew. Was he on his way to London yet or was he staying with friends a little longer before setting off? It was my fault that I had not questioned him closely as to his plans – mainly because I had wanted to live in the present and not think about the future. Had he told his friends about our weekend or had he mentioned nothing apart from visiting his old home and working on his family history? How honest was he prepared to be about me, I wondered?

That evening Robin suggested we go out for a meal in our local pub and I was only too pleased to agree. When I was in Cornwall my sleep in those last few nights had been fitful and restless at best. I think I was too excited to really relax and unwind, so after working so hard on my return home I prayed for a dreamless night's rest. Usually *The Plume of Feathers* provides an "all you can eat" menu, and we always wash it down with a large glass of their best red wine. As we ate Robin asked me all about my extra few days in Newquay and I described them to him in detail. It was surprisingly simple but that was because my husband hadn't inherited a jealous bone in his body. He immediately suggested we invite Andrew and Fay for a future weekend. I dubiously agreed but, remembering how Andrew had reacted when I had arrived home, I was not sure if he would accept. Later, some boisterous friends came over to join us and, while Robin enjoyed a noisy game of darts with them, I sat back and contentedly watched the world go by.

The next morning I was up bright and early. Somehow I vaguely hoped Andrew would find some way to get in touch – maybe a quick chat on our mobile phones or perhaps sending a hurriedly scribbled postcard. There was no earthly reason why he should contact me, of course, and he certainly hadn't promised to before he had driven off; but I found it difficult to accept his last hug meant little more than. 'Thanks for a good time, Jenny. See you around!' The honest truth was that I missed him dreadfully.

Lots of mail landed heavily on the mat that morning but there was nothing, as I had half expected, from Andrew. I comforted myself by imagining him still in Dartmouth, maybe surrounded by his golfing cronies, or possibly returning to Yorkshire to pick up Fay and take her to London. It is easy to supply excuses when one wants it hard enough and I always did have a vivid imagination. I filled my time with necessary chores and added a few that I had been meaning to do for ages. I immersed myself in a pile of ironing while enjoying Sarah Kennedy chatting brightly on the radio. I next took advantage of the good weather to tackle our large back garden which had decided to turn itself into a jungle while we had been away. Finally, I prepared a huge pot of curry, half of which could be put in the freezer for a later date, before I made my daily pilgrimage into Rose's next door bungalow. I helped her drown a few cups of strong tea and demolish a plate of melting shortbreads while she regaled me with the usual lurid newspaper headlines. Why did she read such a scurrilous rag, I always wondered? We discussed her favourite television programmes and then she criticised all the current soaps – most of which I honestly thought she secretly loved but would never admit to!

Catching up with my routine chores had made me late with her shopping. First thing every morning I normally fulfilled my daily function by demanding her shopping list as well as settling down to listen to her night's dreams. She dreamed long and intensely most nights and we usually made sense of them by discussing what she had read in the newspapers, or had seen on the television, the previous day. As the news that affected her was invariably bad, often her dreams turned into nightmares. Their one redeeming feature was that they always included her late husband, who she had adored, and I usually managed to cheer her up by asking what he had been wearing and what he had been up to.

That evening I left Rose speedily and wandered indoors as soon as Robin's car entered our close. While he had a quick shower I reheated the curry and started laying the kitchen table. It wasn't Force policy to discuss police work away from the station but Robin would often relay any general gossip that was going the rounds and, if it was interesting, what he had been dealing with on his shift that day. Sometimes it was boring, mundane routine, or he would be moaning about the amount of paperwork generated by even a simple incident. That night it was serious – a schoolgirl had gone missing. We discussed some of the possible suspects – from her stepfather to her jealous teenage boyfriend. Occasionally Robin would find my slant on an enquiry interesting. As a woman, a member of the public, and having worked in the medical sector dealing with mental problems, I sometimes could throw some light on a possible motive. That night he was baffled, irritable and tired so I joined him on the couch and we watched our favourite television quiz programme until we both dozed off and it was time to make our way to bed.

Another day put behind me, I decided the next morning. I mentally shook myself crossly at my infantile attitude but it didn't stop me going swiftly to examine my computer in case Andrew had decided to write while he was away. Nothing. And nothing on my mobile phone or in my mail. Daily, my ebullient feelings were seeping away as time slowly passed. This mooning around was foreign to my nature. I couldn't confide in anyone as, since I had married Robin, I had never felt like this before and it seemed disloyal to my husband. How could I admit *that* to anyone? He didn't deserve to be treated so badly even though the guilt was only in my mind. Up until that time I had always been 'good old Jenny', up for most things and always to be relied on for a laugh or assistance. Where had their kindly neighbour disappeared to? I mused about it over a cup of coffee in the garden and came to the conclusion that I must forget about Andrew for the time being and concentrate on one day at a time. I would immerse myself in my surroundings and make myself useful.

As I returned from the shops I espied Petra's mum, Lorna, lugging home several huge bags filled with groceries. She only lived around the corner, so I drew up and pushed open the car door for her to get in. Naturally, as soon as we arrived at her place, she invited me in for coffee. I was only too pleased – it was either finishing the last of my back garden chores or being up for a good natter. Coffee and a pleasant gossip won hands down!

We staggered in loaded with two bags each and I helped her fill her kitchen shelves before we made ourselves comfortable at the breakfast bar. As she filled our mugs she told me she and her husband were hoping to visit her parents in Norfolk shortly.

'Petra adores going home and my parents *do* make such a fuss of her,' she said. 'And Derek could do with a holiday – even if it *is* only draughty old Blakeney and not terribly exciting.'

I silently agreed with her as I knew their new house had stretched them to their financial limit and doubtless a proper holiday was out of the question for that year, at least.

'Who will be looking after boisterous Rex and Jimmy the Gerbil?' I asked. Not too many of our neighbours would be willing to help out. Rex, their dog, was only just emerging from puppy-hood and their gerbil would chew for England if he escaped his cage.

'Not only Rex and Jimmy, I'm afraid. You know Petra and her mania for collecting all sorts of animals? Well Mrs Robertson asked for volunteers to look after two goldfish during the school hols and our Petra was first in the queue. She was only entrusted with one, but then she got around her Daddy to provide him with two mates, for company; so Gertie and Gumdrop have joined George in our entourage. I just cannot see my mother coping with all that lot. Their feed and habits are a logistical problem which goes beyond the point of human endurance and, frankly, transporting them to Norfolk horrifies me.'

'That's fine, the more the merrier,' I stated. Other people's animals can be great fun in small doses. 'Robin and I will be delighted to walk Rex with our old Crumble and I promise to keep Jimmy under lock and key. As for the three goldfish, well that's easy, no exercise and a sprinkling of food once a day should satisfy them. So get off to Norfolk and enjoy yourselves.'

I left there feeling satisfied I had filled in some more of my free time before I would be able to chatter to Drew once again. As I entered my hall I heard the telephone ringing stridently. I raced to answer it, my heart hammering. It was the Head Teacher of our small junior school opposite. Would I help out at their annual jumble sale the following Saturday? As a school governor I was delighted to be of use and promised to sort out some of my old clothing, some discarded paperbacks and a few useless souvenirs that friends always insist on bringing back from their holidays. Robin also had some old running gear stuffed in the back of his wardrobe, I had noticed recently – so I added that to my mental list.

I also added, for good measure, 'I'll go and see the old folk too, and maybe get them to part with some of their heirlooms.'

Good-oh, I thought, Robin will be happy to de-clutter our

place and I will be delighted to eliminate some of that senseless dusting. As I was already on the phone, I decided *now* might be the time to check if our local rambling association was planning any decent autumn walks in the near future. I had rather neglected them recently and maybe now was the time to impress Drew with my energy and current interests. I learned there was to be a short walk the following Wednesday around Branscombe, an unspoilt village bordering the sea where one could walk for miles without meeting another soul. The walk sounded interesting and, as long as the weather stayed fine, I agreed to go with them and mentally crossed off another lonely day. I also tried to ignore the fact that this was becoming an obsession.

Bit by bit I managed to find an outing or complete a necessary chore until such time Andrew decided to resume our e-mails or put an end to our correspondence once and for all. Once a month I helped arrange flowers at our local church. I wasn't terribly artistic but I enjoyed both the chatter and the coffee in equal measure. Sometimes on a Tuesday or Thursday I was roped in for dusting or polishing the same church which, in lots of ways, was easier but not so much fun. There were only ten small bungalows in our small crescent but most days one or other of my neighbours wanted shopping collected or maybe a lift down to the shopping centre instead. Some liked to have the occasional lunch in the warmth of our local garden centre and I encouraged them by offering lifts and doing escort duty. It gave me a reason to have a decent meal too and, quite honestly, I mostly enjoyed their company and was certain they all appreciated meeting and chatting. I mused that this retirement routine could become a bit of a bore if one had no fixed plans in mind. Most of my neighbours lived alone and needed some encouragement not to stagnate and become recluses. I must admit, for the first few weeks, after I had left the hospital I had revelled in what felt like a permanent holiday. That was until reality kicked in and I had shaken myself mentally and decided to get to grips with my life from that moment on. I considered I was lucky I still had a husband who did a responsible job, we could both make plans for our future together and we were both healthy enough and had the resources to do, within reason, whatever we wanted.

As the days passed I made sure I was always busy. I planned

a shopping spree with an old school chum who had moved to Taunton. I hadn't seen Jess since the previous Christmas and now seemed a good time to visit the shops there. We would have a nice leisurely meal, and I'd listen to her invariable moaning about her slightly thoughtless husband, hear tell of her grandchildren, who she minded daily after school, and commiserate with her going on a rigorous diet but barely being able to shed a couple of pounds.

I had heard it all before and this time was no different. 'I try so hard but, when the children come in from school and I am offering the milk and cookies around, I can't resist helping myself too.' I silently agreed when I caught sight of the bulges over and under the stretched waistband of her skirt. I remembered when she had been the trendiest girl in our school. I wondered if she did.

The most important thing, I decided, was that she looked satisfied with her lot – a grumpy, awkward husband and unruly grandchildren notwithstanding! *My* stories sounded boring by comparison, mainly concerning lonely old neighbours and how I tried to employ a loose rota to visit them, listen to their needs and resolve their various complaints. My present life was as different from hers as it was possible to imagine. I had gradually morphed into a District Nurse and she had become a Managing Director of a large and rambling family empire. We giggled at our changed circumstances. Such a vast difference from the Upper VI and cramming for our school exams!

At the very end of our day together I reminded her I had seen Chris and casually mentioned I had also spent a couple of days with Andrew. Jess probably had enough family matters of her own buzzing around in her head for her to take more than a cursory interest. I was only too aware it was all water under the bridges of time, so I did not elaborate. Why should she be interested in my ex-husband and an old ex-boyfriend, I thought?

Old Fred, who was my other next-door neighbour, also kept me busy for the next few weeks. It seemed he was forever asking me to open cans of beans for him, put his rubbish out as his lumbago was suddenly worse, replace spent light bulbs (I could never convince him long-life ones were cheaper in the long run: I'm sure he thought it was some deep plot of the government to force him to spend more money!) and working out how to charge the battery on his new mobile scooter. One morning we both spent hours zooming around our close on it – much to the annoyance of all the other old dears. I felt it was the nearest he could get to one of his beloved sports cars that he had been driving until only a few years previously, but I must admit we did career around like a couple of juvenile delinquents!

So it came as a great shock, when I was listening to the early news one morning, to realise almost seven weeks had elapsed since Andrew had slipped out of my life. Crumble was nudging me to take him out for a walk, but I begged him to wait for a minute as I mentally checked the dates once again. I then took one last look at my computer. Silent as the grave, as usual, I noticed. I was suddenly perturbed. *Andrew* was the one who had always encouraged me to use my PC from the very beginning – so why wasn't he making sure that I did? He had urged me on when I was inclined to flag and say I would prefer to send a letter. He had laughed and told me I was old-fashioned. Something was obviously wrong. I went over in my mind the three days we had spent together. We had been inseparable, we had laughed, we had teased one another, we were both so happy and I remembered his final words as I alighted from his car that very last time. He hadn't struck me as a man who was terminating a friendship. His hug had spoken differently and I refused to believe he had wanted it to end right there, that sunny afternoon.

Crumble and I climbed the steep hill into a copse of trees as I racked my brains to try and find a clue that would guide me. I was well aware there were many miles between Devon and Yorkshire: and I also knew there were a fair few between York and London. Traffic was always unpredictable – had he crashed, had he been killed? Or maybe he had an accident that afternoon on his way back to Dartmouth. Who would ever tell me? No one. He could have died in a collision weeks previously – and I would never know. I shivered at the thought. Crumble waited patiently as my mind fumbled for some explanation.

Maybe Fay had been the problem, perhaps she had become suddenly unwell and the whole jaunt had been called off; but my common sense immediately kicked in and told me he would have informed me if that had been the case. No, it had to be him. It had never occurred to me to ask for his mobile phone number when we had been together. He had mine but, as I never had occasion to ring him, I had never enquired. I had his home number – but suddenly I was nervous of even trying it. I walked back home in a thoughtful mood.

That evening my cousin Dee rang from London. She reminded me I had half promised I would go up and visit them soon. Suddenly it sounded like a brilliant idea. I missed her and her husband Paul but, although we spoke on the telephone constantly, a meeting would be even better. Perhaps my best friends Meryl and Adam would also be around and I could combine the two visits and make a mini-holiday of it. I also hadn't seen my two strapping godchildren since their last trip to Devon the previous spring, and I missed them. Robin was all for it. He had been working hard for weeks on a particularly complicated case and he promised, on my return, he would put in for some leave to enable us to spend time together, sailing, before the weather deteriorated.

'Or would you prefer to go on a canal?' he asked, 'or how about we hire a boat on the Thames and maybe pick it up at Shepperton and meander slowly through the locks to Mapledurham? Or do you fancy somewhere new to explore? How about the Broads? It should be quiet this time of the year and we could enjoy the mists and mellow fruitfulness.' Immediately I felt better. Just planning something out of the ordinary always cheered me up. I left Dee arranging a Departmental Store crawl around London, based on Harrods and the Mayfair area; Meryl was working out which National Trust houses I had never visited in Essex and Robin began poring over an old map of the Grand Union Canal.

I would sort out the whole conundrum of Andrew while I was away, I decided. And Dee could assist me. Once I had made up my mind as to my course of action, I felt a lot calmer and went happily to bed as soon as the TV news had finished.

Chapter 6

*

The next two days were hectic. It was almost as if some of my mischievous neighbours knew of my planned escape because they thought up all sorts of reasons to delay or postpone my departure. Mr Montague fell out of bed in the early hours of Thursday night. When our telephone shrilled I was in the middle of a muddled dream where Alexis's two lads, Owen and Cameron, were teaching me to sail a brown-rigged ketch in a lumpy sea off Maldon in Essex. I groggily stretched out to answer it and there was Mr Montague's polite, cultured voice informing me he was half in and half out of bed, and could I give him a helping hand, please? I must have sounded as if I had half a dozen nuts and bolts in my larynx as I grated out I would send Robin along straight away. Of course Robin had no intention of rousing himself when he realised it wasn't a police matter, until I made him the civilised offer of tea and biscuits on his return – and hustled him out of the door, grumbling.

The next morning when I visited Rose, I noticed she looked a little wan and wide-eyed. I excitedly told her about my unexpected mini-holiday. I prattled on thoughtlessly about my favourite London stores, like Harrods and Harvey Nicks and how many grand, stately homes there were in the south east, but she wasn't her usual responsive self. Normally she would have been delighted to hear my news but this morning she appeared subdued and quiet. I asked her if anything was wrong and she immediately straightened up and smiled. I noted, on her shopping list, she had added two bottles of brandy which, even to me, seemed excessive for someone who already enjoyed a regular pre-dinner drink.

I laughed and said, 'I won't be gone long, honey.' I was aware she didn't answer me.

Fred also buttonholed me later that morning to discuss a new bed he thought he needed. He showed me an advertisement in our local paper and I promised, on my return from "The Smoke", to take him to a suitable store and we could examine these electric marvels together. I agreed they must be an arthritis sufferer's dream. He wasn't too pleased he would be forced to wait but I gently pointed out that he had already waited eighty-seven years and another couple of weeks shouldn't make that much difference. He subsided, muttering, and, to cheer him up, I promised to bring him back a few cans of ale from the off-licence.

Margaret, the vicar's wife, rang to say she thought she was getting the 'flu, so would I be a darling and collect Megan from school. That was no chore as Megan was the happiest and chattiest seven-year-old one could ever hope to meet. I suggested I bring her home to my place and supply her with her favourite meal – beans on toast – before ferrying her to her ballet class. That would enable her dad to complete his early confirmation class and then pick her up.

I relayed all this to Robin over the meal I had managed to throw together after spending most of the day either running errands or listening to other people's troubles. I was slightly perturbed about Rose. She suddenly wasn't her usual happy, interested self and also, as she was on the wrong side of eighty, I was aware she was much frailer than she would ever admit. Robin promised to keep an eye on her while I was away. Quite often he had got into the habit of visiting her on his way home from work, and joining her for her favourite tipple before dinner. I knew she missed her husband dreadfully and loved to have a man around who she could chat with and pamper.

Robin took himself down to The Plume of Feathers for his weekly game of darts. I had been planning to go to bed and relax with a good book but decided to take one last look at Rose instead. She was in her dressing gown, curled up in her favourite armchair and deeply absorbed in her usual soap. I slipped in the back door and joined her. As soon as the programme had finished we settled down with a steaming pot of coffee between us for a long talk. I had time then to tell her all about Andrew and our Cornish adventure.

We had never had any secrets from each other and, over the years, I had often unburdened myself to her. She would have made the most understanding mother, I always reckoned, as she was forever interested in what I was doing – or had done in the past – and was seldom censorious. Often one of my reminiscences would trigger off an even more intriguing one of her own and I would listen, fascinated, as she recounted how she had manipulated her father and her lover until she was allowed to get married at seventeen. I also realised how very little changes through the decades. We all love and suffer angst and, even though we are certain our own lives are unique, they usually aren't.

She had often heard my teenage stories about Andrew, our time together in Cornwall and the solid correspondence that had glued us together for six years. She recognised a similarity in her own love story except that she had married her prince and had been happy ever after: and I had made a stupid mistake and had vaguely regretted it ever since.

Since her husband had died, Rose had lived alone and veered towards semi-reclusiveness so, when I introduced her to my ex-husband Chris on one of his visits to us, it probably enlivened a few days of boredom. He certainly gave us loads to chatter about and, surprisingly, she had been as indignant as me when he had forcefully insisted I would *not* be renewing my old friendship with Andrew. She never went as far as urging me to disregard his instructions but she certainly had not discouraged me either!

I had always made it clear to Robin that I wanted to meet up with Drew again and Rose now questioned me closely as to how our three days had gone. So, over steaming beakers of coffee, I now admitted I was worried sick as Andrew had failed to contact me – especially as it was now almost two months since our return. She agreed it was strange and suggested I write or telephone. I explained I was reluctant to do this as I had no idea how much he had told his wife and I could possibly be causing trouble. Suddenly I sensed she was not listening to my replies. I wondered if she felt ill or if something was worrying her.

'No, my dear,' she replied. 'I will miss you when you are away – like I always do – so hurry home and you can tell me all about Dee and Paul as well as your friends who live in the wilds of Essex.'

I laughed at her exaggeration: no way can affluent Epping be described as *wild.* Or even labelled *beyond* for that matter! But I *did* sense she was rapidly becoming tired, so I kissed her goodnight and returned to my cosy bed and my new absorbing paperback.

The next morning I caught the 10.53am train to Waterloo. Always a good time to travel as it was usually quiet with few passengers glued to their laptops or chattering away on their mobile phones. To be bombarded with loud voices making irrelevant observations or to be constantly nudged in the ribs by laptop users who spread themselves over their own seat, and over half of yours too, is my idea of commuter hell. So it was refreshing just to watch the passing countryside, tackle the *Telegraph* crossword or bury myself in a book. At Waterloo I managed to catch the correct Underground train and then find the right bus and, once again, I was lucky to miss all the hectic hordes that descend on and abdicate London, all within a narrow time scale, twice a day. It meant I arrived at my destination – Chingford – feeling reasonably relaxed but starving hungry.

Dee had set out an appetising ham salad accompanied by thick crusty bread and a delicious, slightly rough, red wine. The second I arrived we set to and demolished the lot, along with a great deal of banter on the merits of Devon as compared to Essex. To my mind Devon won by a whisker. Paul disagreed. We then all settled down in front of their ancient television with a pot of coffee and half a bottle of brandy. When it was time to ring Robin, to tell him of my safe arrival, we were all feeling rather mellow and expansive. Dee was sprawled across the settee with her feet in Paul's lap. He was massaging them and humming to himself. I was lying on the floor, on a huge downy cushion, with my legs hooked across an old chaise longue. Their cat, Penelope, sat purring proudly on my midriff staring, as if mesmerised, into their crackling log-burning stove. Needless to say we all made our way to bed fairly early that first evening.

The next morning I clambered out of bed as soon as I awoke. I knew that if I snuggled down once more there was no way I would want to arise from their deliciously cosy guest bed and I was determined not to waste a second of this unexpected holiday. I was gently scorching the toast as Dee and Paul crept down the stairs, both yawning hugely. I offered to boil them some of the eggs

I had brought from our local farm, but both rejected the idea and held out their plates for some of my hot buttered toast. I shoved another four monster slices in the toaster and poured their coffees as we all seated ourselves around their massive kitchen table that does sterling service at every mealtime. Because Dee refuses to be bombarded by the radio in the mornings, we each took our favourite part of the newspapers and settled down to digest the food and the headlines.

Paul dragged himself off to the shower, complaining he would be late for work, and Dee followed him as I cleared away. My cousin and I aimed to be in London's West End as early as possible to maximise our shopping trip. It was a cold day, but sunny and dry, as we bustled into Selfridge's ground floor perfumery department. I wandered around sniffing perfumes I had barely heard of and made a mental note to remind Robin of them in time for Christmas. Dee talked knowledgeably to as assistant about a new cream that could, hopefully, work wonders for those of advanced years. I listened respectfully.

From Selfridges we made our way to Knightsbridge to enable me to stare wide-eyed while absorbing all the exotic offerings on display in Harrods Food Hall. The delicious smells alone made me salivate and yet I noticed a great mix of customers, all sauntering nonchalantly around the counters, obviously at home there, as if in their local supermarket. I was awestruck to notice that some of the prices would have kept Robin and me in food for a month. How the rich live, I mused. Shopping always makes me hungry so I treated Dee to a hot salt-beef sandwich, on her recommendation, and then spent my time staring surreptitiously around at other fashion-conscious customers seated close by. It was a real eye-opener and would enable me to tell Rose what was in, and what was *not*, in our capital city.

We then took ourselves off to Marks and Spencer's huge store at Marble Arch to drool over their excellent lingerie. I took the opportunity to stock up on some completely non-essential, delightful underwear for myself and something a little more traditional for Robin. I even remembered to purchase two teen bras for Rose. She is so small and delicate and I knew she would be delighted that I had remembered her.

We wandered back towards Oxford Circus, on the way refreshing ourselves with afternoon tea by following a secret crack of a passageway that leads off Oxford Street and opens out into Gee's Court and St Christopher's Place. Hardly any visitors ever penetrate this serene oasis of gentility and it is a pleasure I can seldom resist on my sporadic visits to London.

Finally, I insisted we walk along Bond Street and window-shop to our heart's content. Dee was delighted to agree. She said we had both spent enough for one day and window-shopping in one of London's most exclusive streets would bring us down to earth. I peered into the dazzling windows of Asprey, Cartier and Tiffany and agreed with her. Eventually we made it to Piccadilly Circus, after a quick detour to Fortnum's, so it was a footsore duo, festooned with carrier bags, that caught the Underground back to Walthamstow Central and retrieved Dee's battered old car from the car park.

Because I, for one, was shattered by our day out, I suggested I take her and Paul to their local Indian restaurant for a meal. They were both pleased with the idea and I felt it would repay them slightly for the laid-back kindness they'd always shown when I visited them. There was an immediate rush for the bathroom and we all dressed up to celebrate, knowing that none of us would be expected to cook the next meal, clear the dishes away or even wash up!

Over the meal that night I gently broke the news to them I would be leaving after lunch the following day. I had rashly promised my friends in Essex that I would spend a week with them.

'But why go so quickly?' Paul asked. 'You always do this to us. You arrive in a rush and it seems no time at all before you are off to visit friends, or other places. We hardly get time to chat before once again you are packing your bags.'

It was true. I should have given them more time but it was typical of me – always trying to stretch myself to impossible limits. The fact that I rang Dee frequently from Devon, and we would chat for hours, hardly excused me doing this to them. Once I had retired I had imagined there would be all the time in the world. Not so. Other people had often complained retirement had never worked out as they fondly hoped – and they were right.

I had been waiting for the right moment to discuss Andrew and my dilemma as to why he had vanished from my life. Dee had met him all those years ago, at various family celebrations, and she had been avid to know more when I told her there was to be a reunion. I had talked to her since I had returned from Cornwall, of course, but I had played down my interest in case Robin had overheard and misunderstood. I also felt vaguely guilty and, as the weeks went by and I became more and more perturbed at the thought of an accident, I was embarrassed to voice my worries.

Now I explained to my cousins that I felt it was impossible to send an e-mail via *my* computer. I had no way of knowing if Fay or Andrew's family were aware I even existed. I also shied away from sending a letter for exactly the same reason. I felt it could be a sensitive issue and if, in the worst-case scenario, anything *had* happened to him I shuddered at the thought that one of his sons – dealing with his affairs – would find a message from a woman he had never heard of.

'I feel there is something terribly wrong,' I admitted quietly. 'I hate being so melodramatic, but none of this is like the Andrew I knew and loved. My mind has gone over it time and time again, as to what may have happened, and I never arrive at a reasonable solution. So, Paul, would you let me use your PC to send a short e-mail and try and put my mind at rest? You will not be implicated in any way, I promise.' I sat back to gauge their reactions and saw only concern on their faces.

The moment we arrived home, Paul walked into his study and switched on his computer. 'It's all yours, Jenny. Make it a good one.'

I sat at his desk with a swiftly beating heart. It was almost as if I had decided on a strategy without consciously acknowledging it, even to myself. Within moments I quickly typed out:

FAO Andrew Lanyon. I am researching my Cornish family history and I have been given your name. I understand you are connected – on the matriarchal side – to the Kittow family. I would be grateful for any help you could give me. Cheers. Paul Fletcher.

Since I had first used a computer I had always begun every e-mail I had ever written by leaving two lines of clear space at the top of the page. I had also spaced everything out as in a letter – because it pleased me to use this format. This time I squashed the message right up at the very top of the page. It looked uneducated and crude to my untrained eye but I knew, if Andrew saw this message, there was no way he would associate it with me and, if someone else was reading it, there was no possible way it would matter. How diabolical was that?

I walked back to join Dee and Paul in their sitting room. I felt I had at last done something useful towards unravelling my disturbing mystery. I joined them in a nightcap. Surprisingly, that night I slept the best I had for weeks.

The next morning Dee and I sat around in our dressing gowns and put the world to rights. Both Paul and Robin still worked, and I knew my two cousins preferred to go abroad for their holidays, but I thought it only fair for them to consider visiting us, for a change, next spring. Dee promised to do her best to persuade Paul and, with that, I had to be satisfied. We prepared an early lunch and then it was time for me to be off. I waited until I was on the Central Line Underground train out of Leyton Station before using my mobile phone to ring Meryl and Adam, warning them I was on my way.

Ashley, their eldest son, was standing waiting for me at Epping Station barrier, with a big smile on his face. He proudly swept me home in his new car to Meryl, who was waiting patiently on the doorstep to greet me. Once again there was a great flurry of chatter and laughter as I was shown upstairs to "my" bedroom to unpack. Their house had always been delightful; purchased as a tumbledown cottage on the occasion of their marriage. Adam and his father had re-designed and re-modelled it until it emerged as a four-bedroomed desirable residence set in its own pleasant grounds. I remember being in awe of Adam and his father's expertise. They had removed the roof and two external walls, had extended the ground floor to include two more rooms as well as a double garage; then added two bedrooms above, making all four bedrooms en suite, before completing their transformation. To me it was the height of elegance and modernity. It represented the sort of home a middle-aged couple would aspire to and, to Chris and I who were newly married and had hardly a penny to bless our cramped Victorian maisonette with, it became totally unattainable. To their credit I had long ago decided that the fact that Meryl and Adam had never thought to improve their property from that day on confirmed they both knew what they wanted and, once they had achieved this, they were content.

Meryl provided her usual satisfying spread and Adam, Ashley and Richard, plus their two newly introduced partners, joined me in demolishing it. I enjoyed a lovely warm bath and was tucked up in my bed long before midnight. All I had to do was report my safe arrival to Robin and Dee and the rest of my holiday was mine to do with as I liked. And enjoy it I did! My friends and I have the same love of stately homes and, frankly, there is a multitude in this part of the world. Adam became our chauffeur. He was never adverse to venturing up into Cambridgeshire, or down towards the River Thames and Kent.

We roved from Chartwell and Knole in Kent to Wimpole Hall and Anglesey Abbey in Cambridgeshire; the choice was enormous and we were interested in everything – from the undulating wall our cigar-smoking Prime Minister tried to build at his home in Chartwell, to the grand royal palace of Knole with its 365 rooms, 52 staircases and seven courtyards. The rooms, furniture and furnishings left me breathless as I stared in awe at the magnificent paintings and tapestries. Knole felt almost like a village in its own right, placed within acres of ornamental gardens, surrounded by extensive grounds and enfolded in a deer park. We *had* hoped to visit Squerryes Court – a gem of a manor house – but time ran out on us. We returned home pleasantly spent and weary.

Our visit to Cambridgeshire was far less grand. Adam drove us to Anglesey Abbey which had started life as an Augustinian Priory, but had been transformed by an unassuming bachelor of American lineage in order to show off his burgeoning collections – from miniature jewelled crucifixes to rare books, carved oriental figures to bizarre continental clocks. It was cosy and intimate and as different from magnificent Tudor Knole, or even Churchill's practical Chartwell, as it was possible to get.

The following day we strolled around the gardens and park of Wimpole Hall, an eighteenth-century mellow Georgian mansion. We wandered through acres of rolling parkland towards a romantic Gothic tower that was shrouded in mist. We walked across a Chinese bridge that led to a grand lake, most of it designed by Humphrey Repton or the inventive Capability Brown. On entering the house I was entranced by the chunky barrelled ceilings, deeply ornamental and encrusted with intricate plasterwork. I found it difficult to drag my eyes down to admire Sir John Soane's architectural designs – like his elegant Yellow Drawing Room or James Gibbs' gilt-embellished chapel and the library that housed over 12,000 books. I had visited Sir John Soane's Museum in Lincoln's Inn and now I was able to admire his architectural genius in an amazing setting. I fell in love with the Lord Chancellor's Room that he had created. Imagine sleeping in such a sumptuous, palatial bed, I mused. It was draped in red and gold silk hangings with sheaths of golden feathers surmounting the top finials, and one could imagine it being slept in by an Indian princess, or a maharajah, at the very least.

But what fascinated the three of us most was the Bath House. Like a swimming pool in miniature. It appeared modern but we were told it had been designed by Sir John Soane in 1792. Originally it had been outside in a draughty courtyard but was now, much more sensibly, indoors. It had a winding wooden staircase that led down to an enormous white, oval plunge pool that holds over two thousand gallons of pale blue water – and very inviting it looked, too. The water was heated by a basement boiler and I could imagine swimming in it would be pure luxury.

Meryl and Adam have always been indulgently amused by my enthusiasm for beautiful architecture and gracious living. Back in the car Adam teased me that I should have been a heroine in one of Jane Austen's novels but, by the time we arrived back home, even *I* had been mentally deluged with too much elegant conservation and grandeur. We walked in wearily and flung ourselves down on the comfortable sofas in their drawing room. I offered to make afternoon tea and disappeared kitchenwards. Meryl checked their telephone for messages as she always did on re-entering the house.

She shouted to me, 'Dee wants you to ring her, Jenny. She says it's not urgent – but today will do.'

She handed me the phone as I returned with a loaded tray and began to pour out for all of us. I immediately dialled my cousins' number. There was no reply so I smartly replaced the receiver as there was no point in leaving yet another message. We demolished the sandwiches and cake and sat around discussing the merits of each house we had visited during the past few days. I loved hearing their opinions as they often differed from each other and, occasionally, I agreed with neither of them. Adam, ever the historian, preferred Chartwell but Meryl and I argued for the royal grandeur of Knole. I suppose women always lean towards romanticism and beauty, but I had to agree with Adam that Chartwell had given me a far deeper insight into the mind of one of the greatest politicians of our time, and the unique history crammed within those walls was fascinating.

There was one day left before I returned to Devon. We had promised Adam, for a change, a day out in Maldon which was one of our favourite Essex seaside towns. It is situated on the Blackwater Estuary and Adam laughed and said maybe it would blow some of the National Trust cobwebs off, which made me feel ashamed of my unbridled passion. Adam's hobby, since he retired, was bird watching and the tidal salt marshes here have always been ideal for all sorts of wildlife. He also mentioned that the famous Thames sailing barges were having one of their rare open days on the Quay and suggested we could do both and maybe invite Robin's sister Alexis, who lived close by, to join us. I knew Owen and Cameron, her two teenage sons, adored sailing and would be pleading to come too. It sounded like a brilliant end to a happy week.

I had insisted on taking my two best friends, plus sons and partners, out for a decent meal that last night. I am sure Meryl was delighted to relinquish preparing and presenting gourmet food for the seven of us. It was soon decided a Chinese meal would suit everyone and I happily agreed. We booked a table in the town centre and I went upstairs to get ready. The telephone interrupted us yet again.

'It's Dee, for you, Jen,' called Meryl, and I raced downstairs to answer it.

'Is everything alright, darling?' I asked.

'Yes, fine,' she reassured me. 'But I *do* have some unsettling news for you. You remember you commandeered Paul's PC to send off that e-mail to Andrew? Well, the answer came back promptly the next morning – soon after you left. We both decided not to spoil the rest of your holiday by passing the message on – so we waited until now. Andrew obviously didn't recognise Paul's name.

He immediately replied that he would supply any information he could about his ancestors. Sorry, darling. I hate to be the bearer of bad news. It's a two-edged sword, isn't it? You either discover he has been stringing you along from the second he met you or some member of his family tells you he is very ill, suffered an accident or, much worse – is dead. Neither way was going to bring you much happiness, I guess. Please don't be too upset, sweetheart. Take heart that you found out before you made an absolute fool of yourself.'

I could feel rage boiling up inside my head and rippling through my body as I stared blankly at the wall. Somehow I had guessed something was terribly wrong; but it was the last thing I wanted to hear that Andrew was taking me for a complete fool.

'I cannot believe it of him, Dee,' I muttered. 'Drew was the most honest person I have ever known. Sometimes he would put himself in a bad light when he was being brutally frank – even to the point when friends would turn against him and dislike what he was admitting. Those three days were the happiest I have ever spent. We lived and breathed as one; I have never been so close to anyone in my life. It was like coming home to a comfortable, warm bed, sliding in and relaxing totally.'

My words shuddered to a stop and I gasped as the tears ran down my face. Until that second, when I had unburdened myself to Dee, I had no idea quite how I felt about Andrew Lanyon. Now I did. It came as a shock and I also felt ashamed to admit the depth of my feelings for him.

'Now you know differently, Jenny. He has now proved – beyond a shadow of doubt – that it was all just a game to him. It's no good thinking back fondly to when you were children - he's grown up since then. He's a double-crossing, two-timing skunk,' Dee said firmly. 'A skunk who had no thought for you whatsoever. Thank goodness it didn't go any further and you didn't do anything really silly – like sleep with him.'

I nodded miserably and, after thanking her and saying goodbye, I replaced the receiver slowly. I retraced my footsteps up to my room and locked myself in the bathroom. Now my first thoughts were that Meryl mustn't guess the depth of my anger or misery. She knew nothing about the past weeks as I had deliberately not mentioned my worries to her. I wasn't sure quite what I felt. Was it anger at being duped or misery that a good friend could do this to me? Either way, I had to put on a brave face and pretend to enjoy my last night with my best friends and their family. I doused my blotchy face in cool water and put on extra makeup until I was satisfied no one would realise the extent of my confused feelings.

Looking back, I consider I did a good job. I managed by asking lots of bright questions of both Ashley and Richard and sincerely listening to their answers. I had known the two lads since they were born and I loved them dearly. I knew for certain they would both pick nice, sensible girls for partners and I made it my business to draw the two of them out about their occupations and interests. Marianne was in her last year at university and Carol worked for a solicitor. The seven of us chatted avidly and I totally blanked out all thoughts of Andrew. I would sort that out tomorrow I decided with a wry grin – like Scarlett O'Hara.

I left Meryl and Andrew waving from behind the ticket barrier at Epping Underground Station. I managed to immerse myself in Adam's *Telegraph* as I bagged a seat for myself on the swaying Tube. I then swapped it for a raunchy 'whodunit' when I caught my train from Waterloo at midday. I firmly put all thought of Andrew and Cornwall to the back of my mind, knowing there would be time enough to give vent to my stormy feelings later – or maybe even the next day. Later, I placed earphones in my ears and tuned in to my favourite Katie Melua *Collection* album.

Robin was standing patiently at the barrier as the train chugged slowly into scruffy little Honiton Station. It was so comforting to see him. He may have wondered why I hugged him back so strongly; but I am sure it reinforced his strong conviction that, as I had returned, all was well in our small world. He had a meal waiting and I took pleasure in his thoughtfulness. It served to soothe the rawness I had been feeling since I had heard Dee's brutal summing up of Andrew's character.

As soon as we had eaten I cleared away, shoved everything in the dishwasher, and made my way into Rose's house to see how she had fared since I had been away. She had been on my mind in a vague way and, as she was in her eighties, I suppose I needed reassurance as to her state of health. I also wanted to give her the two bras I had bought her. It was always a pleasure to see her eyes light up with glee at even the simplest gift.

Although her husband had loved her dearly all their married life and there was never a shortage of money, he seldom remembered to discover her wishes or preferences during those last few years and, consequently, she existed on dated clothing from a couple of decades previously. Everything she possessed was old-fashioned and some of her clothes were truly shabby. She would often recount long ago memories of evenings in nightclubs, when she would be wearing an elegant cocktail dress, or attending a sumptuous dinner where she would waltz in a magnificent ball gown. Sometimes she would bring one of these dresses from the back of her wardrobe and stare at it with glowing eyes. To me they looked crumpled and tawdry but, to her, they were as lovely as the day her husband had bought them for her. As she had never worked, and she and Cedric had been childless, she could so easily have been spoiled. But the fact that her whole married life had been devoted to her beloved husband meant it never crossed her mind to ask for more than what she thought she deserved – which I guess she considered was very little.

They also, for some reason, never kept up Christmas so that festive season, when Cedric was alive, would slip by every year without presents or decorations. If they received Christmas cards she would slit open the envelopes, read the cards, replace them and then add them to a neat little pile on her sideboard. Two years after Cedric passed away Robin and I dared to ask her to our house to celebrate Christmas with us. We had placed a small mound of wrapped packages for her under our tree and, even if she managed a small portion of the meals I prepared and only a little of the alcoholic drinks on offer, I felt she was only just entering the world that most of us take for granted.

I watched her unwrap the two delicate bras and study them closely. I could see by the way her eyes lit up that she approved. What worried me more was her ashen paleness. She had always been slight, bordering on gauntness, but now I saw she looked positively emaciated. Had she looked like that before I went away? There were dark circles beneath her eyes. I asked if she was OK and she responded vaguely. I said nothing but I decided that, first thing the next morning, I would inform our doctor and ask him to call in casually, as if on a regular visit. We spoke about my two short stays with Dee and Meryl and Rose asked all the usual questions about shopping in London, her old stomping ground, and enquired which stately homes we had visited. Although she appeared interested, I had a suspicion that she was not really listening to my responses. As I neared the end of my narrative she cut me short to ask for refills for our brandy glasses. I topped hers up but, as I could see she was weary, I collected her shopping list for the next day and slipped away, leaving her curled up and snuggling deep into the corner of the sofa. I glanced down at her list as I walked out of her back door and noted another request for two more bottles of brandy placed under her meagre food requests.

I obediently drank my cocoa with Robin on my return, but my mind was buzzing most of the night worrying if Rose was really ill or was my overzealous imagination working overtime. It slightly blunted the edge of my wrath about Andrew's thoughtlessness for not getting in touch. I would deal with that later, I vowed.

I put my computer on hold first thing the next morning to enable me to ring the surgery and ask to speak to Rose's doctor. He was also *my* doctor but, as I had worked closely with Dr Sanderson at the hospital for years I felt, as her next-door neighbour and friend, it was acceptable to voice my concern about her. He listened as I explained.

'It's nothing I can put my finger on, Dr S, but she certainly hasn't looked well for a week or so – and her sudden preoccupation with so many glasses of brandy each evening is certainly not like her at all; completely out of character. I will be in most of the day so, if you want me to, I can accompany you and maybe we can sort her out together.'

The doctor knew her as well as I did, and also of her prickly dislike of admitting illness of any kind. 'I want to make sure she doesn't meet you at the door and say she feels fine,' I explained to him. He seemed relieved to agree with my subtle strategy.

He said he would come as soon as his morning surgery was over and I promised to keep an eye out for him. As soon as I had settled my immediate problem with the doctor I turned to my desk and fired up my computer. I am ashamed to say Andrew then took the brunt of my smouldering resentment. It had been building up ever since Dee had rung me in Epping to tell me he was alive and well with, apparently, not a care in the world. On my train journey home, when

I had time to think quietly and alone, my thoughts had crystallised into a burning resentment. I felt his insensitive behaviour bordered on cruelty. As a lad he had been kindly and courteous and, during our few days together, I had seen no reason to alter my opinion of his pleasant nature. As a boy he had been incapable of telling a lie and now, it appeared, he was incapable of even basic truthfulness. Why promise he would be in touch? He must have guessed I would be worrying. How he must have been amused at my naivety, my blunt truthfulness as to why I had ended our relationship and how much I had really loved him. I shuddered at what my honesty had revealed. I remembered him talking eagerly of how he had felt at that time. I had believed everything he said and now I wondered if his honeyed words were just that – empty assurances.

I rattled off a steamy e-mail to him without a moment's hesitation. It is so strange that, when adrenaline gets to flow in one's system, every other emotion surges out and one is able to be clear and concise. It was almost as if the message had already been composed in my head and was waiting for the opportunity to sear itself onto the glowing screen in front of me.

Andrew

Well, thank you for letting me know of your return to the UK – as you so solemnly promised. I'm sure you had such a whale of a time with your American friends it put all thoughts of promises right out of your head. Did you regale them with stories of how you had met this pathetic old flame in Cornwall? Did you amuse them with tales of times gone by and what we both used to get up to? How we loved each other? Did you tell them how we corresponded daily for six years? Silly, childish letters full of dreams and hopes; and how lucky you were to escape this awful woman's clutches? And how fortunate you were to finally meet the love of your life, Fay, who rescued you and enabled you to live happily ever after.

Thank you again, Andrew, for revealing your true nature to me. I am obliged to you. Good luck with the rest of your life. I am so pleased I found out about you in time – before I made an even bigger fool of myself. To think I ever loved you! Or trusted you...

Jennifer Mackenzie

Fury coursed through my body and the words tripped off my fingers. I didn't even bother to check my typing for errors. I sent it the second I signed my formal married name. I immediately felt a sense of overwhelming relief. A feeling of liberation. It was if I had been enmeshed in a childish fairytale thrall and now, by composing and sending this letter, I was free to carry on my life as before.

Before I could have second or third thoughts, I received a telephone call from Fred, my other neighbour, who wanted to check I had not forgotten about his new bed.

'No, of course not,' I cheerfully explained. 'But I am a little busy at the moment, Fred, as I have only just arrived back. Is it OK if I call in later and we can discuss it?'

He grudgingly agreed and I went back to tidying the sitting room while keeping a sharp eye out for Dr Sanderson. I had vacuumed most of the bungalow and was finishing off my second mug of coffee before his battered old Volvo turned into our close and drew up at the kerb. I slipped outside and took him through Rose's side gate and garden to save him standing outside her front door and being the victim of our neighbours' beady eyes.

'Hello,' I called as we walked in. 'You have a visitor, Rose. Come in Dr Sanderson,' I said loudly as I ushered him through her kitchen.

We both walked into her front room. Rose was once again curled up on her settee and I suddenly had a frightening feeling that she might have been there since I had bid her goodnight the previous evening. Our two empty brandy glasses were still sitting forlornly on her coffee table, I noticed, and she was still wearing her faded dressing gown with her slippered feet tucked under her. I swept the glasses off the side table and muttered something about making them both a cup of coffee. Rose looked up at the doctor dully and, as he eased himself down beside her, I backed into the kitchen and switched on the kettle. As unobtrusively as possible I placed a tray of coffee at their disposal and then slipped out of the house.

Forty minutes later David Sanderson tapped on my door and I could tell by his sober face that the news wasn't good. I had been hoping I had misread the signs but his opening words dispelled that hope.

'I examined her fully, Jenny, but it is impossible to do a full check in a home environment. I really do feel it would be sensible if she went into Exeter Hospital and had all the appropriate tests done so we can rule out anything nasty,' he said, diplomatically. 'She has agreed, so I have arranged for a hospital car to pick her up in about an hour. I wonder if you could pack an overnight bag for her? Thanks for calling me in. I know how much she hates the medical profession – and dislikes hospitals in general. Maybe, if you could accompany her she would feel a little less scared?'

I agreed to make everything as painless as possible and returned to Rose with a heavy heart. Strangely, she never said a word about me inviting her doctor around without her permission. I think by then she was feeling so ill that it was a great relief to have the whole decision taken out of her hands. I went in and gave her a smile and a comforting hug.

She glanced up at me and said, 'I knew something was wrong. I have had this pain in my tummy for weeks, and then I couldn't go to the lavatory in the mornings. I kept meaning to ask you to go to the chemist and get something for me, but every day I hoped it would get better. Oh, Jenny, I am so frightened.'

I tried to do my best to reassure her; but she was a very private lady who had been protected and cosseted by her husband all her married life. She had never worked, never been ill and never needed to visit a doctor. Her only contact with the medical profession had been the few months leading up to the death of her husband and that had shocked her deeply. Luckily Robin and I had been on hand to take her to register the death, help her to arrange his funeral, stand by while she paid all the bills and help sort out his straightforward financial affairs. We had then tried to settle her back into the life she was accustomed to and, since then, I had tried to keep a close eye on her well-being and endeavoured to make sure she ate three decent meals a day. Sadly, she lost all interest in the outside world once she was widowed. She probably found my odd taste in National Trust houses somewhat bizarre but she would listen to my descriptions of these places and carefully study the colourful books I invariably brought back from these excursions. I had hoped it would make her feel like an armchair traveller. Likewise, when we went on holiday, I would try to take as much video footage as possible and keep up a running commentary while filming, in the hope she would feel as if she was on vacation too.

I quickly packed enough clothing to see her over the next few days as I had no knowledge as to how long they would keep her in hospital – or how extensive the tests would be. I added a dressing gown of my own to the pile as we both decided the one she normally wore was a little faded and shabby. Luckily Robin had given her a pair of slippers for her birthday, so I was pleased to find them and remove them from their wrapper. The car arrived at the door shortly after and I noticed, with a lump in my throat, how she walked down the path with her head held high – as if taking a ride in a hired car was a normal experience for her.

She was admitted as soon as we arrived, so I guessed the nursing staff had been given prior warning. I noticed she had been allocated a single room and, within minutes, she was undressed and in bed looking exhausted. A young houseman came in shortly afterwards to enquire and record her medical history – or lack of it! He was a pleasant enough chap and I was relieved when she smiled at him and politely answered all his searching questions. That was my cue for leaving her. I told her she was in good hands, kissed her on the cheek, promised to visit the next day and made myself scarce. The doctor gave me an approving nod as I stood in the doorway and waved.

I had to return home on the train, which was somewhat annoying, and I vowed to bring my own transport the next day. As soon as I walked indoors I remembered Fred and my solemn promise to take him to sort out the new bed he was suddenly unable to do without. Too late now, I thought. I retraced my weary footsteps and went in to see him and explain, but obviously some other neighbour had informed him that Jenny had gone off with Rose to an unknown destination, so my explanation was no surprise to him. He was usually a crusty, self-centred old rogue; but I guess this time the news had circulated around our close, probably striking terror into the older inhabitants by reminding them of their own vulnerability, which made him grunt and accept my apology with very little moaning. That was so unlike him – but it saved me having to stress how ill I suspected Rose might be. Fred and Rose were of a similar age so why frighten him? Anyway, I had no idea if her condition was serious or not, so I strove to make light of it and mentioned it might only be for a couple of days and, as he was a typical man, I knew he would shy away from any intimate details as to the state of her health – which I had no intention of divulging, anyway! I just prayed I wasn't being too optimistic. I told him I would be going in daily to visit her until she returned home and, surprisingly, he meekly agreed to wait before we made further plans. I then returned to my kitchen and hurriedly prepared an evening meal for Robin and myself.

To Robin I could unburden my heart and I did. I told him how meek Rose had been when Dr Sanderson had walked in through the door behind me. How she had hardly moved at the sight of him and how I had this awful certainty that she had been resting on that settee all night – unable to take herself off to bed. I knew she must have felt really ill to allow a doctor to examine and question her. She was a reserved but feisty lady and normally she would have ushered him from her house, denying any illness with a pleasant laugh, in the shortest possible time.

Robin understood my fears because he had come to know Rose quite well in the intervening time since Cedric had died. Like most ex-nurses, I had always looked on patients and hospital work dispassionately. One has to. Men and women enter hospital sick. We never knew them earlier in their lives when they were fit and healthy. Now they are scared, vulnerable shadows of themselves and all hoping the medical profession can cure them and return them to a life before illness invaded their bodies. It is only when relatives, or friends, describe how they were in earlier periods of their life that one is able to visualise the healthy beings they once were and see them in a different light. Sometimes it is only *then* that one is able to help and encourage them. Invisible barriers of dislike and distrust disappear as the nurse and patient join together to fight their malady and – hopefully – to win.

All our neighbours had become good friends, or acquaintances, over the years. Now we both saw them as human beings first and some as little frail folk second – ones who might need a helping hand. If any of them were ill we were *all* concerned and I felt, in this instance, our concern might be justified.

We both decided to take ourselves off to bed as neither of us had any stomach that night to watch superficial TV programmes.

Snuggling down, we picked up our books and attempted to read, but actually all I really needed was a comforting hug and my kind, understanding husband to soothe away my fears until I quietly fell asleep on his shoulder.

Chapter 7

*

Sadly for Fred, he had to wait for his bed. I went in to visit Rose in Exeter daily. She had four sisters, all older than herself, but as they were spread over a large portion of the UK, one could not expect them to spend hours travelling to the West Country. That was if they were even *able* to travel or could summon up the transport to do so. Most evenings, as soon as I returned home, I would telephone them, one after the other, to keep them up to date with Rose's progress. For some reason she had chosen me as her next of kin. I had protested as she had other distant, younger members in her family who surely would expect to take on that role. But Rose was adamant and, much to my surprise, the doctor in attendance explained it was the patient's choice and it had nothing to do with actual kinship. I gracefully gave in to her request with the stipulation I would only do it as long as it did not offend the other members of her family.

First of all the news was fairly hopeful. She had a twisted gut, the doctors decided, and twice they carried out a procedure which left her wan and heavy-eyed, but buoyed up with the hope that she would now be cured. Nothing much was said for a few days; but soon I noticed a change come over the staff which coincided with a change in her medication. I was sensitive to their mood and noticed a distinct reticence to discuss her condition when they spoke to her. Eventually they suggested a blockage of the bowel and talked about an operation. They sounded positive it could be cured. Rose listened quietly and said very little. She looked forlorn and childlike in her white bed.

Finally a young consultant came and sat next to that bed. I went to move away but Rose motioned me to stay. She had been given a scan the previous day. The young doctor broke it to her as gently as possible. It was cancer. They could operate and there was a good chance it would be successful with the addition of other backup medication. Rose sat looking at him until he came to the end of his comforting speech. Then she told him she wanted no operation, no chemotherapy and no radiation. She did not raise her voice or cry, as one would have expected. Her final words were, 'I will manage.'

I doubted it. I had heard other patients voice the same brave sentiments, thinking they could withstand the onslaught of CA. They cannot imagine when the pain is new, and only just taking hold, how at its worst it can rule every second of one's day. Even with the strongest drugs the management of this invasive disease is unpredictable; and this was from a woman who never even resorted to a couple of aspirin tablets for a headache!

The young consultant moved away with a benign smile. I am sure he was surprised, and unbelievably relieved, at her dignified response. Most patients cry and collapse when they are told what is in store for them. Usually a nurse or relative will be on hand to console and comfort them. Nurses dread witnessing this sort of revelation and it is made worse when it is to a patient they have nursed for some time, often one they know and like.

Rose accepted the diagnosis philosophically, having no idea what was awaiting her, and I was the one who crumbled and sat with my head in my hands. She ended up by leaning over and comforting *me.* I was the one who was shattered. She, who had always appeared frail and clinging, comforting me - the younger, sturdy, resilient one. Not so, I suddenly realised; *she* had always been my deeply embedded rock protecting me from turbulent times. She had listened and sensibly advised, she had laughed and seen the brighter side of life when I had been pessimistic and cynical. What would I do without her? How would I manage without her rational, shrewd and practical outlook on life?

I looked up at her from my bedside chair, unable to stop the tears from coursing down my cheeks, and she calmly handed me a fan of tissues. I took them and scrubbed at my face, ashamed of my reaction but unable to hide my feelings. Once I had got over my emotional outburst, she made me pull the curtains back from around the bed and accepted her cup of afternoon tea as if she were in her own drawing room. I gulped and breathed deeply, and hoped no other patients were watching my disintegration. We then talked of Megan, the vicar's mischievous daughter, and how she was growing out of everything – shoes, school uniform and even her bicycle. Rose had promised to try and talk Megan's mum into letting her attend senior ballet classes, and we laughed ruefully as Rose remembered her own dancing lessons and I told her of my hopeless efforts at learning to play the piano.

That night I returned home and found it difficult to compose myself sufficiently to telephone Rose's numerous family members and pass on the sad news. They didn't say much. Maybe they could see the probable results of the hospital tests long before I faced the possible reality and outcome. Robin, tired out after a long day of hard graft with little reward, came home later than usual and was greeted by a thoughtful wife who had dutifully produced a decent meal to cheer us both up. It didn't work. I unburdened myself to him over dinner and we talked, until it was time to go to bed, about how Rose would cope with dying.

The ward team at the District General Hospital did not give up on Rose and a senior specialist came round the next day to try and persuade her to accept any treatment they thought was necessary. She was her usual pleasant and polite self but explained to them, with a wry smile, she considered she was long past her sell-by date and she was sure far more younger patients, suffering from the same dreadful disease, would benefit from their expertise. He went away after giving her a warm smile and a light pat on the arm. I sat silently in the corner and didn't comment.

Four days later Rose was shifted into our local hospital. In lots of ways it was much easier for me as it was only a ten-minute stroll away from where I lived, and I also had a feeling she felt much happier in a more homely environment. The authorities knew she was coming back to the smaller hospital to die and I tried to make the single room they offered her into a little bower. I bought some large pot plants and placed them outside her ground floor windows so she could see their bright colours from her bed. I also went out and found the prettiest nighties I could buy. Pastel colours are always flattering and Rose brightened up considerably as I played the fool and strutted round her room, holding them up to my chest. I found two cosy dressing gowns and two pretty bed jackets to match them and she admitted she had never looked so good even when she was first married.

Visiting hours were so much more relaxed in the cottage hospital environment and the staff also made time to chat as they raced about their duties. All our neighbours did their utmost to make it a special time and we produced a loose rota of friends to visit as long as Rose was up to it. Robin sneaked in early one evening with a bottle of brandy under his coat. Rose's eyes lit up and I know for certain the medical staff looked the other way when he gave her a small tot each night before she went to sleep.

Gradually, as the days passed, I guessed Rose was getting extra medication and I soon sensed she was relying on it and watching the clock. One afternoon I went in and she seemed fine for the first ten minutes. We talked of our local primary school open day and spoke of decent weather to make it a success. I went on talking about amalgamating the cream teas along with an ice-cream counter in their airy hall that doubled up as the school gym, morning assembly room and welcomed our monthly PTA meetings. I suddenly realised Rose had ceased listening to me as she was staring at the clock and glancing towards the doorway. I asked if her injection was due. She nodded vigorously and I went quickly down to the nurses' station to summon someone. My friend Melissa was in a nearby ward dressing a patient's leg. I knocked on the door and waited politely. Mel pulled a face when I passed on the request.

'I only asked her twenty minutes ago and she said she was fine, Jenny. I am a bit busy at this minute, doing this dressing. Can she wait until I am free?'

I nodded, but I was uncertain if Rose really *could* wait until then. And then, of course, I was loath to walk back into Rose's room with the bad news that her medication was on hold until I could get a nurse to prepare it. I stood there – feeling uncertain and an intruder – as I waited for Melissa to finish. I wanted to make sure she didn't get called away by another bell and also that she didn't forget as a welter of equally important chores took precedence in her mind. As we walked back down the corridor my friend gently caught my arm and quietly complained that she had asked at the due time but that Rose had airily said she didn't require it, thanks. How many times had patients annoyed me by suggesting they didn't need their medication – only to start shouting five minutes later? Brightly, Mel went into Rose's room and no one would have guessed at the minor drama I had averted. I didn't want her to be treated as a special case just because I had once worked in this hospital. I knew how some friends and family could become demanding in this way about a patient with the mistaken attitude they were being helpful and vigilant. Constant complaining and finding fault with the nursing staff did not make for an untroubled relationship; it could also upset the patient when they imagined the nurses would rather not attend to them to avoid even more unfounded accusations.

That afternoon, as soon as I arrived home, I telephoned Dr Sanderson and explained about Rose's sudden intolerable pain. He decided to put in place a procedure that would supply her with constant small amounts of medication which, in turn, would dull the pain and lessen her discomfort. I was so relieved. It is so distressing to see someone in agony, and knowing full well there is nothing one can do about it.

Buoyed up with the outcome of my talk with Rose's doctor I decided to ring her family to remind them time might be running out. I did not want to sound callous but I also did not want them to accuse me of not keeping them fully informed. I struck gold on my first call. I called Rose's eldest sister. Her daughter answered the phone and I explained my predicament. Norma, her mother, was almost ninety and confined to her bed most of the time. When I used to ring her each evening, Hazel always sounded the nicest of all Rose's family. She readily agreed to bring her mother down to the West Country as soon as possible. Knowing that speed might be of the essence, we agreed on a day early the next week. Hazel's husband Michael would be only too pleased, she explained, to drive them down from Cheltenham and then the two sisters would be able to spend an afternoon together in comfortable surroundings. I was pleased and relieved at the simplicity of our arrangements. I promised Hazel a decent meal for the three of them after their visit to enable them to take their time getting back to Gloucestershire. I was sure it would be a great effort on behalf of Rose's elder sister but I wanted them both to take advantage of some time together – even if it would be for the last time. We decided that I should not divulge our plans to Rose in case Norma was unable to make the journey; if so, the disappointment would be all the greater.

Hazel offered to ring around the rest of her family and explain how Rose was feeling and what we were hoping to do. It was a great weight off my shoulders as my responsibility was suddenly lessened. I got on and prepared our evening meal with a lighter heart and I was bursting to tell Robin the news as soon as he arrived home. He agreed with me that her family should be kept in the picture even though most of the news was devastating. Rose had been the youngest in her family and I was sure her four siblings were saddened at the thought she would probably die first.

Much to my delight Tuesday dawned bright and sunny. I arrived at the hospital earlier than usual to make sure Rose was wearing her prettiest nightie and bed jacket. I unobtrusively tidied up around her bed and sprayed her with some of my favourite perfume that I had brought in from home. Rose made no comment. She appeared acquiescent and sleepy and I desperately hoped the whole day would not be a sad disaster.

They arrived just before lunch. The hospital had been very kind and had offered to supply a simple meal for the two old dears – to be eaten in the sanctuary of Rose's room. I had fetched sandwiches in for Hazel, Michael and myself. I planned we would eat them in a quiet corner of the hospital's reception as there was no café, or restaurant facilities for the public on the premises.

They came in with beaming smiles and I liked them immediately and felt comfortable. Michael was pushing Norma in a wheelchair and I was relieved to see she was brightly looking around observing her surroundings. We walked along the corridor and all of us stood expectantly at the double doors of Rose's room. Norma cleared her throat loudly and Rose slowly opened her eyes and blinked sleepily. Suddenly she hauled herself upright against the pillows and stared. Norma put out her arms and Michael steered the wheelchair forward.

They clasped each other as if they would never let go. I retreated unobtrusively as the other two stood and waited to greet their favourite aunt. They placed the two sisters closely facing each other and Hazel said, as she came to join me ten minutes later, they were holding on to each other as if neither would let go and both were talking for England.

We found some comfortable seats and I produced my scratch picnic. I had spoken many times to Norma and Hazel on the telephone but I had never met them face-to-face. We spent the next couple of hours getting to know each other while Mike, as I was told to call him, read the *Telegraph* and threw in the occasional comment as it occurred to him. I really liked them. They were obviously a lot better off than Robin and myself – judging by the expensive four-by-four they were driving – but they were down to earth and pleasant as only really nice folk can be. Eventually I suggested that if the two sisters were happy to be left together, Hazel and Mike might like a mini-tour of our historic town. We had a small museum and many antique shops which lots of visitors seemed to find amusing and it seemed a good opportunity to take a stroll down the length of our High Street while the two sisters were immersed in each other. It also gave me the chance to sit on a bench and tell Hazel everything that had happened since Rose had first been taken ill. Mike had found a fishing tackle shop and was well away chatting with the owner. Afterwards we went into my favourite café and sat watching the world go by until it was time to return and collect Norma. Once again I left the family to their sad farewells and politely waited outside.

That evening the five of us sat down to a fairly subdued meal. I had done the best I could but my heart hadn't really been in it to provide an elaborate spread. They were all polite and pretended to enjoy every mouthful. Robin tried to lighten the atmosphere but I knew we were all thinking of Rose, left scared and alone, in her stark hospital room with only the bustling nurses for company.

We said our goodbyes and, as soon as I had dealt with the dishwasher, I telephoned around and spoke to the rest of the sisters. I knew Hazel would telephone the next day, to bring them up to date, but I wanted to put their minds at rest as to how the day had gone, and what a pleasure it had been to see the two sisters engrossed in each other.

Robin must have been tired because he went to bed with a good book. I was wandering around aimlessly, plumping up cushions and generally tidying up. I sat down, for want of something better to do, and turned on my computer. I had neglected it since Rose had been rushed to hospital all that time ago. In fact I had forgotten it even existed. I tried to work out how long it had been and was astounded, when I glanced at the calendar, to realise it had been weeks. I leant forward and pressed MAIL and, within seconds, the screen flashed up a list of names. I looked at it, not comprehending what I was seeing. Dozens of names the whole depth of the screen – all duplicated, all from Andrew. I clicked onto the first one and saw an apology. The second appeared to be the same except it was more fulsome. Once I accepted they were all different dates and times I knew I had unleashed an avalanche of regrets. After such a devastating day I was unable to take in what I was seeing and I stretched forward once again and turned the machine off. I would deal with that tomorrow, I decided, and slowly made my way to my husband and our rumpled bed.

* * * * * * *

The next morning I luxuriated with a long lie-in in bed. Andrew could wait until a more suitable time. I knew every one of our neighbours would be avid to hear how I got on at the hospital, but I felt too lazy to stir and snuggled deeper under the covers. I then padded around the kitchen and brought a tray of fruit juice, muesli and coffee back with me. I visited most of the folk in the close and then prepared to make my usual trek to Rose's bedside. All I could see was a slight mound under the covers; she was apparently asleep. I slipped into the seat next to the bed and clasped her nearest hand. She squeezed gently back and I felt enormously relieved. I coaxed her to eat some lunch but her heart wasn't in it. I felt she had given all her strength the previous day and the mundane routine of eating was beyond her.

That evening, when Robin came to visit, she barely acknowledged him. He said he sat silently with her, his hand covering hers, as she curled up like a child under the sheets. He returned home, obviously dispirited, and I explained I also felt useless and found it nigh on impossible to keep up an act of cheerfulness when all I really felt was despair. We sat and half watched a silly, light-weight television show; but I guarantee neither of us could have described any of it afterwards.

The next morning I lost my nerve somewhat, so I enlisted the help of Margaret, the vicar's energetic wife and her ten-year-old daughter Megan. I asked them if they would like to accompany me to visit Rose later on. I felt she might have been getting bored with too much of my company and hopefully a change of face might brighten her day. Megan skipped along beside us as we entered the hospital. Although only young she was a self-assured child; she entered Rose's room confidently and threw her arms around her adopted "auntie" without a backward glance at her mother. The child had painstakingly spent the previous evening copying a colourful painting of a ballet dancer. She must have found the original in a book because it looked suspiciously like a Degas model to me! She generously handed it over to the frail figure in the bed. I was so pleased when Rose appeared to sit up a little straighter and take more notice when she arrived. Megan was one of her favourites and soon they settled down to chatter about the forthcoming ballet classes that she had begged her parents for. Rose had added the weight of her recommendation to Megan's and it looked as if it had finally had the desired effect and she would be getting her heart's desire.

Both Megan and Rose had a short attention span. The child soon retired to the corner of the room to study her comic and the sick patient settled back to doze. Margaret and I sat conversing quietly. Eventually we took our leave as we did not want to tire Rose unnecessarily. Sadly it was the last time I was to see Rose awake and attentive. When Robin and I returned to the hospital that evening she was in a deep sleep. Maybe they had increased her medication because, the next morning, she had descended into a light coma. I returned home and, with a heavy heart, reported back to her family. Only one relative, a niece by marriage, had queried why I had been chosen to inform the rest of them. With great relief I offered to shed the responsibility in favour of her and her husband but, as they lived many miles away in a prestigious part of Tunbridge Wells, she refused with alacrity. The rest said very little but I could not help feeling I was an interloper, as well as useless and ineffectual. The distances were so great and they must have felt so far away. I wandered around the house not knowing what to do. I took myself off to the sofa and curled up with a cup of coffee for comfort, when I remembered a promise I had light-heartedly made to Rose months previously. I was to inform her Devon family solicitor if anything ever happened to her. Had she guessed, even then, I wondered?

I slowly uncurled my legs and took myself off to their offices. Mr Frobisher had been recommended to us by Cedric when we first came to the West Country. He was a placid, benign man with a large prospering country practice and I had liked him from his first handshake. He had dealt with the conveyancing of our property and a colleague had processed our new Wills. This time our meeting was far more sombre. I explained Rose's medical history to date and he nodded and made a couple of notes after asking me to keep him informed of any news. Strangely, I left his office feeling a lot calmer than when I had first entered it. Once again I had shared responsibility with another in authority and, consequently, felt better for it.

Isn't it strange, time can speed up or slow down to suit our moods? It was early autumn and the bright sunny days all served to enhance the beauty of the world Rose was leaving. I walked around in a virtual dream as events took their rapid course and I was swept along with them. I still visited religiously, but I never knew if she recognised my presence or not. I kept vigil and reported back to her family daily. The whole nightmare became an ordeal of distress that went on and on.

Until one day it all stopped. As usual I was sitting beside the bed loosely holding her hand. The sun was shining obliquely through the window and making a pattern on the floor as it filtered through the trees. Suddenly I sensed Rose had left me. I replaced her hand carefully and quietly walked out to the Nurses' Station to report that I thought she had gone. I'm sure I sounded calm and in control, but inside I felt cold and desolate. I walked away to allow the nurses to summon a doctor and do all the things it is necessary to do at this time. I went and sat with the other patients in their Sun Lounge. I could hear muffled talking but I had no understanding as to the meaning.

I spoke with the doctor and staff and suddenly there was no

reason to be there. I walked back towards town and made a detour to Mr Frobisher's office to do as I had promised. His secretary gave me a cup of tea while I waited until he was able to see me. He briefly took down details, which I am sure he would confirm later, and asked me in his dry lawyer's voice if I would be willing to arrange the funeral? It seemed a strange request to me but I hesitatingly said I would, as long as her family did not object. I went home in a daze and spoke to the funeral directors. Unfortunately we had used them quite a lot recently. My parents had died within a short time of each other two years before, and five years previously Cedric had suddenly left us. Rose and I had both used the same undertaker and, in an odd way, the man in charge had become almost our friend. Des was young and slight and not the least like one would imagine a funeral director to be, as he was neither obsequious nor insensitive but kind and helpful. He also had a dry sense of humour, which I appreciated. I did not see him as the man who dealt in the disposal of the dead but as an efficient and thoughtful man who eased the path for his clients and made their ordeal bearable.

Robin and I carried out the solicitor's instructions, collecting the death certificate and presenting it to the Registrar who, in turn, gave us half a dozen copies to be handed back for the solicitor to deal with. We then telephoned the undertakers. I gave him all Rose's details, including her solicitor's name and telephone number, and left him to arrange a suitable date and appropriate venue for the funeral. Des promised to ring us back once it was all settled to allow us to inform Rose's family and our own immediate neighbours. He had it all planned within the hour. After lunch we visited our neighbours and told them the sad news.

That evening I left Robin watching a television sports programme and reluctantly took myself off to Rose's bungalow. I had been asked to gather up anything of value and I wasn't quite sure where to begin. As her solicitors were the only executors I supposed they were responsible for anything of worth in the property. I opened every cupboard but found nothing I considered valuable. In her dressing table I discovered an ornate chocolate box stuffed full of jumbled jewellery. I had no idea as to the content's value so I laid it to one side to take in the next day. I remembered her and Cedric had often talked of two pre-war Rolex watches but, as they were nowhere in sight, I reckoned they had been given away to her family along with other jewellery Rose had told me she had distributed to her nieces a few years previously. All through the house I had stumbled over small caches of money. In out-of-the-way places I found jars and envelopes containing pound coins. There were a few in her knitting bag and a mound in her sewing box. Every coat pocket yielded up some and there were even a couple beside her bedside clock. I had gathered them up as I went along and stacked them in a pile on a side table ready for bagging up later. I felt I was being excessively nosy when I finally picked up her handbag. Her purse held a couple of twenty-pound notes and a wallet contained about a hundred pounds. I scooped it all up and took it back with me. In all there was £382 and I carefully wrote the amount on the front of the package.

The next morning I handed over the money, some insurance policies and the chocolate box to Mr Frobisher's secretary. She insisted on making a list of the items of jewellery, even though there were some damaged or broken items, and then diligently counted the money.

'You have stated there is £382 in here,' she dryly pointed out. 'I only make it three hundred and eighty one pounds in this envelope.' She looked at me expectantly.

I mumbled an excuse and rushed back to the bungalow. I fell in the door and there, in a patch of sunlight on the patterned carpet, I spotted that rogue coin. I picked it up and sighed with relief. I wasn't to be accused of thieving after all! I raced back and handed it to her. She took it and didn't comment. I walked across the road, shattered, and visited our local florist and spent a much more pleasant hour choosing the flowers that I and my neighbours wanted to send Rose off with.

Later that night Robin pointed out I could have opened my purse and handed over a pound coin to make that secretary's accounts balance. I had been in such a state it had never occurred to me. I smiled tremulously. Robin has this theory that all the bureaucratic, official paperwork that one has to generate so quickly after a death helps to take our minds off the loss of our loved ones. It is always a difficult period with lots of hold-ups, pitfalls and minor mistakes and, while we are immersed in it, we have scant time to grieve. That comes back, like a tidal wave, afterwards.

* * * * * * *

The day of the funeral dawned cold and sunny. I had arranged to take Fred and two other neighbours to the crematorium at eleven o'clock. Megan would be staying at school for lunch, so Margaret had offered to transport four of Rose's most mobile friends to the service. Robin took time off from work and met us there.

It felt like a wedding with everyone taking sides – either groom or bride. We sat on the right and all Rose's family congregated on the left. I had telephoned Hazel in Cheltenham to ask if she would take charge. I felt this was a diplomatic move especially as Rose's niece-in-law might make some more scathing comments if I appeared to be running the show. Hazel's mother, Norma, was the eldest of the sisters left and I had hoped she would attend. Hazel said her mother had decided to stay at home but that she and Mike would willingly take over as soon as we arrived at the hotel afterwards. I breathed a sigh of relief. I wanted no confrontations with irate members of their family. I wanted the day to run smoothly as Rose would have wanted it, had she been there.

My lot did me proud. They sang the three hymns firmly and I was relieved that Hazel and I had chosen some good old recognised favourites. The congregation on the left appeared amazed at the number of folk who were at the service. They were probably puzzled as to who we all were and surreptitiously kept looking askance at us, I noticed. They watched as Fred sang lustily and then subsided politely to listen to the retired vicar's short résumé of Rose's life. She and Cedric had never been churchgoers as long as Robin and I had known them, so Hazel and I had composed a brief two pages of notes for him and included a few intimate details and jokes to enliven them. They were all anecdotes Rose had laughingly mentioned during our chats and I felt no compunction in mentioning them in front of her family as I'm sure they could have included loads of their own. The curtains closed and it was all over....

We dutifully shuffled out and obediently walked to the crematorium garden to admire the flowers that were heaped under

Rose's name. It was a relief to get back to our car and lead the way to the country inn Des had chosen for us. As we entered I immediately stepped back and Hazel and Mike welcomed us all as if we were their guests and I felt that was as it should have been.

Robin and I, with our eight neighbours, loosely seated ourselves around three tables and Rose's family occupied the rest. I couldn't help noticing the older members of her family were shepherded in by their children, who seemed comfortable with each other but it also appeared obvious that the husband and wife duo, who had telephoned to enquire what business it was of mine to be arranging this funeral, didn't seem to fit in with any of the others.

The pub had put on a decent spread of buffet food, as promised, and Margaret and I busied ourselves filling their plates with appetizing delicacies and satisfying them with suitable drinks. Robin diplomatically went across to the two cousins who were sitting alone and began chatting with the husband. As the wine, teas and coffees flowed so everyone relaxed and became more animated. The aftermath of a funeral usually brings with it a lightening of the atmosphere and I was delighted to see people mixing and talking together.

I had met only a couple of Rose's close family at Cedric's funeral. It had been a completely different occasion. All his family, even his three younger siblings, had predeceased him and it appeared that most of his friends had passed away, too. I always had the impression that Rose's family considered he had been too old for her. He once told me he had met her at ten years old and married her at seventeen. He earned an excellent salary and drove fast sports cars and Rose told me she had been headlong in love with him. So much so she managed to influence her mother to persuade her father to give his consent. They had married and left in a flurry of veiled criticism and, possibly because of that, she had remained devotedly by his side for the rest of his life.

Finally it was all over. The tables were littered with plates and glasses, chairs had been shifted, the easier to talk with others, and we were all replete. Margaret, Robin and I went around and wished everyone going back across the borders of Devon a safe journey and then we ushered our neighbours out and into the cars. I felt as if I had run a marathon as I sank into my seat alongside Fred, after settling in Elsie and another neighbour. I had done my best and I hoped it would please Mr Frobisher that I had tried to fulfil all his wishes. I hoped it would have pleased Rose, too.

Robin and I hardly watched any television that night – apart from our daily dose of the News. Our talk was mainly of how such a difficult day had gone. I think our old neighbours had been satisfied with the funeral arrangements for their good friend. Without Margaret and her shepherding capabilities none of it would have run so smoothly. Fred hadn't disgraced himself and annoyed any of the ladies with his usual loud complaints and I hoped Rose's family thought it was a pretty good turnout from such a small community. The retired vicar had spoken to the whole of the congregation with a pleasant deference tinged with friendliness. Anyone not knowing him would have imagined he had known Rose for years. Obviously the collaboration between Hazel and I had proved seamless and even the acerbic couple from Tunbridge Wells looked fairly mollified after Robin went across and introduced himself. I had watched him exert his usual charm as he drew the two of them out and I noticed, in no time at all, the rather dour nephew was telling family anecdotes about his favourite auntie. Hazel and I hugged as we were all leaving the inn. I hoped we would remain in touch as I felt I had made a friend. We promised to ring each other early the next week and I went home satisfied.

When we finally ran out of conversation that night Robin and I made our way wearily to bed. Just as I was wrapping my arms around my pillow and snuggling down, Robin finally dropped his bombshell.

He quietly said, 'I'm not sure if you will think this is good news or not, Jenny.' I raised my head and looked at him enquiringly. 'Two days ago I was asked if I would go up to Newcastle. There is to be an enquiry into the conduct of certain high-ranking police officers in their inner city force. I don't know much about it but I think it's pretty powerful and serious stuff. I would be on secondment for as long as the investigation lasts. It might be over quickly or it may drag on for some time. I'm surprised my name was put forward at all. I feel there are others who are probably more suited to the task but, I must admit, it is a compliment and I would love the chance to tackle it. I explained to my bosses about this funeral, Jenny, and I asked for two days to think it over. They agreed, but the two days are up tomorrow and I have to give them a firm answer first thing in the morning. What do you say, Jen? I will quite understand if you would prefer me not to accept. It's the last thing I would have wanted; but it may lead to promotion on my return and I would love to be given the opportunity to have a crack at it.'

Put like that, what could I say? I was proud he had been chosen, proud his obvious dedication to the police service was at last being acknowledged. I sat up and hugged him. We talked about it far into the night and I knew there was no way I would stop this husband of mine from doing something he had set his heart and mind on.

Consequently, I tossed and turned most of the night. A multitude of thoughts were cascading through my head. How would I manage without him? With Rose gone my life would be duller and emptier from now on. Who would take her place as my confidante in future? I would miss Robin but he had his own busy life to lead while Rose, undoubtedly, had always been there for me alone. Don't be silly, I chided myself, you will be fine. Then my mind skittered back to the funeral. Was there anything I had omitted to do? Had I fulfilled all Rose's wishes? And, finally, who would be moving in next door, I wondered? Would I like them? And, more important, would they like me?

Chapter 8

*

I remembered my promise to Fred and we went out and purchased his electrically adjustable bed the very next day. I took him into Sidmouth and tried to make it a special occasion for him. He watched while I bounced, sat up and lay down on a selection of beds in the store. I think he was rather intrigued as to how they worked. He was astounded at the prices of course, but when I told him he would have something none of his neighbours possessed, he was finally persuaded. I then took him down to the elegant sea front and we sat beside the beach, in the sunshine, and munched contentedly on a huge ice cream each.

As soon as we arrived back home, and I had decanted Fred into his favourite chair with a mug of tea, I started packing for Robin's Grand Trek (as we had whimsically named it). If I could manage the bulk of it then he could put in all the extra items that he wouldn't be able to do without for however many weeks the job took. He had promised to ring me as soon as he arrived and then telephone me each evening on returning to his lodgings. I didn't want to act like a clinging wife but I hated the thought of his being alone and friendless up there in a strange city.

Normally, when police personnel go to another station, they are greeted by the incumbents, shown the ropes, which usually include their local favourite watering hole, and made generally welcome. This time it might be slightly different. I was not sure of the procedure in such a sensitive area and I wondered if Robin could easily be on his own with very few colleagues of his own rank. Until he arrived, he said, he had no idea of the size of the group or where the rest would be travelling from. It all seemed a bit vague to me but possibly Robin either knew more than he was letting on or it was so secret he hadn't been told much himself. Either way I would have to wait and see.

I stood on our doorstep in my dressing gown early the next morning and waved him off. As usual, he wanted to get an early start and, as Newcastle was a fair distance, he was eager to be off. I shut the front door and wandered back to bed with another cup of tea. There seemed little reason to get up and I sat in bed sipping my drink and reading an intriguing detective novel. The long day stretched in front of me. I met Lorna in town for coffee and then did a little desultory shopping. I longed for Rose and a good chat. The garden looked unnaturally neat with its closely shaved lawns and neatly edged borders. I felt like an umbrella without the rain or a school teacher without a class. Useless!

I was eating my evening meal when Robin finally rang. The four hundred miles had taken their toll. He had been introduced to his colleagues and shown where they would be working. Finally they were taken to their various lodgings and he had just slung his case on the bed and was sitting with his feet up.

'Well so far so good, Jen,' he said wryly. 'There are two of us in what looks like a decent guest house and we will be going down for our evening meal in a minute. The sergeant with me is from Milton Keynes. He seems a nice enough lad and we thought we'd eat and then go out for a drink after. Get our bearings a bit before work starts tomorrow. Sleep well, darling. I will be thinking of you snuggling down in our cosy bed. Night, sweetheart!'

I knew I wouldn't hear from him for another twenty-four hours and sighed with frustration. I wandered around the bungalow not knowing quite what to do. All the hectic excitement of the previous two busy days had now left me feeling a bit lost and slightly redundant. As I said goodbye to Robin that morning I had been conscious of a latent elation in him. I could feel it smouldering beneath the surface of his usual calm, I envied him his mission and wished I could be involved in something similar. He had pointed out, by the very nature of the remit, it might be a difficult and sensitive undertaking and there was no guarantee they would be able to bring it to a satisfactory conclusion. Even so, I knew he was keen to show his abilities to his superiors.

So there you have it; call it ennui, apathy, boredom or a vague annoyance at being left behind – I felt life was unfair. Whatever it was, it probably tugged me enticingly nearer to Andrew and, instead of settling down in front of the television or picking up a good book, I walked over to my long-neglected computer and fired it up. Within seconds I found the Mail Box and came across the dozens of e-mails Andrew had sent. The screen was filled with them. I opened up one at random and found they all replicated a similar message:

Jenny. Please, please forgive me. Andrew

Jenny, I couldn't get you out of my mind while I was in the States. The fun we had and just how great it was to be together once more. Don't go out of my life once again...

Jenny, please stop punishing me. What can I do to make you forgive me? I really, really am so sorry. Love Andrew

Jen. You have no idea how I hated to leave you that afternoon. How jealous I was of your Robin and your life in Devon. I know I should have written but, when I returned, I didn't dare let myself think of you in case it was all a dream on my part and just a bit of fun on yours. Please forgive me? Your Andrew.

And two of the last ones, which were more desperate, more explicit:

Jenny you have no idea how jealous and bereft I felt that day I took you back to your home. It killed me to leave you. Did you not notice? Honey, I have always bitterly blamed myself for letting you slip away from me, as I did, all those years ago. Now I have almost done it again. Please say you will keep in touch? Tell me you'll write occasionally. I give you my word I will never annoy you; but just promise me you will correspond occasionally and I will be satisfied.

And the final one was even more frank:

Jenny, sweetheart. When I saw you that day, sitting on the steps of that church waiting for me, my heart did a great bump in my chest. Same old smile, same gentle voice, same old Jenny. I nearly swooned when I stretched out my arms to kiss you – and you let me! And those three days! Every morning I couldn't wait to finish my breakfast and be with you. I stood outside your hotel like a lovesick teenager even though I knew the whole day would rush by too quickly and be over so soon. Did you not sense my feelings? The evenings were the best. I could sit and talk and watch your face. I was in heaven. Darling, can I telephone you sometime? I know you were hurt and furious with me; but I was too scared to write in case it was all a dream. That was my biggest fear – that I had imagined the whole thing – and you felt nothing at all. Just let me know if I can ring you. It will make my day. Your Drew xx

Of course this all came at the wrong time in my life. The sad thing was it was my own fault. *I* had precipitated it by getting in touch with Drew. What had started out as a casual enquiry had descended into madness – a madness I was unable to control.

I was an ageing, vulnerable woman. I was as susceptible as the next person to flattery and admiration. Sadly, I had lost my best friend and had no one to talk to, no one with whom to discuss this new turn of events. I had nobody to apply their common sense or to staunch all this romantic rhetoric. No opinions but my own to consider. Added to that, I had been separated from my husband just when I needed him to be there for me. I needed routine and comfort and, I suppose, love. Unfortunately it happened at a time when he was too busy to notice. It is easy to look at this time in my life with hindsight; but there I was – alone and unsure of myself, hurting badly – and here was this loving, kind man offering to make everything better. It was the perfect antidote to a sustained hurt and bereavement that I was only just beginning to comprehend.

I am ashamed to say I began my first love letter, via an e-mail, to Andrew that evening. I sent it and within minutes had my answer. He asked permission to telephone and I sent my number without a qualm. For the next seven weeks he rang me every night around midnight and we would chatter for sometimes up to an hour. This was on top of the dozens of e-mails that winged their way backwards and forwards through the ether, daily. It was a good thing neither of us was employed because an employer would have dismissed us. We wasted hours writing thousands of loving words. It was like an avalanche that tumbles down a mountainside and covers all in its path.

Looking back, I must have had blinkers on because it never occurred to me that, although I was living a solitary life now Robin was away, Andrew most certainly wasn't! How naive can someone be, I have asked myself since. I never puzzled out how he managed to sit for hours in front of his computer and then how, in the middle of the night, he was also able to spend hours on the telephone as well. In fact, I am ashamed to say, I never thought of his wife, Fay, at all.

As long as I was able to spend early evenings in conversation with Robin I felt I had fulfilled my promise given before he went away. He told me what little he could about the work he was doing. I learned there were only about ten of them in total, with two senior officers in charge. They were divided into two groups and each section carefully cross-checked with the other, daily. Other than that I knew nothing about their work or their findings. It sounded sensitive in the extreme and Robin spent most of our time chatting casually about Newcastle in general or us in particular. Ross, the lad he was bunking with, was a likeable chap who accompanied him to various eating houses every night but, other than that, there seemed little enough to do apart from visit the local pub for the occasional pint.

As everyone knows, life never stays the same forever. It is always constantly changing – for the better or worse. It fluctuates like a see-saw and we are usually on the way to pleasurable contentment or slipping sadly down towards something mediocre or barely tolerable. Andrew soon made it clear he wanted us to be together again as soon as was humanly possible. Now was obviously a perfect time as one of the first things I had told him was that Robin was away and therefore I was a free agent. He appeared to be one, too. He suggested we meet somewhere that suited us both. We expended many words, both by phone as well as via our busy computers, deciding a destination. At that time I persuaded myself it was a fairly innocent and simple decision to ponder over – but of course I knew it wasn't.

Andrew's first love had always been Cornwall – and Polruan in particular. As I lived reasonably near the Cornish border it seemed a sensible destination to me too. We had already spent some time in Polruan and Fowey and now he wanted to visit Portwrinkle. It was a tiny fishing village roughly halfway between Looe in the west and Millbrook and Plymouth in the east. He warned me he had discovered there was very little there apart from some coastguard cottages where his mother's father had been stationed when he first arrived in Cornwall. Andrew was hoping to complete a little more of his maternal family tree and this seemed as good an opportunity as any. It did cross my mind to enquire why he hadn't been before, but I smothered it and agreed instantly. The next night I told Robin casually I would be visiting a school friend in Essex and would probably stay for a few days. I told the same story to my neighbours and only felt better when I had stocked them up with enough food to last them a week. I didn't see either Lorna or Margaret, which relieved me of telling any more lies to two good friends.

I caught the train from Honiton and changed at Exeter for Plymouth. I was like a kid going on holiday for the first time. We pulled into Plymouth and I stepped off the train onto a blustery, almost empty, platform. Paper and dust were whirling around in the wind and I suddenly wondered if I shouldn't have come. I started yanking my case towards the exit, looking anxiously around, and within seconds Andrew came towards me with a big grin and his arms outstretched. He hugged me and immediately I forgot my apprehension. He packed me expertly into his comfortable car and slammed my suitcase into the boot. We were off in no time and making our way towards the Tamar and the Torpoint ferry. He had obviously made this crossing numerous times and this allowed him to relax and talk about inconsequential things at the same time. I am sure he was trying to put me at my ease because, for some unknown reason, I suddenly felt stupidly shy. It must have been obvious when he read my e-mails and we had talked endlessly on the telephone for hours that I was as enthusiastic about meeting again as he was. Suddenly all that determination had evaporated and I scrabbled around to make sensible conversation, feeling as if my tongue was glued to the roof of my mouth. I knew it was only a short journey to our destination and I was panicking as to what would happen when we arrived, what we would speak about, what would we do, and, more importantly, what on earth I had let myself in for.

Andrew went on chatting as if there was nothing amiss and gradually I began to calm down, and look about me at the deep lanes bordered by wild bushy hedgerows. Suddenly we turned left at Sheviock and made our way down towards Crafthole and Portwrinkle. The tiny village nestled at the bottom of a hill overlooking a small harbour. There were two beaches of shingle and sand and it all was pretty plain and basic. Andrew had booked us into a fifteenth-century inn. He admitted that he had chosen it because it boasted a four-poster bed and he thought nothing could be as romantic as a medieval inn with a bed to match. I burst out laughing at his absurd definition of a romantic setting. We found it eventually and signed in, with me feeling highly embarrassed and staying unobtrusively in the background, and were shown the way to our whimsical room. Well it did have a four-poster bed, right enough, and it *did* look pretty antiquated, but it certainly was not glamorous or picturesque. As soon as we closed the door we fell on the bed and laughed. And that was all it took to dissipate the embarrassment and awkwardness I had felt since we met. Andrew brewed a very modern pot of tea and we wandered around inspecting the room, its cavernous cupboards and the decidedly shabby en suite bathroom, as we were drinking it. Neither of us mentioned it was all a little tawdry and not quite the romantic retreat we had both envisaged. We chatted brightly and ignored our surroundings, including the massive bed that we had swiftly vacated and which took up most of the room.

It was a great relief when Andrew suggested we go out to eat. I was scared that, if we stayed in to dine, our first meal might be as mediocre as the room. Seven o'clock saw us sitting down in a bright pub, entirely different from Andrew's medieval choice. The landlord was welcoming and the clientele were jolly and talkative. We appeared to be the only visitors in the village. Straight away we were quizzed as to where we had come from, where we were staying and for how long. We stated our destination, which produced knowing grins around the bar along with the prompt offer of a bed from Mine Host – which made our hearts sink. We ate at a pleasant, secluded table and after the first few mouthfuls, when our conversation was stilted, we settled down and enjoyed a really delightful meal. Of course, it helped that Andrew had chosen a decent wine, which left me feeling mellow and relaxed. We politely declined the proffered bed a second time as we sat and finished with coffee and a liqueur. I remember leaving about eleven o'clock in a decidedly genial mood.

We stumbled into the now dark inn, made our way down uneven corridors, past mullioned windows and up and down a couple of stairs until we reached our oaken door and Andrew produced the huge wrought-iron key with a flourish. I was at the giggling stage by then and ordered him to take a shower while I got ready for bed. In reality I lazed back against the pillows and waited. I hadn't planned this; in fact I had never done anything so wanton in my life. I calmly lay there as if I were sunbathing on a beach. Andrew came out of the bathroom in a cloud of steam, his towel wrapped tightly around his waist. I watched him placidly as he pulled up short.

'I thought you would be in bed,' he said sharply.

I stretched out, catlike, and grinned. 'And I thought you might like to have the pleasure of undressing me,' I answered sweetly. Where had that come from, I wondered fleetingly?

I could see, from his face, he appreciated my humour. He took his time, released his towel and shut the bathroom door all in one sinuous movement. Then he proceeded to do just that. I had drunk enough that evening to neither feel embarrassed nor awkward as he eased buttons and zips. He then gently removed my bra and pants and I helped by wriggling down in the bed until it seemed the most natural thing in the world as we melded together, under the billowing duvet, and I remember very little more until I awoke the next morning.

It took me a matter of seconds to stare about me and get my bearings. The hangings around the bed framed my view of the room and suddenly it all looked homely and cosy. Around the edge of the tapestry curtains was a thin rim of sparkling daylight, so I guessed it was morning but I had no idea of the time. I arose from the bed, trying not to disturb Andrew, and crept into the bathroom to use the loo and clean my teeth. I did it as quietly as I could because it felt odd to be doing this with a strange man breathing deeply and gently a few paces away from me. I went across and eased the curtains back to enable me to glance at my watch on the dressing table. 6.40am – I sighed with relief that we had not overslept, and prepared a tray of tea. I turned round and found Andrew, fully awake and sitting up in bed, watching me appreciatively. I pulled his shirt off the chair and threw it around my shoulders. It made me feel a little less conspicuous. I padded over to the huge bed and placed the tea beside him. I slid under the covers and we sat shoulder to shoulder drinking it. I wondered how I had registered in his estimation the previous night. Was he sorry he had suggested this rendezvous? I had no way of gauging his response because the preceding hours were extremely hazy in my mind. I'm certain *I* had enjoyed it, and I felt he may have done too, but the overall effect had been vague due to the amount of alcohol I had drunk through sheer shyness. I hoped I had not made a fool of myself.

To prevent me compounding any mistakes I may have been guilty of, I brightly smiled and jumped out of bed.

'I bags the shower first,' I said brightly. I went in and firmly closed the door. Unbidden, a thought entered my mind. How am I ever going to sit on this loo and open my bowels with this man only a door's width away, I pondered. I don't ever remember being uncomfortable with Robin but, as we had been married so many years, I expect I had probably forgotten those first few weeks of marriage.

Mundane showering and dressing masked any discomfort either of us felt and, by the time we had reached the breakfast room, we were as indistinguishable as any other guests there. Andrew described the coastguard cottages his grandfather had manned. It had been the sole reason for our journey to Portwrinkle. He had a couple of dog-eared sepia photos in his wallet and he passed them across to me. I studied them closely and saw a weathered man, with a shock of fair hair and a dark jersey, smiling into the camera. The building behind him was probably his home as well as his workplace, I surmised. We asked the waitress and she called the owner over to help us. Yes, the cottages were above the beach and easy to find. He gave us directions and we collected all our gear for the day, including my camera, and went to search for them.

There were a handful of them in an unbroken line. They were squat, weathered and attractive with a clear view of the sullen sea and beach below. We chose a middle one, at random, and knocked on the worn door. We heard a movement inside and immediately the door was pulled wide. A man stood there with a smile of enquiry on his face; a comfortable, elderly man with a shock of grey hair and a rough navy jumper. Fleetingly, I saw Andrew's grandfather of the photograph.

'Yes? Can I help you? Do you want to stay at one of the rented cottages?' he asked. 'I'm not sure if any are free, but I could find out for you.' I glanced towards Drew and stepped back a pace.

Andrew explained clearly and concisely our interest in the row of cottages. He told how his grandfather had been the coastguard in Portwrinkle for some years. He hesitantly said he might have been the chief coastguard; but possibly that was family exaggeration, he added. Immediately the man's face lit up. He generously motioned us to come inside and as we walked into the slightly untidy main room, he went on to say we had, by instinct, chosen the right cottage. *He* now resided in the Chief Coastguard's house, and had done so for some years. He waved us over to a deep settee and went out to his kitchen to make us coffee. I sensed he might be lonely and was pleased to chat. We looked round appreciatively. It was lovely to find what we were searching for so quickly, and also to find a man who was willing to talk to us.

He returned carrying a tray of coffee and biscuits, shutting the kitchen door with his foot, but not before a huge tortoiseshell cat had sneaked in with him. The cat looked owlishly around and then chose my lap on which to make his home. I rubbed behind his ears and listened carefully to what John, the owner, was telling us.

'At one time there wasn't the technology that there is today. These lookouts were the eyes and ears of the country. Coastguards were an integral part of the coast and you will see the remains of their workplaces and homes everywhere you go – especially down here where the sea was a way of life and can be likened to the motorways of today. So much was transported by this method as well as the human fodder of troops for the many wars we persistently waged. Invasion was also a possibility, from the time of the Spanish

Armada onwards, as well as vessels being swept off course, going aground or being wrecked here. It must have been a hard life and sometimes a lonely one. After a while men were permitted to bring their wives and families with them and that would have eased it a bit, I feel. Your grandfather, whether he was the chief here or one of his assistants, would have been an important man and I was delighted to actually live in this historical building. It makes me feel I belong to a grand tradition.'

Drew and he both yarned on for ages as it turned out they had both served in the navy. I drowsily stroked the cat and half listened. Eventually we were offered a tour of the cottage. I declined, as my burden was asleep, and I thought no man likes a woman to take a close interest in their housekeeping skills. They disappeared up the stairs and all I could hear was some low conversation punctuated by the odd laugh. As they came back I noticed Andrew was holding a large red book rather carefully. It was the official records that went way back almost to the beginning of the eighteenth century.

I gently put the warm cat down and Andrew and I pored over it with reverence. Yes, family reminiscences had not exaggerated – Andrew's mother's father had indeed been a Chief Coastguard. There was his signature – R Tuckenhay. Andrew quietly told me his grandfather's name was Russell Tuckenhay and their family originally came from Devon. His daughter, Andrew's mother, had met his Dad in Looe and there must have been some magnetic attraction because she had returned only once to her family home in Portwrinkle before she married him and went to live in Polruan.

We handed the precious journal back and said our goodbyes to John. He waved to us as we walked down the hill to visit the beach. I am so pleased we did go and see this friendly man that day because, less than a year later, when we returned to pay another visit to our friend, a stranger opened that scarred front door. We were told bluntly that John had died. When we asked about a red Coastguard account book we were met with an incomprehensible stare.

No, there had been nothing left in the house when these people took over. We turned away...

That afternoon we decided to explore to the east of the tiny village. We had a hurried snack and then took the car and made our way down towards the hamlet of Freathy and Whitesand

Bay. Whitesand Bay was one of the largest beaches in Cornwall, seldom stumbled across by visitors as it was tucked away behind Millbrook and Antony, with the deep indentation of Plymouth, with all its tributaries that divide Devon from Cornwall, further to the north east.

Here there was nothing but mile after mile of sand edging the English Channel. Andrew laughed and reminded me of Whitesand's one moment of fame. A huge vessel was wrecked off the beach and shed its load of wood along the whole length of the sands. For ages the locals had a bonanza; they could gather as many planks of timber off the beach as they could shift and gossip had it that many a household in that secluded corner of the West Country now sported a new kitchen, a table or even a solid wood front door!

The beach was deserted until we turned inland at Rame Head where there was a primitive hermitage chapel crowning the headland. We walked up to admire the fortitude of any hermit making his home here and then drove further on to the villages of Cawsand and Kingsand. Most people only discover them when they come across on the Cremyll ferry from Plymouth. That day we chatted with some half dozen lads who appeared to be at a loose end as they congregated near the church. They told us about Mount Edgcombe House and Countryside Park but we decided we had done enough exploring for one day.

We went back that night and had our meal at the Finnygook Inn. I drank a reasonable amount of wine but I made sure I was aware of my surroundings when we finally got to bed. All day we had laughed and exchanged confidences and I now felt more able to go to bed with a man I had fallen in love with and who was not my husband. I might have made a point of ringing Robin daily, but other than that I was living for the moment and sadly Robin did not figure in that moment. I was unable to blame Andrew or Cornwall or my sudden loneliness. I knew I was breaking every moral rule; it seemed I had pushed morality behind me for the time being, along with my good sense. I felt ashamed – yet exhilarated. I was unable to say no when Andrew drew me towards him and I revelled in his lovemaking.

We lay beside each other afterwards and I questioned Andrew as to why he was doing this. Did he love Fay no longer or was it just a fling to amuse himself? He looked at me with a shocked face.

'At home in Polruan I felt secure. I was loved by my family. I suppose they indulged me – being the youngest. They allowed me to go my own way, hence the *Arethusa* on the River Medway in Kent at such an early age. I knew I could always go home and my Dad, with my two brothers and Deborah, would welcome me with open arms. The prodigal son returns, and all that,' he said ruefully.

'I still don't understand how you managed to get from the Merchant Navy to the Diplomatic Service in one fell swoop,' I said.

'I didn't. I told you how I decided to leave the navy when we split up? Well, I had no idea what I wanted to do, apart from not wanting to return to Cornwall with my tail between my legs. I heard I could probably get a decent job ashore with GCHQ in Cheltenham. I had gone up there for a few days to attend an interview. I had just come away from it and I thought I was halfway to being accepted. I was in a really good mood when I passed through a park on the way back to my digs. I saw Fay sitting on a bench. She was sitting absolutely still, crying. The tears were coursing down her cheeks but she was staring straight ahead. There was no one around so I gingerly sat at the other end of the seat and asked if she was alright. She turned her dark blue eyes on me and shook her head. I suppose I was lost from that moment. I took her out to a café and that was that. She told me she was attending a language college in Cheltenham because that was what she was best at and her parents wanted her to have a career. She also told me her boyfriend had let her down but she never explained that boyfriend was a married tutor with whom she had been having an affair. I later learned that on that particular day she had given him an ultimatum – leave your wife or we are finished. He had obviously thought better of it and took the safer option to stick with a wife who he certainly knew and probably trusted. I now know that Fay was the sort of girl who would strive for an almost unattainable goal but, on grasping it, found maybe she didn't value it after all. I wonder now if her middle-aged tutor summed her up better than I ever did and reached the right conclusion,' he said thoughtfully.

'So what happened then? I questioned.

'I was ripe for it, I suppose. Our liaison took off at a rate of knots and we were sleeping together within the week.' I winced. 'It was a tempestuous affair – a whirlwind romance, I suppose you would label it, Jenny. I stayed in Cheltenham; couldn't tear myself away from this fiery, self-opinionated, spoilt young girl. I was offered the job at GCHQ but she persuaded me to turn it down. She talked of my aspirations being too low. I should aim higher she said - she pointed out her father could probably get me entrée into the Diplomatic Service. I was naive and impressed by her certainty. She spoke by telephone to her family daily and raved about me, my intelligence and resolution. I'm sure, now, it was only her hormones talking, but she convinced her parents as to her serious intentions and, within two months, I had been inspected and accepted and was on my way to be trained in diplomacy in the service of my country.'

'Golly!' I commented. 'What did your family think of that? One minute you are roaming the high seas and the next you are swanning around the world as an Ambassador.'

'Not quite, Jenny. I was only accepted initially, provided I could make the grade. Strangely it was my cadet training on the *Arethusa* that served to hinder me. The school had been set up originally to help lads from poor homes. I had the devil's own job to prove my family owned a reasonably well-established boat-building business. Standards may be a little lower these days but I still needed to prove I had been educated to a reasonable standard and knew how to hold a knife and fork correctly before I was admitted to the hallowed courts of St James. Of course Fay became agitated as the wheels turned so slowly. I'm sure, in the end, her father pulled some strings and so I began my career on the lowest rung of the civil service diplomatic ladder.'

'So where did you live?' I wanted to know.

'I started work in London – and difficult it was, too. Fay wanted us to be engaged immediately, and planned marriage shortly after. Her parents seemed to agree. I was reluctant and pleaded to complete one thing at a time. By then we were having lots of rows and in a high dudgeon one day she stalked out and chose and purchased her own engagement ring. That's the first time I have ever admitted *that* to anyone, Jenny.'

I looked at him with sympathy because I still felt it was up to the man to set the pace. In my world a man woos a woman and Andrew should never have allowed this headstrong girl to decide his life for him. 'So you completed your training, got married and then what?'

'I think Fay's father must have pulled a few more strings because I was sent on secondment to the British Embassy in Stockholm. Surprisingly, I missed my home in Cornwall. Life in the navy was easy-going and secure. Out in the diplomatic world I was uncertain, fearing ridicule and I made few friends. Those friendships I made were only superficial because most of the staff was only passing through. And don't forget, I was still only a very lowly clerk trying not to make too many mistakes, but Fay was back where she belonged, in the thick of Diplomatic life and cushioned by her parents' position. She had a habit of mentioning various fairly well-known people who she had met or been out with. I heard them mentioned so often I stopped listening but it was still hurtful. One boast was the Sultan of Brunei's nephew who she had dined with twice, and I often wondered if she was regretting getting tied to a simple Cornishman. She was pregnant at the time but that never stopped her. We attended most parties – usually with me working – and her enjoying herself.'

'So her language career went out of the window,' I surmised.

'Yes. She was pregnant and that was more than enough to cope with, her mother decided. I remember we were entertaining an important Arms Trade Mission one evening and I had been trying to gather some sensitive information most of the day. Fay was annoyed because she said I was neglecting her. I went across in my dark unobtrusive suit to be with her. She made a point of turning her back and raising her glass to a dashing young captain of the Household Cavalry. He was acting ADC that night and must have been well aware how his Life Guard's uniform, with its three shoulder pips and various campaign dress medals, suited him. The Blues & Royals are an elite force and my beloved wife flirted with him all evening. By the time she allowed me to take her home she was well and truly drunk and I had to cadge one of the Embassy cars to drive us on the short walk to our flat. I left her sprawled on the stairs and went on up to bed, I am ashamed to admit.'

There seemed little to say after that and I turned on my side. Drew took me into his arms, as if he, or I, needed comforting. I snuggled down and we must have been very tired because we both drifted off to sleep.

The next morning was our last. We packed up the car and decided to go west towards Looe. On the way we passed Downderry and Drew pointed out where *The Gypsy* had been wrecked in 1901. We spent a lovely day wandering around Looe's Banjo Pier and fish market – where we watched a lively auction – and after lunch we visited the Museum. It was only small but full of interest. I found the khaki World War I field stretcher so poignant: I could imagine a soldier being gassed, maybe with only a cloth to cover his face for protection, being rushed from the field to try and save his life. Andrew spent some time talking to the Archivist about Looe Island – from the smuggling era until the present day. It had certainly had a chequered history.

We made our way slowly down some steep stairs and Andrew found a Scold's Bridle. 'Illuminating', he said. I decided it was macabre, gruesome and cruel. The Cat-o'Nine-Tails was worse, I thought. I could imagine a sailor being flayed alive or being keel-hauled for some minor misdemeanour. We both decided life was hard in those days.

By the early evening it was time to return to our respective homes. After a meal in one of Looe's many inns we made our way back to the car. I felt shattered but, when Andrew insisted he escort me back to Honiton, I refused. He would have a very long journey back to York and I was quite capable of getting a train from Plymouth. Also, I might have been tempted to ask him to stay the night if he took me to my empty bungalow, and I'd be risking my neighbours seeing us and wondering. I was conscious how much worse it would be to betray Robin in our own home and our own bed.

I managed to get my way and he saw me off in Plymouth. I sat most of the way on the train with my eyes closed, drained both physically and emotionally, and pondering on the revelations Andrew had divulged about his marriage and wondering if I would ever get over this ridiculous infatuation. I should have quit worrying if I had known that something of far greater importance that would change my life forever was waiting on the mat at home to shock and astound me.

Chapter 9

*

By the time the train slowly crept into Honiton station it was late and I was running on stupor. I slung my bag over my shoulder, grabbed my suitcase and wheeled it outside. The station forecourt was deserted so I had no option but to trudge doggedly up the slope towards home. There were a couple of street lamps on in the road outside the close but all the bungalows were in darkness. I hoped they were all snuggled up and cosy in bed. I bumped my case down the shallow path and fumbled for my keys.

The front door resisted my push. Lots of mail was jammed behind it and I was forced to carefully ease it open wide. I tiredly bent down to yank everything out of the way. There were two local papers, a few circulars and a number of letters, I noticed wearily. One was large and quite heavy. Probably for Robin, I guessed. I tossed them all on the table in the kitchen while I made a well-deserved cuppa – which I drank standing up. I was too tired to even open my suitcase, so I left it in the inner hall and took myself off for a shower and bed.

The telephone shrilled while I was deeply asleep the next morning. I had forgotten to set our trusty radio alarm and was shocked to see it was past eight o'clock by my wristwatch. It was Robin, avid to hear about my "holiday". I mentally pulled myself together and vaguely alluded to the few days, without mentioning anything much in particular. He was warmly interested, as usual, and I felt my face reddening with guilt as I sleepily lied, by omission, to him. Yes, of course I'd had a good time. Yes, it was a lovely rest. No, we hadn't done much and *of course* I was pleased to be back (and that *was* a downright lie!)

Not wishing to discuss these mythical friends of mine, I changed the subject swiftly. How was his job going? It seemed the charges were partly substantiated but none of it was as bad, or as serious, as they had first expected, Robin informed me. A bit of a storm in a teacup, he admitted wryly. A couple more weeks might wind it up he hoped, and I sighed with relief. Once home, surely things would return to normal? He had been my rock for so many years – beloved and warm. Like a worn pair of slippers that were comfortable and comforting – I could rely on my husband and I longed just to be with him. Andrew became a distant mirage as we talked. Minutes passed until he reluctantly said he must get to work and I, even more reluctantly, slid out of bed.

I padded into the kitchen to prepare my breakfast. The sun had come out and I was mentally preparing myself to go the rounds of my eight neighbours' homes. I wondered if Mr Montague had managed *not* to fall out of bed while I had been away, and what moans Fred would have about his new electric miracle. I'd promised to ring Lorna and Margaret on my return but decided the telephone, and any answerphone messages, could wait until I was ready to face the day.

I took my laden tray back to bed and picked over the great pile of correspondence. I discarded over half as junk mail and the rest were mostly bills. I put the two newspapers to one side and slit open the large, heavy white envelope as, surprisingly, it was addressed to me. I pulled apart a huge wedge of closely written foolscap pages and began to read the first few lines... and then I read them again. This was rubbish. A joke. It couldn't be right. I forced myself to read them a third time until it finally registered with me that my next door neighbour – my lovely Rose – had left me half her estate at her death. The rest went to a charitable organisation for dogs. I started to read the letter yet again just to make sure I hadn't made some terrible mistake. No, everything Rose and her husband had ever possessed was to be valued and sold. All the money realised, plus their savings and investments, was to be divided between two beneficiaries; and they were informing me I was one of them. Now it all became clear why Rose's solicitor had asked *me* to register her death and arrange her funeral. They were the executors of her Will but, as I was to benefit from her largesse, they saw no reason why

I should not help them complete their assignment. Once I had fully understood the implication of the letter, I lay back on my pillows and considered exactly what this would mean for me and Robin. We would now be relatively well off and, as we were both in our retiring years, it could make our future life together extremely smooth and pleasant.

Suddenly I was jolted out of my reverie. But what of Rose's *family*? What about her four sisters? Surely they were far more entitled to receive the fruits of Rose and her husband's labours? The Will should have been made in their favour, I strongly believed; they were related to her and I was only a neighbour and a friend. We had always been close and reliant on one another – but why me? I had only known her for just over a decade and she had been part of a large family all her life. What would these people think and, more importantly, what would they say? Her nieces and nephews must have had expectations even if her ancient siblings didn't want, or need, this inheritance. I was sure someone in her family must have assumed they would be her heir when she died. And what about Norma, her oldest sister, and Norma's daughter Hazel? Only a few short weeks previously they had travelled all the way from Cheltenham to see Rose in hospital. We had taken to one another immediately and, although we had only known each other a short time, I valued this budding friendship. What on earth would Norma, Hazel and Michael think about this Will?

I also remembered the implacable niece-in-law who had questioned me as to why I was in charge of the funeral arrangements. I blushed at the thought of what she would be saying as soon as she was informed that Auntie Rose had left her favourite nephew nothing. Surely a woman like that would be prepared to contest this Will? The thought of arguing in court sent shivers down my spine. I would rather return the money than go through that, I decided.

Who could I tell about this bombshell? No one, I resolved, until I could telephone Robin on his return from work that evening. I forced myself to get out of bed and made myself presentable to face my neighbours. I listened with half an ear to Fred's usual grumbles about window cleaners and the shopping that Margaret, the vicar's wife, had kindly delivered to him. The biscuits weren't his favourite bourbons and the jar of coffee she had chosen was far too large. He didn't mention his new bed so I didn't either! I walked in through Mr Montague's front door and found him contentedly watching his usual diet of morning television. I made him a strong cup of tea and chatted for a few minutes but, as his eyes kept straying towards the flickering screen, I made myself scarce and went on to finish my round before going off to the shops to re-stock my depleted larder.

That afternoon I found more than enough to keep me busy in the garden. Petra and Megan came skipping by, wrangling amicably as usual. They stopped to finish off a nearly empty box of ice creams that had been languishing in my freezer. While they were munching they innocently asked me where I had been as they hadn't seen me. I told them my usual tale of having spent a few days with friends, but I found myself faltering and hesitating. I was not exactly lying, as Andrew had always been a friend, but I felt distinctly guilty to be telling these embroidered fairy tales to two innocent children who trusted me implicitly. I was relieved when they left me – still bickering.

The rest of the afternoon dragged by and eventually I went indoors to make myself a tray of tea and tried to settle down with a library book. I remembered my promises to ring both Margaret and Lorna on my return, but I was reluctant to speak to either of them with such a momentous happening hanging over my head. They would never forgive me for not telling them my unbelievable news, so I decided it was better to keep quiet until I had first unburdened myself to Robin. The clock's hands crawled nearer and nearer to six o'clock when I hoped Robin would have arrived back. At five minutes past six I shakily dialled his mobile. It rang four times and then it went to voice mail. A sweet young girl's dulcet tones said she would take a message. I grimaced and cut her off. I forced myself to wash up my dirty tea things but before I could grab the tea towel my land-line was buzzing merrily.

'What is it?' asked Robin's breathless voice. He had obviously run upstairs. 'Are you OK? I was just parking the car in an impossibly tight spot when my mobile started flashing. I raced to my room as the traffic is pretty noisy at this time of night and it was easier to do that than trying to answer you.'

I took a deep breath. Where to start? 'I received a letter this morning from Mr Frobisher, Rose's solicitor.'

'Oh, yes?' Robin sounded puzzled.

'Don't panic, darling.' I reassured him. 'It's good news. Well, I think it is. It said Rose has left us half of her estate and everything she owned. Oh, and the other half is going to a Dogs' Home,' I added for good measure. There was a deep and echoing silence.

'What! Say that again, slowly.'

I repeated what I had said, word for word. The silence lengthened once more.

'So you are telling me Rose decided to cut out her family from her Will and has given us, and the Dogs' Home, everything she possessed?'

I nodded and then realised he couldn't see me. 'Yes, it looks that way. She couldn't have been thinking straight, those last few weeks. How could she leave them nothing and us everything?' I asked. 'The cancer must have affected her brain and her reasoning. Mind you, I don't even remember her calling Mr Frobisher to her bedside when she was in hospital, so when could she have done it?'

'Have you received the Will?' asked my astute husband. 'See when it is dated.'

I quickly scanned the legal document once again, and then I saw what he was getting at. 'It is dated over four years ago,' I said. 'But, Robin, there is no way we can accept this windfall, surely? I feel the family will never forgive us.'

'No, I agree, darling, but you must admit this puts a different slant on things. If she had done it last week I am sure there would be grounds for her family to contest this Will. But, as it was written long before she was ill, she must have decided this was the way she wanted her estate divided. Better telephone Norma and Hazel and ask them what they think. Norma is the eldest of the sisters and she will put everything into perspective, I am sure. If she is not able to discuss it, then I am sure Hazel and Mike will be only too willing to tell us their feelings on the whole affair.'

I was shattered by everything that had happened to me that day. My whole world had been turned upside down by a simple letter accompanying a printed document. If we had received a similar letter from a long-lost relative of ours then we would both have been rejoicing, I had no doubt. But, because of the circumstances, all I felt was apprehension and worry. Instead of unbounded happiness I was anxious and bothered. I agreed with Robin that I should contact Rose's eldest sister and her family in Cheltenham to ask what they thought of the strange turn of events and what they would advise.

I heard a distant knocking and Robin informed me Ross, his fellow police officer, was ready to go out for a meal. They had been working hard all day so we murmured a rushed goodbye to each other and I sat there fondling Crumble's ears, completely oblivious to the television programme that was playing before my unseeing eyes. Finally, after mulling over our strange change of fortune, I turned the set off and persuaded Crumble to come with me into our bedroom. I dragged his bed to the bottom of mine and watched as he flumped down with a sigh of resignation and a groan of arthritic pain. It helped because, for the first time since I had been alone, I had the most disturbing dreams; none of them happy and most bordering on nightmares.

* * * * * * *

The next morning I was awake as soon as it became light. No lying in bed with a good book today. I showered, made my breakfast and ate it at the kitchen table. After my second cup of coffee I judged it was time to ring Hazel and tell her my news. She answered on the second ring. I apologised for being early and then went on to read out the solicitor's letter that we had received. I then tried to explain, with many stops and starts and throat-clearings, what Robin and I both felt.

'It isn't the glorified rejoicing you might imagine, Hazel. We are both worried that this isn't right and we are sure your Mum, and the rest of your aunts and family, will agree that we have no right to this money whatsoever.'

There was silence on the other end of the line and I longed to see Hazel's face. What on earth was she thinking? Was she feeling a sudden revulsion for this couple who had snatched a substantial nest egg from her family? Suddenly her warm tones filled my ears.

'What on earth are you talking about, Jenny? You gave Auntie Rose and Uncle Cedric great happiness the last few years of their life. You were always there for them, you took them out for days, you even took them out for meals – a thing they had never done in their lives before – and you helped them as if they were family. You asked and gave your opinions as if you were of a similar age; you treated them as equals and I know they flourished under your care. Did you not know that they were always full of their "Jenny and Robin" every time Mum rang them? My family, on the other hand, aided and abetted their parents when they tried to stop their great love affair. Did you not know Rose was ten years younger than Cedric and, at seventeen, she eloped with him because her father refused to countenance his favourite youngest child marrying a man he disliked intensely? Consequently, they never set foot in the family home ever again. Rose was always very protective of the hurt they suffered and they lived a really solitary life. That was until they came to your corner of Devon. They blossomed and I know my mother, as the oldest, breathed a sigh of relief. Go and spend the money with our blessing, Jenny. None of us needs it and – quite honestly – none of us deserves it. I will explain to the rest of them and I can assure you there will be no nastiness from any of them.'

I was not quite so sure as to the reaction of Rose's niece and nephew of the snobby address and the demanding manner but, on hearing Hazel's amiable words, a great emotional weight slipped from my shoulders. She and her mother didn't mind after all. Suddenly I became relieved and relaxed. Hazel and I chatted on for some minutes until I told her maybe it was time I told the rest of the neighbours.

'Don't bother for a while,' she advised. 'Let everything settle. Old people are often wary of change and, if you blurt out your good fortune, it could scare them unnecessarily. They all rely on you and are happy in the knowledge that they only have to call and Jenny is on hand to help them. Let them keep their comfort for a while.'

We said our goodbyes and I sent my regards to her mother and Mike. Little did I know how Hazel's advice was to colour my thinking as well as changing my life in the not-too-distant future. I decided to tell my best friends Lorna and Margaret, in confidence, when the opportunity arose. I was still trying to come to terms with the fact that there was an empty home right next door to me. The loss of Rose had left a hole in my life and Robin, being so far away, had compounded that emptiness. Now I hoped someone would soon fill the property – even if they were unable to fill my heart.

My self-imposed rounds were almost non-existent that morning. No one was desperate for help. I scribbled down two shopping lists as my neighbours dictated them. I knew all the right sort of questions to ask as to sizes and preference, so no one became irritated with my obtuseness. I had soon purchased all that was needed and swiftly delivered it. At a loose end afterwards, I settled back to watch even more daytime television. But I couldn't concentrate on it because, insidiously, I realised that everything could change shortly. I felt exhilarated but scared as well. Did I feel it would be *our* money to spend, or had Rose expected me to nurture it as she and Cedric had always done? I longed for Robin to be home so we could discuss this at length. I wondered how he was coping at work. Did he have the phlegmatic ability to erase all such thoughts or was he as excited and anxious as me?

My nervous energy made me wander around aimlessly. I fingered various objects scattered across the room and picked up a book twice; but I was unable to concentrate. Eventually I drifted towards my laptop. I fired it up and waited to see if there were any messages. About two dozen appeared. Two e-mails I immediately recognised – one from Dee, my cousin, and the other from Meryl and Adam. I diligently read what they had to say and promised myself I would answer them later. There were three special offers from the supermarket and these I deleted. I took a deep breath and, one by one, opened the rest.

Of course they were from Andrew, as I knew they would be. Writing was a medium he loved and he made these letters resonate with longing. I felt that each one was a mini love letter. He told me how much he missed me, said that I had left an ever widening gap in his life, he stressed that if he was only able to speak to me he would feel happier and more content. He pleaded to be able to telephone and asked my permission. It was a heady experience for a middle-aged woman, one who has always lived a pretty dull life, to be fêted like this as if they were something special. Maybe other women had experienced this sort of loving affection. I never remembered rousing any sort of fascination in a man's estimation, outside of my marriage, that is. Occasionally, at the hospital, a sick patient might come on a little strong and I would be more likely to scotch any sign of misplaced tenderness or warmth with practical common sense – or possibly a jest – just to hide my extreme embarrassment. That was me and, up until then, it had served me well.

Now I was vulnerable and lonely, with my best friend dead, and the inheritance she had left me causing great upheaval as to thoughts of my immediate future. I know most people would have been rejoicing at their good fortune but then I am not most people, I told myself ruefully. I leant forward and touched the reply button. I gave Andrew permission to ring me at any time. I then abruptly switched off the television set and rang Robin to tell him I was taking myself off to bed. It was obvious Ross was having coffee, or maybe something stronger, with him because he accepted my brisk statement and amiably wished me a good night.

I lay in the dark and stared at the ceiling. Eventually I must have dropped into an uneasy sleep because it was with great fear that I awoke to hear my bedside telephone loudly shrilling. I leaned over and answered it – sounding like a cross between a frog and a fog.

'Hello, sweetheart,' softly breathed in my ear. I rolled over in a muddle of concern and heaved myself up in the bed. The clock glowed eerily at almost midnight.

'What?' I muttered, dazed. Then I awoke completely and clutched the telephone tightly to my ear. 'Oh Drew, I have been in bed for hours,' I said groggily. 'When I said ring me, I never expected it to be in the middle of the night. It's almost midnight and I was sound asleep.'

He chuckled and proceeded to talk to me as if it were the middle of the day. Second by second I became more aware and receptive to his words. We laughed and giggled softly to one another and when an interminable number of minutes had passed, he finally said it was time that we both put down our phones and get some sleep, I felt sad and bereft at the thought I would be cut off from him. By then I was wide awake and wanted more. The line went silent and, once more, I persuaded myself to settle down again as I tried to return to my previous drowsy slumber.

And that is how my life continued for the next week. During the day I ran errands and chatted to anyone who needed to talk. Every evening Robin rang as soon as he arrived back from work and immediately after he'd returned from his evening meal. We talked a little but I was more and more disinclined to discuss anything very personal, apart from how his work was progressing and what I had been up to that day. I am sure he was sensitive to my coolness and reticence. He said nothing. Maybe he put it down to us being apart and my feeling of abandonment. What he didn't know was that every evening, around midnight, Andrew treated me to a cocoon of loving words, to comfort, delight and pleasure me. I began to live for these interludes and consequently Robin reaped my lonely, sterile and forlorn feelings. However I tried, it was always difficult for me to respond to Robin's kind enquiries as it was easy to accept Andrew's warm love and attention.

It all came to a smarting head as the weekend drew nearer. I asked Robin abruptly one evening, just as he was recounting to me a story about the guest house cat and some missing sausages, exactly when I could expect him home for good. He answered, I felt, evasively and I became even more clipped and terse. 'You must have been given a date, Robin? Or is this *jolly* going on forever?' I asked, sarcastically.

The line went quiet for a few seconds and then I heard Robin draw in a deep breath. 'No, darling, the main object of our inspection is finalised and being put to bed right now. Most of the police on secondment will be returning to their own patches and the whole enterprise will be wound up.'

'But?' I asked. 'There sounds like a definite "but" to me.'

'I will be coming home too,' he replied. 'Trouble is, I am not sure for how long. But one thing *is* certain – we will discuss it properly face to face.' I knew, by the tone of his voice, that I would have to be satisfied with his answer and my reply was just as abrupt – I immediately smacked the telephone back on its rest to show my hurt and displeasure. I noticed he did not ring back, which only served to increase my distress and resentment. That night I was especially receptive to Andrew's endearments. I needed someone to smooth my ruffled feelings and he did just that.

Robin, good as his word, returned early on the Saturday. I stood in the doorway as he dragged in his case and various unwieldy bags. I went into the kitchen with a stiff back and an unyielding attitude. I made a pot of tea and returned with it to the lounge to hear what he had to say. In the intervening two days all sorts of thoughts had been tumbling through my head; from him preferring the excitement of Newcastle and wanting to remain up there, to his meeting another woman and needing to make his new life with her, to his just being fed up with our simple, quiet, rural backwater and deciding to caste off our mundane marriage at the same time.

I am ashamed to say that during the next few days, as each thought took hold, I only dismissed it as a new one entered my fertile brain. And, as usual, the things I had most been dreading were all a figment of my lurid imagination. I settled back and waited for the bombshell to explode.

'Jenny, I was unable to discuss this over the phone,' Robin began. 'Out of the fourteen-strong contingent that went up north only five of us are to remain. Yes, there were some irregularities that needed investigating and these have now all been straightened out but, in the course of this investigation, we have discovered far more serious crimes that may have been committed by officers right at the very top of this force. These will be examined in detail but in a far more sensitive way. I have been chosen as one of the team. Ostensibly, we will be setting up a new department while, actually, we will be probing and examining something that could be far more sinister.'

I looked at my husband, amazed. So *this* was what it was all about. My first instinct was to be immeasurably relieved. None of my worst fears were realised. He wanted me to be proud of him – and I was – but it also meant our separation would now last a lot longer than we first anticipated. In my delight, I was prepared to sacrifice everything. I was not a selfish woman, and I was genuinely pleased for Robin: it just meant I would go on being lonely for a while longer. I knew I could bear that.

We spent a thoroughly indulgent weekend. None of my neighbours received a visit. I rang Margaret and Lorna and, between them, they promised to tell all of them that Robin was home – just for the weekend – and, if they needed anything, to give *them* a ring. We took advantage of their kindness to laze around and do very little. On the Saturday we took our dinghy out for a long afternoon's boisterous sailing and met our friends for a meal round the pub. I did no housework and barely any cooking. I suppose I wanted to make Robin's short leave as pleasant as possible. I am sure I was also trying to smother my overwhelming guilt and the only way was by cramming fun into every moment of our time together. In fact I almost forgot Andrew, and the excitement he could generate just by his nearness, as I basked in the warm glow of relief to be with Robin once more.

Of course it didn't last. I saw Robin off in the early evening of the Sunday. We had cleared away the messy leavings of an impromptu party that had developed when our friends, Kevin and Hazel, had come round unexpectedly and now I was left with the dreary remains of the washing up. I tidied around and then went up to bed. I had a free night and, surprisingly, I dropped into a dreamless slumber but, the next evening, I was awakened by my usual midnight call. And so the subtle pleading began once more.

This time Drew suggested we visit the Cotswolds. He knew my love of history and what more magical than the love story of William Shakespeare and his Anne Hathaway? Many years before, I had gone with a hospital friend to visit Stratford-upon-Avon; it had only been a brief visit as she was not terribly interested, and I had always wanted to return and absorb the whole area once again. William was a young lad of eighteen when he met and fell in love with Anne, a farmer's daughter, who was eight years his senior. In my heart I always thought she must have been the love of his life. At twenty-six she would have been considered middle-aged, I am sure, and, as she lived on a farm, she must have been fully aware of the effect she had on her young swain. In those days sex before marriage was not frowned on as it was centuries later. Maybe it was considered a good union; William' s father had his own business and was also a wool dealer who later became an Alderman. They lived in a substantial town house so maybe he was the perfect catch for a prosperous sheep farmer's daughter.

Whatever, he married her and they had three children, a daughter and twins, in quick succession. He obviously took his vows seriously because he accepted his responsibilities and decided there was nothing for it but go to London and make his fortune; William then stayed faithful and looked after them and his parents, for the rest of his life. The thought of going to visit his home seduced me immediately. Just to soak up the atmosphere and surroundings would be superb. I was sure Andrew calculated my willing response before I did!

He told me he was looking at a hotel in Bourton-on-the-Water. 'You'll love it, Jenny - it's the most romantic place I've ever been to. It's elegant, quiet and sleepy with a wide stream flowing gently down the main street. There's a beautiful bridge, everything is built in honeyed Cotswold stone and I guarantee you will not want to leave. Please say you'll come for a long weekend? We will do Shakespeare until he comes out of your ears, you can wander around to your heart's content and I can book for us to go to the theatre, if you like.'

Would I like? Of course I would love to be taken, to be cosseted, to be indulged, to be loved. I promised I would mention it to Robin as soon as he rang the next evening. He sounded relieved at my enthusiasm and easy capitulation. Once again I remembered that Andrew had a wife and this time, I promised myself, I would question him as to the state of his marriage when we were alone once more. What was she doing when he went off for these mini holidays? Did she not question him as to where he went – and why? Didn't she care? Or had she a lover of her own?

The next evening, when Robin made his routine call, I mentioned casually I was at a loose end and therefore I would be going off for the occasional weekend whenever I felt so inclined. I decided not to use false alibis, and involve my friends or family from then on, but to be truthful and above board. Attack, we are told, is the best form of defence and I employed my feeling of boredom and loneliness to good effect. Either Robin would take exception to my unwillingness to wait at home like a dutiful wife or he would accept my explanation. Looking back now, I am sure he was immersed in some deep probing of a delicate nature and had little time to question *my* flimsy motives. We chatted about everyday trivia for half an hour until I was certain he had no inkling of my real reason for spinning such lies.

I was able to report back to Andrew four hours later that he could book anything he fancied and I would join him whenever, wherever. That night I slept deeply and peacefully which proved one does not need a clear conscience for one's mental health and well-being.

I was not quite so fortunate with Lorna, who came by as I

was pegging out the washing the next morning. She chatted for a while about Rose's bungalow being up for sale in the estate agent's window. We both hoped our new neighbour would prove as friendly as our last. Then she mentioned she had a hospital appointment the next Friday and asked if I would look after Petra when she returned home from school, just in case she wasn't back. I may have reddened somewhat, I definitely stammered when I told her I might be away the whole of the next weekend. She looked at me appraisingly and asked if I was off to Newcastle to spend the weekend with Robin. I shook my head but was unable to meet her level gaze. I muttered I was fed up and had decided to take myself off to somewhere nice. She nodded and said that was fine – she would ask Fred to keep an eye on Petra. She also offered to take care of Crumble, which made me feel even more guilty. I was misleading her and then trading on her generous nature. Relieved that my explanation had been accepted so readily, I thanked her and we parted amicably.

The next day I had a telephone call from Margaret. We chatted for some minutes about nothing in particular and, it was only when I put the phone down that I realised there had been nothing she wanted to know or ask me to do. So unusual in a vicar's wife, who was expected to organise a dozen things and plan half a dozen more. I immediately had the feeling she and Lorna had been chatting about me and were concerned at what I was up to.

From that moment I decided I must supply more convincing answers in the future if I was to persuade my two friends of my credible and innocent intentions. I ignored the fact I was constantly lying and totally in the wrong, of course. I might pull the wool over Robin's eyes with ease; but their womanly intuition might take some fending off.

Chapter 10

*

I was determined that I would be as independent as possible, so when Andrew told me he had booked us into an hotel in the Cotswolds for the next weekend, I told him I would make my way up there under my own steam. He wasn't too pleased but eventually agreed and suggested he met me at Evesham. I raced down the road and then spent ages in the booking office of Honiton's train station trying to work out a suitable route. In between serving other customers the ancient clerk said I would have to go via Clapham Junction and, as there were the usual rail works in progress that weekend, it looked as if I would take all day to reach Evesham. Andrew was testy when I mentioned it that evening and reminded me we barely had four days and I would already be wasting one. In my eagerness I had accepted the inevitable and had resigned myself to spending most of one day travelling the rails of the southern half of England. I looked once more at the atlas to see if there was an alternative.

Friday seemed to take forever to arrive. I was up ridiculously early and arrived at the station almost an hour before my train was due. The platform was deserted so I took myself into the booking hall and went for a casual chat with the lad on duty there. Needing someone to relieve my pent-up tension, someone who didn't know me, I explained I needed to be in Evesham as soon as possible. He listened closely to my explanation of how odd it seemed to travel so many miles east only to turn sharply and then race north. With a few taps on his screen he suggested an alternative route. This was via Exeter and Bristol and appeared to be shorter, quicker and cheaper. I asked how his elderly colleague had not come up with a similar solution. He shrugged, said he worked in many stations in the area and, anyway, it was his job to know these things. I dutifully handed my ticket over plus my credit card, trusting he knew what he was talking about. He cancelled it and issued me with another and, quite soon, I was on my way in the opposite direction.

I gaily texted Andrew and told him the good news plus the revised time I was supposed to be arriving at Evesham station. Within seconds he had telephoned me back to say he was on his way and would be awaiting me, with arms outstretched, as soon as my train came to a halt. I guiltily looked around hoping no one had heard my end of the conversation. I found myself staring down the long jerking carriage at our local pub landlady. I smiled and waved gaily and she immediately left her seat and made her way down the aisle. I shifted my handbag and she lowered her ample bottom onto the seat next to me. I then spent the whole of the journey to Exeter Central station making up some fictitious story to cover my illicit weekend. Normally I would have been alighting at Central station too; instead I was forced to make up a few more lies explaining why I was going on to the main line station. Oh what a tangled web we weave!

After various changes that all went smoothly I was decanted at Evesham station and, as promised, Drew was there to enfold me in his arms. He had arrived two hours earlier and had spent his time wandering around the market square with its abbey buildings and gateways, found the riverside meadows and had even made time to visit the small museum. He briskly escorted me off the platform and straight into The Royal Oak for a meal. We sat close together, we bent our heads and laughed and touched our feet under the table – all innocent fun – but I guessed we positively glowed. Occasionally I noticed the man behind the bar glancing our way; I recognised we must have seemed an ageing and intensely odd couple to him but, as neither of us knew him, it mattered not.

As soon as we had finished our meal Andrew hustled me away to our destination. I had the distinct impression he was impatient to be alone with me. I began to feel like a delectable box of chocolates just waiting to be opened and plundered. I found mischievous amusement in taking a close interest in the road and villages as we travelled south. I especially noticed Broadway, a golden Cotswold stone village of handsome town houses mixed closely with very old humble cottages in a grass-lined main street. I pointed out the muddled, unevenly tiled roofs and received a cursory glance and a grunt for my troubles. Artists must have had a field day in such a beautiful place.

Stow-on-the-Wold surprised me because it was a more austere market town, built on a high plateau, and with none of the golden charm of the other Cotswold villages. I saw signs to Upper Slaughter and then Lower Slaughter and Andrew assured me they were beautiful riverside villages and we would be exploring them, along with Stratford-upon-Avon, within the next couple of days.

Suddenly we were entering Bourton-on-the-Water and I watched, entranced, as the village unfolded before me. A grassy sward that lazily meandered alongside a softly flowing, shallow river with a low, wide bridge flung casually across that allowed visitors to pace from one side of the village to the other. The sun was warmly shining and the whole area was lit up like the most perfect painting. Andrew must have known where he was going because he turned off the main thoroughfare and made his way towards what looked to me like a seventeenth-century coaching inn. We pulled into a sheltered courtyard and were welcomed inside a reception hall with dark beams and a huge oaken fireplace. I stood back as he introduced himself and went through the formalities. We were shown to a luxurious suite of rooms with more beams, a deeply encrusted ceiling sporting all sorts of forest animals on a deep plaster frieze and a huge stone fireplace. Through a door, I glimpsed a massive four-poster bed hung round with embroidered crimson brocade curtains and crisp white linen sheets. The room had darkened linen-fold wood panelling with deep wardrobes flanking an exquisite dressing table. It was all softly lit and was as inviting as any stately home I had ever visited.

As soon as the porter deposited our luggage, and the door had closed softly, Andrew turned to me and pulled me gently into his arms. I heard him breathe a deep sigh – perhaps of relief – and I had the distinct impression he felt we were now safe. I marvelled that I was able to raise such a deep emotion within him. Here, to all intents and purposes, was a sophisticated man who was used to conducting himself in the most elegant of surroundings, conversing with cultivated people; and yet all he appeared to want was a simple, ordinary person like me.

After Cornwall, and the patently scruffy inn he had chosen in Portwrinkle, Andrew obviously wanted to impress me with this luxurious hotel that boasted every amenity. There were dark red roses spilling out of a crystal vase on the low coffee table placed in front of the stone fireplace and, beside a cooling bottle of champagne, was a box of expensive chocolates on top of some glossy county magazines. On either side of this lamp-lit glowing tableau were two deep matching settees, but neither of us chose to sit down. I stood transfixed as my eyes travelled around the room from the mullioned windows, through the wide doors to the billowing opulence of the four-poster bed, and then on through another door where I glimpsed an en-suite bathroom.

'Did you arrange this all for me?' I asked in amazement. He nodded wordlessly and I was touched beyond measure. We sank down on the bed and I lay back passively as he undressed me. He carefully lowered himself on top of me as if I was the most precious treasure he had ever discovered. I buried myself deeply within his arms and savoured a magical emotion I had never felt or encountered before. To be loved in such a special way was novel and moving for me – I wanted it to last forever. I strove to blot out all other feelings: I needed to yield and yet welcome him at the same time. I must have displayed my innermost thoughts because Drew took his time, watching my face as he delicately aroused me again and again. His shy smile proved he was matching me second by second and I was constantly and greedily begging him for more. Eventually it was all over and we lay side by side, our hands entwined, as our bodies adjusted to returning to the real world. Eventually Andrew went across to the side table and made us both a cup of tea. Afterwards, we languorously slid out of bed, donned the thick towelling dressing gowns provided and began exploring the rest of our cosy sanctum.

The bathroom was as modern as the other two rooms were original. Bright lights, mirrors, sparkling white tiles and brilliant chromium, with a large sunken bath, a Jacuzzi, a huge walk-in shower that could have housed an elephant, twin hand basins, piles of fluffy towels and every toiletry requisite one could need – or imagine. There were no taps or knobs – everything appeared to operate through hand signals breaking beams, so we experimented and were delighted with the results. We played around in wonder. Finally we dropped our luxurious dressing gowns in the middle of the floor and, just like two mischievous children, gambolled between the bath and shower, splashing each other and giggling.

That night we both slept deeply and serenely. I awoke the next morning refreshed and rested after a long and arduous day. We both discovered we were ravenously hungry and therefore, when Andrew and I presented ourselves in the Breakfast Room long before, I suspect, many of the other residents were even awake, we were the only occupants. The hushed surroundings didn't deter us from eating a hearty breakfast; rather it enabled us to discuss quietly our plans for the day. Our first port of call was the Memorial Theatre where Andrew purchased two tickets to see *King Lear* that evening. Like most other visitors to Stratford, I wasn't terribly enamoured at first sight by their contemporary theatre. I hadn't expected to see London's replica of *The Globe*, but I was surprised that no Shakespeare devotee had insisted the Bard's theatre shouldn't resemble a public library or, at best, a red brick university. Luckily it overlooked the River Avon and every effort had been made to provide a pleasant promenade here with gardens, in which to stroll, and it enabled me to dream of earlier times or search out a cosy café – or restaurant.

Andrew bought all the necessary entrance tickets and then left it for me to decide in which order we would view the various houses that had sheltered England's most famous son. I remembered, when I had visited many years previously, I had arrived with a nursing friend who had little regard for anything Shakespearean. She had invited me to accompany her on a weekend to the Cotswolds – and Stratford-on-Avon just happened to be on her list of "must visits". My friend was driving and, when she showed no interest in any of the old Tudor buildings, apart from me photographing her outside Anne Hathaway's delightful cottage (which she considered was "cute"), I had difficulty in hiding my longing to spend the rest of the day submerging myself in the Bard's surroundings. Never had two work mates been so incompatible and, realising this sad fact, I never accompanied her on any subsequent trips.

This time I was like a child left unsupervised in a sweetshop.

I dragged Andrew to where Shakespeare was supposedly born in Henley Street and I walked reverently through the rooms, absorbing every detail and soaking up all the information I was offered. Luckily there was no pressure to rush through at speed, as I noticed so often when Robin and I walked through a National Trust property. Robin was always delighted to give me a surprise and take me but he seldom saw the point of lingering in rooms full of beautiful objects and furniture that would immediately capture my attention. Consequently, I always obediently followed his steady pace forward in the knowledge that, given the choice, I would have lingered and he would never have come.

Drew and I bent and studied, stood just gazing at rooms, and quietly talked. As it was so early, we were able to absorb the undoubted atmosphere almost on our own, and we made the most of it. From there I suggested we go to Shakespeare's house in Chapel Street where he had died in 1616. By then he was an established playwright who was well known, honoured and fêted in London. None of it had appeared to go to his head. I could never imagine him bragging: indeed he had married a lady older than himself, fathered three children and kept his wife and his parents comfortably provided for during the rest of his life. Not bad for a lad from Warwickshire! We took ourselves outside and wandered in the small Elizabethan knot garden that was saved long after the original home had been destroyed a century later. Next door we found the Tudor gabled home of Shakespeare's daughter. It had a display of medicine – which interested me enormously – and a lot of Elizabethan and Jacobean furniture which we hoped was possibly original.

After our intensive culture lesson Andrew decided it was time to head for the High Street and some welcome refreshment. We found a small café which offered delicious snacks and sat in the bow window resting our aching feet and reviving our flagging energy by watching the world saunter by. After devouring a delicious array of sweet and savoury bites, helped down by numerous cups of tea, we felt refreshed enough to carry on with our tour of all things educational. But first of all we succumbed to a busy gift shop that tempted us with its bright lights and sparkling presents. Andrew's birthday was due in a short while, so I persuaded him to let me buy a beautifully elegant, white porcelain mug depicting views of Stratford delicately line-drawn in pale blue with touches of gold on the rim and the curving handle. He laughed delightedly and said he would think of me every morning as he drank his morning coffee. He bought me a souvenir edition of *A Midsummer Night's Dream* – his favourite he said – as well as *King Lear* which we would be watching that evening. I also chose some postcards to send to some of my friends and neighbours.

Andrew decided we would take a leisurely stroll to Shottery where Anne Hathaway's cottage was. She had lived there until her marriage to William and, as we walked along a country lane, I imagined how this village must have looked in their day. Were there footpads prowling around the countryside and would it have been a dangerous walk when the evenings were drawing in and most God-fearing folk would have been safe indoors? I daydreamed of him visiting Anne every evening. Maybe he had written a sonnet or jotted down a vague idea for one of his future plays. I like to think he was besotted with this farmer's daughter who was possibly more worldy-wise than he, being his elder by eight years. Did her family consider him a "good catch" due to his father being today's equivalent of a councillor or even mayor? The family business was wool dealing, a staple commodity in Tudor England; but the young Shakespeare, although well educated, had no job and relied on his father's generosity to keep him, his wife and their three children until he was able to find gainful employment. Was there finally a bitter row, with his father suggesting it was time his son went out and found a job? Or had it been the cold reproach shown by his father that forced the sensitive young man to desperately seek his fortune in London? We shall never know but, thank goodness, he did seek his fame and fortune and it was in the theatre. His decision immeasurably enriched literature all over the world. It is a fact we use his sayings constantly, and his descriptions enhance our language daily.

We stood outside the charming thatched farmhouse surrounded by its riotous cottage garden flowers. The very mellowness suggested great peace. We walked inside and found it virtually empty. Either the hungry hordes were still crowding into restaurants or they were in town buying up souvenirs. There were no coach parties, no Japanese tourists and no parents trying to control their unruly, bored offspring. We walked around, hand in hand, and imagined the two young lovers together. I looked at the Tudor furniture, the uneven flagstones in the kitchen, the utensils, the wide hearths, the small lattice windows and tried to imagine it as a lively, loving home. I am ashamed to admit Drew and I sank down on a settle that had been placed in the bedroom and quietly dreamed, as we stared at the small chunky four-poster bed, of life more than four hundred years before.

It was the most perfect introduction to *King Lear* that evening: the simple story of a misguided king who puts his faith equally in his three daughters. One, Cordelia, is the Cinderella of the play and the other two, Goneril and Regan, are the horrible, scheming Ugly Sisters. It is a lesson in mistaking flattery for love and regarding truthfulness as disloyalty. I enjoyed every minute of it and the Royal Shakespeare Company received a standing ovation. Andrew and I both walked out of the auditorium sated and happy.

On the way back to our hotel I must have sounded thoughtful and absent-minded because, when we entered our room, Andrew asked me outright what was the matter. This gave me the opportunity to ask all the puzzling questions that had been clogging up my conscience as our affair had intensified over the past months. We both took a shower and tumbled into bed and it was there I voiced my concerns to him.

'Andrew, what has been bugging me for several weeks is the partnership you share with your wife, Fay. I take it you are still married and live together?' He nodded. 'You tell me her main interests seem to be her women friends – lunching, shopping with them and playing bridge. Yours, on the other hand, are golf and your two grown-up sons and *their* children. That seems to be *it* apart from a few men friends who you meet up with occasionally. You obviously prefer to be with *me* or you wouldn't be in this bed right now! You may think it none of my business but during the past few months I have spent more time with you than I have with my husband and this is obviously putting my own marriage at risk; so I consider I have the right to ask these very searching questions.'

He settled back against the pillows and placed his arm around me as he considered his reply. 'Yes, Jenny, of course you have every right to ask. I have so loved being with you, talking, laughing and finding out about each other that I had forgotten this isn't all about me and *my* feelings but concerns both of us. I think I must be under some sort of magic spell. Everything goes out of my mind when I telephone you. When we talk I never want it to end even though it is often well past midnight. I spend all my time daydreaming of us being together and planning possible escapes and, when I see you, joy overwhelms me and I can think of nothing else but you. It is as if the rest of my normal life is wiped out by your nearness and, quite honestly, I don't know what to do about it.'

'What on earth happened, Andrew? You married a girl who you presumably loved; you had two children in quick succession with her – and then what? And what has *now* caused you go from being a loving husband, father and grandfather to my besotted swain? Or are you going through an old man's crisis and this is all an impossible dream that you are unable to extinguish?'

Andrew sat for some moments with bent head, marshalling his thoughts. Eventually he leaned back and started to speak. 'No, it is none of those things, Jenny. I married Fay in an awful hurry, I admit that. My family were miles away and had enough to cope with. Deborah had to nurse my Dad who was failing rapidly, the boatyard was going through a slight slump and it was not long after that my elder brother, Mark, died suddenly. I had no one to confide in but I know, now, that was a poor excuse. Fay's parents were loving and kind, but I realise their daughter's happiness was always their prime concern. We lived together before we were married and we had lots of rows and reconciliations during that time. Even on the day of our wedding we were barely speaking to each other but, as we always seemed to land up in bed and our sex exploits appeared to compensate for our bitter quarrels, I thought sex would forever be a solution. Don't get me wrong. The children were loved and welcomed by us both. I felt I had become a man and revelled in being the head of my family.'

'I don't think Fay felt quite like I did. She loved the children and enjoyed showing them off but, basically, she had lost her carefree, single status and I think it irked her. She was still on the periphery of diplomatic life, courtesy of her father, but there was no mistaking the fact that her husband was still a lowly assistant to an attaché and advancement seemed to be slow in coming. I beavered away taking courses in, of all things, Russian and Mandarin Chinese, as I had been advised, and I suppose I may have been too immersed in my difficult studies. One day Fay announced she would have preferred a mate with a university degree. In a high dudgeon, I suggested we return to the UK and I would show her what I was capable of. Within two months she had her wish. I applied and was accepted at York University and we returned to Britain. I know her parents were worried and concerned. They lent us some money but basically we were on our own. We found a small house to rent and I worked most nights in a bakery to supplement my grant, but there was no doubt that we were poor and that never sat terribly well with my wife. Looking back, I suppose I was too tired to do anything properly. Studying all day and sweating around hot ovens most nights made Fay's comments even more acid. I'm sure I told you that she then decided to return to her parents in Washington for a holiday and, as I was sitting my finals, I agreed to them going.'

'Well what was wrong with that? I asked. 'A holiday was probably a good idea and it must have been easier for you to study when you knew they were being well looked after?'

'Of course I felt like that initially but, once back, I'm sure Fay sank back into the ordered, smoothly running routine she would have been so used to. A nanny had been engaged to look after Peter and Mark – which I thought was excessive – but it enabled Fay to sightsee and shop with friends while joining in the diplomatic social whirl. I would telephone constantly and listen to reports of their hectic lifestyle. Time passed rapidly and suddenly I noticed she dodged any question of returning home. I was unable to pin her down to a date: there was always one more glittering reception she needed to attend; one more day at the races, or another picnic with her new acquaintances.'

'So what did you do?' I asked yet again.

'I waited and hoped. Her mother, whose dress sense was excellent, had encouraged Fay to visit some of the better known designer boutiques that abound in sophisticated Washington. Her father, while she was with them, had agreed to a generous dress allowance and I am sure she longed to show off all her attractive, elegant new clothes. For her twenty-third birthday it was suggested that she sat for her portrait with one of the foremost artists in the capital and Fay was unable to say no. She posed in an exquisite ball gown, looking fragile and serene.'

'Her picture was hung in the hallway of her parents' home and she swiftly became the toast of the Washington elite. A heady situation for an impoverished university student's wife who had been forced to cook, clean and be in charge of two boisterous children in a small terraced house. Her social life had been non-existent in England and now she had a full calendar and many friends.'

'So how did you persuade her to return home?' I queried.

'I tried everything I could think of, including an appeal to her good nature, saying I missed the children and I was certain they missed me. Nothing worked. I began to suspect she had met someone else. Most mornings she would spend horse riding, she would join friends for lunch and often spent the evenings either playing bridge or going to the theatre or cinema. I am sure she was always escorted and, with the threat of having to watch every penny removed, I am certain she would have been blooming and her good humour restored. She was probably her old ebullient self. In desperation, I appealed to her father. He refused to discuss it, saying anything she chose to do was fine by him and his wife. I knew her mother would be even more adamant on the subject so I didn't bother trying. They adored their daughter and doted on their grandchildren so my demands were ignored completely.'

'So, what *did* you do?'

'Nothing. I knew I couldn't take on the whole of the Foreign Office so I simmered and fumed. Eventually the Americans came to my aid. One has only a certain amount of time in their country if you state you are only there for a holiday, on entry. Her time ran out and Fay was forced to return home. I am only guessing at this, but her parents could have possibly sorted the whole issue out and, if she had been willing to divorce me, they might have been able to erase a diplomatic blot on the family's unblemished record. But, without her agreeing to this extreme course, she could not have returned to the family fold and I know her father would not have broken the law unless she had been willing to cooperate. I gather at no time has she ever wanted that – so I won!'

'Did her parents never like you?' I queried. And, if not, why on earth had they encouraged the marriage, I wondered.

'Oh it wasn't like that at all. When Fay was wildly determined to marry me they had no objections at all. Their beloved daughter was the centre of their universe. In fact they were delighted for her and hustled us both to tie the knot. And, to be fair, they never showed the slightest animosity to me whatsoever. What they thought in private was another matter but their demeanour was always disguised by a pleasant, urbane courtesy.'

'Anyway, she returned home in a fury, thinking I had some hand in her embarrassment Her dislike of me turned glacial. It didn't occur to her that her parents' fear of nepotism had helped to cause this impasse. It was me she blamed. The happy homecoming that I had dreamed of vanished and the only time I was vaguely content was when I was out at my first teaching post or when my two boys were clamouring for me to play with them. I *did* notice, a few weeks after her return, a post card behind the bread bin that began *Cara Mia* and ended with an unreadable signature. It may have been left there deliberately I decided. So, perversely, I ignored it and noticed it had disappeared a few days later. We limped along over Christmas that year as I watched her discontent turn to bitterness. My income always fell short of her demands so she cast around for a more lucrative form of employment. Her eyes alighted on the Army – her father's first career. She learned I could hold a respectable post with them, as a teacher abroad, and constantly nagged me to enquire. So I, once again, agreed to apply to see if the armed services required my teaching expertise. That's how I went off to teach in Hong Kong, Jenny. I accepted the "King's shilling" – "Queen's"now, of course – and began teaching out there almost immediately. Just previous to that my Dad had died so there seemed little reason to remain in the UK. We were both unhappy and I desperately hoped the change of scenery would help our marriage survive and, indeed, it appeared to brighten with the sunshine and the uproar that is Hong Kong.'

Andrew heaved a great sigh and I glanced at the clock. It was past two o'clock. He turned on his side and was asleep almost instantly. I, on the other hand, spent most of the night gazing at the ragged clouds racing across the sharp radiance of the moon.

****

199

The next day we went north on the Fosse Way and found our way to Warwick Castle. The day was cold but sunny and I shivered as we slowly walked across a meadow to see what all the visitors outside the castle were watching so avidly. It was an archery display with a yeoman's commentary. The man who was conducting it was dressed in medieval costume with an earthy, acerbic language to match. He had the crowd roaring with mirth as he poked fun at his monarch *and* his officer-in-charge. Andrew stood behind with his arms wrapped closely about me; I leaned back against him, appreciating his warmth. We then learned the food was awful unless you made friends with the buxom cook and the toilet facilities left much to be desired. He was rude about the French archers' proficiency in battle and how they sometimes twanged their arrows one way and ran the other! I hoped there were not too many of our friends from across the Channel in the audience. Afterwards we were told that British technique had always been far superior to our enemies; and finally he coaxed a few stalwarts to try their hands. That gave his audience an even bigger laugh.

We dragged ourselves away and walked under the Portcullis and through the main gate. From then on we were spoilt for choice. We saw yet another crowd in the distance and followed them across a narrow bridge and the *River Avon*, to visit Fire Island and *The Trebuchet*, a massive wooden structure built to capture a castle. The object was to fling a huge boulder against a castle wall until it crumbled. We watched as the weapon of war was prepared. The crowd stood silent as the tension mounted. Suddenly the arm swung up and an enormous rock came flying through the air and landed with a crump that shuddered the earth under our feet. It was awe inspiring and one could imagine it being used at the siege of Calais and the fear it would have generated as it was drawn into place outside the city walls.

We made our way back towards the castle: there was falconry in one direction and colourful jousting, on huge *Destrier* horses, in another. We watched and winced at the hand-to-hand combat and smelt the mouth-watering smells of the open-air medieval village where food was being cooked in huge black cauldrons over crackling fires. We went inside and found our own mouth-watering food in the restaurant and then it was time to view the castle interior.

What a feast! We followed a lively group of school children around and, in the Great Hall we marvelled at the armoury displays and the huge life-size models of horses. Their sheer size awed me. We peeped into kitchens with spits and ovens big enough to roast an ox. We saw a breathlessly beautiful dining room (with two peacocks peering through the windows like a pair of nosy neighbours), various withdrawing rooms, and the bedrooms of lords, ladies and servants. We saw the lifelike display of Madame Tussaud's waxworks figures and were surprised when the Earl of Warwick spoke. Naturally, everyone lingered close to Henry VIII with his six wives and tried to decide which one was which.

We went again outside and visited The Mound, the oldest part of the castle – built in 1068 on the orders of William the Conqueror. We gazed into the distance and I could just make out Shakespeare's Stratford-on-Avon. I was tired by then and I expected our tour was over but Andrew, ever desirous of a grand finale, declared we were going to sample The Dungeons.

And we did – with a vengeance! Our lady guide obviously followed a routine of patter. It was obviously a tried and successful ploy to choose a man who can take a bit of ribbing and respond to any teasing. She immediately picked on Andrew to be her scapegoat – much to the relief of the rest of us! He amiably made a fool of himself, to everyone else's delight, and we were duly amazed, informed and scared by turns. We stumbled outside absolutely replete with historic tales of heroism and nasty deeds.

On the way back we called into a Craft Fair ostensibly to have a pot of tea. I spied a cache of earrings on the way out and I stopped to admire them. Earrings are a great love of mine, especially those unique to the artist designing them. They don't have to be expensive but they have to enhance the wearer. Drew joined me and then kept presenting me with ones he preferred while I had fixed on a turquoise and silver filigree pair. He certainly was not on my wavelength for once and so I, feeling a bit hard-done-by, said nothing and we left to continue our journey south on the straight-as-an-arrow Roman Fosse Way to Bourton-on-the-Water. On the way back I mused on the revelations he had made about Fay. We are *all* thoughtless at some point in our lives and this incites us to sometimes make mistakes, especially when we have been married for some time and often have busy lives and subsequent preoccupations. I was fully aware I could hardly criticise as I was in a similar position. I found it easy to understand Fay's delight in returning to a life she enjoyed, surrounded by her parents' love and attention as well as the heady excitement that had been lacking in her life since she had married; but it was her calculated and cruel attempt to prevent her sons seeing their father that made me shiver. I had always imagined that, once one accepts the responsibility of children, one's own desires take second place. Apparently this was not so for Andrew's young wife Fay. What amazed me was her parents' acceptance of the situation, even possible encouragement, and her husband's desire to appease her.

We had quite a simple supper as we were both tired. We had enjoyed a long day and I, for one, had a lot to think about. It was quite early as we made our way to bed in our luxurious suite. Andrew, I noticed, made love pensively and I sensed his melancholy thoughts. I tried to be warm and attentive to comfort him, but I was unable to prevent myself discussing what he had revealed the previous night.

'I hate to say this Drew, but when Fay attempted to kidnap your lads and refused to return to you with them, do you think they have remembered any of the drama of what went on at that time?'

'No, I don't think so', he said thoughtfully. 'The nanny her parents employed probably kept them well amused and children are very adaptable, you know. I expect, apart from asking where Daddy was a few times, they would soon have forgotten their very quiet and ordinary life back home. Peter may have fretted a little but Mark would have been too young to have understood, or to have missed York.'

'What about the *Cara Mia* postcard from Washington that you discovered?' Like a dog gnawing a bone, I was unable to leave it alone. 'Did Fay ever mention it? And did you ever admit you found it?'

'No, what was the point, Jenny? Fay was already brittle with annoyance at being embarrassingly turfed out of the States and to cause any more waves would be courting disaster, and my little lads didn't need any more upheaval in their lives. What was more to the point; whoever the foreigner was, Fay had obviously encouraged him. I was unable to blame him for trying and anyway there was the whole of the Atlantic between them and I knew my wife was not the best correspondent – so I expect they soon lost touch.'

And with that I had to be satisfied. I turned on my side and drifted into a deep sleep. The next morning – as it was our last day – we were up early. Over breakfast Andrew mapped out his plans for us for the day. He suggested we explore Bourton itself and then go off to the nearby Upper and Lower Slaughters and walk from one to the other. In the evening it had been recommended we watch the sun go down over the Vale of Evesham. The hotel receptionist said it was a popular destination and our waiter suggested a decent restaurant. I threw a slight spanner in the works by pleading to return to the craft fair we had visited the previous day. I then had to admit I had really wanted those unusual turquoise and silver earrings. Andrew looked at me in amazement. I could see he would normally have been exasperated if anyone else had admitted they liked something and yet had done nothing about it. Perversely, I had wanted him to sense my interest and buy them for me. When he didn't, I just turned away. How stupid was that? Robin, of course, knew me so well he would have half-expected me to do this very thing. I knew that Andrew was immediately contrite at not guessing my wishes. He put his hand on my back and motioned me to the car. All the way back, he grumbled incessantly about "women who can't make up their minds and women who waste petrol on unnecessary journeys". I just nudged him good humouredly until he finally stopped glowering and burst out laughing. My main worry was that the fair had been a one-day event but luckily, as we pulled up at the hall, I saw people wandering in and out. My next concern was maybe I would be unlucky and my precious earrings had been sold. No, they were there nestling in their little silver box. Andrew purchased them and put them carefully into my hands saying, 'Well that was a pleasant forty-mile round trip. Jolly expensive jewellery, I must say.'

The rest of the day went as planned. On our return we wandered along beside the banks of the shallow *River Windrush* and strolled across the low bridge with the rest of the Sunday crowds. We stared in antique shops and sat in the sun on the grassy sward and licked delicious ice creams. We tossed up between Birdland or The Model Village and the village won. We picked our way between the 1930s, perfectly scaled down, reproduction of the village all in golden Cotswold stone. We marvelled at the unbelievable detail. The shops, the gardens, the roofs, the local church, complete with music, the river, even a turning waterwheel.

We then went, finally, to Lower Slaughter and followed the same *River Windrush* towards its twin village of Upper Slaughter. What two perfectly awful names, I thought, and what a beautiful leisurely stroll it turned out to be. It is only a mile or so between two of the loveliest villages in this part of England; but the shady trees, grass and softly gurgling water make it a heavenly lovers' ramble. The crowds had disappeared and we had the peaceful place to ourselves. We walked with our arms entwined, cocooned in happiness.

We made our way back to the waiting car and found Lower Swell where we had a pint and a pasty at their local pub. We sat inside and I thrashed Andrew at dominoes. This was to teach him that I might often find it difficult to make my mind up about certain things – but I'm still mustard at dominoes!

We returned to our hotel and, while Andrew sought directions to the restaurant they had recommended, I dressed carefully for our last dinner together. I showered, perfumed and creamed my body and chose clothes that perfectly complemented my delightful turquoise and silver filigree earrings. When we slipped out of the hotel later, I felt like a million dollars and I am sure my mischievous grin said it all. Drew eyed me appreciatively as he shepherded me towards his car.

It was the most perfect evening – he couldn't have stage-managed it better – and I have no idea where we visited: I was on a dreamy cloud all that night. We began with an aperitif that the waiter brought out to us on their sheltered veranda as we watched the sun go down in a hazy glowing ball of fire, across the Vale of Evesham and the Malvern Hills. We then went inside the restaurant to a sumptuous three-course meal. We ate with our heads close together as we talked about all the lovely places we had visited in such a short space of time and all the exciting things we had seen. *The Trebuchet* fascinated Andrew the most – I think it was the awesome noise of a huge rock being catapulted at such enormous speed and distance – but he also spoke of our walk from Lower to Upper Slaughter and said it would remain in his memory forever.

I admitted I enjoyed Warwick Castle's Dungeons most, especially to hear Drew being teased unmercifully and loving every moment of it; but the place I knew I would always remember was our stroll in the sunshine across the common to Anne Hathaway's cottage. For some reason, since we were in our teens we had both been in tune with each other's likes and dislikes; we had always enjoyed each other's company and now we had met again, nothing appeared to have changed. It was a great temptation to imagine this would always be the case and I was apprehensive as to where this would lead us.

As soon as we arrived back at the hotel I rang Robin, as I had remembered to every evening, and informed him I would be returning home the next day. He asked me if I had enjoyed myself and I admitted I had. He sounded warmly interested and I felt a great flush of guilt at his concern. To change the subject, I quickly asked how *his* work was progressing and suddenly I had the impression he sounded more carefree. He said there should soon be news and with that we ended our conversation.

Fay was not the subject of our talk that night. She had invaded our precious space long enough, I decided. And so we talked of days gone by; of Polruan and boats; of rowing across the harbour to Fowey when there wasn't a breath of wind to hoist a sail; of swimming out of Ready Money Cove and racing up the alleyways of steps above the town. Of sitting down at the Boatyard to a scratch lunch that Deborah would provide. We would all be hungry and it would be a case of grabbing a freshly baked roll, splitting it open, stuffing it with ham or cheese and munching it with tomatoes from the garden. There was always a huge bowl of seasonal fruit on the side with a large jug of cider to wash it all down. For the first ten minutes or so we would all be intent on satisfying our appetites, but gradually we would relax. Mark and Hugh would inform their Dad of any Boatyard gossip, Andrew might be joining in but often kept his own counsel, Deborah would often instil a bit of common sense or settle an argument while I would shyly add the occasional comment – but only when asked.

'You used to say very little at those family meals, Drew. I'd see you tying incessant nautical knots with the piece of string you always carried in your pocket - but what were you really thinking about?' I asked.

'Often I was back on the *Arethusa*, Jenny. I missed the comradeship even though it was a hard life when I first started. Did you know I begged to be allowed to go on her? No one in the family liked the idea, especially as it was for poor boys really. Boys from broken homes, boys whose fathers had died and their mothers were finding it difficult to raise them, naughty boys who had the choice of that or Borstal. It had been the brainchild of a William Williams as far back as 1843. He had spoken to some young lads on a train bound for deportation to a Penal Colony in Australia. He started asking questions and it appeared most had committed only minor misdeeds, usually to feed their starving families, yet they knew that, once in Australia, they would never see them again or be allowed to return to England. Williams was so troubled that he spoke to his best friend, Lord Shaftesbury, who was the youngest MP in Parliament at that time and they devised a plan to halt this drain on Britain's starving young poor. They purchased old sailing ships, vessels that had seen out their time, and placed them around the coast at such places like Newcastle, Plymouth and near the Thames. Places where poverty and overcrowding was endemic and opportunity for improvement was lacking. All over this country philanthropic men, often Quakers with a conscience, have done something similar down through the years – in such places like York, Bournville and Port Sunlight. They considered the poor were no different from themselves – just unfortunate. It was a very novel idea and Lord Shaftesbury in the 1800s, was one of the first. He stopped small boys having to climb chimneys, he shortened working hours for women and children in mills and mines, he even went as far to provide affordable housing. And his Acts of Parliament made sure this was cemented in law and could not be overturned by rich men who were making fortunes. As a small boy, I read about him in our public Reading Room back home and, burning with fire and zeal, I wanted to be part of his legacy.'

I was quite swept away by his enthusiasm. I nodded and said, 'Well go on then, what exactly happened? You've often spoken vaguely about those days but you have never told me exactly how it was.'

'I suppose I was a bit cocky as I had just passed to go to Grammar

School. All I could think was, if I got bogged down in this elite educational system in Fowey, no one – and certainly not my Dad – would allow me to leave and spend time on a Boys' Training Ship. It had become my dream by then so I decided to strike while the iron was hot. Somehow I pleaded until I managed to get Mark and Hugh, but more importantly Deborah, on my side. Eventually my father agreed to let me try, with the proviso that, if it proved unsuitable, after one term I would return and resume my studying in Cornwall.

'I went up to Kent in the September of that year. I changed trains a few times, completely alone, and arrived early one evening at a Kentish station called Strood. All the other passengers alighted and went their merry way until there was only me and another young lad lingering forlornly on the windy platform. That's how I met Rod. His given name was Roderick, but he always threatened to thump anyone who called him that – so none of us ever did! I sympathised, as I thought Andrew was a bit prissy and much preferred Andy.'

'We stood there and stared at each other. Later, I learned this was a test of initiative: the staff made a point of never meeting any train or conducting anyone to their new berths on the *Arethusa*. We hesitantly asked, and the Station Master directed us to the nearby bus stop.'

'Two eleven-year-olds travelling alone – unheard of today – but we did it. And from that moment Rod and I were firm friends. We fought off older, seasoned boys together – once standing back to back on the deck, throwing punches as six older lads taunted us, while threatening to dump us overboard in the river. That was a favourite pastime so, soon after I arrived, I started swimming classes for the non-swimmers, until throwing scared lads overboard from the top deck wasn't half as much fun as it had once been. I'd always been able to swim like a fish and I taught as many as wanted.'

'It was a tough life. Reveille was blown on a bugle at crack of dawn. We slept in hammocks and rolled out immediately it sounded or the *Nozzers* were roughly tipped onto the deck. They often had us scrubbing the decks, the old-fashioned way, with salt stone blocks and seawater, followed afterwards by physical jerks to get our blood singing – that's when we weren't doing lessons. We always called the ship *The 'Are* (as in 'Arry without an H). She'd originally been named the SS *Peking* but then all the training ships in the fleet were re- christened TS *Arethusa* and we were so proud of her. She was a four-masted steel barque and was berthed on the western bank of the river near Upnor Castle. Sadly, in 1975 she was sold, taken to the Seaport Museum in New York and the River Medway lost a stirring bit of history. But our most exciting times were when we "Dressed the Ship Overall". It was always for a special occasion like when the Commander of the Nore would slowly pass by, with great pomp and ceremony, to salute and review us or the various open days when all our friends and relatives would visit and we would entertain them. We would always proudly climb the masts and line the yardarms. It was truly a magnificent, breathtaking sight.'

'I suppose it was a hard regime but I loved it. Some lads hated every moment of it and escaped back to their homes again and again. I was in my element just messing around in boats and absorbing all things nautical. Most of the lads who felt like me joined the Royal or Merchant Navy, or ended up in other branches of the armed services. A few joined the Army or Royal Marines and in my time two went to the RAF. Rod and I, when we were older, managed to join the local yacht club. We used to hang around the Club House and helped berth or cast off the odd dinghy – until one day an ebullient family, whose house happened to overlook the *Arethusa*, took pity on us and invited us aboard their lovely sea-going yacht. From then on we often crewed for them over a free weekend and loved every moment of it.'

'I stayed until I was sixteen. That's when we met, Jenny, just before I was due to start my Merchant Naval training at Plymouth Polytechnic. Living in Kent gave me the best memories of my life and, even though I enjoyed being back home with my family in the West Country once more, when we met I was poised to train as a Radio Officer, join a ship and "see the world".'

I leaned back against the pillows and snuggled against him. So I had snagged him in passing and then lost him again six years later. It all made sense now and I once again bitterly regretted my childish actions at that time. I settled down and shortly we were both asleep – worn out with honest revelations on his part and a deeper understanding on mine.

The next morning arrived all too quickly. I felt groggy from trying to absorb all of Andrew's early history and slightly grumpy that our perfect idyll was shortly coming to an end. We both ate breakfast in a thoughtful silence and I stood ready to leave as our baggage was transferred to the car by willing hands. We then started the short journey back to the market town of Evesham. We were early, as usual, and sat on Evesham Station like a couple of refugees awaiting transportation. We clung to each other and spoke low, hurried words together that neither cheered nor satisfied us. Finally a clean, bright train swished into the station and we swiftly exchanged one last hug and one lingering kiss before everyone bounced aboard and I was left, trying not to cry, peering at Andrew through a shining pane of glass as he disappeared into the distance.

I can remember nothing about the journey; it became a sorry blur. I arrived home several hours later to be greeted by an empty house but lots of news – some good, some anticipated and some awfully sad. But all of it gave me food for thought.

Chapter 11

*

I walked into my empty bungalow feeling bereft, tired and dejected. I was beginning to recognise this sorry state and knew it was the result of having had such a happy time with Andrew. I went into the kitchen and made myself a reviving drink before sitting down and checking my flashing answerphone. I had various messages. The most interesting was from Robin who sounded upbeat and happy. He said he had some good news but it would keep until the next day. I wondered why he had not tried my mobile when I was travelling but maybe he had and found there was no signal. I looked across at the clock. It was too late to disturb him and so I curbed my impatience and forced my fingers to refrain from dialling his number. There were various messages from both Lorna and Margaret, all roughly giving me similar news. I listened grimly to their sad tidings.

Mr Montague had died in his sleep two nights previously. He had left us as he had lived - quietly and without fuss. I mourned the gentle man. We had met his wife when Robin and I first came to reside in Honiton. She had been in poor health at that time and he had tended her considerately and lovingly. When she faded away he became a shadow of his former self and appeared to settle down to a life of waiting. Well now he had joined her, I surmised. The funeral was to be at the end of that week and I was thankful I had returned in time and was able to attend.

The second batch of messages concerned Fred. Grumbling, irascible Fred had moaned once too often. His daughter and son-in-law had decided enough was enough and had arranged for him to go into a local care home. His younger daughter was living in New

Zealand and obviously she had *also* been fed up with hearing his grievances every time she made an expensive telephone call home. She had been in complete agreement with her family and poor old Fred hadn't stood a chance. One of the messages was from him and I listened while he complained and groused about his usual tribulations and said sharply that if I had been there the family would have not have dared to, 'Kidnap me and force me into an awful home'. I felt guilty because there was probably some truth in the accusation. I promised myself I would take the car and go and visit him first thing the next day.

I slept badly that night. I was aware that the original ten people in our close had been whittled down by half and that in future there would be little for me to do by way of shopping and helping the ones who were left. Feeling pretty useless was not a state I relished. I was sure I would feel happier and more content when new blood had arrived and I once again had neighbours to pass the time of day with, and possibly, share a morning cuppa.

Margaret and Lorna had kept their news blessedly short but I still felt, at the back of their messages, there was a latent questioning about where I had been recently – and why. My conscience was gnawing at me and I longed to explain to one of them about Andrew and me; but I knew Rose was the only loyal confidante I had ever had and there was no way I could burden either friend with such a dilemma.

The next morning I arranged flowers for Mr Montague's funeral and then went straight on to visit Fred in his new abode. I was shown into the lounge quietly, without Fred catching a glimpse of me, and immediately saw him waving the local paper in the air and arguing loudly with the man sitting next to him. Good old Fred, I thought; he was doing what he loved best – annoying everyone around him. I turned to the carer and said I hoped they could manage him as he could be a bit exuberant. She gave me a wise smile and I guessed they had dealt with much worse. Reassured, I put my hands on his shoulders and gave him a swift kiss from behind. He glanced up but didn't stop his tirade so I knew he was fast settling into his new environment.

I had bought him some boiled sweets and a bar of chocolate, which he put carefully on his table along with his glass of water and newly discarded newspaper. I dragged a chair around so I could sit in front of him and then spent the next half hour hearing about the shortcomings of the staff (I hoped they weren't listening!) and the few brief visits he had received since his "incarceration". I gently remonstrated with him after he admitted his daughter had been in twice before they returned to their home in Somerset and that both Petra and Megan had come in after school, accompanied by their mothers. Luckily I was able to escape as soon as the morning drinks trolley was brought round and left the room immediately before Fred realised there were only shortbreads on offer and no digestive biscuits. I could hear his muted complaints all along the corridor and I smiled ruefully as I let myself out of the heavy front door.

I had waited in vain for Robin to telephone me first thing that morning. I felt slightly hard done by: I had spent the past few days being cosseted and demonstrably loved and suddenly no one seemed to care. I decided if this news was so important why hadn't he bothered to contact me? I had listened carefully for the phone while I showered and ate my breakfast. I even kept my mobile on while I visited Fred. Maybe it wasn't such good news after all and he was wary of telling me. The rest of the day I spent shoving washing in the machine, going to the library and taking Crumble for a long walk up on the Common. I hoped it made up for him being left alone with Rex and Petra instead of me. He gambolled happily across the grass and burrowed under the low furze to find non-existent rabbit holes, so I guessed his world hadn't been too disrupted. In fact, with Rex to play with and Petra on hand for lots of walks, he probably hadn't missed me at all.

I was making myself a huge sandwich when Robin finally kept his promise. After the lovely meals I had enjoyed on my mini-break I couldn't be bothered to cook anything special, as I would be eating alone. I had just placed a bowl of soup, my sandwich and a large mug of tea on a tray to take into the living room when the telephone finally did ring. I shoved the tray back on the kitchen worktop and ran to answer it. Robin sounded as warm and nice as ever and I felt slightly ashamed of my earlier grumpiness. He started asking about the Cotswolds. As usual, I was pretty reticent about recounting even more lies so I was relieved when he told me his news.

'I should be home within the next three weeks, Jenny,' Robin informed me. 'Everyone has worked really hard and the results finally came thick and fast. I don't think anyone wants to stay longer than necessary up here. Although we have been treated fairly decently, they must hate being investigated by another force and unfortunately we were from various forces so they must feel even more open to gossip and innuendo.'

I settled back against the settee cushions to take it all in. Naturally I was relieved Robin would be returning soon; but the thought of relinquishing those soft midnight chats from Andrew every night left me feeling forlorn and lost. How stupid was that? I had a kind and loving husband so why would I yearn for another soul mate, and at my age? And what were Andrew's intentions as far as he and I were concerned? How far was he prepared to take this affair? Did he want a full-scale liaison or was it just a sudden fling that would finish as soon as one of us became tired of it? Robin must have heard the hesitation and doubt in my voice because he suddenly became quiet.

"Are you still there, Jenny?' he asked.

I cleared my throat and marshalled my thoughts. 'Yes, I'm still here. Of course I'm delighted with your good news. As soon as you get back we must celebrate with a grand party. And it will certainly be nice to relinquish the gardening to you – *and* the window cleaning. Give me a break.' I then went on to tell him about Mr Montague's death and Fred's banishment. He laughed at the thought of Fred causing mayhem in his new home and we reverted to ordinary gossip about our friends and neighbours.

****

When the telephone rang on my bedside table well after midnight I lay and stared at it for a few moments; but choice is a two edged sword and I couldn't resist answering it. What would I say, I wondered? As usual, within seconds my truthfulness got the better of me and I was giving Andrew an update on my news. He was silent for a short while and I found myself flushing with embarrassment. Did he think I was trying to force him to reveal his true feelings for me? Did he imagine I would coerce him into saying something he might later regret? I had no intention of forcing myself on him under those circumstances. Our lovely times together were so precious and they would soon come to an end. Could I bear that? Once Robin was back I knew I would rarely be alone again. I had become used to being with a lover who was exciting, great fun and who, for some obscure reason, adored me. A pint of lager would describe Robin, as opposed to a flute of bubbling champagne that would depict Andrew. I became alive with Andrew, while feeling only comfortable with Robin. I craved for one and sadly not the other. I longed to be touched, I found I responded to stimulation and I was wanton and bold as I had never been before in my life. Once I had been stagnating gently and now I was alive with unexplored sensations. I wanted Andrew more at every meeting and died a little at every departure. I knew I loved Robin warmly, but with Drew I felt a dangerous yearning. Would I ever be able to return again to my simple Devon routine? Would my savage tumult be obvious to everyone – including my husband? I waited fearfully to see what Andrew's response would be.

His Cornish burr warmed and comforted me. 'Jenny, please don't tell me this is the end for us. I don't know what has happened, but I am unable to carry on my life without thinking of you constantly. Every waking moment you are in the forefront of my mind – as I drop off to sleep at night and as soon as I open my eyes every morning. I dream of you and wish it were reality. It is like a forest fire. I keep expecting it to abate but it grows fiercer the more we speak and the more we are together. I touch you casually and then immediately want to hug you closely. Every second of every day I want to take you to bed and bury myself in the sweetness that is you. I can't get enough of you. I keep pleading for one more meeting but I am an addict who is never satisfied. Please help me, Jenny, as I really don't know what to do.'

I breathed a sigh of relief. So it wasn't just me and my vivid imagination. Andrew felt just as I did and, like him, I had no idea what to do about it. We whispered far into the night and eventually agreed to one last meeting. Neither of us cared where it was – that was immaterial. We decided on London and Andrew said he would book somewhere suitable within the next few days. I agreed, feeling guilty and joyous all at the same time. I slept very little in the few hours that remained of that night and awoke the next morning feeling heavy-eyed and lethargic.

As I was pushing my muesli around in its bowl the next morning, the telephone shrilled. I expected it to be Robin and shrunk a little at answering it. But it was Lorna sounding slightly brisk and businesslike. Would I meet her in Sidmouth for a light meal that lunchtime? I was delighted to agree. There was little for me to do most days with half of our close empty and it was a relief to have some definite plan as to how I would spend my day. We met in a favourite, cosy restaurant where they served home-made meals with a motherly attention.

I sat and nursed a glass of cold white wine. Lorna sat opposite me with her usual glass of rosé. Our conversation was a bit stilted as we waited for our salmon cutlets to be served. The music was nostalgic '50s and quietly soporific. I drifted off in a reverie – probably due to so little sleep. Lorna brought me back with a jerk.

'Are you OK, Jenny? I feel you have lost weight and I wonder if anything is worrying you? We have seen so little of you recently and I keep thinking you are ill. You aren't, are you, darling?' I shook my head and tried a smile. 'Well something is up – I feel it. You hardly ever come round to see us now. We catch a glimpse of you in passing and you'll often wave – then disappear. The kids used to spend half their time with you but they rarely talk of you now. Petra and Megan mooch around bored and, when I suggest them trotting round to see you, they mumble you are probably out – and I wonder where their favourite auntie is off to this time.'

I hung my head in shame. It was impossible to confide in Lorna, good friend as she had always been, so I made up a load of placating lies and switched the chat to the homecoming of Robin. I could see I had almost convinced her as we discussed a party for the "prodigal" on his return. I also promised to do her cleaning at the church that week as she wanted to start her Christmas shopping without her daughter in tow. I had literally forgotten the season of goodwill was imminent and managed to turn the conversation to presents and suitability. I could imagine her going home and telephoning her best friend Margaret with the reassuring news that I was fine and we had enjoyed a fruitful lunch.

That night Andrew rang on the stroke of midnight to say he had booked us into a decent hotel in Kensington for a few days. I guessed I would be "visiting" my cousins Dee and Paul and wondered how I could do it without Robin realising that I would actually be residing in a far different part of London. Looking back, maybe we should thank our lucky stars that mobile phones have been invented. They may often be a curse but they can also be a great lifesaver when one is desperate.

I honoured my promise to Lorna and did my stint at our church the next day. None of the cleaning was difficult and only entailed a duster and some spray polish after a general tidy round. Luckily, I was alone and able to scoot around and not get entangled in an afternoon session of tea and biscuits with gossip and a few laughs thrown in – as so often happens with my easy-going friends. I then filled up the freezer and made the bungalow look respectable before I rustled up some clothes to take with me to London.

The next day I caught an early train for Waterloo and arrived on a dusty concourse three hours later. Andrew, as promised, was waiting under the main clock and we grinned mischievously as we fulfilled the classic rendezvous of lovers. We caught the Underground to Earl's Court and then dragged our cases across the busy road and into a quiet, typical square surrounded by large cream-coloured houses that once housed the affluent middle-class citizens of London. We were ushered upstairs to our room which overlooked the square's rectangular garden. A few trees and some grass were enclosed by wrought iron railings and an ornate gate and, at one time, this must have made the inhabitants feel as if they had their own private bit of countryside on their doorstep. I could imagine Victorian and Edwardian nannies pushing their charges around the square, unlocking the gate and meeting under the shade of the trees on summer afternoons. It was all pleasant and quiet and belied the bustle of the Brompton Road and Earl's Court Road a few hundred yards away.

Andrew snuggled me in his arms as soon as the door closed behind our affable porter and we christened the comfortable bed immediately. But we both knew our time was short and, after taking a quick shower and composing ourselves, we made our way towards Hyde Park and the museums. I was given the choice and decided on the V&A first to be followed by a change of scene at the Brompton

Oratory. I had no idea of the size and complexity of the V&A so, after studying the floor plans and turning down a free guided tour, I chose the Henry Cole Wing because it gave me the chance to see the Frank Lloyd Wright Gallery – mainly because I adore his 1930s architecture. We then went on to gaze at some exquisite Holbein and Hilliard portrait miniatures followed by a plethora of John Constable paintings – all of which I had never dreamed of ever viewing. I was ecstatic and, with a contented smile, Andrew drew me towards rooms containing Spitalfield's silks, Hugenot silver, delicate carvings in a pale lime wood by Grinling Gibbons, huge Chippendale furniture, rooms by Robert Adam that took my breath away and paintings by Angela Kauffmann and Gainsborough. As soon as he could see I had had a surfeit of beauty and design he took me away for sustenance. We went to the V&A café and I gratefully rested my feet as I ate, drank and tried to talk at the same time. I had had no idea of the vastness of this one museum and I longed to take a quick glance at everything. Andrew gently explained that was physically impossible so, when we were both filled and rested, he took me next door to The Brompton Oratory.

I had no idea what to expect as it was a place I had only heard and read about. It appears I had chosen London's most flamboyant Roman Catholic Church. Begun in 1880 by a young architect called Herbert Gribble and filled with Italian Baroque treasures that normally one would only find on the Continent, I immediately fell in love with its soaring beauty, its pungent smell of glorious incense and its sheer atmosphere.

We walked back to our hotel with our arms around each other as we both spoke of the happiest afternoon I had ever spent. Andrew took me to a nearby tiny bistro for our evening meal. Each table had a glowing, dark red, shaded lamp which made it an island of intimacy. As we sank a bottle of red wine which accompanied the most perfectly cooked French food I had ever tasted, I tried to thank Andrew for a most marvellous day. My life back in Devon was mostly unvaried and pretty mundane, so this unfolding London panorama of beauty, inventions and ideas was a revelation to me. That day I had visited just two interesting and varied places and my ignorance made me feel very humble. I knew there was so much more just waiting out there for me to explore – for us both to explore. Not just in London but all over the country – all over the world. Some people glance casually but do not see; others long wistfully for what might be out there and yet never get a chance to reach out for it; and yet others get the opportunity and catch hold of it with both hands. I wanted to belong to that third category. I also wanted to ask Andrew what he wanted from life and what he precisely wanted from me. He never spoke about Fay or their relationship. He had shown me some photographs of his comfortable home, set on the outskirts of York, and he had spoken glowingly about his sons and their children, who all lived on the other side of the Pennines, but he had never mentioned anything of his day-to-day family life. I knew he played golf, roamed extensively across Yorkshire in his car, walked a lot, explored every museum, stately home and worthwhile church in every town he visited and made sure he saw the latest films, shows and entertainment on offer. That was the sum total of my knowledge of him and his life. Presumably he lived with his wife but he never mentioned her and it was as if she didn't exist. I wanted to know the structure of their partnership as so much seemed to be missing – and I knew this was the perfect time to ask.

I had my opportunity as soon as we returned to the hotel and our spacious room. We both showered and sank gratefully into bed. It had been a long and exciting day but now I needed to talk and ask all those questions that had been building up in my subconscious for the past few months. I now had the perfect opportunity.

Andrew held me tenderly in his arms. 'Drew,' I murmured as he went to draw me closer, 'I want to know about you and Fay. You never speak of her unless I ask a specific question. What does she say about you leaving her so often? Does she not know, or care, where you go? What excuses do you offer when you go off for days at a time? And where are you when you telephone me so late every night? Does she not live with you now? Do you have separate households? I find it all excessively puzzling. I don't know anyone who lives like this. None of my friends would comprehend this way of life and I need to know the truth before I make an even bigger mess of my own life.' *There, I had said it.* I settled back to listen to his reply.

'Jenny, I have been scared and yet longing for you to ask me about my odd life. I will try to answer all your questions. I will also attempt to put it into context – how it all happened and how I see it. We have a large and lovely home. It's modern and set amongst many others of its size and type. My neighbours are charming, mainly affluent and I am comfortable with them. I have lived there many years and Fay and I have built a suitable life within the community. She has her girlfriends – mostly divorced or widowed – and they designer-shop avidly, play bridge seriously and lunch often. I, on the other hand, meet with my men friends at our clubs and pubs, play golf and take myself off – usually alone – to explore, paint or simply wander. Fay and I present a united front to the world, our family and our neighbours. We attend social events together, we host dinner parties and attend many others. We visit the theatre together but usually I go to the cinema alone as we share a different taste in films. We see our children occasionally, but only at my instigation. Fay seldom suggests us going over to visit them but, once it is planned, she accedes with good grace. If, on the other hand, I invite them to come for a short holiday with us, as long as it doesn't clash with any previous engagement of hers, she accepts and makes them welcome. We have a lovely time and I always wonder why I don't suggest it more.'

I stirred impatiently. I felt Andrew was not getting to the crux of the matter. He was talking vaguely around what I wanted, and needed to know. What about the relationship between Fay and himself? I went to ask him but he forestalled me.

'OK I know what you are longing to ask. What about Fay and me? Well, to put it baldly, we lead two separate lives. We live in the same house. Luckily it is fairly large so it is possible. We have separate bedrooms; mine incorporates my study. I have built en-suite bathrooms to each, so we never need to come in contact with each other. We rise at different times. I do the dutiful husband bit and take her in a cup of tea every morning and, apart from pulling her curtains back, I leave her alone until lunchtime. I shower and have my breakfast with the cat before going off to get the morning papers. I do things that need doing – like cutting the lawns or trimming shrubs – but mostly I look at the calendar and, if I am not needed, take myself off to amuse myself for the day. If I am around she provides lunch for me but, other than that, she also does her own thing. We shop together, if necessary, or, if she has a previous engagement, she presents me with a list the previous evening and I go and do her bidding the next day.

'It's all good clean fun, Jenny. Most evenings she provides a meal at six o'clock on the dot and, while I clear away and shove everything in the dishwasher, she takes herself off to her sitting room and plays games on her computer, often until past midnight. She downs innumerable glasses of wine – I try not to notice, or count, how many – and then makes her way to bed when it suits her.'

I went to speak once more but he held up his hand to stop me.

'Please let me finish what I was saying. I feel if I don't get it all off my chest now, I will never dare speak of it again.' He continued, 'When I have completed my chores, and made the kitchen look presentable, I go into our other sitting room, flop down in front of my own television, close the door and take myself off to bed when it suits me. And shall I tell what is really amusing, Jenny? We often choose the same programme! I can sometimes hear it through the wall. In the beginning I would wander through – ask her if she wanted a coffee or something – and she would barely look up from her clicking fingers and distractedly nod towards her usual brimming glass of red wine. If I sat on the arm of her chair she would pointedly sigh and I would usually beat a hasty retreat.'

'I know she drinks too much; I also know she has an unhealthy obsession with the same game. Her goal seems to be to outwit a machine. She usually starts straight after lunch, stops while she cooks and serves dinner, and then goes on until the small hours. When she occasionally wins, instead of being satisfied, she will start another game immediately and go back to being immersed in her tactics. The whole time the television plays in the background. I have tried coming in and asking if I can watch another programme, such as football or athletics, with her but she insists I don't touch it. And all the time her head is bent over the laptop keyboard.'

'Does this happen every night?' I was aghast at the thought of a married couple sitting within feet of each other and yet, for hours, having no communication whatsoever.

'Pretty much, unless we go out with friends or have them at our place for the evening. When that happens, she gets herself ready and then goes straight back to her laptop and doesn't stop until there is a ring at the doorbell. Then she is all smiles and welcoming or she calmly picks up her handbag and walks out of our house to join them.'

'How long has this been going on for?' I asked. 'You say she has lots of girlfriends. Is she like this with them as well?'

'Good grief - she is a different person with them. The phone will ring and she will giggle and laugh while planning shopping sprees, bridge parties or girlie lunches. It must be ten or fifteen years since she first took an interest in computers; and it was shortly after this her game-playing began. Strangely enough, every new fad, and there have been a few, has developed a compulsive element – but it is her excessive drinking that worries me the most.'

I had one last question that was burning a hole in my tongue. 'But how do you manage to ring me every night without her hearing?'

'It's simple, my dear. We haven't slept together for years. Eating together we are chaperoned by either the lunchtime or early evening television news, so we rarely need to speak. Our lives are almost completely separate. When I retire to bed I don't even bid her goodnight. I could speak to you all night, if we so wished; she cannot hear and probably couldn't care less if she could! I make golfing, or some previous commitments, my excuse if I want to get away. She barely registers my explanations and I am given carte blanche. She obviously stopped loving me years ago and her coldness has killed off any love I might have felt in return. I am sure she feels she has her reasons, but I have long ceased to question those reasons. So that's it, darling, the sorry tale that is my life. Are you now able to imagine how my heart lifted when I heard your warm voice on our answerphone all those months ago?'

I sat back and tried to absorb all the revelations Andrew must have been hiding for years. I found it difficult to understand how anyone could live under these circumstances. It would have been impossible for *me* to carry on in such a way and if my relationship with Robin had sunk to this sorry state of affairs, I would have insisted we discuss the situation and then, if no solution was reached, I would have demanded we live apart until such time we sorted out our differences or divorced.

When I asked Andrew how he had allowed it to happen, he shrugged. What did his sister-in-law, Deborah, and Hugh, his brother in the States, think? He admitted he had always kept the true state of affairs well hidden from his loved ones. And his children – were they aware?

'They grew up in a permanent state of tension – Fay was never the easiest to please – and they probably accepted our family situation from an early age. I always tried to keep the peace, by doing mostly what Fay wanted, and as a family we must have appeared fairly normal to anyone else. Now they have families of their own and they probably neither know nor care that nothing has changed in our relationship.'

That night I slept fitfully. Questions and Andrew's explanations buzzed around in my head. Looking back, I now know that moment was the turning point in our affair. Suddenly it was personal. My best friend and lover had been deeply hurt and humiliated. This was not just a family tiff - it had been going on for years. I was incensed and furious with a woman I hadn't even met. Up until then I had been an onlooker: abruptly my viewpoint switched and I became an indignant defender – Andrew's furious champion. His war became my war and, sadly, from that moment on Robin, and my marriage, took a back seat.

The next morning I looked tired and pale but, as Andrew didn't look much better, we decided to get out and do some of the exploring we had promised ourselves when we first made our plans. Neither of us had ever visited the British Museum. I am sure there are lots more popular places that head any London visitor's *wish list* but, to my mind, this was the hub that held the key to all things British. I felt this place encapsulated all that we hold most dear and I longed to see it for myself. But, before we lost ourselves in its archives I wanted to take a quick peek at Sir John Soane's Museum near Lincoln's Inn. The Inns of Court were another area I had never visited, along with Dickens' Old Curiosity Shop near The Royal College of Surgeons. Here was my opportunity.

We travelled by Underground to Holborn and walked down Kingsway. The museum faces Lincoln's Inn Fields, the city's largest square, laid out in the 1640s. After the uproar of the main road this was a haven of peace and quiet. We were welcomed into an elegant hallway and it felt like a hushed, select private home and not like a public museum at all. Sir John Soane was the son of a bricklayer and eventually rose to be architect of the Bank of England. On the way he collected an intriguing mixture of art and antiquities. Everywhere was crammed with surprises from underground crypts and cloisters where we found tombstones dedicated to his wife and son, cantilevered stairs, domes and skylights to hidden racks of pictures hiding more false walls and more pictures. There were cameos and miniatures alongside statues of every kind and racks of convex mirrors. All this was squeezed into an elegant home of the 1800s. Every corner was a surprise, every family room a revelation of good taste. It was a mixture of the working environment of a man with far-ranging interests, a collection of eclectic works of art and a graceful town house. We loved it and were loath to leave. But leave it we did, to enable us to visit the pinnacle of my ambition – The British Museum.

Time was passing, so as we left Lincoln's Inn Fields we asked a passer-by to direct us towards the British Museum. With a smile, as I take it this question is posed constantly by visitors, he instructed us to take the *scenic* route. So we made our way back towards Holborn Underground station and crossed over towards Southampton Row. As directed, we found a narrow alleyway on our left and this turned out to be a continental promenade with the grand name of Sicilian Avenue. It is a fascinating short walk between slender Greek columns and brought us out almost opposite Bloomsbury Square Gardens.

We had been told to skirt clockwise around this Square and we would end up in Great Russell Street. Suddenly we caught sight of the Museum in all its glory. I had imagined a building similar in looks to Buckingham Palace encompassing a rather dusty exhibition with a jumble of art and antiquities all shoved into small dark, airless rooms. Not so: this edifice was pristine, magnificent and huge. I stood gazing at it open-mouthed. It reminded me of a citadel in an ancient Greek city and I wondered if this is how the Acropolis in Athens had once looked. We ascended the steps and walked into The Great Court. This modern Greco-Roman atrium was a light, massive and airy space. It rose up towards a huge circular glass dome composed of hundreds of triangles held up in the middle by what looked like a truncated lighthouse. This, in turn, was encircled by two sweeping staircases that rose upwards to the right and left. These staircases echoed the shape of the glass roof which reminded me of a billowing sea lit by a reflection from the sky above. The floor was paved with massive creamy flagstones and these were enclosed on both sides by Greek columns – as if surrounded by Greek or Roman temples. In my bemused state I was unable to decide if these columns were Doric, Ionian or Corinthian – as if it mattered!

Armed with a very necessary map we took ourselves off for sandwiches and coffee before beginning our explorations. In the same way that most visitors always search for the Mona Lisa in the Louvre in Paris, so we made our way towards the Elgin Marbles. I have always felt their title a misnomer and, as a child, I imagined them as little round glass balls! They were, in fact, sculptures snatched illegally by Lord Elgin from the Parthenon in Athens in 1801. The marble friezes were obviously out of place in this mausoleum and would be better suited to a warm Mediterranean setting where one could gaze, and appreciate them. Set atop slender columns they would be breathtaking.

Like everyone else, we also went in search of the famous Rosetta Stone and marvelled how this intricate inscription, carved on a black basalt slab, provided the key to unlocking so many mysteries of the ancient world. Andrew decided he would like to see the Oriental Collections and I was only too pleased to agree. The Japanese art I found most delicate and the Chinese miniature landscapes and snuffboxes the most interesting; but it was the porcelain that enthralled us. We wandered around exclaiming at the beauty and colour of the intricate designs.

Strangely enough, the highlight of the visit for me was the Clock Room. We almost missed it as we were tired and weary; luckily our attention was captured by the sound of hundreds of clocks all clicking away. We entered a veritable throbbing hive of machinery. From simple pocket watches to ornate grandpa clocks – all chiming, whirring or booming – a carillon of melody and of constant movement that held our rapt attention.

As Andrew commented, 'Simple things obviously please *our* simple minds.'

I suppose our busy holiday had taken its toll on the pair of us. We had attempted too much, too quickly. There was so much to see and so very little time to squeeze it in. Andrew caught me yawning and decided it was time to return to our pleasant square and even quieter hotel. We made our way down the grand sweeping staircase and, as we walked through the Great Court and under the impressive portico, I looked back with longing at an amazing and impressive architectural monument that houses over four million exhibits and welcomes visitors from all over the world.

On the Underground back from Bloomsbury to Earl's Court I silently reviewed our day. Personally I preferred Sir John Soane's fascinating museum. It felt like a home; it had character, which the huge impersonal British Museum lacked, and I found the mixed hoard of simple relics interesting and intriguing. Years of love had been lavished on it and yet this very rich and influential man had offered the fruits of his labours to all who were interested. And people still were. Unlike London's largest repository, this was not the culmination of generations of collecting moguls but the life's work of one man who came from a working-class family, made it to the top of his profession – architecture – and yet still had time to look, to admire and to purchase.

I tiredly re-lived the past few days. Cosy lavish meals interspersed with exploring whatever took our fancy and, at the end of each day, deep and satisfying love that left me sated and content. Andrew had encouraged me to relax and enjoy myself and had offered to take me to see and do anything I wanted. It was a rather heady mixture of indulgence and gratification. I hoped I had been sensible enough to keep all my plates spinning back at home. I had telephoned Robin regularly and spoke brightly of Dee and Paul. Luckily he had never asked to speak to them himself, for which I was eternally grateful. I was ashamed to be deceiving him so deeply but it seemed I was unable to stop myself. It was almost as if I was in Andrew's thrall; luckily I believed his domination stemmed from love and from not a need for power. At least I hoped it did! Once I laughingly called him Svengali and was surprised when he became upset. Drew never rang Fay, I noticed, but after listening to his amazing revelations now I fully understood why.

I arrived back at the hotel in a daze and after eating a simple meal in a nearby tavern, I slept for twelve hours without a thought of making love or even getting up to visit the bathroom. I awoke blearily to find Andrew, shaved and neatly dressed, sitting at my bedside reading the Times. His smile beamed out immediately and, as I struggled to sit up, he reached forward swiftly and yanked down my cosy bedclothes.

'Get up woman,' he growled. 'Who do you think you are? Sleeping Beauty?' I grinned back and tried to dodge him smacking my behind as I climbed out of bed and, by the time I had taken a quick shower, I was as eager as him to eat and begin our last day together. We walked down the stairs hand in hand and were greeted by our usual waiter with coffee pot at the ready.

Andrew had decided we would take it easy for our last day. He suggested a walk in the open air beside the Thames might be fun. On the way he spied a delicatessen and after telling me to wait outside he returned with a cardboard hamper which he cheerfully swung as we walked the mile or so to the river. We made our way down to the Chelsea embankment and turned left close to Battersea Bridge. Our guide map told us there were four more bridges to pass if we wanted to go all the way to the Houses of Parliament and Westminster Abbey. The day was sunny but slightly blustery as we strolled along one of the most elegant promenades in London, holding hands, while a light breeze ruffled our hair. On the left of the road we noticed numerous pale blue plaques commemorating all the important people who had resided in this part of London. It was interesting to read about the good and the famous but soon we tired of it and crossed over so that we could wander past all the many houseboats that were moored alongside Chelsea's ornate banks.

I had no idea where we were heading and was surprised when Andrew turned into Swan Walk and the Chelsea Physic Garden. This garden is enclosed by Cheyne Place and Cheyne Walk and must be on one of the most expensive plots of real estate in London. It was founded in 1673 by the Royal Society of Apothecaries in the reign of King Charles II and, over the years, has nurtured every herb known to man as well as cedar trees, cotton seed from our American colonies and Britain's oldest olive tree. We wandered around walled gardens and rockeries until we came to the statue of the garden's benefactor – Sir Hans Sloane, a physician to George II and naturalist – who had gifted the land and his herbarium of eight hundred species to establish this amazing herbalist's dream in the centre of London.

At the back of the garden is a café and we went in for coffee before going on to the different exhibitions above it. We stayed until well past midday when Andrew decided it was time for lunch. We walked on until we could see the Chelsea Pensioners' Home. From their back walls there was a huge triangle of green here that stretched right down to the Embankment and the Chelsea Bridge. We had found the Ranelagh Gardens and I soon discovered what was in the cardboard box Andrew had toted all the way with us. We found a comfortable bench in the Gardens and he unpacked it. Tiny pasties and sausage rolls with miniature salmon and cream-cheese bagels were packed neatly on top of a bottle of Chablis, two plastic glasses and some pale lemon napkins. We spread it out on the bench and were soon demolishing it. For dessert he presented us both with a huge slice of moist carrot cake. Why are picnics such fun, I wondered? We sat in the fitful sunshine and raised our faces towards the heavens and enjoyed the peace and quiet.

By then I was flagging, so Andrew decided to retrace our footsteps until he could signal a cruising taxi to return us to our hotel in South Kensington. Once in our room, we slipped off our outer garments and stretched out on the king size bed and once more I unashamedly fell asleep. It seemed no time at all before I was being urged to get ready for our evening entertainment. Andrew had booked two seats for *The Lion King* and had kept it as a last-minute surprise. I scrambled into some suitable clothes and we were off to the West End for an early evening meal before taking our seats in the Dress Circle to watch an enthralling musical.

I loved every moment of that evening. The singing was sometimes gustily enthusiastic and, at others, strangely poignant. We came out tired but satisfied. What a truly wonderful few days. We caught the trusty Underground back to Earl's Court and I sat with my head on Andrew's shoulder and relished his arm tight across my shoulders. In bed we made the most of our last hours together. We whispered promises and spoke of all we had done and what we hoped to do in the future; we snuggled closely down under the smooth sheets, entwining our legs and arms, pretending this would go on forever.

The next morning we were woken by the strident ringing of our early morning alarm call. We hurriedly got out of bed and Andrew showered as I packed both our suitcases. It gave me a sense of being close to him just by providing this intimate service. When it was my turn to use the bathroom, he checked every drawer, the wardrobe and under our bed. Maybe it gave him a similar feeling. We wanted to leave fairly sharply as I had a dental appointment that afternoon and he had promised to return for a family birthday party.

Breakfast was a frugal affair because both of us were not up to having a leisurely chat with each other or the waiter that morning. I suddenly found it difficult to speak and, by the look of him, Andrew may have had a similar feeling. He settled our bill and asked the porter to bring down our cases. We went back to our room to pick up our coats and gave each other a deep and long-lasting hug. Neither of us knew when we would meet again. Andrew pressed his face into my hair and I knew he was crying softly. Luckily there was no time to talk. I was heading to Waterloo Station and he was bound for Kings Cross after he had seen me off. Both tube trains were packed as they rushed us through the eight stops taking us to Waterloo. This meant we had no privacy to do anything but clasp hands. Andrew relinquished me at my platform gate a few minutes after ten and by twenty past my South West train was gently sliding out of London. I deliberately switched off my mobile and buried my head in a book but, when I stepped off the train in Honiton at 1.15pm precisely and went straight to my dental appointment, I had not turned, or read, a page.

Chapter 12

*

That evening Robin rang and joyfully gave me a firm date of his return in three weeks' time. I hadn't heard him so upbeat for months. He was soon talking about a holiday, as he considered we both deserved one. It made me feel ashamed as my life had been one long holiday in various hotels at nice locations ever since he had left me. He suggested Lanzarote and I was only too pleased to fall in with his wishes. We had been there before and had both enjoyed it. He promised he would book two weeks somewhere on the island. He had always loved being in charge of our holidays and because of the way I felt at that time, I was grateful to have it taken out of my hands.

He asked about London and I waffled on vaguely, but it was quite obvious that the only thing on his mind was his return to Devon and a subsequent relaxing break. At around midnight Andrew rang to check that I had returned safely, although I had already texted him as soon as I stepped off the train in Honiton, and I gave him my latest news. He said little about Robin returning at long last, but sounded plainly upset that we would be going on holiday immediately Robin came back. I tried to put his mind at ease but I could feel he felt many miles away and not in charge of his own destiny – or mine. Our whispered conversation drifted on and on that night. It was as if he hated to replace the telephone and lose contact with me.

The next day I forced myself to get up bright and early, collect Crumble, and return to my usual busy routine. There was laundry to put through the machine, a garden that was looking a trifle unkempt and some empty shelves in my fridge to be filled. I kept myself going until lunchtime and I had just sat down with a ham sandwich plus a bowl of soup when Lorna's shadow passed the kitchen window. I jumped up and let her in joyfully. I made another mug of soup while she sorted out a sandwich for herself. We sat around the kitchen table, with our feet up, and both dredged up our latest news. I told her about visiting various London museums and *The Lion King* and she spoke of the end-of-term school concert in which both Petra and Megan had bagged leading roles, she was relieved to tell me.

'They were both pretty good, even if I do say it myself, and finally brought the house down with their rendition of two nosy, gossipy housewives tearing their neighbours' reputations to shreds,' Lorna admitted with a rueful grin. 'Hope they haven't been listening in to us when we have verged on the slightly bitchy.' We both sniggered, remembering some of our odd acquaintances and their quaint ways.

'Won't be long before we will be sorting out tea towels for the three Wise Men, gold lamé for the Angel Gabriel and wondering if it's possible to make Mary and Joseph look more authentic,' I mused. 'Christmas will soon be here.'

'And I just hope this year Miss Beech won't insist every child dresses up in some outlandish costume to represent all those animals Noah wanted to take into his Ark. Do you remember those *three* rabbits and the *one* giraffe fiasco? And as for the elephant costumes... I remember they were only finished on the night because the sleeping bags you insisted dying pale grey wouldn't dry,' she answered.

We sat back with our feet raised and smiled reminiscently. Actually it had all been good fun and neither of us would have missed it for the world. I then told her about our planned holiday. She agreed Robin needed a break and the best time would be before he got stuck into routine work back with the Exeter police. Lorna hoped to go back to her parents for the holiday. It was cheap and I knew her parents longed to see them. Once again, I promised I would look after Petra's menagerie. The sad news was that Gumdrop and Gertie had both departed their watery world – possibly because her daughter may have overfed them, Lorna mentioned.

'George, the oldest of the three, has survived but maybe he hadn't been as greedy as the other two. Luckily the two goldfish that replaced them, Petra ruled, would be Gertie and Gumdrop *also*. Said it was in remembrance of the other two. Her Dad and I heaved a sigh of relief until she came home from our neighbour's carrying a hedgehog that she felt sure should be named Horatio. So, sorry love, you'll be lumbered with a spiny lodger as well as three goldfish; Rex, who's getting more arthritic every month and Jimmy, the genial gerbil.'

'Thank God for that!' I murmured. 'I can never keep up with them all and Petra gets so indignant if I muddle their names up.' I walked to the calendar and printed *HORATIO HEDGEHOG* at the top, to make sure I stayed in Petra's good books. Crumble, at least, would be pleased to have Rex along on our walks and the rest of them shouldn't pose any problems, I surmised.

One bit of good news, Lorna imparted, was that various people had viewed Rose's bungalow recently and it looked as if one was interested. She has been round twice the previous week. I prodded Lorna and she reported that, although she didn't know her name, she looked roughly our age and the two children had stated that she had a nice smile. I smiled also. It would be a relief to have a kindred spirit next door, one who was able bodied and who we could both relate to, I decided.

We then went on to talk about dates for our respective holidays. I tried not to think of Andrew fretting and feeling impotent up in Yorkshire but, every time I did, I felt a warm frisson of pleasure steal over me. To be loved and wanted imparts confidence and I was human enough to bask in it. As we were chatting a car pulled up outside Rose's property and a slim, tallish lady alighted. Lorna and I arose as one and went out to intercept her. I went up to her with my hand outstretched and I noticed she shook it firmly. Lorna murmured a hello and I introduced Lorna as my best friend. We talked for a few minutes and learned her name was Hilary and that she was moving down from Ealing in west London. She had recently retired and had always fancied living in the West Country. We praised it up and both mentioned all the advantages – not least the more reasonable property prices and a less stressful way of life. I asked her in for a cup of tea but she declined, saying she needed one last detailed look round before returning to the estate agents and making a final decision.

Lorna and I returned to my place and we both decided Hilary seemed pleasant enough and, if she took the bungalow, it was a distinct advantage not to have another frail eighty-year-old claiming our attention. Lorna returned to get the family's evening meal and I settled down for a guilty chat with Dee and Paul in London. I knew Lorna would tell Margaret of our conversation with my, hopefully, new neighbour-to-be. *I* just waited on two telephone calls – one from my thoughtful husband in Newcastle and another from my ardent lover in York.

The first came as I was eating a casserole I had prepared that morning and the second as I was drifting off to sleep at almost midnight. I was alert for the second. I switched on my bedside lamp and smoothly raised myself in bed cradling the telephone into my neck. Oh it was so good to hear Drew after twenty-four hours. I asked how he had spent his day and he mentioned shopping and taking the car to the car wash. None of it sounded half as exciting as the time we had spent in London together and I breathed a sigh of relief. Fay, he told me, had been at a bridge party with her usual exclusive group of women friends for most of the afternoon and I shuddered at the thought. It was all too organised and cultivated an atmosphere for my liking. Imagine dressing up to impress, listening to the latest gossip and trying to win at a game that I barely understood and had never craved to excel in. Why Andrew loved me was a puzzle but slowly it was dawning on me that maybe the fact that I was an easy-going ally with no pretensions was appealing to an intelligent man who was restricted and bound by so many conventions. The life he led was probably as different from mine as a shop assistant's would be from a High Court Judge's. We had never discussed it and I decided it was irrelevant, anyway.

'I almost rang you earlier but decided you might be busy, sweetheart,' he said softly.

I felt immediately relieved. Lorna had never been an inquisitive friend but even she would have been intrigued, however bland my conversation would have been with Andrew. How can one have a fond and tender chat and make it sound as if one was only talking to the Gas Board or checking one's refuse bins had been emptied that week? Even Lorna, good friend as she was, would have been puzzled just listening to the tone of my voice and could not have failed to notice the delighted smile on my face.

'I know there are only days to go and I have been cudgelling my brains as to what we will be able to cram in during this time. I have to go to London for just a day next Wednesday. I can probably cancel my official trip by putting it off until another time, and we could meet there and spend the whole day together. What do you say? Would you like to go, Jenny?'

Would I like to go? Of course I would *love* it; and my heart did a little twisting beat in my chest. It was almost as if I was a failing junkie on the road to ruin. I was unable to refuse him anything and, in fact, I was rejoicing already to grasp an excuse to be together – even if it was only to be for a meagre few hours. I thought swiftly. What excuse could I come up with this time? I was fast running out of plausible explanations and I knew my close family and friends would soon be guessing my reasons and working out exactly what I was up to.

I took a deep breath and silently apologised to all these people. 'Yes, I promise I will find some way to take the train to London next Wednesday morning,' I vowed.

Somehow, I had to invent a reason to revisit a place I had only just returned from. My trouble was, up until then. I had always been so open and honest with my friends and family; and now I found it difficult to lie and invent fictional reasons to do something that would have been quite simple before Andrew and I had met. Within a few months I was watching my words, making excuses for my actions and generally being careful with the very people I loved and admired.

'This time I will catch the 6.20 train out of Honiton and be with you at 9.15am.'

Drew promised he would be waiting on the platform to meet me and then went on to discuss where I would like to go for the day. He suggested the Tate Modern and I agreed immediately. Country bumpkins like me rarely get a chance to do the things Londoners take for granted. We look avidly at the papers and vaguely wish we could visit an art exhibition or see the new production of *La Traviata*; but it is only a fleeting longing and is soon submerged by household chores or local events. And probably, if we did reside within commuting distance of these exciting occasions, we would still forget to do anything about them until it was too late. That is human nature – the unattainable is impossible and the achievable is often shelved in favour of more pressing priorities.

I asked what Fay was doing as we spoke.

'Well as it is past midnight she is probably downing her last large glass of red wine and getting ready to close down her laptop and go to her room.'

I was appalled at their separateness. Possibly Fay was satisfied with this arrangement but obviously Andrew wasn't – or why would he constantly be seeking my company? In my estimation, a good relationship should be built on loving, or at least liking, one's partner, with a mutual sharing of happiness and a desire for it to continue. Anything else was a sham and a façade. Obviously some marriages run into difficulties, with spouses preferring to be apart when there is no common ground for conversation, shared interests or civility. Most people I have known who have gone through this, separate for a short time and either resolve their difficulties or make it permanent by divorcing. That had happened to Chris and me – we began our married life as a loving couple but, during the following ten years, we had gradually trodden divergent paths until our partnership became an empty shell. A constantly philandering spouse is heart-shattering and, as I was not prepared to accept his endless womanising, I gave him an ultimatum. Shamed by my courage, Chris didn't take much persuading; he decided it was much healthier to acknowledge this and we dissolved our partnership swiftly and amicably. Happily we still stayed friends which, strangely, shocked some of our acquaintances and family.

Andrew and Fay had an entirely different approach. Their own personal feelings appeared to hold no relevance in their marriage. They pretended to the outside world and, Andrew admitted, even to their closest friends and family, that everything in their garden was rosy. Together, and on show, they were a happy devoted couple; but, the second their front door closed on the world, they were two strangers who ignored one another, only spoke when necessary and lived completely detached lives.

I am certain this would have broken my spirit. I could not have gone on pretending. To be disliked, ignored and used in this way would be alien to my open nature. Once, I asked Andrew how long this had been going on for. He shrugged – he was unable to remember. It had happened gradually, he reckoned. I asked if he had never confided in anyone; someone like Deborah or Hugh, his surviving brother, and he admitted it had never occurred to him. He said he had grown to accept that most marriages descended into this banal, cold partnership even though, had he bothered to look, some couples must have been contented with their lot. What about when his children were growing up, I asked? Didn't they get upset? No, they were pretty inured to their mother's moods, especially as their father studiously ignored them. Later, both lads went on to university and had never returned to the family home. Not unexpected, I surmised.

We had finished our conversation long before, but these thoughts were still searing a corrosive path through my mind and I spent yet another night worrying about troubles that were beyond my control. The next morning my *white night* had taken its toll and I arose looking decidedly wan. I knew vigorous action was the antidote for my see-sawing emotions so I went to visit my few remaining neighbours who were still in the close. I was only too pleased to run a few errands for the twin sisters who quietly lived in the far corner and, by 11 o'clock, I was also helping at an impromptu coffee morning and making small talk with some of the stalwarts of the Mothers' Union.

As I walked down the path to my front door I saw two boards in the gardens to either side. One said *To Let* and the other *SOLD*. With a pang of nostalgia I fleetingly thought of times gone by. It was the end of an era and had left me bitterly missing my lovely friend, Rose; but also, in a strange way, I longed to speak to crusty old Fred who would never have reason to moan at me again. That reminded me – I owed Fred a visit. I swiftly fixed a snack lunch and got ready to go and see my old ex-neighbour.

The sun was shining on the neatly raked gravel in front of the Home. I carefully parked the car and rang the huge, jangling doorbell. The pert young girl who opened the door had a smile on her face and I felt what a welcoming establishment it was. I went inside and she took my coat. Most of the residents were in the warm sun lounge listening to some gentle music or playing cards. Fred's face lit up as I walked across the room. He tried to disguise his happy response by mentioning "they" had lost a pair of his navy blue socks and he was fed up with all the "foreign food" they were serving up constantly. The "foreign food" turned out to be lasagne and that had been dished up four days previously, I discovered. I asked what they had been given for lunch that day. It turned out to have been cottage pie with apple crumble for the second course. I hid a smile. Actually I had sampled some of the Home's catering and had been frankly impressed by the standard. But what did I know? If Fred hadn't been moaning I wouldn't have recognised him. I did notice his belligerent shouting had been toned down to a disgruntled rumble – so that was progress. And, of course, instead of me, Margaret and Lorna dancing attendance on him, and catering to his every whim, he now had to compete with eleven other residents for the carers' attention.

A sweet little old lady was sitting next to him and he introduced her as Mrs Jewell. Her eyes twinkled at me and I wondered if the proximity of a delightful lady may have gone some way to sweetening Fred's demeanour. If so, I applauded their good sense! I plonked down my goodwill offering, a huge box of Liquorice Allsorts – Fred's favourites – and an assortment of peppermint toffees. Apart from Fred commenting they could break his teeth, he accepted them gracefully. And I noticed the attentive Mrs Jewell was offered both. I waved a fond farewell from the door but Fred had already turned his attention back to his attentive neighbour and was again moaning about the awful "foreign food".

Wednesday dawned dry but cold. I decided there was no point in mentioning I was off to London once more. It was only for the day and I would be back at home probably before they even noticed I wasn't around. I could just as easily be shopping in Taunton or Exeter and, as I was not in the habit of discussing my itinerary for either place, I thought no one would even detect my absence. I decided to take myself off quietly. I deliberately did not take my car to the station but timed it perfectly to collect my return ticket and caught the 6.20am train to Waterloo. This time I had no case as I would not be staying overnight. I had prudently packed a clean pair of knickers and my favourite perfume in my handbag, along with my toothbrush and paste in case we ate a pungent meal and I needed to repair the damage. Oh, how we lovers want to appear perfect in the eyes of our admirers!

I had dressed as elegantly as possible but staying warm was my priority as I didn't want to arrive looking pinched and pale. I knew I would probably be sitting in a fuggy compartment with many other commuters, mostly businessmen, all bent on using their laptops or chattering incessantly on their mobiles. So many travellers at this time in the morning seemed to do half their office work before they even arrived at their destinations while, often, the other half was devoted to keeping up with their social life. It is amazing what one hears on some train journeys. Where people at one time aimed to keep their personal life separate and workplace practices private, these barriers seem to have been lowered today – sometimes to such an extent it can often be embarrassing. I certainly didn't aim to sit and listen to their gossip. I had hoped to squirrel myself away in a window corner with my trusty *Telegraph* crossword and a good book for company. The train started out fairly empty but by Salisbury it became filled to capacity and I was pleased I had a comfortable seat as well as a cup of coffee.

It has always been a slow and boring journey from Devon to London, and this particular one seemed endless. Finally, when we pulled into Waterloo Station, I was one of the first off the train, like a cork out of a champagne bottle. Drew was waiting by the barrier and immediately hugged and kissed me soundly as soon as I edged past the ticket collector. I gave him a beaming smile and we made our way down the crowded Underground stairs looking towards each other and grinning inanely. Personally I didn't care where we went and I waited passively as he purchased our tickets and studied the shiny white direction boards to decide our route to Blackfriars, via various lines. I stepped on and off trains, often buffeted by warm winds and Londoners, all in a hurry to be somewhere else, and it was a relief to come up into the open air once more. We made our way down St Paul's Walk where I could see the white dome of that impressive cathedral rising behind a glittering array of buildings away to my left. Andrew swung me round and there was the River Thames, backed by a broodingly sombre Bankside Power Station, on my right. We followed the crowd to the slender Millennium Bridge which connects these two so very dissimilar edifices, and crossed. The bridge, contrary to my expectations, didn't appear to be swaying unduly as we joined the crowds all eagerly making their way towards the suddenly famous Tate Modern.

I'm not sure what I expected after so much previous hype from the media, but it was a revelation to enter this vast echoing building. As far as I could tell, little had been done to alter its appearance since it had first been designed and built by Sir Giles Gilbert Scott in 1947. It was built, not for beauty in those austere times, but out of necessity in a country that had almost been brought to its knees. And now it still looked like a massive factory outside, with its dark red brickwork and tall angular tower, and the steel girders and concrete floors gave it the feeling of a huge industrial complex inside. We entered by way of the Turbine Hall, which had originally housed the electric generators, Andrew informed me. The space was five stories high, and what could have been a quarter of a mile long. The whole area left me totally awed at this giant space under one roof. I don't think I had ever been in such a raw, echoing plant, with these immense proportions, in my life.

What *did* amaze me was that one end was piled high with cardboard boxes. It was as if a thousand people had moved house on the same day and used this huge, empty space to store their unwanted boxes. They were haphazardly piled on top of each other with no sense of order, some leaning at odd angles and heights, often with small boxes shouldering much larger ones, until my fingers itched to tear it all down and stack it neatly again. So this was Modern Art? I said little but stared around – wide-eyed. I felt like a typical "Devon Dumpling" who had been dropped into another dimension and had no idea of any measurement I could apply to what I was viewing.

We walked up echoing, metal, open plan industrial stairs and walkways and I wondered, with a grin, if the visitors might feel more at home in overalls and steel-capped boots. We passed huge metal tubes that reminded me of the underside of hidden flumes in swimming pools, where the boilers are often squashed into a corner. I never discovered their purpose or if they were part of the exhibition, but it certainly enhanced the industrial theme still further. There were seven floors and soon we were both abysmally disorientated as we turned this way and that to visit various galleries. Luckily most of these rooms were small with white-painted walls which displayed the artwork sympathetically and we were able to admire and comment comfortably.

I began to flag after about our fourth gallery and Andrew decided it was time for coffee. We discussed what we should do next and both agreed the whole place was far too vast to absorb more than a fraction of what was on display and would have to be left until another day. We decided, while we were munching our cheese scones, to visit a new exhibition of an unknown (to us) French artist's work. It would only be on show at the Tate Modern for a few weeks before moving on to some other venue. We eagerly made our way down and joined the queue of art enthusiasts. I have to admit that, to this day, I have no idea of the artist's name. It was certainly Gallic sounding but he was definitely no Matisse, Monet or Renoir! We walked around and I heard reverent "aahs"and "oohs" from the viewers. The chap had painted, at a guess, in the 1920s but there was none of the flamboyant, zinging colours of the South of France or the amazing clarity that typifies the beautiful coastline of the north. No Mont-St-Michel shrouded in mist or Ile de Noirmoutier on a stormy day. No earthy peasants, no oyster boats, no elegant châteaux and no Parisian rooftops. This was no eye-catching modern art, like Picasso or Mondrian that appealed to my senses rather than my eye.

Every painting contained a horde of dun-coloured matchstick men. Grey, brown, fawn and black had been used to clothe them, with every tone in between. Most of the men wore bowler hats as one sees portrayed by very young children and, if I had been told a five-year-old had produced the work, I would have looked on it with kinder eyes. The daubs were infantile and, although I studied every picture on display, I could see nothing to enthral or beguile me. Andrew and I never said a word as we looked closely at every title while reading the short resumé printed at the side of each painting. Finally we walked outside and I stretched mentally from all the culture I had been subjected to.

Drew, with candid eyes, asked my opinion of the whole exhibition.

'I enjoyed it. It was a shock, but one I think London can stand. It is way out, different and controversial and as the various successive exhibitions are staged, our understanding of what we have always considered to be "art" will probably also change. But that last French exhibition of paintings is, to my mind, diabolical. Childish daubs in dreary colours. I hated it, Andrew, and I could see no merit in it whatsoever. But what really upset me was the reverence and awe some of those people showed. Talk about The Emperor's New Clothes! I felt I should be shouting out, telling the whole room to open their eyes and see it for what it is.'

I waited, with my head down, for him to disagree but, after staring at me for some seconds, he burst out laughing and hugged me to him.

'Oh you are brilliantly refreshing, darling, and I love it when you are so incensed and dare to speak out. No, I totally agree with you and I began wondering what those stupid old fogies would find to admire next.'

I had no idea that my lover had planned another treat and it was awaiting us both. He had booked a hotel near Kensington Gardens. We took the Underground to Lancaster Gate just so we could look at *Peter Pan's* statue, he said. It was erected in 1912 in memory of J M Barrie, *Peter Pan's* author, who used to walk his dog beside The Long Water which divides Hyde Park from Kensington Gardens. We stood and admired it, completely alone, with our arms entwined. I loved the fairies, rabbits, mice and squirrels that chased each other around the base of the statue and knew this was another day I would never forget.

We took a taxi to our sumptuous hotel that overlooked the Gardens and, once in our room, shut out the view and sank on the huge bed to do what we had been longing to do since early that morning. The loving was good but scarcity of time puts an awful constraint on ardour and we eventually had to force ourselves away from each other, relinquish our warm caresses, however reluctantly, and shower in our grand bathroom. So my clean panties came in useful, after all!

Andrew had booked a table for early dinner in the dining room. We ate sparingly but well, as we had to leave in time to catch our respective trains. We dropped our key off in the hotel Reception as if we were off to the theatre and would be back later. We took the tube once more to Waterloo as I had to catch the 8.20pm train and, as it was the last one, we could not afford to be held up by traffic.

We made a last-minute dash up the stairs and I just managed to get through the barrier and fling myself on the train before the doors slid to and it was off. Andrew and I stared at each other through the window as the train slowly drew out of the station. There had been no time for a farewell kiss or hug. I felt out of breath and bereft all at the same time and it took me a few minutes to pull myself together and make my way towards the train's front coaches, find a seat and calm myself down. Half an hour later Andrew texted to say he was aboard his train, also. He would be home before me but he would daydream about me, and our wonderful time together, all the way back to York. I smiled with contentment and followed Andrew's daydreams with some of my own. I was stunned to think that a huge, ugly power station, that had cost the country more than £134 million to convert, could be used as a massive art gallery. To my eyes it still appeared to be a vast shell of an industrial complex but obviously nearly five million visitors per year would disagree with me as they went there in their droves and appeared to derive an immense amount of enjoyment from it. I had been shocked, amused and interested. I, who knew nothing about modern art, was quite prepared to learn and apparently millions of other people wanted to appreciate this modern culture too. My dream also dawdled through the second half of our day and my cheeks grew warm as I relived our short time of tenderness and rapture in bed together. The meal that followed brought our lovely day to fitting end – we laughed and chatted and were in perfect accord with each other. It was the leaving of each other, so abruptly, that had hurt me. I felt as if I had been physically wrenched away from Andrew and it wasn't a pleasant sensation. The train's drinks trolley interrupted my reverie and forced me to settle down with my book and an excellent cup of coffee.

I stumbled off the train at almost midnight and, because I was so tired, I took a taxi home. Crumble met me at the door and there was mail on the mat. I shuffled it together and put it on the kitchen worktop as I brewed myself a cup of comforting, hot chocolate. The answerphone was flashing, I noticed, as I sank down on the settee. I had forgotten Robin completely the whole day, I admitted to myself guiltily, as I leaned over to listen to my messages. Yes, sure enough, he had rung three times and patiently asked where I was. I decided it was far too late to ring him back – and, anyway, I felt too tired to explain or make up some excuse to cover my escape to happiness. I took myself off to bed vowing I would telephone him first thing in the morning and put things right.

But the next morning I had something far more important to think about. I got up hurriedly and took a cup of tea back to bed with me. I glanced through the mail – mostly bills, luckily none of them too high, a couple of circulars inviting us to a pension symposium and an offer on solar heating. I binned the last two and slit open an official looking, weighty letter that was at the bottom of the pile. It was from Mr Frobisher, Rose's solicitor. He had already told us half of Rose's estate had been willed to me but had divulged no details. Robin and I had discussed what this probably meant in terms of money, but we had no clear idea of how much she and Cedric had been worth. It was the last thing we had ever thought about. They were our friends and money was never mentioned. If we had been in trouble I know they would have both offered monetary help and we would have supplied the same but, as this had never arisen, the subject had never come up.

I knew Rose had never worked since she had been married and I knew also, when Cedric died, she had been entitled to almost his whole pension. He had held a very good position with Britain's foremost airline so I knew his pension had been substantial. The sad thing was, after Cedric died, Rose spent as little as possible on herself. She had been cosseted all her life but I don't think she ever wanted material things as her only interest was basking contentedly in his love. She had always enjoyed her nightly brandy and at the end, her hand may have been a bit lavish, but other than buying only the most basic foodstuffs, Rose spent very little on herself. She never bought a new pair of slippers, underclothes or even simple commodities like tights, hand-cream or perfume. I used to get all her shopping and often tried to tempt her to add a box of chocolates or luxury biscuits to her shopping list but the answer was always a polite refusal. Consequently, when it came to birthdays or Christmas time, I used to scour Marks & Spencer's for suitable lingerie and try to include a pair of attractive slippers or warm pyjamas as well as some pleasant-smelling toiletries. We had always bought many little gifts for Rose because, surprisingly, she and her husband had never celebrated Christmas since they had been in Devon. I believe it went back to Cedric's brother dying unexpectedly one Boxing Day, when their Christmas spirit had been quenched forever. Luckily, Robin was like a kid as the time drew nearer. He had few others to spoil, apart from his sister and his two nephews, so he indulged himself and found masses of small presents for me – some acceptable and some not – and scattered them under our tree. I made sure I gave him half a dozen in return so it had been easy to add a few more to delight Rose and make her feel at home.

Crumble kept getting under my feet that morning. Maybe he was hoping I wouldn't leave him alone for another whole day. I had left brimming bowls of water in various places, given him double rations and left the patio door discreetly open while I had been away. Normally Lorna would have had him but I couldn't face making yet more excuses, so I cheated and he had to suffer. He had been getting progressively slower during the summer, I noticed. I bent down, made a fuss of him, and promised loads of long rambles as I studied the solicitor's letter yet again.

Every time I looked I kept expecting the amount to be reduced. It seemed an indecent sum to me. It would almost purchase our house outright, I surmised. Mr Frobisher reported that a Miss Hilary Browne of West Ealing had paid the full asking price on Rose's property, providing she could move in immediately, and, as she was a cash buyer, he was able to agree and wind up the estate forthwith. He enclosed a copy of the estate's account of assets and liabilities plus his company's charges and professional fees. My eyes widened at the last amount.

At least the solicitor's letter gave me something to talk about when I telephoned Robin. He was just off for work, probably knotting his tie as he devoured the last piece of toast - I knew him so well. He had been trying to ring me again and again with urgent news, he said, brushing aside my excuses. I held my breath as he told me – had his homecoming been cancelled once more? No, he would be coming back a week earlier than expected. He had booked us two weeks in the Canaries and he wanted to tell me the good news. I'm sure I made all the usual replies, with my mind in a whirl as I was trying to re-order my thoughts. Immediately he rang off I rushed upstairs and threw two suitcases on the spare room bed and began filling them with toiletries, sun tan lotion and our swimming gear.

The next five days passed in a blur. I washed, pressed and packed, found our passports, booked Crumble into our friendly kennels, as two weeks were too long to trade on Lorna's good nature, and tried to get my house and mind in order. I explained to Andrew as soon as he telephoned that night. He went very quiet.

'Does that mean this is the end for us?' he queried.

'Yes – no – I don't know.' I was distracted, excited, worried and sad. Did it mean that our marvellous relationship would cease? Would everything return to normal once Robin had come home and would I never see Drew again? I tried to explain I would use the next two weeks in Lanzarote to sort my mind out. I would laze around in the sunshine and think, I promised. I had said nothing about my inheritance from Rose. It was a delicious secret that I knew would change me for the rest of my life. A year previously and I would have shared every thought and idea with Robin. We could have revelled in it, deciding how to make that huge amount of money enrich our lives – forever. Now I was being drawn in two different directions and the see-saw of my emotions left me wallowing in uncertainty.

I had decided not to mention the money to Andrew as soon as I found out. I didn't want it to colour our relationship or to affect the way he thought of me or any future plans we might make. I wanted it to be decided on our simple love for each other and not on some exciting possibilities. With Robin I had a different set of worries. I didn't want to be swept away with future plans; I needed to think carefully. This money suddenly became the cornerstone of our life, the key to my future maybe and I wanted to be sure what sort of future I envisaged and with whom. Was it sturdy and loving Robin or exciting and equally loving Andrew? A year before I would have been amazed and amused by such a scenario. Now I was in a swirl of indecision. This two-week holiday, I hoped, would sort out my mind and finalise the rest of my life. It was a lot to cram into a short space of time, but I would.

In the midst of my haphazard packing and chaotic thoughts, Hilary moved in next door. She appeared calmly efficient and capable. I offered assistance from cups of tea to shifting awkward furniture, but it was all politely declined, so I backed off with a slight feeling of relief. I guessed we would never become bosom pals, more over-the-fence/pass-the-time-of-day neighbours. That was fine – I had more than enough of my own worries to cope with.

****

Robin arrived home one wild and windy evening two days later. His car was full of worn, crumpled clothing and junk from Newcastle. Lots of leaflets about the history and sights of the town, a couple of presents he had picked up in an antique shop one Saturday and loads of discarded paperwork that needed shredding. We unpacked the car and went off to bed.

The holiday came as a great relief. We arrived in the midst of warm sunshine on the Sunday lunchtime. Robin had chosen Playa Blanca because we had stayed there before. The small fishing village had expanded since our last visit but it was still a pleasant place to stroll along the attractive walkways and, at Playa Flamingo beach, we would choose a busy café for morning coffee; it was easy to sit and people-watch and plan the rest of our day. But mostly we lounged around the heated pool under a parasol with books and magazines and amused ourselves. We swam a little but stretching out and relaxing was our aim.

I spent a lot of time, in between dozing, thinking deeply and trying to reach some decision about the rest of my life. There was no doubt Robin was attentive; we laughed, talked and explored – visiting the huge local market that visitors from all parts of the island flock to see, taking the boat to Papagayo and enjoying the six primitive, golden sand beaches with the naturists. Finally, to round our holiday off, we hired a car for a couple of days and visited Timanfaya National Park with its very active volcano, the beautiful Jameos del Agua with its underground lake and pale blue and white lagoon, and the amazing house of Cesar Manrique which was built over five volcanic lava bubbles. The rooms were simple, yet grand, and were connected by white tunnels; there was a delicious garden set around a white lagoon with a tinkling fountain and a leaning palm. It was all so beautiful and calm and I always enjoyed my every visit. These three places were amazing and I fleetingly wondered if Andrew had been – and if he loved them as much as I did.

We returned to Devon relaxed and fully energised for the Christmas season. I rushed around buying presents and writing my way through a mountain of cards. Why do we always feel we have to give an update on nearly every card we write, I mused? Is it because our lives are so hectic and full that we feel guilty about not keeping in touch with old friends, so guilty that we are obliged to tell and explain what has been occupying us for the past year? Sometimes it is one's *only* communication and, if we don't take this one opportunity, then maybe our friendship will lapse and we will lose contact forever. So there I was scribbling madly – just to stay in touch.

I pondered if I should send Andrew and Fay a Christmas card. I had no idea if or how Drew had described me to her. Quite honestly I didn't much care, but I felt some recognition of our renewed friendship wouldn't go amiss. I scribbled our names on one before I could change my mind and put it ready for posting. Andrew had curtailed his regular evening calls, of course. He now only rang when Robin was on nights but he had also increased his day calls when he knew Robin was busy working. Somehow I managed to field these in company without too many raised eyebrows or pointed comments. Often he would time his calls on my mobile when he knew I would be taking Crumble for his daily ramble. But these days Crumble seemed to be feeling his age and often I turned back from a long walk so he could drop down next to the radiator in the hall and regain his breath. At other times, usually in the company of Rex and Petra, he would boldly dash around as if he were still a puppy. But these feisty exhibitions were getting rarer, so I tried to make sure his walks were well within his capabilities and that he never failed to enjoy them.

We arranged the Christingle Service which as usual, in the warm glow of candles, brought a lump to my throat. Our Carols by Candlelight went without a hitch and not too much coughing or sneezing either. But our Nativity was the best production we had ever staged. It certainly had the largest selection of animals I have ever seen. We managed to steer clear of elephants and giraffes but just about every other species known to man was represented –

with a friend's twins insisting on being two ladybirds! Robin and I were trying not to laugh as all the children marched down the aisle solemnly, as if they were on their way to The Ark. I dared not catch Lorna's eye as she was trying to adjust a tea towel on the tousled hair of a wriggling shepherd and to hand one of the Wise Men an ornate tea caddy for his myrrh.

In fact Midnight Mass was almost ordinary by contrast. Lorna and I strolled home alone at well past midnight. Robin was working and Lorna's husband had offered to child-mind both Petra and Megan. I had promised to go back for a drink and a sausage roll afterwards and, as we were divesting ourselves of our outer clothing, my mobile started its usual music. They both looked at me expectantly and I snatched up my phone, murmuring that it might be Robin and quickly disappeared into their hall. Of course it was Drew and he wanted to wish me Happy Christmas. I answered him so briefly that he got the message immediately. I also probably blushed crimson and disguised it by marching back in their family room and crouching close to their blazing log fire.

The year came to an end with a noisy fancy dress party thrown by Robin's best friends Kevin and Pete plus their partners, as well as the annual dinner and dance we were expected to attend, hosted by the Exeter Constabulary. It was a busy time of the year and I am sorry to say Andrew and my telephone momentum dropped as we both attended celebrations many miles apart. I looked forward to the new year with anticipation but I was still uncertain as to my decision about the two men in my life.

Chapter 13

*

The New Year that started with music and festivities petered out into the usual round of shopping, cleaning and predictable evening TV. All of my neighbours were either away or self-reliant and not needing me. It became very cold and I made excuses not to stir far from my warm house. I dragged Crumble out to walk on the common most days but he obviously felt the iciness as much as I did and would sink down with a relieved sigh as soon as we came indoors. I kept the central heating at a cosy temperature and basically we both vegetated. I am sure I became a very boring, introverted human being.

The only cheerful break in my day was when Lorna or Margaret made the effort to come round and spend an hour with me, or when Andrew telephoned. From call to call he asked when I would be available and planned his calls accordingly. I must have been very unresponsive towards Robin during this period as I only became animated and happy when I had a call from Yorkshire, I am ashamed to say. But, strange to admit, although I was reticent in bed at this time, and Robin must have been mildly puzzled, I clung to him during the day - especially when he was going off to work or out with his friends.

Winter limped along with Andrew whispering all sorts of enticements in my ear about Caribbean holidays that included lots of sun and sandy beaches, and I became more and more depressed. Finally March came roaring in like an express train, green leaves started appearing on sullen trees and Andrew talked about an April holiday in Cornwall. Could I manage to get away?

I deemed it impossible until Robin went into overdrive regarding a teenager who had gone missing from a nearby village. She had been joining her old friends for a school reunion that was to last over a weekend. She never turned up and, for a day, nobody noticed her absence. Once the police were informed they sent every available man to the area, but it was as if she had vanished off the face of the earth. She had left her parents' home after lunch, her mother had kissed her goodbye and she had waved to both her parents as she reached the end of their drive. That was the last sighting anyone in the village or surrounding countryside had of her.

Robin was really perturbed. There was no nasty stepfather to interview, no boyfriend who had been given a recent brush off, no clues on her computer – nothing to give them a lead on a well-liked, well balanced teenager who appeared not to have a care in the world. So when I mentioned I might go down to Cornwall for a few days, Robin was too deep in his mystery to take more than a cursory interest.

I hugged him tightly before I left. Don't misunderstand me - I was aware of what I was doing; I was also ashamed of my duplicity and in my mind I was constantly apologising, but it was almost as if I was unable to refuse Andrew's relentless cajoling and unable to take a firm stand to preserve my marriage. I, who had divorced a womanising Chris, was doing exactly the same thing to a man who had never done me a day's harm in his life. I was guilty of hurting a man I liked, admired and loved – *but not enough, a small voice insisted on reminding me.*

I played a game with myself – if I saw someone I knew, maybe I would call this madcap escapist holiday off. I saw no one at the station and noticed no one I recognised in my carriage. We arrived in Exeter St Davids and I changed trains for Plymouth. The only person who spoke to me was a man who bumped into me as he emerged from the Gents toilets and ran for his train. I climbed aboard my train and sat with my head down and steadily read *Pride & Prejudice* for the umpteenth time, not taking in a word and barely registering the stations as we arrived and departed. At last we were near Plymouth. I quickly wandered along to the toilets to make myself presentable – even nervously spraying myself with my precious *Obsession* perfume in the hope it would disguise my fear. The train crept into Plymouth station and I spotted Andrew immediately; he was waiting by the barrier with an enquiring half-smile on his face. I suddenly realised he was feeling the same consuming torment and shyness as me in case his dearest wish was not to be granted.

The reluctant train ground slowly to a halt and I stepped down on the platform, bumping my case behind me, and ran into his warm and welcoming embrace. As we hugged I felt our breathing slowing down and I was suddenly aware of a sense of euphoria and determination I had never felt in my life before. He hustled me out of the station and carefully settled me into his sturdy BMW and we were across the Tamar Bridge and into Saltash, and therefore Cornwall, before I had time to look around me and take note of the route. I settled back with a sigh and placed my hand on Andrew's knee for comfort. He glanced at me with a mischievous smile as we cruised on with gathering speed towards our secret destination. At Trerule Foot we dropped down towards Looe and I sat up in expectation of seeing the sea, but suddenly we turned right in the direction of Pelynt and swept through the quiet village. As Andrew drove unerringly onwards I noticed a sign that pointed to Lanreath. I knew then I was finally lost in this part of Cornwall, so I settled back once more to await our final haven. And haven it was. Suddenly we came to a tiny picturesque waterside village snuggling deeply into the banks of a river. We pulled up outside a pub and Andrew got out of the car and stretched. This was it, he informed me. We were in the village of Lerryn. Suddenly the name Lerryn struck a chord in my memory.

'Didn't you bring me here once in *The Shy Curlew*? We had sailed up to Golant and you said you thought we might just get up the river as far as Lerryn. We only stayed a short while, because you were worried about the tide, and then it was time to return.'

'Goodness me, you must have perfect recall!' Andrew exclaimed 'How on earth can you remember what we did in our teens?'

Little did he know, but I remembered just about everything that had happened all those years ago.

'Yes, this is the tidal limit of the Fowey River,' Andrew explained. 'Dad would sometimes bring me here as a special treat, if the tide was right, and it always seemed to be a magical place to me. We would wander along beside the river to look at the geese and a pair of swans that always seemed to be in residence, and hopefully I might spy a shy kingfisher, flashing his gaudy plumage, as he streaked along the riverbank. Farther back, in the woods, we occasionally caught sight of an egret or buzzard – but that was rarely. In the spring the bluebells always formed a crisp carpet and I would eagerly collect armfuls to take back to Deborah. Sadly, they were always drooping by the time we arrived home.' With that he turned away and heaved our suitcases out of the car. 'Right, let's introduce you to your home for the next few days,' he said as he led the way into The Ship Inn. It was an oddly shaped building that looked as if it had been two or three separate cottages, set at right angles to each other and built of random white stucco and granite; they now appeared to have been bonded together and had emerged as the village inn.

We entered a slate-floored area and found Mine Host drinking a pint with another man and laughing uproariously. They turned to us with interest and I noticed Drew's voice took on a soft Cornish cadence as he enquired after our room. We were taken to a warm, comfortable bedroom already lit by soft lights, and immediately I felt at home. We were asked to come down to the bar as soon as we had settled in and we would be shown the dining area.

After I had tossed all our clothes either onto hangers or stowed them away in various drawers – trying not to be intimidated by Andrew's ironical grin – I grabbed his hand and we swiftly made our way back downstairs. In the dining room we were shown to a comfortable table and proceeded to order and eat a very enjoyable meal. No one disturbed us and it was as if we sat within an enchanted circle as we quietly talked and laughed. We had coffee and brandy out in the bar and it was in this mellow frame of mind that we climbed the stairs to our welcoming room to make up for all the time we had spent apart during the past few weeks.

The next morning I was awoken by bright sunshine shining across my face. The previous long night of intense loving and deep sleeping had given me boundless energy and I sprung out of bed to make us both a cup of tea, while Andrew groaned and turned over. Back home that would have been Robin's job and I was amused at this role reversal. Andrew and I then curled up in bed, because it was so early, and planned our day. After our last holiday, when we had so feverishly visited as many places as it was possible to fit in, Andrew asked if I approved of doing nothing in particular, wandering around, enjoying the spring sunshine and going where our inclinations led us. I would have agreed to absolutely anything: just being by his side, able to touch him, ask questions and talk about anything and everything was my idea of heaven – so, of course, I enthusiastically and willingly assented.

We made our way downstairs hand-in-hand – like a pair of teenagers out on their first date. We had eyes and ears only for each other and barely glanced at our waitress when we came to order the full English breakfast accompanied by a large pot of coffee. While we waited Andrew perused *The Times* and I pondered dreamily if happiness and a good appetite often relied one on the other. Whether it did or not, we sat and demolished twice the amount of food that I am certain neither of us would ever consume for breakfast at home!

We set out that morning suitably wrapped up and booted. Andrew had decided to initiate me into the charms of Lerryn and, although the village and river was bathed in bright sunshine, it was still only early April so we were prepared for anything. There was quite a selection of small craft scattered across the river, all lazily swinging at their moorings, and the few modern houses were hidden amongst the weathered cottages, and all looked as if they were piled haphazardly above each other on the opposite bank of the river. The almost still reflection of the whole glowing scene must have made Andrew's fingers itch to buy some paintbrushes and transfer the whole setting onto a canvas. I breathed deeply and he hugged me to him.

We walked briskly along the riverbank towards where the rivers Lerryn and Fowey converge. I had noticed my companion glance once or twice to his right and wondered what he was searching for. The birds were trilling and I could hear cautious rustlings in the undergrowth that bordered the path, so I knew all the wildlife was aware and awake and were also taking advantage of such a glorious day. We strolled along for about a mile or so and the only animal that crossed our path was a small vole, and *he* scuttled off into the damp grass that bordered the river and disappeared with a mellow 'plop'. We had almost reached the main river opposite Penquite when Andrew decided it was time to retrace our footsteps. As we neared Lerryn once more I realised what he had been searching for. Suddenly stepping-stones were appearing, as if by magic, out of the river.

'What a brilliant bit of timing,' Andrew commented dryly. We stood and chatted for a short while as we waited for the river to subside some more and he pointed out Ethy Woods, a large dark green copse, on the far side.

'We will explore them later and I will explain why they were *so* important to me as a child,' he said cryptically as he shepherded me across the stones to the other side. We wandered up the far bank and made our way towards a small bridge that stood above the village. It was perfectly proportioned and, to my delight, it was of the *packhorse* design, with sharp angles that stood out from the main structure; this allowed people or animals to safely shelter from passing traffic. There were two arches and, as it peaked towards the middle, it faintly reminded me of the *Rialto Bridge* in Venice.

'A village green, a picturesque pub, a quiet river, stepping stones and an attractive bridge. What more could one hope for?' I asked.

'Only a decent companion who can appreciate it,' came back the instant reply. I grinned in agreement. 'I mugged all this up before we came,' he explained. 'This bridge dates back to the 1280s and the Mill, which stood close by, was built around 1346. It crushed iron ore; there were also lime kilns in this area and sailing barges that easily made their way upriver, in those days, so it would have been an extremely busy place. Of course smuggling was also prevalent, as it was all over this part of the world, and they even have a Brandy Lane to commemorate it!' he said with a laugh. 'Legend has it that there was also a cave in the woods with a tunnel to Ethy House cellars.'

'Ethy House?' I asked.

'Yes, that's where we are going next, to Ethy Woods and, as we walk and enjoy a perfect day, I will tell you a most marvellous tale. You know Kenneth Grahame's *Wind in the Willows*?' I nodded. 'Well legend has it that he actually finished this children' s classic while he was living here. That's probably where the story began about a cave in the woods leading to a cellar. Remember how Badger knew about a secret passage to Toad's home and how it enabled the four friends to chase out the nasty stoats and weasels who had taken over the Hall? Of course, as a child, my father read me the story. He also insisted this is where it was written so I always imagined Ratty, Mole and Mr Badger living right in this very spot.'

'And what about Toady?' I asked. 'Where did *he* live?"

'I'll show you in a minute. Over there is Ethy Wood and the locals have always said Kenneth Grahame chose Ethy House as Mr Toad's large and pretentious home. Personally I think it is more likely he would have modelled it on one of the large houses that line the banks of the Thames around Marlow where he lived as a child – possibly Mapledurham House which is a very grand, impressive Elizabethan mansion. That is all conjecture as Ethy House has long since disappeared but we do know Grahame certainly resided here at roughly the time he was in the process of completing his masterpiece.'

'I bet you didn't know,' he went on 'it came from stories he made up for his young son, Alistair, who he nicknamed 'Mouse'? What started as stories turned into letters sent to amuse Alistair who was with his governess far away in Littlehampton. He was apparently a precocious child, often having ungovernable rages, and these stories appeased his appetite for more tales of the Riverbank. Gossip has it that the new Governor of the Bank of England didn't take too well to Mr Grahame and he had taken extended sick leave in Cornwall. He and his wife stayed first in Falmouth but soon made their way back to Fowey, where they had been married, and finally ended up the river in this very spot. It was here these stories became the basis of his enthralling book that children have loved ever since. I *do* know that as soon as my Dad told me, I made him read it again and again until our copy became extremely tatty and, every time we sailed up from Fowey, I spent ages looking and looking for quiet Mole, grumpy Badger and sensible Mr Rat. And I am sure it was from that time that I felt 'messing around in boats' was the only thing worth doing.'

We spent ages wandering around the wood but, sadly, *I* heard no pattering of tiny feet or spied any furry animal sculling against the tide as it rose; but we did catch sight of a kingfisher as it flashed through the dappled shade under the trees. Tired but content, we made our weary way back to The Ship Inn and downed a welcome cream tea. When asked, the Landlord proudly told us that the pub had stood there since 1762 which impressed us both. We made our excuses and then went to our room for a well-earned rest. I hate to admit that neither of us did much resting as Andrew gathered me in his arms as if he was determined to show me what real love was all about.

That evening we came down for our meal as the last diners were finishing theirs. If they glanced at our flushed faces I'm sure they would have seen a satisfied glow and drawn their own conclusions. That night there were no whispered conversations or smothered laughter - we slept like proverbial logs and it was not until 7am the next morning that either of us opened our eyes and faced the world. Breakfast was as satisfying as the previous day and we brightly chatted over it as we planned our day. Andrew decided, as time was running out, that he would like to take the car and get back to Polruan and Fowey. I knew he missed his home and, although I was wary of bumping into any of his friends or distant family, I agreed to accompany him. Deborah had long since moved towards Mevagissey and was busy mothering lads in a public school there, Hugh was with his family and firmly established in the USA so, apart from some odd quirk of fate, we should be fairly safe I surmised. I warned Andrew that if he was greeted anywhere in either town I would fade away into the background and, with that, he had to be satisfied. He laughed at my concern. I was surprised as there seemed a very real possibility of us being seen together and it causing trouble for him. It wasn't until sometime later that I learned the likelihood of that was extremely remote.

The day was bright but slightly blustery and as we arrived and parked way above Polruan I rejoiced to see white caps dancing out in the bay. We took the footpath around the cliffs, down Battery Lane, past The Old Blockhouse and back through town towards the foot ferry without passing a single person. Two motherly ladies waited alongside us for the ferry that came bustling across from Fowey's Town Quay. I think it was their weekly shopping day as each nimbly stepped on board clutching a couple of huge canvas bags apiece. They briefly greeted the boatman and then settled back comfortably for a satisfying gossip. As neither glanced our way I guessed Andrew's parentage was unknown to either of them. At the last moment an elderly man joined them with his huge curly-haired dog. We both shuffled along to give the dog more space but, as he spent the next ten minutes chatting and laughing with the skipper, we realised he knew neither of us either.

We stepped ashore and I looked around cautiously. The few people in sight were attending to their own affairs so we both strolled across the Quay and made our way, by common consent, towards Fowey's Ship Inn and ordered coffee. The place was almost empty and neither the barmaid nor any customer looked even remotely interested in us. It was too early for the lunchtime regulars, I guessed, so we settled down for a good long chat. I knew the fourteenth-century inn had once been the family home of the Rashleighs. Placed as it was right next to the parish church, the one where Kenneth Grahame and Elspeth were married, and situated in the centre of the town, close to the hub of commerce and the governing bodies that ruled Fowey, it was an ideal place for the rough and rollicking men, Andrew told me, who became known as the Fowey Gallants.

'I thought that was the local sailing club,' I mildly mentioned.

'Yes, it is *now*, but when they were given that name, between the fourteenth and seventeenth centuries, it referred to an unwieldy band of privateers and pirates whose swashbuckling antics caused much consternation around the country. In the beginning, when we were at war with France and Spain, they were given licence by the monarch to attack and seize any vessels on the high seas or in the English Channel. For such men, most of whom my family were related to, like Thomas Tregarthen, John Trevelyn, Nicholas Carminow, Sir Hugh Courtenay, the Rashleighs and the Treffrys from Place House, it must have been as music to their ears! When the French attacked Fowey in 1456 Elizabeth, the wife of the second Thomas Treffry, repelled them – with her servants – by pouring molten lead from the roof down on them. If their womenfolk dared do that, imagine what the men of Fowey were prepared to do? To be told one can play havoc with another country's navy, remove any spoils of war the ships would be carrying and it would incur no punishment, must have been a revelation to them. Indeed one captain, John Wilcocks, seized fifteen ships in 1469 alone! These were men who had a deep kinship and affinity with Raleigh and Drake and would have basked in their reflected fame and glory.

Obviously, when this carte blanche was granted, they became a law unto themselves – answerable to no one. Don't forget they were in an inaccessible part of this realm, far from the capital and their sovereign. Communication was almost non-existent, with messengers taking weeks to complete a journey - or possibly never being seen again. This state of affairs couldn't be allowed to continue and, when England finally made peace with France, Edward IV decreed that men from Dartmouth were to stop this blatant piracy. They arrived, ships were seized, the harbour chain was removed and several Fowey men were arrested and hanged.'

Drew sat back and smiled at my absorbed attention. 'Don't worry, Jenny, I promise I'm not about to hijack the next cruise liner that passes this way or steal any gold bullion. You are safe with me! Let's go and stretch our legs and find something to eat before I take you to the Museum. I am hoping to find something more about these nefarious country gentlemen as well as the town's numerous fishermen-turned-pirates. I know they were finally stopped by the sovereign at a much later period. At school we were told it was something to do with a group called The Hanseatic League. I am hoping their history is recorded somewhere here and that it won't be too dull for you. But let's go for a wander and find a decent meal first.' And with that he pulled me out of the settle and dragged me out into the spring sunshine.

We wandered down towards the castle and then strolled back to find a sunny, sheltered corner in the Old Grammar School Garden until it was time to eat. Last time in Fowey we had discovered a small bistro that offered soup and the usual Cornish pasties. As both were homemade we enjoyed them enormously and washed them down with two halves of locally brewed cider. Feeling pleasantly satisfied, we made our way back towards the Quay and entered the Museum. Drew explained to me it had once been the Town Hall and this particular room was the old Council Chamber. The middle-aged woman on the desk listened intently and, on his asking for information about the Hanseatic League in relation to the Fowey Gallants, she appeared puzzled (like me she had only heard of the local sailing club!) and then, in mitigation, admitted she originally came from Surrey and knew very little about the town's varied history. She offered any of the hundreds of books and historic papers that were stored there and suggested we take a look at them. Andrew sat down eagerly and it was not long before he was finding all sorts of gems.

He quickly made a summary and it appears that between the twelfth and the seventeenth centuries a commercial and defensive confederation of merchant guilds came into being. Starting in Lubeck, Germany, it eventually spread across the Baltic, through the Low Countries and down as far south as Britain. It had been created to protect its members' economic interests and offered diplomatic privileges to all those merchants trading along its routes. We know they traded in timber, furs, flax, honey, cereals, cloth – probably in anything they were able to buy or sell. To show how important they became, in 1157 Henry II freed them from London tolls and soon they owned warehouses in places as far apart as Berwick, Kings Lynn, Boston, Bristol, Norwich and York. Their collective bargaining power was immense. Sadly, all one can deduce is the Fowey Gallants either didn't recognise their special status or dismissed them as fair game because, whenever they got the chance they would attack them, impound their cargoes and "escort" the ships back into Fowey harbour. Obviously all the spoils were divided between the various privateers and, like the smuggling trade many years later, it would all disappear from sight and no one would know a thing about it. A few empty ships might lie abandoned in the harbour for a short while but most were probably re-named and re-deployed to attack a few more innocent merchantmen on the Gallants' behalf.

I had been relegated to another table and was manfully ploughing through scraps of relevant information when I suddenly struck gold. 'Hey listen to this, Drew. Eventually the King was told of your ancestors' nefarious attacks and, in a towering fury, sent a Royal Messenger to sort it all out. He was supposed to bring the wrongdoers to justice, recover all the stolen goods and return them to their rightful owners, thereby appeasing the Hanseatic League. But I don't think it went to plan. The messenger, whoever he was, had his ears cut off and was sent packing! Talk about thumbing your nose at your Sovereign Lord! I wonder if that was when the King demanded that the men of Dartmouth teach your lot a lesson?' I asked.

We both sat back and grinned at one another. By then it was getting late and time to retrace our footsteps. We caught the Polruan ferry just as it was about to leave and were back on the other side of the river in no time at all. We trailed up the steep hill to collect the car and I must have felt particularly tired because I curled up on the front seat and dropped into a deep sleep. And I didn't wake until Andrew gently ran his hand over my hair to remind me we were back outside our Lerryn hideaway.

We had our evening meal early that night and I must have found my second wind because, when we were snuggled down between the sheets, I again returned to questioning him about his seemingly odd relationship with his wife. I hated prying but felt I was entitled to a reason why they disliked each other so much and yet still remained together. I also knew my partnership with Robin was on the verge of collapsing and therefore I was determined to be clear what Andrew felt about his marriage and if there was the slightest chance of resolving his problems. I took a deep breath and began.

'You say you and Fay lead completely separate lives. *She* has her own friends and you have yours. You have told me, if *you* don't speak, she can go hours without uttering one word of her own accord. She sits almost all day playing games, a topped-up glass of wine at her side, and it is often well past midnight before she retires to bed. Do you *really* have separate bedrooms and sitting rooms?' I asked. 'And even at meals, which are always accompanied by the television, you say you rarely communicate unless one of you demands the salt. May I also ask why you both mark your solitary events on a calendar, or leave brisk notes for each other, instead of discussing them face-to-face? That's what normal married couples do, Andrew, or didn't you know? What you are describing is the way colleagues at work conduct their *business* affairs and certainly not the way husbands and wives carry on their humdrum lives. Where's the fun, where's the togetherness, what's the point? OK, so she left you once and tried to abscond to the States, accompanied by your children, before circumstances forced her back. You also told me she possibly had an affair at the same time she was in America with them, but that was years and years ago, Andrew, and surely you both got over that once she returned to Britain?' My voice had risen with amazement and indignation at the sterile arrangement he was determined to still call a marriage. 'Every time you contact me, I ask myself why me and not his wife? I think, why don't *they* enjoy a life together, have fun, disagree, cry, get bored and do all the things most couples do? And next I query what you see in me, and why I am so special. But perhaps I'm not and anyone could take Fay's place and it doesn't need to be me at all?' There, I'd dared to say it. It sounded so odd – even to my own ears. I sat back and waited for his explanation. Surprisingly it was nothing like I had bargained for. I didn't know I had thoughtlessly forced open *Pandora's Box.*

'Oh, Jenny, you don't know the half of it,' Andrew answered, so quietly that I had to lean to catch his whispered words. 'Remember that Fay was a beautiful, but spoiled girl, who had never been thwarted in her life. Her parents indulged her because they loved her so much. She was precious to them, as she was their only child and I believe her mother was unable to conceive again, but it obviously never occurred to them that the man she married, and any family they might have, would have to live with her tantrums, her demands and be constantly forced to accede to her wishes and even change their lives to accommodate and please her.

'I went back to studying once more. Going to university meant a great deal of hardship and work. I attended lectures during the day and worked in a bakery at night; but I was prepared for that because it culminated in my degree. I had just settled down to teaching in York when, once again, Fay pulled the rug out from under our feet and demanded I obtain a better job. I was puzzled as I thought she *wanted* a schoolmaster for a husband She did, but she was scathing about my salary, my prospects and our surroundings. Suddenly she longed for a warm climate and a more exciting way of life. I think she remembered, with longing, some of the officers she had met when living in various embassies around the world. To cut a long story short, to appease her, I applied for an Army posting to Hong Kong and was accepted. It was a different way of life from what I had known in the Merchant Navy and the Diplomatic Service but, after an initial induction period, I settled down and began to see it was a good move after all. And Fay was happy at last. The children were only three and four but they both began to thrive in the pleasant atmosphere she generated – and I learned to relax too. Mess do's, reasonable accommodation, servants to cater to her every whim and lots of exciting new friends. For me there was sailing, which I had missed since my Medway school days and Cornwall, so perhaps I too became caught up in the excitement of making new friends as well as weekends competing against other members of the yacht club. I taught both the kids to swim, along with any other children who were interested, and they became like little dolphins in the safe, warm water. I suppose I also became too complacent.'

'Sounds idyllic,' I muttered.

'We made lots of friends that first year. Most of them were married couples, often with families, and teaching was an enjoyable career in such pleasant surroundings. There would be the occasional single chap – often labelled by the rest of us as Merry Bachelors – and one such became my best friend. He was ADC to my Colonel and had kindly shown me the ropes on my arrival. Ernest often made a threesome at our table - he would usually join us for any Mess do's and many an inebriated evening we would spend happily together. His wife was in the UK, he told me, looking after her aged parents and would only join him if anything happened to them. Fay took up bridge with a vengeance and attended coffee mornings with all the other mothers and wives. Peter and Mark settled down with their ayah and were lovingly spoiled by all the rest of the household. I thought everything was going well until one day I arrived home early after an important meeting had been cancelled.'

'I walked in the door ready to surprise them all with a trip to the beach. I thought Fay looked startled and saw a flash of annoyance pass across her face. I bent down to rummage through a drawer for my swimming togs as she stated they were off swimming with Ernie. I grunted assent and dug a bit deeper for a decent beach towel. Making herself very clear, Fay then said, "The children and I will be picnicking on the beach with Ernie." The silence stretched as I gradually realised the implications of such a statement. I straightened up and turned to her. I could hear Mark grizzling about a toy Peter was trying to take off him as Fay looked at me defiantly. I gazed at her silently. She then admitted to me they were in love, had been for ages and any time he was able to get off they tried to spend together. For a short while the whole of my world dissolved and then the shouting began. I bundled up the children and thrust them at their nurse who appeared, as if by magic, and quietly removed them. I then told Fay to telephone her boyfriend, mention their jolly was off and say I would sort him out later.'

I sat, open mouthed, as Andrew explained what must have been the worst jolt of his life. The silence stretched as he contemplated the rumpled duvet. 'And then what happened?' I asked.

'She told me Ernie would have left and be on his way. I stared moodily out of the window until our bell jauntily sounded. At that I descended the stairs. As soon as I opened our door I saw my best friend had guessed what had happened. I tersely told him to get out of my house, get out of my sight and leave my wife and family alone. He stepped forward to remonstrate with me but then realised there was no point and returned to his parked car. He drove off, with a spatter of gravel, leaving silence in his wake.'

'I climbed the stairs and then, as I said, the shouting began in earnest. Two days later she said the affair was completely over. I went back to work not absolutely convinced. But, as time passed, I began to believe my marriage had survived. I also ignored the Colonel's ADC as if he didn't exist and he avoided me like the plague! Everyone else politely ignored the pair of us.'

With that, we both settled down for sleep. I must admit it was a long time in coming to me that night; I mulled over Andrew's revelations and I was awake long before dawn appeared the next morning. I think that night was the turning point in *our* relationship: I suddenly saw the man I had always admired enormously, and had grown to love without restraint, was as frail and human as I was. He had been hurt unbearably but he had managed to keep his family intact and I admired him for these qualities.

The next morning it was raining. Suddenly the weather had changed. Gone was the bright sunlight making the dewy grass and river sparkle while lighting up all the small craft at their moorings. It was now sombre and dark as a mist came down amongst the trees and hid the weathered cottages on the far bank. I had been given the choice of destination for our final day together. My mind had been toying with the idea of Newquay's huge sandy beaches. I longed to walk the cliffs, watch the surfers at play and breathe in deep lungfuls of salty air. Sadly it was not to be, so I settled for the Eden

Project. I had been there a few times since it was first built and had been amazed at the progress that had been made and how popular it was with holidaymakers. I had heard visitors from as far away as New Zealand mention it with awe and, on a cold and drizzly day, I knew it was the ideal place to stay warm and enjoy all that was on display in those gigantic biomes.

It had been built in 2000 but *I* had viewed it before it had been opened. Robin and I had joined a coach party from Honiton to see this new phenomenon that had been built in a fifty-metre deep crater, an old kaolin pit, near St Austell Bay. Our coach had come trundling over the hill and, for the first time I had viewed what looked like some glass-domed igloos. I now know they are not glass but hexagonal plastic cells supported effortlessly on steel frames. I can remember wondering what all the fuss was about as they simply looked like big greenhouses to me. Suddenly I had spotted what looked like a tiny fly on the roof of the biggest dome and, as we travelled nearer, I had begun to realise what looked insignificant to me at a distance was really a human being perched on the roof of the most gigantic building I had ever seen!

That day we arrived before most of the crowds. We parked our car in the huge car park and, shunning *Perky,* the blue train, we made our way towards the entrance. Lots more had been done since my last visit. The whole edifice was now nestling cosily under a skyline of trees and looked as if it had been there for generations. The raw scar had been healed and, in truth, this *was* Cornwall's answer to the Garden of Eden. Even though it was only April, I noticed a glowing frill of lemon around the buildings; a veritable meandering stream consisting of hundreds of daffodils. Even in the absence of sunshine these dazzled my eyes. We wandered past a lake, lots of vegetable plots and sculptures. I spotted a massive bee and didn't approach any closer. After being badly stung as a child, I pretended indifference but was quietly in terror of the furry brown-and-yellow insects. I forced myself to walk nonchalantly past and stared instead at a large robot. It was made of discarded rubbish and I smiled to see, in its toothy smile, old computer and mouse gadgets. As we walked inside I saw a perfectly sculptured mettlesome horse made of driftwood, looking ready to gallop away. I directed Andrew towards the Mediterranean Biome first and, as we strolled around, we admired thousands of plants taken from their natural habitat and placed in this controlled and gentle climate. A hundred years ago this would have been awe-inspiring to the stay-at-home British public, but today, when most of us regularly holiday abroad, we view flourishing plants that are often impossible to grow in our country and it has made us a little blasé even in these stunning surroundings. Now the Tropical Biome, to my mind, is vastly different. It always attracts crowds who perhaps have never seen a rainforest and it all looks so authentic – with steep climbing walkways and a massive gushing waterfall. Andrew and I steadily made our way to the top and leaned on a rustic bridge to survey the whole moist, misty vista. It really was stunning and it was not difficult to believe, in the steamy heat, that a Malayan jungle had been transported to the West Country.

Soon after, we realised it was past midday and time to eat. We made our way to the restaurant and enjoyed a pleasant, light meal. Sometime later, feeling benign and well rested, we decided we might need educating. We made our way to The Core and joined a school class of boys and girls as they walked through booths, studied a multitude of displays and learned all sorts of interesting facts from all around the world. Tired but happy, we then decided to make our way back to Lerryn – both satisfied to have dodged the squally showers and to have had a marvellous day into the bargain.

As we made our way through winding lanes back to the Ship Inn, Andrew - ever the schoolmaster and raconteur - told me a little of the life story of Kenneth Grahame. 'Originally born in Edinburgh, he lived in Scotland until he was five years old and then moved to his grandmother's house in Cookham Dean on the River Thames in Berkshire along with two young brothers and a sister,' he said. 'He was educated at a school in Oxford and hoped to go to university there, but the family couldn't afford the expense and at seventeen he entered the Bank of England as a clerk. One wonders if he had been lonely as a child, but apparently an uncle, the curate of Cookham Dean's church, introduced the children to the river and boating. Grahame certainly must have been bright and resourceful because he rose through the Bank's ranks fairly quickly and, at thirty, he became its secretary. He was a confirmed bachelor, a big and clumsy man and, in 1899 at forty, he briefly courted an Elspeth

Thomson, mainly by post, and married her.'

'Golly what an odd couple they must have been,' I commented. 'Passionate ardour via the postman!'

Andrew grinned, 'We are told she became disillusioned almost immediately, but a year later she bore him a son prematurely, christened Alistair and fondly known as 'Mouse'. Sadly Alistair was born blind in one eye and, we are told, was a difficult and precocious child but, in a studio portrait, he looks a delightfully chubby, handsome little boy and soon his father was amusing him with bedtime stories. Eventually his father translated these stories into letters for 'Mouse' while he was far away with his governess in Littlehampton and these finally became the first draft of his classic children's story. Two things may have contributed to his retiring from the Bank of England. The new Governor wasn't enamoured with his slightly eccentric secretary but, more sinister, he was involved in a shooting and it is not clear who the gunman was aiming for. Anyway, Grahame retired on grounds of ill health when he was forty nine and immediately published his *Wind in the Willows*.'

Andrew went on to tell me the couple must have fallen in love with Cornwall as they chose Fowey's St Finbarrus parish church in which to marry. They later returned to the Green Bank Hotel, Falmouth, where more letters were sent to 'Mouse', but soon moved back to their favourite haunt, Fowey, for a month. They finally arrived in Lerryn and stayed for a short while. I had listened intently because their story had become extra special to me. The setting where Andrew had spent his childhood became the magic place where *we* had met and fallen in love. Silly, I know, but that evening I walked back into The Ship Inn basking in a golden glow.

We ate our meal chatting about the Eden Project and all we had seen, interspersed with our thoughts on Kenneth Grahame and his strangely interesting life. I must admit we made our way up to bed distinctly early that night. We were to be abruptly parted again the next day with neither of us able to see a solution to our problem.

Lovemaking over, we curled up together and, half asleep but still unable to let it go, I asked some more searching questions about Fay and her lover, Ernie. Andrew mumbled some unsatisfactory answers until he said, 'And I wasn't entirely blameless, I suppose.'

I sharply asked him what he meant. 'Susan, next door neighbour....
hardly knew her... came in next day to borrow something... sugar...
tea.... found me crying.' I quickly asked him what he was talking
about and the answers became even more indistinct. '... tried to hide
my face......pulled me into her arms...ended up on our sofa... my
head buried in her lap...' I waited, hardly daring to breathe – and
then he said it, 'We ended up in bed together.'

I lay in that huge, comfortable bed frozen with shock. All the
talk about Fay having it off with Andrew's best friend and then he
informs me he was doing exactly the same with hers! Hong Kong
sounded like a decadent shambles to me. Were none of these people
faithful to their partners and marriages? I shuddered at the casual
infidelity his words had uncovered that night. Andrew had slid into
a deep, sound sleep and his even breathing sounded loud to my
ears. I carefully slid from under the sheets and curled up tightly
against the wall and the foot of the bed. I was to stay that way for
most of the long night. The moonlight shone fitfully on my face as
racing clouds passed across the cold light. I shivered and drew my
feet up and away from the man who had just shattered my illusions,
and my love, forever. What an idiot I had been, I chided myself,
and if only I could creep out of this room and get away from the
enormity that was his squalid revelation. That was impossible. Our
beautiful hideaway was hidden in the depths of Cornwall. There
was no public transport and no way of making my escape.

The next morning I was up before Andrew had stirred. There
were no cups of tea brewed and offered in the early light of dawn
and, when he clambered out of bed, he met me coming out of the
shower. I quietly pushed past him and dressed in the first clothes I
came across. I packed my case swiftly and efficiently and went and
stood looking out of the window. *He* chatted away as normal while
he grabbed handfuls of socks and ill-folded shirts to slam them
into his holdall perched on the other side of our bed. Obviously he
never noticed my silence, or he misunderstood it, as we marched
downstairs for breakfast and, luckily, the usual greetings and
ordering kept me from having to make conversation. I ate very little
and still he failed to notice. After settling our account we both slid
into the car and drove out of the village. We were well past the
Polperro turn off before my silence, even to me, began to grow

oppressive and it was only then that he placed a gentle hand on my knee and told me to cheer up. I ignored him by turning my face to stare out of the window and started counting chimney pots. Finally he must have realised something was very seriously wrong.

'What's the matter, sweetheart?' he asked. 'Don't feel sad - we are on our way back to civilisation. There will be other meetings, I promise you, and maybe next time we can arrange for a much longer holiday.' I turned to face him and simply stared. He immediately pulled the car up at the side of the road and took my freezing hands in his comforting warm ones. 'What?' he stammered. 'What on earth have I done?'

And it was only then that I unfroze my voice to explain exactly what he had admitted to me only a few hours before. He sat with his head touching the steering wheel and then, as if he was in a daze, drove on towards our destination – Plymouth. He asked me to wait until we were nearer the station and then he promised to explain, truthfully and at length. I sat back in my seat and forced myself to stare ahead and tried not to think. We pulled up at the old Plymouth North Road station and he parked the car and disappeared inside to buy us both a takeaway coffee. I curled my hands around the cardboard cup for warmth and comfort as he began his explanation.

'Please don't think I ever took my marriage lightly, Jenny. Maybe Fay had become tired of me but it had never crossed my mind she would hurt our children in any way by threatening our marriage. Oh I knew she would often act provocatively and, with an ironical twist of reasoning, I would try to ignore her shallow flirtations for what they were – nothing. Our real friends soon grew to know her ways, usually when she had drunk too much, and would gently steer her back to me. I suppose Ernie was lonely and she probably found him an easy conquest.'

'After me shouting at her and confronting him in our hallway, it went quiet for a few days until Fay approached me and said their affair was over. They had obviously talked it out and maybe she had decided she had too much to lose or possibly he couldn't face telling *his* wife back in England. Anyway, she promised me it was finished and asked me to forgive her. I said very little. The hurt had gone deep but *I believed her*. In the meantime I realised what a fool I'd been involving Susan in my troubles. I told you she was a neighbour, but she and her husband had never been particular friends of ours. She was motherly and kind and not really Fay's type at all. She didn't play bridge, had older school kids and didn't mix with our set at all. So one afternoon I forced myself to knock on her door and told her what an idiot I had been. She took it very nicely and kissed my cheek for old time's sake. I, of course, felt an absolute heel!' I nodded coldly, but Andrew continued.

'Within a week Fay was smoking. Only a few cigarettes a day, even though she knew I hated the whole concept of smoking. I must have been feeling particularly belligerent because I insisted she never did it in the house and never in front of the children. She agreed. Things went very quiet but I still could not quite settle back into my easy-going routine. I took to coming home at unexpected times and one day I came home and heard her talking quietly on the telephone to her lover. Suddenly I knew why she had taken up smoking. Ernie smoked heavily and it was to disguise any vestige of smell on her clothes or body. I had been duped. I stood in front of her, stone faced, as she fell over her words to finish the conversation. Then, defiantly, she told me she was expecting a baby and it was almost certainly *his*. She also called my two lovely little boys to her. She went down on her knees, took them within the shield of her arms, and said if I stopped her going to him I would never see them again. I stood transfixed as Mark glanced towards me, looked worried, and then both children started crying.'

'What happened after that is pure guesswork. Three days later she told me she had lost the baby. I accepted her statement. She was never a liar. I have no idea if, in the interim, she had gone to my 'best' friend and informed him and he had still refused to break up his marriage for her. He may have originally told her to pass the baby off as mine but that was never Fay's way. Maybe it was his rejection that made her throw herself on *my* mercy. A miscarriage, after all the upset she had suffered, was to be expected I suppose and in one way I felt vaguely sorry for her. A spoilt daughter all her life and now she had lost a child, the love of her paramour as well as the loyalty and love of her husband.'

'And then what happened?' I asked as Andrew stared vacantly out of the car window.

'The next morning I went and spoke to my commanding officer.

In confidence, I explained what had been happening to my family. He expressed real concern and within three weeks his ADC had been sent back to 'promotion' in the UK. I was well aware and under no illusion that my post as a headmaster was more difficult to fill than his and therefore I had been appeased while he had paid the price. Two years later I insisted we moved on to Germany. I don't think Fay ever regained her facile gaiety and, quite honestly, neither did I. But, more importantly, I don't think she ever forgave me!'

Chapter 14

*

Andrew had to see me onto the train. I probably looked as bad as he did: I was completely shattered at his disclosures. I sat in a deserted carriage and stared unseeingly at the passing countryside. No sleep for the past twelve hours - listening to explanations and revelations that stretched my loyalty and understanding to its limit had taken its toll. One minute hearing about a wife's cruel infidelity, then it being counterbalanced by equal unfaithfulness on Andrew's part and finally his telling me the horrifying fact that his wife was willing to take his children away if he stopped her leaving with her lover.

I mused – it was almost as if the miscarriage had proved the perfect solution. I disagreed with Andrew's acceptance. I felt certain Fay had secured an abortion in a mad effort to stop her world rapidly falling apart. Her boyfriend had turned his back on her, she had already told her husband she was expecting another man's child and her options had finally run out. I knew as a nurse that it is difficult to dislodge a healthy growing child if there has been no history of miscarriage. It seemed highly unlikely to me but there was no way I would ever discuss it with Andrew as I hated to add fuel to his already burning fire of puzzlement.

I changed trains at Exeter and waited for what seemed like a long time for the Honiton connection to arrive. I was unbearably tired but needed to see a friendly face so, on the way back home, I called in to see Lorna. She welcomed me with a cup of tea and gently told me some sad news. Fred had suffered a severe stroke while I had been gone and wasn't expected to recover. I mourned his budding friendship with the chipper Mrs Jewell. I told Lorna I had been hoping they would be good for each other. I promised I would visit immediately after the weekend although Lorna warned me he was unconscious. His family had asked if the Home was prepared to look after him and they had agreed, providing he didn't need expert nursing. And I knew, if it were possible to ask Fred, he would have hated to be shifted into a hospital bed on an impersonal ward in our District General Hospital.

Petra joined us as soon as she came in from playing with Megan. We hugged and then she discussed all the animals and fish at length – even Horatio the hedgehog whose name I had miraculously remembered. After looking at Lorna for permission, I decided it was time to warn Petra that Crumble was getting a bit old for his usual long walks with Rex on the common and soon it would only be an amble round the close and back to his comfy bed. Lorna helped by reminding her that Crumble was very old while Rex was only middle-aged and that appeared to satisfy her. I knew I was putting off the time for my meeting with Robin but finally, as Derek arrived home, I forced myself out of their scruffy kitchen armchair and made my way back to the bungalow.

The place smelt cold and a bit dusty as I walked through the hall to the sitting room. For something to do, and to break the ice with Robin, I rang him on his mobile and asked him to bring in a takeaway. I couldn't face getting food out of the freezer after deciding what he would like for dinner. Personally, I didn't feel like a meal at all which was stupid because for the past four days I had eaten everything that was placed in front of me. Robin came in like a March wind – his arms full of Chinese food and a case stuffed with work. I asked about the young girl who had gone missing and was told, with a grim smile, that she had turned up two days later with a drippy boyfriend in tow and a very flimsy excuse about them going to Blackpool for a dare. In April? It all sounded like a cover-up story to me but it was so similar to how I was conducting my own secret life that I didn't hotly comment as I would normally have done. Instead I smiled compassionately, because no one knows how much untold upset this sort of thing causes the police or how many personnel are channelled away from important work to begin searching once an incident like this is reported. Adults are given far more leeway, and time, to sort out their own problems; but a child, or teenager going missing, is taken extremely seriously and causes far larger repercussions for the law.

'Anyway, her parents were so relieved to see her that they refused to let us question her too closely,' Robin said with a resigned sigh. 'I personally asked the abashed boyfriend what the hell he had been thinking of – but I got the impression she was the ringleader and he just went along for the ride. And staff shortages, plus routine normal paperwork, made us only too pleased it was all sorted almost immediately and we could get back to catching burglars and tax disc dodgers.'

I could see he was jaded and tired. Guiltily I accepted that my being constantly away didn't help. I dished up our Chinese meal and then watched as straight afterwards he took his unfinished day's work into the sitting room and prepared to sit at his laptop until it was finished. I cleared away and washed up before taking him in an extra coffee. I kissed him and asked him, to save me disturbing him with the evening's television programmes, whether he would mind if I went to bed and read. He absently agreed and I took myself off for a long soak in the bath followed by a good book.

That night I lay in bed and faced exactly what I was doing to my husband. I was aware I was making him unhappy and either I relinquished him completely and threw myself on the mercy of Andrew, a man I quite honestly knew very little about, or I pulled myself together, stopped being unfaithful in thought as well as deed, and got on with my comfortable, fairly contented, life. I might have known Andrew intimately between the ages of sixteen and twenty but that did not guarantee I really knew him all these years later. I loved him – yes – but was that a residue of the old passionate ardour I suffered from as a young woman, I wondered. New lives had intervened for both of us; one that both partnerships had crafted to suit themselves. Did I want to throw all that away for an uncertain future? Either I left kind and considerate Robin and threw myself on Andrew's mercy or I went back to a perfectly pleasant and undoubtedly happy marriage. My conscience nagged constantly; Robin deserved more of me.

I shifted miserably in the bed. It would be Robin's birthday at the beginning of May and I now decided he should have a decent one, whatever the outcome of my tortured doubts. I wondered if he would like to sail our boat to the Isle of Wight for a long weekend. We had long promised ourselves that treat. I could arrange for it to be made ready at fairly short notice and it would certainly blow the cobwebs away! Then an irresistible picture of Cornwall rose unbidden in my mind – of Newquay with its magnificent beaches, endless rollers, blue sky and cliffs. I couldn't promise the blue sky but I could deliver the rest and, if I could ensure all our friends would come as well, I knew instinctively that Robin would dearly love it. That settled, I went to sleep and didn't awake until after Robin had crept out of the house early the next morning.

First thing, as soon as I was presentable, I rang the Home and arranged to visit Fred. The Matron warned me he was deeply comatose but I still felt I needed to see him, if only for a short time. I noticed the driveway shingle had been recently raked as I pulled up outside the shiny, black front door. The carer's face lit up as she welcomed me in, and then fell as I asked to be shown up to Fred's room. I saw only a shallow mound under the bedclothes. The curtains were drawn and his breathing was shallow and laboured. All I could do was clasp his hand and sit close to the bed. I chatted on about the few old neighbours that were left behind in the close, I spoke of the weather, I told him about Lerryn and Kenneth Grahame and how beautiful the slow-flowing river looked in the sparkling dew of morning. There was no response. I noticed that every half hour or so, a nurse would glance through the doorway so I knew they were taking very good care of him. Finally, I stood up and squeezed his hand as I kissed him goodbye and made my way down the stairs with a heavy heart.

I was surprised to find Mrs Jewell sitting dejectedly in the Quiet Room. Obviously she missed her new friend, too. I gave her Fred's fudge that I had brought back from Cornwall and she absent-mindedly patted my hand. I took my leave of her before she could ask for the latest news of him. I didn't want to add to her distress.

As soon as I returned I rang Robin's boss and asked if Robin was entitled to a long weekend off for his birthday. I swore him to secrecy as I wanted it to be a complete surprise for him. I also asked, diplomatically, if he and his wife would like to join us. He had always been a good sport and agreed immediately. He promised to ask his wife. I was then able to contact most of his work colleagues;

Ross, his police roommate in Newcastle; Alexis, his sister and some of our mutual friends. Both Lorna and Margaret regretfully declined – Margaret because she was unable to leave young Megan and her vicar husband. Lorna moaned that Derek was unexpectedly snowed under with work, but then she was also unable to leave Petra or any of the animals as well. She promised faithfully to look after Crumble and, with relief, I found another problem had been sorted. I left Dee and Paul, as well as Meryl and Adam, until last as I knew they would surely be up for it. Who wouldn't? A free few days in Cornwall with food and entertainment thrown in was a spring blessing. As I ate my scratch lunch I made a list of probable names. If most people could get away, I reckoned there would be eight or nine couples and roughly three or four on their own. I went ahead then and booked the usual small hotel we always used when we visited Newquay. As it was pre-season they were delighted to open the place just for us. I secured a really good rate but warned them the numbers could possibly rise or fall with unforeseen circumstances. They accepted philosophically. They also asked if we needed entertainment. I asked what was on offer and I decided a magician would suit everyone on the first night, a 'Who Wants to be a Millionaire' quiz on the second – that we could run ourselves – culminating on the last night with a singing guitarist playing 60s to 80s music, plus an impromptu darts tournament for anyone who was bored.

The hotel was in the centre of town but also in the enviable position of overlooking The Island. I tried not to remember that was where I had booked when I had spent my first few days with Andrew. Luckily I had chosen separate hotels for us both, much to Andrew's amusement, so there would be no awkward moments when I walked in with friends.

I hadn't spoken to Andrew since I had returned home. Our only connection was through our mobile phones during the day. I would tell him when I was free either during an evening, when Robin would be returning late, or when he was on nights. Once we got into an established pattern he would ask me – from call to call – when he should next ring. But, after that evening in bed when I tried to sort my feelings out once and for all, I was curiously diffident to set the whole affair in motion once more and I hesitated to contact him. His texts never stopped coming although he seemed to be aware of my tardiness and, ever polite, he waited for me to get in touch. Eventually I told him I was arranging a large birthday bash in Cornwall for Robin and they ceased immediately.

Conversely, now we weren't in contact, it gave my mind freedom to dwell on the life Fay and her husband led. I now knew why he was able to ring me sometimes in the evenings when I would hear muted music or the television playing softly in the background. They would be sitting in separate sitting rooms and he would be taking little risk. Midnight would be no trouble at all. He would wish her good night, take himself to his own room and his solitary bed, while she would be playing her compulsive computer games and drinking herself into oblivion. Six large glasses of red wine a night seemed like an awful lot of alcohol to me and I wondered at the state of her liver. He assured me she treated him like a pane of glass the rest of the time, except when they had visitors when she immediately became devoted and helpful, and his only daily chores were to awaken her at a suitable time with an early morning tray of tea and to feed the cat regularly.

He had amused me somewhat by saying, 'We have been known to pass on the stairs in the mornings. Me emerging from my en-suite shower and Fay entering the family bathroom.'

Everything was arranged for Robin's party and my only task was to tell him the good news. No one cancelled and most people appeared to be looking forward to it. My friend Jess was having difficulty in persuading her husband to bring her. I had never known him that well and had always considered him a rather difficult man with a ponderous, negative attitude to life. She said he hadn't been well recently and she hesitated leaving him. I rang her for a long chat and she finally agreed her husband was quite capable of looking after himself for a few days and, anyway, her daughter-in-law would always be willing to keep an eye on him. I promised that Robin and I would make a detour to Taunton to pick her up early on the Friday morning and deposit her back four days later. We ended up laughing and reminiscing about days gone by when Jess had been a flighty teenager making eyes at all the boys and I had been too shy to join in.

Lorna went in alone to sit with Fred for an hour the next day and sent word of no improvement. Two days later he slipped away in the early hours of the morning and we both mourned him. The funeral, conducted by Margaret's husband, was a week later. It was a low-key affair with just a scattering of his family and with only Lorna, Margaret and me representing the rest of our neighbours and friends. I felt as if my world was shrinking and clung even more to Robin when he arrived home from work obviously jaded and harassed. I encouraged him to spend the odd evening with his mates at the local pub and I always managed to tag along. It saved me looking longingly at the telephone and wondering what Andrew was doing. Was he bored by the television or hosting a dinner party to pass the time?

Our trip to Newquay came around very quickly. I was sorry Lorna and Margaret were unable to come but relieved I was leaving Crumble in good hands. Robin loaded up the car and I took the dog for his short amble. We were all ready to go but I found a reason to go back indoors and give him one extra cuddle. He raised his head with a big yawn and thumped his tail for me but I was certain he knew I was leaving him alone. I comforted myself knowing Petra or Lorna would be round shortly as we raced off to Taunton to pick up Jess.

Things weren't much better there. Jess's husband, never the happiest of men, looked lugubriously up at the sky while dragging her suitcase out to the car and predicted rain within the hour. She kissed him and we drove off rapidly before he could make any more dismal predictions and put a damper on our holiday.

The three of us managed to get settled into the hotel before the general mob arrived and I spent the next hour sorting out, with Reception, who was going where and making sure friends were near to one another and that everyone was happy. Mounds of luggage was all dumped in the foyer as friends shook hands, hugged one another or waited to be introduced. The hotel announced there was a free buffet laid out for us in the dining room. Promptly we made our way there en masse by following a smart waitress. We soon devoured the light refreshments that had been provided for our enjoyment and that thoughtful gesture from the management seemed to set the easy-going tone for the whole weekend. Robin stood up and explained, after my prompting, that everyone could meet for breakfast between 8am and 10am; guests were then free to go their own way the rest of the day but he asked them to be back for dinner every evening at 6.30pm sharp. A notice was placed in Reception about the after-dinner activities each night and I noticed various friends studying it and passing amused or rude comments. That was just what I wanted and hopefully no one would be bored.

My cousins and our best friends found their rooms and unpacked and, at our request, made their way back to our large bedroom for a get-together. It was so lovely to be with them once more and we ended up sprawling on our bed, on the chairs, or the floor and nattering to our hearts' content. Dee, hunched up on the window seat, was watching the surf as it crashed up against The Island and threw spume through the fragile bridge that connects it to the cliff opposite our hotel. Paul, Adam and Robin were arguing about football and Meryl, Jess and I were discussing, of all things, the price of shoes.

I had booked Merlo, a magician, for the first night. He came on as soon as our meal had been promptly cleared away and we were lounging around with drinks of our choice and a mellow mood had settled over us all. He was brilliant. He appreciated the adult audience of friends and colleagues and started his act with lots of funny patter and jokes that had the men roaring with glee and the women looking a bit pink. Gradually he got the measure of us and he then chose his accomplice with care. Hazel, who agreed to be his stooge, came and stood beside him on the raised dais. Kevin, her husband, was busily telling everyone how hopeless she would be, while we all attended closely as watches and bracelets disappeared and turned up inside uncut loaves of bread. Cards were chosen, lost and then found again. Money was taken, marked, destroyed and then appeared again in a friend's pocket on the other side of the room. We watched amazed. Robin's boss almost lost his trousers as his braces disappeared and his wife nearly tumbled out of her chair with laughter. Hazel got her own back on her husband being so rude when Merlo bound Kevin in chains and then left him sitting on the floor trying in vain to extricate himself. That night we all went to bed chattering and laughing and, as Robin and I settled down for sleep, he thanked me and I could have cried at his being so grateful.

The next morning dawned bright and clear. As can sometimes

happen at the beginning of May, the sun came out and it felt as if summer was only just around the corner. To my cost I know that is often a false impression, but after a hearty breakfast most of us took ourselves off to enjoy the delights Cornwall has to offer. Meryl and Adam went off to visit friends in Mevagissey and Dee, Paul, Robin, Jess and I all went for a walk across Great Western and Towan beaches. There were lots of surfers in their black wetsuits and we spent ages gazing at their amazing antics as they rode the waves and then paddled out madly to catch the next one – and the next. Surfing consists of dreams, I consider; it is the perfect wave, caught at the optimum moment and can always be eclipsed, bettered and exceeded again and again. It is the Holy Grail of water sport and I can watch it endlessly.

We came to the Harbour and made our way across the rippled sands and tethered anchor ropes towards the granite steps cut into the cliffs. Whenever we came to Newquay, Robin and I would always have our morning coffee at the small Harbour Hotel that perches above the small bobbing craft anchored within the encircling protection of the chunky quay. There was a glass-covered verandah where one can sit in cosy comfort, and look along past the various coves towards Watergate Bay. We drank our delicious coffee and did just that.

After a snack lunch we all squeezed into our car and visited Padstow. I would have liked to have shown them Prideaux House which stands just outside Padstow and overlooks the Camel estuary. It was built in the 1500s and is still a comfortable family home with elegant, encrusted, high white ceilings, a fabulous library and a Great Chamber which is famous for its biblical tableau.

Sadly everyone opted to wander around the gift shops and admire the chic boutiques which seemed to multiply every time we visit. This is still a bustling fishing port with a small fleet and a jumble of slate-roofed cottages around the harbour, interspersed with picturesque narrow alleyways, quays and boat slips. It is said St Petroc landed here, five hundred years after Christ was born, in an attempt to bring Christianity to Britain. Sir Walter Raleigh chose to live here when he was Warden of Cornwall and the famous Captains Hawkins and Frobisher sheltered in the harbour on stormy occasions. There are also elegant Georgian and Victorian villas that have been turned into very attractive restaurants and cafés. And of course Rick Stein, with his renowned fish restaurants and café, is extremely well patronised.

I told my friends about the Doom Bar – a sand bank that has gradually built up across the estuary and is still a danger to craft today. We had missed Padstow's 'Obby 'Oss Day which takes place on the eve of May each year. It is a strange ceremony and no one can say exactly what it represents apart from a fertility rite. It takes the form of a sort of circular wheel worn as a sort of skirt by a man and covered in material. It is prodded and pushed through the streets and hundreds come to see it. Robin and I had never managed to be in Padstow on the right day – unlike the Helston 'Furry' or Floral Dance which we had seen quite often. We had an ice cream as I told them the history of the port and then, on the way back to Newquay, we travelled by way of Trevone, Constantine, Treyarnon and Bedruthan Steps to enable them to admire the magnificent unspoilt coastline that abounds all along Cornwall's northern seaboard. We had spent so long in the sunshine lounging around on Padstow's waterfront, with me telling them tales of days long gone, that we were almost late getting back.

We all rushed away to our rooms to shower and change for the evening meal. Everyone had explored in different directions, it seemed, and they were all excitedly telling their neighbours what a good day they had had. I was sure it was all due to the pleasant weather and I was grateful – Cornwall can be dreary in the rain because its pleasure mainly relies on outside entertainment and consequently there are very few Eden Projects, ten pin bowling alleys or stately homes to shelter one from inclement weather. Robin stood up and tapped his glass as the last person took their last mouthful of delicious food. He announced we would be having a superior, 'Who Wants to be a Millionaire?' type quiz. Pete and Denise often devised this sort of competition down at the Police Club and we had all been roped in to play from time to time. Everyone groaned and Kevin quipped, 'Well, as long as the Boss doesn't win we shall know it's not fixed!'

The tables were cleared and we all gathered round in various poses of indolence. Most people went to the bar for drinks to fortify themselves and the rest of us tried to look intelligent. Peter got up and Denise handed him the questions. He swore she hadn't had a hand in setting them so we all grudgingly allowed her to take part. Actually, to my surprise, it was good fun. The Boss got booed by his staff as a matter of course every time he ventured an answer and shortly into the evening we were *all* teasing the poor man. His wife made up for him, I noticed, and gradually she was quietly making her way through the heats and taking on all comers. It ended with her and Adam fighting it out to the last and, whether he was being his usual gentlemanly self or not, she ended up with the bottle of Champagne and he won the bottle of wine. Honour was satisfied between the men and the women with lots of boasts that the next night we would beat the pants off the men at darts – easily.

Robin and I made our weary way to bed just before midnight. It had been another successful day, I considered, and I hoped he was really enjoying the run-up to his birthday the next morning. We snuggled down and I must have dropped off to sleep almost immediately because I didn't wake up until my husband nudged me with a cup of tea and a beaming grin on his face. I remembered to murmur *Happy Birthday* as I buried my face in the steaming fragrance.

We strolled downstairs just past eight o'clock and were met with a rollicking chorus of 'Happy Birthdays' and back-slapping. Robin's plate was piled high with gaily wrapped presents and he was forced to open them before he ordered his food. Joke handcuffs, police helmets, wigs and even a urine bottle were unwrapped but there were also some decent ones as well. My cousins presented him with a cashmere scarf, and the expensive wristwatch I had bought on the promise of my inheritance money was oohed and aahed over; but it was Robin having to sit and eat a full English breakfast in a red glittering wig, with a child's police helmet perched on top, that fascinated most people.

The meal finished very late that morning. I am sure the staff were itching to get away but they took it all in good part and joined in with the fun. I rang home to make sure Crumble was fine and Lorna took the opportunity to wish Robin a happy birthday and remind him we were due at their place for a meal on the Monday evening to celebrate even further. Robin asked me what I wanted to do with our day. Meryl and Adam had offered to take Jess with them to the Eden Project and my cousins asked to join them.

Personally, I hated the thought of returning after spending such a lovely time there with Andrew, so I looked at Robin enquiringly. Would he like to visit the Lappa Valley Railway out at Newlyn East, I wondered, and then maybe go on to Truro for lunch? I knew how he loved all sorts of trains and engines and, as we hadn't visited this miniature railway for years, it might be interesting to see what improvements had been made. Robin was delighted and we went off happily together.

In fact the Lappa Valley incorporates *three* miniature railways now. We took ourselves the short journey inland from Newquay, down past Kestle Mill and Trerice, a small National Trust gem of an Elizabethan manor house, to Benny Halt Station. The line had originally been built around 1850 to transport minerals but luckily, when it became derelict, someone had the foresight to open it once more to amuse people like us. We climbed on board to be transported the one mile it takes to travel to East Wheal Rose mine, passing on the way two lakes where colourful canoes bobbed around islands in the sparkling sunshine. We then took the Woodland Railway on a high-speed replica train around a circular track, past the maze, a towering mine chimney and a derelict engine house. Finally, we got on the branch line to Newlyn East. The ·whole valley is relatively small so we opted to walk back towards Benny Halt and our parked car. This way it enabled us to enjoy all the carriages and puffing engines as they bustled by crowded out with excited families, waving and all having a whale of a time.

Truro was staid by contrast. We chose to have our lunch in the shadow of its cathedral, a modern, muted, flint-grey Anglican church, the perfect size for such a small city and only completed just before the First World War, in 1910. When I enter the town I am always amazed at the dramatic impact of the twin spires when they appear, as if by magic, behind streets of shops and houses. The square around the cathedral is often bedecked with hanging baskets and is serene and tranquil; this blends in easily with the surrounding streets that are a mixture of cobbles and Georgian elegance, with market stalls and even a modern Marks & Spencer's. We found an antique shop, a veritable Aladdin's cave and, after I bought an old fishing rod that Robin coveted, we strolled along the banks of the city's meandering river until we finally arrived at Lemon Street on the Quay feeling sad it was time to depart.

There was no way we dared be late again. A special meal was being laid on and we wanted everyone to enjoy their last evening. We were back just before five and found lots of our friends sitting in the spacious lounge enjoying the last rays of the evening sun. Everyone dressed up that night and as we trooped down the main staircase we discovered the dining room laid up for a splendid gala meal. The management had pulled out all the stops; their food was exceptional and it was presented with a flourish. The wine flowed and we were all pleasantly buzzing as we sat back to enjoy our singer accompanied by his guitar or keyboard. True to his brief he gave us songs from the 60s, 70s and 80s with our guests lustily joining in the refrains. Ross, who had roomed in Newcastle with Robin, and his partner decided to show us West Country "bumpkins" a fast-moving jive. Everyone generously clapped and they sat down pink and perspiring. It seemed no time at all before we were taking the floor for the last waltz and shortly afterwards our troubadour took his leave. We had promised the grand finale was to be a darts match – women versus men – and, after the previous night, everyone was determined *their* side would be the winners of this contest.

Well, to give the females their due, they tried hard but I suppose it was a foregone conclusion that the men would wipe the floor with us. Dee, with great encouragement from Paul, held on as long as she was able but even *she* finally succumbed to Ross who, in the end, made it look so easy. They genially shook hands while we all dutifully jeered and Robin handed him a bottle of decent brandy which, like the true gentleman he was, he shared with us as a nightcap.

Gradually we made our way upstairs to our rooms, talking and laughing, in two's and threes and I was truly satisfied it had been a lovely break for us all. Robin cleaned his teeth and moved around in the bathroom as I pushed aside the curtain and stared out of the window.I wondered when next I would be seeing The Island by moonlight. It was glinting through the moving clouds and lighting up the frothing white foam that stirred around the base of the cliffs. It was a calm night but suddenly I felt unutterably sad.

The next morning everyone made an early breakfast in an effort to be away sharply. We stood on the hotel steps and waved them off until it was finally our turn. We dropped a relieved Jess off at Taunton for lunch; her husband, looking none the worse for a couple of days alone, came out and collected her belongings. I was relieved also when we pulled up at our bungalow. I felt a bit like Jess as I raced inside to see Crumble. He raised his head and thumped his tail, which allowed me a deep sigh of relief. Lorna had left a message on the answerphone reminding us of Robin's birthday dinner that evening and, within no time at all, it was as if we had never been away.

****

Two days later my world came to a juddering halt. Robin, coming downstairs to get an early breakfast before work, found Crumble curled up and in a permanent sleep. He returned with a cup of tea and tried to break the news gently. But how do you ever tell anyone their best and most faithful friend has left them forever? I lay in bed shuddering and crying, scared to even venture downstairs and look at Crumble for myself, while Robin put his warm arms around me. I finally remembered not to burden him with my desolation. I knew my husband would be feeling equally wretched, but, as he had to go to work and face an outside world, I knew I had to pull myself together and show I could cope. I heard him make a quick phone call to Lorna, or maybe Margaret, and then a second one to the vet. Once everything was in place he made his way quietly out of the house and I was left in peace.

Lorna came about an hour later and by then I had showered and dressed. I noticed Robin had closed the kitchen door and she tactfully kept it that way as she ushered me into the sitting room to await the vet's arrival. She competently let him in and supervised the removal of Crumble while I crouched in the corner of the settee holding a mug of coffee to my chattering teeth.

I thanked her for her thoughtfulness and, ever Lorna, she replied, 'You would have done exactly the same for me, honey, I know you would.' It was true and I noticed, as we went out through the back door on our way back to her place for lunch, she had removed Crumble's bed, bowls and toys that usually littered my kitchen floor. I stayed with her and Petra until Robin managed to leave work a little earlier that day and then we walked home through the persistent rain together, both of us feeling bereft and sad.

I woke up the next morning alone. For a few seconds I had forgotten Crumble's death and then it hit me all over again. I stretched out my hand for Robin's warmth before I realised his side of the bed was empty and cold. He had thoughtfully allowed me to sleep on while he got ready and set off for work. I struggled into my dressing gown before noting it was past nine o'clock. I sat in the kitchen stirring a solitary mug of tea, which was all I could face. Of course I would learn to accept my faithful companion's life had run its course. It comforted me to know he had died in his sleep, knowing we were close by, although it didn't make it any easier to bear. Trouble was my world was undoubtedly shrinking and, like so many human beings, I needed to be wanted and to be of use to someone.

The day afterwards, I succumbed and contacted Andrew. Call me shallow and self-centred – I was probably both – but I needed to talk. OK, I could have dialled any of my friends and spoken to them on the telephone but I chose to send an e-mail to Andrew on my computer. It all came rushing out as if I had lanced an abscess – the holiday in Newquay, everyone's enjoyment, the coming home and finding my dog still alive, although old and tired, and delighted to see me. *Then the awful morning when he wasn't.* I begged Andrew to please take me away. I missed my four-legged friend; I was unable to enter our kitchen without glancing towards his corner; no one thumped their tail, no one yawned and no one nudged me when they were hungry. I begged for his comfort and care and told him I didn't want to be alone for even another hour. Andrew must have wondered at my sanity but, ten minutes later, he called me on my mobile phone. 'Just tell me where and when and I will arrange it, darling,' he promised.

'Can you? Won't Fay be suspicious?' I asked.

'Leave all that to me. Work out where you want to go and I will be there. Wherever it is, I promise to meet you the second you alight from your car, train or plane.' It was a reckless assurance.

I sat back and felt calmer now Andrew had offered a solution to my panicking hysteria. What on earth was the matter with me? It was not in my nature to be unreasonable and now I was being stupid and paranoid. We managed to finish our conversation – never easy for us – with me promising an ever-wary Andrew to suggest a place that I could visit without raising my husband's suspicions. I could – all too easily.

My story was all in place by the time Robin arrived home that night. As I prepared the meal I worked out a convincing scenario. I had telephoned Cassie to establish an alibi. She was always pleading with me to visit. She had been one of my oldest and best friends: we had trained as hospital probationers together and she had been the one who saved my reason when Chris, after marrying me, had made a fool of me by having an affair with another nurse on our ward. Luckily she now lived midway between my London cousins and Meryl and Adam's place in Epping and fortunately Robin didn't know her well because we had rather lost touch since I had divorced Chris. Cassie had married an intern but it hadn't lasted long and now she appeared to be quite content with her golfing cronies, evening classes and holidays.

Dee and Paul had always extended an open invitation for us to visit them at any time. My concocted story was this: I would take a train up to Waterloo, mention I would be staying at Dee's house for one night before going on to Cassie's flat in Woodford for a few days and then, if I needed to tack a couple of extra days onto my holiday, I could mention I would be going to stay with Meryl and Adam in Epping. It was all pretty vague and I knew Robin would hardly worry and, as long as I rang him regularly, he would never question my whereabouts.

It was indeed a tangled web I wove. I outlined my plans as we had dinner that night. I knew he was concerned about me and I took advantage of his worries to tell a fistful of lies. He, kindly as ever, immediately agreed to my taking a few days off and the next morning I texted Andrew and it was arranged. He suggested we stick to the truth as near as possible by actually going to Essex; later on that day he rang to say he had booked a small, secluded hotel in South Woodford. The picture he sent, via his computer, showed a mock-Tudor black-and-white hotel festooned with hanging baskets. I wouldn't have cared if it had been a prison of a place, with bars at the windows, as long as I was getting away from sadness and bitter loneliness.

The week Andrew chose began on Sunday 3rd July, 2005...

Chapter 15

*

So Andrew wasn't obliged to keep his promise to meet me because I made my own way by train, Underground and bus to Dee and Paul's house that Sunday. Robin was working and therefore was unable to take me to Honiton Station. The whole journey was uneventful but nonetheless I was tired by the time I alighted from the bus in South Chingford.

I walked up their long road and almost fell into their arms when they opened the front door to me. As usual, Dee had laid on a huge spread and we all lazed around as I gave them all the news from Devon while munching and sampling their delicious wine. For once I was relieved to take myself off to bed at a fairly early hour after informing Robin of my safe arrival. As I snuggled down in their cosy back bedroom, I hugged to myself the thought of meeting Andrew the next afternoon and tried to forget that both my cousins had tried to persuade me to ring Cassie and put my "visit" off for a couple of days. There was no way I could agree, so I made up some rubbish about her going on holiday shortly. She often visited an apartment her relations owned in Cyprus so I hoped I wasn't telling an outright lie.

The next morning I arose bright and cheerful. I think Dee was surprised at the miraculous change in me. I hummed as I made the toast and put a huge pot of coffee on the kitchen table. She came down in an old belted dressing gown and scowled at me.

'You sound chipper,' she commented. I filled my mouth with crunchy toast, nodded absently and agreed. Luckily she had to visit her dentist shortly after midday so I took the opportunity to get myself ready and be on my way. I tried not to appear too eager. My cousin is more astute than a traffic warden on the prowl and I didn't want to raise her suspicions. I promised to give Cassie her love and we parted at Chingford Mount where I awaited my bus and she went off to her dental appointment.

I had never been to Kings Cross Station in my life but I discovered it was a fairly simple journey to take the Victoria line from Walthamstow Central; it also meant I arrived in the main line station almost an hour early. To amuse myself I went for a leisurely coffee then sorted out which platform the York train was expected on. I stationed myself outside WH Smith's and watched as other commuters from other trains bustled past me at the normal speedy London clip. Suddenly I was surrounded by three lanky schoolboys. They all clutched clipboards and were obviously doing some sort of study.

'Can you spare us a few minutes, Miss?' the ringleader asked. I glanced at my watch and nodded. They wanted to know whether I lived in London. I disabused them of that one and admitted I came from Devon. They asked if I had ever been to that particular station before and I said I only knew Waterloo, London Bridge and Paddington. Various other questions followed while they all diligently wrote down my answers.

Suddenly I glanced up and there was Andrew standing watching us with a delighted grin. I sent a mischievous smile back and they all turned apprehensively. I then explained this was the gentleman I had come to meet. Andrew explained we wanted to be off before the rush hour began and waited politely as they all thanked me for my time. As they walked away he commented, 'Gosh what is it with you? I can't leave you on your own for five minutes before men are buzzing round you and chatting you up!' I protested vehemently but his answer was to sweep me up and go and find an Underground map that would explain the complicated system of lines that would get us out to the wilds of Essex. It wasn't half as difficult as it first appeared but it did involve changing trains a few times; and more than once we had to make our way down a flight of stairs to find the right platform. Refusing help and being fiercely independent, my usual way was to bump my case down one stair at a time, by kicking it smartly with my foot, while Andrew would simply pick up his case and carry it to the bottom. At one particularly difficult changeover there were quite a few commuters pushing past me when a burly lad took my case out of my hand, swiftly took it down the stairs and deposited it neatly at the bottom. I called out my thanks and he grinned over his shoulder as he shot off in a Londoner's usual hurry.

'See, told you so,' Andrew told me triumphantly. 'You only have to look willowy and helpless and men are swarming around to help.' I told him to shut up as I pushed him along the platform and we squeezed aboard the train that came racing in as we spoke.

Sadly the elegant mock-Tudor hotel wasn't quite as genteel as it had appeared on Andrew's computer. There were no bright hanging baskets festooning the façade and, on entering the reception area, we found it empty and had to ring for service. We were informed it was 'under new management so please forgive any disruption'. It looked deserted to me. The manager showed us to a downstairs room that looked a little the worse for wear to my untutored eyes but, apart from asking for a couple of extra towels to supplement the two that were in the bathroom, we could find no real fault. It was clean, if a little threadbare.

I unpacked both our cases – once again under Andrew' s sardonic gaze. 'What? I asked. 'What am I doing that amuses you so much?'

'I am not used to anyone doing this sort of thing for me. I pack and unpack my own bags - always have. I book the holidays, get the tickets and, if passports are required, I get them out, make sure they are up to date and then look after everything. It would never occur to Fay to bother with such mundane tasks. If I forget anything it is my fault so I always try and remember everything. You are like a darling mother hen, Jenny, who does everything for her chicks. It is so funny and refreshing and I love you for it.'

It had never occurred to me before that there was no necessity for me to do this sort of thing. I was used to accepting responsibility for what I considered were housewifely duties plus a few extra ones like writing cheques, making telephone complaints and sorting out regular house maintenance. Especially now when I had retired and because my partner was still working, I felt it was my role to make our lives run smoothly. I didn't bother to enlighten Andrew as to my philosophy – to me it was only common sense and a supportive attitude that makes a good partnership.

We went out for a meal and Andrew chose a lovely Thai restaurant. I admitted to him I had never tried Thai food and I was looking forward to the experience. Before we were seated Andrew encouraged me to have an aperitif at the bar. I thought it was a rather a large gin and tonic. I didn't realise that, for that night only, they were doubling up the measures. Add that to a bottle of decent wine that accompanied the delicious meal, which I enjoyed immensely, and it was a very drunk woman who walked back to the hotel that night. I had only been even *slightly* drunk about twice in my life and it each time it was due to circumstances and an empty stomach. This time I had been relaxed and happy; I had enjoyed a good meal in delightful company so I suppose this was the perfect occasion for me to really push the boat out and let my hair down. Luckily I always giggle and laugh and am hopeless at doing anything even remotely sensible. Poor old Andrew had to escort me back to the hotel which, luckily, was only a short distance away. We went into our room and, amid chuckles on my part and grim determination on his, he had to undress me, see me into the shower and then tuck me up in bed. I am not sure if he had ever offered the same service to Fay.

The next morning I awoke to bright sunshine stealing through the shutters and, with no sign of a hangover and only a hazy idea of the previous evening, I hopped out of bed. Andrew seemed relieved I had returned to normal, once more, and was probably amazed the only thing I craved were two cups of tea and a cuddle before breakfast. We came across the empty dining room, quite by chance, after wandering up and down corridors and were welcomed by a Polish waitress who served us with a perfectly adequate breakfast. Andrew, who couldn't resist brushing up his language skills on anyone who would listen, tried to converse with her in rusty Russian and a smattering of Polish. It was lovely to see her face light up; she immediately rushed into the kitchen to get her friend and the three of them held a long conversation with many laughs and queries while I sat, enthralled, watching them.

Over the last of the coffee we planned our day. I suggested that to start with we go and take a look at Sir Winston Churchill's statue that I knew resided in the middle of Woodford Green. He had been the revered MP for the area and, after the end of WWII, his constituents had proudly erected a monument to commemorate his leadership at that time. Afterwards I proposed we could take the Central Line Underground to Bond Street and maybe wander round my favourite departmental store – Selfridges – then, for a touch of culture, perhaps we could go and look at the Wallace Collection which is tucked away to the north of Oxford Street in Manchester Square. It seemed like an awful lot to do in one day but I knew it was perfectly possible and I also knew Andrew loved to be entertained and stimulated.

We walked to Churchill's statue. It still looked as impressive to me as when I had seen it in the 1960s, set on a village green and surrounded by plane trees. We strolled back and made our way by the fastest route possible, by Underground, to Mayfair. Oxford Street was as busy and crowded as ever. We crossed over and walked the short distance to Selfridges, entering by the swinging doors. The delicious smells of the perfumery department wafted towards us as we stepped inside. I absorbed them with relish and would have lingered but Andrew was hungry, so we made our way straight to the restaurant and devoured a pile of salt-beef sandwiches washed down with cool apple juice. Then I took him on my favourite meandering walk. We started on the top floor and came down, by way of the central atrium and moving staircases, to the basement. There is not much one is *unable* to purchase in Selfridges and this way we saw and were aware of all their fascinating merchandise. We were tempted by all sorts of gifts but, with an eye on my watch, I dragged Andrew away before he could become saturated with the variety and novelty of the place. We went north and arrived at the Wallace Collection in a matter of minutes. Hertford House is an elegant eighteenth-century home that still retains its charm. When I had been a nursing probationer I would often make my way here to enjoy the art of Rembrandt and Rubens, the delicacy of Fragonard, Canaletto's Venice and the unbelievable Sevres porcelain. Entrance was free and I always felt it wanted me, as an appreciative audience, to enjoy the quiet atmosphere and to admire what the owners had so lovingly collected. There were other rooms of arms and armour but, as long as I was able to meander among the exquisite furniture, look at the paintings and china, I could return to the real world and be contented. We stayed a little over an hour and then I suggested we go and find a little restaurant that I hoped was still open. I explained it was quite a walk. At Oxford Street we turned left to Oxford Circus and then walked to almost Tottenham Court Road.

Andrew would have agreed to anything that day, I am sure. I explained we were going to a Hungarian restaurant in Greek Street – which raised a twisted grin on my companion's face. It had always been popular with publishers and journalists and I hoped he would find the Soho atmosphere and good authentic food to his liking. It was certainly different! We sat downstairs and were not disappointed with either the food *or* the wine. Later that night two weary tourists made their way back to South Woodford and, although neither of us were drunk, we curled up in each other's arms and sunk into a dreamless sleep as soon as we arrived in our room.

The next morning, over breakfast, I admitted to Andrew I had never seen Canary Wharf. When *I* had been living in London, Fleet Street was a mecca for huge newspaper offices, famous moguls and journalists. Now it had moved, lock, stock and barrel, down the Thames to be joined by the world's biggest banks. I longed to see this transformation. We looked on the Underground map and getting to Canary Wharf appeared to be as easy as visiting Mayfair the previous day. Once again we would take the Central Line from South Woodford station as far as Stratford. At Stratford we would change to the Jubilee Line and get off four stops later. All pretty simple, we decided. We would wander around the whole new area and, depending how much there was to interest us, we could move on to Greenwich to look at *The Cutty Sark*, the Royal Observatory, the Queen's House and, if we had time, the National Maritime Museum.

Everything went to plan until we arrived at a modernised Stratford station. It's now a massive junction that deals with various London Underground lines, including the Docklands Light Railway, as well as National Rail serving Essex and East Anglia. It had changed so much since I was a child that I was totally lost. Andrew went off to find a toilet and I wandered along the platform trying to get my bearings. A huge British Rail train quietly chugged slowly past me. A kindly driver leaned out and asked if I was lost.

I grinned back and asked for directions to Canary Wharf. Andrew came back to see me looking up to a towering cab with its driver leaning down giving me directions. I thanked him, he waved his hand and slowly moved on.

'Told you!' Andrew said triumphantly. 'I leave you for five minutes and find you being chatted up by some beefy train driver. What did *he* want?'

I explained he was only being helpful but he didn't look convinced until we found the correct platform and were on our way to our destination. The buildings at Canary Wharf are now as well known as the skyline of New York. Everything was very clean and spaced out by elegant plazas, walkways and water features. It was all very new and very bland and, once we had walked around it, neither of us had any inclination to linger so we made our way via the Docklands Light Railway to *The Cutty Sark* in Greenwich.

Andrew took an amateur's interest in *Gipsy Moth IV* which is moored by Greenwich Pier. He wandered around marvelling at how one man, Sir Francis Chichester, dared sail this small yacht single-handed around the world. Since then it has been replicated but never with such simple navigational aids. We then went aboard the most famous Tea Clipper in the world. *The Cutty Sark* was built in 1896 and was the fastest ship of her time. Speed was of the essence and danger was a secondary consideration when she raced around Cape Horn in an effort to bring this luxury commodity, tea, to our shores. Her fastest record was 363 nautical miles in one day. Andrew paced around the deck, as well as peering into the gloom below and, I'm sure, was imagining himself working aboard such a greyhound. I took one look at the rigging and shuddered at the thought of going aloft in gale-force winds.

We then walked up to the Queen's House. It was a Palladian villa built for the Royal Family in the seventeenth century and designed by Inigo Jones, first for Anne of Denmark and later for the wife of King Charles I, Queen Henrietta Maria. Little was left of it now apart from the vaulted crypt which was fit for any queen and beautifully decorated. I wandered around absorbing the atmosphere until Andrew dragged me into the Royal Naval College. There we stared in wonder at a beautifully painted chapel and hall. All the façades of the buildings were in a matching golden stone with cupolas and minarets and one could easily have been standing in Venice looking at similar palaces. It was the Palace of Westminster, St Paul's Cathedral and Blenheim Palace all rolled into one, and one knew instinctively that great architects like Wren and Vanbrugh were instrumental in the sumptuous designs long before Buckingham Palace was even considered as a Royal residence.

We had to drag ourselves away to visit the Royal Observatory with all its instruments for time-keeping, navigation and astronomy. We looked in awe at John Harrison's clock which revolutionised navigation for sailors and, giggling like a pair of kids, did what all visitors do - we straddled the Greenwich Mean Time brass line which was the original line of zero meridian longitude from where all world time is measured.

Andrew suddenly decided we had done enough indoor visiting for one day and should give the National Maritime Museum a miss. He suggested, as an alternative, we took a boat from Greenwich Pier right back to Westminster and the heart of London. It was a breezy but warm day and I was only too pleased to agree. We supplied ourselves with sandwiches and strong coffee and made ourselves comfortable on the upper deck to see what the River Thames had to offer in the way of sightseeing. It was the best decision he had ever made. We cast off and I snuggled against my thoughtful escort as the mighty Thames unfolded before our eyes. We saw warehouses and historic buildings all lining the waterside. Andrew buried his face in my windswept hair as we munched contentedly and enjoyed our picnic accompanied by a short and pleasant commentary. Suddenly a cheer went up and I glanced up as a banner was thrown out of a warehouse window and unravelled before our eyes. *LONDON IS CHOSEN TO HOST THE 2012 OLYMPIC GAMES.*

As we drifted nearer the capital, more and more impromptu signs and flags appeared. People were cheering on the tow-paths and waving excitedly – and we shouted and waved back.

Trafalgar Square was a sea of excitement as we arrived. We followed a crowd into a hall and discovered an official announcement was to be made accompanied by television cameras and sound equipment. This was proof it was all true and just by chance we were in the heart of London to celebrate with the crowds. As the cameras prepared to roll we ducked out and walked towards the fountains. People were singing and frolicking in the water and it felt as if the whole of England was rejoicing. We found ourselves outside The National Gallery and by common, unspoken, consent we walked up the steps and went to view our Nation's art treasures. Even in The National visitors were laughing and chatting like old friends. We wandered around having no clear idea what we wanted to see, noticing famous art we had only seen in books before – Dutch, Italian, French, Spanish, modern, impressionistic, religious. We looked with open minds and uncritical eyes. That was until we opened one silent, heavy door and stood alone in a hushed gallery. In front, and towering above us, was an immense George Stubbs painting. Like Constable, this painter is the quintessence of English art. We had discovered *Whistlejacket*. We both stood there open-mouthed as we took in this beautiful specimen of a horse. Looking back, I find it strange how a simple discovery like that enhanced what was an almost perfect day for me and has left a deep and enduring memory ever since.

Everything after that was an anti-climax. We went into a bar and had a celebratory drink and then we found a decent restaurant and ordered a meal. London was en fête and soon they would all need feeding and watering and we didn't want to be caught in the middle of a stampede for food. We caught a fairly early train back to Woodford feeling benign and replete from a really perfect day. In bed the happiness and love spilled over until I felt I was drowning in it.

****

The next day began pretty much like any other. The exhilaration generated by the 2012 Olympics news had simmered down and now the only cloud on our horizon was that the two of us would be leaving each other later that afternoon. Andrew would be speedily travelling back to York from King's Cross, while I would be making my way from Waterloo on the slow, meandering train back to the West Country.

Andrew glumly handed me his clothes so I could neatly pack them away before beginning on my own suitcase. We had decided to go up to London one last time and then return after a quick lunch to collect our baggage and go our separate ways. We had no plans for the day and were really just marking time until we would have to leave. We had argued as to who would see the other off until Andrew insisted he couldn't trust me on the loose with all those predatory males around. I tried to produce a tentative grin but it wasn't terribly successful.

Breakfast was a fairly silent meal apart from the two Polish girls wanting one last chat as they served us. They had very little free time or money to explore on their own, they had told us, and always enquired where we had been the previous day. I would answer in simple English and Andrew was delighted to translate for them by practising his knowledge of Polish and Russian. That last morning we spent rather longer than we had anticipated chatting and laughing so when we came down to Reception, to ask them to store our luggage, the desk was empty and we had to wait patiently for them to answer the bell.

Consequently we arrived at the entrance to South Woodford station later than usual. We found the doors closed and only one passenger pacing up and down outside. We asked what was going on and the woman, with a deep frown, said, 'Oh this is pretty normal. Very seldom are staff around to ask but often, when there is a power surge or trouble further back up the line, they stop the commuters entering the station for safety reasons and we all have to mill around outside until everything is back up and running again. It is frustrating but London Underground never seems particularly bothered.' She went on to complain about the price of a yearly ticket and how the Central Line needed to improve its services. We listened politely and commiserated. I was pleased I had left my London travelling troubles far behind me. After ten minutes she appeared to come to the end of her patience and, with a final rattle of the gates, she stalked away – either to try again later or perhaps call in sick. We stood around for quite some time while various other travellers wandered up, took in the situation, and turned away to find an alternative mode of transport. It obviously did happen with some frequency on this line as they all seemed resigned to this state of affairs.

Eventually, not knowing quite what to do, we retraced our

footsteps up the hill towards our hotel. As we passed a large fruit and vegetable shop, with many of its wares spilling out enticingly onto the pavement, we heard an exceptionally loud radio. A woman reporter was speaking in a measured, shocked voice. We stopped to pay attention to her. London had been bombed that morning. She was telling listeners about an attack deep in some of London's Underground stations. It had begun at King's Cross. We stood immobile as we tried to understand and take in her words. The owner of the shop came towards us, white faced. I asked if we could come inside and he stood aside and gestured us in. We stood mesmerised, among the apples and earthy smelling potatoes, and listened as an inhuman story began to unfold. Andrew stood with his arms wrapped around me and I laid my head on his shoulder and cried. At that moment it was *my* town, these were all *my* people and suddenly unknown terrorists were trying to slaughter them. The reporter's voice was unemotional and clear. As far as they knew, at approximately 8.50am that day, three trains on different routes had been bombed deep in the bowels of the earth and now rescuers were fighting their way in to try and reach the dead and injured. I, who had travelled on those lines for years, appreciated their difficulties and the danger of their tasks. And supposing there were more bombs all primed and ready to explode, I muttered. Suddenly the reporter said news was just coming in that, almost an hour later, a double-decker bus in Tavistock Square had also been blown apart. I shuddered and Andrew tightened his arms around me.

She went on to say that first accounts of the multiple accident spoke of a possible power surge on the grid and originally it had been thought this may have caused the explosion. But it was soon confirmed to be a deliberate act of terrorism in an effort to bring London to a standstill by spreading terror and death at the height of the morning rush hour. The explosion on the number 30 bus in Tavistock Square had happened at 9.47am. Had this attack been deliberately planned to coincide with the hundreds of travellers stranded outside closed stations all clamouring for transport and therefore vulnerable?

We listened and heard the capital's mobile telephones had been deactivated by the police in an effort to prevent the planned possibility of them triggering even more devices. The horror mounted steadily. Later this was amended to a possible overload due to usage but I preferred to think the Metropolitan Police had a plan in place that morning. Sure enough, when I tried to ring Dee and Paul, I received a recorded message refusing my request. We thanked the greengrocer for his generosity and left him looking shrunken and shell-shocked.

As we made our way towards the hotel I found it difficult to think coherently. We didn't know who could have planned these atrocities. At that time it was the least of our worries as we had no idea if it was the beginning of a terror campaign which would engulf the whole of London and then spread further to every other major town in the UK, or a one-off co-ordinated attack that had run its course. The Kings Cross explosion had taken place at 8.55am that morning. We had heard how the station was now closed and the ticket hall and waiting area were being used as an emergency hospital clearing station for the dead and injured. I immediately knew Andrew would not be able to use his return ticket and I was fearful for both of us using any other London station. In my mind it seemed perfectly logical that the next places to be blown up would be other large mainline stations like Waterloo, Paddington, Euston, Liverpool Street and so on. I also tried to make an educated guess as to where any other bombs would be placed. The command centre appeared to be Russell Square where all the services, under police direction, were co-ordinating the city's rescue efforts.

Andrew had always accused me of having too vivid an imagination and that morning it was working overtime. I was madly trying to outguess these terrorists and I knew, if I were planning this attack, I would then send men or women into every major hospital that was trying to deal with these casualties to set off more bombs and spread even more chaos. I also felt the police, who had apparently cut off all public telephone communication, would throw a large cordon around London to stop any terrorists escaping and, in the middle of it all, Andrew and I would be trapped. I was determined this would not happen.

It seemed crazy to be thinking like this on the quiet, leafy streets of Woodford. I told Andrew that we had to get out while we could. I also begged him to stay with me until such time as we were able to get well away from London and into the relative safety of the suburbs. From then on I hoped we could then think again and make a clearer decision as to what to do next. So we returned and smartly collected our luggage with all the staff clustering around and wanting to chatter about the awful events that were being reported. We spoke for a few minutes and then wished them well. As we emerged from the hotel I knew it was imperative to inform our families and friends as to our whereabouts and that we were safe. I tried Dee and Paul once more – to no avail – and then spoke to Lorna. Robin was on night work that week and I was determined to not wake him as there was nothing he could do to help. So I rang my best friend and explained. Her voice cracked with concern but I managed to convince her I was safe and was making my way towards the West Country. I promised to ring as soon as I had any news and she promised to drop a note into Robin's house so he would not be unduly worried by the news. That was the best I could devise. Andrew obviously spoke to Fay but I had no idea what excuses he had made and, as he didn't comment on her response, I never asked.

We then walked back into the centre of Woodford and found a car rental outlet. As soon as we entered we were told they had no more vehicles on the premises. We enquired for their nearest branch that might be able to help and asked them to telephone ahead and reserve a car for us immediately. They suggested Enfield. I had never been to Enfield in my life and stood irresolute as they told us it was relatively easy to get there. They directed us to a bus stop and, within a few minutes, we managed to find a bus going in the right direction. We swung on board and a kindly driver put us off at the place nearest to our destination. By then it was drizzling with rain and I suddenly realised how refugees must feel when they are forced to flee from a war zone. We walked and walked and I could feel panic overtaking me yet again until, just by chance, we spotted a taxi rank and with great relief clambered into a welcome, dry and warm cab. Andrew showed the card we had been given by the rental company and suddenly I felt safer.

As we alighted at our destination, I saw a group of people clustered around a bus stop. I noticed a young WPC and, as we unloaded our cases, I walked up to her and asked did she want to examine our baggage. She stopped talking and turned to face me, 'And why would I want to do that?' she asked. I looked at her, astonished at her naïve stupidity; I raised my hand in disgust and I turned towards the car rental shop. She was the only person I met that day that was not alive to the terror that had descended on London.

The calm atmosphere of the showroom allayed all my fears and I sank down on a comfortable chair with a sigh. I left Andrew to make the arrangements. I could hear him quietly talking to the clerk while explaining our predicament. I sat back and closed my eyes. Suddenly he was bending down to speak to me.

'Jenny, we are in a bit of trouble. I didn't bring my driver's licence down with me from York. I have to go and see a branch of my bank to prove who I am and then get my own bank to vouch for my good character etc. They will supply a pass for me and this company has agreed to give me the use of a car, so I can run you to somewhere safe, and then I will be driving it back to York and leaving it with their branch up there. I just have to go down the street a short way to speak with my bank, and then we will be off. Is that OK?'

The manager kindly appeared with a cup of tea as Andrew disappeared into the continuing drizzle. I sat and waited. We were given a small Ford Ka and to me it was as good as one of the most luxurious cars the company had ever supplied. We were sent off with a basic map and explicit instructions on how to reach the M4 motorway. As soon as I saw the signs for the A406 North Circular road I knew we were going in the right direction and that shortly after we would be joining the M4 that would take us towards Reading and the south west.

Sadly it didn't quite happen like that. All the roads that led towards Heathrow Airport were blocked that day. We sat patiently in queues that hardly moved and then, as we edged nearer the airport, we saw people - obviously desperate to catch their planes - alight from cars and make their way along the motorway, dragging their luggage behind them. The refugee problem had begun again. We reached Reading at about seven in the evening, both tired beyond measure. We had tried to keep each other's spirits up as we listened to the continuing news that unfolded hour by hour but, by then, all we needed was a bed for the night and a decent meal. We pulled into the first motel car park we saw. Amazingly we were given the last double room in the place. We went straight into the restaurant and devoured a huge meal before we even removed our suitcases from the car or went to look at our room. It was adequate in pine and pale beige but, apart from that, we barely noticed the decor. While Andrew was showering I telephoned home and spoke to Robin at last. He offered to come up immediately to get me; but I managed to dissuade him by saying I was in reasonable accommodation on the outskirts of Reading and, unlike a lot of other people that day, was fine. He rang back an hour later to explain that Margaret's husband, the vicar, was due to be in Winchester early the next day and he would make a detour and come to rescue me. Andrew listened to my one-sided conversation with stony eyes, I noticed, but once I had rung off he expressed relief that when it was time to leave me, I would soon be in safe hands. Suddenly I understood that he didn't hate Robin – he was just deeply concerned for *me*. I had no idea if he telephoned Fay again or what sort of excuses he would have made for not returning home that night. It was obvious, from our pale and strained faces, that we needed some rest. Neither of us had done anything strenuous the whole of that day; maybe it would have been better if we had. A few minutes earlier at those station gates and we would have been involved, if not in the actual bombing, then close enough to offer any aid we could. I am sure they required every able nurse in the vicinity to offer help and I knew Andrew would have been right behind me. I slowly turned down the covers on the bed and we slipped in between the cool sheets to watch on the television, again and again, ambulances, dazed walking wounded, blackened firemen and horrifically injured people being rushed out of smoke-filled London Underground stations. The commentary droned on and on. Andrew must have finally switched the set off – but I don't remember.

I must have plummeted into a profoundly troubled sleep because again and again, all through the night, I awoke with a start to remember another terrible account of what it had been like to be trapped underground. Stories of soft sobbing, heavy bodies pinning people down, blood warmly flowing and not knowing if it was yours, blessed rescuers grasping victims' hands in the dark and helping them to step over great gaping holes in the floors of smashed carriages; but most of all the trying not to breathe in, and choke on, the gritty dust and smell of burning. I was just feeling my way along the black tracks in the impenetrable darkness, petrified the current had been switched back on, when I awoke with a gasping sob. Andrew's arms were around me in seconds and it was then I finally broke down and cried. He switched on the bedside lamp and made us a pot of tea. We both clutched the warm and comforting mugs and stared at each other. I sat up amidst a heap of rumpled and twisted sheets, clasping the hot drink, my teeth chattering. It was just after three o'clock but neither of us attempted to return to our troubled dreams that night. We lay back and seriously discussed our future together. All the light-hearted plans we had made were like kindergarten dreams now. Did we want to spend the rest of our lives hundreds of miles apart, only talking to each other whenever we could sneakily snatch a free moment? No! Did we want to spend every waking minute together? Yes, of course. Did we need to touch, look, laugh and cry together? Did we long to shout to the world that we were in love and were we brave enough to face our families with the most awful news they would ever imagine? Suddenly, after experiencing a heart-stopping disaster together, our barriers were lowered and here we were revealing to each other our innermost thoughts.

'Fay hasn't loved me for years – if she ever did. I go through the motions when we are in company but, when we are alone, all pretence drops away and it is as if I don't exist for her,' Andrew admitted. 'I really believe she hardly sees me as a human being at all. When it started I was hurt, but now I have learned to live within myself. In fact I have built up a life that is padded out with friends and family so I have probably become as equally selfish as her. And now I have you again, Jenny, I know what I was missing.' I listened – wide eyed.

'Robin loves me in his way,' I said. 'He is protective and kind and has always been my best friend as well as my husband. I started off by being grateful when he rescued me from Chris's casual promiscuity. On the way, maybe I confused love with comfort and kindness. If I hadn't found *you* again, Andrew, I might never have believed this very special euphoria I always feel when we are together. This rapport is now more special than life itself. I cannot explain it but I recall it well from when we first met all those years ago. Until now I had never questioned the subtle difference between the love I have always felt for you and what Robin and I have shared for years and years. It frightens me to remember that, if I hadn't got in touch with you again, I would never have discovered this unique bond we now share. It scares me to think that if Chris hadn't taunted me that evening I would never have dared to try and find you.' I stared at him horrified.

Andrew broke into my musings. 'Jenny, what I feel for you is far too precious to abandon. Darling, we will make plans and I promise you faithfully that, eventually, we will spend the rest of our lives together!' I sank against him and we both gazed at one another shocked and dazed at revealing our innermost thoughts.

Suddenly my heart stopped racing and a great calm descended on me as I sipped my long cold cup of tea: confidence and certainty seeped back into my soul and I knew I could now face whatever the future would hold. Perhaps, with hindsight, it was lucky I was unable to peer into this future we were glibly discussing with so much trust and belief – but at that moment I felt Andrew and I could take on the world.

****

The next morning we parted as the sun rose. News was half listened to as we showered and I repacked our cases. No more awful happenings had disturbed London through the night although the police had not ceased their vigilance and enquiries. The injured were being patched up and looked after at various London hospitals and the dead were slowly being identified. Sadly, many families and friends were searching for loved ones who had not been heard of since the previous day and some of the stories were frightening and horrific. We had listened numbly. Andrew didn't stop for breakfast. I made him a warm drink and stood lonely, in a chill breeze, as he backed the small black car out of the crowded car park. His hand waved from the open window until I could see him no longer. I then forced myself to go back inside to eat a sustaining breakfast and wait patiently for my chauffeur to come and rescue me.

Margaret's quiet husband arrived mid-morning and we both spoke dully of the previous day's happenings. Suddenly it all felt like an evil dream and I wanted to discuss it no longer. I think I must have slept in the car because as I climbed out hours later, in front of our bungalow, it was as if I had been away for several months and was bemused. Robin had taken the day off work and I fell into his arms at the end of our path. He hugged me as if he would never release me and I inhaled the warm clean smell of his jumper and tried not to cry. Within minutes several friends came by and, while Lorna made them all drinks, I went through the events once more. They made it easy for me and, without deliberately lying, I told them exactly what had happened that previous morning.

Eventually we were alone and all I wanted to do was go to bed. I unpacked slowly and got into a comforting bath while Robin brought me some hot soup and told me to snuggle down. I dropped into a dreamless sleep and didn't wake until late the following morning. The next two days I thought of nothing. I didn't want to watch the news or discuss events as they unfolded. Finally, we learned a total of fifty-six people had died that morning – including the four suicide bombers. How the police knew who they were, as well as piecing together mangled bodies and identifying individuals, sickened me. Luckily, my wild imaginings of a large terrorist group who would go on to bomb all the other London stations as well as the emergency hospitals proved groundless, thank goodness. But two weeks later, when another terrorist police suspect was challenged and killed when he refused to stop, at another London Underground station, one understood the terrible fear and alarm that festered within the city's minds at that time.

Andrew contacted me within a few days. Fay had barely noticed his return and had no interest in where he had been anyway. He had delivered the car back to the company's Yorkshire headquarters and only the paperwork proved he had been in the centre of London when he should have been elsewhere. Bridge parties and Fay's friends meant far more than her husband, it seemed. Gradually our lives returned to normal and, with my fears receding, I became immersed in our love affair once more.

This time, instead of planning more and more short breaks, we indulged in long-term plans for our future. In the beginning

Andrew wanted to return to Cornwall. I dissuaded him because he had made his life in the north of England: that was where his children and grandchildren lived. I knew how much he loved and enjoyed their company so I felt that dragging him away to the south west would have been a cruel and heartless act that would affect both them *and* him. I said I was prepared to go and live reasonably close to both families and, as Andrew felt most at home in York, I would willingly go and join him there.

Then another idea he aired was that we should go and live abroad. That frightened me immensely. Holidays – yes; but to actually give up one's base in the UK and step into another country for the rest of our lives seemed the height of stupidity to me. We were both reasonably well but Andrew had a few health problems and to leave the British welfare state and throw oneself on the mercy of a foreign power, and their health regimes, was deliberate rashness to me. We were both well into middle age so obviously we could expect health problems to rear their ugly heads at some time. Could we take out enough health insurance, I asked, to cover us for all eventualities? And if one of us became ill, could we explain in a foreign language the extent of the ailment; but, more important, would we be able to understand and trust a foreign doctor's diagnosis? Andrew listened but was constantly muttering about Cyprus, Spain, France or the Canary Islands as a suitable base for us both.

Then he spent ages talking about our finances. I was always a bit hazy about my end of the partnership. Maths had never been my strong point and he was either trying to pin down what I would bring with me or guessing wildly. *His* financial affairs were clear and concise and he had everything listed and accounted for. I had not told him about Rose's legacy. I wanted to surprise him with a considerable amount of ready cash as well as my half of various investments that Robin and I had acquired over the years.

And so the rest of the year ran its course. Only two incidents need to be recorded because, in different ways, they affected *me*. First of all Robin was promoted. I was delighted for him. He had long deserved promotion as he had always given diligent and active support to whichever department he was seconded to and now it had been recognised. The second event was sad. My good friend Jess lost her husband. It was unexpected and sudden. We had all found him rather pompous and old-fashioned with his crusty, negative attitude to life but none of us, and certainly not Jess herself, had ever expected him to take to his bed and die so suddenly. I drove over to Taunton as often as Jess invited me, but my bubbly good friend had become much quieter and more pensive, I noticed with concern.

The fact that at long last Robin earned the promotion he so richly deserved eased my conscience just a little. Somehow I had to tell him I would be leaving him and I hoped his new job, plus the added responsibility, might to some extent assuage any grief he would suffer. For good or ill Andrew and I decided we would spend Christmas and the New Year at home and then leave shortly afterwards. The 1st December arrived so quickly that year. I forced myself to source and buy presents for all our usual friends and family, and heaped them around our Christmas tree, while madly trying to arrange the huge party we gave every year. I heaved bottles of booze, an oversized turkey and as many vegetables as I could carry out of the car as I worried about what I might have forgotten or overlooked. It all became a chore with most of the fun missing. I abstractedly wished neighbours a Merry Christmas while secretly visiting my solicitor, my bank manager and speaking to our investment broker. I swore all of them to secrecy and it said a lot for the sorry state of our society today when none of them showed undue surprise and the whole enterprise went perfectly smoothly. I made sure our separate, current bank accounts had exactly the same balance and I simplified our bill paying facilities so Robin would have no troubles in the foreseeable future. If I had been planning a war I could not have executed it better.

Everything was arranged. I intended to speak to Robin on the 8th January. The next day a letter would arrive from my new solicitor, and my bank and broker would have everything seamlessly in place – or so they assured me. For months Andrew had begged for reassurance that I really *was* determined to leave Robin. I found it difficult to convince him of my commitment. He seemed unable to accept I had made up my mind and there was no way I would ever change it. I knew that he would only believe my constant steady promises when I had left Devon and was well on my way with him to Yorkshire.

Christmas passed in a haze. I was obviously getting through the days on autopilot. I smiled and joked with our friends. I visited all our old neighbours and tried to ignore the fact I would probably never speak with any of them again. Petra and Megan kept me up to date with what their longed-for presents were and the three of us guessed at the likelihood of these materialising on Christmas morning. We went to a couple of seasonal dinner-dances with Robin's boss and a horde of his colleagues and, as I glided round the room to a caressing waltz or discoed madly to a scintillating rhythm, I found my eyes filling with tears knowing this could never happen to me again. I used a cold as an excuse not to go to Midnight Mass for the first time in years. Somehow I couldn't kneel at an altar next to Lorna and welcome in a new baby. Our tree was as sparkling as ever and, as Robin handed out all sorts of lovingly chosen or daft, crazy presents in his Santa suit, I gazed at all my good friends and tried to absorb that fragile moment to tuck it away and keep it in my heart – forever.

We saw in the New Year in the traditional way but, as I had never been into whooping up the beginning of another twelve months, my quietness didn't raise any eyebrows. As the clock chimed midnight Robin and I hugged before kissing and as we did so I felt a text from Andrew buzz in my evening bag. There were then only seven days left...

Chapter 16

*

On the morning of the eighth day of January I forced myself to drink the tea Robin had brought so cheerfully to my bed and slowly made myself go downstairs and face my breakfast. The tea scalded my throat and the cereal would not be pushed down. I had promised to take both Petra and Megan to school so it was a relief just to escape the house. I left Robin cleaning the car and talking to a neighbour's tabby cat.

The children skipped and chatted all the way through town and I absent-mindedly answered them. I checked they both had their school lunches in their backpacks, plus any current homework, before I waved them off at the school gates and received blown kisses in return. On the way back I called into the supermarket for milk and a daily paper for both Lorna and myself. Lorna would have kept me chatting but I made the excuse that it was Robin's day off and maybe he wanted to go out.

As I turned into our close, Robin was just finishing by standing back and admiring his handiwork. He grinned at me. 'How about a ride somewhere?' he enquired.

'I need to talk to you,' I said quietly.

He walked up the path immediately behind me and dumped his bucket and cleaning leathers in the porch. 'What's up?'

I sank down on the sofa. It was his usual seat but I was so agitated I never even noticed. He went and perched on the arm furthest away from me and waited. I looked at him, mutely willing him to understand what I was going to say and not start arguing the moment I opened my mouth. All the time, in my head, I was reciting *you don't have to do this. You don't have to say anything.*

If you don't life will go on as before and no one will be any the wiser. The temptation was almost unbearable and I sat looking at my hands and tried to stop them shaking.

When I finally got the words out I managed to listen to what I was saying. I sounded most reasoned and logical, with my voice only cracking occasionally as I strove for breath. Eventually I ran out of steam and raised my eyes to Robin's face. He had sat through the whole of my explanation, not moving and not speaking. Finally he got up and went and stood by the window.

I'll leave immediately,' he stated softly. He went to turn away...

'No, that's not what I meant,' I said hurriedly. I went to stand next to him and I noticed he moved a few inches away. 'It's my fault, my mistake and I will be leaving shortly. This is your house – our house – and I never want for you to leave it. I will be going away as soon as I can, so there is no reason for you to leave – ever.' He shrugged my hand off his sleeve and swiftly walked out through the front door.

I have no idea where he went or if he spoke to anyone. He didn't return until it was dusk. I had made a meal of sorts and placed it on the kitchen table in front of him. He pushed it away – not in anger, I don't think – and went and sat in the sitting room to watch the television. I busied myself doing all sorts of unnecessary tasks until there was nothing left to do – so I forced myself to go and join him. We said very little and I am certain neither of us saw any of the moving images on the screen. At 9pm we went to bed and I feel sure we both lay and stared at the ceiling in the darkness. I know I did.

The next morning Robin waited for me to wake and then asked me my plans. I stumbled to answer while he patiently stood by the door. When my words petered out he nodded abruptly and left for work.

I arose, had a shower and placed a case on the bed. My mind was blank. I had no idea what to take; no idea what to leave behind. There was a whole lifetime of chosen clothes in my wardrobe but a void in my mind. The telephone shrilled twice that morning. I ignored it. I didn't go out and I ate nothing all day. Finally the first case was full and I turned automatically to the second. I selected half a dozen sweaters at random, jeans, trousers, boots and shoes and a couple of pairs of socks. I scrabbled for some slippers and added a neat pile of underwear. My mind was on autopilot. When Robin arrived home much earlier than usual I was at a loss as to what I should prepare. He patiently went and fried eggs, bacon and chips. We ate in the kitchen, saying nothing. I drank copious amounts of water but touched very little else. I wanted to ask who he had told, as I was sure he needed to confide in a friend. I didn't dare and he never explained. After the early news he glanced at me and asked, 'When will you be off?'

'The day after tomorrow, if that is OK?' I asked tentatively. He nodded and quietly went to bed. I followed him at midnight. I am sure it was another *white night* for both of us.

The next day I threw into my case a muddle of clothes, jewellery, medicines, shoes and a few odd things as I thought of them. I remembered toiletries as an afterthought and then shoved in a bottle of perfume. Was this the best I could do after years and years of love, affection and harmony? None of it mattered to me and yet all of it was a part of me. I included two books and then realised I would have to take a third case as I had not thought about a top-coat, scarves, gloves or an umbrella. I packed my passport, credit cards and cheque book. This was forever and I had not prepared for dealing with it, unlike the meticulous planning I had undertaken with my solicitor, broker and bank manager. This was a bewildering tangle. I neatly placed my three forlorn cases by the front door and took myself off to face Lorna.

I knew by her shocked pale face that she had heard, but she still welcomed me into her arms as soon as I tapped on the window and went round to the back door. The warmth of her body was a comfort until I eventually pulled away and she thrust a cup of hot chocolate into my hands. I sat on their worn old armchair, next to the cosy range, and explained. She listened without interrupting until I came to the end of my explanation. We sat and talked it over and I was surprised she never chided me or tried to speak in Robin's favour. Her loyalty was unshakeable but I knew this was because Robin would have wanted it to be like this – and she was also honouring his friendship, as well as mine.

'Will you explain to Margaret?' I asked. She nodded. 'And to all the rest of them? I don't want *any* of them to ever blame Robin. He has never done anything wrong and the blame will always lie fairly and squarely on me alone.' She nodded again.

Petra and Derek came thumping in the back door together, laughing and teasing each other. I immediately got up and returned home after giving Petra a long thoughtful hug. Both she and her Dad watched me go out of their house, looking puzzled and sad. I waved until I got to the corner and then gulped back tears as I walked home wishing Crumble could have been there just once more to welcome me. I texted Andrew to tell him everything was in place for the next day and then sat around until it was time to prepare a meal and face another awful evening.

It was a relief when the final day dawned. Robin had taken time off work – which I appreciated and hated all at the same time. No one can maintain awful tension indefinitely, I now know, and we suddenly found our voices and spoke as if nothing had happened between us. He went out and bought fish and chips for lunch and afterwards we sat side by side on the sofa and he actually put his arm around me. I sighed and sank against his chest and he held me firmly. We had the television turned low for comfort and I was lulled into a feeling of sleepy ennui. At four-thirty, as it became dark, Robin asked when I was leaving. I had no idea. It all depended on Andrew's journey from York to Devon and I said I was awaiting his call on my mobile. Another half hour dragged by as it stubbornly remained silent on the coffee table in front of us.

Just after five o'clock Robin stirred in irritation and suggested I ring Andrew. He told me he would ferry me to wherever I wanted to go. I knew how he felt. It was like waiting for a catastrophe to happen and the relief when it did would outweigh the anguish of waiting. I slowly went towards the kitchen and dialled from there. My call was answered immediately. I asked tentatively, 'Are you anywhere near here yet?'

'Good grief, I was just waiting for you to ring me and wondered if you had changed your mind after all.' He sounded testy and tired.

I breathed a sigh of relief. 'Why didn't you ring and *say*?' I queried. 'I thought that was what you had planned. But never mind, tell me where you are. Robin has promised to drop me off with my cases. I think the best place to meet would be the railway station. That is in the centre of town and is always well lit even on a dark, cold night like this.'

'I don't know where I am. I am in Honiton – in a car park – it's dark and there is no one around to ask where anything is and I have no idea where to find your station. Quite honestly, Jenny, if you hadn't got in touch I was preparing to retrace my journey back to Yorkshire and put it all down to experience!'

I walked back into the other room and gave Robin a brief resumé of our conversation. Within two minutes I had donned my coat while my husband loaded up our car and I was off to face my destiny. Robin pulled up sharply outside the station. As predicted, light was spilling onto the frosty forecourt as he swiftly unloaded my three cases, gave me a brief hug and shot away leaving me standing forlornly beside the kerb. I waved as he swept past me but he never responded.

I got out my mobile and rang Andrew again. 'I am outside the station and waiting for you,' I informed him and attempted a joke. 'I am sorry darling but, as I have three heavy cases and only two arms to carry them with, I am afraid you will have to come to me. Just drive around and you will soon spot the station. Honiton isn't a big place, you know, with very few car parks, so it won't take you above five minutes, I'm sure.'

Actually it took three! Andrew's large car turned towards the brightly lit station precinct and he was out and clasping me to him eagerly. His face looked pinched and wan and I suddenly understood how all his exuberance at the beginning of his journey might have seeped away as he got deeper into southern England, along with his feeling of absolute certainty that I would be waiting at the end of his journey. I guessed, rightly, that he had missed a meal on the way down and sitting in his cold car for a couple of hours on his arrival may have quenched his exhilaration.

'I don't suppose you want to eat in the town,' I said. 'Wherever we go someone will recognise me and come up and want to be introduced to you. Devon folk are a nosy lot on the whole, and I don't want you to be an object of avid interest, so I have booked a table at The White Hart at Corfe. The inn is just short of Taunton where I have booked a hotel for the night. Can you hold out until then, darling?'

And that was what we did. I directed him towards Taunton and within half an hour we were eating a decent meal in an old-world tavern with blazing log fires and a welcoming attitude. Andrew cheered up immediately at the sight of hot, succulent food and suddenly we were both ravenous. We ate and drank, chatting quietly. Suddenly all our doubts were as cobwebs and I tried to forget Robin's face when I had sat him down and revealed my devastating news four days previously.

The hotel was also an excellent choice. I had telephoned The White Hart weeks before, certain they had accommodation, only to be directed to a luxurious hotel only a short distance away. I followed the explicit instructions and ten minutes later, as we parked the car, I saw through a window a rosy, softly lit, welcoming room gleaming with firelight. It would have made a perfect honeymoon retreat but all Andrew and I needed, as we sank down into the luxurious, cosy bedding, was a deep and dreamless sleep. I was now on the threshold of the first day of my new life...

****

The next morning we arose in a leisurely fashion, sampled a hearty and sustaining breakfast in a delightful Georgian dining room and were on our way before the mist had completely lifted over the Somerset Levels. We had a light lunch near Bolsover and reached York in the early afternoon. Andrew had booked us into a hotel near Beningbrough Hall, which I later learned was to the north west of the city. It was close to the River Ouse and reminded me of the low-lying dykes and fens that I remembered around The Rodings in Essex. The day was wet and cold with a thin miasma of drizzle that spread in every direction so, when we arrived at our destination, I was delighted to enter a warm manor house and be welcomed by a buxom, smiling owner in twin-set and pearls.

On the way north Andrew explained that he had searched for suitable accommodation months before, as soon as Fay went off with her girlfriends on their yearly visit to a luxurious health centre for a few days. He had come across this place just by chance and, though it was situated in the country, it was not too remote from the city of York itself. Personally I would have followed him to an igloo if he had deemed it necessary! The farmhouse, for that is what it had been, had quite a few en suite bedrooms but also boasted a number of chalets in the extensive grounds for guests who preferred to have breakfast in the main house but cater for themselves the rest of the time. We were never shown the hotel bedrooms - instead we were conducted to an attractive small building set in the grounds. It could be described a studio: the accommodation consisted of a main bedroom – with a sizeable alcove that would provide us with a sitting and dining area – a well-equipped small kitchen and a decent en suite bathroom with a large shower. There were two massive wardrobes for our clothes, I noted, with lots of space for storage and in the sleeping-cum-dining room there were deep armchairs, a reasonable table plus a large television. Not quite home from home; but I was relieved we weren't to be squashed into a prison cell of our own making. One feature I failed to note was the heating. *That* was supplied by electric fan heaters positioned on every wall.

The proprietor left us to unpack and invited us to dinner that night to help us settle in. We agreed immediately. Andrew had mentioned no definite leaving date but I guessed there would be little pressure on us to depart due to the isolation of the hotel and the inclement winter weather. Maybe the whole place would come alive in the spring and summer but very few would be spending time here, I reckoned, within the next three months.

We unpacked my three suitcases and Andrew's two. Once everything was put away and arranged, with the cases either placed on top of the wardrobes or shoved under the bed, there seemed a paltry number of possessions for two people to commence their life together. I also discovered the fan heaters, once switched on, would only run for an hour and then would turn off – automatically. The significance of this did not strike me as a nuisance until we had been in residence for a few days.

It was a pleasure to shower, dress up in some comfortable clothes and make our way round to the hotel lounge. We had been invited for drinks at 7pm sharp and I noticed as we walked into the dining room that the large oval mahogany table was only laid for four settings. As we lowered ourselves into our seats I saw a large man stroll in to join us. Andrew jumped up to shake his hand and then turned to introduce him to me.

'This is Gordon, who I often meet at my golf club,' he said. I smiled obligingly and held out my hand too. 'Good heavens, old chap, I had no idea this was your place,' he continued.

I then sat and listened as they discussed the club, the house and mutual friends as we politely ate the meal that his wife served up. I could see both he and his wife were studying me covertly between courses and eventually, as we sat down for coffee in the sitting room, his wife positioned herself near me and asked how long I had known Andrew.

I was delighted to inform her it was since we were young children and I could see her re-evaluating me. She made a few more pertinent inquiries and I wondered if she was a particular chum of Fay's or if she only vaguely knew of her. I could imagine, once we had left their house to return to our chalet, that she and her husband would be deep in conjecture about the two of us. And that the next morning, passing on such a snippet of gossip would be her first chore of the day. I found it faintly amusing as none of these people were remotely connected to me, but, nonetheless, I wondered at Andrew's reaction to the unexpected meeting.

Luckily when we ran through the cold mist to return to our snug rooms I found Andrew as diverted by the situation as me.

'Who would have dreamt that old Brophy would be our landlord until we fix ourselves up with somewhere decent to live!' he exclaimed.

I agreed and then asked him something I had been longing to mention since Andrew had collected me from Honiton station. 'What happened when you told Fay you were coming to Devon to hook up with an old girlfriend and what did she say when you mentioned, for good measure, that you would not be coming back?'

Andrew sat on the edge of our bed as he removed his shoes. 'I cheated. I told her in five minutes flat and then I walked out of the door. There's no way of breaking news like that gently, Jenny. Soon everyone will know that I have dumped her – even quicker now Gordon and his wife have met you – but quite honestly maybe this bit of gossip has come at an opportune time. It will save a lot of speculation and wondering than if I had disappeared into the sunset – never to return.'

I wondered how Fay had taken the news. Drew had not waited to find out. Was it a cowardly exit? Only he could judge that. And was it better, or worse, that their friends and neighbours would probably know before their immediate family now? I felt distinctly sorry for both Fay and Robin. The shock must have been shattering for both of them. Would they deal with it in a similar fashion? I had no way of knowing, but all I was sure of was that Andrew and I had the better deal and I felt incredibly sad for *both* of them.

The next morning dawned dank with intermittent squally showers. I had roused a couple of times in the night just to switch on the fan heaters once more when our bedroom became distinctly chilly. I could imagine, while the weather remained miserable, this could become an awful chore. We awoke early and had our ritualistic morning cuppa in bed. Andrew was his usual amorous self but I hustled him out to have first shower instead. As the water ceased I heard a disgruntled moan, 'Oh God, these towels are cold and damp! Brrr! This isn't funny,' he grumbled.

Grinning at his thoughtlessness of the previous evening, when he had walked out of the shower with two fluffy bath towels wrapped around himself, I called, 'Use one of my hand towels and stop moaning, you big baby. I'll teach you how to keep everything reasonably dry.' I didn't mention that personally I find huge bath towels unwieldy as I have a habit of trailing them wherever there is water. I also had been brought up by practical parents who expected one to mop oneself down with a flannel before going near a dry towel. Andrew grunted his thanks.

We arrived slightly late for breakfast with glowing faces – there is nothing like ardour to put a sparkle in one's eye – but sodden shoulders. We were advised to use the back door in future, which would save us a trek around the house. We thanked Joan Brophy for her excellent dinner of the previous night and tucked into her equally good breakfast. No other residents joined us so we surmised that either they had gone out earlier or the place was virtually empty. Our happiness knew no bounds – we now had all the time in the world to savour our new surroundings while experiencing the warmth of fun and laughter. No surreptitious phone calls, no pretence about meeting friends, no lying about our whereabouts: this wasn't a holiday where we had to squash in as much enjoyment as possible, but a time of rediscovering each other and experiencing a never-diminishing tenderness.

That day Andrew introduced me to some of the delights of

York. By mid-morning the rain ceased and the puddles magically disappeared. We started, as everyone probably does, with York Minster which towers over every building within the city walls. He had a special pass, courtesy of living locally, which allowed him to conduct me around and show me some of the rare wonders within that sensational building – medieval stained glass, the soaring nave with its roof bosses a metre across that one can only examine with decent binoculars, that glorious heart-shaped West Window, the newly restored Rose Window and the scintillating, colourful choir screen with its intriguing statues of the kings of England beginning with William the Conqueror. I wanted to see more but Andrew, knowing not to overload me with too much history, decided to take me for a light lunch at St William's College restaurant.

Set around a cobbled courtyard, it was a fifteenth-century Tudor building that transported one back in time and I became absorbed in my surroundings. He proudly explained how it was closely connected with St John's College at York University and I listened intently. Afterwards, for light relief, we visited Mulberry Hall and I marvelled at the cornucopia of luxurious and beautiful gifts displayed in a delightful setting. The day had flown by.

On the way back to our fenland hotel I dozed and, once back inside our cosy bolt-hole, I dropped into a deep sleep wrapped in Andrew's arms. That evening I had my initial taste of first-class Asian cooking: it was a great shock. I realised how my life had always been sheltered. My parents ate simple English food and I suppose I had carried on the tradition. In my busy job I had very little time or inclination to experiment with food; Robin and I were mostly on shift work so meals were often rushed and usually simple. When we went out it was mainly to local pubs with occasional forays to the more expensive restaurants and, by chance, none of them were Asian. Andrew and our waiter, who appeared to know him well, advised me to try chicken korma. I didn't realise this was the standard dish that every novice starts with until they are able to sample the delights of much richer, spicier and hotter food. Andrew laughed as I spluttered over a tiny spoonful of *his* fiery dish. It left my tongue burnt but numbed and he teased me that his grandchildren regularly ate such food with gusto. I went to gulp half a glass of iced water but he advised me against it, saying it would only make matters worse. I subsided, breathing heavily, with my eyes smarting. Oh dear, would I have to get used to this torture, I wondered? What saved me was a huge revolving dish of accompanying mango chutney, plain yogurt, cucumber raita, coconut cream, plump raisins and various breads. I could have eaten them on their own!

I think Andrew would normally have only eaten one course, plus a decent bottle of wine, as one was spoilt with the selection of accompaniments to any curry, but he turned to me and politely asked if I would like a dessert. I could choose between a sorbet, pearl tapioca, a lemon soufflé and a lassi. He explained the last was a thick milkshake and, intrigued, I chose that. It was delicious. Maybe I had redeemed myself.

The next morning, after another mouth-watering breakfast, I asked if we could go into town. I needed lots of writing paper, envelopes and stamps. I knew eventually I would have to face reality and contact my friends and family and now was the time to start. I had no idea how Robin would go about telling them, and anyway it was not his problem – it was mine – and I knew it was up to me to explain and put their minds at ease. There were some that I could maybe telephone but there were so many others that would be horrified at what I had done and they would be desperate to hear from me. It was the last thing I wanted to face but I knew there was no alternative. I cringed at the thought but I was also aware I couldn't disappear off the face of the earth without leaving a contact address or telephone number and telling my nearest and dearest that I was alive and well. I also had to speak to my husband and tell him my whereabouts and I suggested Andrew contact Fay and his two boys to also put *their* minds at rest. My suggestion fell on deaf ears and, no matter what I said or how I pleaded, Andrew refused to contact anyone. He sat on the bed and lost himself in a whodunit he had brought with him.

I finally gave up and went to sit at our small dining table armed with an address book and a list of telephone numbers. I wrote over two dozen short letters that day, all giving a similar version of my escape to Yorkshire. On the top of every letter I printed my new address and, at the close of every one, I insisted it was nothing Robin had ever done or said, he had been the perfect partner all our married life, it was just me who was at fault and I needed them to give him all the support I was unable to supply in the future. I begged them to try to understand but I was absolutely certain few of them would.

Then I started telephoning. I had written to my cousin Dee as well as to Meryl and Adam but I needed to contact them as soon as possible by phone as well. I knew they would be worried by my silence and would be imagining all sorts of terrible things happening to me. Also Lorna would need to know I was safe and I trusted her to explain to all my neighbours as well as to our mutual friends. I couldn't face telling Margaret – don't ask me why. Did I expect her to preach to me or berate me for my stupidity? I have no idea, but I knew Lorna would keep her up to date so I put her on the back burner of my conscience.

I knew that shortly we would both have to bite the bullet and get down to some serious letter writing – such as reporting to the official concerns that needed to know our whereabouts – like our banks, our solicitors, pension offices and the Inland Revenue for starters. For the time being we didn't need to arrange any contracts with the gas, water and electricity companies and, luckily, our mobile telephones took care of any communication problems; but eventually all these chores would have to be faced.

I decided not to nag Andrew about not getting in touch with his family and, the next morning, when he asked what I would like to do, I glibly said, 'Swimming. I would love to go swimming.'

So that's what we did. Andrew knew of a large swimming pool quite close to York and, as we entered its warm, steamy atmosphere, I felt myself gently unwinding and relaxing. We had the huge place to ourselves and we both giggled and laughed as we splashed through the foot pool and I gently lowered myself into the welcoming water. I have always been a novice at swimming, never progressing much since I had taught myself to swim at the age of eleven. There had never been anyone I could implicitly trust to hold me up and not to duck me under as a joke and it was only the cheeky young scamps at our local pool, who would shove one in for fun, that gave me the determination to avoid this at all costs. So I had learned the breast-stroke, with my head held high out of the water, but I had never improved or advanced. In the Mediterranean, where the summer seas were calm and warm, I would laze around for hours in the shallows – swimming and floating – but never seriously doing much else.

Now *I* wanted to be as proficient in water as Andrew was. He was a natural. Born in Cornwall of seafaring folk and always at home in the sea meant he had a head start. In Hong Kong he had taught his own children, and anyone else's, to revel in the sea and they became like seals and totally competent. Now I longed to learn. To swim down towards the bottom of the deepest part of a pool – with my eyes open – was my goal. Drew shrewdly gave me confidence when he praised my breast-stroke style. Then he had me ducking under the warm water for a few seconds at a time. Each time I would panic and bob up like a cork but still he would put his arms around me and swear I was doing brilliantly. Whether my head actually dipped *below* the surface of the water to any extent is debatable. I tried until I became breathless. We then swam up and down, doing lengths, with me doing my awkward stroke and my partner swimming underwater to prove how easy it can be. When a group of schoolchildren joined us two hours later we took ourselves off to the showers feeling pleasantly tired and, when Andrew showed how much he loved me as we changed together in our boxlike cubicle, I'm sure I emerged looking bedraggled but sated.

That night we took fish and chips home and ate them avidly, on lap trays, as we watched some game show on television. Every day proved an adventure and my blood was singing with happiness and contentment. Every night we were ready for bed early. If it hadn't been for the fan heaters that needed constant attention every hour through the night I would have been totally satisfied. Luckily Andrew never stirred, apart from occasionally grunting when I had to slide under his arm while trying not to wake him and, for that, I was thankful.

On the Friday night I decided I should ring Robin to make sure he was alright. He answered on the second ring and then sounded taciturn and clipped from then on. Yes, he was eating properly; he'd done some washing but had not attempted to iron it yet; Lorna had popped in for a chat and Derek had been over a couple of times but he had seen no one else. He didn't ask if I was OK or what I had been up to so I never bothered to say. He told me he had made a note of my new address. When the small talk had dried up I reluctantly ended the conversation and put the telephone down. I had insisted Andrew remain in the room the whole time because I wanted him to hear what I said. I wanted no misunderstandings – ever – it was important everything should be open and above board.

As far as I knew, Andrew hadn't spoken to Fay or his two sons. He may have texted them but I deliberately didn't enquire. It wasn't like him to be secretive and I hoped my being so open would encourage him to act the same way. It didn't.

The next morning dawned bright and clear and, for once, I breathed a sigh of relief on the way to breakfast. Joan was affable and asked our plans for the day. Andrew mentioned Knaresborough and I listened intently as they discussed it. They both decided I would like the place. It had some odd quirks, Joan said. Drew said I was sure to like the windows – which puzzled me somewhat.

The day lived up to its promise. We arrived in what looked like a typical market town. We parked the car and made our way towards a small ruined castle perched on what turned out to be a rocky outcrop overlooking a deep gorge: at the bottom of which a meandering river wound its way towards an arched, grey stone viaduct. As we watched a tiny train chugged its way across as if for our own personal amusement. There were steep, dark woods lining either side of the broad river and I stood and stared in wonder. I could easily have been in the Dordogne, in France, it was so picturesque. We made our way down towards the tiny ribbon of buildings that clustered along the waterside. There were skiffs moored at the water's edge and a tea-rooms that were open. By common consent we went in for coffee. Because it was so sheltered we were able to choose an outside table right by the river and sit down in comfort. The pale sun felt warm and I shrugged off my jacket and sat enjoying the peace even though it was still only January. I was told that, in summer, the slow-moving river would be alive with these colourful skiffs and it would look even more Continental. Andrew, with his legs outstretched, pointed across the river towards the trees and told me about Mother Shipton's Cave and Petrifying Well. It all sounded a bit frightening but he assured me it was not and promised to explore it with me the next time we visited. He explained that the dripping water contained huge quantities of minerals that would turn any object hung under the cliffs to stone within a short space of time. Everything imaginable was there from hats to old boots and umbrellas. A teddy bear would take three or four months to solidify and visitors came from all over the world to witness this miracle.

We then walked along the right bank of the River Nidd, under the viaduct and viewed some black-and-white houses. Walking back towards the castle Andrew guided me up through the steep Bebra Gardens to view the Courthouse Museum and then we returned to the Market Square and he took me to the oldest chemist's shop in Britain. It was a pharmacy as long ago as the 1720s and is now a fascinating mixture of a chemist, a sweet shop and an emporium with a charming café upstairs. We enjoyed a light lunch and then I was taken on a short tour of Knaresborough's town windows. I stared open-mouthed at zoo animals apparently poking their heads from windows, Blind Jack leaning out playing his fiddle, a fighter pilot staring into the distance to see if he can spot a distant plane. We walked up and down streets and I kept tugging at Drew's arm and saying, 'Oh look at *that* one!' while he grinned at me enjoying my enthusiasm. I had never seen anything like it. Andrew explained he had no idea when it had first begun here in Knaresborough, but it is known as *trompe l'oeil* – a painting with a clever use of perspective that deceives the eye and convinces the viewer it is real. We strolled down one cobbled street and I caught sight of an open door – that wasn't! It led to a pretend garden that, if I hadn't known we were in the middle January, I would have believed to be full of warm sunshine gleaming on blossoming spring flowers. As we turned the corner I spotted a window cleaner balanced precariously on a jutting windowsill and I marvelled at the ingenuity of the artists. When we had exhausted the sights we walked back to the car and returned home. I chatted incessantly all the way.

The next few days were taken up with sightseeing. We visited York's Art Gallery and I fell in love with a warm painting of St Anthony which I swore had been executed by Rembrandt himself. We visited two museums – one in the picturesque gardens of the ruins of St Mary's Benedictine Abbey with its pale stone tracery of cloisters. I stared entranced at Roman and Viking artefacts, but what caught my eye was an engraved, shining ring of the purest gold I have ever seen. We went back to the Minster again and again. One morning Andrew led me through thronged streets of excited visitors, past a Roman Bathhouse and a thriving market, pointed out the Shambles, showed me the Yorvik Viking centre and took me past elegant, Georgian Fairfax House. He tried to give me a potted history of each one but, eventually, I had to beg him to stop. I was muddled, excited and saturated with historical facts until my head was spinning. The next day he assured me the York Castle Museum, at the base of the mighty looming Clifford's Tower, would be a complete, and different, surprise.

'You will love it, Jenny. I do. It's a relaxing, time-travel experience; you can walk along cobbled streets thronged with carriages and peer into authentic Victorian shops as the street goes dark and night falls; you can look at period living rooms from Jacobean, through to Victorian, stare at wartime kitchens and be taken back to the sort of sitting rooms we remember as children. They have a 1960's juke box, children games, dolls' houses, Roundhead pikes, costumes that our great grandparents would have worn, World War I and II uniforms, prison cells and slot machines. It's such good fun and I never tire of it. I return again and again'.

One night we went out for an early meal and went on to the Theatre Royal to watch an Ibsen play. And then Andrew remembered he had tickets for the pantomime so, on another night, we joined crowds of adults and children who booed and hissed and cheered as soon as the curtain rose. We came out of the theatre laughing and that night didn't seem half as bad as I struggled to wake up every hour in an effort to dry our towels and undies draped in front of the fan heaters.

The washing problem was one I failed to solve. I could rinse out our socks, pants and my lingerie daily and Joan would change our bed linen and towels twice weekly; but it was our heavy winter top clothes that proved difficult. I had been neatly folding our worn sweaters, shirts, vests and trousers and stuffing them into a bin bag that I had stowed against the wall under our dining table. I knew eventually I would either have to resort to a dry cleaners or beg the use of our landlady's washing facilities and wash and iron them myself. But before that, Joan half solved my problem for me.

Our landlords had been pleasant, in a distant way, and in fact, at the end of the third week, we were asked to yet another hotel dinner party. But this one was also attended by a selection of Andrew's golfing acquaintances – plus their partners. I wondered if we were still objects of gossip and if this was the golfing fraternity's way of taking a canny look at us and working out if I was suitable material for their circle. During the evening I said very little but I reckoned I was under surveillance and wondered if Andrew and I had passed muster. I suppose I still felt a little awkward asking Joan for a favour when we had been accepted, socially, into their circle – it seemed presumptuous to ask to borrow her washing machine – so I postponed it again.

One evening we arrived home in a flurry of uncertainty about whether to go out or stay in for our evening meal. Drew switched on the heaters as a matter of course and I noticed the bed had been changed and there was now a pile of clean, fresh towels. As I stooped down to remove my shoes I saw our black bin liner on its side. I automatically bent down to straighten it when I realised it was only half full. Intrigued, I pulled it open and emptied it onto the bed. Everything that belonged to Andrew had been removed and the only clothes remaining were my skirts, trousers, sweaters and blouses. I sat down and laughed uproariously.

'Well that's a turn-up for the book,' I spluttered. 'Joan is obviously more concerned about *your* welfare than *mine*. I wonder where she has taken your dirty linen and what she had done with it. Perhaps she fancies you, darling,' I teased.

Andrew, who had been making a hot drink, came in enquiringly. I showed him the half-empty bag and we both saw the funny side of this odd gesture. The next evening we came home to a large, neatly ironed pile of Andrew's clean clothes balanced on the foot of our bed The following morning I quietly thanked Joan and offered to pay her for the service but she dismissed my offer airily, never mentioning why she had decided that only Andrew was worthy of clean laundry. If she thought this subtle insult would upset me she failed in her purpose as I had decided I still had enough fresh clothes for the time being and would manage. I strolled out of her kitchen, bestowing an amiable smile after informing her we were hoping to go into York and walk along the banks of the Ouse towards the

Millenium Bridge. Our plan was to get as far south as Bishopthorpe and the Palace.

And that was what we did. It was a crisp, cold day so we wrapped up warmly, parked the car just outside York city walls and, walking briskly south along the river bank, we crossed over the arching modern bridge that had been erected to welcome in the new century. It may have been cold but it was a sunny day and we met lots of other people also out for a stroll – many of them walking their dogs. We passed houseboats and all sorts of craft lining the banks of the river; chattering contentedly, we soon reached our destination. I was taken to a warm pub in the village and we thawed out in front of a roaring fire while devouring a "ploughman's and a pint". Andrew then took me to the gates that guard this modest Palace. He told me it has been the official residence of the Archbishop since the thirteenth century. Discreetly hidden away on the banks of the river Ouse, there was little to see apart from a romantic gatehouse. I had the impression it had once been the vibrant centre of cathedral life but, like the Sleeping Beauty, had succumbed to drowsiness.

We found a bus stop and made our way back into York. It was still fairly early so Andrew introduced me to York's Coppergate Shopping Centre and we strolled around window shopping until it was time to return home. I must have been more tired than I realised because I was in bed and asleep before the start of the BBC news that night. I was still aware that the temperamental heating needed a constant boost from me if the place was to stay warm and dry out our damp towels. Andrew would drop into a deep sleep as soon as his head touched the pillow and I often wondered exactly what *would* rouse him from his peaceful slumbers. I managed to wake shortly before midnight and not long after 3am. I remember easing myself out of bed for the second time and shivering as I walked around barefoot throwing switches. I must have decided it was also time to use the loo because, when Andrew found me over an hour later, I was sitting perched on the toilet, my head on my arms, which were being held up by the adjacent basin. It was a miracle I didn't tumble onto the floor!

He gently led me back to bed and took me in his arms. I promptly sank into a deep sleep. The next morning he explained he had woken and realised I was not beside him. He reached out and found my side of the bed was cold He had thought I was ill and came to find me. I think it had shocked him to realise that every night, when he was happily asleep, I was mindful and willing to sort out our heating dilemma. By the next morning he had decided it was time to leave our fenland retreat and, from then on, he searched for somewhere more suitable and comfortable for us both to live.

Chapter 17

*

How Andrew knew Martyn Frayn I never discovered. He would certainly have never been accepted as a member of Andrew's golf club so it must have been by reputation alone.

I later learned he had been born near Liverpool docks into a poor immigrant Irish community. His dad had left home one day and never returned, which left his mother to bring up him and his older brother as best she could. As soon as they reached an age they escaped and gradually made their way eastwards across the country until they fetched up in Bradford. The brother cobbled a life of sorts for himself in a factory, and settled down with his sharp-tongued whippet of a wife, but Marty had obviously caught the wandering bug by then and carried on towards Hull. How he managed to end up in York I have no idea.

He later told us that he was at a loose end one cold winter's day – probably looking for work – when he saw an auction advertised. Hoping to spend some time in a warm room, and maybe cadge a cup of tea, he followed two rather scruffy men who swept past him and up some steps. It was a house auction and Marty, who had occasionally slept rough and never owned a property in his life, felt he couldn't then turn tail and sneak out. So he put on a brave face and joined the two men near the back of the auditorium. The place was half empty and bidding was either non-existent or slow. He sat, nursing a mug of tea and trying to look knowledgeable and intelligent, while gradually people began to drift away. He had guessed, rightly, that the hall would be moderately warm and he was loath to leave. Eventually it was just him and his two neighbours. One of them bid low on a back-to-back terraced house and then made his way out of the building after securing the small scruffy dwelling at an impressively low price. Finally the tired auctioneer announced the last lot. Silence greeted him as he tried to wheedle some response from the last two of his audience. The other man laughed, raised his hand and followed his friend out the door. Marty told us that without considering his rashness he had offered less than a quarter of the asking price and listened with his mouth open as the Auctioneer accepted, copied down his name and address, gathered up his paperwork and walked away. We were in a bar talking late one night and I had leaned forward, intrigued by Marty's story and asked what had happened.

'I didn't sleep all night. I kept imagining the police arriving at my digs and dragging me away to prison. That morning I found a job as a night-watchman and that afternoon I went into the first bank I came to and asked for advice. The manager listened in amazement, then asked some searching questions as to how much rent I paid where I lived and finally offered me a mortgage.' His cheeky grin said it all.

Our Mr Martyn Frayn was an engaging rogue. He may have looked like a young, suave José Mourinho, in his navy blue Crombie and his designer stubble, but he was an astute businessman even so.

'That's how it all started. I did the place up during the day and worked all night. I sold it within three months at a fantastic profit. I went to another auction immediately and bought another, larger, similar run-down property. But I had learned: from then on, after giving each house a coat of paint, I let it out and pocketed the rents. That way I make money enough to buy my next bargain and yet I still own each freehold.'

Andrew and I were bewildered at his truthfulness. He proudly admitted the size of his portfolio to date and I could see Drew mentally calculating his worth. Marty obviously liked and trusted us – maybe we were nothing like his usual mates – because, as soon as he met us, he offered us accommodation in one of his nicest properties. It was a Victorian villa just beyond York's city's walls and, on viewing it, we accepted with alacrity. It housed a pair of Japanese students and seven Polish couples. There was a rather scruffy woman who he introduced as his housekeeper and, from her eagerness to please her employer and us, I gathered we were not the type of resident she was used to. All the tenants had use of the kitchen with a washing machine, dryer and iron in the utility room. Marty took us to the small breakfast room that overlooked the walled garden and stressed to the housekeeper it was strictly for our use only. I could see us rising even higher in her estimation. All I was conscious of was the warmth and cosiness of the whole property. And when I was shown the Edwardian bedroom and en-suite bathroom I fell in love with the place all over again.

****

We terminated our vacation with Joan and Gordon and I, for one, was not sorry to see the back of them and their Spartan holiday home. Their false heartiness had grated on my usual easy-going ways. They had assumed a dual role of equality and service and yet I felt we were being watched and assessed under the guise of friendliness. I didn't want to have to ask and be granted favours, because we were paying them well for their trouble. When we went down their drive for the last time I sank back in the car and breathed a sigh of relief. Andrew glanced at me and gave me an understanding grin. It was as if a huge laden blanket had been removed. Our adventure was now ready to begin...

Once we moved into the house – Alexandra Lodge – I immediately noted it was the nearest place to a living museum I had ever seen. It had once been an elegant, double-fronted Victorian villa of some standing and it still retained its old-world charm. A large vestibule led to a dark hall with a graceful sweeping staircase at the far end. Deeply carpeted in red, it led up through the gloom to the first floor. The housekeeper used the two ground floor front rooms, I deduced – probably so she could keep an eye on her tenants' movements. The impressive bannisters began with a thick swirling mahogany roundel and, as I set my hand on it and progressed slowly upwards, I guessed how minor royalty must have felt. The kitchen and utility rooms, situated towards the back of the house, were pretty basic with patterned black-and-red quarry tiles. All the appliances were of the latest design, I noted, so it appeared Mr Frayn did not skimp on satisfying his residents. There was a large scrubbed deal table in the outer room (for breakfast?) and the cupboards contained serviceable crockery and cutlery plus a fair selection of pots and pans. The microwave oven sported an *out of service* sticker so I wondered which of the foreign tenants might be responsible for not understanding the instructions! Our tiny breakfast room was just behind the kitchen with a pleasant oval table, chairs and a dresser – and more *objets d'art*. I rejoiced in our view of the walled garden and the privacy that eating alone would give us. All the corridors had memorabilia hung on the walls and placed in glass-fronted cabinets: there were also old photos, small statues and interesting paintings.

Our room looked like a period stage-setting for an Edwardian melodrama. A huge crystal chandelier hung from the moulded ceiling; it highlighted a mahogany half-tester bed – its deep overhang curved and sensuous – and showed off the crisp cream Victorian *broderie anglaise* bed linen to perfection. The huge window sported fresh white fine voile nets with long dark velvet drapes held back with massive tassels. I breathed in sharply when I saw what looked like two French *armoires*. They were hugely spacious wardrobes with many cupboards and deep drawers which, once filled, were big enough to crawl inside and get lost amongst the hanging garments. Whoever had dressed this room knew their period and when I first saw it I expected Lillie Langtry herself to lightly trip in through the door and introduce herself. Highly polished brass door furniture was probably original plus ornate, caste iron radiators which were all set off by a smooth, dark cream, deep pile carpet which completed the illusion of Edwardian life.

The bathroom held an even bigger surprise. Apart from a cream roll-topped bath, with claw feet and massive taps, there was a life-size statue of a voluptuous nude standing seductively beside it. Andrew immediately christened her Ariadne and, what really amused me, was the way he tossed a towel over her head every time he went in for his bath.

'Can't have her lascivious eyes devouring me,' he muttered.

But what dominated that room was a huge, stained-glass window. All vibrant blues and reds – it depicted St George getting ready to slay the dragon and, when the early morning sun poured into the room, the whole place beamed with light and I felt I was drowning in colour.

We settled into the life of Alexandra Lodge without a ripple. I adored the warmth and splendour of our new surroundings. No more did I have to wake again and again throughout the night and drag myself, shivering, out of bed. That torture was a thing of the past and I relaxed and brightened considerably. Talking one evening in bed we discussed about how we wanted to spend the rest of our life. Andrew leaned towards renting our own property but I was aghast at that suggestion. I had brought enough of Rose's inheritance money with me to pay for approximately half a reasonable house. Andrew and I both had investments in our own right but I was concerned Rose's nest egg would be frittered away on rent therefore preventing us having enough cash to buy anything: then we would be reliant on Andrew getting his divorce and splitting what he and Fay owned down the middle. I had insisted Robin kept our house and I didn't want Andrew's decision to leave Fay to add extra stress to what must have been hell for her. I would have preferred her to retain her family home, too.

So we kept our priorities practical. We considered three bedrooms would suit us perfectly. I leaned towards a bungalow but knew, because they take up a lot of floor space, they are usually far more expensive than a property set on two, or even three, floors. Other than wanting to buy my own property, I had no preference for the type of place we should choose and I was quite prepared to view whatever was on offer in the York area. Andrew recommended we choose somewhere within a ten-mile radius of the city of York itself. He appreciated the social life that was generated within the environs of the city and I was only too willing to go along with his superior knowledge.

With that in mind, we set out the next morning to walk into town and search out a realistic number of reputable estate agents. My goodness, there were dozens! We began our walk by strolling under picturesque Bootham Bar and then took it in turns to "leap frog" each other all the way down Petergate and past the Minster. Sometimes, if Andrew recognised the names of golfing cronies, he would venture inside these agencies in the hope they might be a little more helpful towards someone they knew. By lunchtime we had acquired armfuls of useful literature. So, as we ate, we went through the pile with a fine-tooth comb and discarded any property unsuitable, unfit or far too expensive. In bed the previous night Andrew and I had disagreed on garaging, but my criteria to every estate agent I visited stressed a decent-sized garage with each property. Robin and I had always garaged our current car and, as I knew Andrew had a double garage attached to his old home, I at least wanted something that would house and protect his lovely car.

That afternoon we slogged around as many other agencies as we could discover. Some of the literature was duplicated, but lots looked reasonable, and we became moderately excited at the prospect of visiting them all within the next few weeks. As we walked back to our comfortable Edwardian rooms I felt we had made some progress and was pleased to discuss where we should go for our evening meal. But as we entered our new home we found a letter waiting on the hall table.

It was from my friend Jess in Taunton. A sad, unhappy little note telling me how she missed me – even though I had only departed Devon a short time previously. I had attended her husband's, Hugo's, funeral, along with other friends, but it wasn't the same as being only a few miles away and meeting occasionally. We had all gently laughed at Hugo – even Jess – and now she felt ashamed at her teasing attitude. Hugo had been much older than us and his crusty, pessimistic view of life had caused much derision from his sunny wife and offspring. Now Jess said she missed his stolid presence – even in bed – and that now his dour utterances would have been preferable to this awful gap in her life. I telephoned immediately and promised to write as soon as I returned that evening. Andrew listened intently and I knew he was thinking of his own family predicament. Had Fay informed their sons? And, if not, it was high time he sorted it out for himself. There were also friends and family – like Deborah in Cornwall – who knew nothing and should be told. I knew it was a huge undertaking and he was well aware it would be an awful shock for them all. I was also certain it was the very last thing he wanted to do and I knew there was no way I wanted to influence his decision. I remembered, a few weeks earlier, forcing myself to open my mouth and begin telling Robin. At that *second* I had the choice of either going through with it or saying nothing. The temptation to do nothing was almost overwhelming. *That* was what Andrew was facing. The fact that he had already told Fay and left her somehow made his task more daunting, I felt. He had half done the job and then his determination had ground to a halt. Now he had to bite the bullet and explain to the rest of them.

After we had returned from our evening meal Andrew suggested we separate and use either the downstairs breakfast room or our bedroom to speak to or write to our friends and family. I insisted he use our bedroom; it was more private and comfortable, knowing I would be fine in the cosy downstairs parlour. I wrote a long letter to Jess and then made short calls to Lorna, my cousins in London, and Meryl and Adam in Essex. I stressed on the telephone that we were warm and happy and told them we had started house-hunting. We had decided on alternate days to view properties and the other days Andrew had offered to show me Yorkshire. It would give us time to evaluate our findings without saturating us with too much searching for the perfect home.

When Andrew came down to get me I was curled up in an armchair reading. He looked pale and tired, not his usual exuberant self but, as he was clutching a mug of welcome cocoa in each hand, I stretched the kinks out of my back and went and found some shortbread to accompany his peace offering. We took it up to bed and talked quietly about our respective problems. He said the two boys had taken his admission very well considering they had no inkling that life had been unhappy between their parents in the latter years. Neither of them had heard from their mother and both promised to ring her forthwith.

Mark, his youngest son, admitted, 'We knew things suddenly became shaky when we were younger. There was lots of shouting which stopped as soon as we walked in. We loved Hong Kong but, when we suddenly left for Europe, we noticed you still spent time with us but ignored Mum rather pointedly. So, when Peter and I were sloping off to Uni, it did cross our minds you might decide to split up. But, every time we arrived home with our grotty washing, everything seemed as calm and ordered as ever; so we imagined you were both fine and happy with things as they were.'

I have no idea of Andrew's response – and I didn't ask – as I felt that was personal between a father and his two sons. To me it seemed pointless to air one's dirty linen in public and trying to get people to take sides in any dispute has always smacked of manipulation to me, and I abhorred it. I am sure Andrew felt this way too. Why rake over old raw situations? Andrew and his wife had managed to cobble together their differences so did it matter if it was for the sake of their children or for each other? Now one of them wanted to go forward and leave the other behind. Was that so awful? They both had made comfortable, separate lives for themselves so neither would be left alone. Fay had her friends for lunching, bridge parties and designer shopping. She appeared to enjoy all three pastimes and, as Andrew had mentioned, when they phoned she became another person who gossiped and laughed until the call was finished. He had his two sons and their families, his golfing cronies, various clubs and me. It should have been a reasonable solution and I looked towards the future when we, plus our two ex-spouses, could at least manage a semblance of normality between ourselves.

In bed, munching our biscuits with steaming cocoa, we settled down to map out our next few weeks. We took the sheaves of property lists from various estate agents and Andrew talked me through the nice areas as we tried to hammer out our priorities and what sort of house would be suitable. We reduced it to half and then both went through what was left and decided two or three viewings every other day would be a sensible strategy. Andrew put them in some sort of order and then he talked of interesting places he wanted to visit with me, as a break for us both, and scribbled down yet another list. I grinned at his enthusiasm and agreed all work and no play would make us both dull.

Thence we set up a routine of ringing up estate agents to make appointments for the next day while exploring the environs of York *that* day. It all worked rather well and I had forgotten Andrew's previous objection to saddling ourselves with buying a house. I had the usual nesting instinct of a middle-aged woman who enjoys comfort and stability so that renting, as a long-term proposition, didn't appear a sensible option to me.

****

The next day I was told the Railway Museum was the perfect place to begin our tour. I knew little about trains – apart from the London

Underground – and I was avid to learn. As we walked through the streets Andrew would catechise me as to its name and where it led. One day I made the mistake of mixing up Bootham Bar (one of the picturesque gates that allow visitors to enter the walls of York) with Micklegate Bar as we were making our way towards the Minster. Another day, I told him I had walked across Lendal Bridge and turned right into Lendal *Street* when I should have known it was simply Lendal. I often forgot the names of bridges too and would hesitantly guess either Scarborough or Harrogate. Andrew would raise his eyes in derision. As I had never visited either place, and had no idea in which direction each lay, I suppose it was excusable; but often, in desperation, I gave well-known thoroughfares a pet name. Thus Coney Street became Rabbit Run to me and The Shambles I called The Muddles.

The National Railway Museum was a fascinating day out for me. We strolled to it the next morning. It was situated behind the railway station with all its constantly shunting trains and, as we squeezed under a narrow, busy railway bridge and into an industrial area, I felt it set the right mood for our visit. We entered huge great echoing halls, which encompassed three hundred years of locomotive history; they had a replica of Stephenson's Rocket close to Japan's modern "Bullet" high-speed train. Some locomotives barely looked like trains at all: one looked like a monstrous black menacing leviathan. I saw the Hardwicke, built in 1895, and learned it was capable of reaching speeds up to 67mph on the run from Crewe to Carlisle. Now that is a pretty fast speed even today and, in the late nineteenth century, it must have frightened passengers unbelievably. Especially when motoring was sedate by comparison and lady passengers wore dust-coats, while their elegant hats would be secured by huge voile scarves. The blue Mallard was built before I was born but it looked so attractive and streamlined that I considered it rivalled any train we see today. It had been the proud holder of the world speed record and was in use until 1963. I noticed most people sighed when they saw the Flying Scotsman. Just the name made it special. Spoilt for choice, I also looked in awe at the elegant Duchess of Hamilton – all green and gold brass – but my favourite was the Royal Train. It was so much fun to peer in windows and look at the staterooms and bedrooms. To see the dining room laid up for a meal and to imagine what the Royal Family would be talking about while they were sedately served food by liveried footmen, maybe glancing out of the windows as the train sped through their kingdom and perhaps catching sight of the occasional family patiently waiting beside the track, dying to catch a glimpse and wave at their revered sovereigns. It conjured up all sorts of romantic notions as I, and probably lots of other people, looked in the windows and dreamed.

We stood and stared in awe at the massive turntable that enabled even the largest engines to swing round manually by just a few sturdy engineers or footplate men. But what really caught my imagination was the upstairs area set aside for all the railway memorabilia. We wandered around looking at hand-signalling levers that were huge and yet worked with smoothness and precision at their operator's touch; penny platform tickets and ticket machines that produced cardboard tokens showing a charge of 1d; all sorts of chunky signs, in the distinctive navy enamel with white edging, that reminded us of times long before Dr Beeching had his wicked way and insisted so many productive branch lines should be axed; lamps of all sorts and sizes; tags that were personal to certain railway staff which permitted them to do all the jobs only *they* were allowed to do, like "snatching" mailbags from stations without slowing as the swift trains went thundering across the countryside. In those days mail was sorted as the locomotive raced towards its destination through the night. A letter posted in Cornwall by evening could be dropping on a doormat in a tiny backwater town in Essex, or in a Glasgow tenement, before 8am the next morning. My goodness that was a simpler, more trusting time when staff were so proud to tell the world they worked for the London North Eastern, Great Western, London Midland & Scottish, or Southern Region railways. We stared at British Rail posters which extolled the beaches and countryside of the British Isles. They now are sold at auction for tremendous sums and yet, in their day, they were plastered casually on the walls of stations, or in the fuggy railway carriages, just to titillate the appetite of the British public. It was a truly memorable day out and I reckoned we would be returning often to the Railway Museum.

The next day, by contrast, we began our house-hunting in

earnest. I am not sure quite what Andrew felt about it but I was excited at the thought of owning somewhere we would eventually be able to call home. I suppose women have a natural nesting instinct that longs for comfort and happiness. I had partially achieved this with Robin and I was certain it was awaiting me, and would be even more delightful, with Andrew. It's not as if I needed to produce excellent banquets for my man, live in the lap of luxury or show off to friends and neighbours. I have quite simple tastes but I wanted to set my mark on a place I could finally call home. My goal was to shut the door, draw the curtains and relax with the man I loved. It also wasn't because I am nosy by nature and wanted to see how folk lived up in this part of Yorkshire. I don't have an envious bone in my body and my taste runs to the simple and modest. I just wanted a happy and pleasant house that I could call mine.

We had decided that our priorities should be three bedrooms plus decent living accommodation, a fairly large garage to take Andrew's spacious car; but we preferred not too much land surrounding the property – so it would never become a burden. I leaned towards a bungalow as I had already lived in one before and we were approaching an age where running up and down stairs can become tiring; but I realised, only too well that possibly a decent chalet bungalow could provide all we needed on the ground floor as well as an extra spacious bedroom above and be more attainable in price. I had no idea what I was wishing for and that it would be almost impossible to find. The difference between the south and north of England is that chalet bungalows are built from scratch in the former and are usually converted two-bedroomed bungalows in the latter. The first day we had selected three quite nice looking properties – none of them bungalows *or* chalets – from our massive pile and had booked sensible, spaced-out, appointments to enable us to enjoy our "no pressure" viewing.

The first house looked exceptionally impressive in the brochure. Large and double-fronted, it stood on a slight rise with a small surrounding garden and at first glance it appeared the perfect place. We were welcomed in enthusiastically and made to sit down for coffee. Andrew, ever the prosaic one, asked how long it had been on the market and was surprised to discover it had been up for sale for quite some time. Eventually the vendors were forced to show us around and then we learned why. It was a sunny, south facing, modern house but it was also a "one room deep" house. Yes, it had a wide frontage with the central hall leading one way into the kitchen which opened out into the dining room. Go in the other direction and one entered a fair-sized living room. The builder had solved the problem of where to put the stairs by placing them at the far end of the sitting room. This took us up open-plan stairs to two bedrooms above, both with en suite bathrooms. It was like some small Victorian cottages where there are almost no passages and bedrooms lead from one into the next. So, when the master goes to bed, everyone in the household has to be tucked up in theirs! This made it totally unsuitable for us. We tried not to show our disappointment and chatted amiably once back downstairs. We admired the kitchen layout and the diamond-paned double glazing, but it was obvious to the owners we had no further interest in their property.

We slid back into the car with sighs of relief and went and found some lunch to cheer ourselves up. Andrew said, brightly, that the other two couldn't be as bad so we set off, after a satisfying snack, in the fond hope he was right. Well they *were* – but in a different way. The first was olde worlde and was set in an untidy garden. The only drawback was the garage, if you could call it that! It was more the size of a garden shed and would hardly hold a bicycle let alone a large BMW. The house was old and rambling and I was totally disenchanted from the outset. We looked around in a perfunctory way and, as the owner – a middle-aged man in a drooping cardigan – wasn't in the best of moods, we didn't linger unduly. I gathered his wife had left him. Obviously he preferred life as it had been and had no wish to help out his disenchanted spouse by selling the family home and was consequently as unhelpful as possible.

The third property was in town. It was a sparsely furnished Victorian house with huge, bare windows and yellowing, grubby paintwork, lopsided cupboards and dark doors that didn't fit too well. High ceilings meant it was cold and I never found out if the central heating was faulty or simply switched off. The vendor, a teacher at one of York's inner schools, appeared distracted and followed us around with a dusty book in his hand. We soon made our way out politely, with him following us to the door.

'Did he think we were going to pinch the silver?' asked Andrew cynically. 'Gosh what a strange lot of people we have met today. Either they had no interest in selling – as one could see from the state of their houses – or they were so eager to snare us they would have fed us a five-course meal to keep us there.' I must say I agreed. After our high hopes of the morning I felt we had been let down badly. As with most estate agents, we were subject to a catechism when we reported back to them that evening. We both found it quite difficult, each time, to give a fair and balanced assessment of our findings without giving offence to the owner or the agent. Occasionally, to test the response, we made a stupidly low offer. It was always accepted. This I found disturbing. Sellers were obviously desperate.

Two days later we ventured forth again. This time Andrew had chosen villages to the north east of York. I must admit there were quite a few names that put me off by their very sound. Isn't that stupid? Why should such odd sounding names like Earswick, Nether Poppleton, Warthill, Fangfoss, Bugthorpe and Pocklington sound any worse than our odd-sounding names in the South West? Well they did and it affected my willingness to view certain houses, I noticed.

This time we had chosen bungalows that had converted extra space in their lofts. Reading the brochures, each one sounded fantastic. Well the first was spacious and immaculate downstairs and I turned to Andrew with shining eyes. *This* was more like it. We were then taken up a steep staircase and into a loft area. There was a landing of sorts but one had to squeeze under and round a huge beam just to get into the new conversion. The young couple had obviously done it themselves without the help of a builder, and had very little idea of what was structurally possible. The en-suite bathroom was unfinished and there appeared to be little insulation. We looked around with jaundiced eyes and I could see Andrew comparing it with his previous luxurious house just as I was thinking of my immaculate little bungalow in Honiton. I wondered if they would ever sell it and move on to pastures new.

The second one was in a pretty village. The bungalow looked perfect – modern red brick with sparkling windows. A youngish husband opened the door and invited us in. He told us his wife was disabled and he had spent years altering the place for her convenience. Sadly she had gone off with another suitor and he was left with a property he was desperate to sell. We looked around but my heart wasn't in it. I hated the thought of an unhappy house – which is what this one seemed to be – and, ridiculously, I felt all the minor alterations that I would see every day would affect my relaxing and being happy there. As we left he offered to accept more or less any price we were prepared to pay and I ended up crying and holding his hands in an effort to comfort him. When we had eased away from the kerb Andrew admitted the ghost of his wife would probably haunt us forever if we dared to take the place. I was relieved he felt as I did and knew there was no way I could make it a home.

After a scrappy lunch we went to see the last place on our list. It was slightly nearer York and, as we pulled up outside, I looked appreciatively at a substantial single-storey house with a sensible garage attached to it ,The little old man and his jolly wife asked us in with beaming smiles. I thought *Oh this is better.* And it was in some ways, but there were too many small rooms placed at awkward angles. The kitchen was exceptionally small, the layout was appalling and the appliances dwarfed the room. The owner had also built a brick fireplace in the lounge and I could see Andrew hated it on sight. It was difficult because, as soon as we entered, they took a liking to us both. The rotund man was an ardent DIY enthusiast and he even offered us all his tools so we could continue where he had left off. Their daughter had decided it was time she offered them a home and, as they didn't want to disappoint her, they were willing to relinquish their beloved cosy home and start again, with her and son-in-law, in Cumbria. We looked at the three bedrooms but I could see none of it suited our taste and, after eating a mound of exquisite little sandwiches and home-made cake, we eased ourselves out of there saying we would think about it and let them know.

'That's the bit I hate most,' I admitted, as we got back on the York road once more, 'having to tell bare-faced lies to save hurting their feelings.'

'Trouble with you is you are too soft and the next thing you know they are telling you about their private lives and you are trying to think of ways to help them out, Jenny. Just go and view these places and then come away without committing yourself. Don't be so nice. Mind you, *I* hate speaking to the agents when we get home. They are avid for our money and it is so difficult not to be brutally honest and upset them.'

I nodded miserably. Perhaps we were doing this house-hunting at the wrong time of the year. Traditionally spring is the normal option and then more people would be viewing property and we could lose ourselves in the crowd.

The next morning brought communication from our respective ex-mates. Robin sent a short text saying I had a dental appointment the following week and Fay's text said briefly *RING ME.* Andrew picked up his mobile phone and dialled her immediately and I was quietly horrified at his attitude.

'What is it?' he asked abruptly. He listened intently and then muttered tersely 'I will be there in an hour to sort it out.' Apparently this didn't suit and he agreed to return home at 7.15pm sharp that evening.

'What is it? I asked, worried. It appeared she had insisted on internet banking when Andrew left her and had made a few mistakes. She now needed him to sort her finances out, but as she was off with friends for the rest of the day, she required him to appear at the exact time she stipulated because an hour later she would be going out again. I sighed with relief as I had imagined some awful catastrophe, but she obviously hadn't taken it very seriously – hence the specific time.

'Come on, don't look so worried,' said Andrew, grasping my hand. 'I am going to transport you to Whitby for the day.' And that's what he did.

Well I didn't get to meet Count Dracula but I enjoyed most of the other sights! On the way into the harbour area we passed a huge, three-masted barque which set the tone for the resort. Captain Cook served his apprenticeship here and there was a small museum dedicated to him close to the harbour. It was a sunny but cold day, which didn't stop lots of visitors milling around this attractive medieval town. It was on two levels, like a stage setting, with the River Esk and harbour cutting it in half and accentuating the two-tiered effect. The lower level was a maze of winding, often cobbled, streets which ended in a large sea wall. This was topped by a lighthouse and backed by a wide, flat, sandy beach. Overlooking the town was a fishermen's church and behind it the most picturesque, ruined abbey I have ever seen. We climbed the 199 steps up to the church and stood, breathing heavily, as we surveyed the streets below us. The church was Norman and surrounded by leaning gravestones. They sparkled in the crisp sunshine. Inside, it had a "Methodist chapel" feel to it regardless of the box pews and white wooden, barley sugar, twisted columns. The pulpit towered above any congregation and I could well imagine the vicar thundering out his sermon.

We made our way towards the abbey. Set on the highest point above the town, its tracery of beautiful grey ruins reminded me of exquisite lace against a pale blue sky. I stood there filled with rapture. We strolled around the Abbey museum but, I am ashamed to say, I took little in. I learned it was sacked by Viking raiders and re-founded just after 1078 on the heels of William the Conqueror's invitation but, personally, I just wanted to stare at this most magnificent monastery. Andrew drew me away, saying he was starving.

There are two ways of descending – one by the 199 steps, the other via a steep, grassy path that follows the sweeping curve down. We made our way to the lower level of cosy taverns, shops and pleasure arcades, but Andrew drew me unerringly towards the Magpie Restaurant. We were both starving and he said it provided the best fish and chips in Yorkshire. Well we had to wait in a queue but it proved his point! After a really satisfying meal we just wandered and Andrew introduced me to the numerous shops selling jet. Apparently jet had been mined here since the Roman times but it was only when Queen Victoria became widowed that she popularised the mineral. And now it was fashioned into every piece of jewellery imaginable – as well as ornaments and miniatures. We browsed in various shops but it wasn't to my taste so I declined a souvenir.

On the way home I purchased a rail ticket back to Devon. I hated the thought of not attending my dental surgery for my check-up and we agreed one night away was a simple price to pay for peace of mind. I provided a snack meal that evening in our pleasant dining parlour so Andrew could visit Fay at the correct time stipulated. I waved him goodbye and returned to our snug rooms. I wondered what sort of reception he would get.

Apparently he had to wait on the doorstep while Fay made a point of unlocking and unbolting the front door. She ushered him in icily and stood behind him while he sorted out her computer. Months later he admitted he never quite knew what to expect on his infrequent visits. Sometimes she would rant and rave, occasionally she would sob uncontrollably, but mostly she was cold and sarcastic. Whenever he tried to talk to her about collecting his mail she refused to discuss it, so he would always return to me miserable and quiet. What happened *that* night remains a mystery. I was snuggled down when he came back and pushed open the bedroom door. I jumped up to make him a warm drink and he sat on the edge of the bed and drained the mug in a few gulps.

The next morning we were back on the "house hunt" trail yet again. This time it was an abandoned young wife. She showed us around her house looking shaken and apprehensive. I think being on her own was a new experience; probably she was used to being surrounded by a comfortable family, and now she was alone and frankly scared. The house was small and quite bare of essentials, so either her partner had removed his share of the spoils or they had only been together for a short while and had been in the process of making a home.

There were only two bedrooms, I had noted, and really it was not quite big enough to fit our requirements, but the first one she showed us was adequate with large fitted wardrobes and an attached dressing table. There was also an en-suite bathroom so that looked promising. She turned away and opened the door next to it. I jumped back in alarm as a huge ball of fur launched itself at me. She explained modestly that this was Rupert's room, her pet rabbit. We both stood there, not knowing quite what to say. It was smelly, lots of pellets littered the floor and there were innumerable scratch marks that proved poor old Rupert wasn't very happy with his gloomy captivity. At our puzzled frowns the vendor went on to explain her mother had offered to take the pet until she sold her property but that she hated the thought of being alone. I gently advised her that probably mum knew best and that I felt certain someone would want her bijou residence; but lots of people would be put off by the idea of sheltered livestock. This time Andrew added his opinion with a kindly arm around her shoulder and she dubiously agreed with us. We came away leaving a forlorn child who needed lots of support and guidance.

After another pub lunch we searched for our next port of call. It was in a leafy avenue and it all looked pretty promising. A slim, middle-aged lady opened the door and I guessed she was either a widow, a contented long-deserted wife or a spinster. Three decent sized bedrooms and two adequate reception rooms interested us immediately. The garage, on examination, was small but Andrew explained to me that could be the least of our worries. We spent ages wandering around a couple more times and then finally sat down, joining her for afternoon tea, and began to talk. I complimented her on the pleasant area she lived in; however Andrew mentioned he had noticed the pub that we had been in for lunch actually backed onto her garden. She answered casually but – I caught Andrew's eye – we had both noticed a slight tension. He pushed his questioning up a notch and finally she admitted that in the summer evenings, when slightly intoxicated drinkers used the inn's garden, things could get a bit out of hand. She pointed out there was a substantial wall at the bottom of her spacious garden and tried to play down the fact that occasionally she'd had cause to call the police. We politely said we would think about it and it was *then* she showed her eagerness to drop the price. Andrew was musing out loud and offered a substantially smaller amount and, to our surprise, we had the woman agreeing with alacrity.

We went home after that quite chastened with our thought-provoking day. To cheer us both up we decided to go out for the evening. We chose a local cinema that was showing *Happy Feet*. I guess we both felt the need to space ourselves away from unhappy folk. Suddenly we had uncovered the sadder side of house selling. Up until then both of us had sold and bought various properties in an upbeat mood of enthusiasm. Now we saw this was not so with everyone. Two or three times Andrew had tested the water, when he was talking with an agent, to see quite how accommodating sellers were prepared to be with the quoted prices. In every case we were surprised and disturbed to find how desperate most owners were and how they were willing to drop their price substantially just to make a sale.

The next day I decided I needed a haircut and, as our shelves were looking so bare back at Alexandra Lodge, that food shopping was a necessity. I told Andrew I needed him for neither occupation and suggested he took himself off to his golf club and made his mates happy. I had been worried that all work could make Jack a dull lover and that his friends, even if they knew he had left home for some unknown woman, would be affronted at his cavalier attitude of ignoring them. Since we had moved on from Joan and Gordon's hotel, as far as I knew, Andrew had contacted none of them and I thought *this* was his opportunity to put things right. I noticed he went with a smile on his face and a spring to his step so knew I had guessed correctly.

I found a male hairdresser who did a lot of talking and then charged me an exorbitant amount for giving him the privilege of doing so, but actually he made an extremely good job of my hair so I was satisfied. Shopping is normally a similar and boring experience anywhere in the UK, so, when I found a Sainsbury's, I went in, did my usual dash around and came out with a couple of brimming bags. I was back home by lunchtime and, after shoving all my haul on the empty shelves, decided to take myself back off to York once more. It was a spur-of-the-moment decision as I was still a little uncertain of what was where inside the walls, so I elected to just wander around and see what I stumbled upon.

I was so lucky because I came across the Roman Bath House in a busy square right in the city centre. I almost missed it because it shared its entrance with a pub and the darkish staircase that led down to the museum looked a bit unsavoury. But, when I reached the bottom, I was agreeably surprised. Very simply laid out, it described what a Roman soldier could hope to find when he was stationed far away in the wilds of the north. I knew the Romans set great store by warm, relaxing baths and cleanliness. To go to a Roman baths would be a social occasion for the average soldier and it was not unusual to mix with ladies once there. This has been proved by various jewels, like the odd earring, that have been discovered in the drainage system!

The bathers would use a simple metal instrument, rather like a blunt butter knife, to remove their skin of grease and impurities and, once in the different bath areas which were warmed to various heats by hot water being channelled under these tiled floors, they would unwind and talk with their friends. The final room was a cold-water experience which must have come as quite a shock after the steamy heat they had grown accustomed to. The place, although small, contained all things Roman and one was encouraged to dress up in a plumed helmet, don a shield, brandish a sword and even take a photo. All good fun and I did the honours by photographing a happy family from Leeds.

Andrew and I arrived home within minutes of each other. He told me he had a satisfactory game of golf which was followed by lunching with his friends in the Clubhouse, and I chatted on endlessly about my Roman Bath experience. And that was the night we discovered the "two-for-one" restaurants. There were two that we grew to like. One was near a large cinema complex and so was always extremely busy and the other was farther out of town. I preferred the latter as it was calmer, quieter and the staff were more laid back. From then on we went and sampled their meals most nights. A good selection of two meals for the price of one, plus a decent glass of wine and a substantial pudding suited us both. It was as if we were on a permanent holiday and it eased our house-hunting chores as well as our exploration days which often took us right to the sea or into the countryside.

We visited five more unsatisfactory houses interspersed with a day out to Castle Howard - which I enjoyed immensely – and a return train journey to Devon, which I didn't. The route was via Birmingham and seemed to take forever. It was expensive as I had booked it at the last moment, to coincide with my dental appointment, and there were no cheap tickets.

I had nervously asked Robin's permission to return home and he'd agreed immediately, saying he would be on night duty but that he would take himself off to Kevin and Hazel's for the duration of my stay and therefore we needn't meet. I let myself into the bungalow in the dark. I had purposefully not told Lorna to expect me and, after making myself a cup of tea, I took myself to the back bedroom and made up a bed there. There was nothing to do so I chose a favourite book and went to sleep. The next morning I was up early. There was laundry in the basket so I set to with the iron and finished it off. It seemed a small price to pay for free accommodation. As I was putting Robin's socks neatly in his drawer I came across a scrap of paper advertising a marriage bureau. With a grunt of astonishment I was surprised that he had wasted no time. But maybe it was some well-meaning friend at work trying to be helpful. I slammed the drawer to, feeling hurt. My dental check-up went without a hitch as normal and, on the way back to the bungalow I remembered to call into our hardware store to select and pay for a new ironing board that Robin could collect. Until I used my usual sit-down one, which I had owned for more years than I cared to remember, I realised how much I had missed it and on the spur of the moment, had decided that I would give a new one to Robin and take the old with me when I finally collected the last of my belongings. I returned home to clean the bath and tidy around before it was time for me to leave. I took myself off by way of Lorna's and stopped by for five minutes. She was surprised and delighted to see me and ran me back to the station just to snatch an extra ten minutes together, while I waited for my train. She told me Robin still appeared shocked and devastated even after weeks of managing on his own. He was trying to do his own cleaning and was worried it wasn't up to my exacting standards.

'He's still not bothering to eat regularly, he often looks lost and forlorn when he thinks no one is looking and I think he is falling asleep watching late night TV and not bothering to go to bed. We are all trying to keep an eye on him, inviting him out for meals and asking him down the pub but, honestly, Jenny, I think he's lost his reason for living and his confidence along with it.'

Other friends as well as his sister, Alexis, had told me in no uncertain terms how bad it was. They had been scathing in their comments and I had listened, shaking, but apart from coming straight back to him – and I knew that wouldn't work because he could never trust me again, and he was right not to do so – there was nothing I was able to do about it. I hugged my best friend for her thoughtfulness and begged her to keep in touch. She saw me off with a tentative wave as the train pulled out.

The journey back to York was a nightmare. Thoughts and fears were scuttling around in my head and it was only when the train decanted me onto the platform at my destination, and I saw Andrew watching intently for me, that I immediately relaxed; and then his arms warmly clasped me to him. In the car going home I broke down and told him the little information I had gathered from my visit. I made it clear that I had not seen Robin. I thought it important Andrew should harbour no misunderstandings. Once more I felt deeply sorry for both Fay and Robin. Andrew and I had each other for comfort – they had no one. And it didn't matter how many friends rallied around them – basically, they were both *alone*.

****

Our estate agents' output had almost dried up and both Andrew and I were becoming disillusioned with our search. I still had the dregs of property details that I had scanned, but as they didn't look very promising I had abandoned them on my bedside table and forgotten them. The next morning I looked up with interest when Andrew threw yet another envelope next to my cereal bowl as I was munching my breakfast. It was a new build to the north of York and, from the photograph, looked hopeful. So instead of visiting the Treasurer's House in York that day we made an appointment to view it pretty smartly.

We discovered a small estate set amongst trees. I personally like new property – one can put one's own stamp on a new house from the very beginning. There is no thinking of immediate alterations and basic decoration just to make it habitable. The house on offer was in a cul de sac just off the main road and, as there were only three neighbouring properties, the secluded aspect appealed to me. The agent met us outside and showed us around and then allowed us to wander at our leisure. I must admit I hate to be followed from room to room with the vendor following behind and stressing the suitability of everything I am looking at. I like to consider and ponder to my heart's content. There were a number of fitted appliances in the square kitchen and further fitted wardrobes in two of the three bedrooms. So the furnishing of it would be minimal, I reckoned. *This might possibly be the one.*

We wandered outside and admired the decent, wide drive and simple grass frontage. The back garden was big enough for privacy and not too large for maintenance, I noted. It would suit us admirably. I turned, at last, towards the garage. Andrew pushed the up-and-over door and it swung up silently. We both knew immediately it was too small and there was no room to extend it. I turned away with a grimace but Drew protested at once that it was OK. He could manage without garaging his car he told me and he spent the next hour persuading me it would be fine. Finally I gave in and we made the preliminary offer on the spot subject to a contract and a surveyor's acceptable report. We returned that night – rejoicing.

The next three days we were delighted to kick over the traces. I was taken to the Dales, to Scarborough and, finally, to the Treasurer's House in York. We ate celebratory meals and generally made fools of ourselves by getting up late and making love whenever we were in the mood. I then realised what a strain we had been under the past few weeks with a less than satisfactory hotel followed by a house full of foreigners who could barely speak our language. Our next problem was Fay. Suddenly she insisted that Andrew return home as often as she demanded, and at a time to suit her – to collect his mail – and then requested he mend a broken pane in the greenhouse and put a new lock on their garage door. It was easier to agree to all her requests than to argue, he said, and I would meet him afterwards and try to ease his feeling of submission and obligation.

Two days later we were brought down to earth with a bump. We received the surveyor's report on the house. There was a medium-sized crack in one of the outside walls and as it was a new build he could give us no idea if it was possibly due to subsidence or just a minor fault in the bricklaying. He and the builder could give us no guarantee that, even if it was put right, it did not presage something more sinister. Andrew and I were old enough to know that it was foolish to complete the sale and we informed the agent immediately. So it was back to the search once more and the end of our high jinks.

That night I was lying in bed feeling depressed. We had started out with such high hopes and gradually, as we progressed through the suitable properties on offer, we realised our dream house might be more elusive than we had supposed. That morning Andrew had received a telephone call from his eldest son, Peter, complaining his mother was beginning to telephone him and his brother constantly and they were finding it difficult to humour and soothe her. He also mentioned Mark was becoming annoyed as it was interfering with his classes at school. I tried not to listen as Andrew sounded distraught for the very first time as he had to plead with his sons to give their mother time to adjust. None of this was helping my melancholy mood as I picked up the diminishing pile of paperwork by our bed. In desperation I went through the untidy sheaf once more. Again and again I had put details of one particular property to the back of the pile. It had looked dull and plain and Andrew had told me it was in a slightly run-down area not far from York's city walls. The next morning, more in desperation than expectancy, I insisted we view it. I could see Drew had no great wish to visit the area but he was prepared to humour me and actually getting out and doing something cheered us both up slightly. The appointment was made for the evening as the owners both worked. We arrived after our evening meal. The road was narrow and ended in a cul-de-sac with a few cars parked on either side of it. Drew commented favourably on the small front garden with a wide drive in front of the garage.

'Well *that* at least could take three cars and the garage looks pretty large, too. Looks as if they have enlarged the modest garage and built a huge extension over the top,' he said. I nodded eagerly as we parked on the large forecourt and rang the bell.

The couple came out of the garage door behind us and invited us in. It was a double garage and, as we walked through towards the small conservatory, I noticed a washing machine and dryer placed neatly at the back of it. This all looked suddenly promising. It was an amazing place. We were taken up a step and into an oblong room that had another bijou conservatory tacked to the end of it. The couple explained that the small sun room behind the garage was a drying room for washing, while the conservatory proper, which extended into the tiny garden, was for sitting in. The kitchen was a large rectangular room with cupboards and appliances on three sides, a huge window and a large dining table at the far end. The sitting room was modest and the hall undoubtedly small, but by then I was entranced. Stairs led up from the hall and we discovered three large bedrooms, and a slightly smaller one that would provide a neat study, a large family bathroom and a smaller room with a shower, toilet and basin. I was gazing around assessing the fabulous potential. Convert the small bathroom to an en suite off the large back bedroom and share the family bathroom with the two big front bedrooms. The study would suit both Andrew and I down to the ground as we could furnish it with our computer equipment. Suddenly, like producing a rabbit out of a hat, the husband pointed towards the ceiling.

'We also have an attic,' he said. 'Our kids used to adore it on wet winter days and, as it is carpeted, it is the perfect place for storage.' With that he reached up and opened the loft cover and pulled down an extension ladder.

Andrew swiftly went up and stepped inside. His head appeared and he beamed down at me while admitting, 'It's all perfect, Jenny. Either of my kids, with their families, could come and visit this house and be comfortable.'

I breathed a sigh of relief. We had at last found our perfect home! Within minutes we had made an offer of the full asking price and promised the vendors we would inform the agents first thing the next morning. We took our leave with satisfied handshakes all round and Andrew gave me an enormous hug once the couple had closed the front door and we were outside, alone. It was a pleasure to return home that night....

Chapter 18

*

The next few weeks passed in a slightly manic dash. Normally cautious when buying even a single item for my house, in case I should later regret my choice, I had no difficulty in calmly selecting everything for our new home with gay abandon. Don't misunderstand me, I was well aware I only had £8,000 with which to furnish the property and I knew, once I had chosen, there could be no mistakes – it had to be *right* - but it was a gloriously delicious feeling to start with a blank canvas and swiftly convert that money into everything we would need.

Andrew watched me with a bemused, shy amusement as he took me to shops I had never even heard of a few weeks previously. I quietly walked around selecting sets of cream bedlinen with matching armfuls of different sized towels plus a dozen flannels along with four bathmats, before spying a pair of perfect bedside lamps. Our trolley then became the repository for everything for the kitchen – sets of saucepans, mugs, linen napkins, every utensil, including a set of knives, a huge selection of simple glassware and tea towels. It went on and on. The home owners had reluctantly agreed to leave all their net curtains behind and I hoped, by dint of turning off lights when we were undressing, we could manage for a short time with only those for privacy. Proper curtains could be dealt with later.

Another Aladdin's Cave supplied us with a huge amount of white, fine bone china and I bought the whole lot – from tea cups to large dinner plates – at an exceptionally reasonable price. At the same time they had an eight-place canteen of cutlery on offer so I snatched it up gratefully. From kitchen clocks to place mats, bathroom cupboards to scales and an argument over a cane dirty-linen bin, which I won by insisting a plastic one was better. As we were going from floor to floor I caught sight of a neat rattan table and two chairs which I decided would be ideal for breakfast in our tiny conservatory. I was told it had actually been ordered for another customer, but my stately progress through the store stood me in good stead and, as I calmly scrutinised everything on offer and made my selection so swiftly, they agreed it was ours and promised to keep everything in storage for us. We paid up and came out laughing.

The next day we approached a building society in York and they agreed to accept half the price of the property as a deposit with the understanding we would pay the balance within two years. For this we would only have to pay the interest on the second amount and when it was paid in full we would then be the proud owners of a large four-bedded house that suited us perfectly. We were amazed at the simplicity of the transaction.

Two other stores were invaded the next day. One sold furniture and, as Andrew played golf with the young managing director of the private company, I just pointed out two double beds and matching wardrobes with bedside tables while he arranged for the chap to come out himself and build them for us. I promised a decent meal at the end of it and he also agreed to keep everything in storage until we had moved. After a celebratory lunch we then went to a well-known retail outlet and this time I bowed to Andrew's superior knowledge and allowed him to select all our white goods – with a fridge-freezer, washing machine, kettle, dryer, iron and dishwasher as one package. I breathed a sigh of relief as the house had a stove built in – one less large bill to pay. I politely stood back as Andrew went through every price he had previously found on the internet and watched him as he convinced the staff it was in their own interest to accept his offer rather than watch us walk away and go to their arch rivals. Surprisingly, he got his way and, to my amazement, they agreed to a hefty reduction as well as offering to store everything until we were able to accept it. I now realise that ready cash and a persuasive tongue gives one great bargaining power...

We then went and bought a cream leather settee and reclining chair that was on special offer as we knew it would be ideal for our small sitting room. And, in a small side street tucked deep within the city walls, we caught sight of a huge dark brown cane four-seater settee with as many large cream heavy sailcloth cushions. It would be perfect in the room off the kitchen that I had christened the *Rumpus Room*. It was in a sale and we couldn't resist the price. I was madly trying to do the maths but still reckoned I was within my budget.

I had forgotten the Wilsons, who were selling. We knew they had not had one offer on their property since it was put on the market a year previously and, until we had come along and fallen in love with it, they had lost all hope. *Now Andrew and I had become too complacent.* We asked if we could go round a second time to take photos and measure up. They agreed but I felt there was a slight coldness that had not been there on our first viewing. Mrs Wilson was alone and, as soon as we arrived, she mentioned the blinds in the kitchen, the rumpus room and across the conservatory window would now cost us £100. I agreed as they looked as if they were newly fitted. I also realised these blinds would be useless to them in their new house but knew it was a small price to pay to keep the peace. As she was accompanying us upstairs she also told us the front room carpet was also almost new and would be removed unless we were willing to pay just over a thousand pounds for it to be left. Before Andrew could comment I bluntly told her there was no way I wanted the carpet unless it came as part of the package. I had decided on our first viewing that the clerical grey of the carpet did nothing to enhance the room and I knew that at the first opportunity I would be looking to replace it. I quietly told her this. She puffed up and started arguing until Andrew stemmed her flow by reminding her, reasonably, that he had imagined the full asking price covered everything and we had certainly not expected to be charged for any extras. She stomped off downstairs and left us to our measuring – probably thinking we would give in once we had considered the alternative. We never did and two weeks later, when we went round for one last look and found her husband alone, Andrew asked if there were any more surprise items that were not included in the sale.

We spoke of the carpet and the husband, looking amazed,

admitted, 'Carpet's over two years old so why would you pay for it, man? We just want to get shut of the place and move to the country with our two grown-up children. Don't take any notice of Beryl – she gets these bees in her bonnet and she will soon get over it.'

We breathed a sigh of relief, but probably out of spite, the carpet was removed along with all their furniture on the day they moved out, leaving us with just the underlay. It didn't matter; we had asked our friend, the furniture store owner, to fit two new pale blue carpets – one in the front room and the other to cover the noisy floorboards in one of the front bedrooms. The rest of the house was carpeted in neutral colours which blended in fine and suited us splendidly.

****

Within two months we were in our dream home. There were still all sorts of necessary items we needed to complete our furnishings. Some we could purchase later and the rest Andrew collected, along with most of his wardrobe, from his old home – like his paintings, his CDs and tapes, favourite books, fishing rods, old unused garden furniture, racking for the garage, his computer and study desk as well as his retirement present from the children, staff and governors of his school which was an impressive leather and mahogany captain's chair. I also went back to Devon and collected a whole van load of things I considered were mine – like the rest of my clothes that might be useful, a couple of favourite oil paintings, my bureau and some retirement gifts I had been given along with my special ironing board and my father's box of tools. Robin had considerately gone away for a few days and I was able to browse and select in peace. Once back it had been so relaxing to wake up together every morning and know there was no deadline to be met that day. All our searching and choosing was over and, finally, that sharing a house with dozens of strangers was a thing of the past.

Shortly before we had left there had been a couple of days when a suspicion of stealing fell over the whole of Alexandra Lodge. One night Marty came up and knocked at our bedroom door. We welcomed him in even though we were both in our dressing gowns and he told us the sad news that valuable memorabilia had been fast disappearing from the house recently. He asked if we had noticed anything missing but, of course, we were so wrapped up in each other that Ariadne, the statue residing in our bathroom, could have disappeared and, apart from Andrew throwing his towel over her every morning, I doubt if it would have registered with either of us. The culprits turned out to be our ingratiatingly servile custodian and her shady friends who always seemed to be prowling around. We had to suffer an evening of the police raiding the house. We heard a lot of shouting and bad language below stairs but luckily we never saw her, or her friends, ever again. Taking her place was a straight-laced young couple with no sense of humour. They ignored the two of us completely and certainly never offered us the exquisite Victorian sheets for our Edwardian bed that we had both come to expect and appreciate. They tolerated us in the cosy breakfast room, but only just. So much for guilty staff, I figured. I guess one can't have it both ways! Marty was resigned to our leaving and wished us well. We spent one uproarious evening with him at his club.

The last week passed slowly. Andrew had telephoned Deborah at her boys' school in Cornwall and said she sounded bemused and slightly puzzled by his news. He reminded her that he had written a letter apologising for his scandalous behaviour, and asked her up for a visit as soon as we had settled in. He said she was strangely reticent in agreeing. I became upset: Deborah had always mothered the three boys and me and, at every visit I had made in those far-off days, we had been the best of friends. Now I wondered if she had forgotten those days and had accepted Fay into her world. I became quiet and withdrawn. Andrew, who always thought deeply, dragged me along to a solicitor's to make new Wills at that time. He explained that if he was suddenly run over, I would have no official place in his life and would be left without funds or status as his new partner.

'And Fay will have no compunction of stripping you of everything,' he said baldly. 'I can guarantee that.' I had shuddered.

So I think it was probably to relieve our gloomy thoughts that made Drew lead me across the road in the centre of York on one of those last afternoons, to look in the window of an antique jeweller's. We were both tired of pricing-up step-ladders and doorbells and perhaps he decided I needed some light relief. The window glittered under the lights and I bent appreciatively towards a selection of jewellery. There was a small tray of rings set with my favourite gem - amethyst - a stone, I had been told, was also exclusively beloved of the Roman emperors who had ruled York. These were all new and each one was made to a slightly different design. I stared at one that was simplicity itself. A wide, plain wedding band decorated with an oval amethyst placed within a raised golden collar. It was elegant – different – and highly desirable. I turned away as a child darted across the road to the shrill shriek of tyres and promptly forgot about any glittering jewellery. The next morning I got Andrew up earlier than usual and, ignoring his moaning, forced him to have an early breakfast in order for him to attend his Probus club. He had been remiss of late and had seldom showed up at the golf club to meet his friends. I was determined all this would stop. I offered to walk with him briskly across the hospital grounds and through the park. I left him at the wrought iron gates and watched as he walked, parallel with me, back along the road, waving madly all the way until we both lost sight of each other. How stupid are old lovers, I thought.

I had just arrived home to do the last of our packing, as well as cleaning up the rooms for our departure, when Andrew's mobile rang. I tutted at his forgetfulness and hesitated to answer, not wishing to be intrusive. I discovered it was Peter, Andrew's oldest son and the father of Rosy, Leigh and Perkin. I told him his dad was at a Probus meeting that morning and suggested I was sure he would love to meet with him sometime soon. Between us we fixed it should be within the next few days and at a place somewhere between York and Chesterfield, where Peter lived. I felt a lot happier afterwards and mused how I could also engineer a rendezvous with Mark, his younger son. I was sure that this enforced silence between him and his lads was definitely putting a damper on Andrew's happiness and hoped this might bring them all into closer contact once more.

The next day passed in a haze of flurry and muddle. We removed an amazing pile of new goods we'd been storing in our rented rooms and staggered up and down the garden path of Number 13. Andrew placed them in my arms so I could unload them onto the front room floor. The space was soon filled knee deep with boxes, carrier bags and cases so we decided it would be sensible for Andrew to return home to pick up the rest of his personal possessions while I stayed behind and cleaned out cupboards to allow us to find homes for all the items we had purchased over the previous weeks. I would also be around so the most important item of furniture could be delivered – our new bed. We had fixed for two beds, a glass table, four chairs and the settee and recliner to arrive that day. The logistics had proved daunting. Some things we could manage without, but not seats, cooking utensils and beds, we had decided!

I scrubbed and cleaned the house although, to do the Wilsons justice, they had left it uncluttered and in good order. I threw clothing on newly bought hangers, stacked crockery on shelves and thrust cutlery into drawers. I placed toilet rolls next to loos and soap near the bath and shower. I found Andrew's shaving gear and gave it pride of place on a bathroom shelf, along with a set of new towels and flannels. I placed our new scales close by. When Andrew returned I had reduced the massive sitting room pile by half and he soon set to and helped me demolish the rest. It is a great feeling to find a home for all one's possessions and we finally stood back with satisfied smiles.

When the men who carried in the beds and settee met the men who had been delivering our table and chairs I was even able to offer them all a mug of tea. I had actually found our kettle, teabags, milk and mugs! That evening we went out for a well-deserved meal because, although I had a stack of brand new saucepans, I had no food to cook in them. Much later that night we were spreading sheets and a duvet on our bed and searching madly for some pillows on which to lay our heads. I wearily went downstairs and finally found them stuffed down behind the cream leather reclining chair. *So I hadn't left them behind, after all.* We stripped off slowly after such a long, physically exhausting day and followed each other into the shower. No messing around tonight I decided with a tired grin. I could hardly think straight and all I longed to do was lie on a comfortable mattress and ease the dull pain in my back.

I gingerly laid myself down and didn't even bother to pull the covers over me. I was dreamily watching the moon, through the net curtains the Wilsons had so kindly left, when Drew quietly went on his knees by my side of the bed. I stretched my arms out towards him and managed a smile. He opened a small box and gently took my left hand in his and placed on it the beautiful amethyst ring I had last seen in the York antique shop. I hadn't known he would go back and purchase it. I was amazed he had even known which one I coveted. I lay still, touching it gently, as his body slid over mine and he took me in his arms and we both dropped off into a deep and satisfying sleep.

We awoke within seconds of each other with the sun streaming through the windows. For a few seconds I was uncertain as to where I was. In my line of vision were fitted cream Regency bedroom wardrobes. Where had I seen them before, I mused? I seemed to have been decanted from strange room to strange room since I had left Devon until, it seemed, I was in a permanent state of bewilderment. Andrew reached for his watch on the floor and we discovered it was almost eleven o'clock. I tumbled out of bed and back into the shower. We stuffed ourselves with bread and jam because we had forgotten the butter and I made a food list while Andrew rang around to all the dealers who were storing goods or furniture for us and tried to make delivery arrangements. The next two days were an anti-climax of buying and forgetting essential foodstuffs, interspersed with deliveries of flat-pack bedroom furniture for the second and third bedrooms as well as a freezer, washing machine, drier, an iron and a dishwasher. One huge delivery van blocked the whole of our tiny cul-de-sac for half an hour and then was unable to turn in the small circle at the end of the road. We watched him, giggling nervously behind our net curtains, as he bumped unevenly back along the pavement and hoped he wouldn't demolish a tree! The telephone was connected on the second afternoon and Andrew and I tossed for who would use it first. Drew won: he spoke to his grandchildren and invited them to come and see him soon. I rang Jess and Lorna as soon as I'd finished a lengthy call to my cousin Dee; but there was little to say apart from the fact that we were in our own home at last, in a terrific mess and trying to make sense of the central heating boiler, the gas fire and even the shower. They laughed and commiserated.

In between deciding where best to install our fitted wardrobes and fixing up Andrew's computer in the fourth bedroom, which we - tongue in cheek - christened The Study, we talked at intervals about the new Wills that Andrew was adamant we must get sorted out immediately. He had booked us in to see a York solicitor and he hustled me along to their prestigious premises within a few days. I felt shy about discussing Andrew's finances although I had always been totally open about my own. If *I* died I wanted everything to go to him until such time as he followed me; and then I wanted my share of my own money to go to the two sons of Meryl and Adam – my Godchildren. Andrew was willing to write a reciprocal Will except *his* children, he considered, should hold precedence over mine who weren't blood related. I was well aware that Andrew had more money in property and investments than me and, when both of us were dead, it might prove difficult untangling our affairs regarding what should be allotted to each group. I understood that clearly. Andrew, who was far more maths-orientated than me, suggested a solution of a 40/60% split. I agreed with him but, unless we both died together, I felt the logistics would take some careful planning.

I am sure this dilemma has been thought about by every couple contemplating divorce and planning a second marriage and must often be asked of solicitors. It is a sticky problem and one that must be acceptable to both parties and administered by competent lawyers. We had two to help us – one of each sex – and each put their respective views. We finally agreed to their suggestions and were shaking hands and leaving when Andrew hesitated with a query.

'Are you sure my lads will get all they are entitled to when I die?'

I stiffened in distress because my intention was to make sure none of Andrew's children would suffer in any way from their father and me forming a liaison. I was determined they would get their just share and more. I wanted to be accepted by them and to cherish them just as their father did – not cause unhappiness by eroding their future inheritance. Luckily the pretty female of our duo swung round and crisply reminded him this had all been agreed when the unequal division of our monies had first been discussed and he accepted this on reflection.

In the car on the way home Andrew mentioned Easter and I was delighted to take my mind off the slight hurt that his last-minute doubts had caused me and suggest his youngest son and family might like to come for the holiday. As Mark was a schoolmaster in Manchester it might be an ideal time for him, his wife and two schoolchildren to come across and spend the holiday with us. The delight on his face wiped all thought of the previous discussion we had been having all afternoon and I hummed later as I cooked a large fry-up in my new kitchen and laid it out for the first time in our cosy conservatory. As a wintry sun sunk in the west we tucked in with gusto and decided what Ben and Camilla might like to do over the holiday. I also reminded Andrew that he was to meet up with Peter over the weekend for a game of golf. I had persuaded Peter to ring his dad with the invitation as I didn't want to be accused of stage-managing a meeting; and I also didn't want to accompany them for the very same reason. A quiet chat between them might clear the air and I felt a golf course would be the ideal venue, while a competitive game in the fresh air would do them both good.

Sticky situations were gradually being sorted out as the days passed and I hoped that Fay would soon accept the status quo and start venturing towards a new life for herself. She had lots of single women friends in whose company she appeared to be extremely happy. Andrew had constantly told me playing bridge, designer shopping and lunching with them seemed to be the highlight of her life and I sincerely hoped this would go on satisfying her. I believed, as soon as *our* new life settled down to a manageable routine, we could begin to enjoy ourselves by going off and exploring York's surrounding countryside; perhaps visiting coastal resorts like Whitby and Scarborough, getting down to our beloved Cornwall and even venturing abroad once more. Andrew had sampled most things but I had never been on a cruise, nor visited any Scandinavian countries, the Far East, Australia or New Zealand. The world was our oyster and I longed for us to enjoy it. Before we had run off together Andrew had tried to persuade me to live abroad and suggested Cyprus, Spain or France but, to me, what we had settled for was a much better option – frequent forays into a mixture of countries as the fancy took us and staying for as long as it suited us. This had become my dream and I wanted fervently for it to be his as well. We now had a comfortable base we could use whenever we tired of travelling and I was content. But maybe I had become too satisfied and smug about my imaginary, dreamy idyll. I had no idea imminent storms could be on the horizon.

Andrew briskly returned from his meeting with Peter with a cheerful step and a smile lighting his eyes. I had no idea what passed between them that day and I didn't want to be told. It also didn't seem to matter who had won their match because, over a satisfying lunch in the clubhouse, both had a long, serious chat I was told. I had the distinct impression Fay was unburdening herself to both sons more often than they cared to hear; but I neither asked, nor was I told, the basis of her complaints.

Easter came round and both Andrew and I were anxious. I was apprehensive that Mark and his wife Rachel might dislike me on sight. I was scared their two teenage children, Ben and Camilla, would despise this woman who had stolen their grandpa. But before I had time to become a fearful, stupid idiot, disaster struck. On Good Friday morning we awoke to a freezing house. The central heating had decided to give up on us so there was no hot water and, most importantly, no warm radiators. Luckily, the two bathroom showers were electric and we had a gas fire in the front room which we kept going the whole time they were there. So, instead of worrying what my new family thought of me, I spent the whole time trying to give them a warm and comfortable three days. As soon as they arrived we went out and purchased radiant heaters for the three bedrooms and the large kitchen where we seemed to congregate. We had most meals out and made our visits to warm places like a ten-pin bowling alley, the cinema and an indoor rock-climbing venue. Late one night we went on a ghost hunt which ended up in a fish and chip restaurant.

As Ben summed it up, as he and Camilla sat in the rumpus room watching television, sharing a blanket and sipping mugs of cocoa, 'I guess this is a bit like the war, Dad?'

And it was at that moment that I realised they were having a great time and I could stop worrying. We waved them goodbye after tea on the third day and went in to call a reputable plumber and check our insurance.

I think Andrew was relieved and happy that his family had enjoyed themselves despite the Spartan conditions we had all endured. In fact the children appeared to think it was a great adventure. I suspected that it was because of this that he suggested we take ourselves off for a few days to Cornwall and I was delighted to pack a suitcase and travel south with him. We spent three days in and around Fowey just messing around in a dinghy we had borrowed from his best friend on arrival. While in the town I was amused and touched when, on meeting any distant family or old friends, Andrew was eager to introduce me to them. Some of them remembered me from the old days and all of them were pleasant and warmly welcoming. But mostly we were out on the river, sailing up towards Gollant and Lerryn and exploring both banks whenever we spied an interesting landing place. Of course we went and paid our respects to the "Q" monument and I made a resolution to try and collect as many "Troy Town" stories and books by Sir Arthur Quiller Couch as soon as I returned home.

By chance, I had only just re-read another famous author, Leo Walmsley, who had written two books about his adventures on that same river in the 1930s. He, along with his girlfriend, had escaped from an extremely hard life as a fisherman in the Yorkshire village of Robin Hood's Bay and, in desperation, had made their way into the balmier climate of Cornwall. With no money in their pockets, they had chanced on a derelict army hut beside a creek on the Fowey River and, as it was offered to them for a tiny rent by the owner of the local boatyard, they decided to make it their home and eventually transformed it into a miniature paradise. Somehow, against all odds, they managed to make a living; they supplemented their meagre diet by fishing – once they discovered an old lifeboat which they repaired; they begged, borrowed and scrounged wood and driftwood to shore up their hut and the author was forced to make most of the necessary furniture. It was a lovely story and it appealed to my romantic side when I first discovered his books while visiting Andrew's family. This time Drew and I were both determined to try and trace the original site of the Walmsleys' home and see if anything remained. We weren't successful but we spent a lovely few days looking and dreaming. Andrew also tried to contact Deborah in nearby Mevagissey while we were there but, as there was no reply, we guessed she must be away on holiday; this seemed strange for a school matron at the beginning of a new term.

Our holiday was soon over and, as we packed up and said our goodbyes to friends and family, we were both sad to be leaving once more. We were bowling merrily back to Yorkshire when Andrew casually brought up the subject of his short golfing holiday. I must admit I had barely been listening when he had mentioned it a few weeks earlier.

'Oh yes, and where will you be going and when will you be off?' I asked, with my eyes on the road ahead.

'It's just over the border in Scotland, it's by the sea and very beautiful. We always go to the same place, at the same time, and there are always the same eight chaps who have been turning up for more years than I care to remember.'

I nodded understandingly; this was the equivalent of a ladies' health spa break and I thought it would do Andrew good to get away from decisions about curtains, plants for the garden and the weekly shop. 'So when is this momentous tournament held each year?' I asked.

'It's always the second week of May.'

I swung round, startled. 'But that's my birthday!' I looked at him searchingly. He surely wasn't planning to leave me alone on my birthday? If it was a jaunt he and his friends planned every year, then since January - when I'd joined him - he could have made sufficient time to explain and make other arrangements. Since we were sixteen years old we had known one another's birthdays so why was it such a surprise to him, I wondered.

Perhaps I had been spoilt for the past decade or so but in my book birthdays, unlike Christmases that we all have and celebrate at the same time, have always been extremely special and should be celebrated as such. I had no intention of pleading my past life but, the fact that Robin and I had always kept both our birthdays free each year and had planned something a little different might not set a precedent in my new life with Andrew, but it showed my ongoing thinking. I had always thought about Robin's day long before it came around and usually planned something that would appeal to him as well as amuse all our friends: for my birthday we invariably planned a holiday far away from our home and work. I always arranged for cream cakes and celebratory drinks to be delivered to the ward and knew my friends and colleagues were joining us in thought if not in fact. During the latter part of my hospital life alcoholic drink was expressly forbidden in any part of the hospital so from then on they had to make do with tea, coffee and soft drinks. I turned back from my musings and faced Andrew, 'I don't know anybody up here, darling. I'll be completely alone.' Another thought struck me, 'And lots of my friends will choose that day to ring and ask what we are doing for my birthday. If they get no reply they will think you have taken me away to celebrate. How can I answer their good-natured enquiries and say you are away for four days with all *your* friends – and playing golf in Scotland?'

Andrew looked startled and bemused. 'Well, explain that it is a long-standing arrangement and that you fully understand the situation,' he said disarmingly.

'But I don't! I'm sure you have the whale of a time with your mates each year, Andrew but, this once, it's different. And I'm finding it difficult to get my head round it, as well,' I added as an afterthought. We spent the rest of the journey both thinking our own thoughts and only speaking when necessary.

The next two weeks Andrew raised the subject constantly and wouldn't let it rest. I had made my point and I felt there was little I wanted to add. I was amazed and bemused at his attitude but tried not to show it. Was it a northern trait and would I have to learn and accept it, I wondered? Andrew, on the other hand, wouldn't admit he was being hard and tried to get me to understand again and again; first by justifying *himself* and then by trying to placate *me*. Once, he even suggested I accompany him and his seven friends up to Scotland. 'Although,' he said, 'there will be precious little for you to do.'

He didn't know it but, at that moment, I almost gave in. Was I being childish and silly expecting him to change the habits of a lifetime? Would Fay not mind if he ignored her and left her to her own devices each birthday? Should I stop being stupid and give in, I asked myself, as warm feelings of love cascaded through my mind once more? I know that if he had followed it up with *'and we will go away together the day I return'*, I would have accepted the inevitable and proudly told everyone who asked me about our plans - and everything would have been fine once more. But the moment slipped by as I listened to yet more excuses.

Finally, exasperated, he snapped, 'For God's sake, Jenny, what's so special about birthdays anyway?'

I looked at him in amazement. Surely he was joking? Birthdays are special to the people they concern. Unbidden, one of those perfect birthdays suddenly came to mind. Robin and I had returned to Sorrento after a lapse of many years. By chance, we had chosen a small hotel aptly named "*Seventh Heaven*". It had been built by a father and son right into the cliffs above the harbour of Marina Grande. Our bedroom window had nestled into the sheer rock face and, as I looked out across a sparkling emerald green and sapphire sea, I'd been able to see tiny boats, beneath me, speeding to and fro between Sorrento, Ischia and Capri. Crisp white wakes had streamed behind them and, as I'd breathed in the warm scented air, Robin's arm had come gently around my shoulders and he'd whispered, 'Happy Birthday, sweetheart.'

We had spent that week with a pleasant couple from Essex. It had been idyllic. We'd explored the mossy old town, entering cool, beautiful churches; we had taken the ferry to Capri and had gleefully done all the things visitors do – like seeing the Farraglioni Rocks, visiting Axel Munthe's treasure trove of a house and ducking into the stillness of the Blue Grotto. We'd licked gigantic ice creams and tried out our excruciating Italian on anyone who would listen. It had turned out to be the loveliest and most memorable holiday I had ever spent. And now my lover was asking what was so exceptional about birthdays. The man, who had been hurt and ignored for years, was asking a woman he professed to love this simple question. I turned to look at him and maybe a small reflection of these thoughts showed in my eyes because, after that, he ceased mentioning it.

So, when the day came for Andrew to be off, he swung his bag into the back of his car and turned to me with open arms. I allowed him to hug me and I kissed him back as he turned away with these final words, 'I will ring you every free minute I get, darling. The days will race by and I will be back before you know it.'

He had obviously forgotten my warning of the previous day. 'Please don't bother, Andrew. I won't answer because I'll have no idea who it is.' He still didn't get it. 'I don't want to have to explain to my friends the reason you are far away in Scotland. I don't want to be embarrassed and appear stupid. Do you understand I don't want them to hate you...?' I said desperately. He shrugged, ducked into the car and was off with a flourish and a jaunty wave.

I went inside to finish my breakfast, cleaned the bath and took out the rubbish. After that I had nothing to do. I sat in the garden but the breeze was too chilly; I watched an educational programme but it didn't hold my attention; I picked up a book but couldn't concentrate. I finally settled down to four days of enforced idleness and seclusion. I was aware I should have taken myself off to town, walked the walls, looked round the Art Gallery once more or taken in another museum. There was so much to do in York, but instead of briskly setting off and enjoying it I chose to sulk indoors and brood. I knew not one neighbour in the street. I was completely alone in the whole county of Yorkshire.

True to my vow, when the telephone rang four hours later I guessed it was Andrew ringing from his hotel and I studiously ignored it. Again and again it rang over the next few days and each time, I walked away. I couldn't bear explaining I was stuck in a house alone and, although it was my birthday, I wouldn't be celebrating in any way. Cascades of cards fell through the letterbox every morning – lots of them accompanied by happy letters enquiring how I was doing – and I drearily opened them all and placed them on every surface I could find. The large number and the loving sentiments they conveyed made me feel lonelier than ever. Late on the afternoon of my birthday, there was a brisk knock on my front door. I arose from watching some mind-numbing programme on the television, relieved at the diversion, and outside, on the step, found a diminutive lady peering round a massive bouquet of flowers.

'Gosh, who's the lucky person, then?' she asked.

'Me,' I said shortly. 'But that's only because it's my birthday and he's off golfing with his buddies up in Scotland.' That was the first time I had admitted Andrew's perfidy to anyone and I felt much better for saying it to a person I was never likely to see again. She handed the monster creation over and backed away with a sympathetic smile and a wave of her hand. I went back inside and placed the gorgeous gift down carefully on the hearth. Andrew had not even left a card for me before he went and the small gift card attached to the beribboned vase bore a strange hand. Somehow the small act of getting someone else to scribble a message made it even more impersonal and hurtful.

The final two days flew by, just as Andrew had prophesied they would. When he finally arrived home on the Wednesday evening I was actually relieved to see him. I had spent the previous two days weeding and making the front garden presentable. The occasional neighbour had walked by and each time I had raised my head and smiled but, unlike Devon, no one came over for an innocent chat or to enquire who I was. They either returned my smile and passed on or pretended not to notice me. Andrew came in quietly, as if not sure of his welcome. I went to him immediately. I hate rows and coldness and usually I am the first to respond to an overture of goodwill. He placed his arms around me and stated, 'Oh God I missed you so much.' He took me out for dinner and we avoided the subject like the plague. Looking back, I now know we should have thrashed the subject out then and there. Someone who could say *'what's so special about birthdays, anyway?'* had a fundamentally different reasoning from mine and I should have asked him if this was just a flip retort, spoken in anger and frustration, or a serious belief that he held.

Part II

Tread softly because you tread on my dreams.
WB Yeats

Chapter 19

*

The next few days were almost a new beginning. Andrew couldn't have been more considerate of my happiness. He brought me tea in bed every morning and suggested some of my favourite meals – and then offered to cook them! I was so happy and relaxed that one afternoon, when I was strolling alone around Fenwick's linen department, I was drawn to the most exquisite *broderie anglais* sheets and pillowcases. I couldn't resist them and I purchased two sets just for the hell of it. I was delighted when Andrew fell in love with them too and we put them on our bed that night just to celebrate!

Because I was happy I even had the effrontery to mention we could do with new double glazing to a few of the windows at the front of our house. The original windows had obviously been replaced decades before. It had been exceptionally well done with draught excluder around every window – a very avant-garde process at that time, I should imagine – but it was old and had seen much better days and I suggested maybe, in the near future, it should be replaced to match exactly the windows in the newer extension that the Wilsons had built. Andrew's response was that we had bought the house because we liked it immensely, so why on earth would we want to change it? I agreed reluctantly because I could see all sorts of minor improvements that needed doing. For instance one was a small section of wallpaper in the spacious kitchen. The Wilsons' dog had apparently spent a lot of time under their kitchen table and his favourite occupation must have been chewing holes in this particular section of wallpaper. One Saturday morning while Andrew was with his friends playing golf, I had taken myself off to a DIY centre and purchased the same textured vinyl wallpaper and matched the exact shade of emulsion. I roughly tore it and glued it into place and then repainted the whole wall until I was unable to detect any gnawing or ferocious scratch marks. So when Andrew returned home flushed with his win over worthy opponents, I met him jubilantly with my own small victory. I told him my next job was to fill in the gap between bath and tiles in our family bathroom. Mr Wilson, although a plumber by trade, was oblivious to the necessity of an elegant bathroom and every time I washed my hair I promised myself that I would remedy his shortcomings as soon as I could buy the necessary filler.

So in this way we both jogged along; Andrew loved meeting his friends and playing golf but he also wanted to introduce me to the part of Yorkshire that he knew and loved. One day he took me proudly to the University where he had obtained his degree. We wandered around the campus while he reminisced about a period of time that he had found particularly hard work but had obviously adored. A student by day and a baker by night: I marvelled at his tenacity and dogged, inflexible will which enabled him to complete his course with a really decent degree and allowed him to go on and achieve all the goals he had set himself.

One pleasant afternoon we spent walking along the River Ouse and picnicking in brilliant sunshine, while on another we travelled up the coast to Runswick Bay – a tiny, picturesque fishing village set in tiers above a calm sea. We wandered around with our arms tightly entwined before finding a tearoom and wolfing down a substantial tea of sandwiches, plus fruitcake topped with Wensleydale cheese, accompanied by a huge pot of strong tea. We both expected this gentle interlude to go on forever but other forces were at work, I was soon to discover.

One night we had just arrived indoors and were taking off our muddy boots when the telephone rang. I walked into the kitchen to put the kettle on while Andrew picked up the receiver. It was Peter, his oldest son, who spoke to his father for some time. I gently pushed the door to and waited for Andrew to come and explain. Apparently their mother had been ringing both him and Mark constantly. Up until then they had taken it in turn to either visit her or have her with them for the odd weekend, but gradually the pleas for help had escalated and both of them were finding it hard to cope with the tedious trivia of her troubles. Andrew rang Fay immediately and, without mentioning Peter's complaints, enquired if everything was alright at home. After a few seconds, Fay launched into a morass of grievances that ranged from his not collecting his mail often enough to suit her, various jobs that needed doing around the house, her on-line banking - that she insisted was *still* in an awful mess – and her car needing a service at the garage. When he suggested he could return the next day and tackle all her problems she sharply told him she would be out and insisted he visited at 3.10pm on the day after. With a sigh he had agreed.

Andrew rubbed the back of his neck and grinned at me as he explained. I pushed a mug of tea in his direction and suggested we take ourselves off for a pub meal instead of cooking the chops I had purchased that morning. We sat in a cosy corner of our local inn as Andrew unburdened himself of all Fay's supposed troubles.

'She's not used to coping on her own. It's not as if she wants me or needs me most of the time but she finds it difficult to break the habits of a lifetime when she ordered servants to do her bidding and her word was law. There is no one now and she feels ineffectual in front of friends.' I nodded. Ever since Andrew and I had run off together I had felt tremendously sorry for both our former partners. Without doubt I considered Andrew and I had the best of the deal. We had been married to them for so long that it must feel as if a limb was missing when we both departed so abruptly. I made a point of telephoning Robin every Friday night; I also made sure that Andrew was always in the room when I did so. I wanted no misunderstandings. It wasn't always an easy conversation, and often I would have preferred to forget my promise, but I felt it was only fair to do this simple thing. It was the one pledge he could rely on week after week.

Andrew hadn't tackled his predicament in a similar way. He rarely spoke to Fay unless she demanded his attention and summoned him to her presence. I had heard one of their telephone conversations and I winced at the cold tone he had had used. I knew she had refused to even think about a divorce and he had been told she had no intention of moving out of the marital home either. When he told me this my reply was, 'Well let her keep it then! We can manage, surely, without turning her out and, quite honestly, do bricks and mortar really matter?' I could see, by Andrew's face, that he believed they did.

He visited Fay on the prescribed day. He told me later he had mended the lock on the side door of the garage and fixed for a painter and decorator to come in and do all her bidding. The car was booked in for its service, with one of the garage lads promising to come out and collect it. The banking issue was sorted once more but Andrew despaired of Fay's aptitude and expertise in that field. While he was there she had asked him to hose down the conservatory roof, so he considered that was one less chore she could complain about. He had also suggested getting the carpets cleaned while they were about it, but she had accused him then of trying to sell their property over her head and he had promptly given up and returned home.

As he was telling me about all the outstanding jobs he had completed I was reminded of a few of our own. On first appraisal our new house had appeared perfect when we purchased it, but as I made a closer inspection – mainly when I was doing the cleaning – I had discovered a few minor things that needed seeing to. The front door had never been used by the Wilsons, presumably because it stuck, and they had made all their entrances and exits through their garage. I objected to that when we had inherited a perfectly attractive front door. Trouble was, it took a huge heave to open it and a mighty thump to close it. I mildly pointed out it probably needed some of the swollen wood to be shaved away and a brisk rub down with sandpaper. I laughed and told Andrew I then promised to paint it a decent colour and ours would be the smartest house in the road. I admitted I had discovered the top window in the kitchen had a faulty catch and, as it could become a security issue, maybe we ought to get it seen to. Finally, like an idiot, I reverted back to my earlier grumble about the double glazed front windows. I probably wouldn't have mentioned it again except that, when I had been cleaning those rooms that week, I realised they really were in a sorry state and needed replacing in the near future.

Andrew stared at me. 'Oh, so we are launching a one-upmanship campaign to not only make over my *old* house but to change everything in this one, too? Is that all women are good for?' he raged. 'Keeping on until men will do anything for a quiet life?' I took a step back. What an idiot I had become. Fay was, as usual, at her best nagging and, instead of cheering him up and comforting him, I was also raising questions about minor jobs that needed to be sorted. I tried to tell him *I* was quite prepared to either put them right myself or get an expert to do the job for me, but Andrew refused to listen. He turned on his heel and walked into the sitting room and pointedly shut the door in my face. I stood there, my smile slowly dying.

It's strange, but when one is at breaking point, often there is no awareness. I had been through a traumatic few months and I had pushed myself to my limits to appear normal and happy. Indeed I *was* happy even when I was rousing myself every hour, all through those first nights, to switch the heaters back on and trying to dry out our clothes! I found myself in a strange environment where I knew no one – apart from my partner – and nothing. Up until a few months ago I had no idea where Harrogate, Leeds or even Scarborough was in relation to York. Tell me to find a street, even within the walls of York, and I would probably resort to a map. Ask me to remember the name of a certain road and I was struggling. That's why I often made up pet names to remind me. I had silent names for all the Bars (gates) in the walls of York so I didn't muddle them up and even to get on a bus or visit the local shops took some forward planning in my mind. I was also concerned about Fay's troubles and his two sons' involvement. No one can be blasé about dislike and I wanted to be tolerated, not actively hated for all the troubles I had brought to their door. I wanted it to be Andrew and me steadfast against the world and – suddenly – my stalwart lover had stepped away from my side.

Suddenly the sobs rose unbidden in my throat. No one must see me crying. That would be the end. I walked across the kitchen, a step down into the little conservatory and left through the gloomy space that was the garage. I eased open the large, wooden garage doors and walked away. I had no fixed goal and just needed to put some space between me and my hurt. I walked along a main road in the sunshine (it could have been raining and I probably wouldn't have noticed) totally alone. Luckily, the road was empty and nobody would know me anyway. In relief I allowed the tears to slowly wash my cheeks. I walked with my head down through old Edwardian and Victorian side streets that led to the racecourse. Only a few weeks previously Andrew had taken me to see where the brave people of York had placed offerings of food when there was an outbreak of plague in 1604. It was Hob Moor and lodges had been built here as a place for exiled plague victims as early as 1550 to safeguard the city of York. The house we had bought was close to the boundary of the Moor and, as there were lots of footpaths leading onto it, we had wandered there one evening. At the end of simple Little Hob Lane we had discovered the plague stone, a small shallow stone basin that would have been filled with vinegar to disinfect the victims' money. It would have held enough coins to pay for food brought to these poor, sick people by the citizens who were brave enough to risk their lives. Plague had swept through England at breakneck speed and this awful outbreak killed over 3,500 of York's inhabitants – about a third of the city's population.

This time - steeped in my own misery - I doggedly plodded on until I reached the awesome execution site of Tyburn. It is right beside the Knavesmire on the Tadcaster Road with a perfect view over the whole of the Race Course. For 400 years public executions were held here until 1801 and would have been well attended The first on record was in 1379 of an Edward Hewitson for rape and the most famous being the Highwayman, Dick Turpin – who would have been hung, drawn and quartered afterwards. The York gallows was known as the *Three Legged Mare* and even today there is a morbid pub in the city to commemorate this event. I shuddered every time we had passed it.

It was near Tyburn that Andrew finally found me. I was still walking and barely took note of his car as it drew up alongside me. Eventually he had to park and take me in his arms before I would even listen to his pleadings. I went back home listlessly and we spent the rest of that evening sitting watching television with our arms desperately holding on to each other. It felt as if we had come across a precipice and had managed to step back from the edge – just in time.

Luckily, I was over it the next day and as usual we were bickering and joking about me always finding minor chores to do around our new home. We were awaiting a pale blue carpet for our third bedroom. The room was in the newer extension of the house and I think the Wilsons must have decorated it for their grown-up son. Dark stained floorboards, a bland mushroom-coloured Venetian blind and no curtains gave the room a masculine, minimalistic and yet very boring look considering the light flooding in from the huge picture window and its bright aspect. I pictured it in muted colours with crisp, white net curtains and we had even picked out pale ash furniture to complement this. I had settled down to painting the skirting boards white, withstanding all Andrew's entreaties to venture out for the day, when the telephone rang. I was on my hands and knees when he came back to say it was Fay and she now needed him to sort out her television. She reckoned she had pushed a wrong button because, suddenly, Sky was not an option. I mumbled sarcastically, 'Well go and sort it out and ask her what else she wants you to do, because you are obviously not willing to help me with this rotten painting!' He muttered something rude as he clattered down the stairs and I stuck my tongue out at his departing back.

An hour later he returned. I was on the last few inches of wood and pushed my fringe off my sweaty forehead to look up and smile. 'Well how did it go?' I asked. 'Was she suitably impressed with your expertise?' There was a silence and I glanced up at him.

'I am going back,' he stated simply.

I stumbled to my feet and glanced involuntarily at the window. Luckily it was closed.

'What do you mean?' I asked stupidly. He came towards me with his arms outstretched. I knew his first thought was to comfort me. I stepped back and put my right hand out – gesturing him to stay away. Until I had made sense of his bizarre words I couldn't let him near me. The skirting board was forgotten, along with the tin of gloss paint, as we stumbled across the landing and into our bedroom. There, sitting on our beautiful bed, he tried to make sense of what he had just said. It appeared he had no intention of returning when he knocked on his front door and Fay undid all the numerous locks. These were the barricades she had insisted on since he left – to deny him access into his own property.

'I put the TV back to rights,' he said blankly. 'And then I am not sure what happened.'

'What do you mean – you're not sure what happened?' I demanded.

I watched him sit in contemplation for a few minutes. I felt so sorry for him. I even wanted to comfort him but I later realised that it was just the shock he had induced in me, along with my natural impulse to love him, that made me feel like that...

Blankly I knew there was nothing else I was able to say or do, so I returned to my tin of paint and finished the chore that had begun in an atmosphere of gaiety and fun only a few hours before and had now ended in tragedy for us both.

****

The rest of that day crawled by. It was as if we had both suffered a major illness and needed to recuperate. I made scratch meals but we were unable to eat them. Andrew motioned towards me with a bottle of red wine but I shook my head mutely. That was no solution. We went to bed but I, for one, didn't sleep. I think I stared at the ceiling for most of the night. That was when I wasn't shedding hot, steady tears; and even then my pride refused to let me disturb the man who was lying quietly beside me.

On waking the next morning (*so I did fall asleep*), I wondered if it had all been some ghastly nightmare, but on seeing Andrew's drawn face and shadowed eyes, I knew it was stark reality and I had to come to terms with it. I wandered into the bathroom for a deep soak and slowly walked downstairs to make the breakfast that I set, as usual, in the warm conservatory. Our mood was sombre so, of course, it had to be a particularly lovely day. The deep pink Camellia that Andrew so loved had just come into bloom the previous day; it peeped in at him through the window and he stared at it as if mesmerised. It gave the whole room a rosy glow. We ate as best we could and made polite conversation.

On the stroke of ten Fay rang and Andrew took the call in the Rumpus Room, making sure he left the door wide open. I heard him tell Fay, although he had promised to return as soon as he was able, it could possibly take a couple of weeks to sort everything out. She must have been appeased because she abruptly rang off.

But in the early afternoon she telephoned again. She had obviously taken advice because, this time, she demanded Andrew return home at once. He quietly informed her he was taking me to give blood in town that very evening so it would have to wait until the next day at least. She immediately demanded when and he then promised he would be back in time for tea - and, with that, she had to be satisfied. We went off to the centre of York for my blood donor session although, quite honestly, it was the last thing I felt like doing. The staff welcomed me as a new recruit and it was all over relatively quickly. I even managed to swallow the obligatory hot drink and biscuit. As we came out into the afternoon sunshine Andrew asked was there anywhere in York I felt like exploring. I looked at him in amazement. The previous day he had told me he would shortly be leaving me and returning to his wife; now he was asking whether I felt up to strolling around and admiring what York had to offer.

Is this man for real I wondered? I shook my head mutely. The busy nurses at the session had almost undone me when they started questioning me about Devon and whether I liked living up in the north of England now. What can one answer? *Up until two days ago I was warmly happy and now I wonder what on earth I have done to deserve my partner deserting me to leave me alone in a strange house, in the middle of an alien city with no one I can actually call a friend. If I died tomorrow there would be no one who would realise for weeks*. I could feel tears thickening the back of my throat so didn't even dare to answer. I nodded without speaking. They probably thought I was an ignorant Devon dumpling who didn't appreciate their magnificent county.

So we went home and watched some more mind-numbing television while pretending to eat the meal I had prepared. I slept that night – probably because I was worn out mentally and physically. Although it was warm I kept shivering until, in the end, Andrew led me to bed and we curled up together like two children lost in a forest. Before I slept continuous questions buzzed around in my mind, but before I could cull them into some sort of serious query, they had slipped over the horizon of my consciousness and a dozen more flooded in. No one can remain in a state of heightened tension endlessly and it was this that finally enabled me to drop into deep oblivion until early the next morning. I awoke to sun pouring in through the net curtains and casting strange patterns on the sheets. For a couple of seconds I had forgotten my troubles and, as the previous two days' drama came flooding back, I sat up in bed with a gasp as my heart hammered. I crept out of bed to allow Andrew to stay deeply asleep. I had a strange feeling that he was unsure as to how we had arrived at this predicament. The situation that he had allowed to develop until it became a fact was something only he could untangle. All I could deduce was that Fay, over the years, had become the dominant force in their marriage and he was so used to obeying her wishes it had proved an overwhelming victory. Whereas *my* newly formed relationship with him had been built upon warmth and love and companionship it was, sadly, not yet strong enough to withstand the impact she commanded which compelled him to do her bidding and, therefore, Andrew and I had both lost out.

He must have felt me move away from him because while I was soaking in the bath I heard him run the shower and we arrived at the kitchen sink together. As we munched our toast he told me firmly of our plans for the day. He had decided we would visit the Castle Museum opposite Clifford's Tower. He had taken me to see both soon after I first arrived, but he said this time we would take our time and look at it in depth. He called it the friendly museum because it encapsulated life through the ages with something for everyone. I agreed because it was easier to acquiesce rather than argue. Who cared where we went, I thought, it wouldn't alter the fact that he wouldn't be returning home with me.

When we arrived the museum was fairly empty. If this had been any other day I am sure I would have appreciated the exhibits but I felt this was just a ploy to pass the time and that it didn't really matter if I appreciated the old fashioned slot machines, primitive toilets through the ages, a jukebox that played my favourite Everly Brothers' music or the selection of children's toys – some of which I could vaguely remember. Of course it didn't! Did I find cooking stoves of Second World War vintage riveting? Hardly. Was I really impressed when the lights were lowered as I walked into an authentic Victorian street scene and stared in shop windows at old world confectionery, haberdashery and hardware? Not really.

Maybe the sight of a cortège of mourners, walking beside a coffin placed inside an elegant glass-windowed hearse and drawn by black plumed horses, was the only exhibit that day that struck the right note as far as I was concerned. I am not sure what Andrew was really thinking as he brightly drew my attention left and right. Was he politely trying to offer this undoubtedly fascinating museum as a bearable alternative to a tearful last day in our comfortable home? If so, it didn't work. At midday he suggested lunch in the restaurant and I followed him listlessly into it and watched as we both pushed good food around our plates and then forgot to eat.

Just after two o'clock I was almost at breaking point and suddenly, as we were walking up a short flight of stairs, I voiced what I really wanted. I wanted him to go. I insisted that he went swiftly and left me behind. I couldn't have borne the charade a moment longer. He looked stricken as I firmly told him to get back to Fay as she would soon be expecting him for tea. He hugged me tightly and with tears staining his cheeks he abruptly turned and was gone. I sat on a nearby bench for about ten minutes – controlling my breathing – knowing I also had to face an incurious world - and then I left to catch a bus.

****

When I arrived home I crept inside the house, feeling like a young snail bereft of its shell. It was still early but I had no interest in preparing a meal – the thought of eating made me feel positively nauseous. I gravitated upstairs and crawled into bed to shut myself off from the world; the telephone shrilled just once that evening. It rang three times then stopped abruptly. I wondered if it was Andrew checking up on me but, as I had no way of knowing, I burrowed even deeper under the duvet in an effort to escape any searching questions.

After a disturbed night, I awoke very early the next morning feeling disorientated and abandoned. I tried to tell myself nothing had changed except that I was now alone and that somehow I needed to sort out my life before planning what to do next. My status had suddenly changed: from a beloved wife, then a cherished partner, to a middle-aged woman who had been deprived of everything she valued. My only tangible assets were a half-purchased property, my two pensions and a few investments that provided me a little extra income. At my asking, Andrew agreed to pay his half-share of the house maintenance and running costs. I had not enquired how long he was prepared to support me in this way, but my deep-seated pride stressed it should be for as short a time as possible.

My maxim has always been *when in doubt DO something*. So I sat in the conservatory sunshine with a cup of coffee close by and, with a pen and paper at the ready, I began to create a plan of action. The list started with: *Tell all my friends and anyone who needed to be told*, and secondly, *Decide on my future*. Under the "future" heading I made a secondary list that baldly stated: *Inform the estate agents the house will shortly be back on the market and let the building society know I will soon be preparing to sell*. All this took up the next two days as I deemed it easier to telephone my news rather than spend hours writing letters or sitting in front of a computer – which, incidentally, was Andrew's! It certainly was easier to speak to the building society and estate agents as it was only another day in their business routines. The building society warned me of a penalty clause I had agreed to. If I paid the loan back under the agreed two years I would be fined a substantial percentage on the amount I had borrowed. Andrew and I had gaily agreed to that at the time as, I am sure, it had never crossed either of our minds we would be reneging on the contract. Elise, our charming young estate agent who had sold us Number 13 in the first place, sounded distressed and concerned on my behalf.

'Are you sure?' she demanded. I assured her I was, with a catch in my voice, and even this tinge of anxiety gave me a sliver of comfort in an uninterested, unfeeling city.

I rang my solicitor in Devon and passed on my news via her secretary. I also stressed I was sure the divorce would still go ahead and asked her to say nothing had changed on my deciding to give our bungalow to my husband. At the end of these calls I felt like a well rung-out dishcloth and treated myself to a glass of wine. On an empty stomach that was probably not a sensible idea but it gave me a modicum of courage that was sadly lacking.

It was far more difficult to telephone all my friends and explain what had happened. Probably because I was unsure myself of the true reasons for my sorry state, I found it difficult to describe what had happened over the past few days. And, stupidly, I wanted to defend Andrew from the stunned reactions I unwittingly provoked. I told Robin at work and his only response was to enquire if I was OK. I reassured him and, with a few more words, we both silently replaced our receivers. I turned then to Dee and Paul, then Lorna, moving on to Meryl and Adam and, by the time I rang Jess, I had perfected my explanation and found I was giving it slightly parrot fashion. After that I made myself speak to Alexis, Robin's supportive sister, and then all of his friends who had obviously come down on his side of the moral fence and had been naturally scornful of my choice of a new partner. I ate constant humble pie by explaining I was the one left with egg on my face and I knew, with certainty, that they were agreeing with me. I finally talked to our friends and neighbours back in Devon who were probably so shocked by my news that they had precious little to say – for which I was extremely grateful.

The next day I decided my abject apologies and explanations were at an end and it was time I got down to putting in place the few small improvements I had mentioned to Andrew. So I started by going down to the local DIY store and purchasing some sealant which allowed me to fill in the awful gap around the bath. I knew I had no alternative but to increase my profit on the sale of this house by a substantial amount – to enable me to pay the building society's penalty clause and my removal fees and, hopefully, to end up with enough money to purchase something small for myself. Sadly, I was still awaiting purchases we had made a few weeks previously and therefore I knew there would be outstanding debts on some items of furniture as well as the dark-blue sitting room carpet. I managed to cancel an expensive bed we had ordered, but I realised any other debt we owed would have to be honoured. I found a double glazing company in the area which promised to mend the faulty lock on the kitchen window and telephoned a locksmith to make an appointment for him to fix the locks on both front and back doors. Before he came I needed to sort out the stuck-fast front door and it also required a decent lick of paint – so I decided that while he was doing one job he could make my house secure by changing the lock on the back door as well.

Later on that afternoon I decided it was time to take a break. By keeping myself busy, with hardly a second to keep mulling over the upheaval of the past few days, I had managed to stop my hands sweating and control my erratically pounding heart. As I made the bed that morning I had discovered an abandoned book of Andrew's on his bedside table and casually opened it. Surprisingly, it captured my attention from the first page. The sun was filling our immaculate little garden. I was surrounded by newly planted flowers under the kitchen window; there was a square of terracotta flagstones, a recently painted shed and a few blue pots bursting with bright blooms and a small statue I had stolen from my garden in Devon completed the picture. I pushed the conservatory French windows wide and intently watched dozens of cheeky sparrows fluttering in and out from their nests in the dark privet hedge that, with a wrought iron gate, surrounded and protected half of my tiny bower.

I should have been so happy as I took a pot of tea outside in the balmy air, placed a small table close by and settled down in a comfortable garden chair preparing to read my newly acquired book. A movement in the darkened room behind me caught my eye and I sat up sharply. It was Andrew, looking hesitant and worried, walking slowly across the room as if unsure of his welcome. Without thinking, apart from the fact he had returned and was there in front of me, I gave a gasp of delight as I threw myself into his readily open arms.

'Sorry Jenny. I rang the doorbell before I let myself in through the garage but you obviously didn't hear me,' he murmured.

I slowly unloosed my greedy arms in order to set another chair beside mine and motioned him to sit down. I placed a mug and a plate of biscuits at his elbow and sat down looking at him expectantly. It was as if we had never been apart. We both sat and watched entranced as the birds peeked at us and then disappeared back into their shadowy homes. The twittering was constant and, with nothing better to do, we foolishly tried to count and calculate how many feathered friends our hedge could accommodate. Looking back, I now realise we had fallen into a time warp. Sadly, it was not to be the only occasion. Neither of us wanted to face reality *or* the future. Andrew may have been wary of my feelings and, remembering the happenings of such a short time before, was probably reluctant to commit himself by putting into words his deepest feelings. I had none of these inhibitions but I *was* scared to examine his motives for returning in case they were not as clear-cut or definite as I desperately hoped.

As always with us, we graduated to the bedroom. It had always been our haven and, as soon as we made love that day, I imagined nothing could stop the inevitable outcome of us being back together once more. I lay back in Andrew's arms and voiced my curiosity. 'What happened the afternoon you were instructed to return for tea?' I asked.

'I was barely welcomed in. Fay looked slightly surprised to see me and, as she still had to undo the many locks securing the front door, I felt like an unwelcome stranger in my own home. It was the usual sort of tea – certainly not celebratory – and we barely spoke because the television was playing rather loudly. Maybe she felt it would be easier that way. I picked up the local newspaper and tried to immerse myself in it. Soon after, it was back to her laptop so I wandered around in the garden until she called me in for dinner.'

Andrew took a deep breath and began again. 'I cleared up afterwards; but the thought of sitting and tamely watching television until late in the evening filled me with dread. I didn't want to hear her tapping computer keys half the night, so I excused myself and went to bed. As I left the room I was told my bed had been made up in what had always been *her* room as mine had been cleared out.'

I could imagine him nodding abruptly. I remembered how once he had confided to me that Fay often snored – so maybe she thought it fitting punishment, I mused.

'Anyway the next morning, as I arrived bearing her usual cup of tea, I was informed there was to be a party that night. She had decided to invite all our friends and neighbours in for drinks and nibbles.'

'Why on earth had she done that? I asked. 'Surely she would know how embarrassed you would feel?'

'Of course,' he said ruefully. 'But, when you think of it, Jenny, that would be the one sure way to make everyone aware of my return – even though possibly some of them never even knew I had *left*! And I probably drank more that night than the last time I was on shore leave from the Merchant Navy,' he admitted.

'Was it awful?' I asked. 'Did you feel awkward and embarrassed? Or did most people politely ignore the fact you hadn't been around for ages?'

I just longed for him to admit to having made the biggest mistake of his life. I thought we would talk it out and find a solution together. I still felt nothing was insurmountable if we tackled it together and, loving him so much, I was willing to put up with any indignity Fay might throw at us just to have him in my bed once more. He answered some very personal questions and I burned with mortification on his behalf. He told me how, at the height of the party, she had become fairly drunk and tried to sit on the arm of his chair to put her arms around him, so he had been forced to ease away and refill some latecomers' glasses.

Suddenly, he glanced at his watch. 'Oh my goodness, is that the time? I had no idea it was so late.' I lay back in the bed, open-mouthed, as he swiftly climbed out and began to gather his clothes together and search for his shoes. He asked permission to use the shower and I nodded dumbly.

'I'm so sorry, darling. I told her I would only be a short while.'

'And so where did she think you were going?' I asked sarcastically.

'She thinks I'm with Paul, my radio buddy. I said he needed help with some equipment and she agreed as long as I was back to take her up to the golf club later as they are having a quiz night and she probably wants to prove I *am* back in the fold.' He stole another glance at his watch and raced off to the shower.

My rising temper forced me to don my dressing gown and accompany him to the door once he had finished his hasty ablutions – even lingering long enough to clean his teeth. My thoughts, by this time, were in such a turmoil that I found it impossible to convey, in a coherent manner, my amazement and disgust at his behaviour during those past three hours. Obviously it was because I felt an idiot. I had simply been duped through my own misunderstanding of the situation. What I had thought was regret and remorse was nothing of the kind. Or if it was, it was not strong enough to bring about a change of heart. It was just Drew treating me as his dearest confidante and nothing to do with him realising he had made a mistake.

Andrew stood outside our front door in the waning evening sunshine and unashamedly clasped me to him warmly. He appeared to find it difficult to let me go – as if he were a sailor returning to his ship or an explorer about to set off on an adventure. In desperation I returned his ardent kisses as if I were staking a claim to his love. As he turned away he remembered his last snippet of news. 'Oh, and she wants to get away for a week – somewhere warm – possibly Turkey. She's also been in contact with our American friends and they are asking about a cruise round the UK.' I stared at him in bewilderment. Why tell me? I don't think he was boasting or trying to make me jealous – he just wanted, as he always had, to tell me everything.

I walked inside and closed the garage doors gently. I then stood in the sombre, empty space and chortled with hysterical mirth until I was almost sick. It was the sort of reaction one can often feel in a tense or frightening situation, like a funeral, when laughter can come bubbling to the surface at a sombre moment. I returned to the most comfortable room in the house, the one we had christened "Rumpus", made myself a strong drink, flung myself across the massive cane settee and settled down to listen to some very loud music.

Chapter 20

*

As soon as I was on my own I began to meet my neighbours. Or maybe it was that I became more aware of them once Andrew had left. The next evening, as I was in the back garden watering my new plants, I noticed two small faces peeking at me through the wrought iron gate that was set in the "sparrow" hedge. I think the gate was put in by two previous families who must have been good friends and wanted a short cut between their homes. The two little faces, looking very much alike and of a similar age, informed me they were twins and before long they were chattering about their day at school and what a bully Rodney, down the road, was. They told me their names were Jodie and Jonty and their mum was a librarian who *read lots of books*. Hearing their giggles, Madeleine, their mother, came out of the kitchen clasping a tea towel and introduced herself. She suggested I put a padlock on the gate if her offspring became too annoying. I told her we were all watching our colony of sparrows and having far too much fun. With a stern warning to them to be good, Madeleine gave me a beaming smile and returned to preparing the family meal. Our other next-door neighbours had introduced themselves to us on our arrival but I had seen very little of them. They had told us their names, which slipped from my memory immediately, and all I could recall was that *she* nursed in the local hospital and *he* was a builder.

Two days later I met Dorothy. I was out in the front garden looking helplessly around as I strove for a plan to neaten and brighten the whole place up. A huge driveway with two small, uneven patches of weedy grass on either side did not make a garden as far as I was concerned. The only decent bit was the low red brick boundary wall flanked by two pillars which looked substantial and pleasing. Three leggy tree-like bushes of indifferent ancestry had been shoved in odd places and, in my opinion, needed to be removed and replaced by a few eye-catching shrubs. I was standing with my hands on my hips and wondering how far I would have to dig down for the removal of the present roots when a woman walked by and asked if I was the new owner. Events of the past weeks made my reply academic but I agreed I was.

'What happened to the Wilsons, then? I've known 'em since they were first married and my kids played with theirs until my girl got wed and moved away. Strange, they never came to say good-bye. Mind you, she could be a bit funny when she felt like it.'

I had no comment to make as I had never got friendly enough with either of them, but I agreed that common courtesy dictated a farewell might have been in order. She went on to tell me her name was Dorothy and, nodding towards the main road, said that she lived a few doors away. I told her mine was Jenny and politely asked her in for a cup of tea. She briskly refused as she was delivering rhubarb, from her garden she said, to another neighbour. I asked her what she thought of *my* garden and she shrugged, 'I've seen better, lass.'

Half an hour later Andrew drove up and told me breathlessly he was on his way to collect fish and chips. He was obviously making a very long detour! He asked what I was doing and I told him I was calculating how much membrane and bags of stones I would need to cover the two areas after I had removed all the grass and dug up the shrubs.

I had already argued with him twice about my plan to sell the house as soon as I was able. He had begged me to stay but failed to grasp I would not have enough money with which to pay off the loan to the building society at the end of the two years. Andrew had confidently expected to receive his half share of the house and investments when he got divorced from Fay – which would have more than covered the shortfall. He also had no idea of the blind panic I suffered every time I thought of the enormous debt I owed and how I would find shelter for myself in the future. I often woke in the middle of the night knowing I might never own the roof over my head ever again.

Now he seemed amazed that I would bother with such an enterprise as re-designing the garden if I was selling the property. I reminded him I had to make a substantial profit on the price I had originally paid for the house. I not only had to pay off the penalty clause but had to find money for selling and buying again plus the cost of the removal.

'Unless you and your wife would like to make up the difference and then I would be only too pleased to stay here,' I answered, facetiously. He stepped back as if I had hit him. 'There's no way I can stay here, Andrew. I have to get back to where I am safest – and that is Devon. I am a stranger up here and there is absolutely no one I can rely on... and you had best be getting back with your fish and chips,' I gently reminded him. Once again, he had lost all idea of time passing and he drove off at once looking dazed and confused.

The next day he turned up early and offered to run me to a decent garden centre that would supply me with what I needed for the garden. When we arrived he explained and showed them my plans. One would have guessed he was my husband, for not only did he arrange for the materials to be delivered but he insisted on paying! For once I allowed him to... He then returned with me and we beavered away the whole morning removing weedy turves and digging up the three stumps that were embedded deep in the subsoil. At the end of our filthy toil I was exhausted and Andrew insisted on taking me out for a late lunch in an Italian restaurant near the York city walls at Micklegate Bar. I almost went to sleep over the delightful meal and, when he returned me home once more, he helped me up the stairs and put me to bed – staying close until I dropped into a deep, dreamless sleep. The next morning he telephoned to say he and Fay would be journeying to Turkey the following day. I was determined not to show my true feelings and brightly wished him a delightful holiday. Adding, a bit snidely, 'Well I hope this time she manages to do the packing for you both!' At the other end of the line I heard a distinct snigger.

The huge bags of chippings were delivered on the first day of their holiday so I had little time to brood over it. I also had a telephone call from Dee and Paul in London. They had been thinking about annual holidays and, out of the blue, suggested I should join them for a week in France. I immediately resisted. I was still worried about money and now I had the added complication of a new garden to think about. I explained that, as soon as it was finished, the property would go up for sale and then I would need to be constantly on hand to show any prospective buyers around.

'Oh come on,' Dee begged. 'Do as much as you can and then take a break. Surely one week won't make *that* much difference?' I knew she was probably right but I didn't fancy the upheaval of falling in with their plans, finding my passport, packing and then catching a train down to London. She suggested we met halfway and could all travel together. Paul added his persuasive voice until I finally gave in. While they were talking a sudden thought had entered my head. I was quietly in the process of getting the house locks changed so, if Andrew returned from his jaunt to see me, what a shock he would get if the house was unoccupied and, on trying his key, he was unable to gain admittance. It was a devilish thought and one I suddenly couldn't resist. For the past few weeks I had been pulled this way and that – unsure of what was going to happen and having no say in my future while being unable to change the developments around me – I felt like a manipulated puppet. If I went away with my cousins things would change, if only for a short while; I would be removed from an unhappy situation, able to discuss it with family who loved me and ask for their advice. For a short time I would be in charge of my own destiny and Andrew would have a taste of his own medicine. It was too good an opportunity to miss and, hopefully, it might give me back a modicum of confidence that had been taken away so suddenly.

We would be leaving at the end of Andrew's week away, so if he came round to the house immediately on his return, he would have a whole week in which to fret and puzzle over what had happened while he had been enjoying himself in the sun. So that last night I packed quickly before I changed my mind and then, early the next morning, took the train from York to Bristol. Dee and Paul were waiting on the platform at Bristol Temple Meads station looking rather abashed. I sensed they wanted to tell me something but it was only at the end of a late lunch that they told me their news. Actually it was Robin who had asked them to go with him to France. It had never been their idea at all and they had suddenly seen it as a way of sorting out our marital problems. I sat in the restaurant stunned.

What on earth had made them think of such a stupid stunt? I tried to explain rationally how it would never work: could never work.

'Look I know you have done this with the best of intentions but you must realise this isn't a women's magazine story where everything turns out fine on the last page. I left Robin not because I didn't love him but because I loved someone else, Andrew, even more. Robin is aware of this because, after all these years, he knows me better than anyone. And he also knows me well enough to be sure that if Andrew beckoned I would go running back to him immediately. He knows that when I decide to do something it will be forever and therefore he will never be able to trust me again. He has said, more than once, that he always thought I was honest and open and now he realises things were never like that at all.'

I put my arms about them because I knew I was imparting bad news and I hated to hurt them. 'Why on earth did you do it?' I asked. 'I love you both but this dream of yours will never work. And the sad thing is I don't want it to and neither does Robin.'

We returned to the car and continued most of the way down to Plymouth with me silent in the back while Dee and Paul tried to talk brightly as if I hadn't spoken. Robin was waiting patiently at the ferry terminal and I could tell by his pallor as he came to greet us that he was no happier than me. I found it difficult not to stare. I hadn't seen him for over six months and he looked really beaten and ill. He had booked one double and two single cabins for us and for this I was grateful. For a few hours I could be alone and not have to talk to anyone. I made my excuses and left the three of them having a drink in the bar as we left the harbour. All I could envisage was a very long eight days...

****

All I have to remind me of those eight days are recorded in about a dozen snaps that Paul took while we were supposedly having a lovely holiday. I remember the ferry docked at Roscoff but where we travelled from there I have no idea. My cousins left their car parked in Plymouth and, once we arrived in France, we used ours. Even something as innocuous as that hurt me immeasurably. I tried to get Paul to sit in the front seat with Robin but he refused so *I* was forced to read the map and guide us to our destination. We must have stayed in Brittany simply because one photograph depicts a small *Hotel Le Bretagne* at night. Two bay trees flank a small entrance. The paintwork is typically pale blue and all the glowing windows have shutters. We couldn't have travelled far, so maybe we stayed near Plouescat because I can see either wide and sandy beaches with surrounding low cliffs and lots of Atlantic rollers in the distance, or tiny coves ringed by a few dozen whitewashed cottages, their small boats pulled well clear of the encroaching tide. We must have visited a minor château set typically by a broad river because there is the usual fairy-tale turrets and stone oriel windows. Paul snapped what looks to be a religious grey stone carving smothered and surmounted by tiny figures and crosses that one finds so often in this part of France. Hollyhocks and roses must have been another safe choice for him. One picture shows three of us sitting at a breakfast table, being served by mine host with croissants, fruit, rolls, jam and coffee. We are all laughing dutifully. I notice there is only one of the four of us – relaxing in the cosy lounge with after-dinner coffee and liquors. Dee, Paul and I are doing our best to grin at the camera but Robin looks exceedingly pensive.

In this way we managed to keep the happy façade in place. On arrival we were offered two bedrooms. One had a double bed and the other two singles. Dee managed to quickly state a preference for the huge double bed which enabled Robin and me to accept the other room. It was bad enough to politely exist in the same room without being forced to sleep in the same bed! We turned our backs as we undressed and I silently shed tears into my pillow. When we were alone Robin never uttered a word: in company he carefully never spoke to me but, to any bystander listening to our joking conversations, I am sure this was undetectable. To all intents and purposes we were two happy couples all having a terrific holiday in the sun. Most mornings Dee would ask me quietly whether things were any better between me and Robin. Always the optimist, my cousin! I would shake my head because, without meaning to, she and her husband had made the situation worse. On the telephone, hundreds of miles apart, Robin and I could be courteous and polite; but put us within feet of each other and the very air was charged with unspoken questions and bitterness. It was an untenable position for both of us and I was relieved when our holiday finally drew to a close and we returned to Plymouth.

We were all awkward as we disembarked and made our way towards our respective cars. My once-beloved husband gave me a long hard hug and then relinquished me to my cousins for our drive east. I waved to him from the back seat and then curled up in the corner and closed my eyes. It was such a relief, not having to pretend to be gay and upbeat, when all I had experienced was a deep sadness for wasted years that neither of us could ever recapture. I sighed deeply and must have fallen into a light doze. I awoke as the car jerked to a standstill. It was time for lunch and we had it on the outskirts of Bristol with the three of us looking wearily tanned. While we were eating Dee leaned forward and grabbed my hand.

'Have you been losing weight, Jen? Robin mentioned it on the first night. He said you looked thin and drawn and was most perturbed. He asked me if more had happened up in York than you had admitted to him. I think he was frightened for you. I told you you had never mentioned Andrew beating you, if that's what he meant.'

I grimaced. 'No, nobody beat me – you can put his mind at rest on that score.' I glanced down at myself. 'Well, maybe I have lost a few pounds. It's not something I think about. Mind you I *have* been very busy, you know. Now it's all gone wrong between Drew and me I've been racing to get the house up to scratch so I can sell it and return to dear old Devon.'

'What's the rush?' asked Paul. 'Surely it's not that important to return immediately?'

'You don't understand, do you? No, there's no rush to go back; no one desperately needs me down south and in fact Andrew has been pleading with me to stay. He has even conceded I might be happier if I moved to somewhere else in Yorkshire – and speaks of Scarborough or Harrogate. But don't you see, that's just to stop me leaving him altogether?'

'So he can bonk you every time he's given a day off,' my cousin answered crudely.

'Yes, probably,' I replied. 'When life becomes boring, or when all his golfing mates might be busy, or when his two boys have taken their families abroad and he's at a loose end, or because Fay is involved with friends, then *that's* the time his thoughts will turn to me. First of all, for my own peace of mind, I need to be well away. Secondly, I need to sell this house before it becomes a white elephant and prospective buyers wonder why it is hanging fire. Summer is here and now is my best opportunity. Also prices in Devon will be rising steadily and I have to find somewhere within my budget and buy it swiftly. I admit I'm scared of being homeless and until I find somewhere – however small – I won't feel safe and secure.'

At last I had captured their attention and they nodded with understanding. They now accepted I should waste no time in extricating myself from Yorkshire. We made our way to Temple Meads station and they saw me onto the next available train. Dee stood on the sunny platform and blew me fervent kisses until a bend in the track hid them both. I subsided into my seat and wondered what I should find on my return. I was in for a great shock.

I wearily pulled my case to within few yards of number 13 and stopped in amazement. What had happened? My garden was neatly finished and looked immaculate. Two bay trees stood in bright blue pots flanking my newly painted lemon front door. The pale chippings had been laid and newly raked into place and there were three large shrubs strategically placed in the midst of them. I had left a hastily dug plot, stored great rolls of membrane in the back garden and abandoned twenty seven huge bags of stones outside the garage doors. Someone – it had to be Andrew – had completed my work for me and then gone one stage beyond by purchasing elegant plants to enhance the whole setting. It was perfect. I stood there and cried. It had all been done with boundless love and yet none of it was for us both to appreciate and enjoy.

I went into the house and found a small mountain of mail. Most of it consisted of postcards from Turkey. Obviously, Andrew wanted me to share his experiences because he told me, in detail, about the resort and what he was doing and seeing. He also made it clear I should have been his companion. I dropped asleep with the cards scattered across the duvet and dreamed of Turkey and France all mixed up and muddled.

The next morning the doorbell shrilled before I had even roused.

I dragged on a dressing gown and stumbled downstairs. After my expert ministrations, the front door opened with ease and I found Andrew outside, grinning widely.

'Not up yet, lazybones? So what time did you get home last night?' he asked.

I mumbled an answer and he slapped me on the backside and told me to get upstairs for a shower while he made breakfast. And that's what we did! Like any ordinary couple we sat down to a meal in the sunny garden and chatted as we ate.

'Gosh you led me a merry dance, young lady.' I looked at him askance but said nothing. 'I had only left you for one week and you turned my whole world upside down, Jenny. I felt it strange when there was no reply to my bell and then, when I discovered my key didn't open the door, I was puzzled. The second day I became frantic when you still weren't home and yet had left all the garden stuff scattered around. It was so unlike you. I also telephoned but there was no reply and I even contemplated breaking in but didn't quite dare. The third day I had a brilliant idea and raided the refuse bins in desperation. I struck gold! I found a ripped-up list of clothes and guessed you had packed to go away for a few days. *That* decided me. Fay had left for Llandudno with her friends for a bridge tournament so I beavered away to complete the job for you. And I did – eventually. I do hope you like the trees and shrubs. The girl at the Garden Centre advised me and I am real proud of them!'

I sat back and couldn't help laughing. He was priceless. Not only had he blistered his hands for me but I had locked him out and then left without a word. No recriminations from this man, just a determination to make me happy. Of course we ended up in bed, yet again. I was unable to refuse him anything because, quite honestly, I *also* needed to be cherished and desired.

The next day Fay returned home, so all communication immediately ceased. It actually took me a time to notice this as my landline had ceased to work, which bothered me much more. I asked my next-door neighbours but they used other companies. In desperation I knocked two doors down and my brisk friend opened the door. I remembered her name was Dorothy and explained my dilemma. She asked, a bit abruptly, whether I wanted to use her line. Of course I did, but I was still rather shy as I found her less than welcoming. I explained my predicament to BT and they said I would be informed when my line was working again and, with that, I had to be satisfied. Luckily I had my mobile for use in an emergency and when Dorothy asked me to sit down for a cup of tea, I smiled tentatively and perched myself on her sofa. Gradually, as we chatted, I discovered her husband had died only a few months previously. She had nursed him at home and I could see she was still very aware and affected by the greatest upheaval in her life. She had adored him and his sudden, severe illness had separated them forever. It was obvious she was still trying to accept it as well as coming to terms with her new status as a widow.

She had a married daughter whom she adored and in return she was well looked-after and protected. Although she lived alone I got the impression she was part of a large and happy, loose-knit family that visited regularly and kept her busy baby-sitting for them. As we talked I gradually began to see another, and much gentler, side of this blunt lady. I realised her brusqueness may have been due to her not knowing too many folk from my part of the south of England. She had visited Cornwall with her husband for a couple of weeks, many years previously, and she still remembered it with nostalgia. I found myself chattering and laughing while we watched a television programme together. Suddenly I felt no longer friendless and from that moment I began to view York and its people with kindlier eyes.

I would like to say that everything went smoothly for the next few months. Sadly it didn't. Just that very evening, I arrived home and patiently awaited my usual call from Lorna. I wanted to tell her that I might have made a tentative friend. It didn't worry me too much that my landline had ceased to work. I knew Lorna would automatically try my mobile. I waited in vain, so by nine o'clock I decided to telephone her instead. It was as if mischievous gremlins had invaded my home: my mobile phone was totally dead, too. I sat back with my heart thumping. *Now I was completely cut off from the outside world.* I couldn't speak to anyone and they, in turn, would be unable to contact *me*. I had been receiving roughly three calls a night on average, so what would my relations and friends think if there was no reply day after day? If I had been trying to ring someone who I knew should be at the end of a telephone line and there was never a reply, I would probably have rung the nearest police station and alerted them. I hated the thought of anyone worrying about me and panicking. It was late and there was nothing I could do, so I made myself a snack and forced myself to go to bed and carry on reading the last few chapters of Andrew's abandoned novel.

I thought my troubles couldn't get any worse but I was sadly mistaken. The last thing I expected was a disturbance in the middle of the night. At two o'clock in the morning the house burglar alarm decided to go off! It had been in place when we took over the house and we had barely noticed it. As far as we were concerned it was just a dusty red box under the eaves of the house that served as a deterrent to any would-be burglar. We had never used it and had no idea even how to set it. At that time in the morning the noise was deafening and soon there were various people peering out of windows and opening their doors to see what the awful clamour was. Luckily my builder neighbour came running in and, between us, we managed to turn the wretched thing off. I made up some rubbish story as to why Andrew was absent and thanked him for his help. I offered him a cup of tea for his trouble and then saw him off the premises after promising to contact the alarm company first thing the next morning. I must have been at my lowest ebb at that moment because my placid forbearance suddenly shattered and I sat at the kitchen table and sobbed bitterly.

Of course, as my mobile was also dead, I was unable to use either telephone the next morning, so I went to see Dorothy, my saviour of the previous day, and she allowed me to borrow her phone as well as her good-natured ears. I told about my mobile also failing me and then asked her if she had heard my alarm going off.

'Heard it? I should think they heard it in Knaresborough!' she retorted. 'I expected to see half a dozen masked raiders race out of your house, at least. We never had those shenanigans when the Wilsons lived there,' she told me reprovingly.

I grinned sheepishly then asked if I could ring the alarm company for them to send an engineer. I knew the rest of the street would not take kindly to be woken so rudely for a second night. I was amazed and surprised at the cost. Back home our alarm was serviced annually and it was always a nominal charge, but after being informed that the Wilsons had never had theirs maintained since installation many years previously, I realised I would be paying for their negligence. Never mind, I knew my house had to be perfect if I wanted to attain a decent price with which to purchase one back in the West Country.

I returned to number 13 to await the alarm company and hoped that one or other of my telephones would return to normal. My first visitor was an irate Andrew.

'Where on earth have you been? I wondered if you had gone on walkabout again! I have been ringing your landline and texting you for two days, Jenny. What's wrong *now*?'

My woebegone face must have half told the story. No communication with the outside world and too much in the middle of the night for all the folk who lived within a quarter of a mile of my house. I tried to explain how the racket of a screaming alarm that would *not* be silenced had frightened me half to death. I explained the builder from next door had raced to my aid.

'I opened the door and, even screaming at each other, neither of us could hear a word. I couldn't even think straight. Finally he pushed past me and started hunting around to find the master control panel. He found it eventually in the glory hole in the kitchen. It was in the far corner nestling behind the ironing board. Even pressing every button didn't stop the awful noise and eventually, in desperation, he resorted to tearing every wire away from the box until there was blessed silence. It felt as if it had gone on for ever but it was probably only about fifteen minutes from beginning to end.'

I didn't mention I was unable to go to sleep when I returned to my bed. The din was still vibrating in my ears and I kept expecting it to start again. I was totally shaken and confused and just cowered down under the sheets.

Andrew looked concerned. 'You are certainly going through it, love,' he commiserated. 'Do you want me to go out and get you a new mobile?' I shook my head. 'Sorry, darling but I have some more bad news. Tomorrow I am off with my American friends to do this cruise around Britain thing. They have been on about it for the past two years and I kept finding reasons not to go. But this time the excuses ran out. It's a ten-day voyage and I promise to send you a card from every port we enter.'

I am not sure what he expected me to say, but with all these sudden troubles to contend with, I was less than enthusiastic. Who cared where they went or what they did? I had more than enough to deal with. Sometimes I felt as if I was fighting for my very existence and I had no time to waste on thinking where my erstwhile lover planned to be for the next couple of weeks. For once we didn't end up in bed – not because I was expecting a helpful engineer, but purely because I had far more important issues on my mind. Small things, like two ridge tiles that needed to be replaced on the roof and the flickering kitchen neon tube that needed renewing. Luckily the money Andrew placed in our joint account monthly had covered all these unexpected bills so far. My latest prayer was *Please God don't let the roof blow off.*

My middle-of-the-night alarm rescuer offered to fix the two roof tiles for me and Jodie and Jonty's mum slipped through the useful gate in the back garden to give me a hand with the long neon tube in the kitchen. Madeleine stood on the stepladder while I balanced precariously on the table as we wrestled to get pins into holes just to force my useless strip light to glow over the stove once more. When asked, I had told both my neighbours that Andrew was unfortunately away. I couldn't bring myself to tell them the truth – that he'd left me – as I knew full well, after listening to so many needy stories when we were viewing all those houses only a few months previously, that I didn't want their pity. Only to Dorothy did I tell the truth. It's a bad idea to admit to prospective buyers one is desperate for a sale. I remembered the sadder the story, the more Andrew would try for a reduction in price. It became almost a game because we had found so few properties we really liked. Finally I had found my dream home only to have it snatched away in a matter of months. Now I needed a buyer to fall in love with it, as *we* had, and be prepared to pay a reasonable sum for it. That's why it had to be so perfect – then none of them would be able to resist.

I carried out one last inspection the next morning before walking into town to speak with the estate agent who had sold us number 13. Over the months, when we had been trailing around looking for property, we had dealt with many estate agents: some were pushy and brash, others were obviously bored with their job and earned a reasonable salary whether they sold or not and a few, a very few, were sincerely interested enough to listen and then steer their customers towards what they desired. I had been privately delighted when the best of these, a pleasant girl with a young family, had seen us through the minefield that is the property market with good humour and efficiency. She looked up with a beaming smile as I walked into her office and offered me a chair. In a few short sentences I wiped that smile off her face.

'Oh my goodness, you poor dear,' she exclaimed. 'Course, I never liked him anyway,' she stated loyally.

'Come off it, Elise, you fancied him rotten,' I retorted, and the dimple re-appeared in her cheek once more.

I went on to explain that an immediate sale was my plan. 'I can't stay here. He's coming to see me every other day and none of it is right or sensible. I think his wife knows he's unable to stay away,' I confided. 'But, as long as he remains with her, I reckon she is prepared to look the other way and pretend not to notice.'

I also mentioned that the fact that I had been so abruptly abandoned was to be kept from prospective buyers. A single woman would be vulnerable and I knew only too well what their reactions would be! I needed their money, not a patronising attitude. Elise saw my point immediately and I was certain she would keep her side of the bargain. She arranged a time for particulars and photographs to be dealt with the next day and I walked back through Low Petergate a lot happier than when I had walked up it.

Perhaps now was a good time, I mused, to try and sell the house while Andrew would be enjoying himself on the high seas around Britain. On my own I could probably deal with these people. Trying to do it as a pretend couple was one step too far for me. My mouth twisted with distaste; telling lies was bad enough but I refused to do it in tandem.

On my own and selling a house. I sat in the rumpus room and forced myself to face a task I had never tackled alone before. Always, there had been a nonchalant Chris or the steadying influence of Robin to ease me through the process. This time it had been Andrew and, because we had nothing to sell and therefore no encumbrances, it had been relatively easy. In truth, it had been a way of getting to know the area around the city of York and I had quietly enjoyed every moment of it. Isn't it a fact that the buying and selling of a home is considered the second most stressful event in a person's life? I curled up in front of a silent television and tried to stifle a rising panic. What had I let myself in for?

Suddenly my mobile telephone started its gay little tune and I stood up hastily. *Where on earth had I left it*? I raced through the kitchen, searching right and left, and crashed open the door into the sitting room. *There* it was on a footstool where I had tossed it in disgust when it has ceased to work. I fell on it in a panic in case the lively music stopped.

'Got you!' said Paul. 'Where on earth have you been? We have been telephoning your landline as well as this one - both ring but you never pick up. Dee kept saying she hoped you hadn't done something stupid and we even talked about contacting the police.' He laughed lightly.

'Stop!' I said desperately. 'Just listen. Both my phones have been down. I have reported my landline and I have been trying and trying to get a signal on this one but it has been completely dead – even after charging.' Then the enormity of my whole predicament enveloped me and I started gasping and sobbing while clutching the precious, tiny object close to my ear. 'Please don't go off the line, Paul. I'm alone and I don't know what to do,' I wailed. Once again a strangled sound that was a mixture of grief and an odd sort of laughter encompassed me. I could feel it rising and sought to control myself:

'Hey, Jenny, calm down. I am going to pass you over to Dee and she will talk to you.' I heard a muttered conversation and then my beloved cousin came on the line. A fresh torrent of tears took my breath away.

'Stop this immediately, Jenny. You are hysterical,' announced my cousin's stern voice. I gulped a few times and managed to control my breathing somewhat. I began to pour out my woes in a muddled, disjointed rush and, somehow, she understood me. 'Look, Paul is going to come on the line now and he will tell you exactly what to do. Listen to him, love, and he will sort all this out for you, I promise.'

And he did! Darling Paul told me exactly how to re-boot my telephone. He explained the simple procedure of removing the battery and card. I trusted him enough to allow him to ring off so I could do so. A few minutes later, as I answered his call, I had a functioning telephone again. I wondered why Andrew hadn't taken the time to show me something similar, but probably my assumed nonchalance had fooled him into thinking I was well able to cope with any problems myself. I thanked my two cousins sincerely for their help. I admitted I hadn't realised how tense and fraught I had been feeling those past weeks. Dee agreed that going away to France had probably been a stupid idea on their part. I disagreed and cheered her up by confessing that, although parts had been embarrassingly awful, being back with them all had been a tonic.

I went to bed and managed a deep, untroubled sleep. I was gradually, one step at a time, surmounting my vast problems. Next was selling my home and severing my links with the man I loved.

Chapter 21

*

Three days later my house was officially on the market. It meant I was getting up at the crack of dawn to shower and clear away the debris of my breakfast. I would then make my bed, clean the bathroom, vacuum around and empty the rubbish. Afterwards, I would check the front and back gardens for weeds and dead-head any flowers that had decided to expire in the night. Once a week I trimmed the huge hedge that encircled the back garden and on another day I would clean the downstairs windows and conservatories. It kept me busy and stopped me from pondering my future. My landline was still dead but Dorothy was taking messages and relaying them to me. I apologised for all the inconvenience but she said she was rather enjoying it.

Most mornings a postcard would announce the whereabouts of Andrew and his cruise ship. He and his American friends had boarded on the east coast at Newcastle upon Tyne and appeared to be making their way south towards Dover. They progressed through the English Channel, calling in at Plymouth before rounding the tip of Cornwall and stopping off twice in Wales. They made a detour past the Isle of Man and visited Belfast. From there they sailed north to Scotland, the Hebrides, rounded the Orkneys and finally turned south again to Aberdeen. I received hastily scribbled postcards almost daily from Dover, Plymouth, Swansea, Liverpool, Belfast, the Isle of Mull, Wick and Edinburgh. Every one stressed he missed me dreadfully and each one I propped up on the kitchen windowsill to cheer me as I tackled the washing up. Each one also strengthened my resolve to remove myself from the temptation of Yorkshire.

Viewings were booked from the first day. I tried to limit them to two a day and kept them well spaced out. I needed to sell and I was willing to show prospective buyers around the property myself. I wanted to stress all the advantages of being close to the city centre, having four bedrooms, a double garage, lots of rooms, two conservatories and yet be surrounded by a low-maintenance garden. By the end of the week I had honed my persuasive skills and most viewers seemed favourably impressed. Feedback from Elise was encouraging and I started to breathe easier.

After a few offers that were so low that I refused to consider them, three serious contenders returned for a second time. One chap was thinking of getting married and brought his fiancée with him on his second visit. I don't think they had any particular time frame so I was reluctant to take him seriously. We left it that they would both think about it and let me know in the near future.

The second was a mother with two daughters. I liked her. She was honest enough to admit her husband had recently left her and she was in the process of divorcing him and selling the family home. She wanted to be near her two daughter's school and the position of number 13 made it perfect. At that time they were staying in a bed-and-breakfast close by; but she admitted it was far from ideal. Two girls of twelve and fourteen are seldom happy in a boarding-house atmosphere. She had a decent job and I imagined, once her own house had been sold, she would be in a good position to purchase mine.

The third serious couple brought their aged parent when they returned for a second visit. They were the proud mum and dad of one toddler and a babe in arms which, this time, they had left with mother-in-law. I showed them around once more and then allowed them to wander on their own. The father asked would I be willing to accept a lower offer and I shook my head. They walked out into the garden and some more detailed discussions ensued. I offered them a cup of tea as I waited patiently. They went away and I wondered if I would ever hear from them again.

The only encouraging thing to happen was my telephone. It was working once more and I breathed a sigh of relief. I also thanked Dorothy for helping me at such a difficult time by presenting her with a huge bouquet of her favourite flowers.

Another week of viewings followed. Some people returned twice more and Elise told me it often happened until they finally made up their minds. I was just getting despondent and wondered if the house was jinxed because, although lots of people had stressed a strong interest, the agents hadn't received a firm offer as yet. I was wondering if I would have to tell Andrew on his return that I had nothing to report. I knew he would be pleased if only because it would mean he could keep me longer in the north.

Then Lorna telephoned to say Robin wasn't well. He had been rushed to hospital the previous night. I telephoned our home immediately but there was no reply. I rang the hospital who said there was little they could tell me for the present. I had no way of knowing if I was suddenly *persona non grata* as far as they were concerned. Lorna promised to ring the second she had any news. I couldn't settle to anything and I am sure I was not very informative with the young couple that arrived to look around the house that afternoon. That evening I rang the hospital once again hoping that Robin had not put a block on any calls from his ex-wife. At my small hospital we occasionally had to vet calls from relatives to whom patients refused to speak. But in this instance I think it had all been my cranky imagination because a very helpful nurse asked me brightly whether I wanted to speak to him as he was now out of intensive care. *Yes, of course I did*!

I tried to sound low-key and nonchalant as she transferred me to the phone by Robin's bed. I also tried to keep the conversation short. Yes, he had woken in the middle of the night with chest pains. He wondered if he was having a heart attack, so instead of dialling 999 he drove himself to our local hospital. The doctor did some tests and then sent him straight off by ambulance, to the District General Hospital in Exeter. Robin said they made a big fuss over him for most of the night with constant tests, blood-pressure readings and a heart monitor machine. He had been told he would remain in hospital until they decided what had caused his rapid heartbeat. They would then find a way of correcting and stabilising it.

'You poor darling,' I said sympathetically, while listening to *my* heart beating unnaturally loudly in my own ears. 'You can't be left alone for a minute without scaring us all to death.'

'Yeah, it was just to get some attention,' he acknowledged. '*And* a few decent meals.'

I breathed a sigh of relief. Maybe he wasn't holding me responsible; although I am sure the worry I had caused could have been a contributory factor to him ending up in hospital. We made a few more mild jokes and I rang off – not wanting to tire him – with me asking him to thank the nurse for her kindness. I needed his carers to accept me ringing as often as I was allowed. Robin had never been ill a day in his life, as far as I knew. Yes, all the childish ailments but nothing since then. I knew his job was difficult with long hours, great responsibility and painstaking attention to detail. And my friends had told me repeatedly that he had never really got over my leaving him. I wondered if he had been eating properly now he was alone. He had always been my best friend and I was distraught at his being so seriously ill. Who could be sure what the cause was? After mentioning my mobile had been out of action, I put the telephone down with a lighter heart than when I commenced the call.

The next day Elise telephoned to say a firm offer had been put in by the couple with the two babies and their dad. The agents had been told they had a mortgage arranged and therefore it should only be a matter of finalising details. She warned me not to get too elated as quite often these prospective buyers would back out if a better deal presented itself. They had also received another tentative offer from the mum with the two teenage girls, on the condition she managed to sell her own property. That impressed me far more as I liked and trusted her. And, lo and behold the couple that hadn't quite fixed their wedding date were also making overtures. Now I would have something to tell Andrew on his return...

****

Lorna rang later the next afternoon. She had conned her way into seeing Robin by saying she was his sister. I wondered what would happen when his real sister, Alexis, turned up – as she undoubtedly would – at the weekend. Lorna then gave me a few uncomfortable facts; ones I hadn't been able to extract from him over the phone. Apparently he had been rushed into intensive care as soon as he arrived, by ambulance, at the hospital. It's usual for a local doctor to telephone ahead and warn the hospital staff. Apparently he had been put on a heart monitor immediately. A house doctor then stood at the end of his bed to check the monitor as his heartbeat rapidly accelerated. Robin admitted to Lorna the audible noise frightened him as his heart beat faster and faster. Finally it must have reached a plateau because just as rapidly, it began to decrease. By then the cardiac team had arrived, but the air of expectancy around his bed had scared him more than the machine when the distinct beat began to reduce. Robin roughly knew what a normal heartbeat should sound like but it went lower and lower and then stopped. He said it felt like ages – but it was probably only a few seconds – before it started again and finally reached a satisfactory level, at which point all the staff clustered around his bed had then breathed a sigh of relief.

I listened with my hand up to my mouth. What I was hearing was so serious; but what upset me most of all was the man I had loved for over thirty years had been forced to suffer in fear and alone. After that first day I heard friends and colleagues had formed a rota so they could visit him constantly – and from then on I began to breathe a little easier.

A week later he was sent home to recuperate and sounded his usual grumpy self. I knew it was due to the enforced idleness. Robin never chose to lie in bed late, even on his days off, so reading books and looking at television had never appealed to him. He would rather be out with friends or at work. I rang as often as I was able – in between viewings and second viewings – and tried to keep him amused and stimulated, but it was difficult when I was so far away. Alexis managed to get a precious week's holiday from her work and came to the rescue from Essex. By then she was barely speaking to me as she considered I was to blame for everything. She told me coldly that, when Robin was asked for his next of kin, he told the authorities no one was responsible for him. When I said he could have still given my name, she pointed out it wasn't *me* he was protecting but *her*.

Because she was only able to stay for a short while, she made a point of immediately speaking to Robin's doctor as well as the hospital medical team to see what the prognosis was. I knew I had few rights as the estranged wife and I was thankful his sister was so thorough and determined. She was told it wasn't an emergency but he would be receiving cardiac surgery shortly. The consultant described it for her in laymen's terms as a fine wire being inserted into the heart muscle to shock it back into normal rhythm. He stressed the majority of patients have no further attacks and, with this, she had to be satisfied. As far as I could tell Robin had not suffered a heart attack but whether it was tachycardia, atrial or ventricular fibrillation, I had no way of knowing. And if it was due to a physical cause we were not being told. I just hoped his miracle treatment was as infallible as his doctor had predicted.

The only good news that week was that I received two firm offers on the house. One from the mum with the two teenage daughters, offering to buy it at the market price but only when she sold her own property; the second from the young couple with the very young family, also offering the full asking price. As they had no property to sell, I accepted with a sigh or relief. Even though I preferred the newly divorced mum I was well aware the other one was a more secure offer and, as they informed the agents a mortgage was already arranged, I felt I was one step nearer to a successful deal. When asked about my partner I rambled on about him being Cornish (true) and that his aged parents had been unwell and he had gone down to the West Country to arrange for them to go into care (definitely pure fiction!). In this way I had an excuse if they were puzzled why he was seldom at home. At some point, I would insist on him meeting them. I knew Andrew would be vastly reluctant to meet the new owners of the house we had chosen together but a malicious streak in me was determined that he should take some responsibility for what he was putting me through and show him the seriousness of my position.

Immediately I cancelled all other viewings to save wasting my, or a prospective buyer's, time which of course pleased Andrew. I decided that, while I was in the huge county of Yorkshire, I might as well see as much of it as I could, so the next morning I took a bus south for Beverley. It was a pleasant journey through the rolling York Wolds and travelling between small, delectable period towns. I arrived at a modern, busy bus station and walked in sunshine from St Mary's, the medieval imposing church in the north, down Ladygate past Dog & Duck Lane, on through Toll Gavel and Butcher

Row to the splendour of the Minster in the south. I considered it a lovely market town, with its great tumbling swathes of bright blooms everywhere against a backdrop of a market cross, cobbled streets, strange white telephone kiosks and a Wednesday fruit-and-vegetable market. Here the modest town cottages surrounding the busy stalls almost hid the towering Minster. Suddenly it loomed over me, looking golden and serene in its parkland setting. Inside it was a haven of peace and sanctuary. Started in 1220 by John of Beverley and completed two hundred years later, the shape reminded me of a French Cross of Lorraine. I strolled through, admiring the windows, the Gothic tracery and the intricate, canopied memorials. Although smaller than York Minster, it was every bit as sumptuously beautiful. I vowed, if time allowed, I would return soon.

Now that both my telephones were working I was able to look at the world with a calmer outlook. Alexis was returning to her job and two sons in Essex while Robin had a firm date for his heart procedure, so I was able to rest easier. The house was sold – subject to contract – and the daily tidying up and cleaning regime had been relaxed somewhat. I still kept an eagle eye on the front and back gardens for any weed that dared show its face; but I allowed the window cleaner to take back his job, once more, of cleaning the downstairs windows.

Andrew would turn up unexpectedly at all times of the day or night. I decided to give him a spare key because, if anything happened to me, no one would be able to enter the house. One of my stipulations, when he deserted me, was that he should leave all his clothes, shoes, shaving gear, toiletries, electric toothbrush, slippers, scarves, hats, sports gear such as fishing rods, hiking boots, and all the books, CDs, player and the new television and photograph albums that he had brought to the house in the beginning. One night he came and begged for his starched dress shirt and dinner jacket. He never said but I guessed he would shortly be attending a formal dinner. Bitterly hurt, I started crying. I had worked my way through all his clothes and was surprised to find a lot were grubby, so I had washed and pressed everything carefully, including three winter jackets, and even mended some of his torn golf jumpers. Stupidly I felt that, if I was the only partner who cared, then I should be the custodian. It ended with him comforting me and promising I could keep everything until the bitter end. How childish and stupid to carry on in this way, but that was my twisted reasoning at that time. I imagined maybe they did not attend that formal occasion or he went out and purchased all new clothes without telling Fay the reason why. I am sure that – between my obdurate stubbornness and Fay's demands – Andrew wasn't having a very happy time. But the day after he had taken me proudly to the Ryedale Folk Museum at Hutton-le-Hole and we had wandered through Victorian thatched cottages and visited the old fashioned pharmacist who had given us a sure-fire cure for chilblains, Andrew telephoned in a jubilant mood.

'Guess what, Jennykins?'

'What?' I asked, rudely.

'How would you like to accompany me to balmier climes?' I asked him what on earth he was talking about.

'In just two weeks I will be taking you away for a whole seven days!' he stated. I made some derogatory sound in the back of my throat and went on clearing the table one-handed.

'Oh yes,' I said disbelievingly. 'So where's Fay off to – Mars?'

'No, a Greek island, accompanied by her best friend.'

'You *are* joking? How will she dare to leave you alone, and on the loose, with people like me around?' I asked.

'Doan 'ee worry, m'dear,' he answered in the Cornish vernacular. 'As long as she is enjoying herself, I can go hang. No, joking apart my darling, we can go anywhere you fancy for a week's rest and relaxation. Now it is up to you to choose your favourite destination. I am coming round tonight to take you out for a meal – so please put your thinking cap on.'

And, with that settled, he rushed off to play golf, get on with some household chores or doze in his warm conservatory.

So I *did* cogitate deeply for the rest of that day. The French medieval town of *Rouen* is one of my favourite exploring haunts; *Venice* is fabulous for lovers, sightseeing, churches and paintings; a Mediterranean beach is splendid for a tanned, lazy holiday and the simple islands of Greece (as long as it wasn't Fay's!) are ideal for absolutely everything. In the UK I had always longed to walk Hadrian's Wall, wander round Portmeirion, visit Bamburgh

Head, Alnwick Castle and Lindisfarne on Holy Island. And I had, sadly, never ventured into the Lake District. Robin and I had often spoken about going, but other holidays somehow had always taken precedence, and we never did get there.

I lazed back soaking up soporific sunshine in my tiny back garden and barely listened as Jody and Jonty sat close to me and tried to count the inhabitants of Sparrow Hedge. As they downed their milk and munched their one-allowed-biscuit-before-tea, I pondered on where I would *really* like to spend one perfect week with Andrew. I roused myself to discuss if coloured beaks or a dab of paint on the sparrow's tails might simplify our task, when Andrew wandered in and joined our conversation. Madeleine called the children home for their meal, as their dad had just returned from work, and immediately Drew, with a bright smile, hustled me off to a reputable pub in Helmsley. He was obviously excited by the prospect of our spending time together...

We sat in a comfortable dining room of oak settles and Windsor chairs where I was spoilt for choice as we studied the pub's extensive menu.

'Well, have you decided where you want to have your wicked way with me?' asked Andrew with a gleam in his eye. 'Is it to be sea and sand, Las Vegas or the battlefields of Flanders?'

Up until that moment I had no idea what I would suggest, but suddenly it was so simple. 'Yes, I know where I want to go. It's to be Cornwall, as ever! But not near your home, this time, Drew. I would like to visit St Ives, wander round Land's End and maybe return to Yorkshire via Mevagissey. If the weather is nice it will be lovely.'

I waited for him to disagree and offer some exotic destination in preference, but his eyes sparkled and he warmly clasped my hands across the table and beamed. 'Fine! I won't book anything up, Jenny. We will make our way slowly to the West Country and stop and stay as we feel like it. A leisurely holiday at a leisurely, gentle pace – it sounds perfect, darling.'

We both sat back and grinned at each other. Little did he guess that I was already scheming in my head. This would give us a whole week to be alone together. Seven days of talking and laughing and making love. Seven days in which to show him what he was missing. No imperial demands, no computer games, no rules to be obeyed and no unhappy whinging when he didn't carry out tasks the moment he was asked. I planned a stress-free holiday – a bit like the six months we had spent together on my arrival in Yorkshire. And he would be back in his own environment where time went slowly and folk enjoyed each other's company.

Surely Andrew wouldn't be able to withstand such a pleasant strategy? I prayed Cornwall would work her wondrous beguiling way with him, that he would see the light and reverse the momentous decision he had made that terrible day in May. I needed to be a mythical Siren, a gentle temptress who would lure my lover back to me by kindness and love. I fondly hoped a few calm, happy days would prove to him life was usually like this – and not the tempestuous battleground that often made up his spoilt wife's environment.

I laid my plans accordingly. Andrew had to take Fay and her friend to the airport, deposit their cat in the cattery and then was free to come and pick me up. I had told all my distant friends and relations I would be in Cornwall for a week and I gave Dorothy my key in case of any emergencies. It seemed as good a time as any to casually explain to my immediate neighbours why so many people were visiting number 13. I concocted a lie, explaining my partner was now staying in Cornwall to sort out his parent's ongoing care and in fact we were being forced to sell the house and move down there to be close to them. Luckily half that statement was true – the half that concerned *my* movements. I knew Andrew would never agree to my admitting he had had second thoughts about our liaison and had dumped me. He would hate to appear an incompetent fool and, in truth, pride on my part made me shy away from any pity they would feel if I told them the stark reality. What would they make of his endless returning? I was able to mention we would shortly be going down on holiday and leave them to spread the news to the rest of the neighbourhood.

Life was just sorting itself into some sort of order when Lorna telephoned with good *and* bad news. The good was that Robin's operation had taken place. Once he was released from hospital he had stayed the next night at their place – for which I thanked her – but the very next day he had suffered another frightening attack. She had telephoned his consultant in a panic, but he had calmed her by prescribing a double dose of medication. Since then Robin had no further ill effects. She promised to visit him every day at home and, when I broke down and cried, sternly told me if our roles had been reversed that's what I would have done. It was true - but I knew I was blessed with a very special friendship.

****

Our week in Cornwall will always be a golden interlude in my memory. Andrew arrived alert and sparkling early on the Saturday morning. He had seen Fay and her friend off at the airport at some ungodly hour. He had then raced home and was waiting outside the cattery as it opened. On arriving back at his house he unearthed his secret list and hurriedly threw all his chosen clothes into a small, battered holdall.

'What I've forgotten I'll buy when I arrive,' he stated airily as I slung my suitcase next to his bag in the boot. It was of little importance to me what he wore so I just grinned and we were off on our grand adventure.

I could hardly believe we were going to spend seven days and nights together, sleeping, waking, eating, exploring and, hopefully, laughing. I sat with my hand resting lightly on his knee. Just to touch him was reassuring and every now and then he gave me a cheeky smile as we chatted on about anything and everything – as it came into our heads.

'I feel as if I am fizzing over like a too-full glass of champagne,' Andrew admitted. 'Time seemed to go so slowly as I listened to Greek Island weather predictions and what was my opinion on *this* sun dress, *that* wrap or are *these* evening shoes dressy enough. As if *I* cared! I only wanted to shout out, "I'm going away with the loveliest girl in the world".'

I laughed indulgently. Fay may have had him while she was cogitating on what to pack but I had him for the rest of the week and my wardrobe was the last thing on my mind. A couple of pairs of shorts, if it was hot, and some jeans if it wasn't, T-shirts and jumpers, a pair of sturdy trainers plus a cagoule in case it rained. For the evenings I had three changes of clothing with some decent shoes and, like Andrew, I would buy anything else if it became necessary.

After stopping to eat a simple picnic, near Tewkesbury, we pushed on steadily southwards. Andrew started to run out of steam around Torquay, I noticed. We got as far as Paignton when I suggested it might be the perfect stopover. We had just negotiated a quiet seafront road when I spotted a small guest house called *Bella Vista* which had made me smile because all one could see was a green field edged by a line of beach huts all facing (presumably) the sea. As we could only see the backs of these colourful huts the view was actually non- existent, but the magic word *VACANCIES* caught my attention. We stopped thankfully and a nice young couple offered us a ground floor room which had an enthralling view of those same beach huts!

Nothing much happened that night except, after a satisfying meal at a nearby inn, we returned home in the twilight to find an elderly couple trying to prise open the French widows to our room. We crept across the bloom-filled gardens surrounding the house and asked them if they were alright. They jumped back in fright and then admitted they had booked a room shortly after us and had walked out without any keys. They had been certain this was their room and were hoping to force the lock without admitting to the owners how stupid they had been. Andrew solved their problem by letting them in the front door and then taking them to the next-door room where they found the forgotten keys thrown on their bed. We all laughed about it the next morning at breakfast before we went on our merry way – ever westwards.

We arrived and looked down at a bright and sunny St Ives about lunchtime. We parked the car high above the town and went and found the Information Bureau which supplied us with a list of guest houses. We wandered around, with a map in our hands, and decided the second one on the list looked pleasant and airy. Modern, and set in its own grounds, with about a dozen rooms, half of them looking towards the sparkling sea, left us satisfied. We had chosen well – a large en-suite bedroom decorated in pale colours with wide, sunny windows fully open to the sea breezes. I unpacked swiftly while Andrew busied himself making a pot of tea. Half an hour later we strolled through the town, enjoying the golden beaches, a few picturesque cobbled streets and the harbour while we searched for the famous Tate St Ives Art Gallery.

A large white building, it is perched right by the sea above Porthmeor Beach. One certainly can't miss it – with its impressive double set of steps leading up to a massive rounded portico. The first thing I noticed, as I entered the huge glassed reception area, was the sea and sunshine being reflected on the encircling walls. It is one of the most exciting, continually changing, sights I have ever seen and, sadly, nothing surpassed that first impression – neither paintings, drawings nor sculptured driftwood. I read the reverent descriptions next to each piece of art and metaphorically shrugged. Most looked a bit pedantic to me with straight lines and primary colours, as if done by self-conscious, slightly precocious, youngsters. My mind immediately flew back to my college days when lots of art students produced this sort of work and believed they were geniuses. Maybe these same students had taken themselves down to the West Country to take advantage of a place where the light is clear and shimmering; but sadly maybe all they managed to produce were these plain daubs of dubious intent which Drew and I were unable to appreciate. The only part of the exhibition that cheered us was the few sculptural works of Barbara Hepworth. These left us both longing to see more and we quizzed the staff as to where her garden was situated.

It wasn't far. We found it tucked away in a cobbled street, in an old part of town, behind an innocuous brick wall. The entrance was through a simple gate with an even simpler plaque stating here was *The Barbara Hepworth Sculpture Garden.* Barbara came to Cornwall with her husband, Ben Nicholson, and four children during the 1940s to escape the war; she found Trewyn in 1949 and remained until her death there, in a fire, in 1975. Trewyn Studio and Garden was a secret, magical haven which took our delighted breath away. We were surrounded by the most amazingly tactile, solid, curvaceous stone, wood, metal and bronze shapes set amidst subtropical plants and trees. It all looked like a glorious stage setting. We walked through the garden in a daze, looking at angles and viewpoints that changed as we progressed. Spoilt for choice, we darted this way and that, calling to each other to look at what we had found. Some bronzes had a green verdigris patina; some stone was dark grey and starkly sharp-edged; other forms were pale and voluptuously rounded with contrasting shades of colour. Many were huge but all made me want to touch, to stroke, to caress. *River Form* was my favourite, with its contrasting pale green interior showing an irregular puddle of rainwater at its heart; but the *Four Square Walk Through* was the most memorable – with its juxtaposition of elliptical curves and towering geometric shapes. Andrew gently put his arms around me and we stood there mesmerised. It was an emotional experience.

The rest of the day was, by contrast, an anti-climax with us exploring the harbour area, wandering around the muddle of small shops and art galleries before lazing on the beach and soaking up the crystal clear light that illuminates the whole of the town. Some of the commercial art on display had used this clarity of light to produce the most amazing paintings and we were both impressed at the exceptional standard of what we saw.

The next day we set out to explore in earnest. We took the coast road to the west, past Zennor and Pendeen where we discovered the Levant Mine was open to the public. This tin mine, whose deep shafts extended far under the sea, was closed in 1930 when over thirty miners lost their lives in a horrendous explosion. It took days before all the bodies were found and brought to the surface by a giant steam engine that still works today.

We went below and were horrified at the awful conditions the men worked in for up to fourteen hours a day. From the deepest dark and dank levels it would often take men three hours to reach the surface before going home to their families. For many their life expectancy averaged twenty-seven years. I shuddered at the inhumanity.

We had lunch in Sennen Cove and then parked the car so we could walk around the cliffs to Land's End. Neither of us wanted to run the gauntlet of the commercial mess that has been foisted on one of the most awe-inspiring places on earth. Luckily one can use the coastal path right round the promontory without sampling the theme park that has grown up behind the sweeping cliffs and jumbled rocks. On a clear day one can see the Isles of Scilly. We passed *The Irish Lady* and walked as far as *The Armed Knight* before wandering back on the path that leads to Sennen. We were truly blessed by sun and light breezes as we captured dozens of photographs of the glorious scenery. I wondered how Drew could have ever left.

Our last port of call was *Chysauster Village* near Madron. This ancient village was built on this site over 2,000 years ago. One can still see the remains of eight courtyard houses with their tiny gardens, stabling for the animals and even sleeping benches for the inhabitants. It was easy to imagine low thatched roofs under which life was communal, hard but gregarious. I wondered who their nearest neighbours would have been and if any of them had ever seen the sea. *We* could speed for miles with great ease, visiting north and south Cornwall effortlessly, while these people were probably confined to within a few miles of their homes – knowing nothing about who or what was over the border, beyond the Tamar.

The next morning was sunny but blowing a boisterous gale. We decided to make our way south towards Penzance and St Michael's Mount in the hope that this side would be sheltered. We wanted to get as far as Kynance Cove and The Lizard after visiting the island. We had both seen famous paintings and photographs of the area and had always longed to explore the coast here for ourselves. Andrew hummed a tune about "going up Camborne 'ill comin' down" and I sat back and just enjoyed being alone together. On arrival at the causeway to St Michael's we found a notice cancelling our hopes due to bad sea conditions so, undeterred, we turned away and made our way towards Helston, famous for the '*Furry' Dance* that progresses majestically through the town every year on the 8th May. At Porthleven Andrew spotted a café offering cream teas and, although it was only halfway through the morning, he persuaded me he could go no further without one. We parked the car up a hill and wandered down to the sea. We found a sheltered corner outside the welcoming café and he ordered an enormous spread. It was fun sitting out of the wind and watching the sea raging in front of us even though I could only barely manage to nibble on a scone. My breakfast had been satisfying enough it seemed. Fortified, we made our way inland past Loe Pool and Helston. We decided to give Flambards Village a miss due to lack of time and, as usual, were drawn towards the coast once again at Gunwalloe. Here, by chance, we found Church Cove. We sat near the tiny, grey granite church being buffeted by screaming winds and looked in awe at the towering waves sweeping the beach. It was the most invigorating experience I have ever enjoyed. This was Cornwall at its fiercest and best. Mullion might be an anti-climax after this, I mused. I needn't have worried because we never got to Mullion, Kynance, the Lizard or even Goonhilly Downs Satellite Station. We had mislaid our rucksack somewhere on our travels. Drew argued with me that there was little of value inside and that he would replace it as soon as we returned to St Ives. Hating to do anything so stupid and being blessed with total recall, I knew we had left it at our Porthleven cream tea "pit stop". I pretended to scold the idiot who was supposedly in charge of it; and crestfallen, Andrew agreed to retrace our journey back along the coast.

I insisted on him waiting in Porthleven's car park as I ran back to the still quiet café. I was greeted by our waitress holding up our battered backpack and laughing. I thanked her and jogged back to the car park with it hidden behind me and grinned at Andrew's worried face. In an effort to cheer him, I suggested we return via the coast route towards Penzance, Newlyn, Mousehole, Lamorna and Porthcurno before turning north to St Ives. Suddenly we were not so upset to be missing the glorious scenery of Kynance Cove. We passed through Penzance speedily, as neither of us was enamoured by busy towns, and found the bustling, working port of Newlyn much more fun. Mousehole is a quaint, steep harbour village and Lamorna Cove is simple, restful and lovely. But the icing on the cake is Porthcurno with its tiny cove of silver sands, set deep beneath high cliffs. It is one of the loveliest beaches in Cornwall, although *that* was not the reason why we were there. I led Andrew unerringly across to the tiny open-air Minack Theatre that stands against a perfect backdrop of these cliffs. It must be the most wondrous spot to perform when there is a sparkling, restless blue sea stretching into the distance. It was the brainchild of Rowena Cade who, with the help of her taciturn gardener and her own hands, excavated, built and improved the theatre over many decades. There are stone balustrades, balconies, tall pillars and archways – all set at different heights and angles with a steep semi-circle of stone and grass seats cradling it snugly against the shelving hillside. Even though Andrew had been born within this county's boundary, he had never visited this area and I wanted him to fall in love with the conception of this very special place.

****

The next day we said a fond farewell to St Ives and the far west of Cornwall. Half our holiday had fled already and it was now time to make our way to Mevagissey. We lunched in Truro and were ensconced in our chosen harbour-side pub just as Mevagissey was quietening and visitors leaving. We enjoyed a decent meal in the bar and then sat at our darkened bedroom window and watched, entranced, as a huge moon arose above the harbour sending ripples of gold around the moored boats that were gently lifting and swinging on the incoming tide. Andrew wrapped his arms tightly around me as we leaned back together on the window seat. I could feel his heart gently thudding against my shoulder and realised what I was feeling was pure, undiluted happiness. That night both of us slept deeply, lulled by the placid, lapping tide and caressed by the breezes that stirred the curtains.

Of course, once there, we explored all the usual holiday haunts. We spent a morning in Gorran Haven paddling close to the harbour wall and hunting around the rock pools near the cliffs for anything that moved. That afternoon we took ourselves off to the *Lost Gardens of Heligan*, a place I had first visited in its infancy. It is a strange story of a grand house that gently fell asleep and became abandoned and, finally, forgotten. At the outbreak of the First World War all the male staff volunteered and, once the fighting ended, sadly none of them returned. The family died out, the gardens disappeared under a blanket of weeds and brambles, and the house became a silent shell. That was until Tim Smit discovered it, fell under its spell and, with backbreaking toil, rolled back the years – like the legendary Prince Charming, he had discovered his Sleeping Princess and had turned an alluring possibility into an awesome fact. I had been the only passenger to alight from a Newquay day trip coach almost twenty years previously. The rest of the coach outing had gone on to spend the day in Mevagissey and it had occurred to me I might have been foolish not to have stayed with them. In those days there was the barest outline of what Drew and I were to discover that day. Originally owned by the

Tremayne family, the grounds were allowed to sleep undisturbed. What we found now was a wonderland of fantasy – an assortment of formal gardens, a crystal grotto, a naturally heated pineapple clamp that produced perfectly edible fruit, a series of lakes opening out to reveal glorious vistas, wicker figures cavorting madly across a green, a productive kitchen garden, and orchards crammed with fruit. The place was a farmer's dream. I shrieked as a large green giant's head, with staring eyes and spiky hair, rose in front of me out of a sea of pebbles and we were then shocked to stumble over a Mud Maiden deeply asleep on a mossy bank. There were surprises at every turn until, with my heart thudding madly, I was forced to enter the sultry, tropical world of a jungle by creeping across a swaying rope-bridge which traversed a deep ravine. There, we discovered an enormous murky pond with giant rhubarb, tunnels of bamboo and even a banana plantation encroaching from every side. It was lush and exciting and our one afternoon gave us little time to explore and appreciate. We came out of Heligan as the gates gently closed and made our way back to our cosy harbourside inn, sated and delighted. Our holiday was proving to be beyond my fondest dreams. In bed, deep and satisfying love; at every turn, new experiences; good food to tempt our voracious appetites and all laced with brimming laughter and happiness. Bliss!

The next day, by contrast, we spent lazing around at sea. Early the next morning Andrew went out and hired a sturdy clinker-built boat. The fisherman threw in all the tackle we would need and we went in pursuit of the humble mackerel. We took a picnic lunch with us and ate it in a gently rocking boat off the cove of Portmellon. Our week's holiday was fast drawing to a close. We had explored with gusto and gazed with wonder at so many beautiful corners of Cornwall. It had been a magical few days and I hoped in my heart it would be enough to convince Andrew we were happier together than apart. I felt he was balancing on a knife-edge of indecision.

On our last day I sadly packed our cases and, as we crossed the Tamar, I silently said my fond farewells. There was no urgency to return to Yorkshire – Fay and her friend were still island-hopping in Greece – and, as there were lots of intriguing places that we had heard of but never visited, we were almost enticed off the M5 motorway a couple of times. We were getting near the outskirts of

Bristol when Andrew asked what I knew of Weston-super-Mare.

'Nothing at all,' I admitted. 'It doesn't sound as alluring as Westward Ho! but, as I've never been there either, let's just go and see what this seaside town has to offer.' In truth I didn't care where we went or what we did. Just to stretch out our holiday for the longest time possible meant I was ready to go anywhere and do anything. Add to this the possibility of finding somewhere special that only the two of us had discovered appealed to us both.

On arrival, we found a simple town with long beaches and a promenade to match. I had been told the tide often recedes towards the Welsh coast and almost disappears; but, as it was rippling in when we arrived, it looked quite presentable. There was a pier; and it was close by that we found a small hotel nestled behind a large garden square. The hotel was half empty so we booked in for the night and were taken to our room. It was delightful, on the ground floor and overlooking a garden deep in greenery and flowers. I unpacked what we needed and went into the en suite bathroom to take a shower. Sadly, the bathroom didn't live up to our pleasant bedroom. Andrew chided me gently, saying it was only for one night so could I not make the best of it? A good scrub around the tiled nooks and crannies would have improved the overall effect and, in righteous anger, I stormed off to complain to the manager.

It turned out the manager was also the owner and his explanation disarmed me completely. He told me how he had held a commission in the Army until his wife gave him an ultimatum to either give up his post or she would divorce him. After great soul-searching, David had agreed and returned to civilian life just as his mother, who owned the hotel, was struck down by a particularly vicious form of cancer. His only option was to step into her shoes until she was well enough to return, but sadly, within three months she had died. Ironically his wife left him anyway and now, two years later, he was struggling with a shabby hotel and managing with cheap foreign labour. He told me redecorating it was like the Forth Bridge – never ending – and he often felt like a hamster on a wheel. Of course, being me, I ended up listening to his sorry tale and promising that when I stood under the shower, I would stay well away from the tiles!

We ate in the hotel that night with David cooking for us and, when we pulled away from there early the next morning, Andrew was chuckling with amusement at my sudden reversal of opinion.

There were no more detours on the way back to York. Andrew dropped me off in the late afternoon sunshine. He carried my suitcase to the front door but refused to come inside. Suddenly his relaxed manner imperceptibly changed and I wondered if he was fearful that, by simply stepping over our threshold, the magnetic power of our love might prove too strong for him and he would be unable to return to another house just a few miles distant.

I walked in and left my case in the kitchen. Within seconds my reason for living had disappeared. There was no one to talk to, no one to plan a meal with, no one to decide what we should do the next day. What did I want to watch on television? Who cared? I felt lost and unsettled, which made me prowl around the house – touching ornaments, fingering books and magazines and then going to stand by the kitchen window to look aimlessly at the garden. The whole building felt dusty and warm. I switched off my mobile and strode towards the front door. I would go for a walk. I needed to get away from being reliant on anyone. I walked the short way to the end of our road and turned right into Holly Bank Road until I found a path that would take me up onto Hob Moor. I strode over a stream, across fields, past a kissing gate, and finally arrived at a large pond set within encircling trees. I stood and looked across to the dappled shade on the other side and suddenly I could breathe again. Somehow I would learn to face this frightening upheaval in my life. I would return to my beloved Devon, take it one step at a time, put myself first for once, and I knew – suddenly with great certainty – I would survive.

I slowly turned and walked back the way I had come. As I entered the house I felt a lot calmer than when I left. The telephone began ringing stridently and I walked into the kitchen to answer it...

Chapter 22

*

'Where on earth were you?' I abruptly heard as I lifted the receiver. 'I have been ringing off and on for what seems like hours. Jenny, I started to wonder if you'd had an accident or had done something silly.'

'Something silly – like what?' I mildly enquired.

'Oh I don't know – something stupid, like taking the train back to Cornwall.'

'Was there something you wanted?' I asked sweetly, once I heard his voice and my heart had ceased hammering.

'Yes,' he answered. 'I came indoors, chucked all my laundry in the machine and then found myself missing you.' I silently thanked God and grinned, until he went on and spoilt it by saying, 'Look, darling, they won't be back until lunchtime tomorrow so, I've been thinking, can I come round so we can spend the night together?'

I kept him waiting for a short time while I nonchalantly explained I had been for a long walk over Hob Moor and, on the way back, remembered to buy some milk. My heart was stupidly rejoicing but I was determined to appear to be considering his request. In the end I burst out laughing and told him of course he could come back – and added, for good measure, 'Well it sounds to me as if you owe me a slap-up meal at a decent restaurant in town.' I smiled as he fervently agreed.

He was back and wandering in the front door before I had finished my pot of tea! In the meantime I had rushed around, opening windows and conservatory doors in an effort to make the whole house appear as pleasant and welcoming as possible. My hopes were high and suddenly everything on my horizon was glowing.

In bed that night we had an impromptu celebration as we laughed and joked like two naughty children let out early from school; but the next morning, although we were up early, Andrew sounded preoccupied and I sensed, over breakfast, he was eating with a purpose. By eleven o'clock I was aware that he was becoming more alert and tense until I suggested tartly he returned home to monitor his telephone and carry out any orders as they were despatched. He, by then, was so uptight that he obeyed me and, as I tried not to show my disillusion, gathered all his stuff together, kissed me gently and swiftly drove off home in his car.

Once again I suddenly realised we had actually discussed nothing relating to our future life together. We were both as bad as each other, I had to admit, constantly clinging to the present and wary of discussing all the difficult plans and intentions we needed to put in place if we were ever to going to make a life for ourselves once more.

****

And that, sad to say, became the pattern of our last few months together. Andrew would race back to see me and take me out, as often as he was able. Fay must have been sick of all the myriad excuses he found to be away from home twice, sometimes three times, a week. It seemed she nearly always had plans of her own: designer shopping to enjoy, bridge parties to attend and meals to sample with her small clique of friends. Very occasionally she would challenge his whereabouts with an abrupt question and he would have to sift through suitable excuses to find one that sounded plausible. I knew he was wary of her moodiness and intimidated by her sudden temper – and a couple of times, he admitted to me, he gave the wrong answer. Once, when she caught him out, he had told her he was at a film the week before it was actually shown in town. I questioned him closely and discovered she had called him a liar but, surprisingly, she never demanded where he had *actually* been. How odd I pondered that when she was proved right, she would abandon the interrogation. I began to wonder if she knew *exactly* what he was up to, but like a cat toying with a mouse, she enjoyed making him squirm. Maybe she guessed the turmoil he was in but, because it amused her, she allowed him a certain amount of freedom – with only the occasional tug at the reins – to prove she was the ringmaster, after all.

Consequently, in spite of her plots and ploys, I had many private, in-depth, tours of most places worth seeing within a hundred miles of the city of York. Knowing I was usually free from any previous engagements now I had sold the house, I would receive a hurried phone call the day before, telling me when I would be picked up the next morning, stating we would be visiting a beauty spot, some fascinating town or little-known attraction. In this way I enjoyed the seaside towns of Scarborough, Whitby, Filey and some smaller resorts like Robin Hood's Bay clinging to the hillside, Sandsend, Runswick Bay and even the tiny atmospheric steep fishing village of Staithes on the border of Cleveland. Inland we visited just about every castle, priory, abbey, grand house and National Trust property in the vicinity. Most of them, I am sure, Andrew had seen many times over, but still he studiously explained to me – an ignorant southerner – about their histories and painstakingly conducted me around proudly and with obvious pleasure that was touching to see. It must have cost him any amount of planning, in thought, inspiration, petrol money *and* entrance fees! Perhaps he had decided, as I had relinquished my whole previous life to be with him, it was the least he could offer in return. He also knew that time was running out for us both and maybe felt it imperative to squeeze every last bit of culture, beauty and interest out of my final months in the adopted county he had come to love so much.

I cannot remember all of these places, sad to say, but some will remain with me forever. Like Temple Newsam, the birthplace of Lord Darnley, ineffectual husband of Mary Queen of Scots. It had a strange benediction crowning its battlements, an art gallery to die for and pleasant strolls by picturesque lakes. Castle Howard also stood in the most magnificent grounds and was Vanbrugh's first commission which began his march to fame and fortune. Ryedale Folk Museum took me back in time to simple farming folk and different values. I felt at home there. Eden Camp, which had been Prisoner of War Camp 83 during the Second World War, still had its Nissen huts all laid out demonstrating what wartime Britain was like - from Vera Lynn singing patriotic songs, to damp air-raid shelters. One such hut depicted a claustrophobic submarine waiting to be attacked and another took us down a coal mine with the young Bevin Boys, most of whom had only just left school. Thirty huts plus one war time "Prefab" made the whole experience so very real. We spent hours there and I loved it all – especially having tea in the prisoners' canteen!

We visited romantic Pickering Castle, Fountains Abbey and Studley Royal Water Garden. In 1132 thirteen monks arrived in this secluded valley to begin a simple life before it eventually became the wealthiest abbey in Medieval Europe. I remember Byland Abbey, one of Yorkshire's greatest monasteries, now a magnificent ruin, with that grand sweep of half a circular Rose Window standing tall in the sunshine. Near Leeds I was shown another monastery and discovered that a wide road, now disused and forlorn, had been driven right through the centre of the towering nave and chancel. What vandalism! Opposite we visited a small museum and were studying the exhibits closely when Andrew was suddenly accosted by a friend. I immediately melted into the background but *he* appeared completely unperturbed – it was as if we were covered by a cloak of invisibility – and afterwards, as we sat in the tiny tea garden surrounded by roses, he cheekily donned his scarlet Arsenal baseball cap just to show me he didn't care.

At Duncombe Park he became so immersed in the elegant rooms and in dreamily wandering round the spectacular gardens, that it was only as we were having afternoon tea he became aware of the time. Suddenly he remembered he was supposed to go out with friends that evening and, in a grand hurry, we had to down our napkins and abandon the tea-pot, sandwiches and scones so he could settle the bill. I was amazed how he could have forgotten a previous engagement and, after listening to him fuss over the quickest route back, I tartly told him to drop me at the stop in his village and I would take the bus home. Which I did.

There were so many other places I remember with great affection – like the Royal Armouries in Leeds and Burnby Hall Gardens. The first we spent almost a whole day walking around, admiring weapons through the ages as well as the magnificent Destrier horses that had to carry men in armour to war and allowed them to joust in peacetime. The second was one of the loveliest and most peaceful havens I have ever visited. Two lakes surrounded with grass walks, specimen trees, a woodland walk, a rockery, secret Victorian gardens, lots of rustic, sheltered seats as well as what looked like a curved Japanese bridge that was reminiscent of the delicate arch one sees in Madame Butterfly or on blue Chinese willow pattern plates. Visitors say it reminds them of the famous bridge in Monet's garden in Giverny, but Andrew told me it was known as Jamie's Bridge. It was close to this spot that we flung down our rug and ate our picnic in the dappled shade of a nearby stripling tree. We then rested our backs comfortably against it as we talked and enjoyed the sunshine. Andrew told me of the owner, a Major Stewart, who became a big-game hunter. Strangely, he was also a conservationist who, when he and his wife moved into Burnby Hall in 1904, decided to improve the estate. And the resulting beautiful park that emerged was the one we had admired and walked around that day. The two lakes were home to over eighty different species of hardy water lilies. Known as the National Collection it was the largest in the world and, when we were there, nearly every water lily was out in full bloom. What a sight! We were spoilt for choice for depth of colour, size and waxy texture. We wandered around and each clump of flowerheads appeared more sensational and exquisite than the last.

There were also fish. The upper lake was home to koi carp - some so enormous, brightly coloured and tame that I yearned to pat them on the head. The larger, lower lake, was full of less exotic fish like the British tench, bream and roach; but all of them delighted in being hand-fed and launched themselves out of the water in an effort to reach the feeder. Andrew purchased a bag of fish food and I spent the rest of that afternoon in a secluded dell, crouching over one of the tiny platforms that jutted out over the water, encouraging and enticing these lovely creatures to eat out of my hand. It was a day I will always remember with great nostalgia.

In an effort to dispel my loneliness, I would frequently ask Dorothy if I could come round and keep her company for an evening. She had lost her husband a short time before we had arrived and I think she found time dragged – as I did. We did nothing exciting – apart from sharing a pot of tea, talking quietly or watching a television programme if there was something interesting on offer.

The only attraction was that we could voice our thoughts and be listened to. I think it cheered us both up.

Three things enlivened my life at this time, not all of them good. The first was that the buyers of our house suddenly weren't as solid as we had been led to believe. They had stressed they already had a mortgage in place and no property of their own to sell. For this very reason I had accepted their offer above the woman with the two children who was in the throes of selling her own house. I only discovered that our buyers had been a shade elastic with the truth when their surveyor found a fault with the lintel over our kitchen window. He had inadvertently let slip they were still seeking finance. When my estate agent taxed them with this, they demanded I reduce the price by a couple of thousand pounds to compensate. My circumstances meant I was in no position to lower the price. Indeed I needed every penny at that time. My lovely builder neighbour came to my rescue and sorted the problem out in no time. Their lies and manipulation certainly did not endear them to me and I discussed it with Robin when I made my regular Friday evening call.

He listened gravely and gave good advice but he also had news of his own to impart. He had met a Scottish lady online and, by the sound of it, they were becoming serious. He was going to meet her and her family the next weekend. I could only feel pleased for him. I knew how *I* had felt when Andrew walked out on me so, after our long marriage, Robin's shocked sadness must have been so very much worse. His news left me feeling bereft but, as he assured me, he would always be my friend, come what may, I could only feel relieved for him. I wanted at least one of us to come out of the whole sorry mess settled and happy.

The third occurrence started with a day out in the village of Aldborough to the north west of York. On the way there Andrew told me we were going to visit a small Roman settlement near the banks of the River Ure, which had originally been on the direct route from York to the wild north of the Empire. The Romans had realised their "scorched earth" policy was effective; but it was of no help in settling the lands they had conquered, so they tried different tactics. They made Aldborough their headquarters and built a stronghold with walls and battlements and, to man it, they took the largest Celtic tribe in the area – the Brigantes – and gently coerced them into their way of life. They Romanised the area and then called the village *Isurium Brigantu.*

When we arrived I found it difficult to visualise a town surrounded by high red walls, sturdy ramparts and tall white towers; and within, a Roman basilica, the Forum and marketplace, and many urban houses with orchards and gardens. On visiting the small museum, however, where we saw almost intact mosaic pavements and all sorts of Roman household pottery, I understood it must have been a very significant outpost indeed. We went to see where the river crossing had been and I appreciated the importance of water for moving grain stores, weapons, armies and merchants to such places as Hadrian's Wall and the ferocious North. The inhabitants of the village had probably worshipped the god Mercury who would have looked kindly on travellers, artisans and tradespeople. Andrew explained that later, in the Middle Ages, a wooden bridge was erected at Boroughbridge to ford the River Ure and gradually Aldborough went back to sleep once more....

When I'd had my fill of all things Roman, we made our way back to the village green and the Ship Inn for lunch, and it was here that Andrew tried, one last time, to get me to change my mind about leaving the north and returning to the West Country. The basis of his argument always came back to the fact that I had given my share of my marital home to Robin. This seemed to annoy him unbearably and he hadn't been able to leave this festering sore alone for weeks. Now he tried marshalling all his charm and persuasion one last time. He'd chosen a hushed, almost empty pub to make one last plea to my good nature and I braced myself to withstand his entreaties.

'Please, please think again, Jenny. We could be so happy together up here. Property is much cheaper in this part of the world and as you don't need to be near a town for work, we could find the perfect bolt-hole for you. The things to see and do are endless and I promise to take you out as often as possible so you never need be lonely. You now know our weather here is similar to yours down south. But most of all, darling, once you leave I will never be able to see you again. I don't want long rambling conversations on the phone, however lovely they are – I need to touch you, sleep with you, wrap you in my arms, walk in step with you over headlands or on beaches by the sea, to sit in a theatre or cinema and be amused, amazed or intrigued. Think about it, sweetheart – we can have everything we want if you take what is due to you – what you worked and saved for all your life. Why act the martyr simply because you consider you are in the wrong and can't bear to hurt your ex-husband!'

I listened, purely because every time I took a deep breath to answer his persuasive arguments, he held up his hand and went on to the next one. Eventually he ground to a halt as he could find no more weapons in his armoury. What Andrew didn't realise was that I'd had countless sleepless nights when I had gone over these very disputes again and again. *Did he not know I wanted to stay? Why did he think I had left the man I had loved for countless years if it was not to be with him? Why was his reasoning so clear on most things but so faulty when it came to us?* Now it was my turn to tell him the way I saw it...

'OK, Andrew. I have heard all your reasons, dredged up over the past few months, about why I should stay up here. So now, perhaps, it's about time I explained *my* feelings regarding this fiasco.' I kept my voice low in an effort not to attract undue attention. Luckily, over the years, I had learned to summarise and demolish shaky arguments: now I knew this was one dispute I had to win. I was fighting for my very existence.

'Once you returned to Fay I was aware, regardless of how she said she'd always loved you, that she was unable to weave any kindness or affection back into your life together. Maybe she finds it difficult to show her feelings, but I suspect this may all be superficial posturing on her part. It's called *dog in the manger* syndrome – she doesn't love you but, conversely, she doesn't want to lose you. Every day *we* were together I was amazed at your happy countenance and beaming smile as soon as you caught sight of me each morning. Was that all false or do you now look at her with the same trust and affection?'

'My almost insurmountable task when you walked out was to ring and tell my family and friends that you had broken your word. You, who had always been so honourable in the past! It seems odd then, that you still treat me with kindness, consideration and love. Why bother when your actions definitely indicate the opposite? I notice a steely determination that nothing I say will shift. Like a pane of glass which I am unable to penetrate. How I longed to go into hibernation – like an animal – to escape the knowing looks and malicious words of people who were delighted I came a cropper; but, strangely enough, this was often easier to bear than the love and understanding so generously offered by the people that truly love me.'

'Be aware Andrew, I'm not the same child who you knew at sixteen, so stop trying to merge the "then" and "now" together. That innocent, naïve girl had no idea what nastiness lurks in the real world. This one has battled through a hard, exacting life and emerged with all her defences intact – still, one doesn't expect to be stabbed in the back by the one person I would have staked my very life on.'

'I am certainly *not* like the "bit on the side" of a philandering MP whose accommodating little wife is in the background and has vowed everlasting love regardless of what her husband gets up to. Actually I don't think this sums up *your* wife at all. In fact, I feel *she* has come out of this stronger than all of us. Whatever anyone thinks, I am *not* a vacillating old woman who is snatching at her last chance of happiness, Drew, so please just listen to my answers respecting your flawed arguments.'

'I will definitely NOT be living in a run-down cottage regardless of how many roses are rambling over the door. I don't need to be taken out and amused. I am not a mongrel dog who needs exercise, you know! I also couldn't care less about your weather. An igloo would be acceptable if we were living in one together. Remember that awful guest house you took me to when we arrived? Did you hear me moaning about the dreary, difficult conditions? No, because I barely noticed them. We were both ecstatic with love – so the surroundings were irrelevant, at least to me they were. And last of all, let's get one thing straight: Robin gets the house, the *whole* house and every penny of what it is worth. It is none of your business how I control my own finances. You can't have it both ways, Andrew – walking away and then telling me how to manage my life. Why is it so important to you, anyway? Would it make you happier if you knew my ex-husband was being punished as well as you? You had your chance, darling and I would have given up anything, done anything, to make you happy. I thought my feelings were reciprocated but I was obviously as wrong about that as about so many other things.'

I sat back and looked at Andrew's ashen face. My last words, I knew, would surely end our relationship forever.

'And there's one thing more. When I was sifting through the paperwork that's been piling up these past months I discovered some that obviously belongs solely to you. You really doodle too much, Andrew. In fact it was your scribble that caught my attention. The letter informed the reader that a long-standing insurance policy would shortly be maturing. It also stated the amount you could expect. From the date on the letter, I gather it had fallen due at roughly the time you returned to Fay. I take it the whole sum had a far greater attraction than a mere half, so maybe that's reason enough.'

Andrew took me straight back to the house. I had spoken harshly; but the shock of reading those words had been reverberating in my head for days. Blame my resentment at listening to a man who I was unable to stop loving, mouthing facile platitudes to comfort me, for the bitter hurt I had been feeling ever since.

****

That evening I had two telephone calls. The first was from Lorna.

'I thought you might be interested to know that Robin brought his new girlfriend home for the weekend,' she said hesitantly.

'What's she like?'

'Well, I only spoke to them both for a few minutes when I was taking Petra for new dancing shoes. She seems quite pleasant – taller than you – and, of course, she has a strong Scottish accent. Petra wasn't keen but that's kids for you - they don't like change and they're conventional in their loyalties.'

She went on to discuss family matters before we said goodbye and I settled back to watch an exciting game of football on the television. Within two minutes the telephone rang yet again. This time it was Margaret who wanted to catch up on what was happening up in Yorkshire, but I noted she also mentioned she had heard Robin had been entertaining a lady friend for the past few days. I grinned and said I knew.

'Golly, good news travels fast,' I commented dryly.

'Well I thought you ought to know,' she said, slightly huffily. I changed the subject by asking about young Megan and the church and then settled down to listen as she told me all the latest news.

I was astounded when, two days later, Andrew arrived as if nothing had happened. It was as if I had never spoken such vitriolic words, never told him exactly what I thought of him and of his silly plans and pleadings. He dragged me off to visit Rievaulx Abbey. We wandered around the almost deserted, extensive ruins with headphones attached to our heads and had a brilliant time imagining how the Cistercians lived and worked with their large number of lay-brothers and servants. It must have been a huge hive of monastic industry set in the most beautiful architectural surroundings. Over a lavish afternoon tea Andrew then went on to mention casually he would be away on holiday for the next three weeks. He was off to visit friends in California. He never said so, but I took it he would be accompanied by his wife because, from that date onwards, I noticed he seldom mentioned Fay's name again – unless I specifically asked him.

Chapter 23

*

I think it was Andrew's casual words, informing me he would be going away once again, that brought me to my senses. My time was swiftly running out and, although not everything had been plain sailing as regards the completion of the sale of our house, it was at last going through and I hoped that, by the end of the year, I could bear to abandon the bright future I had expected to enjoy and manage to return to a far simpler life back in Devon. Robin had promised to move me and my furniture. When I had asked whether I could stay in our bungalow until I found a suitable place to live he had immediately refused. I don't think he was being vindictive: he had obviously given it some thought and decided it was not a good idea. He gave me no reasons and I accepted his decision and never mentioned it again.

To keep myself busy I then decided I would buy a camera. I had been a prolific amateur photographer since I was a young girl. By some oversight I had left my trusty camera behind and now I was about to rectify that. For years anything and everything that interested me had been saved – not just holiday snaps – and now I knew I needed some sort of record of the past year to save it disappearing into obscurity. I desperately needed to be able to rely on this visual aid to bring back the memory of the deep happiness that Andrew and I had both revelled in. I wanted to return to the places we had visited together – and top of my mental list was a tour of all the churches in York. There were so many – lots with a special claim to fame – and it would be easy to visit them as they were spaced within a few miles of my home. So it was just my good luck that one Sunday, as I made my weary way home for tea, I made one of the best discoveries of my time up there. I passed my local church and noticed a few people making their way up the steps. Most were laughing and chatting as they passed between the wide oak doors. On the spur of the moment I decided to join them, for what else did I have to do that was so vitally important once I had satisfied my hunger? I was met by beaming smiles all round and an outstretched hand. Immediately a woman stopped chatting with a rather distinguished-looking elderly gentleman and introduced herself before casually coming to sit by me. I know this is standard practice in church – to encourage new blood – but this was done with such warmth and generosity that I accepted it gratefully. I also realised that, mentally, I was probably at my lowest ebb and therefore extremely vulnerable while such an uncertain future faced me. I was basically living from day to day while trying to ignore a feeling of desperation. Maybe someone was taking care of me that day because, just by the slimmest of chances, I had found an unusual place that was dynamic, down to earth and friendly.

There were only about a couple of dozen in the congregation that evening. I discovered that was par for the course but, to me, that made it even more attractive. Hundreds came to the morning services; in fact it was family-orientated with excited children of all ages walking in with their parents and grandparents before gaily racing off to join their different groups. Morning services were a rollicking, joyful rejoicing and the church would be packed with the lusty singing threatening the stained-glass windows. Evensong was a low-key affair by contrast, and I absorbed the comfort, tranquillity and friendship that was extended to me – like a veritable sponge. It was only the sacrament of communion that I refrained from; sitting quietly in my pew as the rest went forward to the altar rail. I was well aware I had broken various commandments since I had met Andrew and I also knew, given the same opportunities, I would repeat the offences instantly. After a couple of weeks my new friends asked if I would like to attend the coffee mornings that were held for parish residents every Wednesday morning. I hesitated, in case they thought I was in need of charity, and noticing this, they swiftly suggested they were short of assistants. I accepted immediately. I eventually came to the conclusion that the young vicar was amazingly influenced by his modern-thinking congregation who made no bones about what they would like – and normally got their way. I realised this when, during the last few months, I attended a café-cum-religious service in the church one Sunday evening, walked the bounds of the sprawling parish as we visited tiny "snickle ways" I had no idea existed, joined the large teenage flock for a hair-raising question-and-answer session in which they grilled a local journalist about his love life and finally enjoyed a massive Christmas party in the crypt. And every Wednesday morning I proudly manned a tea urn as we dished out hot drinks and cake to all the local people who, like me, were either lonely or just plain hungry.

On other days of those solitary weeks I began my tour of York's various and fascinating churches. I started with the oldest, purely by chance. After wandering by the jewellers in Goodramgate I was musing over the beautiful ring Andrew had chosen for me when I noticed a narrow opening between two medieval shops. Unable to resist. I slipped through and found myself staring at a pretty little church in a tranquil setting. *Holy Trinity* was originally in existence during the reign of William the Conqueror and had been preserved ever since. Enter, and you may feel you are in a time warp – the uneven flagstones and high boxed Georgian pews have been retained, so one can easily imagine the squire, his tricorn hat resting on his knee, nodding off to sleep during a boring sermon. The next three buildings all took my eye because they had something in common – crowns. Not steeples or square battlements but beautiful airy coronets. *All Saints Pavement* was the Guild church for the city's seven lodges and, as thirty-four Lord Mayors had also been buried here, it must have been an important civic church in its day; *St Michael-le-Belfry* holds an important position close to the Minster but has the dubious reputation of baptising the infamous Guy Fawkes who was born close by and, lastly, *St Helen's* was supposedly the private chapel of Helen, the Christian mother of Constantine who changed his allegiance and became the first Christian Roman Emperor. I decided, by then, that I had viewed enough ancient churches and switched my walks to find more modern buildings. I searched for and found *The Salvation Army* church just outside York's walls, in Gillygate. I couldn't really miss the huge industrial looking, red-brick building proclaiming *BLOOD*

AND FIRE over its entrance. After that I decided to try the other end of the spectrum and attended a *Friends Meeting House* service in Friargate one Sunday morning. I searched and found it eventually in a back street close to *Clifford's Tower*. The simplicity, silence and atmosphere of calm acceptance impressed me deeply and I was pleased I had come. In between these pilgrimages I still visited *The Minster* constantly, usually clutching an old pair of binoculars, which enabled me to study those inaccessible, high places that were difficult to discern from below. It always amazed me that medieval Guild stonemasons were prepared to devote their whole lives to enhance the glory of their Lord – maybe in a place no one could see.

I then decided to visit a place I passed almost daily – *The Bar Convent*. It stood on a crossroads, outside the walls of York, near Micklegate Bar. A daring Roman Catholic Church, built at a time when Catholicism was banned in England – and often accompanied by terrible punishment or even death. It was a plain, innocuous building that none would ever suspect was a religious house. Established in 1686, it became a nunnery and school for Catholic girls; and less than a hundred years later, it secretly employed an architect to build a delightful chapel with a miniature cupola. This he cleverly hid away beneath a pitched roof and none was the wiser. I wandered in one morning and was amazed to find a pretty café in an enclosed, restful garden and an extremely interesting museum which was opened to me just by asking. I wandered around for ages, admiring some inspiring art, and finally found my way to the secret chapel. Here I discovered a miniature *Sacré-Coeur*, not in the heart of Paris but hidden away in a convent museum in York. I was then asked by a passing Sister if I would like to view Margaret Clitherow's hand. I must have looked puzzled and hesitant because she walked over to a mahogany cabinet and unlocked it.

I had not been long in York before I had learned the terrible story of Margaret, wife of a butcher and living in the Shambles. I had viewed her simple medieval house, which looked almost Quakerish to my untrained eye, and learned it had become a place of pilgrimage for many. Apparently she was drawn to Catholicism, possibly because she was a sensible, caring woman and she saw how badly Catholics fared at that time. It was rumoured she sheltered priests and may have spoken in their favour. In 1586 the mob came for her – she was dragged outside, convicted by public opinion, put under a hastily taken down stout door and had stones piled on top of her until she died. She was canonized in 1970. And now I was being offered a view of her hand? I stepped back in consternation as I was shown what looked like a withered leather glove! The Sister serenely returned the relic to its dark home and, shuddering, I smartly followed her down to the ground floor with all its sunshine and bustle.

I was sitting on a bench in the shadow of the Minster one afternoon when I began talking to a pleasant couple who were doing a similar tour to mine. They casually mentioned the church of *St Denys*. It sounded intriguing so I asked for directions and went off to find it immediately. I was told, 'Go down past the Minster Yard to Low Petergate and follow the road straight on until you reach Fossgate, then cross over the River Foss and go down Walmgate where you should then spot the church on your right'. I was also told, 'When you reach the city walls you will know you have missed it and need to retrace your footsteps!' And that was how I came to discover this tiny gem amongst so many more famous ones.

I think the nickname "The Unfortunate Church" is probably appropriate as it had been severely damaged in the past. It was struck by cannon shot in the Civil War, then half of it fell into a sewer when the land around the river was being drained which, in turn, necessitated the nave being demolished and the steeple, which had been struck by lightning, was removed when it became unsafe. The church also had a funny little turret squashed into a corner that rivalled Pisa's famous Leaning Tower, which gave it character. It had also inherited a Norman doorway when the original arch was removed from the nave in 1160 and repositioned to where a window had been. And, to me, it was this beautiful, carved doorway that made *St Denys* so special.

St Denys, I learned, is the patron saint of Paris and fishermen. He supposedly walked away from his Roman execution carrying his own severed head. He must also have been pretty special for the Guild of Fishmongers pledged their allegiance and worshipped here. The building was now an unusual, square shape but the original was built on a Roman site, maybe even a temple and, when I walked around, I was spellbound by the oldest stained glass in the city topped by a lovely, fifteenth-century, heraldic roof. The deeply colourful Melrose Window was spellbinding as was also the window depicting St Denys himself. He was shown as a handsome old man with a long, curling beard plus a crown; but the strangest thing of all was his companion. It looked as if he had an animal nibbling his ear. This beast had a spaniel's soft ears and two ram's horns, I noted, so maybe he kept a pet goat for company!

But my favourite of all these religious houses was my "Pocket Watch Church". I found it in Coney Street one day when I was strolling home and, since then, I had visited it constantly. It was the outsize, double-sided, circular clock that caught my attention first of all, mainly because it was relatively low and jutted out, right over a thronged shopping thoroughfare. I am sure this timepiece is well used by nearly every shopper as they jostle one another and are jostled in turn; and I am equally sure none knows, or cares, that they are passing a priceless treasure in this hectic corner of York. I am also certain hardly any of these busy people will bother to turn aside, lower their heads and pass through the small insignificant door to peer inside. The church of *St Martin* has found itself, quite by chance, in an odd place – between a popular cinema and a modern bar. Strange neighbours but, as the church was built centuries before either, it doesn't appear to matter.

St. Martin-Le-Grand was originally founded around the eleventh century. It became the main Parish church in the area and probably would have stood proudly on the banks of the River Ouse. On 29th April 1942 it was destroyed by a bombing raid over the city and remained a ruin until it was restored in 1961. Most of the church was demolished but outside, on the north side, I found a small cloister-like, enclosed garden, a shrine of remembrance to all those who died in two world wars. *St Martin's* was named after St Martin of Tours – the patron saint of soldiers. His Feast Day is 11th November which, appropriately, is our Armistice Day.

To me, a casual visitor, it appeared a bijou chapel proportionately in the shape of a shoebox. So tiny it may barely hold a congregation of forty, but the simplicity of the pale grey stone walls, muted grey flagstones and bleached wooden pews were a masterpiece of design and therefore enhanced its theatrical impact. The roof was flat and coloured a sky blue with touches of gilding and had bosses, heraldic designs and faces peeking down from it. From the door – only a short walk away – this simplicity of design meant my eye was instantly directed towards the interesting fifteenth-century stained-glass window encased in delicate pale stone tracery, before it was irresistibly drawn down towards a glittering gold host of apostles hovering above a scarlet altar cloth. It all sounds a bit garish but, in fact, it was vibrantly stunning. Because I had difficulty remembering so many unusual names in York I called it my "Pocket Watch Church" and seldom walked past it without spending a few minutes inside absorbing its cheerful, relaxing peace.

By this time I knew I'd had my fill of ecclesiastical buildings. My time was running out and I was also aware Andrew would soon return from his trip to the States and probably had every minute of my remaining sojourn planned in detail. I, on the other hand, wanted freedom of choice, so I made a list of places that interested me and I lost no time trying to fit them all in. Top of my list was the restored Windmill in Holgate – so the next day I walked from my house, a map clutched in my hand, to discover the residential road where it stood tall and imperious. First built in 1770, when it ground flour for the surrounding villages of York, it became redundant and then a ruin until it was finally restored in 2012. It was perched on a small mound at the top of a short flight of steps and gave a good view of the Minster and the York Wheel. The main body of the mill was a dull black and peppered with various small white windows at different levels; it had five huge sparkling, white-bladed sails that greeted me by turning slowly and was crowned by a bright white cap with a sharp finial on top. I stood and stared, open mouthed. What an impressive sight and I was so delighted I had at last seen it in all its glory.

My next port of call was York Cold War Bunker. If we had any such places in Devon, I knew nothing about them and I was keen to learn exactly what purpose they had served. Once again I was willing to walk as it was a dry, bright day and, using my trusty map, I discovered this chilling place halfway down a residential road in Acomb. It was, frankly, the last place one would expect to find such an important and sensitive nuclear shelter. A grass mound, a short flight of steps and a bomb-proof door were all that advertised this odd retreat. Not knowing quite what to do when I arrived, I politely waited outside until a young woman appeared, as if by magic, and ushered me in. I was told that between the 1960s and 1990s, atomic warfare became a real threat to our country. I know, as a young student, I had sported a CND badge and attended various sit-ins and marches in the hope that every civilised country in the world would outlaw nuclear war and, in return, Russia would do likewise. Atomic warfare had become a two-edged sword by this time; it may have ended World War II with a bomb on Hiroshima, but once produced and in ignorant hands, it could be used by any country that wanted to dominate the rest of the world. At that time the nation we were most fearful of was Communist Russia. So, all over the UK these secret bunkers were constructed in the hope that, if an atomic bomb *was* sent our way, key personnel could hole up in such places with sufficient provisions to last until such time as it was safe to emerge and fight off our aggressors. Whether this would ever have been a viable proposition is debatable. How could a select few be saved when these personnel would be aware they were abandoning their nearest and dearest to a horrible death?

I was taken ever-deeper underground and viewed the strategic communications system that was in place - this was global as well as national. Detailed maps were laid out and executive decisions could be taken as and when they became necessary. This mini war office looked chillingly bleak to me. I thanked the staff for their information but as soon as the blast proof door was opened once more, I took a deep breath of fresh air and walked quickly away. One fact I have learned in my life is that aggression breeds more aggression – never less – and with it comes fear and misunderstanding. At that moment all I wanted to do was get home to my cosy conservatory and make a comforting pot of tea.

Well, as I had swapped churches for windmills and nuclear bunkers, I decided my next quests would be more cultural. I had walked the walls of York, after overcoming my ridiculous fear of heights, quite a few times. I loved looking into the gardens of the Minster Clergy, trotting up and down steps on the ramparts and trying to work out that the brass sign *Jewbury,* set into the flagstones, was a sign of a long-lost ghetto. There was always something new to see, some view or angle of York I had never spied previously and, this time, I decided that two of the decorative gates – Micklegate and Monk Bar – were to be my next objective. I had noted both housed museums but usually, when I finally got to one or the other, I was either too tired to explore further or else they were due to close for the day. Now was my opportunity, I thought, before Andrew returned and commandeered my last days. I started with Micklegate Bar as that was the nearest and I had always considered it the most picturesque of all the gates. It was set on the London/York road so it would have been the most important entrance to the city, welcoming royal retinues as well as displaying, on the battlements, the gruesome severed heads of traitors and wrongdoers. I visited early one morning and had the place to myself. I learned about the gatekeepers, their families and their workaday lives. It was an interesting insight and I loved the small mundane anecdotes I learned.

The second museum was on the far side of York. I wandered under Bootham Bar, past the Minster down through Goodramgate to Monk Bar. This was the home of the Richard III Museum. Monk Bar was built in the fourteenth century and it was very different because this gatehouse still retained its working portcullis. I was especially interested in the tour we were given as, until that time I had always considered Richard III's life and death to have been shrouded in a mystery that had never been documented, or resolved, by historians. We now know the Welsh Tudors, to substantiate their fairly tenuous claim to the crown of England, vilified him as a murderer of his two young nephews in the Tower of London, and even depicted him as a hunchback in one of the few paintings we have of him. Strangely, to the people of York he was a hero – fighting bravely for his brother, the King, even though he had a spinal deformity which, on donning armour, must have caused him considerable pain. So we know, physically, he would have been fairly frail. These were dangerous times when plots and counter plots may have forced him to become a strong leader insisting on stern measures once these plots were discovered. This still doesn't answer why, on his brother's death, Richard went on to claim the throne of England, even though the country had two young, legitimate heirs – his own nephews. Possibly his advisors insisted on a strong leader and it may have been decided charismatic Richard was the only one for the job. This still begs the question: what happened to the two

Princes? And if, as seems likely, they *were* murdered – was it done on his instigation or without his knowledge, with him being forced to go along with it after the act had been committed? I had read he loved his wife dearly and was a great family man, but as that can never be proved one way or the other, I reserved judgement.

The museum also re-created a modern-day trial and we were asked, after being told a few sparse facts, to decide whether he was a capable, courageous and a beloved monarch or simply a cruel monster. The loyal people of York would have voted the former, but as he only ruled his kingdom for just two years and then was killed ignominiously at the Battle of Bosworth, the rest of us will never be convinced as to either argument. I exited the museum still with my mind fixed on times gone by when gloomy prisons, dank dungeons, beheading and murder were common occurrences if one was important enough. I carried on walking on the remaining ramparts until the walls ended abruptly at Peasholme Green. I wandered down the steps and decided to take the bus from The Stonebow and, luckily, was home in record time to be greeted by a long text that informed me Andrew was bored in the sun – I grimaced because we had suffered cold drizzle for the past two days – and was longing to return.

"Dying to see you, Munchkin. I keep imagining an afternoon in bed with you – no interruptions, no attending yet another beach picnic or making small talk with some important boor at a faculty shindig, where I only vaguely know my hosts, while trying to balance a plateful of indigestible canapés plus a large G&T. Might sound idyllic to you but can't wait to fold you in my arms and talk down-to-earth Anglo Saxon once more! Luv A xx"

Suddenly it was imperative to get the rest of my sightseeing out of the way. I remembered Andrew stressing he would very definitely *not* be escorting me to the JORVIK Viking Centre.

'If you only knew, darling, how the place is the top of everybody's "to-see" list. I have taken grandchildren, adults, pupils, my own kids and anyone else's offspring until I am sick of the sight and the smell of the place. This is the only time I'm opting out Jen, so you'll have to do it on your own.'

I had nodded solemnly, and promised myself that when he was off on one of his golfing days, I would sneak in and return home well-versed in Viking law, dress sense and pillage expertise that would surprise everyone with my depth of knowledge. Now was probably my last opportunity. I chose the next day: it being midweek, there would be less chance of disobedient children and distracted parents. I followed a party of Japanese students and we all clambered into what looked like outsize buckets, or doctored dodgem cars, and off we swung. It was fabulous! I listened intently to the commentary, sniffed the scents and marvelled at the dedication York had shown by preserving this unique past for future generations. The museum has been built over the site that was discovered by chance during some routine excavations. When they dug down they found the unbelievable Viking city of Jorvik as it had been over 1,000 years ago. It was intact, with houses, workshops, streets and backyards and included 40,000 tools, utensils and everyday artefacts as if they had only recently been used.

As we alighted from our mini-buckets I allowed the chattering students to go on and I slowed down to study the exhibits with care. There was so much to see and I darted from one glass wallcase to another, often returning for a second look. Finally, I came to an oblong glass cabinet that held a bleached skeleton. I was drawn to it like a magnet and a young girl, probably a student, was standing proprietarily nearby and asking everyone, as they passed along, if they would they like to know more. I nodded, but it appeared to upset the rest because they frowned and scuttled onwards immediately. My young mentor then began to quietly explain about the bones that had only recently been discovered.

It was an adult young male who was above average height for the period. His bones were straight and sturdy so he had obviously come from an affluent, well-fed family – even possibly a minor ruling-class family. Deep grooves on his wrists and ankles pointed to the fact that he had been imprisoned in later life and shackled – probably in irons. The students had come up with the theory that the lad may have been a prince who had been captured from some far-away land by the Romans, brought across the sea to Britain and then incarcerated in York. Maybe the Romans were confident of extracting a ransom in return for his release, but sadly he had died, fettered and imprisoned, instead. Whether the research team would be able to do some sort of DNA test to determine the colour of his skin or to pinpoint exactly where he had been born was a possibility but, after seeing the poor young man in a completely different light, I was so pleased I had stopped and listened to this history in the making. I stepped out into the sunshine after I was informed my Jorvik ticket would give me free entrance for a further year as well as allowing me to visit Barley Hall – so I made my way towards Coffee Yard, off Stonegate, to take advantage of this promise.

Barley Hall is an authentic medieval townhouse nestling right in the oldest part of the city. It once belonged to the monks of Nostell Priory as well as the Mayor of York. I felt I was going back in time as I walked through an arch and arrived at a large courtyard. I could imagine messengers galloping in, thrusting their horse's reins to a waiting servant, and then making their way to report to their master. The house was almost hidden away but, once I entered the yard, there it stood looking as it must have done at the time of Richard III and, later, the Tudors. It had been restored beautifully – exposing the timber framing and displaying the typical windows of the period. The Great Hall felt rather bleak and empty to my untrained eye, but had a magnificent high ceiling and, as I walked from room to room, I could almost feel the ladies, with long flowing robes and intricate headgear, drifting around me.

The next day I brought to a close my Grand Tour by taking another look at York's Treasurer' s House. It was such a weird and wonderful National Trust House, with its thirteen rooms all aping the style of four different centuries and, as Frank Green was a bachelor, it was never used as a home – ever. Maybe he wanted it to be a stage setting to enable him to impress his friends, or business acquaintances, with his perfect taste or his obvious fortune. It took him thirty years to turn it into the perfect venue with which to display his acumen with various types of antique furniture. My favourite was the great pendulum clock that was so tall it swung between two floors. We were told Frank Green was one of the few experts in this field of collecting but, reading some of the notes he wrote to his staff, I realised he must have been a crusty, domineering master into the bargain. They were expected to obey his every whim, with him even insisting studs were placed on the floor of each room to ensure the servants replaced every item of furniture in exactly the same spot that he had decreed it should go. That would be after they had cleaned under, over or around it, I suspect! What a ridiculous fusspot.

On this visit I did not go to the cellars. For some reason the Treasurer's House had been built right on the site of a busy Roman road and when, in 1953, a workman walked into the cellars, he suddenly saw Roman soldiers marching through one wall and disappearing into another. When questioned closely he admitted he had seen no feet. People said 'trust him to allow his imagination to run away with him' but actually this severely shocked his questioners because, as experts, they were aware the Roman road would have been a few feet lower than the cellar's paving - so it was highly likely he had been telling the truth! As neither Andrew nor I felt any ghostly vibrations, when we had intently stood below stairs and tried to conjure up something similar, I decided the sensible option would be to visit the tearoom for a light lunch before going on to my last port of call.

This was the Merchant Adventurers' Hall in Fossgate – the very heart of the City. York has always been interwoven with "snickleways" and odd, ancient corners so it was strange Andrew had failed to take me to see such an old, important and picturesque building. It had been swiftly erected between 1357 and 1361 and was used as a merchants' trading floor or a modern-day stock exchange. One cannot liken these guilds to the Trade Unions of today as they were far more important. This one building controlled most of the City's commerce within York and, through the River Ouse, the huge River Humber and the port of Hull, enabled them to trade with most of northern Europe. It made its own laws which all the tradesmen in the city were forced to obey, and would have operated a "closed shop" policy.

I walked in through the Fossgate entrance and under a colourful Coat of Arms that showed two winged horses placed on either side of a shield surmounted by a warrior's helmet. I noticed decorations of scrolls of vines, with bunches of grapes, on the wooden timber frames outside the building as well as the surrounding gardens which, I later learned, were placed at the disposal of the people of York after World War I.

The Hall was at its most prosperous in medieval times and I was told it is the best, and oldest, example in England of a timber-built Guildhall with an Undercroft and Chapel. The prime aim of the Guild was to promote business, dispense charity and offer religious succour. I discovered three main rooms as I wandered around. First of all was the impressive towering Great Hall with its massive high beams. The Undercroft, now hung with Guild banners, was used as an Alms House for the sick and poor and the Chapel represented the close religious ties between the church and crafts. There were collections of silverware and jewellery and they had an *Evidence Chest* from the 1300s that would have stored titled deeds. The Chapel was decorated in light colours and felt amazingly restful and different from the other two halls.

As I emerged into the evening air close to the modern Coppergate Shopping Centre I was swiftly brought down to earth once more by the reality of the twenty-first century. Within a few short weeks I had completed something akin to a Grand Tour that young men of noble birth were expected to take as a part of their education before they settled down, back in England, to ruling their Family Estates. In a very minor way I had emulated the footsteps of people like Lord Byron or Jane Austen's *Darcy* by wandering around ruins, museums and romantic churches – albeit in England and not in Venice, the Rhineland or Switzerland – for no better reason than I had excessive time on my hands, an insatiable curiosity and nothing better to do. I probably now had the best credentials of any tour guide in the whole of Yorkshire, I surmised. How sad was that?

As I walked past Fenwick's departmental store my mobile phone, which I had just remembered to switch on, returned to life with two text messages. The first was from Jess in Taunton reminding me I owed her a call and the second was from Andrew.

"Where ARE u? Phoned but no ans. I'm BACK n came straight round. Left parcel in hall but rather have given it in person along wiv crushin bear hug. Oh God have I missed u, Jen! LUV A. x x"

My heart turned a somersault as I read his terse message a second time. I had finished my educational crash programme just in time, it seemed; and now my self-esteem needed cosseting, indulging and caressing to make up for our separation, I considered. Immediately all thought of the aloof response I had been planning, as and when

Andrew finally decided to show his face once more, disappeared as mist fades in morning sunshine. I hurried home busily planning meals in my head, which clothes I should wear to tempt and beguile him while trying to remember every little anecdote I had saved up to tell him. Such was his special magic that I was unable to resist him. It had always welded us together like indestructible magnets ever since we first met as teenagers. The strength of it meant I had always wanted to be by his side, to bask in his love, be accepted in his life and remain with him – forever. I can fully understand why well-meaning friends always felt obliged to point out my stupidity or, more correctly, *our* stupidity. *Their* common sense would prevent it ever happening to them and it was beyond their comprehension that I had allowed myself to be duped and dumped – as they labelled it – and yet still want to return to my lover for more. Did they never think that, when they sternly insisted I stop being pathetic, pull myself together and tell Andrew to buzz off, that I had never tried to make myself do exactly that during those past few months? After much deep thought I eventually came to the conclusion that this intangible "oneness", this strange honesty and integrity we had towards one another other, and had always had – where veneer and pretence have never existed – was what went to make up the steadfast cohesion that ensured we were in love and would always stay in love. This was what made us very special. In other words, we were unable to resist whatever they were condemning us for: and, truthfully, neither of us wanted to.

I walked down the road until I suddenly caught sight of Andrew's car parked in our drive. I ran the rest of the way and, on turning the key impatiently in the lock, I found him sitting at the bottom of the stairs. I obediently bent down to pick up the parcel at his feet.

'Leave it until tomorrow, love. I can only manage another hour here and I want to spend it holding you tightly,' he said with a smile. He drew me into the sitting room. I grinned contentedly back and swiftly went off to forage for some food. I returned with a pile of cheese and crackers, as well as grabbing a couple of glasses of wine, and sank down on the settee so we could sit tightly curled up together for the next hour, munching contentedly and watching the evening news. Suddenly all was fine in my small, and very ordinary, world.

Chapter 24

*

The next morning I awoke early, probably due to anticipation and excitement. It may have been rather childish but life had somehow become so much rosier since I was no longer alone. I fingered the parcel, still on the floor in the hall, as I ran down the stairs, but decided I would leave it alone and the surprise might be all the nicer. I wondered what on earth Andrew had brought me all the way from the States and then wondered some more why Fay hadn't noticed the extra luggage. We hadn't got around to planning anything for the next day, but as the last thing Andrew had said as he had spun off in the car was 'See you, darling' I reckoned it was sure to be somewhere nice.

I took it that his enthusiasm to be off exploring together the next day meant he would have thought of something exceptional. I dreamed of the sea, some romantic castle or a stately home that maybe Drew hadn't visited before. It didn't matter to me in the slightest – I would be certain to enjoy it, no matter where we went. So the next morning I prepared my meal, singing along to a Lesley Garrett aria as I buttered my toast and then settled down in the conservatory to a leisurely breakfast while I waited for Drew to come and join me in a final cup of coffee. I waited, looking around the garden, noticing it had suddenly taken on its winter mantle without me even being aware. The year was rapidly drawing to a close and I would soon be heading down south. Today I decided to let the future take care of itself while I would try and live for the moment. Maybe my turn for happiness was just around the corner. I went on humming along with Lesley as I waited impatiently.

Eventually the pot of coffee cooled and I sighed as I arose to do the washing up. I wondered why he was so late. Lesley Garrett had just finished telling us her name was Mimi from *La Bohème* as I peered up the street in an effort to spot Andrew's car. I went out to the garage to put some bed linen into the washing machine. I might as well make use of the extra time I had been given and do some proper work because, in all probability, I might be otherwise engaged for the next couple of days. I smiled at the thought. I went to the cupboard to get out a large Thermos flask. Perhaps Andrew might prefer some soup in this cooler climate. I was aware it would have been so much warmer in California. I searched through the fridge to find something tempting to make up a decent picnic and then dug deep in the freezer to defrost a joint that we could cook later. Still I waited.

After that I sat down with a book I had started to read the previous day and tried to concentrate but I didn't do very well. Eventually I put the lunchtime news on and tried not to wonder where he had got to. Maybe something serious had happened and he was unable to ring me. I discarded that thought. He would *always* find time to ring me. But he wouldn't if he was ill himself, I realised. Then the next unbidden thought was that maybe something had happened on the way home the previous night. He had left me with a grin and a promise. What's to say he didn't have an accident on his way back home - some idiot driving badly or a lout drunk at the wheel? I went back to the window and looked frantically towards the corner houses – willing him to drive merrily down the street.

I knew I shouldn't ring either his mobile phone or his home number. Then I pulled myself together as I remembered *my* telephone was ex-directory so my number would be untraceable. I walked into the kitchen and dialled immediately. Andrew's quiet Cornish voice, so noticeable over the telephone, answered within seconds. I silently replaced the receiver, collected my jacket and bag and, in a sudden seething rage, walked out of the house. I caught a bus into town and went and saw a gory film that was all the rage that week. I cannot remember the title or the plot but, coldly incensed, I watched it to the bitter end and then stormed home to fling myself on the bed – the bed where we had made constant, joyful love so often. There were no messages on my answerphone I noted as I walked indoors, so no mitigating circumstances had prevented Andrew from making the short, promised journey. Later that evening I tipped the leg of lamb, which I had taken out of the freezer with such cheerfulness that morning, into the bin and made myself a scrappy cheese sandwich. The telephone still remained ominously silent. I could have done with any form of communication at that time – Dee's light tone with Paul's rambling comments on the side, Meryl's family gossip or even Jess's plaintive grumbles would have relieved the acrid anger that lay heavily on my heart and scorched my spirit. Eventually I dragged myself wearily to bed – not to sleep – *that* eluded me. I lay for hours watching the slanting lights of passing traffic until it seemed the whole world finally fell into a deep slumber.

The next morning I was up just as early; but this time I made my breakfast with grim determination and finished it just as quickly. I packed up two rolls and a bottle of water, shoved them into my small backpack and was out of the house by mid-morning. Dorothy waved from her front bedroom window; I didn't allow it to deter my footsteps, sending a sketchy salute back instead. Andrew had often talked about Pickering, I remembered, and I considered it during the long night. He had mentioned a castle, a museum and an exceptional church. In passing, he told me the small, quiet town also boasted a famous steam railway that George Stephenson had built. One could travel, right across the North York Moors, the eighteen miles to Grosmont which housed various locomotives and antique carriages; he said the line passed restored nostalgic stations as well as Goathland where one could alight and visit *Heartbeat* locations, if one was so inclined. That day I was *not* inclined. My bleak mood decided me to keep my visit short and the museum seemed as good a choice as any. I had studied my bus timetable and knew that to get to Pickering I would have to change at Malton bus station. I had visited it recently and knew it wasn't too far away.

I felt cold and damp as I queued in the draughty station for a bus to take me towards the Moors. I wondered if I would regret my spontaneous jaunt as I huddled deep in my warm anorak, but shortly the bus trundled in and we all surged forward. I gave my destination and was showing my bus pass as my mobile beeped. I sat down rapidly and answered it. I hate to annoy other passengers with my trivial conversations so I answered it extra quietly.

'Where are you, darling?' interrupted Andrew's blithe voice.

'Just left Malton bus station – in the rain,' I replied shortly. 'Why?'

'Well I have just turned up at a deserted house with all sorts of plans and you have scarpered, by the looks of it.'

'No,' I replied evenly. '*You* were supposed to come yesterday – and you didn't – so I decided to suit myself for once, and go out on my own.' There was a brief silence.

'Oh. Sorry, darling, yesterday was hopeless. She found me oodles of work to do – cutting the grass, cutting back shrubs that she deemed were overgrown, pushing the weekly shopping trolley while she whirled around like a Dervish and, finally, getting her car seen to.'

'Yes, you sounded run off your feet when I telephoned yesterday,' I retorted curtly.

'Oh, was that you? I wondered who was ringing our number. I was just sitting down to eat a late lunch when it rang,' he answered easily. 'What a shame, I was determined to be free all day today. I made all sorts of excuses and hoped we could spend the whole day together. I have even managed to get the evening off – I'm supposed to be going to a men-only Rotary night – but preferred to book a rather nice meal in the evening, just for us. Oh well, never mind.'

'Well, I'll be in Pickering shortly – so what's to stop you getting in your nice warm car and joining me?' I asked sarcastically.

'Mmm,' he said judicially, 'well Pickering's quite a journey from York.'

'Not half as far, or as difficult, as it has been for me,' I said, even more bluntly.

'And it also sounds as if you are in a bad mood anyway,' he went on.

I didn't deny or agree with him but I must have sounded depressed because he ended the call pretty sharply after that, which made me feel even more aggrieved – as if it had all been *my* fault which, to my mind, was far from the truth. I arrived at the Beck Isle Museum and was surprised to find it a pleasant Regency mansion set close to a bubbling stream. The sun came out as I walked towards it and I saw what a beautiful place it would be in the summer.

I walked in and was greeted by two friendly staff. The building, which looked so compact on the outside, contained nearly thirty rooms, I was told. I set out to explore them at once. Anything from the past two hundred years was often displayed, it seemed. I wandered around various fascinating rooms until I arrived at the Working Print Room. A jolly chap had just finished explaining the old methods while I watched sheets of print roll off the Columbian Press of 1854. In the sudden silence I heard a familiar voice ask if there was a particular lady visitor wandering around. Within minutes I was joined by a smiling Andrew who stood close behind me, wrapping his arms gently around my middle, which allowed me to lean against him while he asked all sorts of intelligent questions about the magnificent, huge printing machine being demonstrated. The museum was pleasantly quiet that day; this allowed us to walk around, hand in hand, looking at a crammed chemist's shop, a very masculine barber's, a village store which was close to a pub – complete with a landlady in a perky bonnet dispensing ale. We stared into the usual dark, Victorian parlour with all its fussy tassels and frills and then walked into a nursery before finding the hardware store and finally the blacksmith's workplace. Andrew looked down at me with a quizzical smile.

'Still fed up with me?' he demanded.

I shook my head and stuck my tongue out. I hadn't completely forgiven him but, as usual, his delightful proximity meant happiness descended on me once more and, within minutes, we were chattering again.

I imagined we would go and picnic in the lovely grounds around the house and was just wondering how far two pâté rolls and a bag of crisps would satisfy our hunger, when Andrew mentioned he had other ideas. I was then hustled into the car to make the short journey back to Pickering Castle. He flashed his English Heritage card at the jovial gate custodian and, with a laugh and joke, we made our way up the slope and into the castle grounds. I was very impressed – the site consisted of a huge mound and various ruined buildings which were encircled by almost intact curtain walls and towers. Andrew dragged me up towards the twelfth-century Castle Keep until he espied a sheltered corner. He then spread out a car rug and this enabled us to sit in comfort and eat our food. He had refused my bottle of water, but after searching his pockets, he brought out two apples and a couple of rather squashed buns which he added to my rather sparse haul. We tucked in immediately. I then sat and looked out over the town, contentedly munching, while he gave me a potted history of the place.

'As you can see it's an ancient market town that happened to be named after a King called *Peredurus*. The story goes he lost a precious ring in the river one day and, in anger, blamed a nearby serving girl. Later that day his entourage were fishing when they caught a pike. Just by chance, it had the glittering King's ring in its mouth. The King immediately apologised, forgave the girl and, shortly after, married her. Hence the river was forever caller *Pike-ring* from that day onwards. And, if you believe that, Jenny, you will believe anything!' He said with a grin. 'But Pickering also has another claim to fame and if you eat up, darling, I will show it to you as soon as we have found a decent café offering a pot of tea.'

We made our way back towards our cheery guard to bid him goodbye. Andrew urged me not to stay long in the cosy café he found in the centre of the town or the light would go before he could show me his final discovery. I immediately pushed my cup away and joined him as we walked towards the Parish Church of St Peter & St Paul. Inside I was stunned by what I saw. I was told originally a Saxon church had stood on the site and I noted that although the nave and windows were obviously Norman perpendicular, many of the side arches looked a rounded Saxon to me. But what surprised me was what I saw spread all over the walls. There were dozens of colourful, lively wall paintings from about the fifteenth century. I had often heard tell that, at the time, few in a congregation could read or write and it was the perfect way for a vicar to teach the Bible to his simple parishioners. This was extraordinary! All *these* walls were swarming with religious and contemporary figures – in the brightest of colours. I learned that, at the stringent command of Henry VIII, most churches had destroyed their idolatrous images and Roman Catholic rites to embrace a more sober religion, of which he had made himself head. Most churches, in fear of desecration or destruction, had either hidden their icons, statues and treasures or - as in Pickering church - had whitewashed the offending walls and paid lip service to the King's commands. Thank goodness, many years later the irreplaceable work had been discovered and restored to all its former glory. I wandered around looking at a jumble of stories showing King Herod, Christ hanging from a cross, a saint – I could only guess at Sebastian – with arrows peppering his naked body, John the Baptist's gory head resting on a table and a virile St George thrusting his spear into the fiery dragon's mouth. What amazing tales would have been told in that church!

The light began to fade and it was time to leave. We had a quick, satisfying meal at a Chinese restaurant on the way home and arrived there full of delicious food and wine. Andrew pushed me up the stairs, where we undressed languidly and fell on the bed. Normally we would have both taken a lazy shower but time was running out for us. I had worked out Andrew would probably have to leave by eleven o'clock at the latest so that would give us just over an hour. I hated this timed, robotic loving. It was a far call from the beginning of the year when we had all night and all day to enjoy our feelings for each other.

I was suddenly startled by Andrew saying, 'Gosh you suddenly look very thin, Jenny. Have you been on a diet, darling?'

I shook my head emphatically. He began to explore my bony angles and I pretended to squirm away from him. Relaxing back on the pillows seemed to accentuate my slimness and, feeling slightly awkward, I pulled the duvet over us both and, with a smile, made him forget my shortcomings. Actually he had accurately summed what had been bothering me for weeks. He was right, I *was* shedding weight at a rate of kilos, it seemed. I was not one to study myself in a mirror but the simple fact that all my trousers needed constant hitching up every time I moved had begun to worry me also. To compensate I had eaten as much fattening fare as I could cram in – usually stuffing myself with cheese and biscuits followed by hot thick chocolate – last thing at night but nothing seemed to make much difference, the weight was slipping off me still. It had become so noticeable that I shunned the bathroom scales next to the bath, not wanting to prove my worst suspicions.

I made Andrew forget his earlier comments and, as he calmed his breathing beside me, I asked if I could open my present from America. He allowed me to slip downstairs and retrieve it, saying, 'Don't expect anything fantastic, Jenny, it's only some odds and ends that took my eye when I was wandering around San Diego and La Jolla.'

I opened the neatly wrapped package and found lots of smaller ones inside. There was a pretty little bracelet with half a dozen cavorting dolphins hanging from it, a beautifully tooled leather belt which, Andrew pointed out, had the initials *J&A* intertwined around it in a pattern, a deceptively simple cameo brooch and a tiny silver heart on a fine chain. I turned to him in wonder, 'How on earth did you manage to buy all these things?' I asked.

'I just made sure I took myself off for walks: no one else was interested, so I often explored alone.' From that I surmised he must have spent a lot of time, in between the fun beach picnics and evening parties, just thinking of how *we* would have enjoyed ourselves - maybe he had begun collecting these gifts to stave off boredom. 'There's two more, darling, so hurry up and open them because I must soon be off.'

One was a small penguin flashlight, perfect in every detail, and the other was a miniscule line drawing of a pelican. 'I got the penguin in San Diego Zoo. Couldn't resist him,' he said with a grin, flashing it on and off in the darkened bedroom. 'The other one I drew especially for you. I was amazed at the vast number of pelicans that inhabit the whole coastline of California. They perch anywhere - one sees them sitting silently, huddled together on palings, under decking, on wharves and marinas, in fact, anywhere a small boat will land its catch you will see them patiently waiting. They are about four feet long, but it is only when they spy a fish under water that they rise up and dive at great speed – like a Japanese Kamikaze pilot – and one sees their wing span can be over six feet. The speed of their dive can stun a fish six feet under the water. That's what I tried to catch for you – a huge bird hurtling out of the sky and diving deep under the sea. Ashore once more, they filter the water out of their huge, cavernous throats and swallow the fish head first and whole. They then calmly re-join their mates to await their next meal. Sorry, darling, I meant to put this in a miniature frame for you but I haven't had time.'

I studied the minute drawing and clasped in to me. This thumbnail silhouette, so lovingly executed, was exquisite and almost made up for Andrew going to America and leaving me.

I slipped on my dressing gown and walked with him to the front door.

'I will see you tomorrow and tomorrow and tomorrow,' he stated extravagantly. 'I promise to feed you up and make you bonnie again,' he said, hugging me tightly. I wanted to say it only needed him to return to me for good and my weight problem would disappear. But I was frightened that he would give an evasive answer; so I smiled as best I could and waved him off.

****

The next morning I returned to reality with a bump. Robin telephoned to give me the date he would come up and help me with the move. He told me he would be going to stay with his new girlfriend, Ailsa, in Scotland over Christmas and he wanted to settle me back in Devon before he left. That meant I would have to find a solution to where I could live while I was searching for a suitable property to buy. Robin had already vetoed our old home as a refuge and I understood and respected his reservations regarding us living together again. In truth I dreaded it more than he did. I would repay the mortgage I had so blithely taken out, but it was only now - when I realised my time in York was limited - that I faced the seriousness of my precarious situation. The purchaser's money paid for number 13 was limited: it would repay the mortgage and only leave a relatively small amount over to purchase a place I could call my own. I would be able to afford nothing extravagant since I had given the bungalow over to Robin and I would end up with only the money Rose had left me in her Will. I wondered if a one-bedroomed flat would be within my price range. I desperately hoped it would.

I explained to Andrew, when he arrived mid-morning, that I would be leaving two weeks before Christmas. He paled and went very quiet. 'Do you want me to remove my stuff immediately?' he pensively asked.

'Please don't,' I answered in panic. I was aware how stupid it sounded but, while I was surrounded by his shaving gear in the bathroom, his clothes in bedroom cupboards and drawers, could lie back and listen to his CDs in the Rumpus room and sit curled up in his comfy garden chairs in the conservatory, I could pretend none of this awful nightmare was beginning to happen. He must have seen the blind panic pass across my face because he gently agreed to all my ridiculous demands.

Instead he began to make brisk plans of places we would revisit again. The words '*before* you go' hung in the air but neither of us acknowledged them as we feverishly pretended all was well and hid our heads, as only naive lovers will do, in the sand. I immediately decided then and there I would enjoy every last minute with Andrew and only when I returned home each night would I start planning and packing up to leave.

So for the next three weeks I was taken to all the well-known coastal resorts again and then on to lesser tourist haunts – like the tough little fishing village of Staithes; neat Runswick Bay with its thatched cottages, many of which were surrounded by picket-fenced gardens; Sandsend where we walked along a meandering, sluggish brook and I coaxed, and snapped, a beaming smile out of Andrew as we crossed the simple bridge. Of course I wouldn't have been allowed to leave before we went, once more, to Robin Hood's Bay. We swung down to the shoreline hand in hand, hunting around the rock pools at low tide, before huffing and puffing our way back up through the steep pathways to devour a huge meal at the top – as a just reward. It was a lovely, exhilarating day with us both living in the present, trying to blank out our future.

And then – suddenly – two events happened in succession. The first was something I could have done without. Ten days before I was due to leave I did my usual trek to my out-of-town supermarket. If Andrew had been around he would have accompanied me, but he was pressure-washing his conservatory roof that morning so, resigned, I walked down to Blossom Street and took the *Park & Ride* bus to the outskirts of York. As shopping is not my most favourite task, I bustled around and packed the two big bags with all speed. Outside, in the car park, there were half a dozen hooded youths amusing themselves by tossing scraps of bread for the gulls. The birds were wheeling and shrieking above the heads of the shoppers and everyone was ducking and scattering in the melee. I quickly pushed past and dashed to catch the bus back to town. I had my bus pass in my pocket along with my house keys, so it was only when I entered my kitchen to empty all my food out on the worktops that I came to the sudden realisation my purse was missing. I panicked, rushed back to the front path, even looking up and down the road, before madly searching once again through obviously empty bags – and even my pockets. With a sinking sensation in the pit of my stomach I imagined I knew what had happened. Immediately I thought of the rowdy lads in the supermarket car park. Could they have been distracting shoppers' attention while they rifled their bags, I wondered?

I would not have been so distraught if there had not been such an excessive amount of money in it that particular week. I always pay any bills by debit card, but only that week I had withdrawn £500 from my bank in order to pay Robin cash for the hire of the van and any petrol costs he would incur when he came to move my stuff. I had stashed it all away neatly in the back of my bulging purse. With a thumping heart I dialled the bank who, in turn, cancelled my cards. I also explained that I would be leaving the area shortly and they agreed to send replacement cards as quickly as possible. I then telephoned the police and reported it to them. Finally, I texted Andrew and told him how stupid I had been. He offered to come as soon as he was through with his tasks. I tried to eat a sandwich for lunch but I was too distraught and only managed a cup of tea.

Half an hour later my telephone rang stridently. I snatched it up and heard Robin's puzzled voice on the end of the line.

'Have you lost anything?' he asked.

'Yes,' I said breathlessly, 'my purse. But how on earth did you know that?'

'I have just had some bus station on to me. They sounded as baffled as me when I told them I lived in Devon but they said if I knew a Mrs Jennifer Mackenzie, to tell her they have her purse in their office. It was handed in by a lady passenger on a *Park & Ride* bus.' He then went on to give me their number and, sounding extremely amused, rang off.

I fell on the phone and dialled their number. The man who answered told me he had my purse on his desk and he would keep it for me. I asked if it was empty. He said yes apart from a few coppers but all my cards were intact and even a doctor's prescription was neatly tucked inside. I asked him, hesitantly, if he would unzip the back.

'Oh my God! There's dozens of notes in here. I'll lock it in the safe for you.' I thanked him profusely with the greatest of relief. I then said I would be down as soon as soon as possible.

Andrew arrived shortly afterwards and, with a laugh and a playful slap on my behind, took me out to Askham Bar to retrieve it. I asked the name of the lady and the driver who had so thoughtfully handed my purse in, but unfortunately, they only knew the driver. I handed an envelope with a letter of thanks to him and some money, to thank him. These two people had renewed my faith in the niceness of the majority of people once more.

The next happening restored my faith in folk yet again. Jess rang from Taunton to ask when I would be returning. She said she was dying to see me for a good girly natter. I must have sounded depressed because she asked, 'I suppose you will be going back to stay in the bungalow?' I admitted I had no idea where I would go – probably to a B&B – it was all in the lap of the gods.

'Oh no you don't, young lady. You can stay with me any time.' I stressed it might be some while before I found a suitable property. She immediately told me not to be so silly – that was what friends were for. I ended up crying quietly down the phone while she tried to comfort me. Until that moment I had no idea how much distress I was endeavouring to hide – from myself as well as the outside world.

****

During that last week *I* took Andrew to the Bar Convent as, surprisingly, he had never really noticed it. I now showed him a peaceful calm corner where one could escape a tumultuous world as we sat in the pleasant garden and had a simple lunch. We went back again and again to the Minster, as well as the Railway Museum, the City Art Gallery and Fairfax House. I couldn't bear to return to the Castle Museum because it brought back the bitter memory of the afternoon Andrew finally left me; but I was delighted to roam around the romantic ruins of St Mary's again and wander along through the Museum Gardens to the Kings Manor. We ambled through the Shambles with dozens of other visitors and made the dash over to Castle Howard. Andrew *had* solemnly promised me a day out at Chatsworth but time beat us to it. Suddenly the next day was to be our last. I was given one night in which to decide where I would like to return to most. I chose Knaresborough as the deep gorge reminded me of the Dordogne and the windows reminded me of typical Yorkshire humour.

The next day dawned cold but bright. Andrew called for me as I was washing the breakfast dishes. Whilst I was getting ready he filched an extra cup of coffee and lounged in our bedroom watching me dress. Knaresborough looked lovely in the wintry sunshine and Andrew tucked my arm through his after parking the car in the usual spot and walking through the town. We had chosen a non-market day, so instead of bustling stallholders lustily shouting their wares, the square was empty. We visited The Lavender Rooms and had coffee over the oldest chemist's shop in England. Then, for fun, we took it in turns to sit on a bench next to a full size bronze replica of *Blind Jack*. Born John Metcalf in 1717, he contracted smallpox at the age of six and lost his sight. This did not stop him becoming an accomplished fiddler, but he was most famous for the turnpike roads he constructed at that time. His statue depicted him with a tight-fitting waistcoat, buckled belt, a coat and high boots – with his inimitable hat on his head. He was cradling a measuring wheel against his right arm. Andrew took a snap of him sitting next to me and ready to chat. I was also wearing high black boots as well as leggings and in the photo we could easily be compatriots.

From there we braved the chill and walked through the Castle Gateway to get the best view in Knaresborough. With the Castle on our right we looked down on the deep gorge and the River Nidd flowing far beneath us and we made our way down towards it and strolled through Waterside and under the viaduct, admiring the elegant black-and-white houses as we went. We walked up to the upper town and the shops, where we meandered around looking in windows. Suddenly I espied a heavy gold Celtic antique ring, which I pointed out to Andrew. He dragged me inside to try it on. I think that particular day he would have given anything to make up for what he was putting me through. Possibly he felt an expensive trinket was a small gift to offer. Sadly it was far too big and heavy for me and, due to its intricate design, there was no way it could be altered. I tried to cheer him up by demanding to see every one of those painted, quirky "Town Windows" that Knaresborough is so famous for. Hand in hand we walked up and down a myriad of streets and narrow alleyways to spot as many as possible. It wasn't only windows but false doorways that beckoned a passer-by, giving the illusion of a colourful town within an already colourful town. I tried to blot out any thoughts that I might never pass this way again as we stood staring up at zoo animals apparently glaring out of windows, Blind Jack entertaining us with his fiddle and a Royalist Cavalier aiming his rifle towards a Roundhead leaning out of the window beneath him. It was a brilliant way to end my sojourn in the north and I turned, impetuously, to thank Andrew for his thoughtfulness.

As a final gesture, probably in a last-ditch attempt towards fattening me up, he had booked an early meal in an elegant French restaurant in Harrogate. I felt a tad underdressed as we were shown to our table but I soon forgot these reservations as the most delicious food was brought to us. Andrew plied me with food and drink as if it was the Last Supper. Maybe, to him, it was!

Regardless of the delectable food, it was obvious he wanted to return home – and to bed. The night had almost turned into the early morning before he reluctantly left. I have no idea what excuse he gave Fay on his return, or even if she noticed his absence; but I watched him, distraught and crying, as he drove away in his car. I stood with my arm raised until he passed out of sight before trudging back upstairs to a tumbled bed where I lay sleepless and chilled until morning finally arrived.

Chapter 25

*

I tumbled wearily out of bed and tried to sort out the final, last-minute packing. Robin planned to arrive around lunchtime. He was determined he would only stay one night and wanted all my goods and chattels packed up and waiting. I had left only one bed made up, which enabled me to strip the other and tidy everything away for removal. Luckily our third bed had been on order and I had been able to cancel it, thereby avoiding another expensive bill. The fitted furniture was staying as part of the deal I had made with the purchasers. I had offered the washing machine, dryer, dishwasher and fridge/freezer to Andrew and, after asking Fay whether she wanted them – and her ascertaining they were almost brand new – he told me she would be delighted to accept them. I was appalled at her insensitive attitude. In *her* place I would have been adamant they would have had no place in either my kitchen or utility room – even if they were relegated to the local tip! Obviously her scruples were different from mine...

Robin arrived quietly at midday. He parked neatly in front of the garage and I showed him the boxes I would be taking. I saw him assessing the racks in the garage that held all sorts of mechanical aids, tins of paint and even some children's toys. In the corner were the washing machine and dryer, along with two fishing rods and, hanging on pegs, some outdoor jackets. He dismantled the smaller television in the Rumpus room but I told him to leave the large one in the sitting room as well as the stand full of CDs and DVDs. I pointed out the neat little table and two chairs in the conservatory were mine but not the garden chairs. I curtly told him everything in the garden shed was to stay. I think he was relieved to know he wouldn't have to manhandle any of the kitchen's heavy machinery and I had packed up most of the newly purchased cutlery, glassware, crockery, pots and pans which I had placed on top of the bed linen to save any damage. All my clothes had been neatly crammed into the original suitcases I had brought with me – all that was left in the wardrobes and drawers belonged to Andrew. I noted Robin deliberately never touched any cupboards or drawers; he stayed well away from the attic where we had stored all sorts of belongings and even looked slightly uncomfortable sitting on any of the furniture. I apologised that I would have to leave him and dash to the local shops in order to buy the food I needed to feed us until the next morning.

I arrived back to find half the van already stacked high with boxes. Somehow, on his own, Robin had managed to dismantle and load one of the double beds as well as the mattress. We beavered away and broke the back of the job until I insisted we stop for a meal. I laid out a spread of cold meats and salad on the kitchen table and we took it back on trays to the sitting room where we ate – both staring at the television. Neither of us said very much. I am sure we were both deep in our own thoughts.

After watching some mindless comedy, which I think neither of us understood nor enjoyed, I made us both a mug of hot chocolate and suggested an early night. As there was now only one bed available I fully expected to share it. Robin soon put me in my place by saying he would rather not. When I scoffed at his embarrassment he muttered, 'I don't think Ailsa would be too keen.'

This, in turn, made *me* feel extremely awkward; I grabbed a pillow and took it downstairs, along with my dressing gown and a blanket, and curled up on the sofa. So my last night in York was an uncomfortable experience and I was certainly up at the crack of dawn the next morning, if only to stretch my back and feel human once more. After a sketchy breakfast we carried out all the large furniture and packed it tightly in the borrowed van and then I did a final sweep round and collected all my small hoard of specially loved objects, like pictures, photographs and books, and Robin was finally able to seal the last box. I made some sandwiches and a flask of coffee because, knowing him of old, I guessed he wouldn't want to stop for an elaborate meal on the return journey.

He came running down the stairs just as I was silently saying goodbye to my house and all the dreams I had invested in it. I was trying not to cry and turned to him with a wry smile.

'You've forgotten some toiletries in the bathroom,' he said abruptly.

I told him they would be staying and he didn't comment. I knew, from what he had seen, that Robin was certain Andrew and I were still living together. He had deliberately made a point of not looking too closely at anything in my house. I had also told him, as well as all my relations and friends – mainly because I felt such an absolute idiot - the very moment Andrew had left me; but the evidence in front of him pointed to a different scenario. Now I was too tired to disabuse him and, anyway, it was unimportant.

On leaving number 13 for the very last time I stood on the front porch and texted Andrew. It was short and to the point. I told him the house was his and his removal men were welcome to clear out the rest of his stuff in the bedrooms, attic, sitting room, kitchen, garage and shed. He was welcome to anything I had left. I said my keys were at the bottom of the stairs and asked him to return the two sets to the estate agent. I then pulled the front door shut behind me for the last time and climbed up into the van. Suddenly I remembered Dorothy – in my rush to leave I had forgotten her and she had been one of the few people in this northern town I could call a friend. I put my hand on Robin's arm and asked him to wait a few minutes and then ran along to her house. She answered the door immediately – as if she had been waiting. I clasped her to me and whispered my thanks.

I ran to the waiting van and climbed back aboard and, suddenly, we were off. No other neighbours saw our departure apart from Dorothy, who stood by her front gate and waved us on our way. I looked back at her gaunt figure as she stood watching us, until she disappeared round the curve in the road. I settled back and watched intently as the familiar streets and landmarks flashed by; soon we were on the outskirts of the town and I tried to talk, as it would be a long journey. I asked Robin about the purse incident. What on earth had happened? He grinned sardonically, explaining how he had been rushing through a snack when the telephone rang asking if he knew of a Mrs J Mackenzie. All policemen are cagey about giving any information so he replied warily. What he found most puzzling was why anyone wanted to discuss me – with him. It soon became clear, when the transport officer explained, but then Robin surprised *them* by mentioning he actually lived roughly three hundred miles away, in Devon. I went on to tell Robin how my purse had been stuffed with notes to pay for this journey, and how shocked they had been when I asked them to investigate and found every one inside the zipped compartment of my purse.

Suddenly my mobile phone bleeped deep in my bag. I fished it out and looked at the message. It was from Andrew and was the first one of many he began to send as we travelled south. It started with an innocuous,

> *"Every second you are travelling farther and farther away from me and I am finding the whole concept difficult to bear. What on earth have I done, Jenny? I love you so much and yet I may never see you again. A xxx"* and so it went on and on – until it became a desperate.
>
> *"Darling, I have just been round to 13 in order to prove you really HAVE GONE. Wandered in and out of the rooms and CRIED. A grown man and I'm crying? Please don't make me plead with you. This isn't the end – I swear it Jen. Just give me a little time and I promise it will all come right. LUV U LUV U LUV U! xxx"*

With each shrill tone I found myself cringing and shrinking deeper into the corner of the cab. Robin deliberately stared at the road and pretended none of it was happening. I hated the thought of my ex-husband having to endure this and in the end, in desperation, I switched the phone off and threw it into my bag; but it took some time before we managed to resume a normal conversation and that was probably because I suggested we eat some of the food I had packed up for us.

We arrived at Jess's house in Taunton just before eight o'clock that evening. We climbed stiffly out of the van as she bustled out and came down the path to enfold us both in a big hug. She ushered us inside and insisted we went and sat near a blazing fire while she heated some soup and handed round delicious slices of sizzling pizza. It may not have been a gourmet meal but it was one of the most comforting welcomes I have ever received. We munched hungrily, cosy and warm, while exchanging gossip at the same time. Jess had made up two guest bedrooms for us and suggested we went to bed early and said the next morning would be time enough to sort out about storage of the furniture. Robin mentioned he had two possible storage units in mind, but I noticed Jess's mother-hen tactics had the desired effect because he was more than willing to get off to bed. Ten minutes later I followed him up the stairs, meanly leaving my friend to wash the dishes and clear away. The next morning Robin borrowed Jess's car to inspect the two storage companies he had found nearby. He came back to say the first was quite adequate, so we took the van round there. I filled in all the necessary forms and gave them the appropriate cheque. The units were situated in what looked like a huge aircraft hangar. Like prison cells of varying sizes, they were all clean, neat and dry. We found our "cell" in the last-but-one-row from the end. There were trolleys available to transport the goods and furniture and we carefully moved it load by load down the aisles and stacked it all neatly away right up to the roof of our storage area. Last of all I squeezed in my precious ironing board, then Robin stepped forward and secured the padlock.

Back at the house we found a nourishing beef stew awaiting us with a note from Jess saying she had gone off to look after her grandchildren and we were to make ourselves at home. As soon as he had eaten Robin announced it was time to leave and reluctantly I saw him to the door, proffering a handful of notes to cover the expense of the hired van and the diesel. He could see from my face that I wouldn't accept a refusal, so he stuffed them in his coat pocket. As he left he thrust a parcel into my hands and gruffly wished me a 'Happy Christmas.' *I* had totally forgotten everything to do with the festive season and apologised for my thoughtlessness. He brushed aside my excuses and, instead, gave me a fierce hug followed by a quick kiss on the cheek, then he ran down the front steps and waved his hand.

I suddenly had a fleeting suspicion that my ex-husband was deeply distressed but, as he was shortly off to visit Ailsa in Scotland for a couple of weeks, my common sense told me I was being stupid and imaginative. I turned away and returned to the cosy fireside.

I had arrived within a few days of Christmas. I felt strange and disorientated and, although I had spent the greater part of my adult life in the West Country, I certainly didn't feel I now belonged. To tell you the truth I suddenly felt I didn't belong anywhere. Luckily Jess made me so welcome and her daughter, husband and their two small kiddies accepted me into their close-knit family as if I was a beloved aunt. I had very little time to gather suitable presents for the whole family but I wanted to show them how much I appreciated their taking me in and making me feel so wanted. I felt like a snail that had had its shell wrenched off, but their sincere offers of warmth and friendliness were an amazing balm to my bruised soul.

I rushed around Taunton's shops and bought presents on the understanding I could take them back if they were unsuitable. It would normally have been good fun, but instead it certainly kept me busy so there was less time to think of what was happening three hundred miles away and make myself melancholy. Jess and I soon slipped into a smooth routine. She liked to do the cooking – which I hated – the housework and washing. I always did the washing-up, when we weren't using the dishwasher, as well as the mountain of ironing that her industry generated most days. I kept my own room clean and neat and tried not to make a mess in the rest of the house. We both enjoyed shopping once a week. But Jess's main occupation was her grandchildren. As so often happens these days, she would go round to their house early each morning to allow both parents to carry on their careers and so retain the whole family's comfortable lifestyle. In this way her usefulness gave her a reason for living, which she had lost after Hugo had died so suddenly, and her mothering instincts satisfied not only herself but her family as well. She adored little Thomas and Ruby and the two tiny scamps gave her their love back a hundredfold.

Although Andrew was so far away he kept in touch daily, either with numerous texts which would arrive from sun-up – when he was unable to sleep - or often at midnight, when he remembered some little snippet of gossip that he needed to discuss with me. Once a day he would find a reason for an hour-long conversation, at least. Often it was when he had taken Fay to visit some beauty spot or a house open to the public. He often said he couldn't tempt her out and she would sit in the car and play her interminable games on her laptop while he went off exploring across cliffs and beaches or wandered around old, dusty houses or even dustier museums. He was obviously lonely. I considered the answer to his problem was simple – leave her – but, in the beginning, many other reasons had got in the way of this ever happening and I was forced to accept them.

Jess was always very kind and she would either disappear when these marathon calls came in, or I would arrange another time when I would be free to chat. Andrew was forced to accept things had changed for us both and that I was no longer available to do his bidding or accompany him on his varied explorations. In this way I accompanied him round the most beautiful stately homes listening to a mellifluous Cornish voice describe delightful works of art, or thrilled to the sound of crashing waves plunging over rocks at Robin Hood's Bay or heard the bell tolling sonorously from Beverley Minster. Sometimes it was a music student singing for their supper in the centre of York. All of it was delightful – but so sad.

Christmas marked a time of relaxation for me. Andrew and Fay were celebrating the holiday with their two sons and their families so he was unable to keep in touch. I usually received a wake-up text each morning from him and another one late at night wishing me a deep sleep and happy dreams. After the holiday, I promised myself, I would do a thorough search with every estate agent in the area I favoured for a suitable property, which would enable me to get out of Jess's hair as soon as possible. I had thought long and deeply and decided my requirements were to find somewhere small and easily maintained, near the sea but close to some habitation and shops. It had to be reasonably cheap and clean. One bedroom would be sufficient but two would be better. I had a finite amount of cash available plus a ludicrous £8,000 to spend on furniture, furnishings and decoration. That was my simple criteria.

Jess and I set out one Saturday to visit the seaside town of Seaton, which was fairly near to Honiton but about forty miles from Taunton. I knew it quite well from previous visits and Robin and I had both liked the quiet little town that had no pretensions of grandeur. Its only claim to fame were trams that trundled up the estuary for a few miles, cliffs on both sides of a pebbly beach and a golf course high above the town. The nearby pretty little village of Beer and sophisticated Sidmouth were within easy distance and, in the other direction, was the Dorset town of Lyme Regis. When Robin's sister, Alexis, and her two children had come to stay we would often take them fossil hunting or swimming at either Lyme or Sidmouth where one could always be certain of an enjoyable day. So Seaton, after lots of cogitating and soul searching, looked as if it might suit my budget *and* my wish list.

We arrived on a cold, sunny day, parked in an empty car park and trawled through the town. There were a surprising number of estate agents around and we took it in turn to visit, at each one setting out my demands and limitations. Most agents wanted to show us flats which were mostly situated over shops. We were told that sheltered housing, although reasonable, was often difficult to find. There were quite a few blocks in the town but apartments seldom became vacant as Seaton was a popular destination for older people, due to property prices being fairly low as well as it being close to the sea. We took all the suitable details we could find and returned home to study them. There were one or two flats that looked promising but, sadly, only a couple of the sheltered housing properties were within my price range, so regretfully we discarded the rest. Jess promised to lend me her car for my house-hunting forays as her family lived close by and she could easily walk to her "Grandma" duties. I was so thankful for her generosity. It meant any journeys would now be reasonable because relying on sparse public transport would have been almost impossible.

Monday morning saw me again in Seaton, bright and alert, ready to begin my viewings. The first apartment I saw was at the top of some steep and winding attic stairs that led out of a busy shop. I wondered how any prospective buyer would expect to get a three-piece suite or a decent-sized table up into the two rooms above. The rooms were directly under a pitched, tiled roof. They were freezing cold – probably due to lack of insulation – and in summer – for the same reason – I guessed the place would feel like an oven. The agent wanted to show me around but one look confirmed my worst suspicions. Sadly the flat certainly wasn't for me. The next place he insisted on conducting me to was similar.

This time there was a separate entrance, but the top flight of stairs appeared to be an afterthought. They were steep and uncarpeted – I felt as if I was ascending a ship's ladder – and the open-plan, top-floor flat confirmed this impression. The windows were ill-fitting and dirty while the present curtains were grey and looked like rags. In no way could I make it habitable and I shuddered at the thought of barely *existing* there. I shook my head mutely and gingerly climbed down again. The remaining "hopeful" was in a sheltered housing complex and my natural optimism returned as we made our way to view it. It was facing the sea so I was eager to see it.

My first impression was the whole complex reminded me of a rabbit warren: flats with twisting corridors and many, many doors. This time I was conducted down to a basement floor. There was a lift but I opted to use the stairs to get some idea of the intricate layout of the whole building. We reached the lower floor and I was told the small garden outside the flat would virtually belong to the owners as few bothered to come round that side of the building. I noticed it looked as if it was perpetually in shade, so I could understand why. The rooms were small and boxlike with a matching kitchen. I mused out loud where I could put my computer and the glassed-in tiny cubicle looking out onto the garden was pointed out. Determined to have a proper look around, in the hope I could make it habitable, I strolled outside into the "garden". I walked the few paces across it and strode up some steps by a high brick wall. I found a small, wrought-iron gate; a road ran outside it and then I found myself looking across a beach. I looked back and realised the whole of the flat I had just viewed would be below sea level if the sea ever washed across the shingle. I was also aware a tidal wave had swept across here over twenty years before and, if it ever happened again, this particular apartment would be flooded to its very ceiling. I politely explained to the new agent and she appeared most amazed that I couldn't see its potential. I returned home that evening depressed and it took a couple of glasses of wine and one of Jess's homely meals before I was ready to cheer up.

I reported back to Andrew when he rang me that evening and grinned as he sympathised and said, 'See, I told you to stay up here but you refused to listen to my words of wisdom.'

The next day I opted to stay in Taunton. I needed some winter boots and it was an excuse to wander around the stores and forget cheap housing and persuasive agents who had no idea of the living conditions most people are used to or what I, personally, required. I've never considered myself a snob but, although I'm easy-going, I expect to live in simple comfort within reasonable surroundings. I arrived home first that day and decided it would be nice to surprise Jess with a cooked meal for once. We spent the evening comfortably in front of the television with a couple of glasses of wine, and ended up reminiscing about so many of our old and mutual friends. Even Robin's birthday party in Newquay felt like aeons ago and I sadly thought what a long way I had travelled since then.

The next day I set out with renewed energy, confidently hoping I would find exactly what I wanted. The agent, this time, was the son of an old colleague who'd worked in the hospital with me. I explained carefully to him why I considered sheltered housing would suit me – his mum's friend. These places have all the advantages of security and on-going maintenance without the high prices that would accompany, for instance, a similar penthouse flat He took me to see one out of my budget range. It was beautifully decorated and set in extensive grounds but was far too expensive. Then we went off to see another that he admitted had been hanging fire for some time. I felt the building had the advantage of a more pleasing position. It wasn't set in beautifully manicured grounds but it was situated on a slight rise and overlooked the sea. I could understand why this particular apartment hadn't sold. It was positioned on a corner and consequently all the rooms were oddly shaped. The bedroom had curving walls which would make it impossible to place a bed or a wardrobe against any of them and I knew this would apply to the whole flat. I enthusiastically told the agent that it was just the sort of place I longed for, except I required square rooms. He reported that two weeks before a two-bedroomed flat had been sold. It was just in my price range so my enthusiasm knew no bounds. On the strength of this he promised to leaflet the whole block and see if he could flush out any prospective sellers. I went home that evening feeling positive and happy and, after a quick meal, persuaded Jess to come to the cinema to celebrate.

The estate agent reported back two days later that leaflets had been delivered to every tenant in Windsor Court and now all I had to do was sit back and wait. It was a great relief to put my search on hold and see something of the surrounding area around Taunton. I also returned to Honiton to spend an afternoon with Lorna and Petra and on another day I helped Margaret with the church flowers. It felt like old times as we chatted together while arranging greenery and blooms; I breathed in the pungent, sharp scent of crushed stalks and immediately recalled times long gone. I didn't visit my home.

Some weekends Jess and I visited such places as Street, which is host to Clark's Village, an attractive factory outlet shopping centre where one can buy almost anything – and we did! At Glastonbury we stared at the Tor and visited the ruined Abbey before wandering around this almost "hippy" town looking at the strangely dressed inhabitants and sniffing at the smell of joss sticks and strange perfumes while handling runes, magic stones and absorbing Arthurian Legends. I also took her to see the National Trust Houses of Knightshayes and Barrington Court as well as the quilts at the American Museum, Claverton Manor near Bath. We kept busy and she seemed to enjoy my company. I certainly enjoyed hers as I remembered how lonely I had been.

The weather improved a little and I became impatient to become settled. Suddenly word came through from my friendly estate agent; a mother had been placed in a home by her family and he had been asked to value her flat. I rushed back to Seaton and was waiting outside the office door a few minutes before they opened. The staff looked at me sympathetically and gave me a cup of coffee to pass the time while I waited to hear the agent's price estimate. Eventually the boss came bouncing in looking pleased with the outcome. He announced a price that was almost to the penny my entire fund and suggested I return with him and take a look for myself. I waited while he telephoned the seller's daughter and she pronounced herself satisfied with his valuation. We wandered round to the building for me to view the flat and I was as tense and breathless as a sprinter waiting for the starting signal.

It was perfect. Only one large bedroom – but it was reasonable, with a square jutting window alcove that would accommodate my computer; a decent-sized living room with large patio doors and a tiny balcony which let in lots of light; a galley kitchen which, as I wasn't a gourmet chef, would suit me down to the ground and a nice square bathroom. The airing cupboard was fitted out with slatted shelves and, although the hall was small, the cupboard at the end was large and useful. It was all clean and pleasant. I breathed a long sigh of relief. Perhaps someone up there was looking down at me favourably after all. We walked back to the office, chatting all the way, and I signed on the dotted line. As I walked out of the building I heard the agent start telling his vendor that a buyer had been found and she was willing to pay the whole asking price. I walked down to the sea and felt like celebrating. The West Walk was empty and even the ice cream kiosk at Fishermen's Gap was closed, so I turned around and went into the first available café. I celebrated with a mug of steaming hot chocolate.

I hummed along to The Beach Boys all the way back to Taunton and went straight round to see Jess, busy child-minding in her daughter's house, to tell her the good news. I stayed there all afternoon to enjoy the company of her and the children and I realised how strained and tense I had been ever since my arrival. Suddenly I knew how an émigré feels once they have been accepted into society in their newly adopted country. It was all heady stuff. I described the flat over and over again to Jess, her family – when they returned home that evening – and her close friends. Was I exaggerating its potential? Large enough for my purposes, easily managed, near the shops, close to the sea but not too close for there to be a danger of flooding and, last of all – the icing on the cake for me – opposite a library! I hoped it looked as good on my second viewing and vowed to take Jess over with me next time, knowing she would be eminently shrewd and sensible if I was looking at it all through rose-tinted spectacles.

We went and looked – and my trepidation was unfounded. It was as nice as I had described it Jess said. Clean, well decorated and carpeted throughout. I could have easily moved in the next day. I'd like to say that from then on everything went just as smoothly. It didn't. I made an appointment with a lawyer and signed all the correct papers and forms. I visited the bank and then waited for the contracts to be exchanged and the deal to be completed. At that point it went ominously quiet. I mooned around Taunton and thought of all I could have been doing. My life was drifting by even though Andrew was speaking to me daily and making excited promises about joining me. I was totally frustrated. In the meantime two more flats, in the same block, came onto the market and I agreed to go and see them although I knew the one I had agreed to was the one I was determined to have.

The other flats were very nice. A different size and layout, both were situated on the other side of the building; but I had made my choice and there was no way I would renege on a deal, as I explained to the agent when he asked my opinion. In the meantime I had heard from the History Society in Fowey who wanted to know if Andrew and I would be coming to their annual re-union weekend in a couple of weeks. I relayed the query to Andrew when he next began his hour-long call. The line went very quiet.

'You know Fay will have hysterics if I even *mention* Cornwall. I can visit anywhere in the world – and she will willingly accompany me – but not there. Not now. Not after what has happened, Jenny.'

Fay had obviously discovered Andrew and I had visited his home-town for two years running and had no intention of allowing a third. 'I will ring and decline for both of us,' I offered.

'No, Jenny. I would like you to go. It will feel as if I am with you – even if it's only in spirit. Just knowing you are down there and doing all the things we love so much – gossiping, wandering round our old haunts, seeing old friends and making new ones. Breathing Cornish air and seeing all the old familiar places once more.' He sighed. 'Just do it for me, love. And perhaps you will get a chance to see Deborah,' he said as an afterthought. 'I *do* worry about her,' he admitted. 'But, every time I ring her she seems preoccupied and I keep wondering if there is anything wrong.'

'OK,' I promised, making up my mind on the spur of the moment. 'I will get myself out of Jess's hair for a week and make it my business to go and visit Deborah – even if it's only to stop you worrying – while I am down there. She may not want to see me,' I warned him. 'But if she does I will report back and maybe it will put your mind at rest.'

Jess seemed sad to let me go even though it was only for a week. I elected to do it the hard way. I thought it might be fun. So she ran me to Exeter in her car and I caught the bus down to Plymouth and, at Bretonside bus station, I waited a short time for the Cornish Greyhound bus to transport me to Polperro and then drop me off at the Polruan Ferry. I had booked into a small bed & breakfast guest house in Fowey and arrived there feeling distinctly the worse for wear. One may sit on a bus doing virtually nothing – apart from gazing out at the countryside or trying to complete a crossword – but the pure length of journey and boredom one endures always tires me unmercifully. I stumbled off the Ferry at last and wheeled my case up towards Place House, thankful I had finally arrived. My room was clean and comfortable and, after a meal at the *Safe Harbour Inn*, I flung myself into bed and slept the sleep of the just. I awoke early next morning to the sound of gulls squawking on the rooftop and, after a satisfying breakfast, I wandered down towards the museum just as the Family History weekend was beginning. I was amazed at the number of members I knew; some were friends from the area around Fowey and Polruan but mostly they were from the rest of the UK, with half a dozen hailing from such far-flung places as Auckland, California and Ontario.

I felt slightly awkward fending off queries as to where Andrew was. People who had been delighted to meet us the previous year were puzzled why I was alone, especially as he was the "local" and I the "foreigner". I found it easier to murmur a vague apology and change the subject by asking them to tell me about their *own* family history. This seemed to work and enabled me to walk around the exhibition and study the photographs and their captions closely. We broke for lunch at midday and then returned an hour later for the usual Society business and then a lecture after on gravestone inscriptions and how to read the impossible and oldest ones that were so often defaced.

That evening we all met at *The King of Prussia Inn* to enjoy some country music and nibble delicious snacks. This time I didn't find it so easy to brush aside enquiries as to why Drew wasn't by my side and charming them all with his company. I decided to be truthful and admitted we had decided to take some time off from each other and, as he was holidaying abroad, he'd suggested I came down in his place. I didn't want to cast him in a bad light, or queer his pitch – these were his friends not mine - and I wanted him to be able to enjoy future Family History weekends.

To lighten the atmosphere and change the subject, I asked if anyone had seen Deborah lately. No one had. An older man, sipping his pint of *Doom Bar*, mentioned he had seen her in Mevagissey some years back but the rest of her old friends and neighbours looked at a loss. I asked if anyone knew her whereabouts but I again drew a blank. What an idiot I was. I should have asked Andrew the name of her school and the address before I left for Cornwall. It had just never occurred to me. I glanced through the telephone directory to no avail. That Sunday was taken up by the exhibition in the morning and a proposed walk around the village of Lanreath in the afternoon. I hitched a lift with an elderly couple who were unsure of the way and we met up with the rest of the group at the medieval church where we listened to an absorbing talk on Tudor gentry. We were told the Folk Museum had been specially opened for us all and spent an interesting hour poking around it at our leisure before deserting to *The Punch Bowl* for a well-earned afternoon tea.

The next morning I was free to do as I pleased so I promptly decided to take myself off to search for Deborah. I discovered a boat that plied backwards and forwards to the fishing village of Mevagissey and hoped that she, or her school, would be easy to find. It was a bright and sunny day when I clambered aboard the bustling, sturdy boat that would take me further down the coast. The breeze strengthened as we cleared Gribbin Head and headed towards St Austell and Mevagissey Bays. We passed the lighthouse and turned towards the harbour of this delightful village that tumbled down the hillside towards the boats at anchor. I stepped ashore and made my way to the nearest café. That was usually a safe bet for obtaining information, I had often found. I munched on a cheese scone to accompany a seriously strong coffee and stared out of the window at the busy scene around the quay. The owner of the café apologised that she was new to the area and sent me along to the Harbourmaster's office. I presented myself to the man who controls all harbour traffic and asked if he knew of a Deborah Lanyon. After an emphatic shake of the head I then inquired about any boys' boarding schools in the area. He rattled off three but, on asking their whereabouts, he stated they were all some distance away towards Heligan or Pentewan. As I was unable to supply the name of the school it was obvious I was on a wild goose chase. I thanked him and left him to his pipe and tide tables. Where should I go? I had three hours to kill and there are only so many narrow alleyways and shops of interest in this pretty village.

I decided on visiting Portmellon a mile further down the coast. I took the footpath out of Mevagissey and wandered along towards Gorran Haven. The view was sublime on such a glorious day. I found a sheltered seat and made myself comfortable. In the distance I could see what might have been a grey seal sunning itself on a rock and I was sorry I had no binoculars. The beach at Portmellon is covered at high water but, as the tide was now at the half, I pottered happily around some uncovered rock pools and discovered two tiny crabs that scuttled away on my disturbing their peace. At one time the tiny cove was well known for the building and launching of small fishing boats. Now all it boasted were a few cottages and holiday homes. It was time to make my way back towards Mevagissey if I wanted a meal. I had half an hour to spare when I got back to the *Fountain Inn*, close to the harbour, so I grabbed a crab sandwich, washing it down with a half of cool cider, before dashing across the cobbles to catch my fishing boat back to Fowey.

The next four days flashed by. I was offered a lift into Looe with the Family History Society's secretary and his wife and I accepted gratefully. They dropped me in Fore Street; I had a quick look around the museum before I made my way back across the river towards Hannafore where I found the footpath that took me over the cliffs towards St George's Island, Talland Bay, the simple, cliffside War Memorial and, finally, Polperro. It was a delightful walk in warm, hazy sunshine and I made really good time. Polperro looked as welcoming as ever as I strode down through the steep Warren and visited The Old Mill House for a quick snack. I caught the bus back to Polruan by the skin of my teeth and spent some time just sitting on the quay watching large and small craft gracefully beating their way towards the sea or finding a berth up river. That evening I sent Andrew my sincere apologies for not finding Deborah. His text was warm and comforting with him wanting to know who I had seen, where I had been and – at the end – how much he missed me.

For the last three days I kept myself busy by visiting Polkerris, Lerryn and Lostwithiel. On my solitary walks I often came across people exploring just as I was. Some of them had been at the Family History weekend and we met with big smiles and warm handshakes, but some were just wandering and enjoying the Cornish countryside and we passed each other with a pleasant nod and a few words. I shouldn't have been, but I admit I was bitterly lonely seeing all our old haunts on my own – no one to talk to, to pass comment with or even to exchange a fleeting smile. Occasionally, when I was in a pub for a meal, old friends might ask me to join them at their table. It seemed discourteous not to, but often the effort of chatting brightly made me feel even more alone. Andrew and I had always felt warm and sociable towards everyone; we liked people and were both gregarious souls – now I felt lost and needy and I hated the thought that these people felt sorry for me. So in the end it was almost a relief when I packed my bags and caught the bus towards Plymouth, Exeter, Jess and home.

Back home there was news at last. The apartment was mine and I could move anytime. I immediately got in touch with a friend who would be able to turn my flat into the home I so desired. He promised to come as soon as I moved in – and I sighed with relief.

Robin also got in touch. He had been trying to sell our bungalow. One woman from Hayward's Heath wanted it desperately but each time had been let down by different buyers at her end. Now Robin was giving up his job, going up to Scotland to join Ailsa, and beginning a new life. He asked if I would keep an eye on the house for him. The shock was immense, even though I had expected it for some time. Originally, I had imagined him staying in our old house forever. All I ever wanted to do was give him a secure, stable base, but of course I hadn't understood the hurt I was also inflicting on him by tying him to the home we had both loved. I wished him well and told him I would do my utmost to get the best price for him. He asked if there was anything I wanted in the way of furniture and explained the rest would be going to the Air Ambulance charity. I mentioned a few minor items and tried not to think that all our lovingly chosen furniture was now to be abandoned.

Robin's second piece of news affected me even more deeply. I had been expecting him to mention this for quite some time; but it still came as a massive shock when he finally put it into words. 'We always knew we would get divorced at some point, Jenny. I need a fresh start in my life. A clean slate so if, or when, I decide to make a new life with Ailsa I am free of all encumbrances.'

My heart thudded in panic. It's bad enough being alone yet I was always aware he was close at hand if ever I should need help. Suddenly Robin was cutting, irrevocably, every tie that had bound us together for decades. I was aware I could still plead with him and maybe even change the course of events for us both; but I *also* knew that I had to him go with love and good wishes - as one quietly slips a mooring rope and allows a boat to gently leave harbour. I forced myself to speak lightly, 'Yes of course you must, darling. Set everything in motion and I will agree to everything you decide. I was totally at fault and accept all the blame. I will even help you with the costs - this way I imagine it will be straightforward and relatively quick.'

He sounded relieved at my acceptance of the situation and, after telling me he was quite capable of footing any bills, we both wished each other goodnight with much to digest.

Jess was sad at my news, but being realistic she knew I couldn't stay there forever. I reminded her we would visit each other often so that very little would change.

Chapter 26

*

I moved into my new flat at the end of May. The removal men swiftly did their work, putting my furniture in the places I indicated, and then left me with a huge stack of boxes to unpack. I was certain I couldn't have chosen better curtains for the sitting room and bedroom than those that were left behind. Already in place, they were floor to ceiling, muted, new and beautifully lined. I have them still and they suit both my rooms perfectly. The carpet looked new also and, as it was pale green, I found it perfectly acceptable for the time being. The furniture Andrew and I had chosen in York was pale cream or white and I decided this was to be the theme throughout the whole flat with the only contrast being a bureau, television stand and nest of coffee tables all in a deep warm yew wood. The glass-and-chrome dining table came with black chairs and that was to be the limit of my colour scheme right throughout the flat.

Terry, my builder-handyman-plumber-electrician *and* friend, arrived two days later and we both set to work. My dream was a new white kitchen, bathroom and doors throughout, bespoke bookshelves and plastic skirting boards. Over the years, in various houses, we had found what we liked and my aim, this time, was for it all to come together to make my perfect dream home. We both decided a new boiler might be in order as the old one had given good service for almost twenty years and now seemed as good a time as any to change it. I wanted no accidents to cause trouble for my fellow residents.

I had previously informed Terry I had a very slender budget so every penny would count. We devised a plan whereby I would accompany him to builders' merchants, decide what I liked and, if it was affordable, he would ask for a discount and I would pass over the cheque. Terry promised to bill me monthly for his time and labour and, if the money ran out, all work would have to cease. This meant our most important issue was to stay within budget – and this we were both determined to do.

Andrew, from the moment I excitedly told him I had found a suitable home for us both, wanted to join me immediately. Thinking about it, I decided it was far more sensible to get the flat as perfect as I could make it, and *then* welcome him with open arms. I knew he was extremely laid back and flexible when it came to accommodation. He wouldn't think anything mattered too much but, once he was living there, all the minor irritations he had previously never thought about would annoy him unmercifully. I also knew the house he lived in was large; five en suite bedrooms, a decent sized kitchen, two sitting rooms, a spacious dining room, a tiny study, utility room and family breakfast room. This apartment, by contrast, was the size of a holiday *pied-à-terre* and, unless it was streamlined, it would never suit my partner who was used to spreading himself around in unlimited, cluttered space. A bit like expecting the Queen to squeeze into a small semi-detached house in Weybridge!

As work progressed I sent snaps to Andrew and received encouraging replies. I worked closely with Terry because, quite frankly, I enjoyed it. He did the heavy work like plumbing and replacing the bathroom and kitchen with simple white units – these we doctored up with elegant handles and dark worktops. I had chosen large cream wall tiles for both rooms with flooring that matched perfectly and this gave the whole place a French farmhouse look. I helped him hang new Regency style doors and, as I had chosen to do all the decorating, I busied myself with taking down every radiator, hanging vinyl wallpaper right through the whole flat and painting that also. It was a mammoth task and one I never dared leave for a day. As I finished one room I began the next immediately. Without this work ethic I knew I would never have the strength or enthusiasm to finish it. Terry made me bespoke white bookshelves that ran the length of my sitting room and installed three mirrored, white wardrobe units that took up one wall in my bedroom. My deceptively simple scheme of cream and white was coming together beautifully – it not only looked clean and new but stylish also.

Everything, I decided, would be divided equally between Andrew and me. I would take over my half of the storage space in drawers, cupboards and shelves and Andrew could lay claim to the rest. Even the huge hall cupboard was fixed up with deep shelves, hooks and neat chests of drawers. I had ample storage for everything including my iron, ironing board, all my DIY equipment, paint pots, stepladder, boxes of paperwork and outdoor coats. My airing cupboard doubled up for suitcase storage, winter shoes, bed linen, duvets, pillows and all the odds and ends that are difficult to place anywhere else. It had taken six months, but I now had a manageable, comfortable home that I hoped would suit us both. I felt almost euphoric when I spoke to Andrew just before Christmas. I told him I would be having a party for all the residents to thank them for their understanding. They had put up with constant noise as well as goods moving in and out of the building at all times. I told Andrew I had chosen a pale, biscuit-coloured carpet and, immediately after my party, it would be laid and then he was welcome to come any time. I heard him breathe a sigh of relief and that night I went to sleep delighted and deeply satisfied.

It was a cold Christmas. I went, laden with presents, to see my friends in Honiton. In our small close I noted quite a few faces were missing. Lorna and Margaret made a great fuss of me but both mentioned I looked tired and a bit wan. I sent almost the usual number of Christmas cards that year but I noticed there were very few from Robin's old police colleagues since he'd left the force and the area. I am sure they blamed me for his departure and this was their way of showing their displeasure. Everything had gone quite flat since Terry had completed his work for me. It hadn't helped that I had finally been granted a divorce. My Decree Absolute arrived in the post and I felt what a hackneyed ending to such a fruitful marriage. It meant for a couple of days I felt lost and useless with very little to do. Working so hard, I had little time to get to know the residents and this I wanted to put right in this season of good cheer. As neighbours they turned out to be a pleasant bunch – mostly older with a very few younger – and I soon learned most of their names when I accepted invitations to various parties as December 25th drew nearer. One couple in particular stood out from the others. I was laughing with them about my constant worry of forgetting my key; or allowing my front door to slam behind me, so stupidly locking myself out of my flat. They agreed most of them had done just that. They then offered to mind a spare set for me and I accepted gratefully. That was how I learned Val and Bertrand's names; that they lived in separate flats and yet spent most of their waking hours together. I heard their respective families were scandalised but the two of them appeared to be light hearted and unrepentant. Just the sort of people I admired for their honesty and determination.

I spent the two days of Christmas with Jess and her family in Taunton. The whole family's welcome was loving and warm and the children's excitement at Santa's visit, plus the mountain of presents he delivered, made my stay great fun. All of *my* gifts were accepted with delight and I marvelled at how much I had accomplished during the past year. Andrew was still ringing me at every opportunity and promising to get away as soon as he was able. I bathed in a glow of satisfaction and returned to Seaton looking forward to a new life.

Robin came back alone at the beginning of January ostensibly to visit his friends; but I had a sneaking suspicion it was to check up on how I was faring. He appeared to approve of my decorating prowess and, after taking me out for two meals, mentioned he and Ailsa would shortly be getting engaged and then married. He had decided against applying for a job with the Scottish constabulary and now worked for the local council in a part-time capacity. Up in Scotland he had inherited a ready-made family. Ailsa had two grown-up daughters – one married with a young baby and the other a career-minded policewoman – so there seemed little point in their waiting. He told me, in confidence, that he had repaid the small outstanding mortgage on Ailsa's home and they were now in the middle of planning improvements on this rambling house that overlooked the sea. He showed me photographs and I could see how immersed he was in his new life. I think he loved being a surrogate grandfather and I rejoiced that life had finally turned out well for him. He had always longed for a family.

Every week I went over to Honiton as promised – to dust, vacuum and generally check all was well with our old bungalow.

Occasionally a prospective buyer would be brought along by the long-suffering estate agent but, as the market was extremely depressed at that time, there seemed little likelihood of a resulting sale. Each time my hopes were raised and then dashed. A month later I was told the original buyer from Hayward's Heath had appeared, yet again, and wished to take another look around and possibly make an offer. Did I want to be there when the agent conducted the viewing? I immediately said yes with the provision that I showed her around on my own. I felt sure I knew substantially more about my own home than a disinterested third party would. And so it transpired. This rather frail lady arrived punctually, accompanied by her elderly son. She had been told I had once owned the bungalow and now was selling it on behalf of my ex-husband. The son asked many pertinent questions and both of them appeared satisfied with my extensive answers. Yes the boiler was new, the walls were insulated, mains water could be switched off at the touch of a button – so saving anyone having to locate the stopcock. The buyer smiled at that and I immediately saw she couldn't imagine herself, on hands and knees, scrabbling around under a kitchen sink unit. She appeared more your *"gin and tonic in the garden"* lady! I also loftily informed her that electricity and water controls had been installed outside the property so her son could wash and vacuum his car, set the garden fountain working, illuminate his flowers or decorate the building with lights at Christmas. I pointed out the automatic loft cover and descending ladder that led the way to a sizeable, well-lit attic area that could store a huge amount of furniture or goods. I finally conducted her towards the French windows where I had set out tea on the low balcony that overlooked our tiny walled garden. We sat in warm sunshine and I knew I had, at last, sold Robin's house for him...

I arranged my grand party just before the New Year, mainly because Andrew was clamouring to come down and I wanted to get a new carpet laid throughout the flat. I tried to estimate how many would come and how much food and drink I should supply. I needn't have worried; just about all the residents attended, but luckily they chose to do it in an unofficial relay. I noticed many of them drifted around from group to group, laughing and joking, as couples divided to speak to neighbours and then re-formed as they moved on. Lots asked to see what my builder and I had been up to so I ended up doing an impromptu tour of every room. I was so pleased because, at that time, I could only muster a dozen or so seats and I had been worried some might feel awkward. Not so; since then I now know that all of us will quietly offer whatever our neighbours need – they have only to ask. These were all relaxed and talkative friends and I had the impression I had joined a warm-hearted club. It boded well for when Andrew joined me. I longed to introduce him as my partner and childhood sweetheart and I suspected he would find them as pleasant as I did.

Val stayed behind and helped me clear up the sad debris that follows every successful party. Bertrand did a sterling job of conjuring up a huge pot of tea and placing it on a low table as we finally sat back, with deep sighs, and put our feet up. From that moment they became my surrogate family. Neither of them were that many years older than me but their concern for my well-being, their including me in all their social activities and outings, their checking up on me almost daily meant I soon felt completely at home in Windsor Court as well as in the town of Seaton. Suddenly I felt useful once more and my loneliness receded.

Robin rang to tell me gently about his engagement party. It had been a low-profile affair with only Ailsa's close family and friends. I sent a card and a small present. I spent ages pondering over the card and then decided simplicity was the best policy and congratulated them both on their excellent taste. With a short note on the bottom stating:

Ailsa, you have picked a good one there!

I wanted them both to accept I wished the best for them both. As I did.

I had my carpet laid with little fuss. I had spent ages choosing it and was pleased that, once more, it complemented my overall colour scheme. I chose a slightly flecked, warm oatmeal tone that I hoped would blend with everything and show very few marks. All the way through my decorating phase I had tried to be sensible yet innovative and from, Jess's compliments, I felt I might have achieved what I had set out to do. It is great fun, and probably appealed to a selfish streak in me, that I had a certain amount of cash which I was allowed to spend, without help or interference, exactly as I wished.

I spoke to Andrew the day after the carpet fitters had left, 'It looks pretty good, love. I have just about come to the end of my money now. The flat, to all intents and purposes, is finished, so that's great. I need a new fridge-freezer and I'd love a modern fire but both will have to wait for a few months as I still need to pay Terry for his last month's work.'

Andrew was very quiet. I felt sorry I hadn't stretched the money as far as I had hoped, but two days later when a cheque for £2,000 arrived I sat looking at it – stunned. Andrew had solved all my problems. I thankfully paid Terry, ordered a state-of-the-art refrigerator and then went to Taunton, with Jess, to pick out a black, wall-hung glass fire. When switched on it warmly gave the impression of flames flickering through a pile of white stones. I immediately loved it as it set off my sitting room to perfection.

Two days later and all my euphoria evaporated. Andrew rang, in great agitation, to say Fay had sustained a nasty accident the night before. They were standing outside the Theatre Royal in York, saying goodnight to friends, when a taxi had skidded across the pavement and knocked Fay down. An ambulance had taken her to the District Hospital and, as far as they could determine, she had only suffered a fractured wrist. He went on to say the tremendous shock had affected her seriously, so they would be keeping her in for further tests and investigations. He had been with her most of the night and was now returning home for a shower and shave. I felt tremendously sorry for her. I know how close encounters with death can affect one's nerves and, although I felt sorry for both her and her husband, I also felt correspondingly sorry for us.

I tried to sound calm and composed and told him to give me a ring as soon as there were any developments. I then raced upstairs to tell Val and Bertrand my sad news. Of course they had no idea of the exact state of affairs between Andrew and I. I hadn't wanted to bore them with my troubles, so although they were sympathetic, most of it made very little sense to them. That night they insisted I join them at one of the local pubs where we listened to an evening of music from a Moody Blues tribute band. Probably Bertrand plied me with a fraction too much wine but, as we didn't have far to return to Windsor Court, I managed to make it home unaided.

Andrew had left a couple of messages on my mobile phone and, after listening to them, I spent most of the night wide-eyed and weeping over a sodden pillow.

Val demanded I went on a short break with her and her partner. They had booked to go to the Isle of Wight for five days and she insisted I join them. She mentioned I looked tired out from my decorating marathon and that I deserved a short holiday to cheer me up. As good as their word, they booked me in with a luxury coach company that picked us up at our front door. I knew I was still reachable, whether in Devon or Hampshire, so after telling Andrew of my intentions, I joined them. I had packed a few books to see me through the holiday and spent most of the journey there and back deep in some detective novels. The rest of the holiday, when I was unable to sleep, I tried to read *Madame Bovary* but, in that, I was slightly less successful.

Andrew and I had been able to have quite a few lengthy chats about the situation when I had been away. I understood he felt unable to leave Fay at such a time. He thought a quiet holiday might help her and planned a short Norwegian cruise. Of course I agreed – what else could I say? I have never been a cold or heartless person. On their return he stopped reminding me he would be down within days and I was too reticent, and far too hurt, to comment on his apparent change of heart.

A few weeks later he raised my hopes yet again by suggesting a holiday on the Isles of Scilly might be the perfect answer to our problems. I responded at once to the idea. I had been there a few times before with Robin, and my glowing reports on what an idyllic place we had discovered obviously lit a fire of enthusiasm within Andrew's Cornish mind.

We planned every little detail, even to a suitable date in June. I told him I loved St Mary's as it was the main island and the hub of social boating activity. I preferred to base myself at Old Town as it was quieter and more magical than Hugh Town which was busy by comparison. He came back to me to suggest the Star Castle Hotel and I immediately vetoed it as being too commercial and right in the centre of Hugh Town itself. It is difficult to explain how it is not possible to purchase the uniqueness of the true Scillonian way of life by choosing a prestigious hotel. His second choice was a modern house overlooking Porthcressa Beach and, once again, I felt it was churlish to explain *I* would prefer a small bed & breakfast cottage, overlooking the tiny bay and church on the beach at Old Town – so I reluctantly agreed.

Once again it went very quiet but I busied myself by getting out and about in the countryside of Devon as well as visiting as many National Trust houses within a very large area. Suddenly Robin informed me of the date of his marriage. He asked if I would mind him inviting my relations as well as our mutual friends. I assured him it was a superb idea, but immediately turned down his proposal for me to accompany my cousins, Dee and Paul, if they were prepared to accept his kind invitation. I knew that would be an insane situation which would not please anyone – least of all me! He had asked most people to take a few days off and was prepared to put quite a few up in a local hotel at his expense.

I was surprised at his generosity but extremely pleased when so many accepted. A few asked me whether I minded. I explained it was not a case of changing their allegiance; I had no wish for people to take sides. My dearest hope was that we should all remain friends. Robin and I had spent most of our adult life in Devon and I guessed he might be missing many of his mates and colleagues. In a strange place we all feel a bit wary and lost and I'm sure Robin was no exception. His previous job had fitted him like an old and comfortable jacket but now he was adrift in a new country, starting a new career and surrounded by few people he knew or could call friends. Ailsa and her family had made him very welcome - he often told me he would go around to her mother's on his days off to share a cup of tea - but it meant his comfortable way of life had disappeared after his five-hundred-mile epic journey. Until he made a new one I felt he needed all the support and friendship he could muster.

Andrew, on the other hand, became extremely uncommunicative. He still rang me as often, usually when he was going out for long walks in the evening, even occasionally in busy stores when he was bored, snatching a quick cup of coffee or driving home from the golf course; but suddenly his chat concerned mundane events and nothing in particular about us. The cruise he had planned had apparently satisfied Fay, but our visit to the Isles of Scilly was never mentioned. Time was passing as I became more and more certain he had forgotten his promise. Suddenly my goodwill snapped and, after listening to him rambling on about a dinner and dance he had attended, on impulse I telephoned a guest house overlooking the bay in Old Town and asked if they still had any vacancies. On their answering yes I recklessly booked a week's holiday for the exact dates we had discussed. From that moment on I became as reticent as Andrew about my forthcoming plans. Our proposed holiday date came progressively nearer and I hugged my secret to me, like a miser checking his resources.

That was until the day before I was due to go, when he rang me and settled in for a long chat. I had been flinging holiday clothes into a suitcase all day and I had just zipped it up, satisfied I had left nothing out. I could hear gulls squawking and, on querying it, Andrew admitted he was in a café near the sea. It all sounded really odd to me. I asked where Fay was and he vaguely stated she was fine. I asked him *exactly* where he was and he muttered Scarborough. But somehow I couldn't leave the question alone and finally he broke down and laughed.

'OK, you win, darling. I'm in Newquay. It's a warm evening and I was bursting to talk to you.' And he started burbling happily on about the holidaymakers.

'Really?' I asked sarcastically. Suddenly I felt a shiver as realisation finally dawned on me. 'So you decided to go to the Isles of Scilly after all?' I asked.

'Yes, I remember you said you often flew from Newquay airport and it seemed like a good idea at the time. We arrived this afternoon and booked into a B&B easily. Don't worry, darling, I have come out for a walk and left her sitting in our room playing with her laptop, as usual.'

I allowed a few beats to elapse as I took the time to get my voice under control. 'Well, I sincerely hope you both have a good time, Andrew. It's lovely over there at this time of the year. But maybe you won't be quite so pleased to hear you might be joined shortly. I got tired of waiting for you so *I* made a booking a few weeks ago. Don't worry – there's little chance of us meeting. The islands will probably hold scant interest to a woman who is not used to walking anywhere and, as you will have to dance attendance on her constantly, I doubt you will be allowed out to explore them yourself!'

With that I slammed my telephone back down and took myself off to bed...

Chapter 27

*

I arrived on St Mary's, the main island of the Isles of Scilly, one warm Saturday afternoon in the middle of June. The ease of using public transport to get to Exeter Airport and then joining the dozen or so passengers waiting for our Islander aircraft made most continental or international flights appear regimented, stressful and overrated by comparison. I sat in my single seat, gazing out of the window, as the north coasts of Devon and Cornwall unravelled beneath me and marvelled at the ease with which one can reach these idyllic islands. As we swooped in gracefully to land, I gazed at all my favourite beaches with loving fondness and relished the thought of the next seven days.

Old Town was near enough to the diminutive airport for me to walk down the sunny, leafy lanes and find my own way to the cottage I had booked. I'd received constant texts since I had slammed down the telephone on Andrew two nights before – they began by cajoling, then making light of his stupidity (his own words) and finally by pleading. I found it quite easy to ignore all of them. As I walked out of the simple Arrival Hall my mobile beeped yet again. Which flight was I due on? He would watch them all fly over, he promised. I glanced down at the glowing screen as I trailed my case down the hill and deliberately switched off my phone.

I was welcomed by the energetic Glenda and shown my pristine room. The window was thrown wide to catch the sea's breezes, which I inhaled with delight while I unpacked my small suitcase. In no time I was down on the slipway staring across the emerging crescent of sand towards the modest church of St Mary's. Here, untold souls were buried and their names recorded in stone for all to see and ponder on. Raging Atlantic storms are notorious for sweeping across these unprotected islands and many a story can be told of the heroism and resourcefulness of these brave islanders but, on a warm balmy evening in summer, it seemed hardly credible. I promised myself I would wander over there early the next morning.

Now it was time for food. My mouth was watering for one of the succulent crab salads the restaurant here on the cliffs was famed for. I scrambled up the path to fulfil my wish. Some of the familiar young staff waited on me that night and, thanks to their usual flair for light gossip and fun, I found myself contentedly enjoying once more the Scillonian easy-going way of life.

Next morning, shouldering my rucksack, I made my pilgrimage to the little grey church across the bay and spent an hour wandering around gravestones, most with intensely sad stories to tell. From there I followed the footpath around Peninnis Head and down towards Porthcressa, past the walled Garrison that is so pleasurable for an evening stroll, and on to Hugh Town itself. It was then only a short walk across the isthmus to reach St Mary's Quay where one could take a pleasure trip to most of the islands, morning and afternoon, efficiently organised by the Boatmen's Association. Most visitors choose to visit one of the five main islands or take various bird and seal-watching trips, go to the Bishop Rock Lighthouse or the Eastern Isles. In other words there is always more than enough to do for avid explorers. I bought my ticket and took a pack of sandwiches on board as I caught the boat for Bryher. A few years previously Robin and I had discovered an artist who had made his home near Rushy Bay and I longed to see if he was still producing the most refreshing art we had ever seen. He was and I wandered around, chatting and laughing with him, until it was time to head back. I sat on the beach in the bright sunshine until it was time to wade out and catch my boat home.

By the next day I had virtually forgotten I was sharing these islands with Andrew when I went off puffin-spotting on my way to the Bishop Rock lighthouse. They were such tiny, darting birds that they were almost impossible to catch on film. A flash of red, black and white and they had swerved past. The Boatman *did* point out a Sun fish and all his passengers obediently peered over the gunwales at the large, spread fish basking a few inches beneath the translucent swell.

The Bishop Rock soon loomed up out of the misty horizon, in shocking immensity. We sat in awe and listened to how this was the third lighthouse built to save seafarers from the notorious reef of rocks known as the Western Approaches – the other two lighthouses were swept away by vast storms and even this one had its iron door, built halfway up the structure, stove-in by the sea's monstrous attack. I was bemused at the heroism of men who decided to risk their lives attempting to build a structure on a perpendicular rock only 30 by 15 metres, covered by water at high tide and which could be swept by waves sometimes forty or fifty metres high. I wondered how many wrecks had been averted by this simple act of selfless courage.

We soon swung away towards St Agnes and the calmer haven of Porth Conger. I stayed on board the boat although I would have loved to wander up the Quay and sample a steaming hot pasty at the Turk's Head Inn. St Agnes is my favourite island but I would save that for another day, I decided, as I was beginning to feel the effect of sunburn – a common occurrence due to the clean, pure air – and I needed some cream to protect my pale skin. As soon as we landed back at St Mary's I made my way to the nearby chemist's shop and was handed a huge plastic bottle with a knowing smile. Andrew then swears I fell over his feet as I slipped past him and turned sharp left to make my way back over the headland to start my anti-clockwise tour of St Mary's itself. This was a ritual that Robin and I had always adhered to every time we visited the Isles. If I did trip over Andrew's feet it certainly didn't register. My mind was probably on a satisfying sandwich back in Old Town before I set out!

Halfway up the coast path my mobile trilled in my rucksack. I fished it out and answered it without thinking, 'Hello?'

'Darling, you were there one minute and gone the next. Where are you? I rushed out after you but you had disappeared like a puff of wind.'

'Where were *you*?' I asked stupidly.

'Leaning against the door-frame; on the step outside the chemist's shop. Didn't you see me? Can I come and find you?'

'No, Andrew. I'm almost halfway back to Old Town now. I'm on the cliffs near Dutchman's Carn – almost at the Lighthouse,' I explained, as if he would know where I was standing.

'Please, Jenny.'

That was my undoing. Sincere beseeching has always been my Achilles heel.

'Stay where you are. I'll make my way back and find you. It will be so much quicker than you searching for me,' I said firmly.

We met in the busy square outside the shop. His face lit up as I walked round the corner. He stepped forward and hugged me so fiercely, and at such length, that I gasped. He ignored the chattering holidaymakers pushing to get past us. He then grabbed my hand as I turned and walked swiftly back the way I had come, and then refused to relinquish it. We passed a large hotel just as we arrived back on the cliffs. I have no idea where it was and I probably would never be able to locate it again. Andrew dragged me towards it and ushered me down some shady stairs and into a dim, deserted bar. The young, plump bartender was busying himself polishing glasses and appeared delighted to welcome us. We made our way to the other side of the basement room and seated ourselves on a comfortable red settle flanked by black lacquered tables. Andrew ordered a bottle of cool white wine and the barman brought it over, with two sparkling glasses, and placed it neatly before us.

And there we sat for the rest of that afternoon, taking it in turn to listen and ask questions, to laugh and marvel, and ask yet more questions. We had not seen each other for months and, like lost men in a desert who discover a spring and cannot stop drinking, we couldn't get enough of each other. The whole time Andrew held me tightly within his arm – as if he dared not let me go in case I might evaporate from his sight once more. I remember him pouring the wine and drinking with his left hand as he stared at me and greedily watched my lips tell of my past months. The wine disappeared and he ordered another bottle. I then asked how he had fared once I had left York. He admitted, in detail, how horrendous the party had been that he'd had to host on his second night back, something of which he had made light of when we were still meeting. He said how his best friend had tried to castigate him for leaving Fay and he also told me how one night – in bed – she had tried to resurrect their ardour, to no avail. I refrained from asking for details, but I suspected it had embarrassed them both. Without thinking, I asked where Fay was now and he vaguely said she had probably returned to the guest house. I had the feeling he didn't know and didn't care and, quite honestly, I sympathised with him. We made plans for the next day with little thought as to what excuse he could conjure up. I suggested he could meet me in Pelistry Bay and described how to find it. I promised to walk him back over the cliffs to where I was staying. He agreed eagerly. I told him to bring food and his towel and, although it was probably too cold to swim, we could paddle in the pellucid, deep blue water. I described the fine white sand here that often sparkled with mica and I told him this beach – so often empty and pristine – reminded me of a desert island. I desperately wanted him to see the *real* Isles of Scilly; not the harbour where the *Scillonian* spills her human cargo, or the heaving pubs where visiting lads roar out sea ditties with a pint of Doom Bar in their fists – I wanted him to sample a time that would remind him of the Cornwall of his childhood – natural, friendly and honest. He smiled his open, trusting grin and then I gently reminded him it was time to return to civilisation.

He insisted on walking me part-way back across the cliffs, like a schoolboy with his first girlfriend. I pointed out all the odd names of the carns and standing stones as we swung along – hand in hand – still chattering and laughing, until we arrived at Pulpit Rock and could see Old Town across the bay. I insisted he turned back here but, as I skipped down towards the grey church by the beach, I saw he was still standing and watching my progress. Each time I turned we both waved...

It was only when I was in bed that night, after enjoying a satisfying meal up at the Tolman Café, I remembered I had never questioned him about why it wasn't *us* enjoying this very special holiday. Why bring a woman who would never appreciate this simple way of life, who preferred cruises and impressing fellow travellers to walking across deserted beaches and messing around in boats? I promised myself, as I drowsily snuggled down in my narrow bed, I would ask him the very next day.

I eagerly ate my breakfast the next morning and collected some pasties, crisps, apples and soft drinks from the café, before making my way up the footpath towards the north of St Mary's. Nothing is ever far away on these islands especially as the views and the rocky outcrops are magnificent every step of the way. I stopped at Porth Hellick Bay to collect my usual pocketful of shells. The whole horseshoe-shaped bay was inches deep in every kind and hue of washed-up shells and I was never able to resist picking up a selection of the very smallest.

Andrew was waiting on the deserted beach when I arrived. He was sitting hunched up, reading a guide book. He immediately wanted to know about Toll's Island and Pellow's Redoubt on it. I had no idea who Toll was but I had been told Pellow was a well-respected Admiral of the Fleet in the seventeenth century who, when a commandant of the island, had suggested a defensive battery here. The kelp pits traditionally burned seaweed and, on this tiny island, supplied elements for the soap-making industry on the mainland. As the sea was still covering the sand bar we were unable to go over and explore. We lay on the warm sand close together and I remembered to ask where Andrew was supposed to be all day.

'I'm playing golf up near Juliet's Garden,' he admitted. I giggled as I was sure no one had explained to Fay it was only a nine-hole golf course and highly unlikely Andrew would bother to waste a whole day of his holiday there.

'And where is Fay, this glorious day?' I asked.

'She's joined a bridge coven – with some fellow addicts – so she will be well satisfied,' he answered with a grin.

As I expected, the June seas were still too cold for bathing, even on that scorching sunny day, so I jumped up and raced Andrew down to the shore for a paddle. Actually we splashed one another to such an extent that we might as well have stripped down to our costumes when, breathing heavily, we staggered up the beach and flung ourselves down on our beach towels. I spread out our impromptu picnic and we tucked in hungrily. We never did explore Toll's island, the Redoubt or the kelp pits but that was because I wanted to show Andrew some of the best views on St Mary's and share with him my favourite place of all – Old Town. He had come across the middle of the island, by way of Cove Vean, and I wanted him to see *Darrity's Hole*, Normandy Down, *White Sheets* and *Little Britain Rock*. We skirted *The Twin Sisters*, *Horse* and *Sun*

Rock and gazed down at Porth Wreck, where we made a detour to look at a 4,000-year-old burial chamber.

I then showed him the small, insignificant monument that commemorates the many sailors of the British Fleet that were wrecked off the Western Rocks one horrendous night in 1707, with the loss of 1,670 men. Many of these men, including their Commander-in-Chief, were washed ashore at Porth Hellick. I also wanted him to marvel at the beach here, now deeply encrusted in seashells. He laughed at the *Loaded Camel* and *Tom Butt's Bed* and then was amazed, as I knew he would be, when we reached the Airport runway. The coastal footpath cut right across the actual runway but, as long as one obeyed a single rule (to stop and wait patiently when the buzzer sounded and then, once the aircraft or helicopter touched down, you could cross with confidence) then the walker's safety was guaranteed. Considering how much traffic used the airport daily I knew how Andrew felt about the islanders' casual attitude to this simple system. The last half-mile was just as beautiful and exhilarating as the rest of the walk. Andrew gazed around him in awe and I knew Old Town and Nowhere were exerting their magic as usual. I pointed out where I dined on the cliffs most nights and then led him to my small guest house that nestled cosily behind the gently shelving beach. I put my head in the door and quietly called out. No reply, so I took Andrew by the hand and, with a shushing movement, drew him towards my room that overlooked the bay. It was only small, with two single beds and a simple bathroom, but was enhanced with antique, highly polished, dark mahogany furniture and matching colourful curtains and bed linen. I swiftly tossed back the sheets and we sank down onto the narrow confines of the bed I had chosen to be mine. At long last we were totally alone and could indulge in showing each other how very much we both cared. I gasped as Andrew gently did what he had craved to do since we had touched hands in town the previous day; and then I threw caution to the winds to join him on a rising tide of fervour until we both attained a climax and, with a deep sigh of contentment, peacefully sank back to reality.

We lay and softly chatted as the breeze softly wafted the net curtains towards our glowing bodies and both forgot time was swiftly passing. Suddenly, Andrew gave a gurgle of what I could only think of as exuberant delight and flung himself across me. Instead of wrapping me in his arms, as he probably meant to do, he catapulted the pair of us straight out of the bed. The massive *CRUMP* that shook the house to its foundations and went on reverberating after we had hit the floor frightened us both. I could see the horror on Drew's face – and that probably only mirrored my own! We waited for pounding feet to race along the corridor and hands to hammer loudly on my bedroom door. We lay breathless – not speaking – until I asked him quietly if he was alright. I eased myself off him – with difficulty. We had crashed between a large bedside cabinet, a huge chest of drawers and the bed. I expected to see blood everywhere – from a bleeding head wound or, at the very least, a broken or dislocated shoulder or arm. I gingerly raised myself off him, with great difficulty, and then put my hands out to help him to his feet. We examined each other minutely – still waiting to hear someone in the house query just what the awful crash had been – but, apart from him spotting a minor scrape on my right elbow, we finally came to the conclusion we had been extremely lucky – in more ways than one. Imagine two middle-aged people having to explain what on earth they had been doing in the middle of the day? I shuddered at the thought of telephoning for an ambulance only to see the knowing faces of the driver and his mate when they entered my dishevelled bedroom. Suddenly we caught each other's eye and howled with laughter. Peal after peal echoed all round that tiny room and I still half expected Glenda to come running to discover what on earth all the noise was about.

We strolled out of the house – still hiccuping every time we thought of our stupid escapade and the consequences from which we had so luckily escaped – and made our way back to the sandy beach. I showed Andrew what I thought was the most endearing part of Old Town – Nowhere – and then dragged him across the beach towards the twelfth century church of St Mary. It is confusing for visitors to learn that most of the Anglican churches on all the islands are dedicated to the Virgin Mary: this one, I felt, was the most picturesque. We didn't stay long. I pointed out the grand monument raised by the grieving husband of Louise Holzmaister, a newly married 23-year old who was on the wrecked *Schiller* bound from New York to join her millionaire husband in Germany. I also showed him the simple burial plaque to Prime Minister Harold Wilson who quietly spent many of his holidays here. Andrew would have lingered but I had to remind him he should be getting back as we still had to walk the cliff path over Peninnis Head. I pointed out *Pulpit Rock*, the cavern of *Izzicumpucca*, the *Kettle and Pans, Tooth Rock* and the *Monk's Cowl*. There were others near the Lighthouse – like the *Tuskless Elephant*, the *Witch's Head* and the *Walrus* but I hadn't time to stop and figure them out It was getting late and a round of golf does not last *that* long.

As we hurried down the overgrown path that leads to Porthcressa Beach I remembered to ask exactly why he had come to take Fay on this holiday. He turned towards me and grasped my hands.

'It was all a mistake, Jenny. I had booked everything and received all the tickets and a welcome confirmation from our hosts. Fay was rifling through my bureau for some stamps – so she says – and came across the whole package. When I arrived home from golf that evening, she met me with the paperwork in her hands. I was speechless that she had discovered I was preparing to leave her. But no, she thought I was making amends and was going to surprise her with a holiday of a lifetime. She even phoned her friends, I noticed, that night and I could hear her delighted murmurings as she showed off to them. I'm sorry, darling, I went along with it. It seemed easier.'

'But why didn't you tell *me*?' I asked, puzzled at his answer.

'Just too damned scared and embarrassed, I suppose. And the longer I left it the more difficult it became until, in the end, I buried it away and hoped you had forgotten and would never ask me.'

I pulled a face at him. 'Forgotten? I was too shy to ask and, in the end, I decided it was more important that you left her and came home to me instead of worrying about a holiday that we could take any time after all that had all been settled.'

He looked crestfallen and only cheered up as we came abreast of the house he had booked us both into. 'That's our bedroom up there,' he gestured. I winced. Fay was probably in that room and preparing to go out for an evening meal at that very moment. I said goodbye and swiftly walked inland towards *Buzza Tower*, the site of St Mary's old disused windmill, then cut across towards the Old Town Road which soon led me back to Nowhere and home. Andrew had mentioned he hoped to visit Tresco or St Agnes the next day so, studying the map while I munched my dinner that evening, I decided I should take myself off in the other direction and visit St Martin's. I certainly did not want to encounter him or Fay in either place!

But the best-laid plans of mice and men can often be knocked awry by contrary Cornish weather. The previous few days had occasionally been fiercely hot but mostly we had been blessed with a warm sun and a slight breeze. That morning, as I struggled to wake from a deep sleep, I became aware of a liquid pattering close by. I stepped out of bed and went and peered from my window towards the sea. An ethereal mist was creeping into the bay and the muted noise that had woken me was a soft rain gently falling on the broad-leaved garden plants. I kept thinking *rain before seven: dry before eleven* as I took myself down for breakfast but, in this instance, it didn't work because, by the time I was booted and cagouled up, the drizzle was as persistent as ever. One always has to have an alternative plan on these isles so, on the spur of the moment, I decided the Longstone Heritage Centre, close to the middle of the island, might be a better bet. It was easy enough to get there. From a road at the back of Old Town I took the Nature Trail that led towards Rose Hill. On a balmy summer's evening it is pleasant to meander up through paths cut deep in the grass on the Lower Moors and watch an abundance of birds and wildlife. But, on a damp morning in June it was not, but at least I knew the various paths and narrow boards would save me from an unsuspected bog – and wet feet. It was a simple journey and, turning right when I reached Telegraph Road, I walked on until I found the right hand turn that led straight to the Centre. From the outside it looked like a large wooden shed but, once inside, I divested myself of my damp waterproof and was welcomed by the appetising smell of coffee and baking buns. The café is surprisingly bright and modern so, of course, I was tempted to sit down. Resisting, I decided to do my homework first and go and look around the tiny museum. I was their first customer that morning so the woman behind the counter was delighted to point the way and I then stepped into the beguiling world of Scillonian memorabilia.

A couple followed me in and, while the woman opted for a

seat and a drink, the man trailed behind me. We strolled around together, discussing the diverseness of the collection, and we were frankly amazed at the thought and work that had gone into it. The amateur curators had assembled photographs and artefacts from the whole community, we reckoned. Families had lovingly given up heirlooms they had probably kept for centuries and it all came together to tell the story of a sturdy island people who were used to being self-sufficient and forward thinking.

We both returned to the café and, while the husband regaled his wife with island stories, I downed a quick cup of coffee and, as a fitful sun had appeared, decided to be off and catch the afternoon boat to St Martin' s after all. As I walked to the door the proprietor asked us if we would like to sign the museum book and add our comments. Both the man and I did so willingly and that's how my offering of: *Absolutely brilliant collection! You should be very proud of all your hard work. Thanks so much for sharing it with me. Jenny Fairburn. Seaton, Devon*, came to be written.

I enjoyed a lovely afternoon on St Martin's. It always seems a distinctively different island to me. A huge crescent with sweeping beaches and glistening sands – so white they hurt my eyes. The boatman landed us at Lower Town Quay and I ate a quick snack at the Seven Stones Inn before making my way up to The Cove and *Rabbit Rocks*, wandering down to Great Bay, Wine Cove and Burnt Hill before cutting inland past *Old Nick's Table* and Little Arthur Farm to get back to Higher Town Bay and the Quay where we were to be picked up. I sat on the beach, leaning against a rowing boat for shelter and enjoyed the solitude. I could easily have dreamed I was on a desert island in the Caribbean. We assembled at the Quay and awaited our boat. The boatman arrived punctually, as usual; then good naturedly waited for a dad and his young son. They had come out with us but had obviously misjudged the time, or the distance, they would need to walk to our new meeting place at the other end of the island. They came puffing up as were getting ready to caste off, full of apologies.

As we came in sight of Halangy Point on St Mary's my mobile phone beeped in my rucksack. I leaned down to disentangle it from beneath my feet and found a terse text message from Andrew. *DON'T – REPEAT DON'T – MEET THE BOAT FROM TRESCO.*

DON'T GET IN TOUCH BY TEXT OR PHONE. SHE HAS FOUND OUT YOU ARE HERE & ALL HELL HAS BROKEN LOOSE. I WILL GET IN TOUCH WITH YOU. A x

It occurred to me he must have keyed it in earlier but had only decided to send it on their return journey. He had obviously panicked, dreading a confrontation. I doubted if Fay had ever seen a photograph of me but, even if she had, the number of visitors disgorged from so many boats every evening meant there would be little likelihood of her spotting me in such a melee. Still, I was relieved we would be arriving later than usual due to our tardy father and son duo with their excuses. The Quay was almost deserted as we came in to land. Most folk had rushed off for a decent meal and, as I stepped ashore, I glanced around but could only see an untidy pile of fish boxes – and not an avenging virago within sight...

****

The next day I decided to go to St Agnes and hoped Andrew hadn't decided to do the same. I was determined this long-awaited holiday would not be spoiled so I walked into Hugh Town, by the direct route, as soon as I completed my breakfast. I had an inkling Fay was not an early riser so I thought it would be a good idea to take one of the first boats out of the harbour that morning. The day had dawned bright and clear and, as it now had tiny puffs of cotton wool decorating the edges of a deep blue sky, I reckoned we were in for some perfect weather. I scrambled aboard, keeping a sharp eye out for any irate travellers to appear; which soon turned into a deep sigh of relief as we cast off in the warm sunshine.

I'm not sure why I prefer St Agnes to all the other islands – Tresco is too commercialised for me with all its golfing buggies and expensively dressed visitors, Bryher frightens me with some dangerously steep cliffs, St Martin's always feels isolated and quiet while Sansom depresses me with its sad, desolate loneliness of the dispossessed – but, strangely, this oddly shaped island has always appeared welcoming and delightful whenever I have set foot on it.

We slid in between *the cow* and *calf* at Porth Conger and alighted under The Turk's Head Inn. It was only a short walk up the hill to the pub and most visitors drop off there for their morning coffee, only to be seduced into staying as they chatter and look down on this enchanting, sheltered cove. I, on the other hand, have a ritual – I walk up through Higher Town and check to see if the sand bar to the Island of Gugh is uncovered and then, if it isn't, I carry on walking until I reach Love Lane. I believe now it is called *Barnaby's* Lane but, as a young local lad called it by this evocative name years ago, in my world it will always be 'Love Lane'. The lichen here grows thick and crusty and, in the hedgerows, wild flowers flourish with abandon. Usually I swing along beneath the dappled shade of the overhanging trees and, in this state of exuberance, come upon the huge sweep of grassland that is known as Wingletang Down. Very rarely are people to be found up here – maybe the odd dog walker – and I can revel in the solitude and space. I can only describe it as a stage setting; close by there are rocks of all different sizes and shapes, as if a giant has tossed them randomly across the grass, and, in the distance, there are more oddly formed rocks in the restless sea – these are often surrounded by a frill of white spray. Imagine all this is placed against a backdrop of cerulean blue sky and you will understand how breathtaking and magical it always feels to be here.

I had brought a picnic lunch and ate it in the shelter of *Crooked Rock* while looking across at the precariously balanced *Punchbowl* with *Gull Rocks* seemingly poised behind it on the edge of the cliffs. Afterwards I wandered down to Beady Pool but, as usual, was unsuccessful at finding any Venetian trinkets. From here it was easy to follow the indented coastline to St Warna's Cove and Castella Down where HMS *Firebrand* was wrecked in the 1700s after foundering along with three other British Ships of the Line on the infamous *Gilstone Ledges*. I always laugh at *The Nag's Head Rock* which I think should be renamed *The Happy Camel* as it always reminds me of an amused, snooty camel! After poking around the Troy Town Maze I made my way towards the Old Lifeboat Station at Periglis where so many seamen have been rescued after their ships were wrecked on the maze of rocks that litter these shores. I try to make a point of visiting the tiny church here. It commemorates many generations of lifeboatmen, mostly of the Hicks family, with its only decoration simple stained-glass windows while outside many of their leaning gravestones fill the tiny churchyard. I was tired by then and it seemed a good idea to make my way back to the Turk's Head for a well-deserved pot of tea and a slice of saffron cake. The boat came to pick us up shortly after and I watched sadly as my favourite island receded slowly into a warm haze. I alighted cautiously back at St Mary's – still being well aware I could be rubbing shoulders with an unknowing Fay – as I joined the dozens all sauntering through Hugh Town. My holiday was rapidly passing – seven days was never long enough for me as I love the islands so much – and I wanted to squeeze every last moment of enjoyment out of the few days I had left.

Up at the Tolman Café that night I was regaled by the daring young local waiters who had been diving off *Gull Rock*, out in Old Town Bay, once their lunchtime duties were finished. They were always full of fun, never obsequious, with lots of laughter and teasing and, surprisingly, they always wanted to know how the visitors had spent *their* day. As usual, we ended up in a huge semi-circle as folk left their tables and pulled up chairs, either downing the rest of their wine or opting for an after-dinner coffee. That was the best part of the evening for me. I loved to hear how others had been enjoying themselves. The lads also forecast good weather for the next day, so I immediately decided to do a round tour of the island – starting in an anti-clockwise direction. I always wanted to explore the ancient village on Halangy Down but we had never seemed to find enough time to fit it in. This time I would.

As predicted, the Thursday morning dawned bright and breezy so I was up with the sun and eating an early breakfast shortly afterwards. In my heart I was relieved that this would be the day Andrew and Fay would be leaving the islands. I hoped he had seen and explored some of the best places the Scillies had to offer and also that he had managed to weather Fay's acid comments. Personally, I felt it would have been easier to tell her the truth and accept her justified wrath. Surely that would have been the honest thing to do and, by accepting her scathing comments, he could regain a measure of pride that he had tried, but unfortunately had not succeeded, in mending their failing marriage? Surely there would be no dishonour in acknowledging a mistake had been made rather than compounding the offence? One could obviously point out I was looking at it from only one side of the argument – yes,

I had a vested interest in the outcome – but when I accepted my marriage to Chris had broken down after ten years, I had faced it and we had both of us acted in a responsible way to do something about it. But, more importantly, we had still retained a link of friendship. I always considered that's what sensible adults did and I was expecting Andrew, Fay and I to conduct ourselves in a similar way.

I was totally unprepared for a relationship that was split three ways. Andrew, as a last resort, may have considered he could keep a precarious balance between the two women in his life, but I was certain neither Fay nor I would ever accept a *ménage à trois*. As far as I was concerned, Andrew had to choose one or the other of us – and then abide by his decision. Anything else was preposterous and, once I had left York and had had time to think about the whole sorry mess, I knew for certain that *I* for one, would never accept second best.

There were two final days of my holiday left and I had planned to walk around the coastal path of St Mary's on the first, and save a visit to Tresco for my final one. I had promised myself a picnic lunch by the *Innisidgen Burial Chamber*, before carrying on round the north of the island to Bar Point which would enable me to take a proper look at the medieval settlement on Halangy Down which nestled under the Island's radio mast. I hitched up my rucksack in anticipation, striding up the footpath towards the airport runway. I climbed up round Church Porth and *Tom Butt's Bed* when I saw a knot of folk chattering on the footpath at the edge of the cliff. As I came nearer three of them broke away and made their way towards me. Like me they sported backpacks, shorts and hiking boots and I grinned at them in the usual way as they came abreast and wished me good day. I leaned forward to fondle the silken ears of their irrepressible spaniel puppy and wished them a good walk. Ten more steps brought me to the remaining couple. Both were staring out to sea, he with heavy binoculars and she as if the horizon held a great interest. For a second it registered that the woman, who was closest to me, was oddly dressed for a stroll across the cliffs. No matter - I cheerily wished them both good morning and went to stride around them. The woman, who was wearing a long, cream-coloured, loose coat to her ankles, swung round and literally glared at me – as if I was disturbing her morning reverie. I smiled again – slightly tentatively – wondering why, on such a lovely day, she obviously hated the world. The man lazily turned, lowered the glasses and answered politely for them both.

For a second the whole scene sparked, as if an electrical storm had scorched my eyes and I found myself smiling at Andrew's shadowy form and then, at my next step, I was past them and moving forwards. To my credit, I never faltered or changed my gait as I reached the summit of that cliff path and started descending towards the beach at Porth Hellick. I knew there was a sheltered bench here, facing the beach, and as I reached it I sank down gratefully and stared out to sea – my mind a jumble of breathlessness and amazement. I had been living in a false paradise. Instead of relaxing I should have stayed keenly alert. It had never occurred to me Fay and Andrew would be tardy in leaving the island. How had they found their way to the cliffs at all? She hated walking and, indeed, she was dressed more for a day at the races, or designer shopping, than for scrambling over rocks above a restless sea. And her baleful glare had whipped the wind out of my lungs and almost erased the happy smile off my face. This woman clearly hated anyone of the feminine gender that day and her angry stare was enough to chase away any pleasantries one would normally offer. But the sheer effrontery Andrew showed when he slowly turned and faced me left me stunned. All I could think was maybe he had been as shocked as me when he turned round and found me confronting him. If so I applauded his serene exterior. I know my heart had thumped in those few seconds like a pile-driver battering concrete. If he had seen me as I made my way up the footpath after crouching down and stroking the delightful puppy while laughing up at its owner, he had showed an amazingly calm exterior with a split-second sense of timing. Was he that clever a liar or had we just been fortunate? I preferred to think the latter...

After collecting my requisite handful of tiny shells on the beach, I made my way up towards Darrity's Hole and on to the *Innisidgen* Burial Tomb that, I'm told, dates back over 5,000 years. Its circle looked so neat, rounded and clipped that it appeared slightly unreal and even modern. Did Scillonians at one time live in it I wondered or was it only prepared for an important chief at his death? There were no window spaces for light or air but then perhaps these people only required security, shelter and safety. I puzzled about their food and drinking water as I munched my tasty pasty, peeled a ripe banana and washed it down with a small bottle of ginger beer. Did they farm animals or live solely on their catch from the sea? I would ask at the Town Museum before I took the boat to Tresco next day, I decided. Gradually I was starting to calm down after my narrow escape with Fay. It looked as if she was still in a towering rage with the whole world – with most of it being directed towards her spouse. I pitied him his journey back to the mainland and in the car during the long trek back to Yorkshire. What on earth could they talk about – or would she harangue him constantly the whole way?

I settled my backpack comfortably across my shoulders and attempted to whistle as I tramped on. After passing Little Porth at the north of the island, the path veered westward towards Pendrathen Quay. I am always amazed when I reach here to find genteel little bungalows, as well as a few farms, so far from the bustling port of Hugh Town, but instead of venturing down their neat, flower lined streets I kept to the coastal footpath which did a wide sweep around the bay and pretended I was totally alone. This area was known as Morgelyn by the locals, which always reminded me of Merlin the Magician and King Arthur. Just inside Crow Rock was Pendrathen Quay which was constructed in 1759 to provide shelter for small vessels from the off islands. I sat there for some time, close to a heap of pungent lobster pots, and admired the view before taking a long look at Bant's Carn It was an immense burial chamber with a square entrance and I wondered who had been important enough to warrant such a grand tomb. The excavated, prehistoric settlement of round houses and courtyard houses were just as fascinating. These date from the Iron Age and, in my mind's eye, I put thatch on roofs and saw corralled animals, sleeping quarters and workshops. It seemed strange to remember that, when these primitive people were surviving like this, sophisticated Romans were living in decorated villas with central heating and baths!

Suddenly I was enormously tired so I turned towards more modern pleasures. I made my way south past the golf course to Juliet's Garden, where I was offered a pot of tea and some hot buttered crumpets plus a civilised conversation with a young crowd of backpackers with their college tutors. I arrived back at Old Town absolutely spent and weary and, although it was still early evening, my only priority was a snug, comfortable bed and a good night's sleep....

I awoke next morning to a welter of text messages from Andrew. He'd had the most horrendous journey back to York, he informed me. Fay had been sarcastic and tearful by turns: he had suffered it in silence and driven on doggedly.

What is there to say, Jenny? I met you and enjoyed every second we spent together – even to falling out of that narrow bed! She will never understand and, in all honesty, I cannot be bothered to explain to her that together WE are relaxed and happy and with HER I am bored, lethargic and sad. I will ring you as soon as you arrive home, my darling. Enjoy your last hours – wherever you are – and I will dream of how marvellous it would have been if we could have spent the whole week sleeping together, eating together, exploring together and laughing the whole time. All my luv D r e w x x

There were others – all in the same vein – and I read them as I was munching an early breakfast. My last day was to be spent on Tresco. I saw my favourite boatman and was delighted he would be taking me there. I listened to his dry, witty banter and was sad I would shortly be leaving the whole of these magical islands yet again. Fraser, the boatman, dropped us off at Carn Near Quay, close by Oliver's Battery, and I wandered up past Appletree Banks and *Figtree Rocks* towards the Abbey Gardens and dreamed of being there with Andrew. Had he seen the *Tresco Children* being tossed in the air at the end of the Lighthouse Walk, I pondered? What had he thought of the Valhalla Museum? Had he loved the gleaming metal Agave succulent fountain that nestled at the bottom of the stone steps? I strolled around in the sunshine feeling wistful and lonely. This would never do on my last day! So, after taking the required photo of the picturesque arches that was all that remained of the twelfth century St Nicholas's Priory, I made my way past Great Pool and Abbey Farm to the New Inn where I had a quick snack before going on to the north of the island.

The north end of the island was totally different from the south. Here there were windswept cliffs that were once protected by Cromwell's Castle and, above it, King Charles' Castle. The first one had a massive round tower and was built in 1651 as a protection from Dutch raiders. The second was older and, to my mind, far more picturesque. I took photos from every angle against a backdrop of a deep blue sea. Bryher looked close enough to wade across here and I stood, transfixed. If I had gone due north from here I would have found Piper's Hole –a narrow crevice that goes deep into the cliffs under the island. I had only visited it once before, with Robin, and I remembered a shallow pool and various rocky arches leading to massive vaulted caverns. As I'd looked around in awe I'd been able to imagine it as a smuggler's haven not that many years previously. We had been offered torches and had used the boat that was moored by the shingle beach but, without these aids, I didn't fancy exploring on my own. Instead, I took a short cut over Tregarthen Hill to gaze at Round Island and St Martin's before wandering down to the beach at Gimble Porth. This soon brought me back to Old Grimsby and the Island Hotel – where I dropped in for a well-deserved glass of cider. I couldn't stay long as I wanted to view the lush sands at Pentle Bay before making my way back to New Grimsby, on the other side of the island, and the boat home. I was too early, as usual, so I contented myself by snapping some flower-filled gardens surrounding the delightful cottages.

That night I had my last delicious crab salad at the friendly Tolman Café and returned home to swiftly pack my bags. I wanted to be away early the next morning to catch my flight back to Exeter and home. In fact I was amazed at the speed of my journey. I tugged my case back up the hill to the Airport and, within a short time, was settled comfortably in the small plane. I watched out of the window as we flew low over the Tate Gallery at St Ives and in no time at all landed in Exeter. The airport bus arrived within a few minutes of collecting our baggage and speeded me to the bus station. I found my Jurassic Coast bus ready to depart so I clambered aboard and, after studying my watch, I reckoned the whole journey had taken less than three hours. Back home, I tipped my clothes haphazardly into the washing machine and took myself off to sit on our beach accompanied by an ice cream cornet; and it was here that Andrew discovered me when he telephoned.

'Good holiday?' he queried.

'Yes, absolutely beautiful,' I said fervently.

'We will visit again, darling, I promise you,' and then he went on to tell me his plans were in place to leave York and come south. 'I have been getting my papers in order and selecting what I'll need in the way of clothes. Actually I have realised there is very little that I can't do without and, as long as I bring my golf clubs, my mobile phone and my shortwave radio I should be covered for all eventualities.'

I lay back on the pebbles and listened to his promises. Suddenly everything was alright in my small world and I knew how a contented kitten feels when it has been fed and stroked and is curled up by a fire. Little did I guess that even the best-laid plans can occasionally go awry and there is very little one can do about it...

Chapter 28

*

I had returned to Devon two days before Robin's wedding. I'd sent a card and a present of money which would enable them to choose whatever they wanted, or needed, to commence their new life together. I had made it clear to my good friends and family that I would be delighted for them to go up and join him for this intimate celebration. I knew it was important for him to have a show of solidarity and support to launch him in his new life. I was pleased that he had managed to resume a life with someone he had grown to love. As usual, Robin had acted differently from all other prospective bridegrooms. He had enquired if Dee and Paul would bring me up with them – which made me break into a peal of laughter. The first wife being present at the second wife's wedding? I think not!

The guests duly returned with reports that all went well - from my good friends and close family - and then I was shown photographs, accompanied by glowing accounts that Ailsa looked blooming and Robin was obviously sublimely happy - from other, so-called, acquaintances who probably hoped I would be overcome with guilt or jealousy. I listened to both descriptions and refrained from commenting on either. My prime concern was Robin's happiness; but most people, I notice, found this difficult to comprehend.

Andrew telephoned every evening, just before my evening meal. Each time he would promise to limit these calls but they normally ran for well over an hour, with him suddenly realising that time had passed all too quickly and he would invariably have to race back home and be late for his tea. Fay was ill-tempered and sickly sweet by turns, Drew told me, so it looked as if his imminent departure would be shelved once again. That was until I received an urgent text one morning, to say Fay would be accompanying her friends for an unexpected Spa Weekend and, if I could manage to join him, Andrew would book an equally long weekend for us both. I answered within seconds that he had only to give me the dates and I would book my journey immediately.

So, at the end of that week, I was speeding up north to be met by a jubilant Drew at York station. It was so lovely to see him again, standing on the edge of the platform as my train pulled up with a mighty sigh. He opened his arms wide and I melted into their strength and comfort with a similar sigh and then we were in his car and on our way before I could even register the bustle or energy that is York.

Our hotel was large, with a honeycomb of uniform rooms that are probably no different from another dozen that grace the streets of Harrogate. We registered, scampered up to our en suite *box*, closed the door gently and fell into each other's arms. I felt grubby after my journey so I elected to take a shower. I was amused to feel Andrew's impatience as he sank onto the wide bed and waited for me to emerge fresh and fragrant. We both sunk on the bed and completed what we had begun in my room on the Isles of Scilly. Later, as we talked and touched, he mentioned there had been a slight hitch in his plans. I went still immediately.

'What?' I demanded.

'I think Fay may have guessed something was up when I suggested I would be going on a golfing weekend. She scotched that idea by insisting I stay at home and mind the cat.'

'You *are* joking?' I said in amazement.

'No, she was adamant that *Marmalade* would not be farmed out just for a weekend and so, to keep the peace, I agreed.' As I sat up to protest he went on, 'Jenny, I didn't care what it took to get you up here. I would have flown to the moon and back, if she had demanded, so I agreed I would feed the damn cat.'

I am not sure what he expected but I erupted in a huge gale of laughter. 'Andrew, you really do take the biscuit! So how do we feed a cat that is miles away?' I asked.

'It is quite simple,' he said seriously. 'I get up at some ungodly hour and race home to give him two big bowls of food and water – tell him not to scoff it all at once and come straight back here for breakfast.'

I still found it difficult to keep a straight face as I teased him unmercifully. 'So poor old *Marmy* has to make his food last all day just so his owner can spend time in bed with his lover?'

'Yes, something like that. Now shift over and get dressed – I want to take you out for a three-course meal. I'm starving and I bet you are too – so jump to it, young lady.'

I arose smartly and we went downstairs to raid the hotel dining room. Funny how making love really *can* improve a person's appetite...

We didn't do much that I can remember for those four days. Drew did his marathon every morning and raced back in time to munch a large cooked breakfast. I tried not to tease him. We walked around the steep streets gazing at the elegant grand houses and the neatly regimented Victorian gardens and delved into various antique shops, but only to marvel at their prices.

We visited the Pine Marten Pub one lunchtime and shared a platter of tapas before we went on to the botanical gardens at Harlow Carr. Seventy acres of woodland trees, gardens, pools and rockeries to enjoy in relative seclusion. I am sure Andrew had visited numerous times before; but he took his time as he guided me to all the best corners and waited while I snapped away diligently and found all the best camera angles.

We did the Pump Room, naturally, although we "didn't take the water". I was told the smell was disgusting. We also visited the Assembly Rooms and enjoyed their coffee and cakes as the palm court orchestra played genteelly. I wondered if Jane Austen had felt like me – cosseted and delicate. I was impressed by the sweeping, red-carpeted staircase and could imagine slender Regency ladies gliding down them in their diaphanous, high-waisted dresses in the hope of attracting a rich, well-connected Lord. Not so different from today, I mused, except that modern girls are much more open about their preferences.

Time flew and, on the last day when we checked out, Andrew appeared quiet and subdued. I'm sure he had envisaged these few days as an extended, relaxing holiday, but as always once we were together, all sensible thoughts faded from his mind: thus my imminent departure came as a great shock. I have to admit we were both as bad as each other. I always planned what I was going to discuss with him before we met and yet, once we were together, all coherent thoughts disappeared and all the concrete questions and answers were never voiced *nor* satisfactory replies ever given. So we were as adrift as we had always been in a sea of uncertainty and confusion – living from day to day and never formulating a plan for the future.

Andrew drove back to York swiftly and I dared not ask when Fay was due back from her luxury pampering weekend. He took me into *The Fox and Roman Inn*, on the Tadcaster Road, for lunch – probably to remind us both of how often we would wander in for meals when we were a legitimate couple. We sat close to one another and chose all our favourite fare. Andrew kept up a pretence of feverish chatter as he endeavoured to make our last hours stretch a little longer. His mobile phone buzzed and we both looked at it in alarm. He curtly answered and I winced for the caller until I saw his face change from patient resignation to radiance.

'What?' I asked.

'She will be later than they expected,' he answered, grinning widely. 'They left late and now hope to be home by early evening. Come on, sweetheart, we are off to an antiques fair that is on at the Knavesmire Racecourse today.' He plucked my napkin off my lap and dragged me up. 'Get your coat on and we will go have some fun!'

And that's what we did. It obviously never occurred to him that we could so easily have bumped into his friends or neighbours as we mingled with the huge crowds on the course. We trailed everywhere and looked at everything. Nothing was beneath our interest as we walked around, hand in hand, pointing out our favourite bargains and discussing their merits. I ended up with an armful of gifts – a tiny gem of a painting of Clifford's Tower, a brass mouse, two silver napkin rings, a commemorative stamp of Prince William that I had long wanted, a Roman coin that Andrew promised to turn into a bookmark and a delicate, screen-printed scarf. Andrew became the proud owner of three ancient postcards of Cornwall, an Edwardian desk set complete with original pens and cut-glass inkstands and – just as we were reluctantly leaving – a highly polished tantalus. Feeling pleasantly tired, we wandered back to the car and stored our treasures in the boot.

He had booked me a last night in an hotel close to where we had lived. Ignoring the magnetic pull of wanting to take one last look at the home where we had been so happy, we went inside and were shown a lovely room with an elegant four-poster bed. The lamps glowed and the whole place took on a rosy glow as we gently closed the door and sank down on that beautiful bed. We tried to pretend there was no deadline, although I was sure Andrew knew exactly when he would have to leave. After he beguiled me with slow and languorous lovemaking we lay together and chatted quietly. I guessed he wanted me to drift off into a deep and natural sleep. This would enable him to slip away without me having to disguise my distress. I watched him steal a surreptitious glance at his wristwatch and put him out of his misery by softly advising him to go. He slid out of bed and kissed me deeply yet tenderly and, within a few breaths, he had gently closed our bedroom door. I slid down in the bed, pulling the duvet over my head, and tried to smother my strangled sobs.

The next morning I received a hurried text wishing me a safe journey, and mentioning he had hardly slept all night. 'Snap,' I whispered as I hurried down for my solitary breakfast. My train came in sharply on time. I intently scanned the faces of the chattering crowds meandering past me as I searched for a certain person, who I desperately hoped might just arrive in time to speed me on my way. My wish was, of course, not granted but, with almost hourly regularity, I received yet other texts informing me I was missed; he hated my disappearing into the distance; he was already making plans and, finally, "*Goodnight, darling. I can't bear the thought of you not lying in my arms tonight. I keep kicking myself for my crass stupidity and wonder how you can ever forgive me. I promise to speak to you tomorrow, when I go for my walk. Sleep well, sweetheart.*" I grimaced briefly as I hoisted my tired body onto the last bus home and puzzled also how I was still able to forgive him.

Early the next morning Val demanded I go up to her flat and regale her with my Harrogate escapade. We were just sipping coffee when Bertrand bounced in. He had been out for the morning papers; now he contented himself by settling back on the settee to study them whilst half listening to my stories of hilarious cat feeding, exploring a snobbish Victorian spa town with its up-market antique shops, aimlessly wandering around draughty streets and sitting in far too many pubs and cafés.

'I did enjoy some lovely gardens at a place called Harlow Carr,' I admitted, 'but really it was a tad too cold to be exploring an English spa town.'

'I have an idea,' said Val unexpectedly. 'Let's get away.'

'Away?' I murmured.

'Yes,' said Bertrand, 'why don't the three of us go off somewhere nice? Somewhere abroad, somewhere warm?'

I glanced from one to the other in bewilderment. My two neighbours enjoyed a pleasant uneventful life together; I knew they never yearned for exotic holidays or longed to leave the West Country – but still they were willing to put themselves out for me. For ages they had listened, and seldom commented, when I agreed to meet Andrew at any destination he chose – wherever and whenever. I would put my life on hold and fly to do his bidding. I often joked about it with them; how I was always alert for the unexpected – a chance meeting in some unexpected place; a friend recognising and challenging Andrew. In the supermarket or a department store, crossing a busy road – there was always tension and I was ready to melt into the background within seconds. Maybe they felt I was being ridiculously super-sensitive on his behalf, but somehow *I* felt it only proved the extent and depth of my love. And now my two dear friends were offering me an escape – where there would be no stress and I could totally relax. I was sorely tempted.

Within days the holiday was arranged. We were to go to Lanzarote for two weeks at an all-inclusive luxury hotel. I told Andrew immediately the final arrangements were made and he said very little apart from that he was thinking of a cruise to a similar destination. I tried not to remember that if we had stayed together, it would have been *us* planning such a holiday. I told him we would be off in six weeks time and he wished us all well.

Two days before we left Andrew rang me one evening and casually mentioned his cruise liner might be stopping at Arrecife, the capital of Lanzarote, after it had called into Cadiz, Gibraltar, Madeira and Las Palmas.

'If you are still on the island, maybe we could meet, darling?' It all sounded a bit improbable to me but I made all the right responses knowing it was highly unlikely our dates would match and, if they did, Fay would expect to disembark from the liner too and Andrew would never be able to extricate himself from any organised excursions. I immediately told Val and Bertrand, expecting them to be amused. I don't think they were.

We left Devon at an unearthly hour on a sharp, frosty morning and arrived to an afternoon of blazing sunshine. And that was the way it stayed the whole holiday. We spent two days exploring the island by coach. We learned about the artist, Cesar Manrique, and his dream for the island to become a veritable paradise. We discovered a smouldering volcano, a blue lagoon set deep in a tropical garden, a house built in five volcanic bubbles, a look-out set high on precipitous cliffs and beaches surrounding the whole island. The rest of the holiday we lazed under sunshades around a warm pool or gorged ourselves on all the lavish fare that was on offer. My friends watched indulgently as I slipped in and out of the pool and waved me off as I walked for miles along a palm-encrusted promenade that edged some delightful beaches. It was right at the tail end of our holiday that Andrew rang with some news. He had texted me every day of his cruise. They had been unlucky with adverse weather conditions and had suffered storms and almost constant rain while at sea. So, although they went ashore at both Cadiz and Gibraltar, their sightseeing was spoilt in consequence. Sadly the captain had decided to give Madeira a miss as the conditions then worsened and they spent two days aimlessly circling the island with their swimming pool emptied for safety reasons. I tried to play down our excellent weather but Andrew realised, as soon as they entered the harbour at Las Palmas, that the Canaries had been enjoying its usual pleasant climate. He reported their whole liner breathed a sigh of relief and bodies, once more, relaxed in the sunshine.

I was splashing along the edge of the sea alone in Los Pocillos when my mobile phone started beating out its distinctive melody. I cautiously fished it out of my pocket to answer.

'Hi, it's me, darling. We have just landed and are disembarking. I will meet you at *San Gabriel's* castle, so be a good girl and grab a taxi and I will be waiting.'

I laughed: after days of warm relaxation I was stupidly somnolent and laid-back, and countered with, 'Gosh I can almost see your beach from here. I can actually see the *Gran Hotel* skyscraper in the distance and I could probably walk along the beach to you. But, don't worry, I will get a local bus and be with you in no time.'

'Don't be silly,' he answered. 'We don't have unlimited time, so get a taxi – I will pay.'

This stung me as I was perfectly capable of paying for my own transport, but I dutifully trotted across the beach and found a friendly taxi driver who was only too willing to take me to Lanzarote's chief city. Andrew was so eager that he spent most of the journey urging me, on his mobile, to get there as soon as possible. Unfortunately, as usual, we hit massive traffic congestion as soon as we reached the outskirts of this busy city. Too many expensive and popular shops crowded the narrow streets which were always alive with noisy cars and buses. My driver kept apologising until he eventually manoeuvred his way through to the seafront and dropped me in front of two massive cannon outside a small castle built on a tiny rocky island. Andrew, with a huge smile, stepped forward proffering a wad of currency, but I was delighted to wave him away. I had paid and tipped my driver earlier.

Drew then enfolded me in a huge bear hug until I thought I would be crushed. We meandered along the beach, hand in hand, until we came to that awful monstrosity that is the *Gran Hotel*. Seventeen storeys high and a blot on the landscape. I explained how Cesar Manrique, a venerated artist in Lanzarote, had an architectural vision of a pure and simple island. Buildings of only two or three stories with no garish colours or embellishments, and how the people took it to their hearts and honoured his concept. I explained that, in 1994, it had burned down in rather suspicious circumstances, but if it was Andrew's choice then I would accompany him to the rooftop restaurant and enjoy a meal with him. Actually, I was able to point out, across the sandy beaches and indented coastline, my low-rise hotel with its landscaped gardens and surrounding swimming pools. I talked about my holiday as we ate.

Afterwards we paddled in the sea and wandered towards Playa Honda where we sat on a shady bench and chatted until it was time to return to his ship. He never explained where Fay was on that bright and balmy day and I never enquired; but I was well aware that, as soon as we neared the coach that was picking up stray cruise-line passengers, he became alert and silent. Our hands slipped free and, apart from one fierce hug in the shadow of an esplanade palm tree, we walked along as passing strangers going their separate ways.

I had refused Andrew's offer of my taxi fare back. He could see I was adamant and therefore didn't insist. As soon as he swung onto the coach and found himself a seat, I abruptly turned and walked swiftly back along the way we had strolled hand in hand only a short time before. The open-air coach station was easy to find and I only had a few minutes of waiting in the blazing sun before I climbed aboard a local bus and was shortly deposited back outside my own hotel.

I raced in to find Val and Bertrand trying to disguise the fact that they had been waiting anxiously for me. They were sitting under two sunshades around the main pool and Bertrand immediately bustled off to order us all some cool drinks. I eased myself down on the extra sun lounger and turned to face Val's enquiring scrutiny.

'Yes I was on the beach when my mobile rang,' I answered. 'Andrew's cruise liner had berthed at Arrecife and he insisted I grab a taxi and get there to meet him as soon as possible.'

'So you obviously did,' she countered, dryly. 'Raced off and then, when he had finished with you, he allowed you to return to us.' I could do little but agree. 'I think it is about time you stopped obeying his every whim and started doing your own thing, Jenny. You aren't a little henpecked housewife, my love, and yet you act like one. This state of affairs has been going on since first we met you in the flats.' I nodded numbly and, by the time Bertrand had returned with a tray of drinks and ice creams, she was lecturing me as to what *my* preferences might be now I had only myself to consider. Bertrand looked distinctly uncomfortable but I could see, deep down, he agreed with every word Val was saying to me. I smiled hesitantly and clasped both their hands – they were only voicing what probably all my friends had thought and yet had been afraid to say to me.

As Bertie reminded me, with an understanding smile, time was passing and there was a big, wide world out there just waiting to be explored. I hugged them both and knew I was so lucky to have such considerate and loving friends. By the time we went into dinner that evening I had compiled a long list of "to do's" offset by a shorter one of "no way's" and we were all giggling at the improbability of some of my desires and pet hates.

'Yes, I'd love to visit the Caribbean or New Zealand,' I agreed. 'But there is no way I want to climb Mount Kilimanjaro or even go skiing. Brr...too cold! I think, for now, I will just stick to exploring as much of the UK as I am able – like Portmeirion, Hadrian's Wall, the Lake District, Scotland's far flung islands and all points in between. I shall also go and visit Dorothy who was so kind to me in York,' I promised myself. 'It will also be easy to take the bus to Plymouth, Torbay, Weymouth or Cornwall. Oh, and Chatsworth House is a must and, if I get to the Isle of Wight again, I would like to visit Osborne House.'

'Surely there must be some hobbies you have fancied over the years?' Val prodded.

'Yes, ballroom dancing, learning to draw and doing the maths exams I was unable to complete at school. I have always been too busy at the hospital, looking after my husband, home and dog or seeing to my elderly neighbours to do any of these things. Now I am virtually a free agent and it looks as if Andrew, for all his promises, is dragging his feet so I will seriously think of just what *I* want to do in the near future.' Val and Bertrand both nodded enthusiastically and we all toasted my new-found ambitions with a large glass of brandy each.

Chapter 29

*

I returned from my invigorating holiday with my two delightful friends fired up with ideas as to how I would kick-start my life once more. I had vaguely acknowledged, as time drifted by, that I had been waiting for Andrew to come down to the West Country and rescue me. From what, I wasn't sure – solitariness, boredom, stagnation, being stuck in a humdrum routine? Whatever it was I knew Andrew felt no urgent reason to oblige and so this was to be the first day of my freedom. I contacted a dance studio and booked to attend a two-hourly weekly ballroom dance class every Wednesday afternoon in Lyme Regis. I explained that I was a complete novice and pretty ancient into the bargain. The male voice that answered assured me I would enjoy myself and I sincerely hoped he was right.

When I shyly turned up the next Wednesday I found a similar mixture of would-be learners. There were a few couples who mostly kept to themselves and practised in a compact group. As time passed I was aware they felt a little superior to the rest of us – probably because they already had a built-in partner and were certainly not looking for any outside input. The rest of us were mostly women who obviously had little to do on a Wednesday afternoon; or possibly needed the exercise. Our teacher, a young man called Ben, in his early thirties, was almost as shy as the rest of us. He demonstrated some simple steps accompanied by some lilting music and so I hoped anything was possible. When he diffidently took me out on the floor I tried to make myself as light as a feather and malleable to his guidance – hoping I could pick it up as I went along. At the tea break, half way through the class, I met half a dozen chattering ladies. Within weeks they became pleasant acquaintances.

Two days later I enquired of my old walking club in Honiton if they would include me once more in their Friday outings. They welcomed me back and the next week I happily joined them on a short ramble around the thatched village of Broadhembury. Afterwards, we went to the pub for a cream tea and, looking around at familiar faces, it was as if I had never been away. They all politely didn't mention my leaving Robin, my year in York or me suddenly turning up in Seaton; but they did appear suitably sad when I mentioned Crumble, my faithful walking companion, had died of old age.

I also looked around to see if there was a voluntary work niche that I would be suitable for in my home-town. Although there were many charity shops in Seaton there was nothing that fired my enthusiasm or caught my imagination. I wandered in and out of them – often picking up the odd bargain – but never feeling I would be much use to them. Instead I took myself on the bus over to see Jess in Taunton or travelled up to London to visit my cousins, Dee and Paul, or occasionally joined Meryl and Adam in Epping for a few days. Thus my days were suddenly busy and I now owned a calendar scribbled full of appointments.

Andrew said very little about my new lifestyle. When he called and I was away from home he refrained from questioning me too closely as to my whereabouts. He might gently probe at a later date and I was always transparently honest, but I think he was well aware that if he was unable to provide what I wanted it was politic for him to keep quiet or he might possibly receive a tart reply! Suddenly I started to take a more active interest in my surroundings.

Then the weather changed. Persistent rain sluiced through gutters, cracks appeared in the sodden cliffs while trees slithered down hillsides and rivers overflowed. A cliff suddenly collapsed onto a lonely beach and a passing girl disappeared beneath it. We listened in horror as her rescuers tried to get to her and guessed, with certainty, it would be too late. In Seaton a crack appeared on a cliff-top road and, within a week, a great chasm gaped where it had been and most of the road tumbled down to the beach below. Behind, a whole community of houses were threatened.

On the Saturday the rain eased somewhat and a watery sun

appeared, so on the spur of the moment I decided to take myself off to Axminster purely for a change of scenery. After wandering round the shops and a delicious lunch I decided it would be sensible to return home as soon as possible as another lowering storm was fast approaching from the west. I had just made it to the station bus shelter, and squeezed myself in with a posse of boys clutching skateboards and mobile phones, when the heavens opened and a deluge of rain thundered down. A bus churned into the forecourt and disgorged a single passenger. He managed to squash himself into a corner as thunder cracked all around us and we realised what a flimsy refuge we had all chosen to cower in.

One by one the lads contacted their parents and mums in cars appeared and rescued them. Eventually the last one deserted us and suddenly I was on my own with a pleasant looking man. He was fairly tall, slimly built with slightly grizzled grey hair and I guessed him to be a couple of years my junior. We both smiled ruefully at each other and were forced to admit that no such liberators would be coming to take us to a place of safety. The speed of the event had taken us both by surprise and it seemed ridiculous to be marooned in a half-open bus shelter because neither of us were foolhardy enough to wade through the swirling waters to reach the comparative safety of the station. Water had gushed into the square and was gradually deepening and swirling around our legs. Our only option was to try and hoist ourselves out of it. With one accord we perched on the narrow metal seat and tucked our feet up out of the way in the hope some public transport would soon arrive to prevent us both being swept away.

Almost three hours were to elapse before there was any sign of the weather easing and I was in despair that life would ever return to normal that day. It was highly likely all buses had been halted due to the dangerous conditions. There had been no trains passing through the station behind us – so possibly they had ceased to operate and maybe the station was unmanned also. Would we ever get home that night, I wondered?

Meanwhile, to pass the time, we had introduced ourselves and were chattering away like a couple of magpies. He was an ex-schoolmaster who resided in Exmouth and had been on his way to Chard to view a house for his daughter who was currently in

Australia. He was in the process of selling her houseboat on the Thames and had decided it would be more beneficial to buy a cheap property, do it up and rent it out to provide her and her husband with an income. Since he had left education he had been dabbling in property renovation for some time, he explained. It produced a reasonable income and an interest at the same time. He liked to solve puzzles and what he didn't already know about modernising old houses he soon learned from the internet or DIY books. I was fascinated by this unique, pragmatic man who held such a positive view of life. He told me he owned a car but seldom used it as his van had proved more useful. He had given it to his son and now often used buses as they served a similar purpose and it was all good clean fun. I gently reminded him that the fun had missed us out that *particular* day, but he grinned and reminded *me* we would never have met but for the abominable weather.

'Look this is daft,' he said. 'I have no idea of your name even. There's me chattering away about my family, myself and what I do in my spare time – while you have hardly uttered a word.'

We shyly exchanged names and I discovered his was Giles, which seemed to suit him. He lived in a rambling house in Exmouth but had worked mostly in Dorset and Somerset as a teacher after following in his mother's footsteps. She had been a headmistress at a small country school and the calling had obviously been bred in him. He'd been married, but it hadn't worked out; regardless, he was still in contact with his ex-wife as well as being extremely close to his two grown-up children.

'Well go on,' he nudged 'what's your claim to fame?'

So, slowly - but gradually gathering courage - I told him in short, succinct sentences about the ten years of Chris's infidelities, the warm loyalty of a long, happy marriage with Robin and the madcap whirlwind of my renewed affair with Andrew. Somehow he seemed to grasp and understand the muddled life I had led. He made suitable comments as I earnestly talked.

'Whew!' he whistled. 'And there was me thinking my life was a bit avant-garde – but yours sounds even more adventurous. Look, Jenny, I'd like to see you again. Maybe we could have coffee or even do lunch sometime next week. Meet me in Sidmouth or somewhere, and let's take it from there,' he suggested with a disarming smile.

I panicked immediately. It was one thing cosily sharing one's life story with a complete stranger under such strange circumstances; but quite another to step into an unknown friendship with a man I had only just met. Did I want to complicate my life yet again? As we continued chatting I began to calm down and, when he said, 'Why don't you give me your telephone number Jenny and, when I get in touch, you will have had time to decide if you want to meet again or politely decline my invitation.' I then realised I was being faintly ridiculous and melodramatic. A few minutes later the rain eased considerably and, quite shortly after that, the first bus surged into the station yard causing wavelets to eddy in every direction. Giles jumped down into about six inches of floodwater and flagged down the driver. As he dived inside he swung round and asked, 'Well what's your number, Jenny?' I gave in with a laugh and immediately the single-decker pulled away.

My Seaton bus chugged in a few minutes later and I was relieved to get home to a comforting bath and steaming hot cocoa. There were stories on the television that night of rivers breaking their banks and sea defences failing. I watched in awe as I realised I had been remarkably lucky. I was just finishing my meal that evening when my telephone burbled. 'So you are not still sitting in that bus shelter then?' a teasing voice asked.

Well it was not the steamiest of liaisons, I can now admit. We saw each other occasionally when Giles thought of it. He had a habit of ringing at the crack of dawn and asking me to meet later that day. I suspect he usually had a few hours to spare from his busy life and decided it was worth a try. Generally I had plans made and was unable to accommodate him at such short notice; I would invariably remind him that, if he had rung a few days previously, I would have loved to go wherever he was suggesting. He was an intelligent and interesting man and we could chat for hours but, sadly, there was no spark between us and I was not unduly sorry when our meetings gradually petered out. It was almost Christmas when I heard from him again. I was in bed and just relishing my early morning cuppa.

'Guess where I am?' asked a warm, friendly voice.

'No idea,' I replied, recognising the educated, Somerset burr and putting my mug of tea safely down on the bedside cabinet.

'I'm at Heathrow airport, soon to be on my way to Australia.'

I must have sounded suitably impressed because he went on, 'I've been a bit of an idiot, actually – I booked a flight out there as a surprise for my daughter and her husband, only to be told ten minutes ago they are leaving today to come over here. So we will be passing each other in mid-flight! Dope that I am – I never thought to warn them in advance.' I pointed out gently it was an expensive mistake and he answered, 'Well all's not lost really. I am still going and I will stay there as long as it suits me. I will explore the New South Wales countryside and try and get a job if funds run low.' Knowing the resourceful man he was I was certain he would be fine and I wouldn't have been surprised if I never saw or heard of him again. I laughed at his predicament, wished him luck and warned him not to run any kangaroos over and get some corks for his hat! I then slid down in the bed and went back to my current novel.

As I became settled in the flats I met and made friends with most of the residents. There were a few single men who had chosen to settle in the building for various reasons and a couple became good mates, but once again - like Giles - there was no meeting of true minds, no longing to be with one constantly and, although Andrew gently prodded me with diffident questions, I had discovered no one who I couldn't live without or constantly needed to be with.

A couple of months after I took up ballroom dancing a new chap joined us one Wednesday. A tall, slim man, strolled into the hall just as I had switched on the central heating and was neatly arranging tea cups and filling the urn for the half-time break. Extremely presentable with light hair, a neat beard and a slight "Down Under" twang. I commented on his accent and he admitted to living in New Zealand for sixteen years. His name was Matt and we had an enlightening ten-minute conversation before the rest of the group came spilling through the double doors laughing and talking.

Luckily one of the other partner-less ladies took him in hand for which I was profoundly grateful: although I found it relative easy to follow our teacher's lead I am ashamed to say my brain froze up when I was expected to remember what Ben had previously taught us. This didn't stop Matt and I becoming the best of friends. We were soon going out for the occasional meal and, when he tentatively suggested we could maybe go and visit a National Trust property, I eagerly suggested Coleton Fishacre in the Torbay area.

It is an elegant 1920s Arts and Crafts country house with a light, beautifully furnished Art Deco interior and grounds that lead down to a secluded cove. I had visited a few times previously and often imagined svelte young "flappers" of that era, lounging around the drawing room while a jazz singer crooned or them lazing on the beach in the erotic bathing costumes of the time and being accompanied by men in striped blazers and jaunty, beribboned boaters. I knew Matt might also appreciate some of the rare and tender plants that hailed from New Zealand and South Africa which might possibly remind him of his previous life.

The day was a success and we started up a loose friendship when one or the other of us would pick up the telephone for a casual chat or to arrange a meeting. He told me about his young wife who had died suddenly and I made no secret of my life in York. I knew he met other women as he also attended a weekly evening ballroom class and would often mention various partners. Maybe he wanted to make me vaguely jealous but it didn't work as we had descended into a pleasant, amicable arrangement and it would probably have remained like that if I had not noticed an almost imperceptible change in his manner towards me. When we were together – eating a meal in an untried restaurant or wandering along cliffs on a delightful day out – we rubbed along quite happily, but occasionally when he telephoned me after his evening meal he would begin a light-hearted conversation which might suddenly change to him lecturing me and, finally, to him losing his temper. I was amazed at his strange behaviour and lightly thought what an idiot he was. Often it would be about a subject I had no knowledge of – usually politics or world affairs – and gradually his irritation would escalate until, one night, he slammed the phone down in disgust. I readily admitted I had no idea of the rights or wrongs of these harangues but I felt I was unjustly being used as a whipping boy and I was puzzled as to why.

The first couple of times it happened he telephoned promptly the next day and was abject in his apologies. These I accepted and tried to put his strange behaviour out of my mind. I had admitted to him I rarely read any particular newspaper and, if I did, I was willing to consider both sides of any argument. Sadly his furious diatribes became more frequent until one day *I* quietly replaced the receiver and, when he telephoned straight back, I made my feelings clear by deliberately not picking up. I think by then he had made another friend as he spoke of a dog-walking lady he had met out in his nearby woods. Without thinking, he had offered her a lift home in his car but her extremely smelly, unkempt dog had obviously not gone down too well and the fact that she obviously adored her pet didn't please him either. Shortly after he complained of twinges of arthritis and I breathed a sigh of relief when he found other things to do on a Wednesday afternoon.

I think Andrew realised I was virtually slipping away, so one rainy morning he convinced me I needed his companionship within the dynamic surroundings of the old walled town of York. On impulse, as the rain turned to a veritable monsoon, I booked a week at a small hotel just outside the walls. It had a small indoor swimming pool and if I couldn't laze on some sunny beach after a long warm dip in the Mediterranean, I might as well take the next best option and get to see Andrew within luxury surroundings.

My coach was due to arrive outside York railway station at 5pm and I excitedly texted Andrew as soon as we left the West Country. For the rest of the day, from when I climbed on board at Exeter bus station, I was inundated with enquiries from him and, at least an hour before we were due in, he was hustling me to tell him whether we were early, late or on time on our journey north. I sat in the coach with an idiotic grin on my face...

"Where you BE? I hopping up and down – to keep warm – but also wishing and wishing you put your skates on and get here soon. People keep looking at me strangely cos I keep standing on tiptoe to peer into the distance to see if you coming over the bridge yet. So HURRY, HURRY, HURRY before I explode," he texted.

I was dead on time and he was standing there, unsuitably dressed in a slightly damp jumper, ready to enfold me in his warm embrace. I remembered to rescue my case from under the coach before it pulled away, then we walked away hand in hand, both talking and neither listening, to find the car to take me to my nearby home for the week. I had no idea what excuse he had made at home but he even found the time to stay for a meal that first evening. We toasted each other in a red Burgundy as we ploughed through a range of courses that probably neither of us noticed or appreciated as we smiled happily at each other.

It was the best holiday I have ever had. Every morning Andrew appeared before I could finish my breakfast. He would come striding downstairs into the dining room with an idiotic grin on his face and beg a cup of coffee from my favourite waitress. He would then snitch a slice of toast off my plate, smother it in marmalade and proceed to demolish it to the last crumb while he told me our itinerary for the day. He would then dog my footsteps back to my room – begging for favours – while I endeavoured to get ready and eventually we left the building laughing and joking with all the staff. I felt as if we were surrounded by a golden circle of warmth and happiness.

First of all he took me to Burton Agnes Hall – a privately owned Norman manor-house tucked away on the Yorkshire Wolds to the south of bustling Bridlington. A gem of a place situated in a quiet and peaceful village. Andrew explained it had never been sold but had passed down through various families and was now lived in by a young family who were still commissioning works of art and obviously thoroughly enjoying their surroundings. The first thing that impressed me as I walked in – after I caught sight of the exquisite carving, plasterwork and panelling of the light and airy Great Hall – was that we were given permission to photograph and touch anything that took our fancy. No ropes impeded our progress and no blinds were drawn to prevent us seeing the cherished warmth of the place. When we hesitated to touch a *Tuscan Obelisk*, a narrowing set of drawers in yew wood in The Long Gallery, a beautiful room with a perfectly carved barrel ceiling, a guide insisted on removing a drawer to show us the immaculate workmanship of the whole piece.

We looked with great interest at the mixture of art that had been collected which included Cezanne, Manet and Gauguin as well as other lesser-known artists from all over the world. I admired a life-size bronze of a small boy standing by his hound as well as some colourful tapestry embroidery that had been commissioned from Kaffe Fassett by the family in 1993. My overall impression was cheerfulness and this was borne out as I walked through the grounds. There were walled gardens with colour themes and giant board games just waiting to be played. It was all delightful and refreshing and the redbrick hall nestled like a gem in the middle of them.

On the way back to York Andrew tossed a wrapped parcel onto my lap. The year before he had presented me with an iPod for my birthday. I had put some of my favourite music on it and had enjoyed it on long journeys ever since. I opened the package with care and found a Kindle reader. It was all charged up and ready to go because he had thoughtfully put half a dozen of my favourite authors on it already. I curled up in the front seat and began reading *Great Expectations* to my captive audience.

The next day Andrew asked if I preferred Whitby to Scarborough. I greedily said I wanted to see both so we made a mad dash to Peaseholm Park and wandered under dappled trees and over rustic bridges before going on to Whitby with its skyline of ruins overlooking the harbour and the bustling crowds below. We strolled across the sands and paddled in the crisp wavelets and, looking at my companion, I wondered why we were still apart. Our attraction towards each other never seemed to diminish: our chatter was constant – we didn't always agree, but we always found fresh conversation and explored each other's minds constantly. Why on earth were we living hundreds of miles away from each other when we both had so much to offer each other and so much love to share? His wife had made it clear she wasn't remotely interested in her husband's well-being. He was a useful appendage when attending dinner parties and social evenings, an arm to cling to, a holiday companion to arrange the transfer of baggage and a chauffeur when necessary – but certainly never the centre of her universe. He supplied what most of her friends and cronies lacked – a male partner – and this slightly elevated her in their eyes and obviously, in her estimation, he was worth keeping.

As we returned to York, Andrew started asking searching questions. 'Where's the one place you have constantly *mythered* me about visiting, above all others?' My mind was a blank. I sat up and thought deeply.

'Hadrian's Wall or Portmeirion. I have always wanted to see where *The Prisoner* was made – it reminded me of Disney World without Mickey', I answered.

'Nope. It's nearer than that and it is one of my favourite Stately Homes. I'll give you a clue. One of its most beautiful and controversial chatelaines was painted by Gainsborough and a later one had a slight acquaintance with Hitler. You will gasp in awe at magnificent ceilings and outdoors you will be entranced by a grand cascade. Got it, darling?' I sat up with a gasp.

'It's Chatsworth, isn't it? You have promised and promised and promised and now you are actually taking me to see it?' I asked in wonder.

'Yep! Be ready early and we will go straight off. We will spend the whole day there and I promise to end it with a visit to the cinema in the evening.'

'Oh, darling, you have made my holiday! Thank you so much - I can hardly believe I will see it at last.' I sat as quiet as a mouse during the rest of the journey.

And so I visited Chatsworth in all its glory at long last. It was as perfect as I had hoped. Drew hired a radio guide for us each to take us around as we slowly paced through the magnificent building. It was privately owned and, unlike most National Trust properties, I was allowed to take photographs – which was the perfect gift to an avid photographer like me. Andrew mentioned the fantastic ceilings and I snapped away at them from every angle. The Great Hall with its magnificent sweep of red-carpeted stairs, the Library - a symphony in turquoise and gilt - the Great Dining Room in eye-watering scarlet with cranberry crystal littering the crisp white damask tablecloth and the Chapel dominated by the *flamboyant* towering cream marble altar surround. I breathed it all in and stared in wonder. But it was also the small insignificant pieces that made my day. The pagoda-like blue-and-white Delft porcelain that looked like Dutch bulb pots but were actually made to take cut flowers, the delicate Parisian silver gilt toilet set, the encrusted silver gilt chandeliers and, in the Sculpture Room, a *Vestal Virgin* who one could swear had a veil of the finest linen across her face although one knew she was carved in marble. Like the faithful dog crouching at the feet of the sleeping *Endymion*. We both gazed entranced at so much beauty surrounding us. I could hardly bear to leave the House.

We walked outside and joined the folk sitting in the bright

sunshine for lunch. Refreshed, we set off around the surrounding grounds. In the courtyard we spied lean bronze hounds that looked, for all the world, like a few strays from the local hunt. We wandered over to the steep *Cascade* and Andrew stood there grinning happily while small children and parents paddled together in the sparkling, tumbling water. The extensive grounds were full of unexpectedly modern wood, bronze and stone sculptures. There were towering fountains and small, hidden lakes set deep in flowery bowers. We concluded our tour feeling sated and satisfied and I curled up in the car and dozed gently as Andrew drove us swiftly back towards York. He had suggested a quick meal near the cinema he had chosen because, as usual, he wanted to cram everything into our time together. We were in the process of queuing up for cinema tickets when his mobile phone shrilled. I never remembered it ever happening before and I glanced at him with startled surprise. As Andrew quietly bent to answer it, I saw his face alter. He promptly moved out of the line and walked towards the door. I followed hesitantly. I could hear a distant aggrieved voice and knew something bad had happened.

'When did they ring you?' he asked. 'Yes I am sure you tried to get me. I have been unavailable all day. I will return home immediately.' I walked to his side expecting to hear that his boys or grandchildren needed his help. He turned towards me with an apologetic expression.

'Sorry, Jenny, I'm afraid the cinema is off.' He looked at me soberly, 'That was Fay to say Deborah is very ill. The headmaster of her school rang to say she has been shifted from her retirement lodge in the grounds to a hospice in Plymouth. Oh dear God, I didn't even know she was ill. I will go down immediately.'

I stood with my heart thumping. *Deborah – not Deborah – she was never ill. She was the one we always went to with our troubles. Like a perfect mum, she was the sensible bulwark who sorted everything out – from Andrew pleading to go to school on a sailing ship to soothing her father-in-law when Hugh produced a modern design which he disliked.* 'I can get the bus back to the hotel,' I offered. 'Don't worry about me – you just get off to Plymouth.'

'Oh, Jenny, I don't want to go on my own. I know it's asking a lot but would you be prepared to forego the last couple of days of your holiday to come back with me?'

'Of course,' I said briskly, the thought of him needing me sending a warm glow through me. 'I'll take the bus back, settle my account at the hotel and pack; you can pick me up on your way back through York. It must be about three hundred miles to Plymouth, so if we put up overnight about halfway, we should be with Deborah first thing tomorrow morning.'

He nodded briefly at the way I had grasped that time was all-important but insisted on running me back to my hotel. I went straight to Reception and asked a startled clerk for my bill to be made up. I explained there was a family emergency and he obliged me immediately. I paid my bill and went to my room to pack. I was just folding the last of my lingerie when the telephone buzzed. I snatched it up.

'Sorry, Jenny - bad news. She has had all day in which to assimilate this while trying to ring me, and the silly cow has decided to make a circus out of the whole thing. She has arranged for us to go down and stay with some Embassy pals in Topsham. I've tried to put her off but she's determined. It's not that she wants to visit Deborah,' he said bitterly. 'But the opportunity of going shopping with Gloria in Exeter and gossiping their daft heads off is too good to miss. I will go on to Plymouth alone. Her plans are made and she is adamant.'

I gulped back my disappointment at not going with him. I felt he needed a loyal friend who would do their best to ease his distress; somehow I guessed his self-centred wife wouldn't fit into that category. I reminded him to drive safely and waved away his concerns about how I would spend the rest of my holiday. 'Just give Deborah my love and a big cuddle. Don't tell her it is from me if you think it will upset her,' I warned him.

I then slung all my clothes back in the drawers and wardrobe and slowly walked downstairs where I asked them cancel me leaving and said I would be staying the full seven days after all. Afterwards I went and sat on a comfortable seat in the bar and ordered a large gin and tonic. Later, in bed, I began to trace their journey throughout the night as Andrew drove steadily on towards a sick Deborah.

I awoke late the next morning and had to force myself to get up.

Suddenly there seemed little point in planning any outings on my own. I had telephoned Dorothy twice when Andrew had left me to my own devices. We had chatted and I had made a vague promises to go and visit, but every time I was swept off on yet another jaunt and I totally forgot. I now selfishly decided that a visit would cheer us both up. I walked into town and bought a cheerful pot plant as I knew she enjoyed her flowers but had been forbidden to venture into her garden by her protective daughter, after a couple of minor accidents.

When I arrived her grandson was there playing on the mat with his toddler son. I stayed for almost two hours and then caught the bus into town to visit the Chinese Buffet Restaurant. Andrew and I often ate there because I preferred it to the spicy Asian food that he adored. I felt closer to him where the staff were always attentive but never intrusive. I wondered how he had found Deborah and hoped he was not too upset. We must have had the same thought process because as I drank my last mouthful of white wine my mobile rang. I found a quiet corner and answered it without disturbing the other diners.

His distressed voice told me he had found Deborah fragile and wan. 'Oh, Jenny, she looked almost transparent and I had to pretend I was not massively shocked. As far as I can make out she persuaded the school not to tell us that she had been failing for months. And there was me gaily making weekly calls and listening to all the lies she was prepared to spin me. What an idiot I have been - I should have guessed when the connection appeared faint that there might have been another reason and that she was hiding something from us. I have come in to the small coffee room of the hospice to give us both a short break and grab a snack. Fay and I arrived at our friends' house in the early hours and I only snatched a coffee and half a slice of toast this morning before I dashed off to Plymouth. The road was busy and I caught all the early morning traffic so, on arrival, I fully appreciated the tranquillity of this place. It is light and airy, fairly modern and there's a lovely tang of polish as you enter. Deborah has a downstairs room with double doors leading onto a sheltered patio. She appreciates that, as her bed is close to the windows and she has a view towards the river. It reminds her of Mevagissey, she says. The house is set in extensive grounds so, although I had a bit of trouble finding it, the peace and quiet makes it all worthwhile. I'll tell you more later, darling, before I return home,' he promised. 'I have an appointment with her doctor and the Matron in half an hour and then I should be fully aware of what's been happening while I've been half asleep.'

He rang me later and wearily told me the doctor admitted, with Deborah's permission, that she had come to spend the last of her life with them. She and the Dean at her school had been great friends for years and it was he who had suggested she come to Plymouth when she explained she didn't want to burden her family with her illness. The doctor confirmed it was cancer and, by the time she had consulted a practitioner, it had spread too far for the medical profession to find a cure. Andrew had then gone straight to her sunny room to talk to her. With little sign of regret she held his hand and quietly told him life had been good since she had married Mark Lanyon and come to live in their Boatyard at Polruan. She had never been sad at having no children of her own because Andrew had more than adequately fulfilled the role of a son while her brother-in-law, Hugh, had been her greatest friend – especially when Mark died at such an early age.

As I listened the tears coursed down my face and I could tell from the break in Andrew's voice he was weeping too. 'She was so matter-of-fact and so grateful for us giving her a home, Jenny. It had never occurred to her my whole family had so quickly grown to rely on her – she became a mother to me, a dutiful daughter to my father and her good sense and fun kept us all together as a family unit. She never understood she gave so much more than she received. I expect that's why she made such a perfect matron to all those little lads at boarding school and I know, from what the Head said, she was in her element mothering them.'

We discussed it until he realised it was late and said he must be off back to Topsham. Fay had arranged to stay until the weekend and he planned to return to Deborah every day until it was time to return north on the Sunday. I swallowed my sadness at having to relinquish his companionship. I told him I would try to carry out his plans for the next two days and then pointed out how ironic it was that *I* was in Yorkshire while *he* was within a few miles of my home in Devon, and that we would be passing each other going in opposite directions sometime over that weekend.

I tried my hardest to fulfil his wishes. I managed to get to Burnby Hall Gardens by taking the bus to Pocklington and then asking to be dropped off. I wandered around the lakes encrusted with jewel-coloured water lilies and fed the massive, brightly coloured koi carp, but my heart wasn't in it. I picnicked under *our* tree near the delightfully curving Jamie's Bridge but there was no fun in the day. No smiles and silly reminiscences, no teasing or watching children revel in a safe, friendly environment. I returned to the hotel feeling faintly sad and bereft. The next day was my last and I was determined to make the long trek to Temple Newsam, a lovely old house owned by Leeds City Council. I started out early and caught the passing Express bus into Leeds. I was kindly shown where to find the local transport that would take me out to within a twenty-minute walk of this Stately Home. I had been told it was also known as 'The Hampton Court of the North', probably because Lord Darnley, the executed husband of Mary Queen of Scots, was born there. I arrived tired and dishevelled and bought myself a souvenir brochure to make sure I appreciated the full potential of this grand place. Sadly it wasn't the same as when Andrew's light voice accompanied me around. I followed other groups and even came across a noisy melee of school children who were being lectured to by their teachers. I trudged around, book in hand, and then wandered over to the Stable Block for a quick snack before making my way back towards civilisation. A young family offered me a lift in their car to the centre of Leeds and I accepted gratefully.

Still feeling slightly out of sorts with the world, I ate my lavish evening meal, finished the last of my bottle of wine and then took myself off to bed. I was due to return by National Coach to the West Country at 11am the next morning and somehow it felt like a relief. I awoke early and ate a brisk breakfast before going off to get some sandwiches and fruit for the journey. I had bags of time but I strode back over the Iron Bridge quickly. I settled my bill in Reception and then went to my room to pack the last couple of items before locking my case. I went on my knees beside my case to smooth a pale, figure-hugging turquoise dress that I particularly liked and Andrew had not even seen. I zipped up the case and clicked the lock before grabbing it along with my coat and handbag and, giving a quick look around, I walked out the door. The staff offered to call a taxi but I laughed and reminded them I was dead mean and a bus would do just as well. I swung aboard an empty bus and was set down at the station five minutes later. The coach was late as usual but, after climbing aboard, I breathed a sigh of relief and took out my iPod to listen to my favourite music. York faded into the distance.

Chapter 30

*

I sat on the coach and looked gloomily out of the window. Luckily I had a seat to myself so I was not forced into making conversation with another traveller. I could think back in solitude. The few days that I had looked forward to with such pleasure had started with great anticipation. I tried to cast my thoughts back to all the warmth and pleasure Andrew and I had enjoyed in each other's company. The tenderness generated as we fell into bed and made love in my hotel bedroom, the quiet talk and laughter that followed as we thirstily swallowed innumerable mugs of steaming tea; exploring the countryside together, visiting old grand houses and absorbing the surroundings as well as their beautiful unique contents, wandering across beaches with the breeze whipping our words away but never the smiles off our faces; how he would glow with happiness and laughter when he first caught sight of me each day; how he would clutch me to him as if he was frightened I would disappear. My expectancy those first few days had built as one day merged into the next. I felt he was on the cusp of affirming he was unable to sustain his false life any longer and that we could be together once more. Then the call that brought our idyllic dream world crashing down.

I could feel the tears gathering in the back of my throat as Katie Melua breathed her magic in my ears. I turned the music off before I made a fool of myself and scrabbled in my bag for my handy book of crosswords. I then forced my mind to search deeply for the cryptic answers to stop me thinking about the whole sorry mess. Deborah being incarcerated in Plymouth was at the top of my list of concerns. It is an established fact that no one enters a hospice to recuperate from an illness. She was obviously dying and she must have reached the extremity of her endurance to agree to being sent away. Somehow I felt even more guilty than Andrew. My contact with her had lessened naturally as the years went by. Marriage at first to Chris and then Robin – neither whom she had met – had reduced me to annual Christmas and birthday cards with the odd letter and occasional telephone call when I thought of it. Somehow I could never dissolve that elusive specialness that she and her family had for me. Also, I admit it now, I couldn't manage to cut myself off completely from Andrew and she was a sure route to him whenever I rang. So, when Andrew and I ran off together a lifetime later, we should not just have telephoned, as we did, and gaily told her we were together once more. How selfish can one get? I know now we should have gone down and told her in person. What on earth must she have felt when we rang? The two of us full of happiness and expectancy while her body was succumbing to a deadly disease.

We pulled into our first rest stop. I wandered in and made use of their free loos and then came back to the coach to eat my sandwiches and sip a few mouthfuls of water. It seemed unfair that it was such a beautiful day. I buried myself in the current novel I had started reading and longed for us to be on our way. The coach swung back on the motorway and we headed steadily south. Did I doze? I'm not certain, but I don't think so.

It was only when we were on the outskirts of Birmingham that I reached in my bag for my purse. I knew, from previous experience, one had to pay twenty or thirty pence to use the facilities in the coach station and, as I needed them, I wanted to check I had change. Like most women who travel, my handbag is one of those with innumerable compartments. My keys and bus pass are in one, my mobile is in another, the third holds my Kindle, iPod and any other reading matter I'll need and the large one contains my cheque and address books, diary, comb and purse. I have been known to misplace one of these in another section, so I wasn't too worried. As we passed The Bull Ring centre I scrabbled around to find it. *Where on earth had I put it*? I went through the whole handbag methodically but found no comforting, bulky maroon purse. I took out and replaced everything item by item but gradually it was dawning on me my purse had disappeared. Frantically I looked around at the other travellers. Could anyone have leaned over, or across, and removed it from my bag? Difficult when it was zipped up and other passengers were surrounding me. We swung into the station and the majority of the bus decamped either to stretch their legs or they were at the end of their journey. I wanted to shout, *'Hey I've lost my purse!'* but realised, if anyone *had* stolen it, this would be useless.

So I sat on the bus – all thought of relieving myself forgotten – and dialled my neighbour Val, back home. She answered on the second ring and I quickly told her of my predicament. She grasped the importance of it because not only had I lost all my money but my debit card and various other cards as well. I asked her to go the few hundred yards to my bank immediately so they could put a stop to anyone raiding my bank account. She listened carefully and then asked worriedly about my bus pass and house keys but I was able to reassure her I had those safe. I felt bereft and shaky. It is surprising how vulnerable and lonely one feels at a time like this. The few stragglers left on the coach were sending interested glances my way as I tried to keep my voice down and not to show panic.

Before the coach had pulled out of the bus station Val rang me back. My bank was unable to stop my card on her say-so but she carefully dictated a number and told me they would do so as soon as I telephoned them. With a sigh of relief I followed her orders and was cheerfully told it would be done immediately and a new debit card would be with me as soon as possible. The rest of the journey became a nightmare of personal recriminations for not taking care of something so precious. I also berated myself for my stupid habit of using my card instead of cash as I had such a large amount in my purse. I have this phobia that I should keep a large float of money on me "just in case" and now it was lining another's pocket by a very substantial amount.

The last hour of the bus journey from Exeter to home seemed interminable and I didn't realise how tired and thirsty I was until I made my weary way up in the lift and walked in Val's door which she had thoughtfully left open for me. She placed a cup of tea next to me and urged me to sit down and tell them exactly what had happened. I gave them a garbled account and, as I was speaking, Bertrand gently stuffed five ten-pound notes in my hand and told me, 'it was just to tide me over.' Suddenly I was crying at the fear and shock I had suffered but mostly at the realisation that I was back among friends.

I went downstairs to my own flat after Bertrand suggested it might be a good idea to telephone the hotel in York on the slim chance I had mislaid my purse there. I agreed, but I was so certain that when I left them that morning I'd had everything with me, that it all seemed a bit pointless. William was doing a split shift that day. He was the one who had totalled up my account that morning and dealt with my payment of it. I told him how I had arrived in Birmingham to discover my purse was missing. He understood immediately and asked me to give him a few minutes to check it wasn't in their safe and then take a quick look round my room, which was still unoccupied. Seven minutes later he telephoned to say he could find nothing. I thanked him and went drearily to bed. I was unable to sleep as the whole night I went again and again through the series of events leading up to my discovery. Saying my goodbyes to the staff/wheeling my suitcase across a traffic free road/ using my bus pass on a virtually empty bus/ talking to a student who was going for an interview in Leeds – he stood all of two feet away from me/handing my ticket to the coach driver as I relinquished my suitcase to be stored under the coach/ making myself comfortable on a double seat. At no time at all could I recall anyone near me. I know pickpockets are adept but I failed to see how it had been done. Had I dozed off on the journey? I honestly couldn't remember. I would have sworn not, but somehow the feat had been accomplished and I couldn't see how. I even cast my mind back to the tiny general store where I had picked up my sandwiches, fruit and water, until I remembered I had taken my card out *after* that, in Reception. I fully remember carrying my handbag, plastic carrier bag, purse and statement back to my room to finish my packing.

As you can guess I awoke hollow-eyed the next morning and was just assembling a late breakfast when my telephone shrilled. A light woman's voice asked if she could speak to a Mrs J Fairburn. I crisply answered she was speaking to her.

'This is York Royal Mail Central Sorting Office here. Have you lost anything?'

'Yes,' I snapped. 'My purse!'

'Well I have it here,' she calmly informed me. She then went on to explain it had been discovered when the local postman, doing his rounds, had emptied a post box. I was totally baffled and asked which box. How could I have posted my own purse in a post box? She said it happened a couple of times a week on average – usually the stolen wallet or purse was totally empty so they had no way of restoring them to their owners. 'Yours isn't and you had the good sense to put your name and telephone number in it. I hope you will appreciate the goodwill and honesty of our crew.' I fervently agreed and she promised to parcel it up and said I should receive it by the next day. I asked if I could reward the man who had so kindly rescued it for me. Her parting words were, 'No that's fine, I'll give him your thanks.'

We were just saying our good-byes when I suddenly remembered to ask the all-important question, 'Er which post box was it actually found in?' *She named the box opposite the hotel I had been staying in for the past week.* I replaced the receiver gently...

Half an hour later Robin rang. He usually checked up on me a couple of times a week since he had taken himself off to Scotland. I don't think he had any real reason, apart from the fact that he had felt responsible for me for more years than either of us cared to remember, and he found old habits die hard. I don't think Ailsa minded and, knowing him, he had always made clear his intentions and she had accepted them.

'You OK? Had a nice holiday?' he asked. I told I had lost my purse on the last day. 'Gosh you really are an idiot. Well no kind person handed it in and telephoned me this time,' he retorted. 'Still, I suppose they wouldn't know I now live in Scotland.' I was still bemused with the latest news, which I hadn't quite assimilated. I went through my movements the previous day for him and then described the telephone call I had only just received. He listened patiently and made a few pertinent observations, as any ex-policeman would, before his parting words were, 'Well work it out for yourself, love. Go back carefully over your movements. Make yourself recall every little thing you did and you will soon see the answer. 'Fraid the money will have gone but at least you will have the satisfaction of solving the mystery - and maybe it will teach you to be extra alert now you are on your own.' And with that he was gone.

I did my shopping and only when I had put it all away neatly did I sit myself down with a pot of tea and forced myself to do exactly what Robin had suggested. I started with my entering the hotel on the way back from the shops. I stood alone at the Reception desk and studied my bill. I then handed William my debit card and replaced it in my purse after he had activated it. I left the Reception area clutching the statement, plastic carrier, handbag and purse. I took out my key and entered my room. I unhooked my pretty turquoise dress from its hanger feeling slightly aggrieved because Andrew hadn't even seen it. I folded it neatly on the bed. My opened case was on the floor by the far wall and I flopped down on my knees and leaned across the bed to gently place this last item of clothing in. Finally I put the crisp, itemised statement on top, zipped up the case and snapped shut the lock. I suddenly remembered what I had done. *My purse had been in my left hand. I smacked it down on the floor as I knelt down AND I THEN FORGOT TO PICK IT UP AS I HAULED MY SUITCASE UPRIGHT AND WHEELED IT TO THE DOOR.* At last I had solved the mystery. No one had stolen it: I had stupidly left it behind. So it had been my fault entirely; but the next thing I had to sort out was how it had jumped from my room and landed in a post box a few yards on the other side of a main road? I raced upstairs to tell Val my news and explain my stupidity. Bertrand, whose loan I reimbursed, was interested in my explanation but mystified as to how Royal Mail got involved. We spent a couple of hours discussing a puzzle that refused to unravel itself.

I was up bright and early the next morning to await the postman. Sure enough he handed me a bulky package and I unwrapped it under his amused gaze. It was probably my lurid imagination but my leather purse felt sticky and grubby as I opened it. I carefully laid all its contents on the kitchen worktop. My bank debit card was there along with various supermarket, Boots the chemist and store cards. My library and mobile phone top-up cards were also in their respective slots. Behind them was a repeat doctor's prescription, a small pink Social Security card that stated I was entitled to a Retirement Pension and a wrapped sticking plaster. Where I normally placed my bank notes I found only dental and hairdressing appointment cards and my bank's telephone number.

There was also a scribbled taxi rank number for emergencies. I then discovered a tiny, foil-covered Thyroxine tablet and two till receipts for items I had purchased whilst up in York. I suddenly noticed that a plastic birthday voucher from Boots for an undisclosed amount (it was only for £10 but the thief didn't know that) had been removed. I opened the coin section and found it, as I suspected, empty and, last of all, I undid the small maroon purse in the centre and looked inside. The two commemorative stamps I had kept for years – one of Princess Diana in a glittering ball gown and tiara and a second of Prince William, taken on his birthday, were gone. They had both been taken. The purse was intact but every coin and note – I estimated there had been slightly over £300 – was missing. I seized the purse and violently scrubbed at it with hot soapy water. It sickened and disgusted me. Some grasping fingers had rifled through it, snatching what they couldn't resist and flinging the rest aside. I shuddered at the thought of ever using it again.

At that moment Robin chose to ring. I drearily answered and told him what had been returned. He was bracingly positive and said I was lucky the thief hadn't obviously been a professional because, if they had, *everything* would have been taken and pawed over and my bank account would have been depleted correspondingly. 'Draw up a personal profile of the person who had the opportunity to do this, Jenny. It will soon reveal the likely culprit.'

I laughed hollowly, 'Who cares! They have my money and I hope it does them no good whatsoever,' I said vindictively. Nevertheless, I couldn't stop thinking of his advice, and, as the day wore on, I sat down and typed up an amateur profile of my own.

When I vacated my room the first person to unlock that door would probably have been a cleaner. Question: how many were on that day? They would have come in with cleaning equipment plus fresh bed linen and towels. The bathroom would have been thoroughly cleaned, the bed stripped and re-made and finally the whole room would have been dusted and vacuumed. It would be *then* they would discover my maroon purse lying abandoned on a maroon floral carpet. Question: did they pick it up and weigh it in their hands? Did they creep into the bathroom and sit on the loo with the door locked in case another cleaner walked in to speak to them? Were they amazed when they opened it up and found it stuffed with ten- and twenty-pound notes? They must have gone through it thoroughly and found a Boots plastic token card that might have some money on it before they discovered two pretty stamps they were unable to resist. Did they think about handing it in to the management: and then did the temptation become too great and they stuffed it deep under their cleaning materials as it would have been too bulky and heavy to shove in a pocket or a bag?

And always, in the back of their mind, would be the chance that the owner, finding it missing, would ring up the hotel in a panic. Maybe the owner was driving and stopped in York for petrol. Possibly a cab had been called on their behalf and, at the station, they needed to pay the driver. All these thoughts would be coursing through their brain. Obviously speed was of the essence. They had to remove the incriminating evidence before they were questioned. (Suddenly I remembered my room was above the kitchens and often any staff who smoked would invariably sneak out of the side door for a surreptitious puff and a chat with their mates. I often saw wreathing smoke float past my window a floor above). BUT any staff who didn't smoke would have no reason to leave the premises or congregate around the back door. So the thief would panic and know they had to get rid of my purse immediately. Adrenaline must have been coursing through them when they had the brilliant idea of posting the damning evidence somewhere safe – somewhere beyond discovery. Where better than Her Majesty's mail box only a few yards across a busy road?

The Profile I drew up was this: The one legitimate person who had good reason to be in my vacated room was a cleaner. I was sure it had been a spur of the moment theft and they had probably been in two minds whether to dare or not. £300 was far more attractive and tempting than sharing it with another. Very possibly they had been female as my Boots token card was removed (what man would know this one card was "cash worthy" amongst so many others?); and then he/she had taken two postage stamps whose value was actually extremely low. They almost certainly smoked or why would they have had reason to be outside? This also had given them the opportunity to leave the premises for five minutes.

That night I decided to ring Carrie, the woman who looked after the staff and was in charge under the owner. I had visited this hotel half a dozen times before and, over time, we had become good friends. A small, exclusive hotel that was almost run as a family concern, borne out by the fact that Carrie's husband and daughter were employed as chef and waitress respectively. I then asked her to keep to herself what I was going to reveal - this was just to alert her and not to start a witch hunt. I admitted I was partly to blame as I had stupidly left my purse behind. No one had stolen it off of me – I had mislaid it. I then told her the saga of Royal Mail getting in touch and returning it the next morning. She sounded relieved and pleased that it had been sorted. I brought her up short by explaining where the postman had found it. She said soothingly, 'I guess someone must have found it in the road where you dropped it, rifled through it, took the money and then dumped it quickly.'

'I don't think so, Carrie. Anyone finding it outside might have snatched it up but their one object, if they had no intention of handing it in, would be to hide it and then go home and search through it at their leisure.'

She sounded dubious, 'Well yes, maybe. But they didn't,' she said brightly. 'They dumped it in a post box.'

'Yes, the one opposite your hotel,' I countered. 'Don't you think that's an amazing coincidence? Any policeman worth his salt would suggest it was an inside job. Are you able to tell me how many cleaners were on that day?' Carrie frostily agreed to check.

'Two.'

'And were they both women?' I asked.

'No, one of each. And before you ask, they were both white. One comes from Romania and the other from Prague,' she answered rather facetiously,

'Which one smokes?' I asked, changing the subject.

'Smokes? The woman. Why?' I then told her my deductions and left her to think about them. I knew, for the moment, she found it impossible to agree with me and her last parting shot was, 'They both came with really good references and often work in the local hospital. We have never had such a complaint before.' At this I metaphorically shrugged.

'Do me a favour and don't report this to the boss. I don't want anyone questioned closely *or* sacked. It will only raise bad feelings and cause a nasty atmosphere. All I ask is that you are aware and alert.' With that I wished her good night and rang off.

Two months later I returned to York for a few days at the request of Andrew. He was most surprised when I asked him to book me into my usual hotel. Little did he know I was laying a ghost to rest. There was no reason to be apprehensive really because I knew nothing like this would ever happen again. They treated me with kid gloves. I was allowed to invite Andrew when I swam in their delightful pool but I was also aware that the owner, who had often been a touch brisk with me whenever we spoke, made a point of asking daily if everything was to my liking. Apart from William, there was a faint air of reserve among some of the staff, I noticed, so sadly I guessed Carrie had been unable to honour her promise to keep her own counsel.

Meanwhile Val and Bertrand were making plans to go abroad once more. Neither had been in good health for some time. Val had suffered two suspected mini strokes and I knew her daughter was worried a major one might be in the offing. So she and Val's family were making plans on her behalf. Bertrand, on the other hand, had been steadily getting more absent-minded as the months went by. Both Val and I had noticed it particularly, but surprisingly his grown up children either refused to contemplate their dad was slipping into the throes of dementia or were convinced we were exaggerating. We had both tried to cushion his escalating forgetfulness regarding where he was, what he had been doing half an hour before or that it was the sixth time within as many minutes that he had asked the same question.

I think Val and Bertrand both knew time was running out as far as their life together was concerned and they longed for one last fling – a relaxing holiday in a warm climate. Val decided they should return to Lanzarote one last time. Bertrand, in his easy-going fashion, was all for it. The three of us had enjoyed a luxurious, laid-back holiday in an all-inclusive hotel and Val was determined to replicate the experience. She kindly insisted I should accompany them and I was only too pleased to accept her offer. What else had I to do with my life apart from staying in contact with my family and friends and making myself useful whenever possible? I had been approached and agreed to occasionally stand in for an English teacher at an adult evening class. I found it pleasurable and hoped the students did too. After reading a brief item in our local free newspaper, which had shocked me immeasurably, I had also volunteered to help set up a food bank in our area. All my life I had lived in a clean, warm environment with enough to eat. Now, in our country, things were changing. It seemed an awful indictment to read how many families were either on the edge of hunger, deeply in debt or had no place to live. My intent wasn't purely philanthropic – I just needed to dam up a gaping well of loneliness in my life and, hopefully, I could be of some use as well. Rambling around Devon's beautiful countryside was fun, as was learning to dance, but I found it vital that I did something useful.

When I gaily told Andrew of my working commitments, my new hobbies as well as my plans to go on holiday yet again, he obviously considered I was either stretching myself beyond my physical limits or exceeding my restricted finances. I assured him I thrived on being busy and being careful with money would do me good. He then changed tack and offered to pay for my holiday. I assured him I was reasonably solvent and with that he had to be satisfied. I noticed he suddenly went very quiet. Possibly he thought I was growing away from him, but what could he expect when our only contact was through long conversations on the telephone, texting or by e-mail? I was tired of begging him to leave York and either join me in Devon or choose somewhere else to live. Once again he had become silent.

Two days later I received a telephone call from York that sent my heart racing. 'I am going down to see Deborah at the weekend, Jenny. I will be alone and I want you to accompany me. Will you?' asked Andrew. *Of course I would.* I was hesitant about Deborah wanting to see me but Andrew chided me for being too sensitive. 'I will be with you as early as I can Saturday morning. I tried to swing it for Friday night but she was having none of it!' I grimaced but said nothing. 'I have promised to leave Devon at the crack of dawn Monday morning. I flatly refused to even contemplate travelling halfway across the UK and back in two days flat. Even my demanding wife was forced to accept the logic of that!'

Saturday morning saw me up as soon as it was light. I reckoned that even if he pulled into a motorway rest stop, it would take Andrew no more than four to five hours to travel down. I prepared a basket of food and then sat curled up in front of the telephone, waiting. The first time it rang it was Dee saying, as usual, *'long time no see'* and the second was Jess who was bored, at a loose end and needed a chat. I devoted five minutes to each of them and then eased myself off the line. He telephoned just before eleven o'clock to say his sat nav informed him he would shortly be in Chard and to put the kettle on. I told him I had a better suggestion – I would meet him outside the flats with a picnic lunch in one hand and a large flask of coffee in the other. 'Atta girl!' was his delighted reply.

We had lunch in the car overlooking Plymouth Sound. Delicate, waxy camellias glowed pink in the winter sunshine as we munched our sandwiches and nibbled the fruit. Although it was warm in the car I was aware, with our free arms, that we clutched each other tightly. Why was it, I mused, that we needed to cling like limpets every time we sat near each other? The steam from our coffee cups misted up the windscreen as I tried to stifle the concern I felt at us making this pilgrimage. Andrew rested his head on my hair and dozed for a few minutes. I sat quietly waiting for him to rouse, knowing the tension had been growing inside him ever since he had heard the devastating news and had to fend off thoughtless questions from an insensitive spouse.

Andrew's directional system led us unerringly to Deborah's refuge. We made our way in out of the cold and I smelt that indefinable tang of cleaning fluids, polish and coffee. The nurse quietly led us into Deborah's sunny room and gently touched her hand. She was sitting propped up within a cocoon of pillows and, even though I had been warned to expect it, I stiffened at how frail she looked. Andrew's light kiss brought a radiant smile to her face and then she half-turned, enquiringly, towards me. Suddenly she accepted us for the couple we had always been. I slipped into the opposite vacant seat, close to the bed, and each of us placed her thin delicate hands in our warm ones. She closed her eyes and we all three sat in quiescent peace. I offered her a lemon drink from a feeding mug and she smiled her thanks. Then Andrew started chatting – he spoke of days gone by and sometimes she roused herself to answer. He told her mild jokes about the family and, once, I added a memory of my own. She turned to me with a grin. But after a while, Andrew's head came closer and they were murmuring together. I looked towards the window and directed my thoughts away from them. Five minutes later my considerate Andrew was tucking her hands down under the sheets and softly kissing her cheek. She had gone to sleep. We crept out and I found myself in the sanctuary of his arms as I soaked his shirt with my tears.

That night as we lay in bed, he told me that, for a few moments, she had mistaken him for Mark, his elder brother. He had accepted the role and told her how much he loved her and it seemed to satisfy her and she dropped asleep at once. We visited again the next day and I could tell she found incredible strength from just resting her hands in ours. We left quite early and I remember looking back and doubting if I would ever see her again. That night I insisted he use my telephone to ring his brother Hugh in the States. He admitted he had already told him everything. 'I told him how ill she is and said I had no guarantee that, even if he flew over immediately, he would be in time. I explained how, being Deborah, she had not wanted to worry us and how she had left it until the very last minute before allowing anyone to contact us.'

'It doesn't matter, Drew, I want you to keep him up to date with everything. Imagine how *you* would feel being all those miles away and not having the latest news. Just go and do it, love. I promise you, you will both feel better when you do. I am going to rustle up some food and I want you to take all the time in the world. I have no interest in the cost. Tell him of her progress and try and put his mind at rest.' With that I firmly walked out of the room.

That night in bed, after we had made a subdued love, he admitted it had been the right thing to do. 'He was chewing himself up not being here supporting me. He's in the middle of a big design job but he said the company would understand and he would drop it immediately if I wanted. He sounded relieved when I told him about you. Not sure if he quite understood what I was saying, but then I'm sure he never could quite understand how we both drifted apart. And of course he and Fay never really hit it off.' I decided not to comment but just hoped Hugh didn't have occasion to ring Fay and pass on his thoughts.

Andrew managed to get down a week later but this time Deborah sadly didn't know us. We sat once again holding her tiny hands and I hope it gave her some comfort: I feel sure it did him.

Two days later he called to say she had slipped away in her sleep in the middle of the previous night. I asked about the funeral even though I knew there was no way I could attend. All of Deborah's family and friends would be present by right. Only I, due to a previous association with Andrew, would be barred. It was hurtful to know I may have comforted her during the last days of her life but that this could never be acknowledged. The day of the funeral I waited until lunchtime and then went and sat in our local church close to the estuary. It is a lovely old building that has probably been here since Roman times. These soldiers, who performed many roles apart from keeping the peace, began a series of salt flats here. Walking back along the river one could still see where fields had been flooded with sea water and then dammed. The resulting dried salt would be removed and stored and then the whole process would begin again. It must have been a lucrative occupation that went on for many centuries because we even had a small, simple memorial near the altar to a salt master who had been born in Looe. This made me feel closer to all my friends in that part of Cornwall.

Because of its tucked-away setting, this small picturesque church was usually deserted when there were no services. And so it was the day I came to pray for Deborah. I knew she had a simple trust in her God and I felt as sure, as she did, that she would now be united with Mark - the only man she had ever loved. She, who had no interest in human remains and burials, had always joked that she would be delighted to hear a few old hymns in Lansallos church and she had requested that afterwards, her ashes be scattered near their family grave. I knew Andrew and Hugh would honour these wishes. And so it was. On a breezy weekday afternoon all her friends from Polruan and Fowey gathered together in Lansallos village church. They were joined by her two brothers-in-law and their families. People who had known her came from Polperro, Looe, London and a few places in between.

What I didn't know about was that a Service of Thanksgiving was held the next day at the Mevagissey boarding school where Deborah had held the post of Matron for so many years. Andrew told me he had been reluctant to attend but his sons had convinced him it would be churlish to refuse and Hugh, his brother, had agreed with them. So it was decided that the whole family should stay on an extra day. He recounted how he and Fay, wearing her most stylish black hat, walked hesitantly into the school chapel followed by his two tall sons. Behind them trailed Ben and Camilla, his elder grandchildren, both looking coltish and uncomfortable. After them came the irrepressible Rosie, Leigh and Perkin stifling giggles and receiving a stern glare from their father. Their Uncle Hugh brought up in the rear accompanied by his American wife who appeared slightly in awe of the occasion. Facing them stood row upon row of expectant young lads in neat school blazers, their hair slicked back with water, and ready to sing their hearts out.

Andrew told me more about the service: 'A short homily by the Head, rounded up with a couple of gentle memories, two prayers and then what looked like the youngest in the school read out how he "already missed Mrs Lanyon" followed by a moving speech by the Head Boy who, in adult terms, said roughly the same thing. The boys lustily sang their favourite hymns and, instead of it being a dirge to a lady who had obviously loved and cherished them, it became a celebration of having her for so many years. Three quarters of an hour later we and the boys marched down to the dining hall and demolished the buffet that was awaiting us. Deborah had obviously brought them up well, as various boys - including one little tacker with a lisp caused by a huge gap where his front teeth normally resided - offered round plates of food and talked intelligently. *Our* children disappeared into the throng and suddenly I was delighted and surprised that I suddenly felt at peace with myself, Jenny. Was that wrong?'

I laughed and said that was exactly what Deborah would have wanted. The gentle merging of her old life with her new would have suited her perfectly. I now knew Andrew would take back to his home some semblance of tranquil composure. As usual Deborah had been the peacemaker.

Sadly I was not too sure what that augured for *me*; or for us, as a couple. From his description of how the day had gone I guessed, for Andrew, that seeing nearly the whole of his family en masse had proved a moving experience. *He had walked away from them once before: could he be expected – or asked – to do it again*? And could one indulged, insensitively cold wife be excuse enough to shatter or split up this whole family forever? I had never wanted such an awful possibility to become reality. I had always wanted the best for his extended family since the moment Andrew and I had left Devon and run off together; but would the man I loved be able to convince them of this? I had never been a marriage wrecker because, as far as I had been led to believe, Andrew's marriage to Fay had been destroyed *long* before I had come back into his life.

Chapter 31

*

For a few days I laboured under a cloud of sadness, tinged with memories of delightful Cornish holidays, until I received an unexpected call from Jess. She sounded strangely different and it was not until she finally divulged what had caused this that I realised the world was still turning and there might be happiness around the corner for all of us – if we awaited it patiently enough. Her news took a bit of extracting until she finally admitted to trailing around the supermarket a couple of weeks before. 'It was the same routine as usual, Jenny, I was reaching for the same boring old food that I stuff in my trolley most Monday mornings and feeling as glum as the weather. I was peering down, searching for my usual muesli when, without looking, I stepped right back and scrunched on the foot of the man who was stretching over me to reach a giant box of cornflakes balanced on the top shelf. I must have hurt him because he went "whuff" and crashed back against my trolley which, of course, I had parked in the middle of the aisle. I grabbed his hands in an effort to stop him landing on his butt and apologised most profusely. We both looked silly and I felt foolish. To get away, I threw my elusive muesli into my cart and scuttled into the next aisle. I looked the other way when he came trailing after me to grab a four-pack of cranberry juice.'

'Yes,' I said impatiently. 'Then what happened?'

'Nothing, until I spied him two customers behind me at the checkout. I ignored him because I still felt something of a clumsy idiot and I think he did too. I was neatly transferring everything to my two shopping bags afterwards when he caught up with me near the door. I smiled again and enquired if his foot was OK. He said it was fine and then, probably as an afterthought, asked if he could he treat me to a coffee in the adjoining cafeteria.' Suddenly it all came out in an embarrassed rush. 'We've met twice more for coffee and he's asked me to go with him to the cinema next week. I said yes but do you think I am being too forward?' she asked. I laughed and told her not to be so silly.

Two weeks later I invited myself over to Taunton to meet this Lothario. Not only had he taken her out to the cinema and theatre but, as well as their regular Monday date at Sainsbury's, he had invited her to a couple of restaurant meals for good measure. It looked as if this man meant business! Jess offered to cook a meal for the three of us and casually asked him along. I found a grizzled, not terribly tall man with blue twinkling eyes and a dry sense of humour. He treated Jess with the deference and courtesy she deserved. No more was she shadowed by the doom and gloom of her previous husband, Hugo, and I felt her family would be as satisfied with him as I was. Thankfully, I knew there would be no more need of constant mercy telephone calls on my part. Jess was home and dry!

Things were also looking up in the holiday department. True to her word, Val had asked her daughter for help and she had booked the three of us into the same Lanzarote hotel we had visited a few months previously. Val, Bertrand and I decided that the internet and children came in very handy! Andrew, when I excitedly told him, said very little apart from checking our dates – to make sure it didn't clash with the Fowey Family History weekend, I surmised. I wondered if he was hoping to get down there also, but I couldn't imagine Fay encouraging this. And, anyway, where would that leave me in the scheme of things? There was no way we could both attend. It would be impossible. I awaited his intentions and when none materialised I booked myself into my usual guest house for the last week in April.

****

Val's daughter treated the three of us like young schoolchildren. She ran us to the airport in good time, minded our baggage while we all trooped to the loo and then shepherded us up to the counter before wishing us a good holiday and waving goodbye. We grinned sheepishly as we tucked our passports away and watched our luggage disappear via the conveyor belt before following the obedient crocodile of holidaymakers to divest ourselves of belts, watches, shoes, bags, mobile telephones and even keys by shoving them into inadequate plastic boxes – while at the same time trying not to panic. Strange how the herding instinct is still very strong and, although we all wandered around the Duty Free giggling and laughing, we were all conscious of the electronic board and its instructions even as we sipped our coffee.

I always feel a great relief when I am airborne. Not because I enjoy flying – I don't – but it means I have surmounted all the escalating hurdles airports now use to confuse and test me and I am aware, once I have arrived at my destination, everything will then be taken out of my hands and all *I* am expected to do is revel in a period of freedom.

On arrival, the three of us sank back into the old pleasant routine as if we had never been away and I took myself off to my poolside lounger with my book, a cool drink and a shady umbrella most mornings. Every hour or so I slipped into the warm water and the only time I vacated my luxury spot was when Val and Bertie collected me on their way to lunch.

We had all seen notices posted around Puerto del Carmen advertising their annual carnival. I had attended the massive Bridgwater Carnival from when I first came to the West Country so I was inclined to be a little dismissive of this one. Bertrand and Val, who didn't appreciate walking too far, had decided they would give it a miss. I said I would decide nearer the time and left it at that. I thought no more about it until my mobile throbbed as I was resettling myself on my tummy and wondering how long I could toast in the sunshine.

'Hi,' said a voice in my ear. 'What are you up to?' I gathered my thoughts together and was giving Andrew a watered-down version of doing nothing and enjoying every minute of it when he interrupted, 'What are you doing Saturday?'

'What, the day after tomorrow?' I asked, puzzled. 'Well, I will be here of course.'

'I'm told there will be great celebrations at your end of the island and wondered if you needed a partner?' I was completely flummoxed by then and all I could envisage was Andrew arriving for a short visit, as he had done previously, on a cruise liner. 'Actually I am nearer than you think, darling, and this seems too good an opportunity to miss', he said with irrepressible logic. Apparently he had been planning it since I had told him the dates of our holiday. Gradually I learned he and Fay were staying for ten days at Playa Blanca, in the south of the island, but he was also hoping *his* penchant for exploring and *her* inclination for not stirring would allow him time away from their complex. 'So make a list of places we must visit and I will do my utmost to accommodate you,' he said with gay abandon.

I turned over in the sunshine to assimilate his astounding news. Val and Bertrand arrived at that moment so I'm sure my explanation was sketchy and muddled. They made few comments and I am not entirely sure they approved. I, on the other hand, went around in a dream, making provisional plans and looking forward to an even more wonderful holiday.

Saturday dawned bright and clear. The wind had dropped, so that boded well for decorated floats, long processions and outlandish clothes. All along the seafront empty, gaudy huge floats were positioned and waiting when I wandered along that Saturday morning. The size of them and their number made me review my first estimate of the importance of this festival. It may not have had the same impact as the Bridgwater Carnival with its November dark velvety skies, its powerful, sparkling lights and blaring music; but it made up for it with the breathless enthusiasm of all the people taking part and all the onlookers who were turning it into a grand fiesta. The whole resort was swarming with holidaymakers and locals who were all striding along the promenade six and seven abreast and, often, twenty or thirty deep. Everyone was happy and I exchanged laughs with gun-toting pretend American FBI Agents, two pink crabs who were unable to walk in a straight line, and numerous Mexicans sporting sombreros, as well as a whole regiment of British soldiers in scarlet uniforms and glossy busbies. They told me the Queen would be along later!

I went back to the hotel to snatch a quick lunch after reporting to Val and Bertrand that I thought they should make the effort to come and watch it, as it looked as if it was going to be an exciting, grand display. I awaited Andrew's call and wondered how on earth we would be able to locate each other in such a confused melee.

My mobile twanged at four o'clock. *'On my way,'* read the text. At twenty past I received. *'Following a convoy of cars. Where should I park?'* I had no idea, as Andrew would be entering Puerto del Carmen from the south – near the old town and harbour – and I was miles away to the north. Also, there was a one-way system normally in operation around the town and I had no idea if it would be suspended for this occasion. At almost five o'clock I received a text which I didn't see until nearly half past, due to the noise of the crowd and music, which informed me, *'Parked in some remote spot and am now walking towards you. I hope!'* Suddenly I was clear on what we should both do. *'Walk towards me with the sea on your right and I will keep it on my left. That way we can't miss each other! OR CAN WE?'*

Suddenly he was there in front of me – his warm smile beaming and his arms outstretched. We clung to each other and I breathed a sigh of relief. What had been a potential disaster had turned into a perfect rendezvous. We found a less crowded spot by the side of the road and watched as the procession unfolded and wound its way past us and into the distance. I loved the hundreds of individual walkers dressed in unique outfits – like the prickly cactus waving his arms, two brightly coloured cotton reels slowly spinning past, a tiny doctor in his green scrubs waiting to operate, two or three Spidermen, a volcano spewing fire, some Smurfs waving as they walked and Zulu warriors lunging at us. A rainbow-coloured fish gasped for air; we waved at various clowns who were followed by a dozen Minnie Mice mums in bright red-and-white polka-dot dresses with black bows in their hair – all pushing miniature Minnie Mice in prams. We saw a swaying camel being led by a pretty little girl and we laughed and pointed out the cleverness and inspiration as we leaned close to snap their pictures. Then came the groups from various villages on the island; pirates with cutlasses, eye patches and huge black tricorn hats, followed by marching bands and accompanied by Caribbean girls, all swaying and spontaneously dancing with the crowd lining the route. Crinolined ladies walked sedately by and snowmen plodded. Suddenly, we espied our British troops, red uniforms immaculate, busbies swaying, with their shining black boots stamping in unison. In the middle was a diminutive little lad representing Queen Elizabeth II. They must have realised our nationality as they came racing across and posed for our cameras. Tiny dogs were dressed up as they paraded proudly with their owners as we all shouted our appreciation and applauded madly. Trick cyclists rode in tight circles around each other and Roman centurions swung by in their leather tunics and impressive helmets – their feet pounding down in unison. And still the cavalcade rolled on...

The cafés, restaurants and pubs along the front were doing a roaring trade, so we slipped into one and found a bench over in a corner. We squeezed in and ordered drinks. The noise was unbelievable with everyone chattering in a dozen different languages and a three-piece band thumping out the latest hits. Some more folk squashed in beside us, nearly sitting on our laps, and we all ended up grinning like idiots and taking photos of each other. Andrew clasped his free arm around me like a vice – not that there was any likelihood of me being swept away – as the whole pub burst into song, arms uplifted and swaying. When the heat and noise became unbearable we pushed our way outside once more and, with one accord, started making our way towards the harbour area where his car had been parked.

The streets were still thronged with revellers but the last float had disappeared and by now people were walking back, costumes a trifle awry, their arms around each other as they tiredly reviewed the whole occasion. Night had fallen and the view along the beaches reminded me of a moonlit backdrop for the film *South Pacific*. It was a beautiful evening just made for lovers – and we strolled along, hand in hand, quietly talking. Luckily Andrew's sense of direction proved accurate and we discovered his hired car standing forlorn and alone in what looked like a deserted building site. Strangely, it seemed to take very little time to return to the quieter end of town where my hotel was situated. We parked in the square and I led him through the back gate, across the gardens and past one of the glimmering swimming pools. The night was still velvety and warm, without a zephyr of wind, as I glanced around the dimly lit bar and tried to locate my two friends. I hoped that, by introducing Andrew to easy-going Val and Bertrand, maybe they would see him in a different light and finally accept our special relationship. I was well aware that they had a poor opinion of this man who took me away from my home and family and then walked out on me for little apparent reason. I wanted them to see the Andrew I knew and had always loved, but unfortunately the pair were nowhere to be seen. I led him upstairs and sat him down on my apartment balcony overlooking the pool, and went and collected two coffees and brandies. We drank them in comfort under a huge moon with the sea sighing down by the palm-edged beach and being lulled by the gentle music pulsing out of the darkened bar. I knew he wanted to make love with the patio doors pushed wide and the sky above a myriad of stars, but I was also aware that if he didn't quickly return to the south of the island, he could be in trouble with the one woman who could make his life a misery if she so chose.

And she did! Twice we made plans to see the home of the sculptor and famous artist, Cesar Manrique, who had designed and built a luxurious home in a series of huge volcanic bubbles in the centre of the island. This man's vision of the island had saved and preserved most of its natural beauty and rescued it from becoming an island of commercial high-rise hotels crammed full of tourists. I wanted to show him *Jameos del Agua* – another natural wonder; a sparkling pale blue and white oasis surrounded by exotic vegetation – as well as the *Green Caves* nearby, all excavated from lava flows. The first time Andrew announced he was thinking of visiting this part of the island Fay said she would prefer to see the *Timanfaya volcano* and then spent the short time they were there complaining bitterly about the blistering heat and the smelly camels. He brought her back immediately to their civilised hotel, sat her in the shade with a bottle of wine and took himself off for a brisk walk, he told me. The second time she languidly said she would join him but insisted they went after a long and drawn-out lunch and then cut short the trip saying her feet hurt and 'what was so special about these places anyway?'

Had Fay discovered our secret, I wondered. That he had managed to meet me on this island on two separate occasions? Maybe she sensed Andrew wanted to be off. She may have noticed an air of excitement about him, no matter how hard he tried to curb it, and was determined that whatever his inclinations were she would scotch them. Val, after asking me about Andrew's holiday plans and getting a negative reply, must have told Bertrand because neither of them mentioned it again. Perhaps they secretly thought we had reaped our just desserts. Andrew rang most days when he found a moment to be alone – usually walking along the tiny indented coves that make Playa Blanca so attractive – but he never spoke about coming to find me for the rest of that holiday and my own pride kept me silent. I felt like a donkey who has been offered a carrot with the promise of more to come – and then the donor never returns. The result was I came home rested in body but agitated in mind and no nearer to my heart's desire.

****

Within a few days of arriving back home, Bertrand's daughter and family came down from Sevenoaks to collect him for a short holiday. The last few times he had gone away Val had accompanied him, but this particular week she hadn't been feeling too well and had decided to stay at home. They rang each other constantly and, although Bertie sounded his usual chipper self, Val was worried he might have been putting on a good act for her benefit. The pair of us went out for our usual Sunday lunch at the pub although it was surprising how we missed Bertrand's bright banter and sharp, predictable jokes. Val had been complaining about breathlessness for the past few months and, on the way back, she started to feel ill halfway up a hill. I sat her on a low wall outside one of the guest houses and offered to call for medical help. I knew she dreaded being taken off to hospital in an ambulance and, as expected, she begged me to wait. A few minutes later colour had returned to her cheeks and she insisted she was well enough to walk, holding my arm the rest of the way. The next day I was ticked off on the telephone by her irate daughter for what she called my thoughtless stupidity.

Sadly Bertrand hadn't fared any better. When he returned home two days later Val was told, in confidence, that the whole family had been shocked to see how his absent-mindedness had escalated. He had often been unable to remember what he had eaten at a previous meal and, when they had taken him out, he had forgotten by the time he reached home. Apparently he had gone for a walk alone one afternoon and then had no recollection as to where he was staying, or with whom, and had been found looking lost and aimlessly wandering, by a policeman. I could imagine how embarrassed he would have felt being brought back home like a naughty schoolboy. Of course none of this was a great surprise to us and Val had even thoughtfully placed notes of his home address, with various telephone numbers, in all his jacket and trouser pockets for this very reason.

I was told by Val's daughter that Val had very probably suffered a stroke warning and that she was planning to take her mother back to the family home in Cumbria. After much soul searching, she also tentatively offered a home to Bertrand but, as expected, his family closed ranks and insisted that between them, they would look after their dad. So, within a few weeks, the flats were put on the market and in a flurry of excitement, prospective buyers were shown around, furniture was disposed of and two cosy homes became neat and alien. With a shock I realised the two people who had become my best friends, who had welcomed me into their homes, included me in their fun and games, asked my opinion and given their loving advice – until I felt they were my surrogate family – were soon to disappear forever. I acknowledged it would soon be a lonely, solitary and much emptier life from then on. Andrew might text, telephone and e-mail constantly, Robin would ring up a couple of times a week to check on me, neighbours would always pass the time of day, my friends and cousin would invariably be available for a chat; but the two lively, warm personalities that lived one floor above me were going to leave Devon and I would miss them unbearably. Possible visits to Val's new home, letters and telephone conversations are fine but no substitute for a front door being on the latch, a warm fire flickering, a cup of tea being thrust into one's hand with an accompanying smile with the knowledge one was welcome. Oh, how I would miss them!

Luckily I was asked to perform an errand of mercy just before my two friends were spirited away, which made things a little easier for me. Derek, Lorna's husband, rang me one evening. He said Lorna was due to go into the big district general hospital in Exeter shortly for an operation. It sounded as if she had been putting it off for some time mainly due to the fact that her parents, who lived in the small village of Blakeney in Norfolk, were willing to come but were unsuitable. They had become frailer over the years and, although the family occasionally went up there on holiday, Lorna felt it would be too much to ask them to come down and take over the responsibility of a convalescing daughter, a builder son-in-law, a boisterous granddaughter, plus half a dozen of her pets, as well as keeping the whole house clean and the inmates fed. I said indignantly, 'Why didn't you ask me before, Derek? You know I will always come over and help you out. Be like old times again. I do miss the old crowd and talking on the phone weekly isn't half as much fun as trailing round to your place, sitting down with our feet up and a steaming hot cuppa to enjoy a jolly good gossip. Put Lorna on the line, darling, and I'll tell her what an idiot she's being.'

He handed over the phone. 'What's up?' I asked. 'Sounds a bit major to me and, because Derek sounded embarrassed, as if he'd rather not discuss anything delicate over the phone, I'm guessing it's a hysterectomy?' She admitted as much and the relief in her voice made me realise that, for all our telephone chats since I had left, we *had* grown a little apart and she had been unsure of my undying support when she needed it most.

Within the week I was installed in a family home once more. We deposited Lorna into the care of the Royal Devon & Exeter Hospital and I returned home praying I would make a suitable substitute caretaker. I had to learn their routine and I usually deferred to Petra to tell me what she and her dad liked and how her mum preferred it done. Petra and I had always been the greatest mates; I suspect this was mainly due to her having the oddest collection of pets imaginable, which instead of making me recoil in horror as most adults would have done, only brought us closer together. Rex, their old dog, lived *en famille* but most of her other pets occupied a warmly heated conservatory and, if it was often a bit untidy and messy, I ignored it as best I could and only insisted we gave it a good clean up when it became absolutely necessary. Petra and I would solemnly discuss if her two gerbils were happy and contented with their surroundings. They had tubes to hide in, wheels to exercise on and we always made sure they had lots of burrowing material when they wanted to disappear. Gertie and

Gumdrop the goldfish had long since died but had been resurrected since and I was distinctly relieved I didn't have to remember any new names. Not so with the hamsters. What had started as a rescue mission in the school holidays of a cheeky black-and-white one called Montgomery was extended when a golden ball of fluff called Rommel joined him. Megan, Petra's best friend, gave her two more for her birthday and, because they were girls, they had their own living quarters. One was scruffy and the other sleek, but they both had delicate pink ears, paws and feet and Derek insisted on calling them Vera Lynn and Ann Shelton respectively, Petra informed me. I coped with the shy green lizard that had a habit of hiding in the greenery or pretended to play dead and I quite liked the yellow canary as long as she didn't fly around the conservatory when I was in there. Luckily Petra had no penchant for snakes or spiders so I was spared sharing my living space with them.

Outside, in the garden, resided Horatio the hedgehog who invariably turned up most evenings when we were in the middle of our meal. He had his own little tin of dried food and another of water waiting for him and we would watch from the window as he would arrive, peer round to see he was alone and then calmly munch through the plateful and wander away, just as sedately, when he had drunk as much water as he required.

I spent a month more with them when Lorna was at last released from hospital and, even if I do say it myself, I think I coped reasonably well. Once our daily visits to Lorna in hospital were over I had more time and it gave me the chance to visit my old neighbours in the close where I'd lived. It looked a little more run-down and tired than I had remembered; but it was lovely to be warmly welcomed in, to hear their latest news and tell them what I'd been up to recently. I also visited Margaret, the vicar's wife, and attended church once more. I was only too pleased to be a stand-in for Lorna when it came to church cleaning and flower arranging and I even managed to get to one ramblers' walk in the Bridport area with my good friends.

But the best part of the whole experience was just sitting with my chum and chatting – usually while we prepared the vegetables for the evening meal. Lorna would make herself comfortable on their shabby couch in the kitchen. Rex would snuggle as close as he dared and we would peel potatoes, shell peas and slice carrots as we discussed anything and everything. She told me how Derek's work had fallen off as people felt the pinch of the recession and stopped thinking about improvements and ónly about necessary maintenance. She was also concerned for her ageing parents so far away in Norfolk. 'When something happens to one of them – and it has to sometime, Jenny – how will I be able to divide myself between Blakeney and here? I keep asking them to think of moving nearer but I think they are too tired to find the necessary energy and enthusiasm. And yet surely they can't expect us to up sticks and try and find building employment close by where they live? Maybe Derek could find work in Norwich, but would it be similar to what he does now or would he have to take anything going? And *is* anything going these days? He would refuse to go on benefits and I know our whole relationship would crumble. It goes round and round in my head and week by week I shelve it when my mother vaguely talks of book clubs and the WI.'

Because we had the time and privacy we needed, I eventually admitted how bad the loneliness was in my flat. She knew how Val and Bertrand had always been around and had been my rock and support. I told her that was fine as far as it went, but one still has to say goodnight, come away and get ready for bed – alone. Nothing assuaged that, and no matter how often Andrew texted or phoned to remind me he was thinking about me, an empty bed was a bitter experience that ate into my determination to stay positive as the months went by. Thoughtful cards, presents and loving gestures when you aren't together can never replace a loving, permanent relationship and I was becoming more and more depressed, I admitted.

I returned home to a Val and Bertrand who were both quiet and a little apprehensive about their coming separation and how they would both manage living with others who would take over the running of their lives. As Val put it, 'Suddenly we won't be in charge of our own destinies - others will decide for us and, like little children, we will have to accept that with good grace.' I knew that, having to wait with them until the bitter end and then wave them cheerfully on their separate ways, would take all the courage I possessed.

That was until Andrew rang me two mornings later. 'How would you feel about accompanying me down to Cornwall for the weekend? I have just received Deborah's ashes and, although I can't face the journey alone, the thought of being accompanied by Fay doesn't bear thinking about. She will turn it into a three-ring circus by arranging to meet our friends in Topsham and insisting the vicar does his stuff as if it were another big occasion. I want to go there, scatter her ashes over the family grave – quietly and simply – just as she would have wanted – and then quietly leave.'

I agreed immediately. I was aware it would be a potentially sad event, and there was no way I would ever admit to it, but a frisson of excitement gripped me. I would have Andrew to myself for two whole days and maybe *this* time we could make some specific plans in peace and quiet, once and for all, and without our usual time restriction. He said he would book us into The Crumplehorn Hotel in Polperro and pick me up, as before, on his way down from Yorkshire. I told Val and maybe she was relieved because I'm sure that putting a brave face on things can be very tiring and so, for a few days, they could both revert to being their anxious selves. What a naïve idiot I always prove to be. Why do I never learn?

On the Saturday morning I must have been deeply asleep because it took a few seconds for me to register that my telephone was ringing stridently. I swung out of bed, catching myself on my bedside table, as I groped around to stifle it. It was Andrew and he was whispering, 'Your mobile wasn't on, Jenny. I had difficulty in remembering your landline number. The trip's off, darling. I came home late last night from a Probus dinner and she smugly informed me it was all arranged: we would be picking up the grand-kids – who are on half term – and leaving before lunch. She told me to ring whichever hotel I had booked into and ask for extra accommodation.' His voice cracked with emotion, 'Ring up and cancel for us, darling, and please, please forgive me.' *I numbly replaced the receiver without even bothering to reply...*

I left it until midday before I rang the country inn that stands at the head of the road that leads straight to Lansallos church. I explained that Mr Lanyon was regretfully cancelling his weekend booking. He understood and fully accepted the full amount would be deducted from his bank account and apologised for any inconvenience he had caused them. I rang off before the concerned receptionist could question me. An hour later I was sitting on the Waterloo train – after telephoning Meryl and Adam, my friends in Essex – having begged a lift to Axminster station from a kind neighbour.

I spent most of the weekend in a state of shock. It had the effect of deadening my brain and thought processes. All I could think of was that this woman – whose self-interest was always paramount – had somehow deduced her husband was poised to abscond and *she* was determined to stop him. Meryl never asked the reason for my precipitous arrival; they both calmly and blandly accepted it and proceeded to entertain me. My mobile was firmly switched off so I was effectively cut off from the rest of the world – and felt the better for it!

Chapter 32

*

I returned from Essex in time to wish Bertrand God speed. I knew, for all his bravado, he was apprehensive about entering the domain of his daughter where she reigned supreme not only over her house and husband, but indirectly over her two daughters-in-law and five assorted grandchildren. I think Bertie was uneasy that he might also be expected to assume the role of childish simplicity and was not sure he was up to it. Val and I waved him off with brave smiles and then walked back inside her flat and had a good cry. I agreed to stay to lunch – as it gave her something to do – and then we finished off the bottle of wine I had brought up from my place while watching, without seeing, some mindless quiz programme on her television.

Two weeks later Val's own family came down from Cumbria and bore their mother away. Her flat had been viewed several times and, although a few tentative offers had been forthcoming, none had been acceptable. The family wanted her safe with them and it brought a lump into my throat to see the way they respected as well as cherished her. Two giant grandsons loaded all her precious belongings onto the disreputable van they had brought with them before gently settling her into the front of their family car and, once again, I waved all five of them off. This time I took myself off to my own flat and sank half a bottle of spirit far more potent than the wine in an effort to numb the feeling of sadness at being alone once more.

Three days later I made my way down to Cornwall to attend the Fowey Family History Week as Andrew had admitted his inability to attend once more. I had no idea if it was guilt or embarrassment but we hadn't had a proper conversation since the débâcle of Deborah's ashes and this time I felt none of the excitement or exuberance of returning to a place I had always loved. He was still texting daily and had sent a couple of letters through the post. One, an abject apology, I threw into the bin, almost unread, as it made me shudder to recall how he had shattered my naivete and trust. I was deeply tired of plans that never reached fruition and dreams that were never realised. The second letter was longer – I felt he had recovered his second wind – and dwelt on our future. I tried to read it objectively as I still-believed in his good intentions but doubted his ability to carry them out. I felt Fay had his measure and guessed his every move before he even thought of it himself. I even began to wonder if she was reading his texts, as he always slept very deeply, because her guessing was uncannily accurate.

As a member, I attended a few of the meetings, listened intently to the speakers, viewed with interest information supplied by other members and chatted randomly while doing so. But, because I felt I didn't really belong, I spent the rest of the time walking the coast around the Gribbin, going up the river as far as Lerryn and wandering around Polruan. It was a lonely experience and it didn't help that the weather was sunny but abnormally chilly for that time of year. I returned to Devon with an audible sigh of relief only to be informed by Robin he was coming down for a few days.

He came alone and stayed sedately with our friends up in Dunkeswell, only venturing down to Honiton, Exeter and Seaton to relax and see his special chums. He had hired a car for ease of manoeuvrability and occasionally he would pick me up to visit these people. Some may have been surprised at seeing us together once more, but I noticed they soon accepted it, by realising our partnership was now dissolved and all that remained was a comfortable friendship. They watched as we laughed and joked together, recognising there was no underlying current of sexuality and there never would be. I was well aware that Robin had never mentioned Andrew's name since I had left York. He had amazed me by asking me to visit him and Ailsa for two Christmases in a row. I had always refused, with a laugh, but only because his relationship and happiness with his new wife was of paramount importance to me and I was determined nothing would mar it. I was also well aware that the slightest hint of Andrew and I keeping in touch would demolish Robin's goodwill immediately and his bitter hurt would terminate our friendship.

A week after Robin left, Jess's gentleman friend rang. For a moment I was at a loss as to who he was. He explained delicately that they had been seeing quite a bit of one another and what did I think of them making it a permanent arrangement? *What did I think about it*? If Jess was all for it, I told him, then I was delighted for them both. I felt slightly embarrassed that the pair had thought to sound me out as to *my* feelings. I felt like a father discussing his daughter's liaison with a prospective young bridegroom. I told him as much and he shyly laughed and explained Jess had made it a condition of her agreeing. As soon as he rang off I telephoned my friend and asked her why she needed *my* permission to marry the man of her dreams? She said her own family looked on him kindly but it felt like indecent haste to be planning a wedding so soon after meeting a suitable partner. I crudely advised her to go and live with him and then, when she was truly certain they couldn't live without one another, to marry him quietly without telling another soul.

'Don't burn your boats yet,' I advised. 'Keep your house for now and let it on a short lease - that way, it will be insurance if you realise you have made a mistake. But I'm betting you're well on the way to the smooth path of happiness at last, darling.'

'Thanks, Jenny,' she said with a catch in her voice. 'I didn't want anyone – and especially not you – to think I'm an old romantic fool who should know better.' I felt slightly ashamed that she had considered me in that way. I had been well aware of her first husband's penchant for gloomy, cynical predictions that gave him a deeply negative view of life and I rejoiced at her being happy with a man who obviously had seen her gentleness and worth and wanted to look after her for the rest of her life. In fact I envied her....

******

I tried to keep busy as an antidote to Andrew's tardiness with his plans and promises. I had decided to take a maths course shortly after I arrived in Seaton. I had always been ashamed that anything to do with figures would alarm and intimidate me and although, given time, I was able to solve any problems that normally arose, I wanted to delve into the intricacy of the science of numbers so I could face them without my usual sinking feeling. I had attended all the evening lectures and used the school's computers almost daily. I finally took the two exams and passed them both; the first with ease and the second by forcing myself to the limit of my ability. I immediately felt more relaxed with myself. In the meantime, while practising up at our local school, I had met some students who were wrestling with English as I had with maths. I had been formally asked by the authorities to help these students with their studies. I had reluctantly refused as I had, by then, begun helping out at a local food bank. It was only once a week, the work was certainly not arduous and I enjoyed being of some use; maybe the need was somewhat hidden but vital nevertheless. I had decided, from then on, that *my* salvation was up to me, even if it meant I would do it alone. I would take as many holidays as I wanted or could afford. I would do my bit in the community but not push myself beyond my limits, I would stop worrying about what Andrew wanted or aspired to – that was *his* concern – and I would try to please myself in all things. Unlike my New Year's resolutions, I would do my utmost to abide by these – until, hopefully, one day they would become second nature. From now on I hoped to enjoy all what life had to offer. Little did I guess my new-found contentment was soon to be shattered.

****

I remember it was a lovely Saturday in late June. The morning sun had prodded me awake and made me only too eager to get out of bed, for once. I ate a quick breakfast and showered before finishing off some chores from the previous day. This balmy weather was too nice to miss and, once the flat had been tidied, I began packing up a picnic lunch to take down to the sea along with my beach mat, loads of sun cream and an exciting novel I'd just borrowed from the library. I'd even toyed with the idea of going for a swim and, as an afterthought, had tossed my costume in. I had my hand on my front door when the telephone shrilled. Sighing, I went back inside and picked up the receiver.

'Jenny, Jenny help me!' For a second I fumbled to place the voice. My mind skittered around as I strove to fix on who it was – then my panic subsided somewhat as I recognised Paul, my cousin Dee's husband, even though it registered he sounded strained and shrill.

'What's up, love?' I asked. 'Everything OK?'

'It's Dee,' he gabbled. 'I can't wake her up.'

'What do you mean – you can't wake her?' I knew something serious must have happened but I was unable to get my head around what he was saying. 'Start again. Now what's the matter?'

I heard him take a deep, rasping breath 'We were out in the back garden tidying up. I'd finished mowing the lawn and Dee was following me around, neatening the edges. She was chuntering on, as she often does, because she hates the job. I was emptying the grass box of cuttings when she gave a soft grunt – more a sigh really – I glanced around as she put her hand to her head and fell across the path. I rushed over to help her up but she had her eyes closed and I couldn't rouse her. I shook her and shook her.' He gave a great gulp, 'Once her eyes slowly opened, I swear, but only for a second – and then closed again.'

'*Ring 999!*' I shouted urgently. '*Have you got your mobile? Just ring for an ambulance.*' I tried to sound calm and reasonable but my voice was escalating. I reined myself in and forced myself to speak quietly. 'Dial 999,' I said again. 'The paramedics will be with you in no time.'

'I have done,' he answered. 'I'm waiting for them now.' *Thank God for that I thought in desperation.* I told him to get a cushion and a blanket and try and make her comfortable.

Then, as an afterthought, I told him, 'Open the front door *and* the gate - it will save time.' It would also give him something to do. I could hear his breath rasping in his throat and I knew he was still trying to rouse my lovely cousin. 'Have you tried CPR?' I asked.

'Oh, do you mean breathing into her mouth and pressing on her chest? I'll try but she's all curled up on her side and I don't like to pull her about.'

'Do it,' I ordered, tersely. I tried to talk him through it and I knew he tried to obey me. I could hear him breathing and talking to her until I heard the blessed sound of footsteps.

'Gotta go!' shouted Paul and my phone went dead. I sat on the floor surrounded by scattered bags and an abandoned sun hat, gasping for air, my hands clasped uselessly to my forehead thinking, *Please God, please God make it all right. Not Dee – please don't let it be Dee.*

There was nothing I could do. I felt useless, so far away. But I knew I had to sit there until I was given some news. I was imagining the ambulance men swiftly entering the house and swinging into action. In emergencies neither would speak much as each segued into a well-ordered routine. They would give Paul a measure of reassurance by their calm manner and disciplined efficiency. I prayed as never before.

I sat by the telephone until it was almost dusk. I had struggled up to make a cup of tea and was curled up in my large armchair when it finally rang. I snatched it up. 'Yes?' I whispered. It was Paul – sounding tired and slow. I knew, before he spoke, my prayers had been powerless. I told him I would catch the next train to London and be with him as soon as I could. In a daze, I collected a few things and went to see my next-door neighbour. He explained to his wife and we left in a matter of minutes. At Axminster station he kindly asked if I had enough money and I nodded mutely, showing him my purse and credit card. I caught the last train going all the way into London and arrived in Waterloo at a few minutes past eleven o'clock. Paul met me outside a still busy Waterloo station and took me straight back to the hospital. They kept the life support machine going until the next morning and then gently explained there was no point as Dee had departed this life. They also explained, with great compassion, that she probably had known nothing after that soft sigh in the garden. I touched Paul on the shoulder and said I would be waiting outside

She looked so peaceful under the crisp white sheets and, as we took our leave of her, I saw Paul look back and hesitate as if there was one last thing he needed to tell her. I was aware the nurses were ready to do their final preparations before relinquishing her body to the authorities. We were told at the desk to go home and get some rest before returning to deal with all the paperwork the next day. It seemed so strange to be on the other side of the nursing barrier. I listened to the medical jargon being directed at us and felt no different from any other bereaved folk who are trying to come to terms with sudden death. I coaxed Paul, because I knew I must, to have some tea and toast in the hospital restaurant before finding the car and making our weary way home through the tail end of the rush-hour traffic.

We went to bed as the hospital suggested, but both of us were so tired and shocked we were unable to sleep and, by mid-afternoon, were making call after call to family and friends. Always explaining, explaining, explaining. That night the tears came for me. I remembered us as children living next door to each other and sharing our mothers who were sisters-in-law; she the giggling little toddler running to catch up with her big cousin and me being sternly warned to take good care of her at all times. Marching off to school together with our new Christmas satchels bouncing on our backs; me hanging around after school when she was given detention; me facing up to the school bully while Dee, white-faced and wide-eyed, hid behind me; even the feeling of unfairness when I wanted to walk home with my first exciting boyfriend and had to accept her tagging along too. I left school and went to college, which gave her space to meet her classmate, Paul, and suddenly they were inseparable. As to our growing-up period – we shared clothes because both our first jobs were poorly paid; we sat in back seats of cinemas and danced all night on a glass of orange juice. She met Andrew one Christmas when I hesitantly brought him home. I had been welcomed down to Cornwall many times and knew it was time for me to entertain him in return. Always reticent and shy, I had rarely, if ever, mentioned our first meeting or subsequent correspondence to my family; and either my parents had never noticed my burning interest in him or had chosen to ignore it. Andrew had arrived at my parents' house a couple of days before Christmas. It had been his first leave from the navy and, as our home was closest, it had seemed an ideal time to invite him. At eighteen he had been beginning his career and had appeared to have adopted a slight veneer of sophistication, overlaid by an inherent shyness yet balanced by his realistic common sense. Dee, at fourteen, had been fascinated by everything about him – his Cornish accent, his honesty and quirky humour. She had asked innumerable questions as to where he lived, why he spoke as he did and what he did on his ship. He had answered her seriously and in depth, which had made her feel very grown up. It had been obvious she was slightly in awe of his intelligence and, from that time, she had been aware of him being central in my life, even though I had rarely mentioned him. In fact it was Dee who had warned Chris off when it was clear he had been determined to marry me.

It had been a magic time for us both. I had gone to college and she'd finished school and obtained a job as an office junior. She'd enjoyed her brief office dalliance with Chris's best friend, the mercurial, charismatic Bryn, until he had quickly dumped her to go travelling around the world with yet more new found friends. It had been as if our age difference had suddenly disappeared, the world was our oyster, nothing had been out of our reach and life and was exciting and splendid. Eventually our contrasting lifestyles had inevitably swept us slightly apart until she'd informed me she was marrying her devoted school sweetheart, Paul, and I had known that she had secured her heart's desire. Shortly after, my pride and stupidity had lost me Andrew, and Chris had been around to sweep up the pieces. Dee had said very little but I'd known she was concerned and apprehensive. I had been aware she was dubious as to Chris's motives. Against all the odds, I'd managed to keep my ill-advised marriage going for ten years before I had thrown in my hand and divorced him quietly and amicably. Dee had been my sturdy supporter through this trying period but once she'd met Robin – and I had married him – she had welcomed him into our family and had soon grown to love him.

Round and round my mind swirled as fleeting memories came and disappeared, to be superseded by yet more. I twisted and fidgeted until finally, after turning over my pillow yet again, I gave in and crept downstairs. Paul was unable to sleep too so I made us both a cup of tea. The next morning we were both wan and bug-eyed when we arrived at the hospital to complete the complex paperwork. Gently it was explained that Dee's body would not be released until an autopsy had been performed. Paul was puzzled and distressed until it was explained that, by law, an apparently healthy person has to be examined as to the cause of death before a body can be released for burial or cremation. They could give us no idea of the timescale for this – which upset him even more. He began weeping silently.

I led him gently out of the hospital and drove him home. I knew he needed to be in his own surroundings to talk out his grief and unravel his feelings. The death certificate and other forms could be left for another day – in fact it would occupy our minds and give us both something to do – but I was also aware this desolate man required peace and quiet and a willing listener. I telephoned the local Registrar and made an appointment for the next morning and afterwards I spoke to the nearby undertaker; I then sat down and told Paul he had all the time in the world to talk and I had all the time in the world to listen.

'What's this sub "something" haemorrhage?' he asked. 'Why can't they say what it is in plain English?' I explained, as best I could, it is a subarachnoid bleeding in the brain.

'That's a bleeding between two membranes covering the brain,' I told him. 'It can come on suddenly – without warning – and occasionally can be fatal.' I said that, in this case, there was nothing he could have done to save her. I held on tightly to his hands and willed him to believe me. He stared at the death certificate and repeated the unfamiliar words to himself. I hoped he was slightly relieved to know no one would hold him responsible for not performing a miracle in bringing Dee back to life He then proceeded to tell me many intimate details of their life together. Secrets which I am sure he had never divulged, or discussed, before. I listened gravely while my own memories marched alongside his and we both tried hard not to break down. As he pointed out, 'Dee would have laughed at us both and told us not to be so soft!'

We both picked at our evening meal that night but fortified ourselves with several glasses of wine. I had purchased some in the hope it would help us sleep and reduce a few of our frightening dreams. The next morning I took Paul up a cup of tea and hustled him out of bed. Keeping busy can blunt the worst despair and I aimed to cram our day with necessary tasks that would give us little time to think deeply. We met the Registrar with the correct paperwork and I was surprised how kindly she treated my cousin – a shocked, bereaved husband – by asking just the right questions and taking her time to listen to his answers. She recommended we take extra copies of the death certificate to save us having to apply for more. She explained that one always misjudged how many interested parties have to be told and pointed out it was so much simpler to have paid for a couple too many, due to photocopies not being acceptable proof.

We went from there to the undertakers where they offered us a pot of tea, which I accepted on our behalf. I then sat silently back while Paul chose the sort of funeral he envisaged for his beloved wife. As I expected, it would be simple with no ostentation. I prompted him by remembering Dee's favourite childhood hymns and, because she had no formal affiliation with any particular religious organisation, the undertaker recommended a sympathetic, retired vicar who my cousin would probably have chosen herself. I left them alone as to the choosing of a coffin. It made me shudder even to think about it and I could see, by Paul's face, he was also imagining her being entombed and confined in such a narrow, claustrophobic box. I clutched my fast-cooling drink and stared into space.

We were too late to find a café still serving lunches but I insisted a sausage roll and coffee for him and a cheese scone and pot of tea for me was not an indulgence but a necessity. While Paul was still shaken from his session at the undertakers, and therefore could hardly be more upset, I decided we should visit our local insurance broker and sort out the various policies my cousins had prudently taken out. The three office staff were also very kind and understanding once we explained our business and, when we left there, I could feel relief and acceptance begin to creep into my cousin's shattered awareness.

Not knowing when Dee's body was likely to be released by the Coroner left us both uncertain as to the duration we would have to wait, so I was relieved that evening when Paul's younger sister telephoned and suggested coming down for a few days and, if nothing had been settled by then, taking him back for a short stay on their small farm near Church Stretton in Shropshire. His immediate reaction was horror at the idea of leaving his home. I am sure, in his mind, he likened it to deserting his responsibilities as well as his wife. I gently took the phone out of his hand, told her to come as soon as she could and, regardless of what he said, convinced him face-to-face that he was being unrealistic and stupid. She agreed and we both decided, as soon as she arrived, I would return to the

West Country. I then turned to him and insisted he could just as easily communicate and plan from a quiet farm in the Shropshire hills as from his London home. He reluctantly agreed after being bombarded by both of us.

Jean, a smaller and more compact version of Paul, pulled up in front of the house two days later driving a muddy, beaten-up Land Rover that looked as if it had seen better days. They hugged and I quietly went upstairs to prepare her room as I guessed they needed time to talk and find comfort in each other. I stayed that night to help her settle in and then made my way by bus, underground and train back to my home with a sigh of relief. It was a comfort to be on my own at last, I discovered. I had baldly told Andrew my shocking news as soon as I heard what had happened. He had texted me constantly but I am ashamed to admit I answered very few of those texts. I felt drained of energy after offering constant support to my cousin's husband and I found it difficult to expend time composing information for my mobile. I noticed, after a few days, he accepted the hint and lapsed into silence after texting: '*Ring when you are able.*'

So I sat on the train and tried to speak with him. Sadly, he had switched off his mobile just when I was able to talk and had the time to do so. I arrived home mid-afternoon and was met by the same neighbour who had taken me into Axminster in the first place. I dumped my case in my tiny hall and groped my way to bed. Apart from getting up twice to go to the bathroom and once to make a mug of tea, I stayed curled up under the duvet, dozing and thinking, until early the following morning. Surprisingly, I felt a whole lot better. I suppose the heavy sense of responsibility had been removed from *my* shoulders. Now it was just a matter of waiting for, and dreading, the unfolding of the final chapter of my cousin's life....

Coming back to my flat was a lonely experience. My two best friends had, of necessity, gone their own separate ways. I had other congenial neighbours but none as close as Val who had taken the place of my mother as my confidante. We rang each other most days but I was not able to thunder up the stairs, knock on her door and be welcomed in with a charming smile. She had her own family now and, of course, they were her first concern and she was theirs. I rejoiced for her but was sad for myself. Andrew's messages were no substitute. His cheerful texts only highlighted my solitary state and, strangely, depressed me immensely. I threw myself into work at the Food Bank, because there, at least I felt useful. I rang Paul most days and he sounded as if he was finding a measure of calm in helping with the unending chores that make up farm life. I hoped it was doing him good. Jean confided to me he had also taken on the job of ferrying his niece and nephew to and from their primary school in the valley.

'Two lively children that are in hot water daily allow no one to opt out for a minute, Jenny. They adore him, scramble all over him and insist he helps with their social life as well as their homework,' she went on with a chuckle. I breathed a sigh of relief. At least one of us was on the way to slowly healing.

Andrew begged for me to take a week's holiday in York. He offered to pay my hotel bill as an inducement. I refused and bluntly explained to him I now had work to do in the West Country while I waited to be summoned back to London for Dee's funeral. Everything must be on hold until then and, anyway, my first priority was to my cousin's husband.

'You have had all the time in the world to decide your future life, love. I have waited and said very little as I'm determined not to influence you, but I see immense procrastination and a million excuses. I'm sure your reasons are valid each time. But there is always some family crisis that threatens either your wife, your two sons, or *their* families. It frightens me that they are always uncannily apt and timely. Almost as if they outguess you and block your reactions – every time. I understand your dilemma but feel nothing is ever going to change if you never take a stand, make a firm decision and then stick to it.' I hated being so cruel but it needed to be said. I supposed it also showed the depth of my disillusionment. I usually had a sunny, positive nature, but at that moment my raw unhappiness showed as plain as day. I also noted Andrew's texting output immediately dwindled to almost nothing. I obviously had given him food for thought; *but was any of it forceful enough to effect a decisive reaction*?

****

Almost five weeks after the event, Paul received confirmation that Dee's body would be released to the undertakers immediately. Two days later we both returned to London. I stayed with a neighbour as I thought it was more appropriate for his sister and her family to use her brother's home when it was time for them to come. The simple ceremony was soon planned to the last detail. Between us we contacted all our family and Dee's friends. We also asked them to spread the word in case we had inadvertently forgotten someone. I was touched and grateful when Robin asked if I would like him to be there. He offered to fly down for the funeral and return to Scotland the next day. He and Dee had been such friends but, selfishly, I also found great comfort in his thoughtfulness. Strangely, the previous day Andrew asked if I would like *him* to attend. *Did I?* What was the point, I asked myself? I was tired of every promise he had ever made had been doomed to failure, so why would this one be different? I could hear the hurt clearly in his voice as he wished me good night.

The day of the funeral dawned bright and sunny and I sent a silent paean of thanks for such decent weather. I had spent a few days sorting and cleaning the house but, in fact, very little needed doing apart from dusting, as Dee had kept it immaculate right up until the time of her collapsing in the garden. Flowers were brought to the door from early in the morning. This should have given us some idea as to the number of people who would attend. The family arrived and mostly stood around in hesitant groups. I think Dee's sudden death had shocked them all. Always bubbling over with fun and good humour, then snuffed out in a moment. They were followed soon after by dozens of friends. Some she wouldn't have seen for years – like old school friends, work colleagues, pub mates, the secretary of the local donkey sanctuary that Dee supported, acquaintances that had enjoyed their company on various holidays and even the manager of her local supermarket. I encouraged Paul to introduce them to each other as it gave him something to do, as well as lightening the atmosphere. By noon most of the sitting room was crammed with blooms of almost every hue. I found it difficult to read the cards of condolence that accompanied each offering without my tears overflowing. The cars arrived soon after and we all trooped out of the front gate, either to get in them or follow in our own private transport. Robin took my arm and helped me into one of the sombre black cars. I looked up for a second and was confronted by an edging of silent neighbours who lined both sides of the road and stretched all the way down the very long avenue. Good friends who stood and quietly mourned as the funeral cortège eased its way through them. I knew Dee had lived in her little house most of her married life but I could never have guessed how she had been loved by so many. Always bright and cheery, ever ready to pass the time of day with everyone, she would have been amazed to see how they all wanted to be there to pay their last respects. I saw two people in wheelchairs and a few young girls with children in pushchairs or clutching toddler's hands. There were even some curtains closed as a typical London sign of respect. Once more my eyes misted with tears as I felt their wholehearted love directed towards a woman who'd always had time for them all.

The service was conducted reverently but lightly. We were told it was a celebration of a life lived to the full, always surrounded by love and happiness. Our pleasant vicar gave a brief history of Dee's life with a few funny reminiscences thrown in, which had the congregation smiling and remembering. Lots of music – some simple hymns from her Sunday school childhood interspersed with beloved melodies by her favourite recording artists. I walked out of that tiny Saxon church feeling relieved and somehow relaxed after the terrible strain of days of uncertainty and sadness; and I noticed that at the local pub where we all gathered, people chatted and laughed and, if there were any feuds, they were all put aside or forgotten. Dee had worked her magic once more.

The next day most of us regretfully dispersed to return to our homes. Paul was being taken back to his sister and brother-in-law's farm and I was relieved my responsibility was now at an end. Robin's presence had affected me like a pair of worn, comfortable slippers and I thanked him for coming and supporting Paul. We had slipped into our friendship mode with great ease and I noticed most of our joint family had finally accepted that this was how it would be from now on. There was little nudging or nodding of heads now, I observed, and for this I was grateful. We left Chingford at midday in Robin's hired car; he kindly dropped me off at Leyton Underground station before making his way to Gatwick airport. I waved as his car sped off in the traffic.

I returned to Devon feeling empty and wan. I had enough money to do almost anything I wanted but I had no plans or goals that I wanted to pursue. I could visit friends, go on holiday or carry on my life as before. Rambling, dancing, evening classes, the church, the theatre or cinema as well as the Food Bank were all diversions but none of them meant anything to me at that time. To be alone and never to be needed, or have another person dependent on you, is a bitter, raw and enervating experience. It had worn me down and I was finding it difficult to cope with everyday life. Ever more tempting was the idea of taking myself off to my bed and, like a hibernating animal, staying there. I'd worked with patients suffering depression and I knew I was well on the way to joining their ranks. I was scared of opting out totally as I knew that was the beginning of the end for me; but I was also unable to rouse myself and face the world. I knew Andrew was concerned, as was Robin, especially as a dull, smouldering and sullen anger was also fuelling my awareness of hopelessness. Nobody wanted me, nobody needed me – so why bother?

I was getting out of bed late in the mornings and, although I showered and made myself look presentable, I was eating very little, not bothering to go out, would forget to turn my mobile on and seldom answered either my landline or any of the letters that dropped through my mailbox. When I *did* speak with concerned friends I tried to act as naturally as possible, while hoping desperately that they hadn't noticed. I still kept in touch with Paul and his family because I knew he needed all our support, but other than that I effectively dropped out of society. My one concession was my passion for books. Every two or three days I walked across to my local library and gathered an armful of books to replenish the ones I had returned. Everything was grist to my mill – serious novels, love stories, even light hearted "chick lit", historical tomes, the most obscure biographies, *any* travel books, classics that I had missed through lack of time or inclination, and even children's books. I watched television until my eyes stung and then found it difficult to drag myself off to bed. As my mother would have declared, 'Don't sit around looking into space – DO SOMETHING!'

I must admit Andrew tried: he had done his best to rouse me

from my lethargy. When I occasionally answered my mobile phone he must have had a list of diversions in his head because he was never short of suggesting I visit York for a few days, perhaps meet him at some destination I favoured, or even go abroad and he would try to join me; but these tactics only served to make me more disagreeable and resistant to every inducement. The nicer he was the more perverse and cantankerous I became. I was like a spoilt brat who kicked the parent who was making a peace offering of a delicious lollipop.

He'd tried to take my mind off myself by talking about every topic imaginable. He eventually mentioned Dee's funeral at long last. It was as if I had been waiting for just such an opening. Pure hostility poured out of me like molten lava. 'How do you *think* I felt, Andrew? A sunny church, lovely innocent childhood hymns, a kind and thoughtful vicar who tried to make us all feel better. On our way in we were offered Phil Everly's gentle rendition of "*The Air that I Breathe*" and, as we made our way out into the shaded churchyard, Frank Sinatra gently begged us to be "*Young at Heart*". Two special melodies beloved of my lovely, uncomplicated cousin - but worse was to come, as only her close family were invited to the crematorium. There were so few of us chosen to see Dee off on her journey. We sat close to each other for comfort and support, in a modern, elegant hall that could have doubled as a new age church or a school's assembly room. There we had to watch as my cousin, encased in an airless, hard oaken box, slid towards a furnace that would devour her. So no, Andrew, I don't want to come anywhere to join you. I no longer believe any of your comforting words and I am tired of being hurt and disappointed again and again. Stay with your clinging, selfish wife and your delightful children. You *chose* them, remember, so think positive - make the best of your life and stop trying to offer me something you are now not at liberty to give. Make your mind up – it's either her or me because you can't have us both – and I, for one, do not want half of you. *She* might find it acceptable to pretend that you are a true and loving husband, but I refuse to go along with such a blatant lie. I have no idea what hold she has over you, but you appear to be abjectly terrified of crossing her in any way. You told me once that, when you walked out, she tried everything and then finally threatened to kill herself and you, believing she would do just that to spite you, returned to her to prevent it happening: then you went home and it was patently a lie. You discovered a stack of estate agents' brochures for single apartments. The shock when you realised you had been duped must have been earth-shattering – and I would have immediately turned tail and disappeared like a scalded rabbit. But you stayed, Andrew. That's why I would rather be completely alone for the rest of my life than carry on with this lunatic charade. So go away Drew, and stay away. I never want to set eyes on you again.'

I heard a sharp intake of breath and the telephone died in my hand. I looked at it, dazed at my hostile outburst. '*What had I done*?' My deep and bitter resentment, that had been seething since Andrew walked out, had finally burst like a lanced, suppurating boil. But, unlike a drained blister, I certainly didn't feel better for it. I slowly sank down on my bed, shattered and horrified at the raging storm that had so suddenly surged over me and taken us both by surprise. My crying came later – desolate and despairing....

Chapter 33

*

Six months had passed since Andrew and I had last spoken. Nothing, not even a text or an e-mail, had passed between us. I can't say it was an uneventful period – it wasn't – lots happened, but nothing pleasant. First off I broke my left wrist in a shopping mall one damp day in Exeter. Wet tiles and high-heeled boots brought about my downfall, and the fact that I was clutching assorted bags of newly bought Christmas presents in each hand, didn't assist my ungainly tumble. Feeling extremely stupid, I pleaded with the well-intentioned passers-by to leave me alone until I could gingerly raise myself and pretend everything was fine. I tottered off home and had to learn to shop, eat and wash my hair with one hand while the other resided in a monstrous, plaster cast. At least I got away with minimal housework but I was also unable to drive and had to rely on public transport – no bad thing, I discovered.

Within a few weeks I was unlucky enough to suffer a whiplash incident when a cab I was riding in clipped a stationary Land Rover parked outside a supermarket. So I not only sported a plaster cast but an uncomfortable neck brace too, for a while. But worst of all, during that time, my flat was invaded by bugs. No one else appeared to be suffering from them so, when I tentatively mentioned their onslaught, I was met with uncomprehending stares or neighbours sidling away from me as if I was infectious. Luckily they were relatively easy to eliminate. The lad who came – dressed in a white spacesuit – removed anything damageable then calmly set off a device as we both backed out of the front door and locked it. I returned two hours later to find my visitors had decided to leave me in peace.

I suppose one could say these silly and irritating incidents may have been upsetting, but they also blunted my mind to the end of my long affair with Andrew. In bed, at night, was the most difficult time for me. I kept busy during the day and usually I would drop asleep with very little trouble most nights; but I developed a habit of suddenly waking up in the early hours – then my mind would start ranging over my life and how I had lost everything I most cherished and had nothing to face in the future but solitude. To all intents and purposes I had become a sterile being: friends and acquaintances abounded but none who I could love as one does a devoted partner. There was no one I could rely on above all others and nobody to sexually perform the act of love which, in its purest form, involves the most glorious abandonment and cements a partnership.

I would lie in my warm bed – unable to go back to sleep – and, being me, I would go through the gamut of my recent roller-coaster emotions. Molten fury at Andrew's insensitivity had finally given way to a cooling down period; then I recognised a bleakness that verged on despair and, as I tried to force myself out of that depression, I went through an odd span of indecision and pure longing to open the door once more and return to our happy and easy-going relationship. Finally, after searching my feelings as truthfully as I was able, I reached an acceptance of the situation as it had formed and reformed through the preceding time we had been apart. I remember when, in desperation, I had allowed Val to become privy to some of Andrew's letters and answerphone messages. She had eventually sighed and admitted we had something special and she could never see it lessening whatever we decided.

"I don't think either of you will ever manage to live completely separate lives, so why don't you go with the flow, Jenny, and accept and enjoy what he *is* able to offer? Take heart, sweetheart, there are not many who get offered this unremitting devotion and ardour for the rest of their lives. Be proud of your commitment towards each other. You have something very special so don't destroy it by striving to change it, darling.'

I still danced, walked when the weather allowed, shopped, cleaned, read and telephoned all my friends with mad determination. It prevented me thinking too deeply and allowed me a modicum of peace. I knew if I contacted Drew he would respond immediately.

Sadly, I was still too proud to make the first move and he was too hurt to attempt it from his end, so we had reached a stalemate. When Chris texted me from Thailand to wish me a Merry Christmas, I hooted with laughter. It seemed everyone wanted to catch up with me and wish me well. Only the one person I longed for above all others remained silent.

A few days after the festivities had ended, I was sitting curled up on the sofa in my cosy dressing gown with my nose buried in a book. I had turned down every Christmas invitation – from Val in Cumbria, Meryl in the depths of Essex and Robin in Scotland – to partake of the season's festivities with them and their families. Even Lorna tried every inducement but I remained firm, making up previous engagements or trying to sound as if my life was one round of parties and fun. I was determined not to succumb to Robin and Ailsa's invitation however many times they had asked. They didn't need me creating even the slightest rift in their new relationship. Val was the most difficult to convince because, having lived in the flats, she knew my situation; luckily the others believed my huge lies and finally gave up trying. I'm sure I would have loved being with Meryl, Lorna, Val or even Jess once more, but deep down I felt I didn't deserve to return to a normal, interactive world. That's why I went to my freezer and picked out a shepherd's pie for Christmas Day and fish and chips for Boxing Day. I knew Santa had passed me by and I accepted it should be so.

I had put my electric blanket on early that night. The weather had turned damp and chilly after lunch and I had decided the best place for me was in my toasty bed with a good book. I had switched off the television and, curled up on the sofa in my dressing gown, was enjoying a hot mug of chocolate while listening to the dulcet purity of Katie Melua's soft voice, when my doorbell chimed. I glanced at the clock. It wasn't much past nine o'clock so still early enough for one of my neighbours to come *a-calling* – usually it was to ask a favour for the next day or to borrow a light bulb. I sighed, turned Katie down, and swung my legs to the floor. They would just have to accept my fleecy dressing gown, I decided, as I went towards the front door.

I walked out into the hall as the doorbell rang for the second time. Gosh, someone *was* impatient. My Christmas decorations

– sparse as they were – were still up and, always a traditionalist, they would remain up until Twelfth Night. I leant forward to look through the security peephole and then remembered it was covered by the usual jolly Santa, with his old-fashioned specs perched on his nose above plump, glowing cheeks. He would be beaming on all my callers but was preventing me from seeing who was outside my door and longing to disturb my peace. Never mind, I reasoned, with sheltered housing we knew no outsider could invade our privacy, so I was confident it would only be one of my neighbours. I just hoped it wouldn't be an emergency that required outside aid. Still, it looked as if my early night might be fast evaporating...

I reached up and opened the door. The small hall outside the lift was brightly lit but my visitor was standing in a patch of shade at the far end. One of the strip lights in the main corridor must have failed, my mind duly registered, as I peered towards the darkness in surprise. All I could see was a man leaning against the far wall, accompanied by a large rucksack or a bulky suitcase of some kind. So, not one of the neighbours was my immediate reaction while my second thought was, '*This will teach you to open your door late at night without knowing who's on the other side.*'

'Can I help you?' I enquired, drawing the collar of my dressing gown up closer to my chin as I tried not to show any unease or trepidation. How had this stranger gained entrance, my common sense screamed at me? Living in sheltered accommodation is a brilliant concept for it allows residents a degree of freedom from the fear of having to protect themselves or their property; but it can be a two-edged sword in certain circumstances. The barrier of a locked front door prevents an unwelcome caller infiltrating our space. They would only be allowed inside with the permission from one of the residents – by their pressing a button. But, if by chance anyone *does* get inside, they would be at liberty to roam up the stairs and through the corridors at will and our safety could be compromised.

'Can I help you?' I asked again, preparing to close my front door smartly.

'I hope so,' the man answered as he straightened up and stepped forward. 'I've driven a hell of a long way through icy blizzards and raging torrents, I've fought off angry black bears and howling hyenas to get to this gentle county of Devon - now I'm just hoping against hope there will be some room at your inn for me and my golf clubs.'

The slight Cornish cadence fell gently on my ears and suddenly it dawned on me that, occasionally, some dreams *do* become reality and delight can sometimes be only a whisper of hope away. I felt a ripple of excitement, stirred by a flooding of pure happiness that threatened to engulf me. I stepped back to show he was welcome and held the door wide.

'I'd best turn the electric blanket off,' I said dryly. 'And, if you are not just passing through, I take it you'll want feeding?' I asked, hoping the response would be favourable. 'And will you be staying long?' I enquired, as casually as I was able.

'Feeding, watering *and* bedding in that exact order, please, but the most important after the bedding is the eternity I plan to spend with you – that's if you'll have me,' Andrew replied with a hesitant grin slowly spreading across his shadowed face.

'I will turn that blanket off immediately,' I answered, with a smile that could probably have lit up a lighthouse. 'I know how you hate a hot bed. The best I can do is beans on toast for you, my lad, and as many mugs of tea as you can handle,' I went on as I sashayed away towards the kitchen. And, feeling like a nubile teenager again, I swiftly tweaked up the volume of Katie Melua's pure young voice to enchant and beguile him as I went off to do his bidding.

Journey's End

*

Many months had elapsed since I had been bowled over by a joy far beyond my wildest dreams and, as the cold days merged into warmer weeks, I gradually began to wonder if miracles do happen occasionally. I am ashamed to admit as the days passed I searched constantly for any signs of disillusionment in Andrew's demeanour; I waited for a lessening of his love and affection towards me; I would laugh with him but was often wary of being too relaxed and liberal in my views; I was always alert to hidden dangers, as if I lived under the shadow of a volcano and now had no idea if an eruption was due, or not. I also tried not to show my trepidation.

Luckily none of these fears materialised and, just as in a war zone where no one can remain on a constant state of alert forever, I gradually lost my dread of the future until slowly, slowly, I began to look outward and forward once again. Fay had retreated into an aloof shell – probable plotting a new plan of attack, I surmised – as Andrew and I slowly began to merge our individual lives into a wholesome, dual partnership once more. And, when Andrew suggested we buy a camper van and take it out on the road, I agreed instantly. I then breathed a sigh of relief. He was never contented unless he was getting on with his life, I had long since accepted. He had made his peace with his sons and appeared to have left his friends behind without a backward glance. Was he really committed to making our resurrected liaison work this time, I wondered? These thoughts came, usually at night, when I found it difficult to sleep.

The camper van was a great success. We had left Devon during the last week of June and, of course, made our way towards the

Tamar. Living so closely together was obviously going to make or break us and I was not sure how I would cope with it or for how long. Surprisingly enough, it was a lot easier than I expected. Once over the border, we meandered around for a while following our instincts and inclinations. There is something exhilarating about being free and we both became light-hearted and content; main meals were a matter of little thought as, going out for them, we didn't have to shop, cook or clean up after them; the weekday wash became a thing of the past as we wore what was clean and then I washed what was necessary. I remembered a friend telling me they spent two months in France every year and how liberating it was not to have to excuse one's shortcomings. I now knew what she meant!

Eventually Andrew came up with a plan of action and we made our way straight to the north coast, near Morwenstow, where Parson Hawker, perched high in his windswept hut on the cliffs, wrote his great ballad to Bishop Trelawney; a refrain that is roared out by lusty young Cornishmen at all their rugby matches. From there, we made our way west through Bude, Boscastle and down to Port Isaac. We turned inland and bypassed Padstow, although I made sure we visited every glorious beach from Trevose Head to Newquay. We then went on, ignoring the Camborne area, and made straight for St Ives where we spent almost a week enjoying the sun, sand and swimming before parking our van in Penzance and taking the boat over to the Isles of Scilly. *This* time there was no sneaking around, no recriminations from an outraged Fay as we thoroughly explored every island and submerged ourselves into the laid-back, simple lifestyle that is an islander's reason for living.

Returning, we messed around on the Helford River. We visited Glendurgan Gardens, Frenchman's Creek (of Daphne du Maurier fame) and Porth Navas. We marvelled at the tame wildlife until I suddenly became aware that Andrew was homesick. The proximity of Fowey, Lerryn and Polruan had become too much of a lure and I was only too pleased to accompany him to visit his friends and a few distant relatives. We spent four days, mostly on the river, after borrowing a small dinghy from an old family friend. We would have been more adventurous but Lawson's boat had seen better days and Andrew wasn't sure it was up to the open sea. Sinking at

Pont Pill was one thing, as I could have probably made it to shore, but off Palace Cove would have been another matter. And I was no mermaid!

We finally had to wish everybody a fond farewell as we had made arrangements to go abroad for two weeks. During the cold, rainy days of February the Greek island of Skiathos was a temptation neither of us had been able to resist, so we had booked ourselves into a taverna – not knowing that shortly before we were due to leave the UK we would be having the time of our lives in a sleepy little village in Cornwall. We packed up the car and decided to depart after a late lunch and, with a few backward glances and the odd salute to loitering villagers, we set off up the steep hill out of town and made our way towards Lansallos.

Of course Lantic Bay was sparkling in the afternoon sunshine and Great Lantic Beach looked so inviting that neither of us could resist parking the van in the nearby National Trust car park and taking the footpath down to the cove. I suddenly had a brilliant idea. I'd wanted Andrew's last day here to be special and this was our opportunity. We filled a rucksack with beach towels, swimming togs and some mackerel that had been swimming in the sea that morning. I shoved in a crusty loaf and a knife, plus some butter and a couple of apples. I reckoned we could make a good evening of it. The tide was just on the turn as we reached the beach, so we spent half an hour swimming around in the shallows and then, to dry off and get warm, we kicked a ball around. When we were breathless and glowing, Andrew showed off his Boy Scout skills by gathering some kindling and lighting a small fire on the beach. Luckily, I'd remembered to bring our fleeces. I spread out the towels and, while he was preparing the fish, buttered a stack of bread and laid out our impromptu meal. The only thing we were lacking was wine but Andrew had thoughtfully slipped in a bottle of ginger beer – which was probably far more appropriate. We lay there devouring the scorching fish with our fingers and munching chunks of bread and crisp apples.

'Mmm! Food of the Gods,' said the chef appreciatively, gulping ginger beer straight from the bottle. I snuggled against him and we stretched out our feet towards the crackling fire.

'Do you think it would be warm enough to spend the night

here?' I asked.

'Not unless you are prepared to climb back up and get a couple of blankets,' said my prosaic lover. Although there was a full moon I decided against it. We lay there quietly talking instead.

'Can I ask you something really personal, Andrew?' I enquired. 'Shoot.'

I took a deep breath and asked the one question that had been playing constantly in my head since he had turned up outside my flat so unexpectedly all those months ago.

'What finally made you change your mind and leave Fay, once and for all?' I hesitantly asked. I wasn't even sure I wanted to know – or would be satisfied with – his reply, but it had been festering inside me and I knew I would never rest easy until he had given me some sort of explanation.

He went very still and quiet and I wondered if he was furious at my temerity. No, he was just marshalling his thoughts. 'I know you often thought me a coward, Jenny. And I know I would regularly back down, when I was first married to Fay, just to keep the peace until, in the end, I suppose it became a habit. I chose to look the other way when she had an affair in the States, right under her parents' noses, with her Italian boyfriend. A few years later, in Hong Kong, I told you she was messing around with my best friend. I took her back that time because she threatened to leave with my children. She arrogantly told me she was pregnant and he was most probably the father. I was devastated and shamed by her cruel taunts. I may have felt a slight sense of relief when she suddenly lost the baby; but I now know this wasn't the solution to our problems. I should have faced the fact our marriage had failed. She doubtless needed psychiatric help and we both needed counselling. But we were both too young and proud to divulge our troubles to anyone – so the pair of us put on a good act until everyone considered we had the perfect partnership.'

'She had always drunk to excess. I suppose it got progressively worse as the years passed, but eventually I ceased to notice – or care. Anyway, it was never too obvious in company as she usually managed to curb herself when we were amongst friends. But, for some reason, dinner parties were her Achilles heel. She must have felt wine could never be as potent when it was accompanied by various courses of a large meal. That's when her good sense could falter and she would sometimes become maudlin and confidentially tell all our friends some of her deeply hidden secrets.'

'Only twice, over the years, do I remember her tearfully mentioning in company she had suffered a miscarriage. Both times most of our friends had been chattering and it had only raised a mild embarrassment among those sitting closest to her. I had always managed to intervene and take her home before she made an even bigger fool of herself.'

'The third time happened shortly after this Christmas. Fay adores entertaining and I'll be the first to admit she's a really good cook. The food was delicious and the wine was flowing freely; the whole company had relaxed and everyone was enjoying themselves. We were halfway through the meal when I noticed she had been sinking two large glasses to everyone else's one, but, as she was on the far side of the table I was unable to curb her intake or distract her attention. I was laughing with two of my golfing cronies about a prestigious tournament, where we had all failed dismally, when I became aware the whole table was falling ominously quiet. Everyone was leaning forward. I suppose it was to enable them to hear the significance of Fay's slurred words.'

'She was reciting the usual fairy tale about Hong Kong and how she had been so happy over there. She mentioned our two delightful young boys and how she had discovered she was again pregnant and that we had both been ecstatic at the thought of maybe a baby daughter. The women, who all knew the extent of our family, looked avidly interested – the men appeared mildly uneasy. Well, she told that well-polished tale beautifully and at the end, when she mentioned the miscarriage, she cried – gently and soundlessly. A close friend leaned across and patted her hand and I saw an arm come around her shoulders, to comfort her. And that, Jenny, was the end of the line for me. I had paid my dues.'

'I wanted to coldly explain to these so-called friends of ours that, in all probability, this baby hadn't been mine – or so she'd said – but the offspring of some sleazy lover who'd been sent back in disgrace to England. I was desperate to explain that this miscarriage had been fortuitous in the extreme as her lover, instead of running away with her, had dumped her and left her to her fate. I was seething and yet felt impotent; by never speaking up, I had colluded with Fay in this cruel fantasy and now I was forever unable to put things right.'

'I found myself standing, as if to replenish my guests' glasses, and quietly slipped outside to the hall and calmly mounted the stairs. I packed a bag within minutes and could still hear a steady murmur of voices downstairs. As I silently eased myself out of the front door I heard a tinkling laugh as some wag finished a joke. I doubt anyone noticed me leaving. I had probably gone before it had even registered and, as I made my way towards York's Ring Road and the South West of England, I chided myself about so much wasted time. It has taken me so long to finally wake up, Jenny, but I have made it at last.'

From the shelter of his warmly protective arms, I stared up at him, puzzled. 'Yes, but why at that particular moment, Drew?' I dared ask. 'After years of pretence, what made you decide it was all over and you'd had enough?'

He smiled down at me, 'You may find this hard to believe, Jenny, but I suddenly caught sight of one of those banal drinks' coasters I had found when I was wandering around Exeter Cathedral years ago. It was half under a discarded napkin; but I knew the sentiment off by heart, anyway.' *"ENJOY LIFE, THIS IS NOT A REHEARSAL."* 'That's all it took, darling. I glanced around at my neighbours and friends eagerly listening to my wife weaving a story of pure fabrication. I thought back to my line of least resistance, and collusion, all our married life; as opposed to your steadfast courage and belief in us. After that it was easy.'

It seemed inconceivable to me that a few words on a beer mat had changed the course of both our lives; but I was willing to accept our good fortune with both hands outstretched.

With our arms entwined we climbed the steep, moonlit pathway and made our way back to the haven of our warm camper van. We stayed in the National Trust car park overnight – illegally I'm sure – but I can now assure you I had my best night's sleep in years. I was under the stars of a Cornish night sky and in the arms of a man who had, at last, completed his own personal way through the woods...

TRICORN
BOOKS